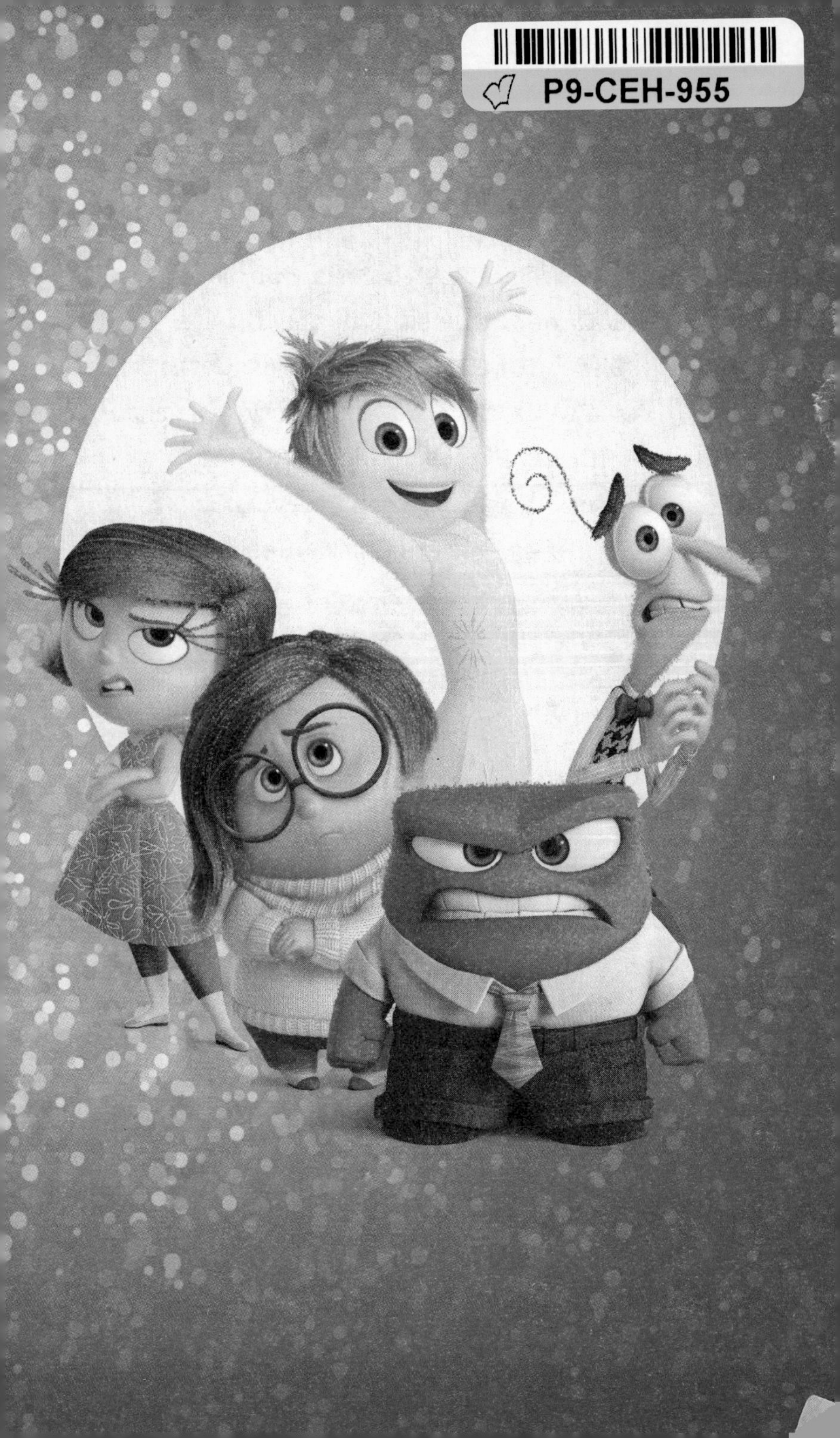

ALSO FROM JOE BOOKS

Disney Frozen Cinestory Comic

Disney Cinderella Cinestory Comic

Disney 101 Dalmatians Cinestory Comic

Disney Alice in Wonderland Cinestory Comic

Disney Big Hero 6 Cinestory Comic

Disney Winnie the Pooh Cinestory Comic

Disney Princess Comics Treasury

Disney•Pixar Comics Treasury

Disney Darkwing Duck:
The Definitively Dangerous Edition

Disney Phineas and Ferb
Colossal Comics Collection

Disney Frozen:
The Story of the Movie in Comics

Disney•Pixar's Inside Out:
The Story of the Movie in Comics

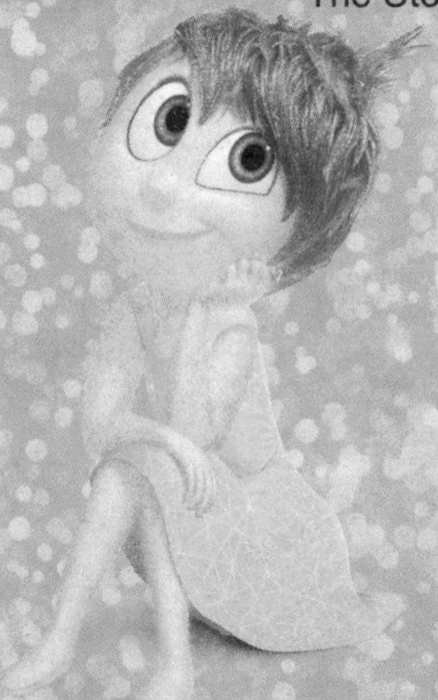

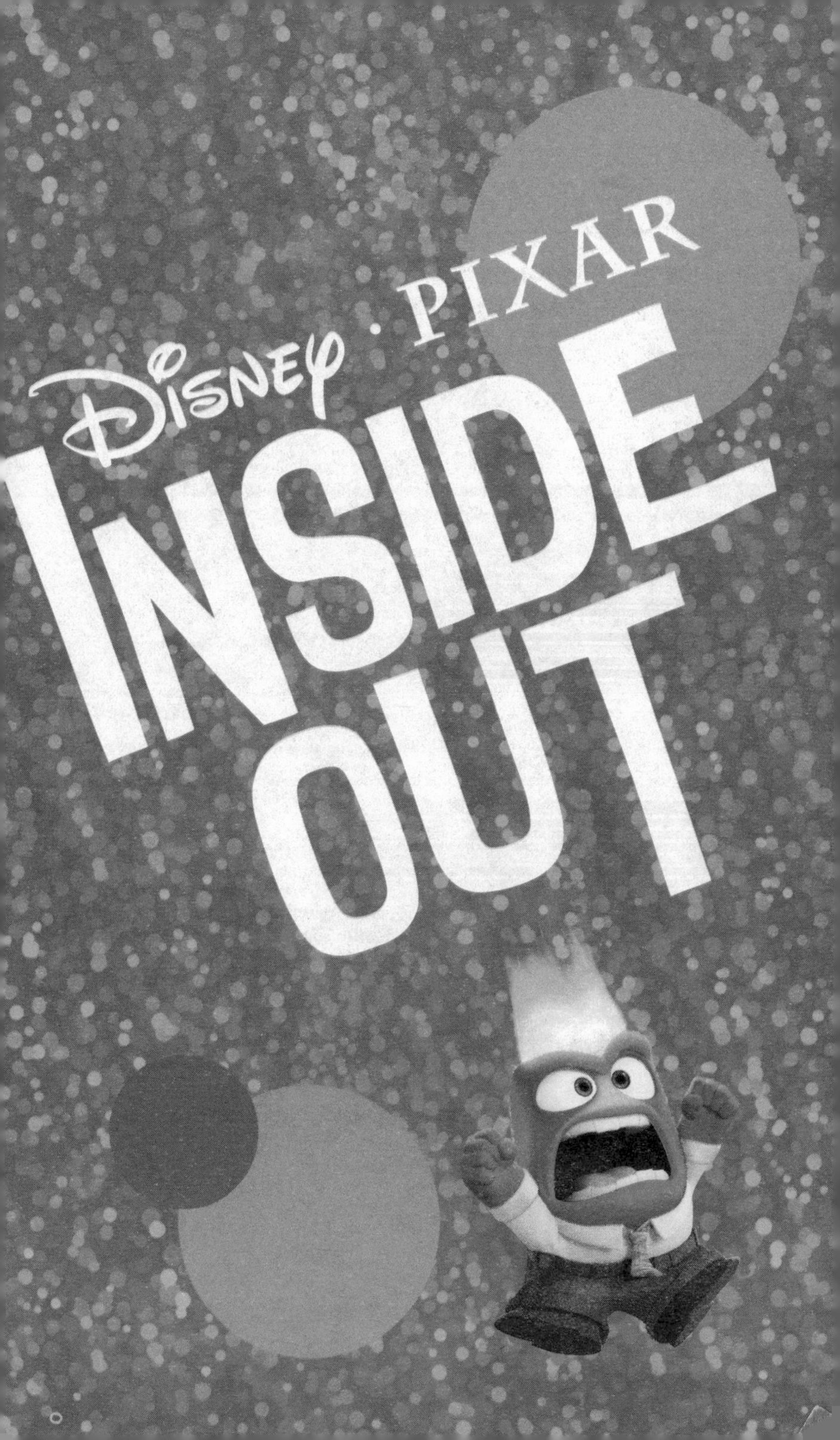
Disney · PIXAR
INSIDE OUT

JOE BOOKS INC

Published in the United States by Joe Books
Publisher: Adam Fortier
President: Jody Colero
CEO: Jay Firestone
567 Queen St W, Toronto, ON M5V 2B6
www.joebooks.com

Library and Archives Canada Cataloguing in Publication
information is available upon request.

ISBN 978-1-9265-1687-5
First Joe Books Edition: June 2015

10 9 8 7 6 5 4 3 2 1

Published in the United States by Joe Books, Inc.

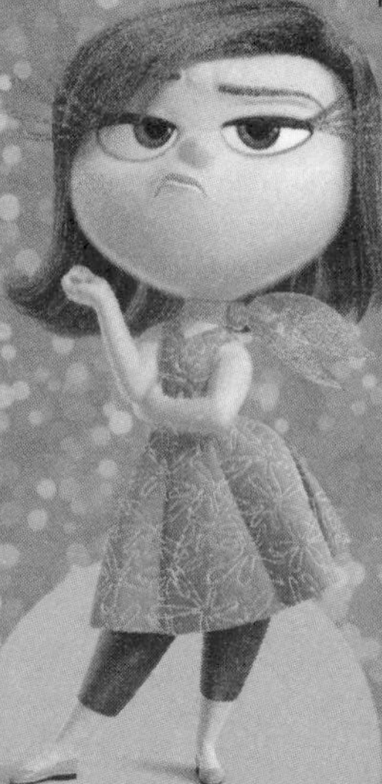

Printed in USA through Avenue4 Communications at Cenveo/Richmond, Virginia

For information regarding the CPSIA on this printed material, call: (203) 595-3636 and provide reference # RICH - 613705

Disney · PIXAR

INSIDE OUT

CINESTORY COMIC

ADAPTED BY
Joelle Sellner

LETTERING AND LAYOUT
Salvador Navarro, Ester Salguero, Eduardo Alpuente, Alberto Garrido, Puste, and Ernesto Lovera

DESIGNER
Heidi Roux

SENIOR EDITOR
Carolynn Prior

SENIOR EDITOR
Robert Simpson

EXECUTIVE EDITOR
Amy Weingartner

PRODUCTION COORDINATOR
Stephanie Alouche

SPECIAL THANKS
Rachel Alor
Curt Baker
Kelly Bonbright
Deborah Cichocki
Julie Dorris
Molly Jones
Behnoosh Khalili
Cynthia Lusk
Victoria R. Manley
Manny Mederos
Beatrice Osman
Nik Siefke
Scott Tilley
Shiho Tilley

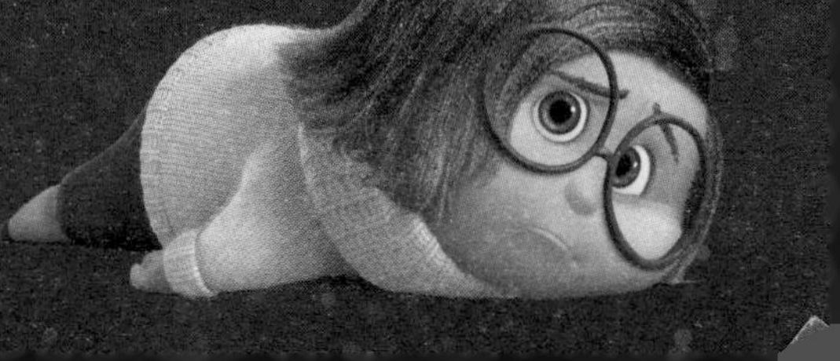

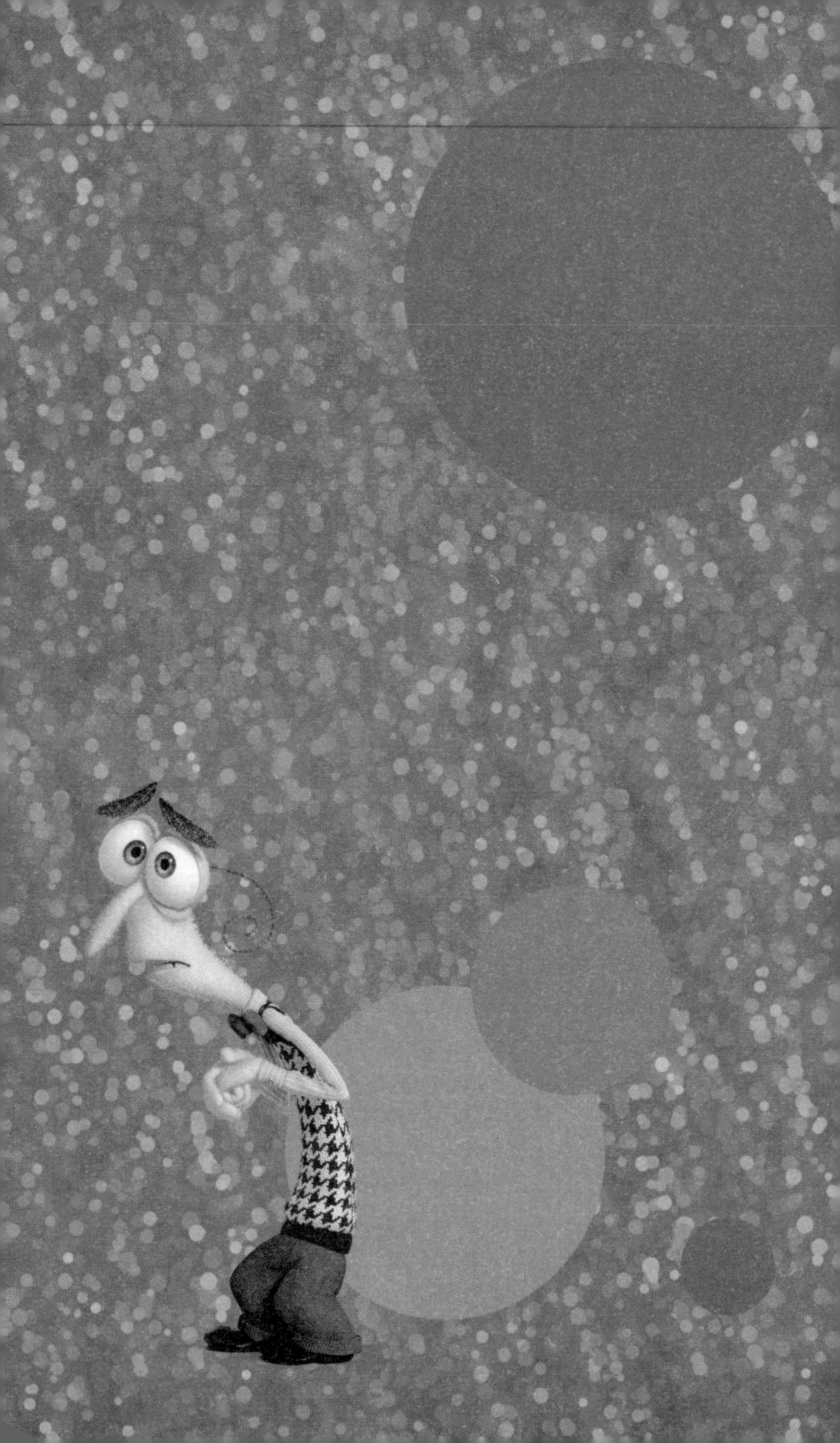

Disney

PIXAR
ANIMATION STUDIOS

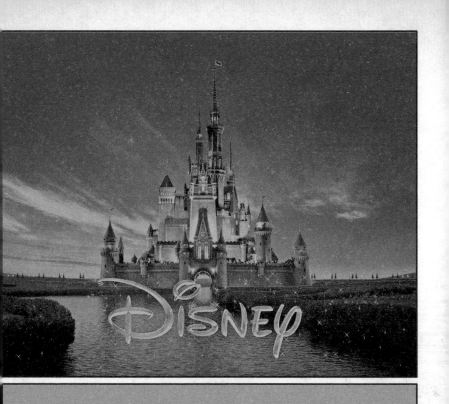

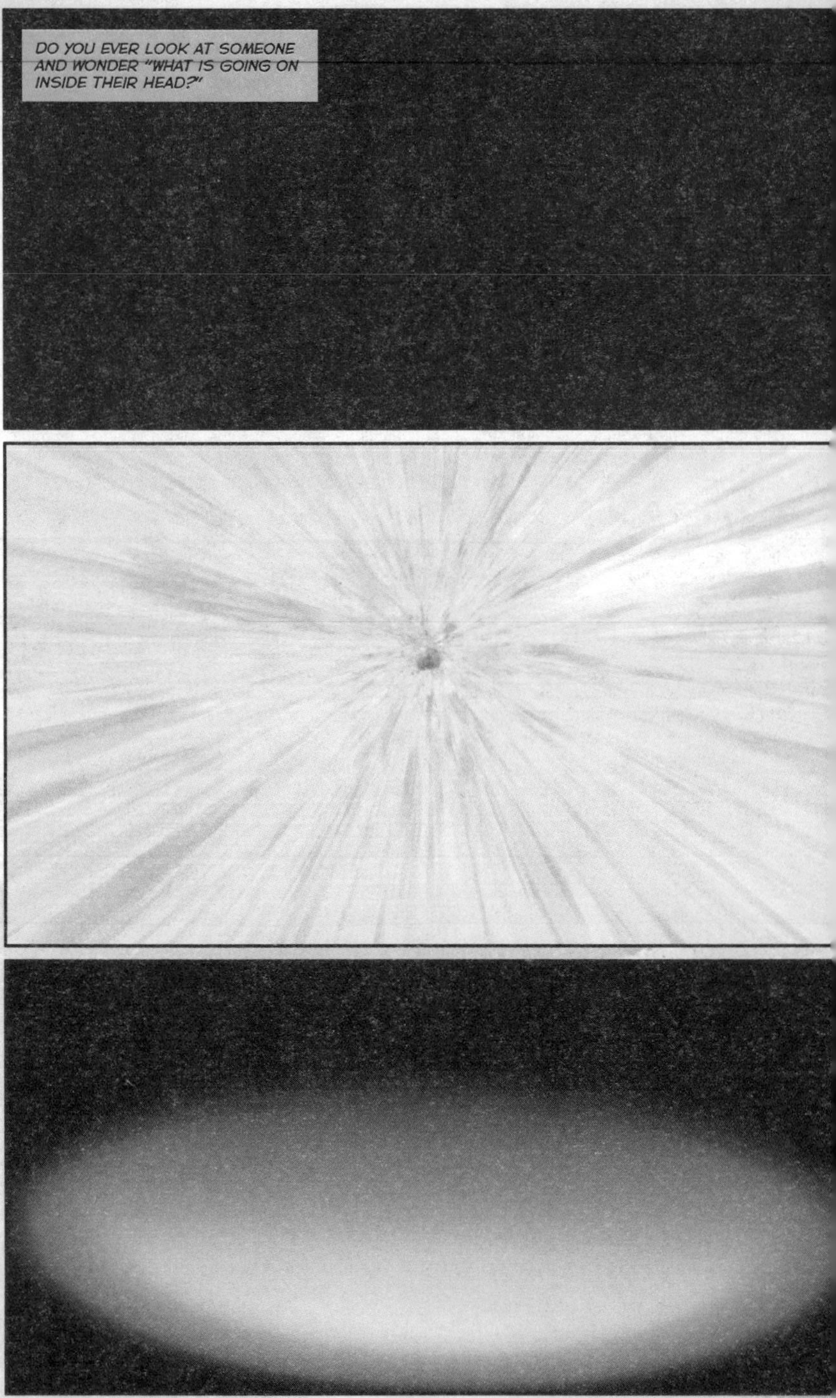
DO YOU EVER LOOK AT SOMEONE AND WONDER "WHAT IS GOING ON INSIDE THEIR HEAD?"

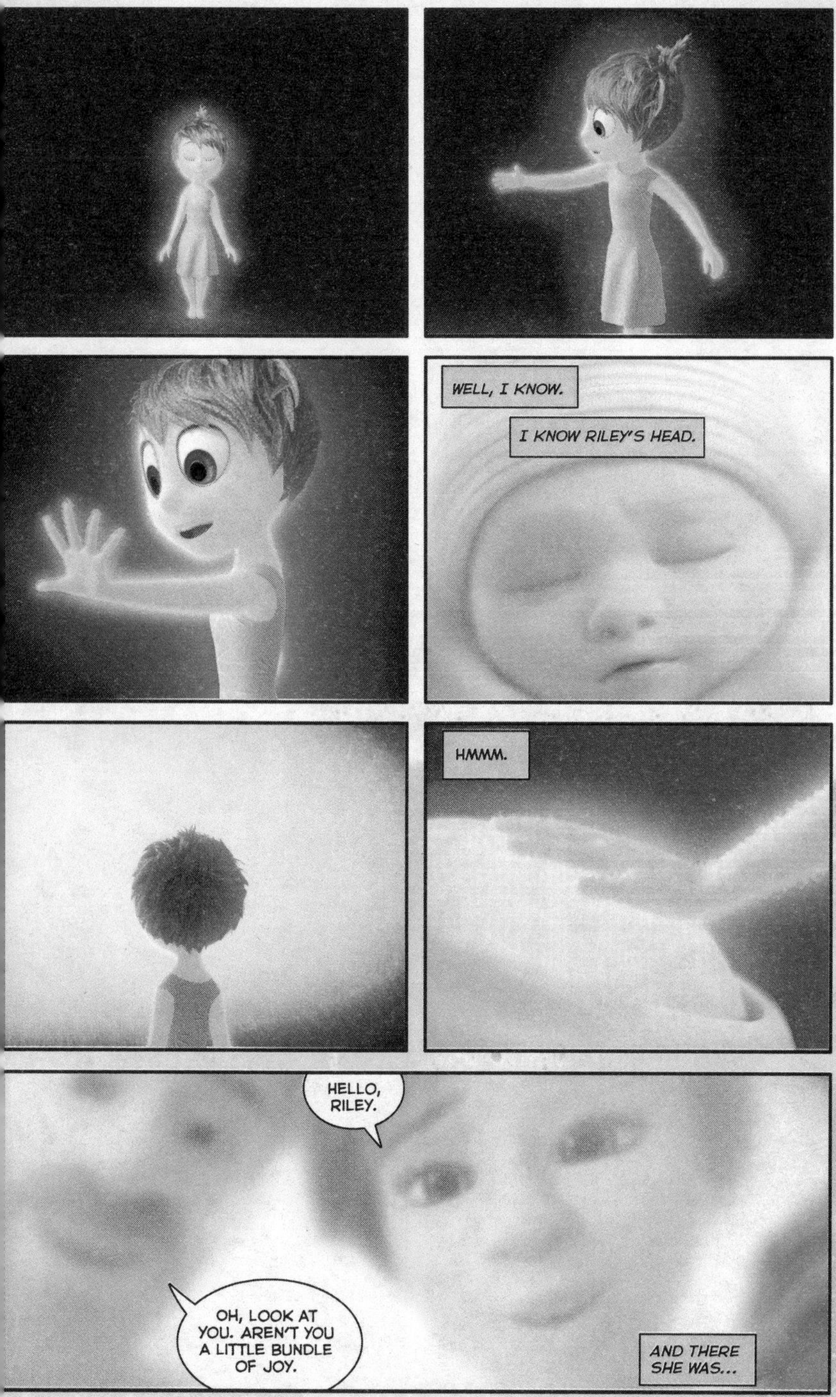
WELL, I KNOW.
I KNOW RILEY'S HEAD.
HMMM.
HELLO, RILEY.
OH, LOOK AT YOU. AREN'T YOU A LITTLE BUNDLE OF JOY.
AND THERE SHE WAS...

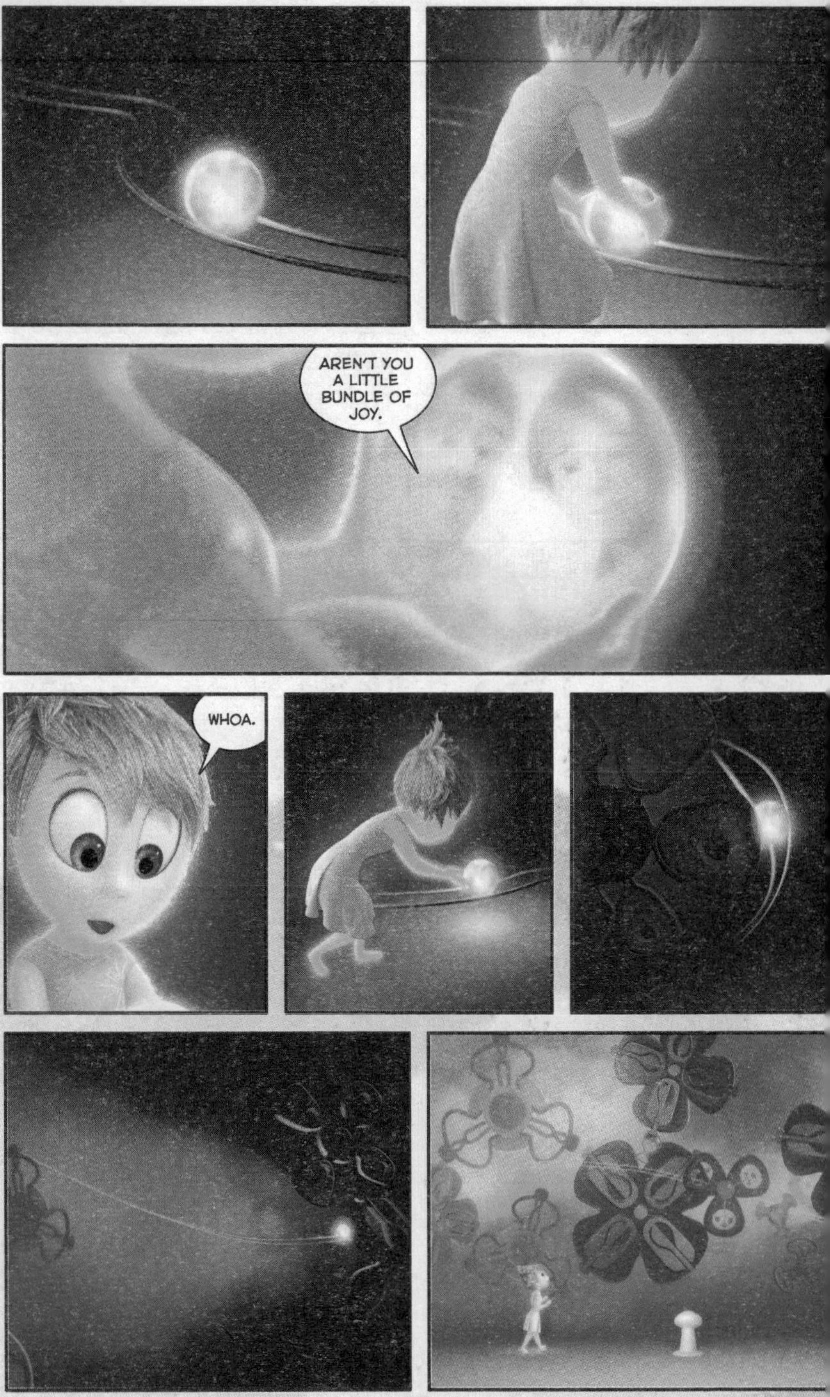
ARE'NT YOU A LITTLE BUNDLE OF JOY.
WHOA.

COOOOOO...

IT WAS AMAZING. JUST RILEY AND ME. FOREVER.

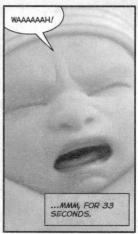

WAAAAAAH!

...MMM, FOR 33 SECONDS.

I'M SADNESS.

OH, HELLO. I'M JOY.

SO. CAN I JUST... IF YOU COULD... I JUST WANT TO FIX THAT. THANKS.

AND THAT WAS JUST THE BEGINNING. HEADQUARTERS ONLY GOT MORE CROWDED FROM THERE.

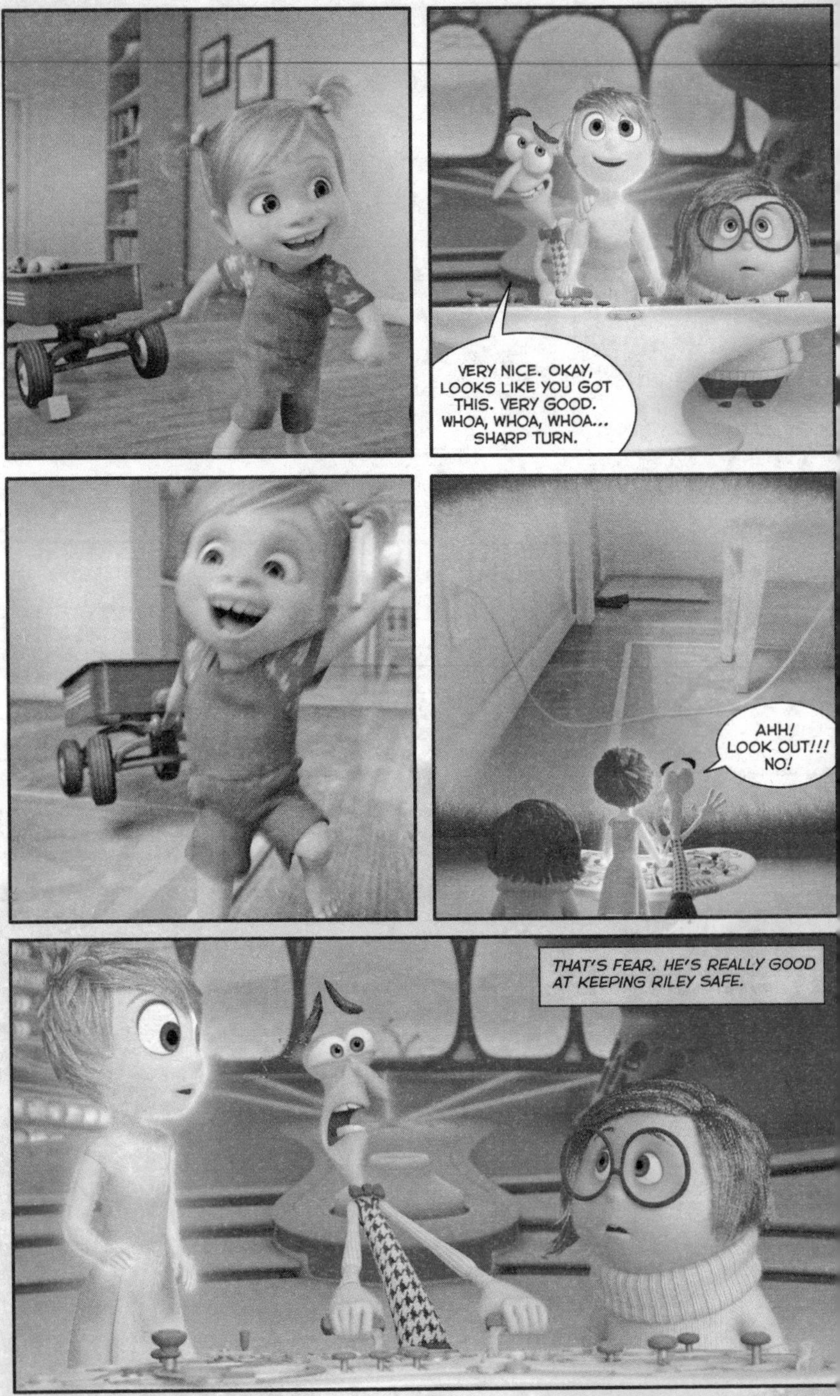
VERY NICE. OKAY, LOOKS LIKE YOU GOT THIS. VERY GOOD. WHOA, WHOA, WHOA... SHARP TURN.
AHH! LOOK OUT!!! NO!
THAT'S FEAR. HE'S REALLY GOOD AT KEEPING RILEY SAFE.

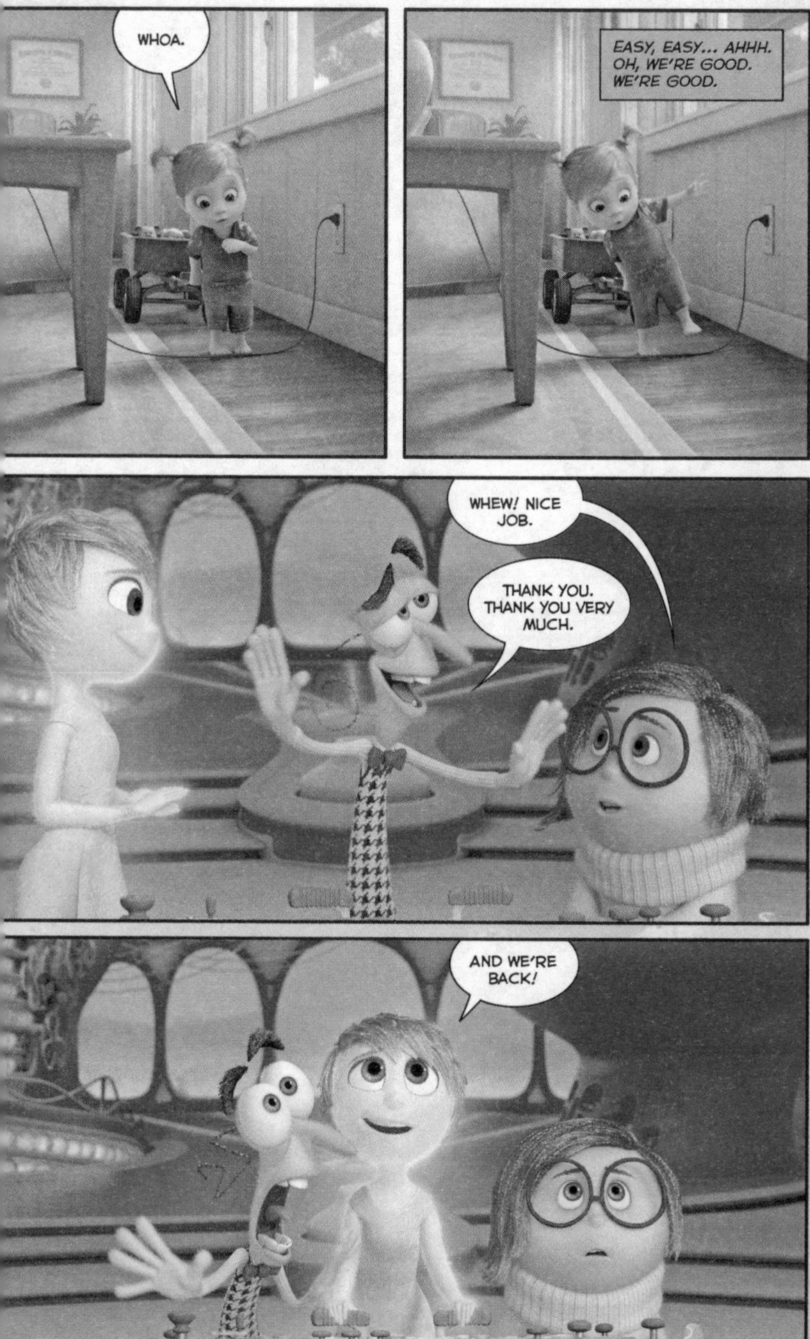
WHOA.
EASY, EASY... AHHH. OH, WE'RE GOOD. WE'RE GOOD.
WHEW! NICE JOB.
THANK YOU. THANK YOU VERY MUCH.
AND WE'RE BACK!

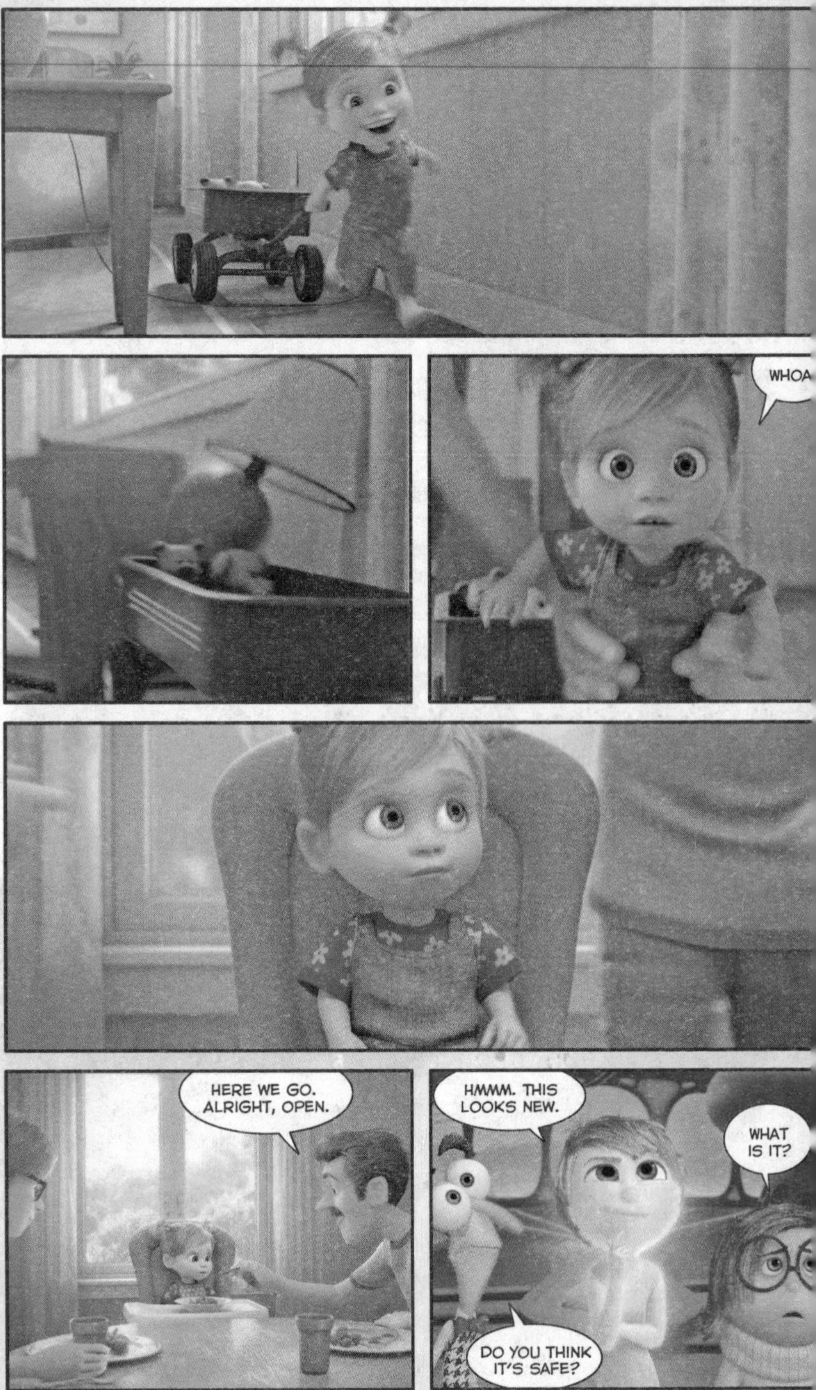
WHOA
HERE WE GO. ALRIGHT, OPEN.
HMMM. THIS LOOKS NEW.
WHAT IS IT?
DO YOU THINK IT'S SAFE?

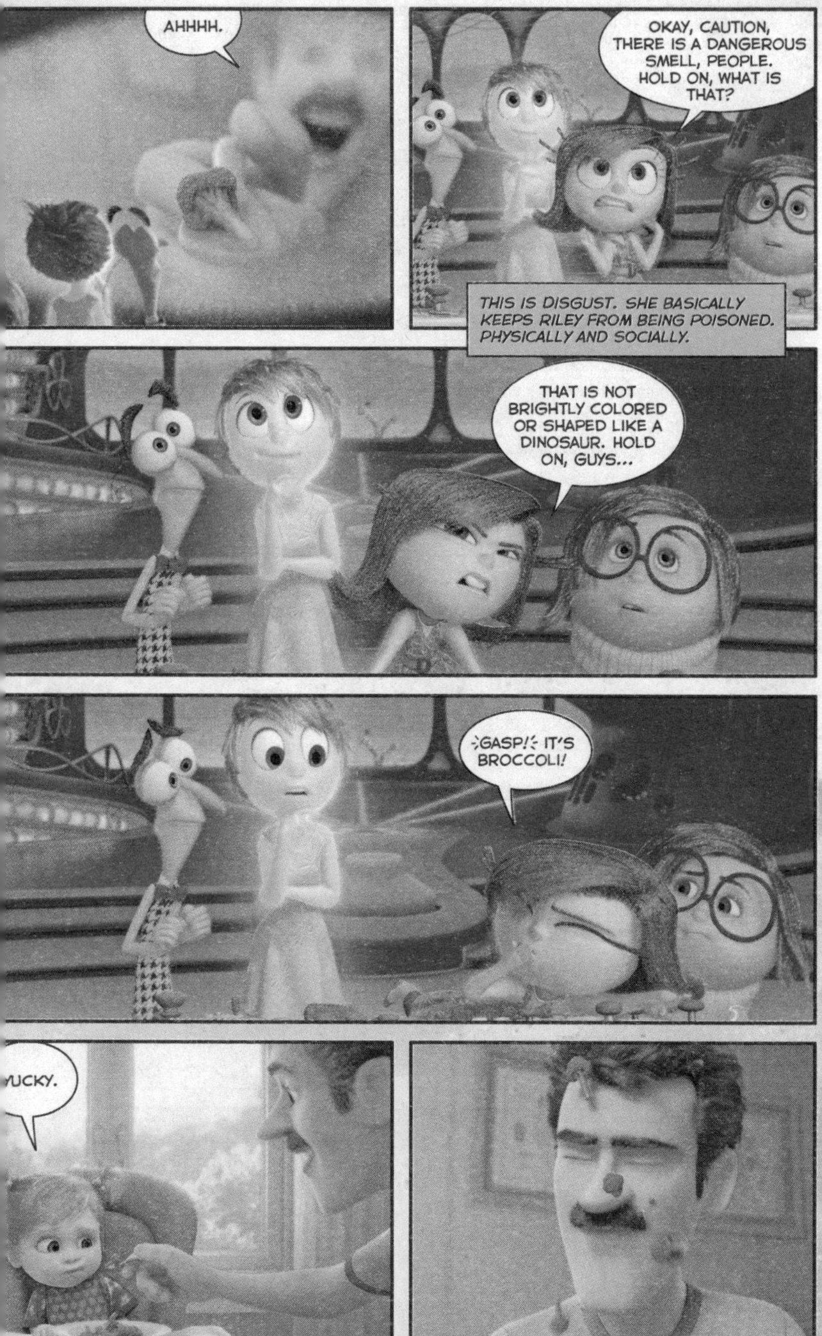
AHHHH.
OKAY, CAUTION, THERE IS A DANGEROUS SMELL, PEOPLE. HOLD ON, WHAT IS THAT?
THIS IS DISGUST. SHE BASICALLY KEEPS RILEY FROM BEING POISONED. PHYSICALLY AND SOCIALLY.
THAT IS NOT BRIGHTLY COLORED OR SHAPED LIKE A DINOSAUR. HOLD ON, GUYS...
GASP! IT'S BROCCOLI!
YUCKY.

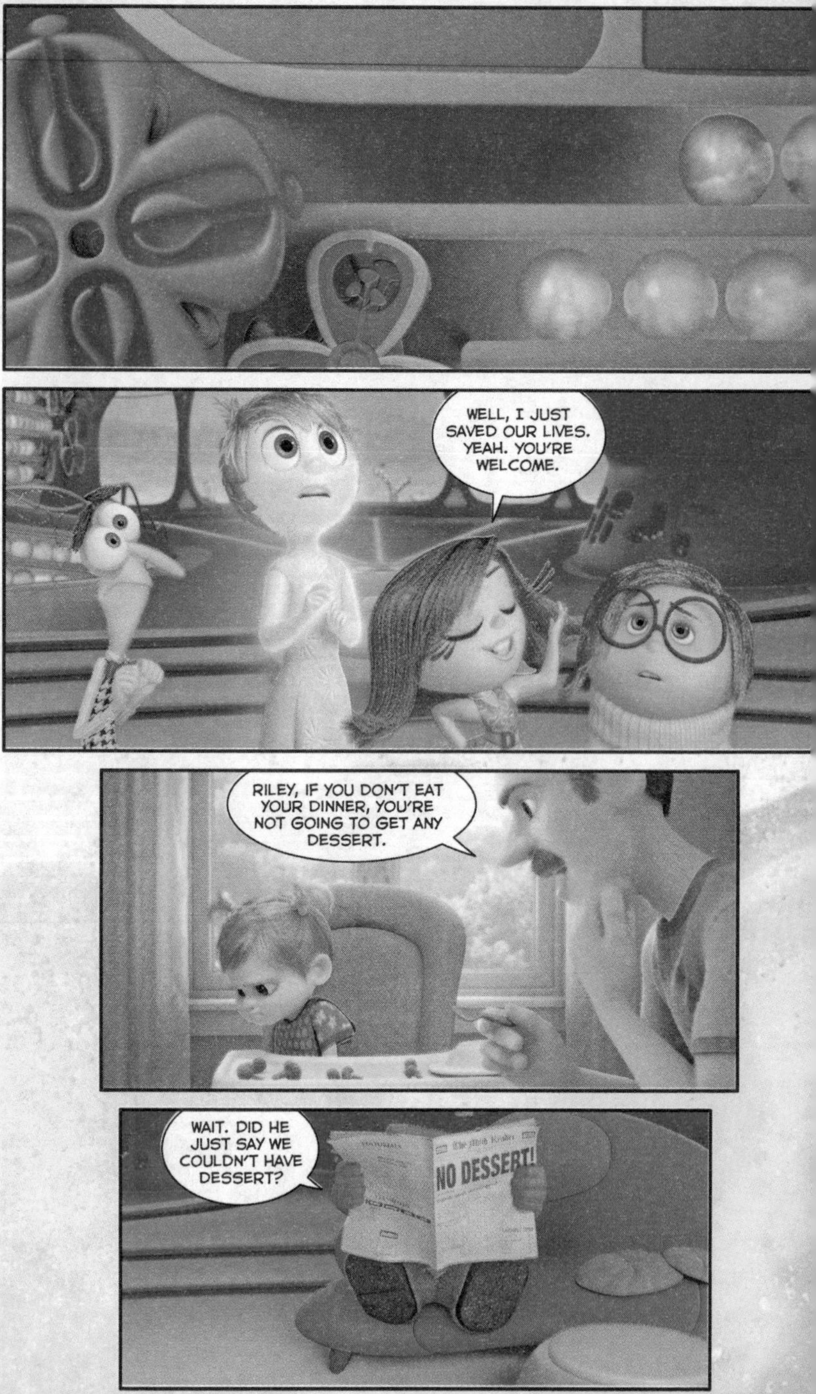
WELL, I JUST SAVED OUR LIVES. YEAH. YOU'RE WELCOME.
RILEY, IF YOU DON'T EAT YOUR DINNER, YOU'RE NOT GOING TO GET ANY DESSERT.
WAIT. DID HE JUST SAY WE COULDN'T HAVE DESSERT?
NO DESSERT!

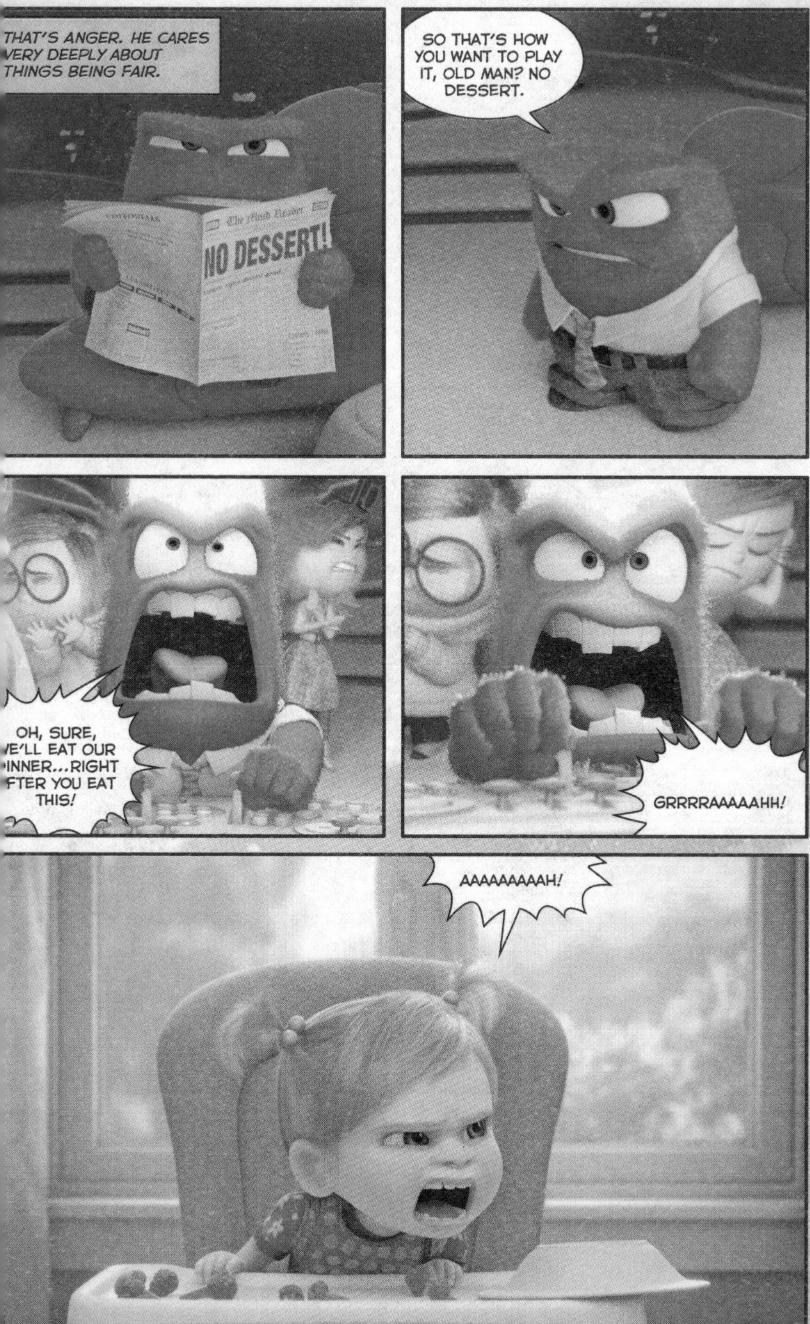
THAT'S ANGER. HE CARES
ERY DEEPLY ABOUT
THINGS BEING FAIR.
NO DESSERT!
SO THAT'S HOW YOU WANT TO PLAY IT, OLD MAN? NO DESSERT.
OH, SURE,
E'LL EAT OUR
INNER...RIGHT
FTER YOU EAT
THIS!
GRRRRAAAAAHH!
AAAAAAAAAH!

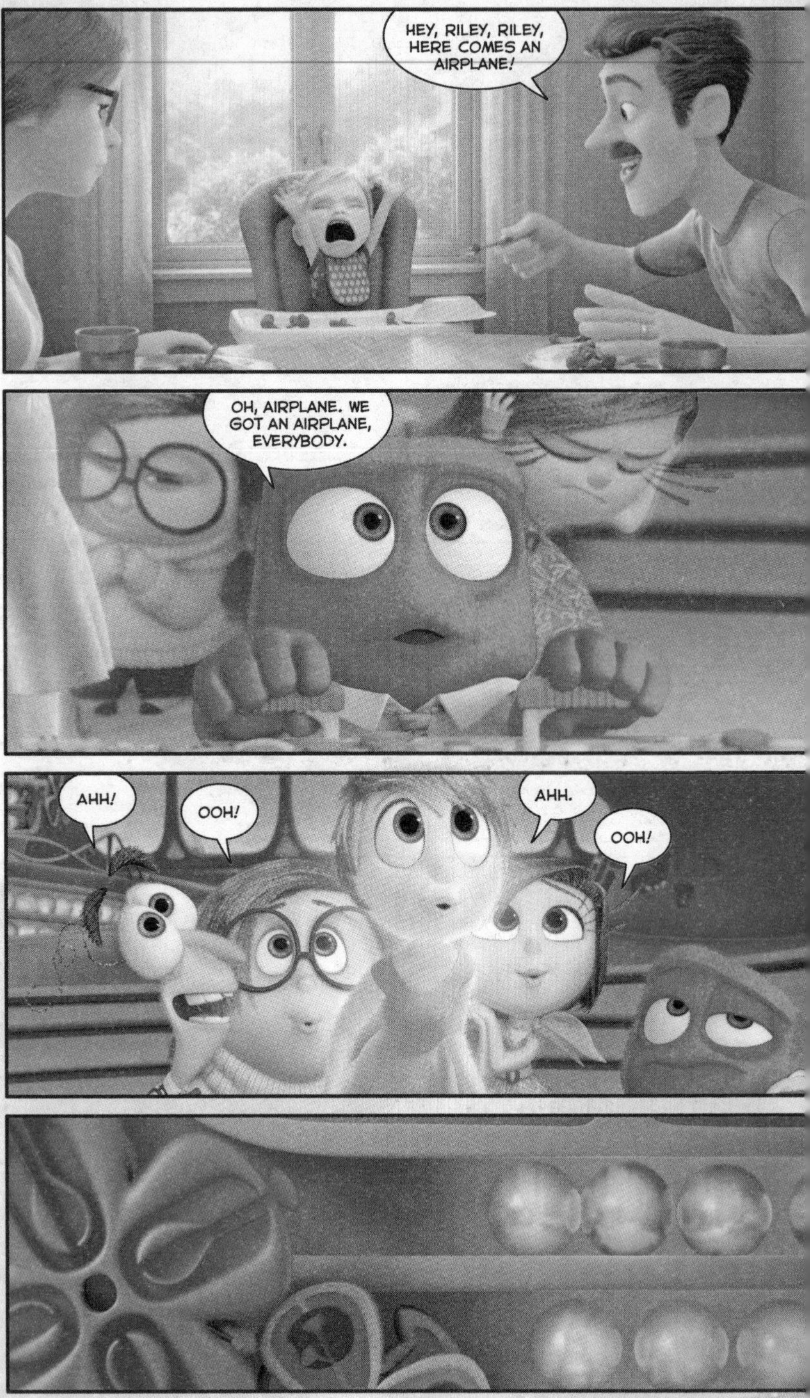
HEY, RILEY, RILEY, HERE COMES AN AIRPLANE!
OH, AIRPLANE. WE GOT AN AIRPLANE, EVERYBODY.
AHH!
OOH!
AHH.
OOH!

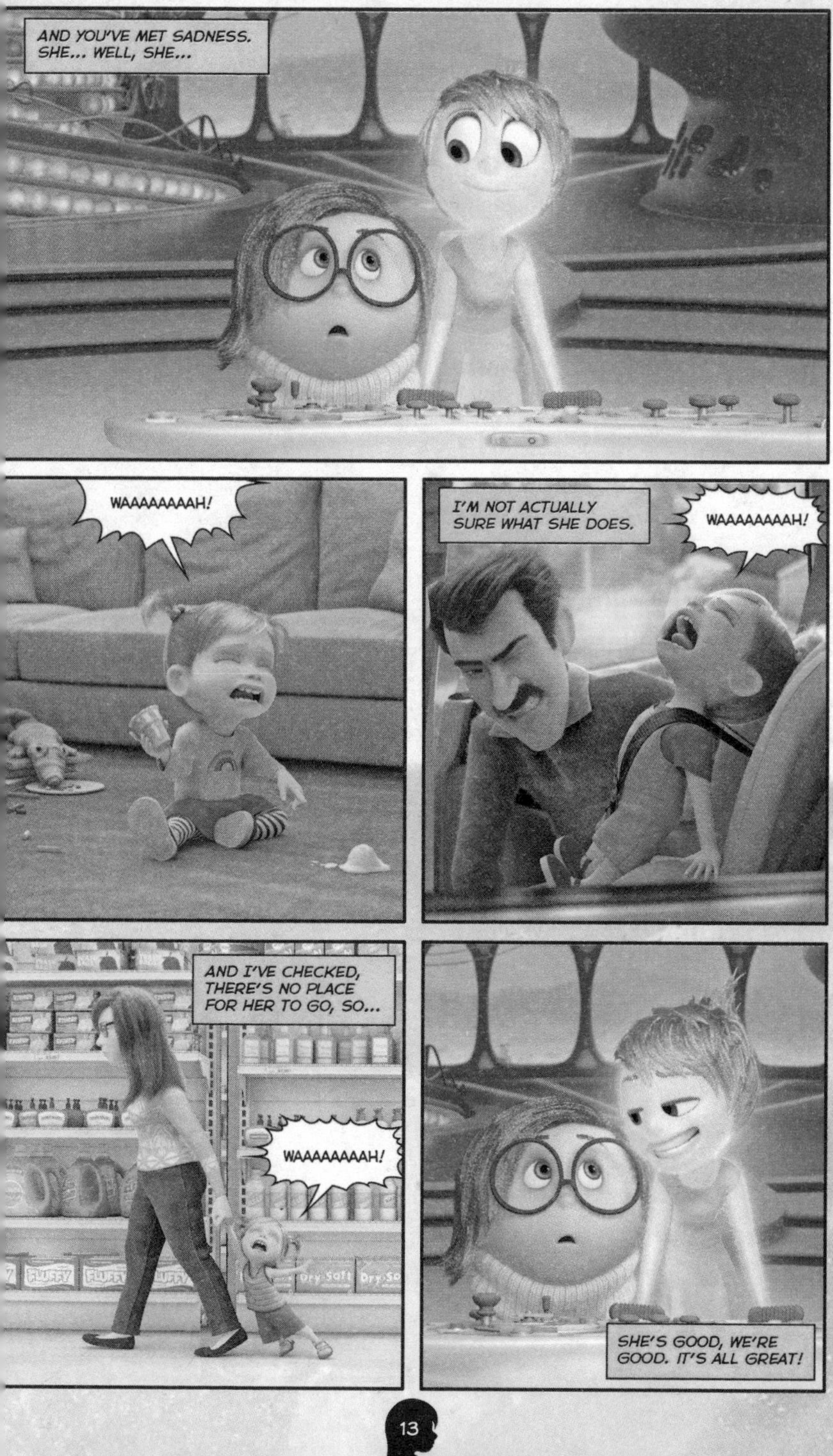
AND YOU'VE MET SADNESS. SHE... WELL, SHE...
WAAAAAAAAH!
I'M NOT ACTUALLY SURE WHAT SHE DOES.
WAAAAAAAAH!
AND I'VE CHECKED, THERE'S NO PLACE FOR HER TO GO, SO...
WAAAAAAAAH!
SHE'S GOOD, WE'RE GOOD. IT'S ALL GREAT!

ANYWAY! THESE ARE RILEY'S MEMORIES...

...AND THEY'RE MOSTLY HAPPY, YOU'LL NOTICE, NOT TO BRAG.

BUT THE REALLY IMPORTANT ONES ARE OVER HERE.

I DON'T WANT TO GET TOO TECHNICAL, BUT THESE ARE CALLED CORE MEMORIES.

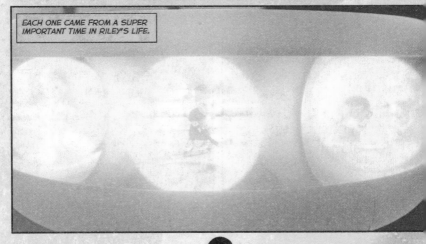

EACH ONE CAME FROM A SUPER IMPORTANT TIME IN RILEY'S LIFE.

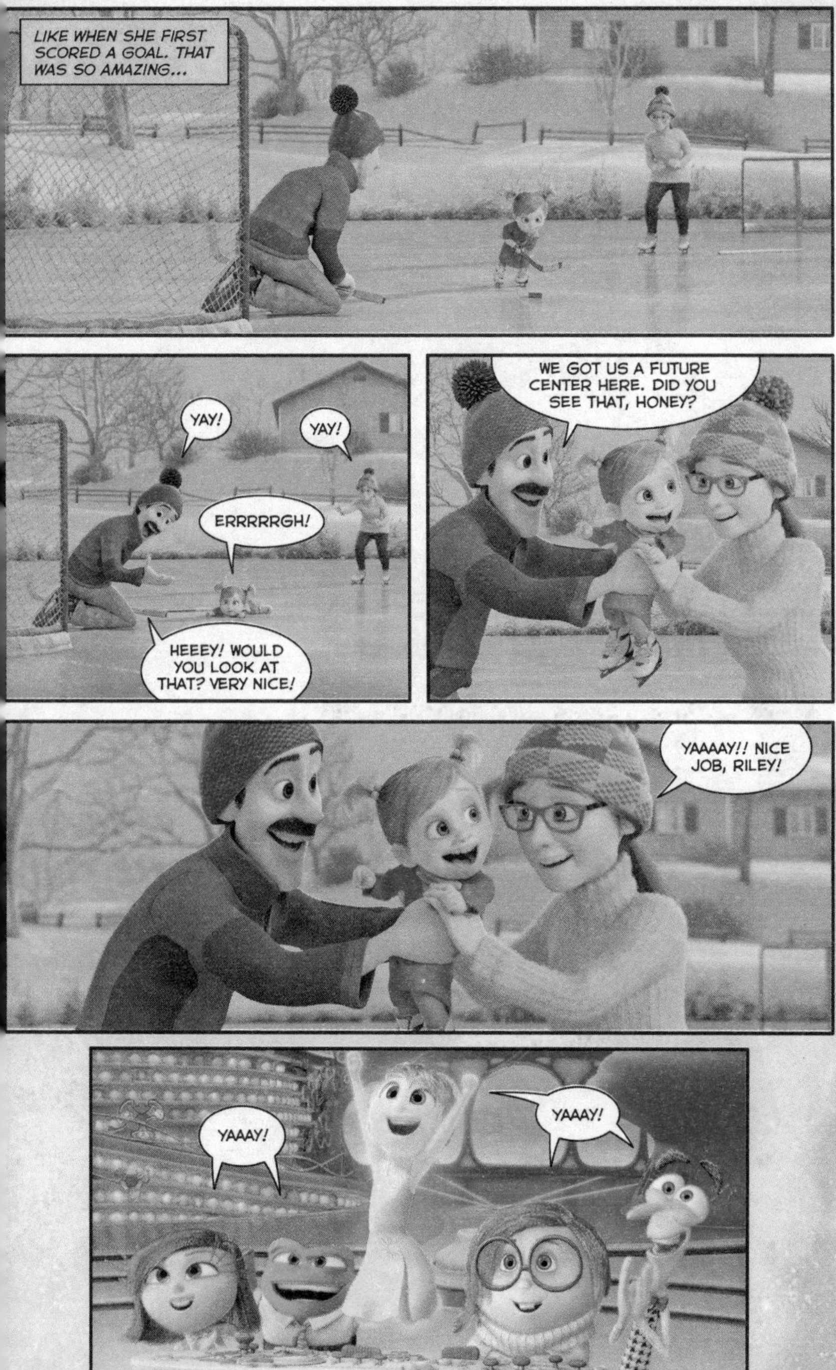
LIKE WHEN SHE FIRST SCORED A GOAL. THAT WAS SO AMAZING...
YAY!
YAY!
ERRRRRGH!
HEEEY! WOULD YOU LOOK AT THAT? VERY NICE!
WE GOT US A FUTURE CENTER HERE. DID YOU SEE THAT, HONEY?
YAAAAY!! NICE JOB, RILEY!
YAAAY!
YAAAY!

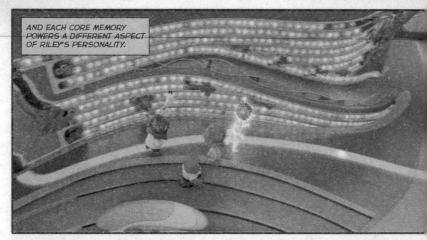

AND EACH CORE MEMORY POWERS A DIFFERENT ASPECT OF RILEY'S PERSONALITY.

LIKE HOCKEY ISLAND!

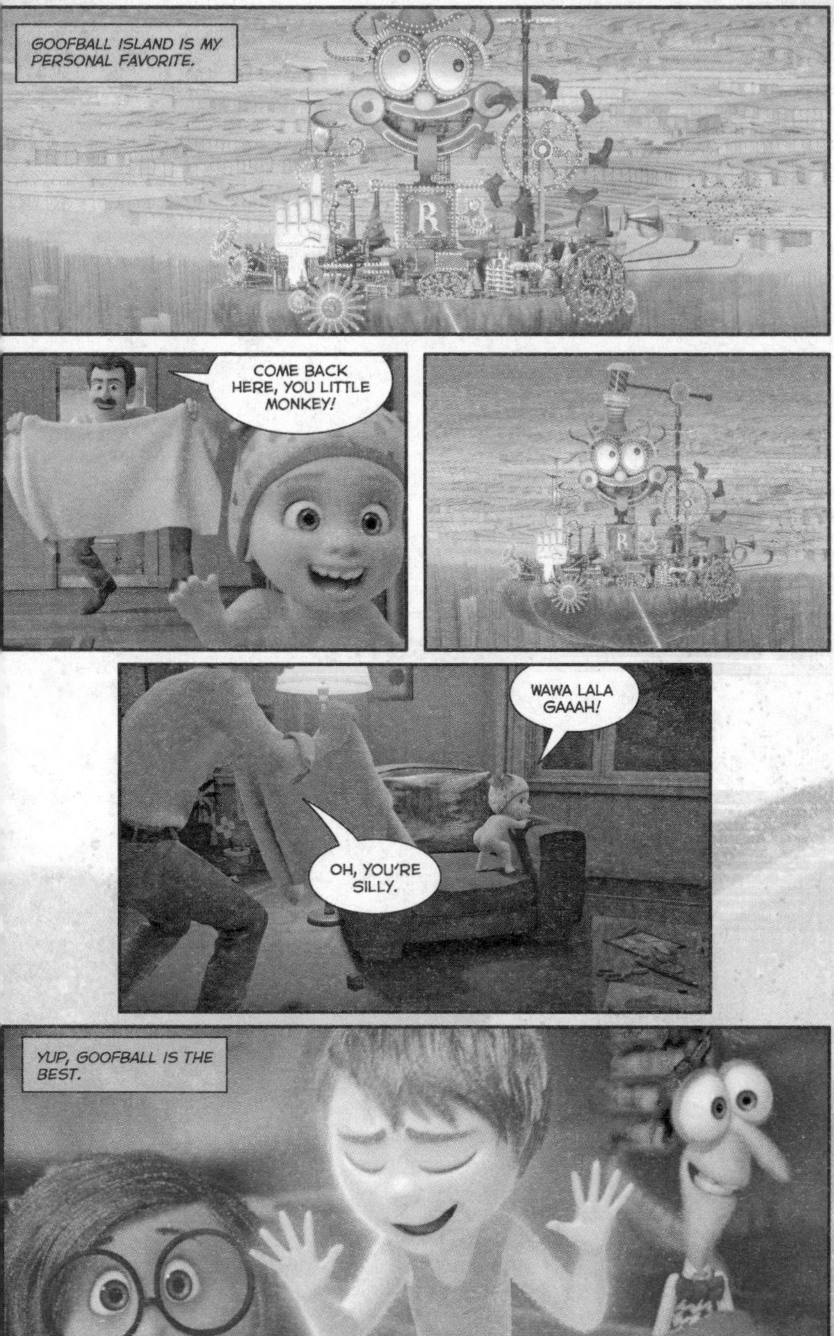
GOOFBALL ISLAND IS MY PERSONAL FAVORITE.
COME BACK HERE, YOU LITTLE MONKEY!
R
R
WAWA LALA GAAAH!
OH, YOU'RE SILLY.
YUP, GOOFBALL IS THE BEST.

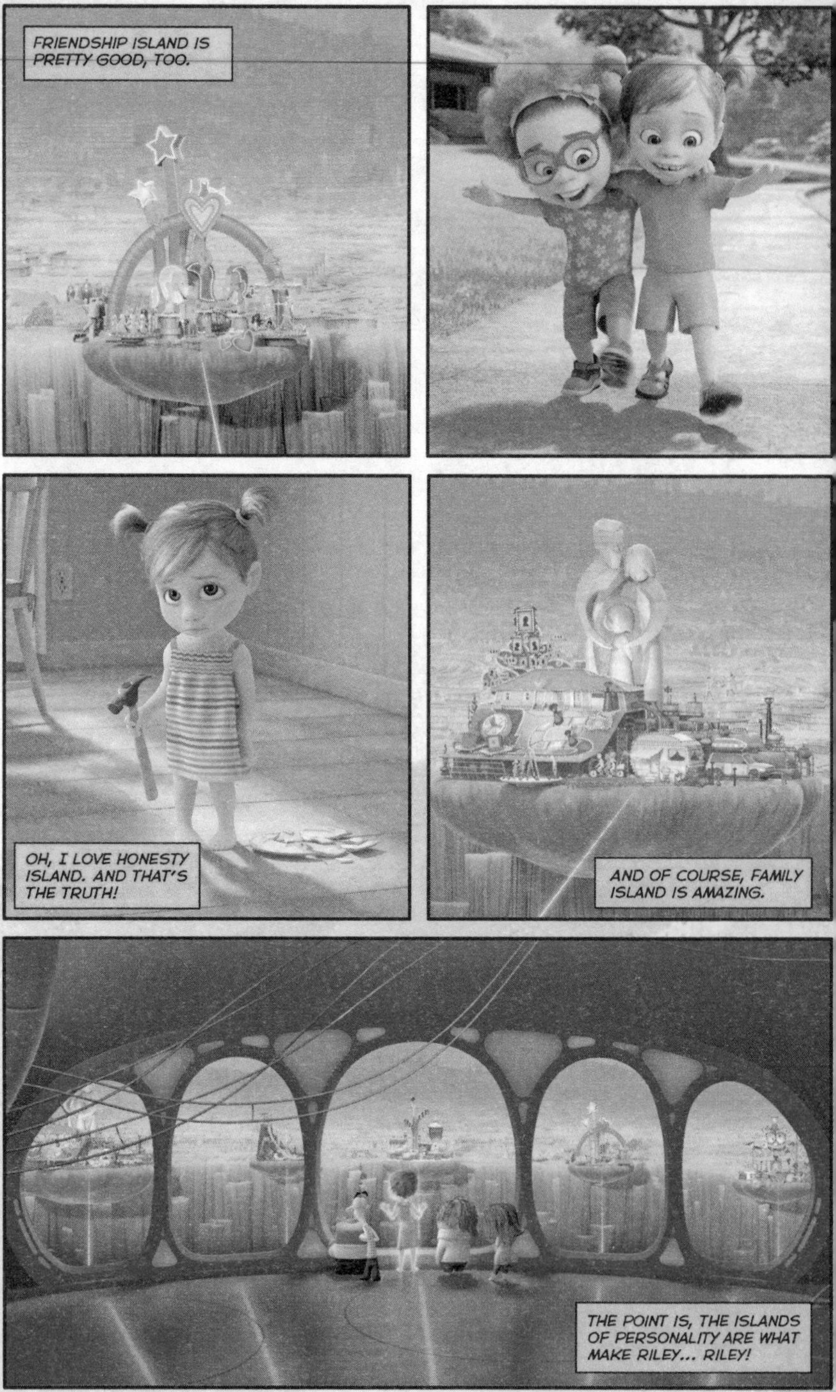
FRIENDSHIP ISLAND IS PRETTY GOOD, TOO.
OH, I LOVE HONESTY ISLAND. AND THAT'S THE TRUTH!
AND OF COURSE, FAMILY ISLAND IS AMAZING.
THE POINT IS, THE ISLANDS OF PERSONALITY ARE WHAT MAKE RILEY... RILEY!

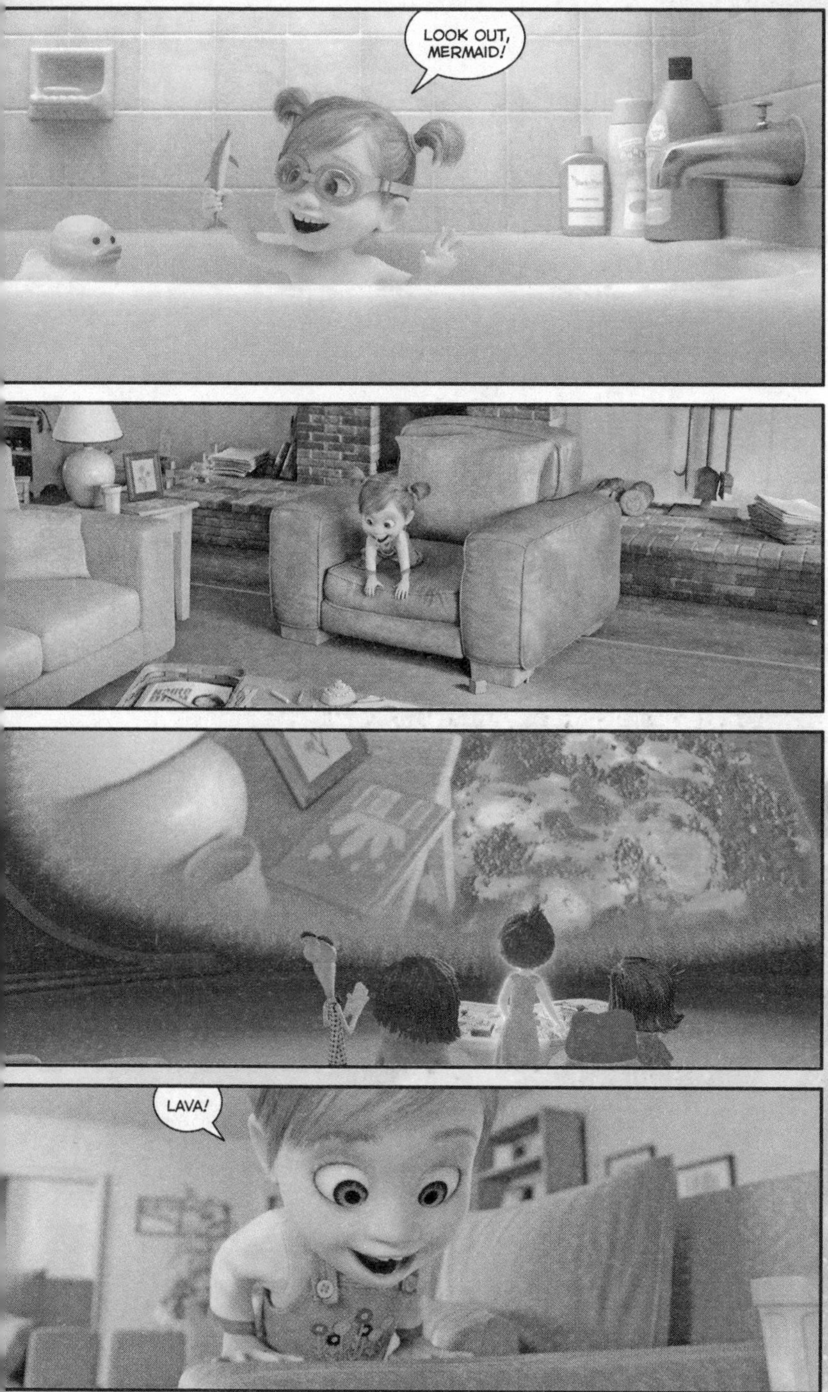
LOOK OUT, MERMAID!
LAVA!

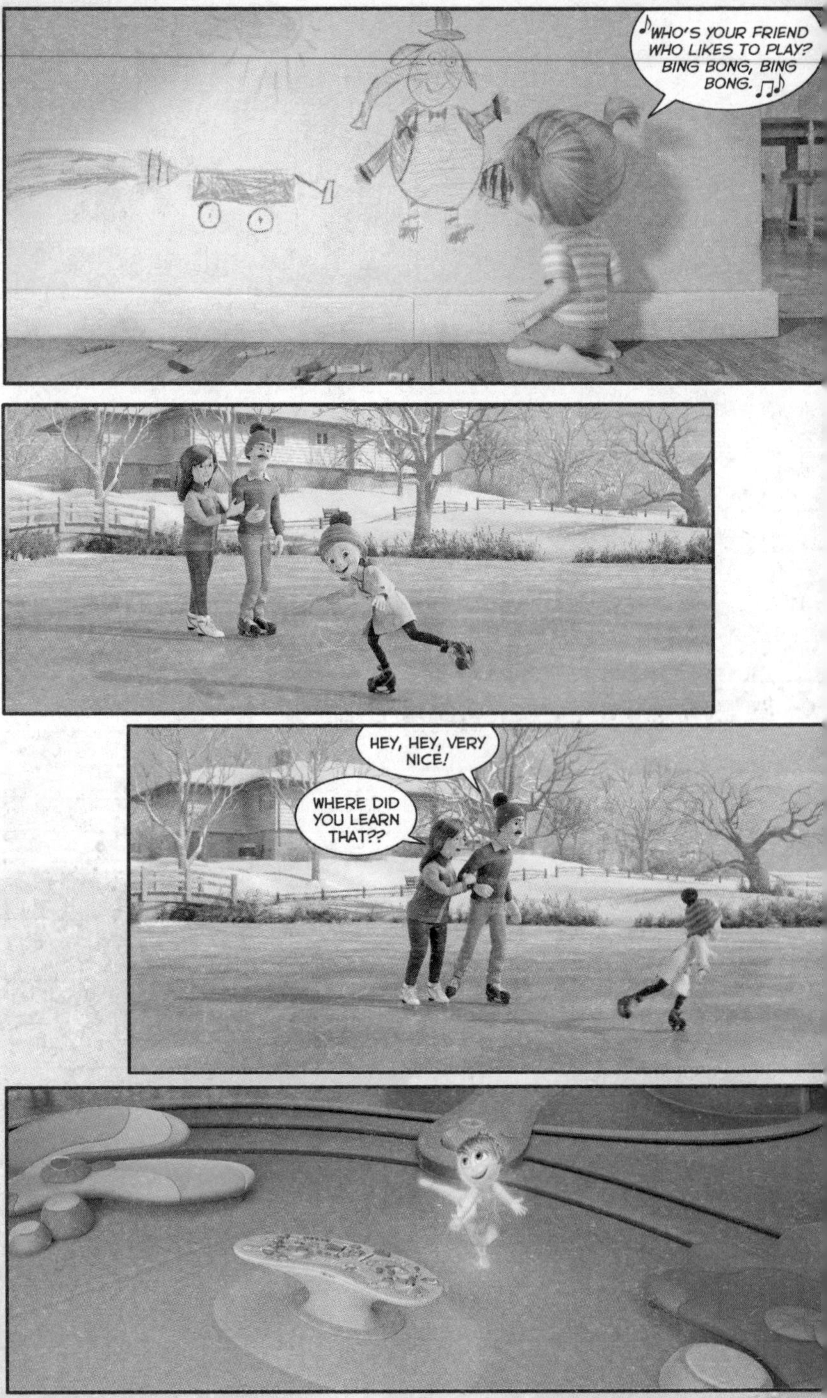
♪WHO'S YOUR FRIEND WHO LIKES TO PLAY? BING BONG, BING BONG. ♫♪
HEY, HEY, VERY NICE!
WHERE DID YOU LEARN THAT??

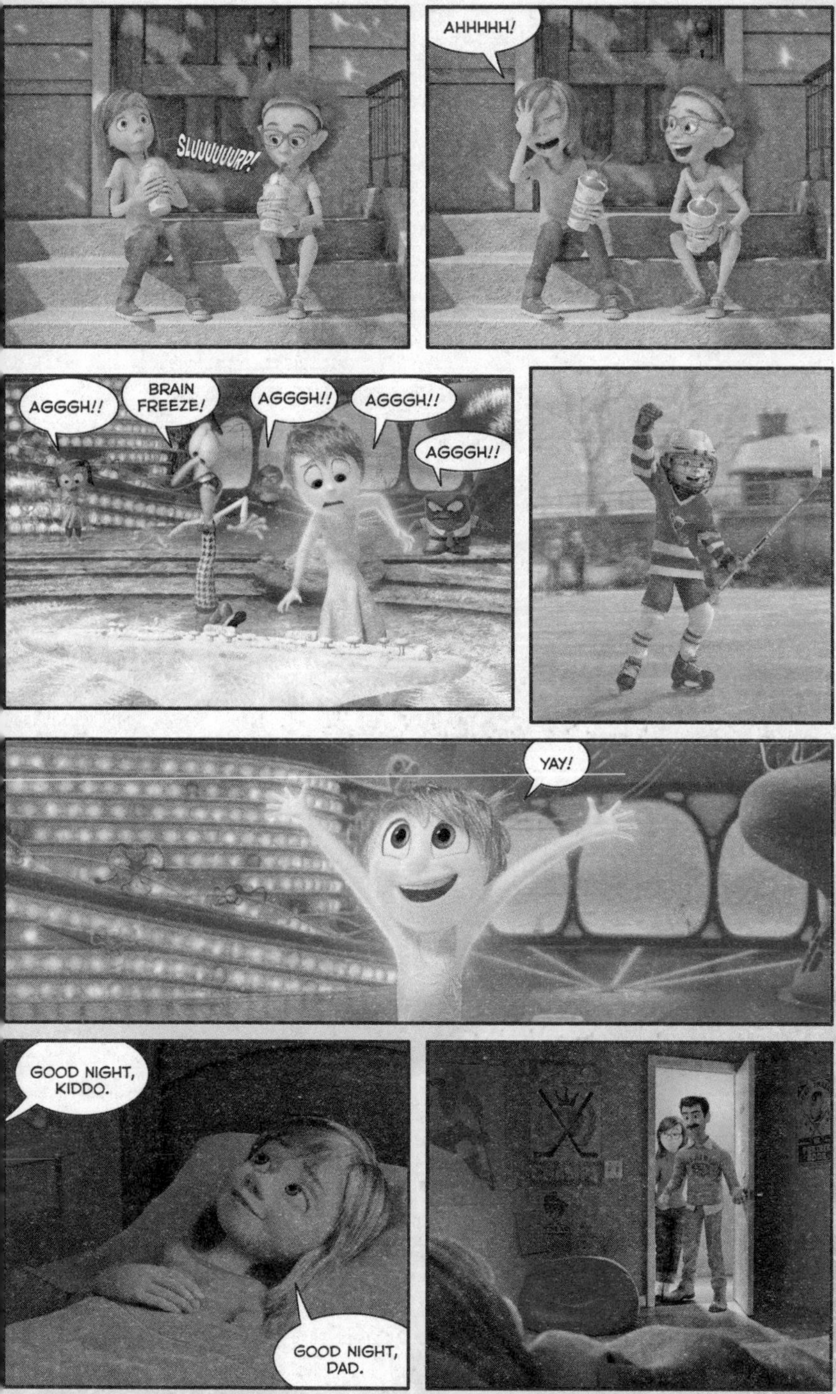
SLUUUUUURP!
AHHHHH!
AGGGH!!
BRAIN FREEZE!
AGGGH!!
AGGGH!!
AGGGH!!
YAY!
GOOD NIGHT, KIDDO.
GOOD NIGHT, DAD.

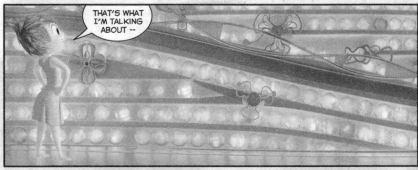

AND... WE'RE OUT!

THAT'S WHAT I'M TALKING ABOUT --

-- WOO! ANOTHER PERFECT DAY!

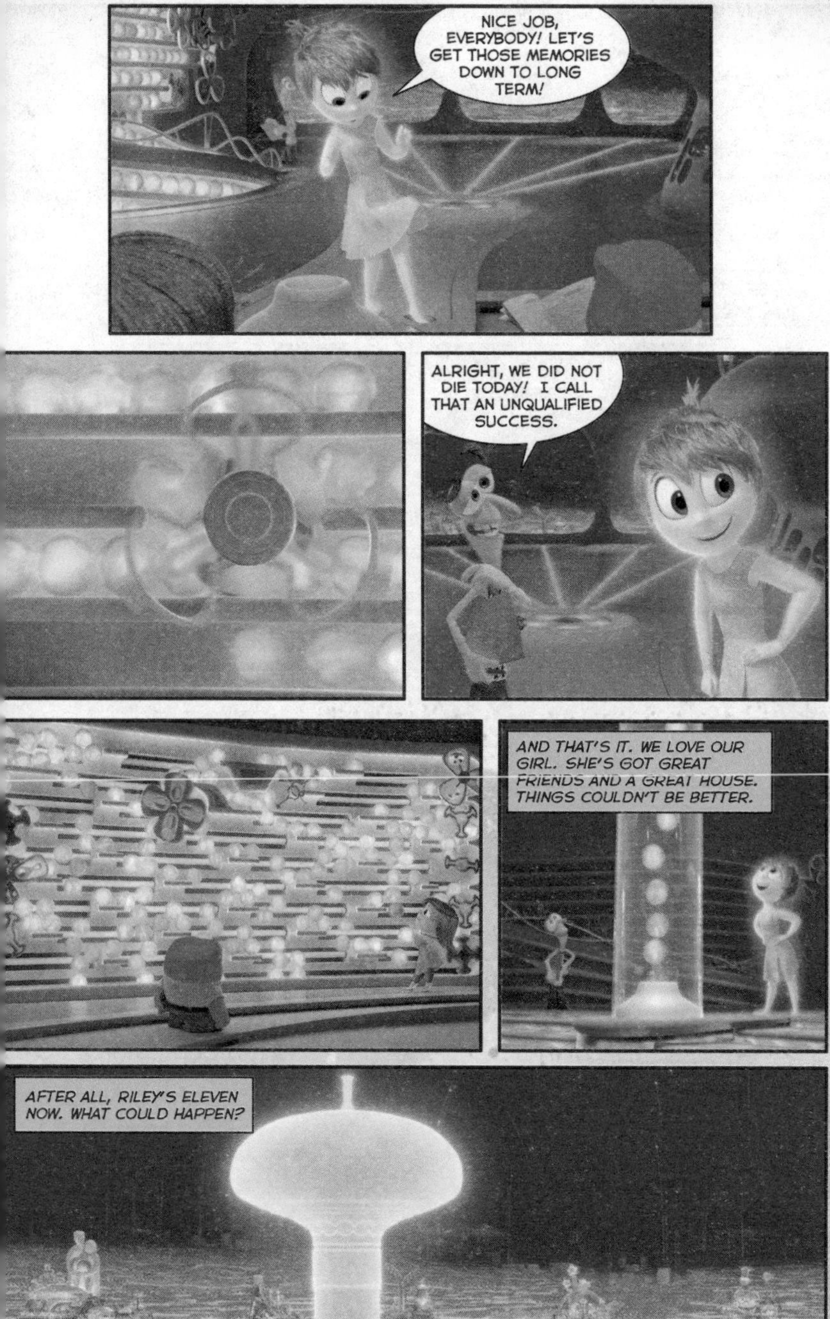

NICE JOB, EVERYBODY! LET'S GET THOSE MEMORIES DOWN TO LONG TERM!
ALRIGHT, WE DID NOT DIE TODAY! I CALL THAT AN UNQUALIFIED SUCCESS.
AND THAT'S IT. WE LOVE OUR GIRL. SHE'S GOT GREAT FRIENDS AND A GREAT HOUSE. THINGS COULDN'T BE BETTER.
AFTER ALL, RILEY'S ELEVEN NOW. WHAT COULD HAPPEN?

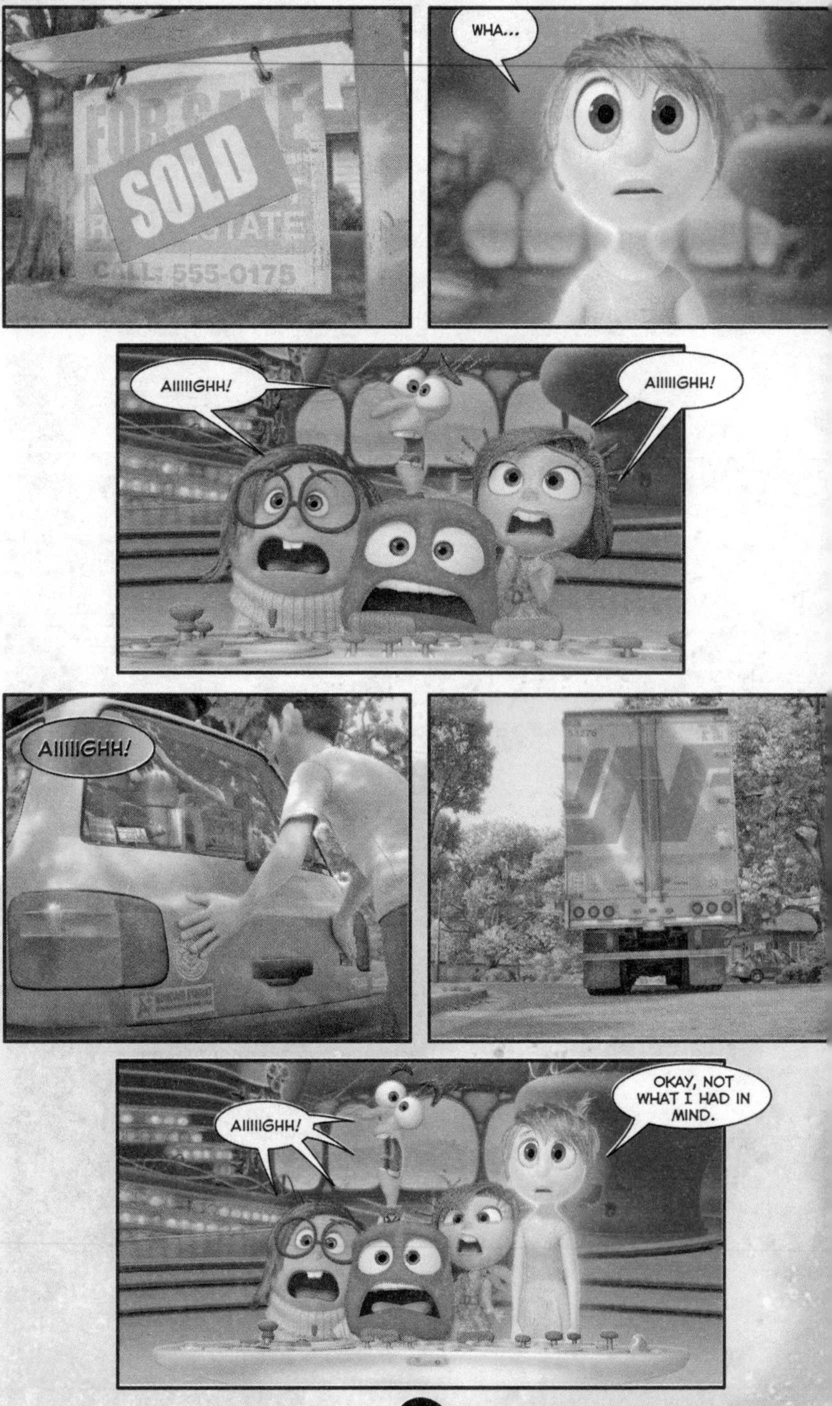
SOLD
CALL 555-0175
WHA...
AIIIIGHH!
AIIIIGHH!
AIIIIGHH!
AIIIIGHH!
OKAY, NOT WHAT I HAD IN MIND.

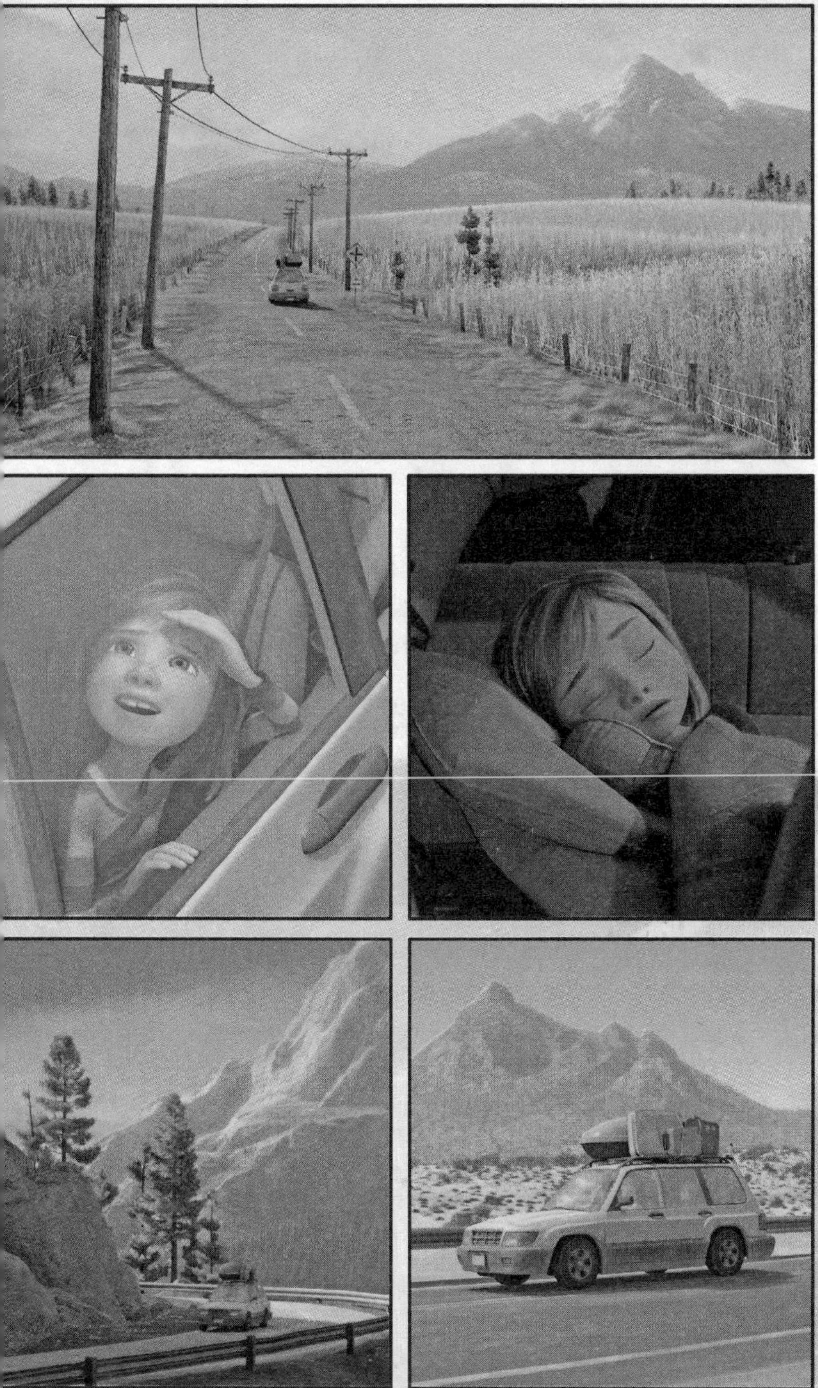

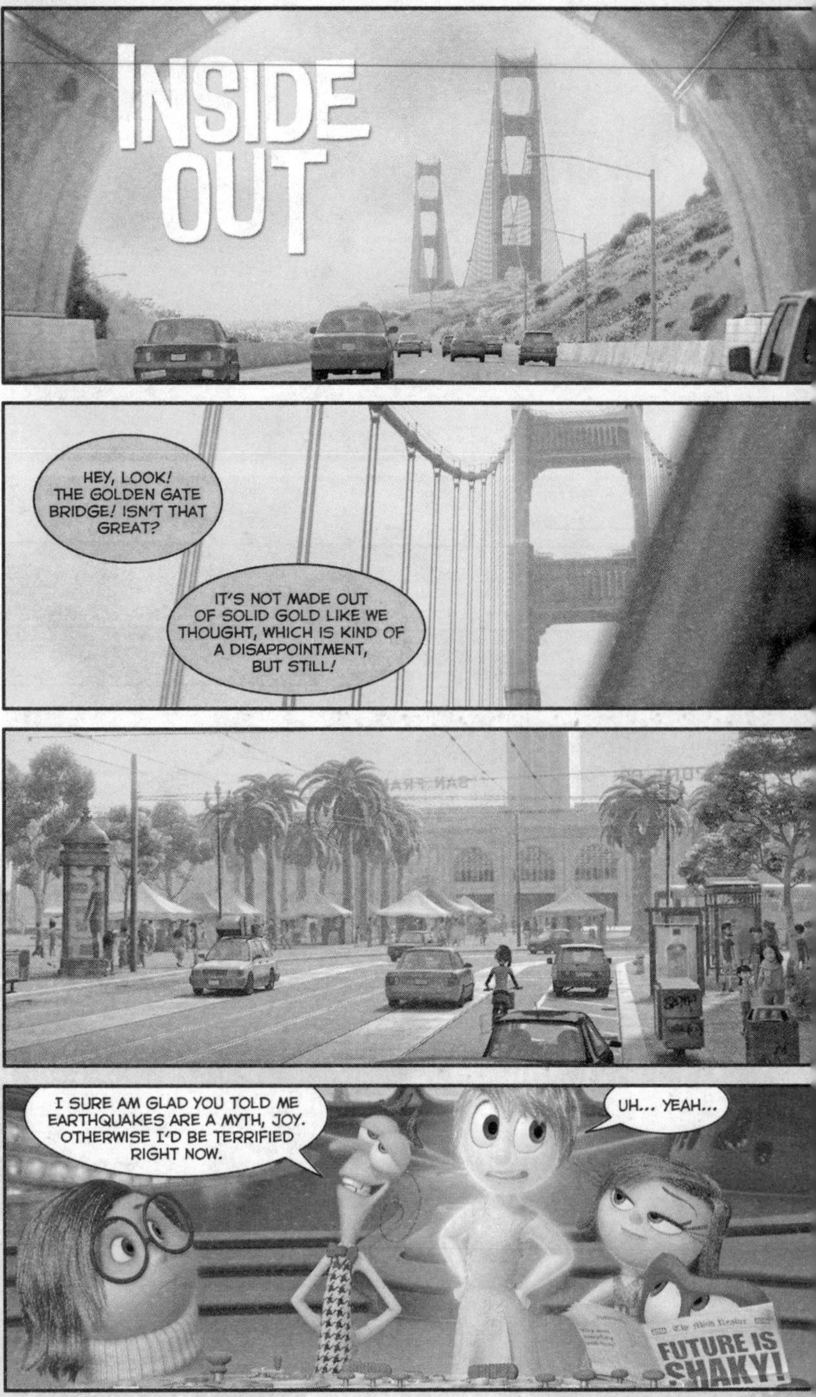
INSIDE OUT
HEY, LOOK! THE GOLDEN GATE BRIDGE! ISN'T THAT GREAT?
IT'S NOT MADE OUT OF SOLID GOLD LIKE WE THOUGHT, WHICH IS KIND OF A DISAPPOINTMENT, BUT STILL!
I SURE AM GLAD YOU TOLD ME EARTHQUAKES ARE A MYTH, JOY. OTHERWISE I'D BE TERRIFIED RIGHT NOW.
UH... YEAH...
FUTURE IS SHAKY!

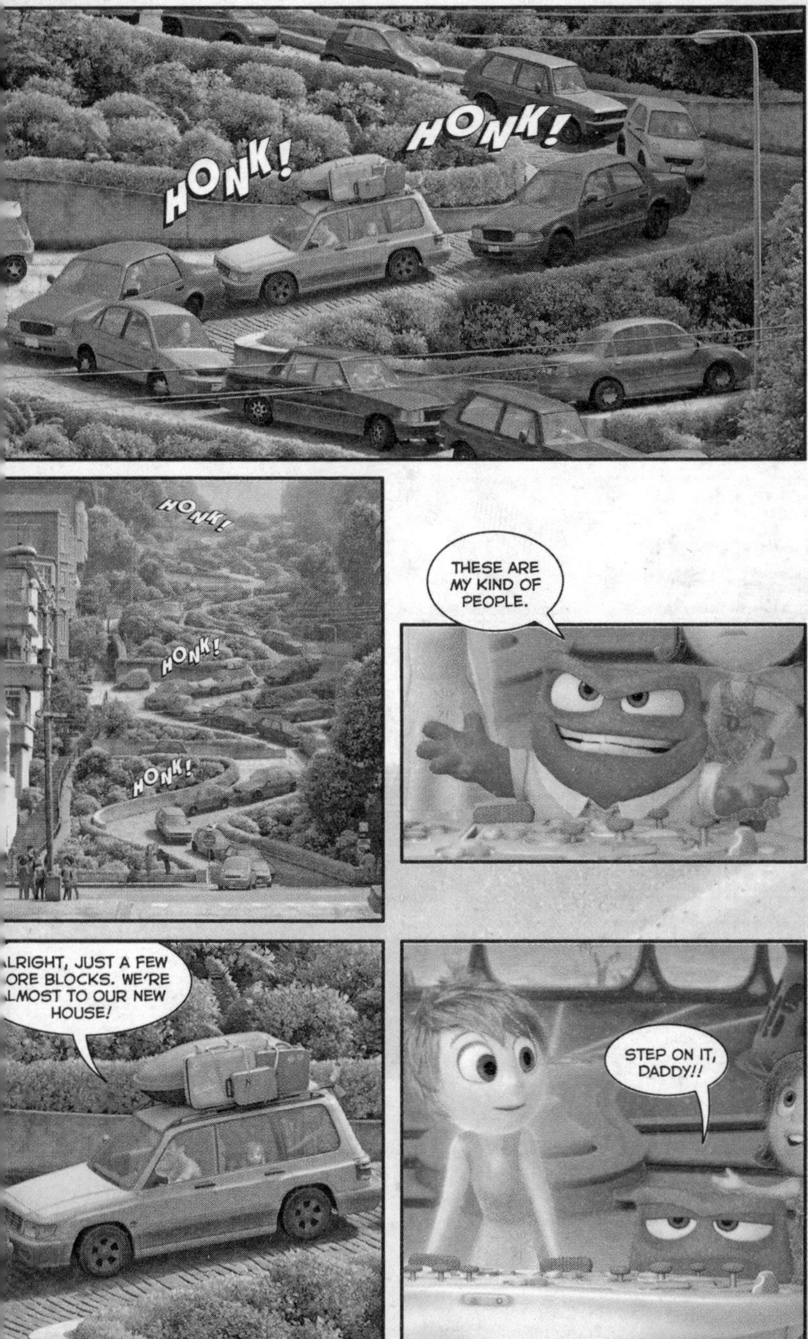
HONK!
HONK!
HONK!
HONK!
HONK!
THESE ARE MY KIND OF PEOPLE.
LRIGHT, JUST A FEW ORE BLOCKS. WE'RE LMOST TO OUR NEW HOUSE!
STEP ON IT, DADDY!!

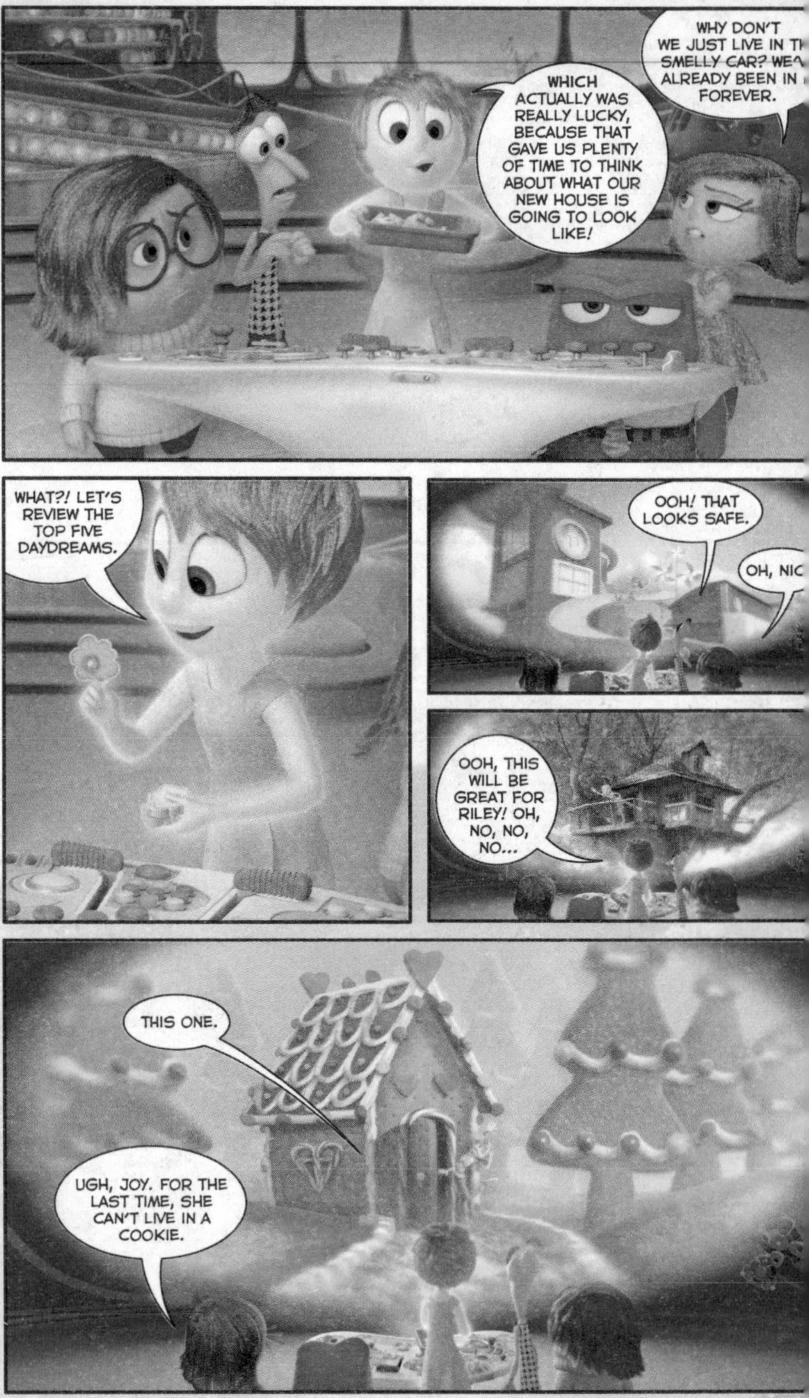
WHICH ACTUALLY WAS REALLY LUCKY, BECAUSE THAT GAVE US PLENTY OF TIME TO THINK ABOUT WHAT OUR NEW HOUSE IS GOING TO LOOK LIKE!
WHY DON'T WE JUST LIVE IN T SMELLY CAR? WE ALREADY BEEN IN FOREVER.
WHAT?! LET'S REVIEW THE TOP FIVE DAYDREAMS.
OOH! THAT LOOKS SAFE.
OH, NIC
OOH, THIS WILL BE GREAT FOR RILEY! OH, NO, NO, NO...
THIS ONE.
UGH, JOY. FOR THE LAST TIME, SHE CAN'T LIVE IN A COOKIE.

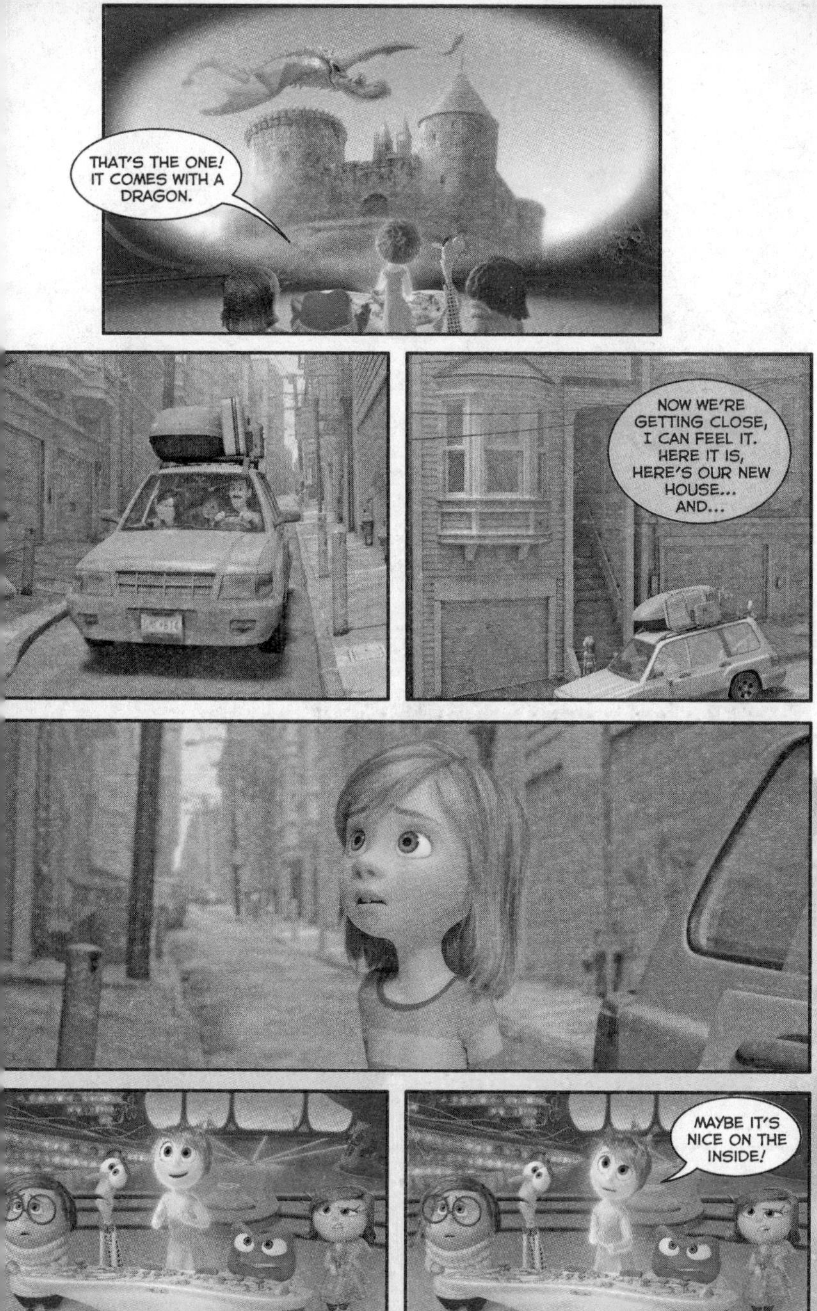
THAT'S THE ONE! IT COMES WITH A DRAGON.
NOW WE'RE GETTING CLOSE, I CAN FEEL IT. HERE IT IS, HERE'S OUR NEW HOUSE... AND...
MAYBE IT'S NICE ON THE INSIDE!

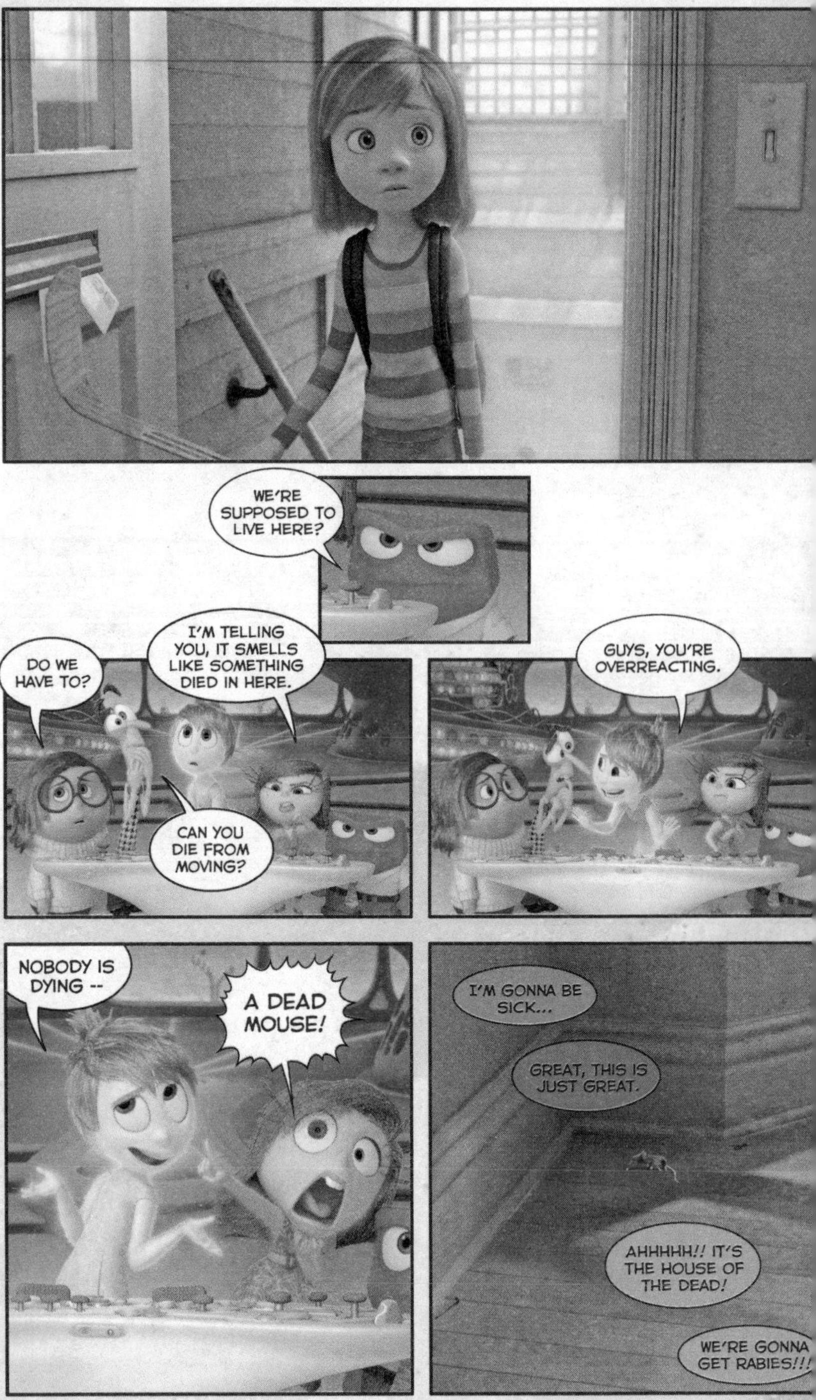

WE'RE SUPPOSED TO LIVE HERE?
DO WE HAVE TO?
I'M TELLING YOU, IT SMELLS LIKE SOMETHING DIED IN HERE.
CAN YOU DIE FROM MOVING?
GUYS, YOU'RE OVERREACTING.
NOBODY IS DYING --
A DEAD MOUSE!
I'M GONNA BE SICK...
GREAT, THIS IS JUST GREAT.
AHHHHH!! IT'S THE HOUSE OF THE DEAD!
WE'RE GONNA GET RABIES!!!

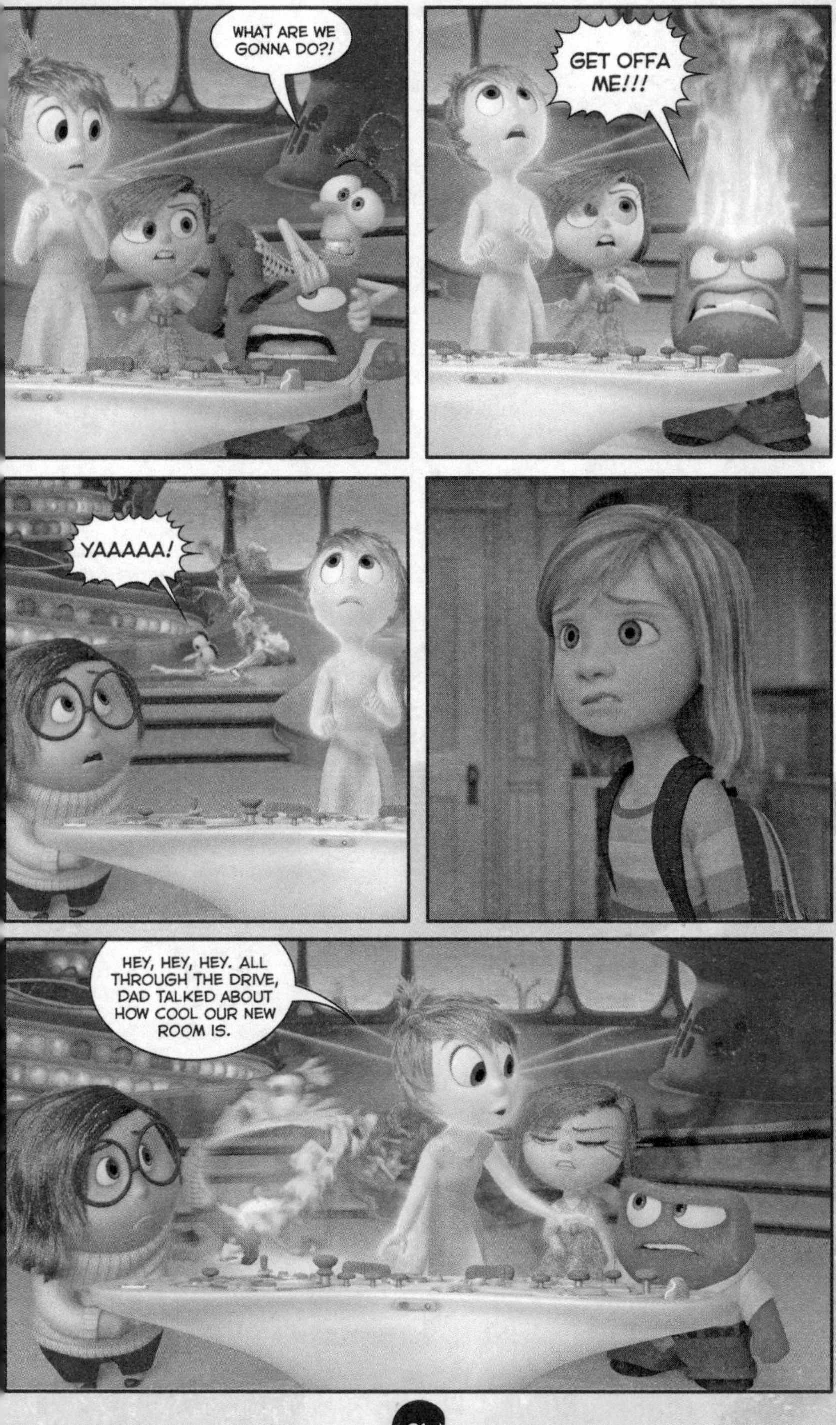
WHAT ARE WE GONNA DO?!
GET OFFA ME!!!
YAAAAA!
HEY, HEY, HEY. ALL THROUGH THE DRIVE, DAD TALKED ABOUT HOW COOL OUR NEW ROOM IS.

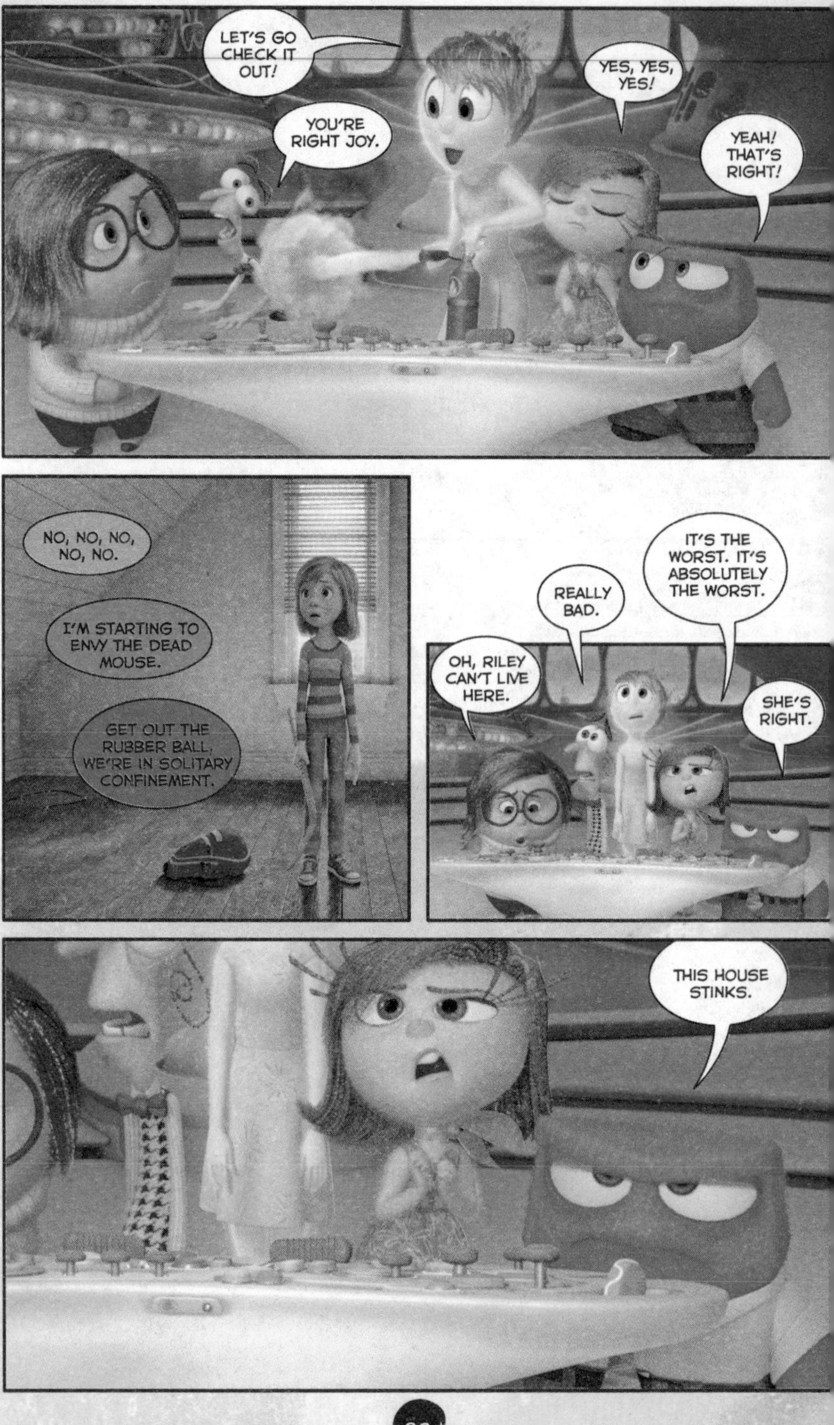
LET'S GO CHECK IT OUT!
YOU'RE RIGHT JOY.
YES, YES, YES!
YEAH! THAT'S RIGHT!
NO, NO, NO, NO, NO.
I'M STARTING TO ENVY THE DEAD MOUSE.
GET OUT THE RUBBER BALL, WE'RE IN SOLITARY CONFINEMENT.
OH, RILEY CAN'T LIVE HERE.
REALLY BAD.
IT'S THE WORST. IT'S ABSOLUTELY THE WORST.
SHE'S RIGHT.
THIS HOUSE STINKS.

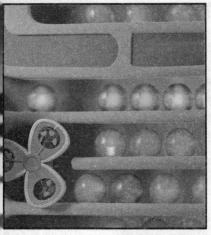

HEY, IT'S NOTHING OUR BUTTERFLY CURTAINS COULDN'T FIX.

I READ SOMEWHERE THAT AN EMPTY ROOM IS AN OPPORTUNITY!

WHERE DID YOU READ THAT?

IT DOESN'T MATTER. I READ IT AND IT'S GREAT.

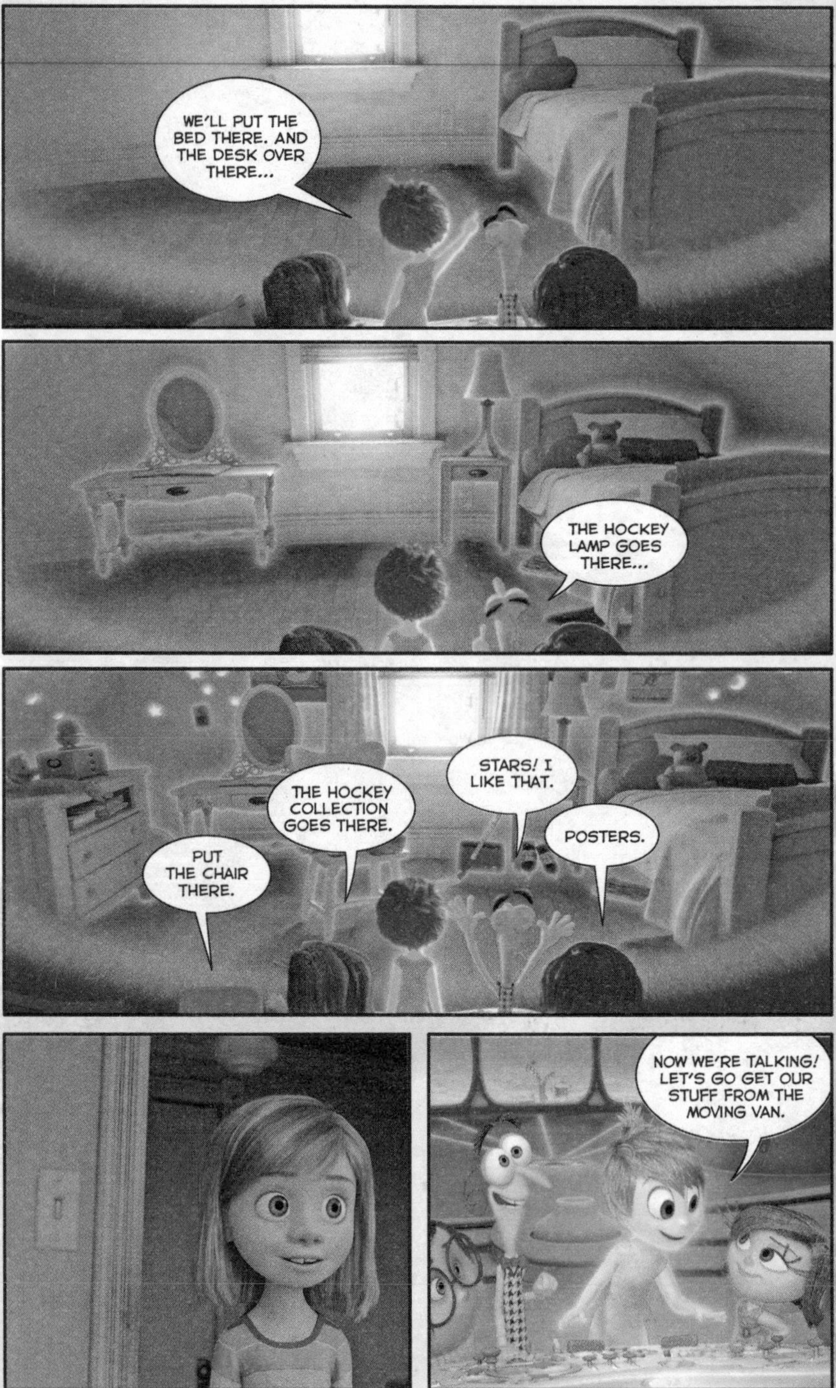
WE'LL PUT THE BED THERE. AND THE DESK OVER THERE...
THE HOCKEY LAMP GOES THERE...
PUT THE CHAIR THERE.
THE HOCKEY COLLECTION GOES THERE.
STARS! I LIKE THAT.
POSTERS.
NOW WE'RE TALKING! LET'S GO GET OUR STUFF FROM THE MOVING VAN.

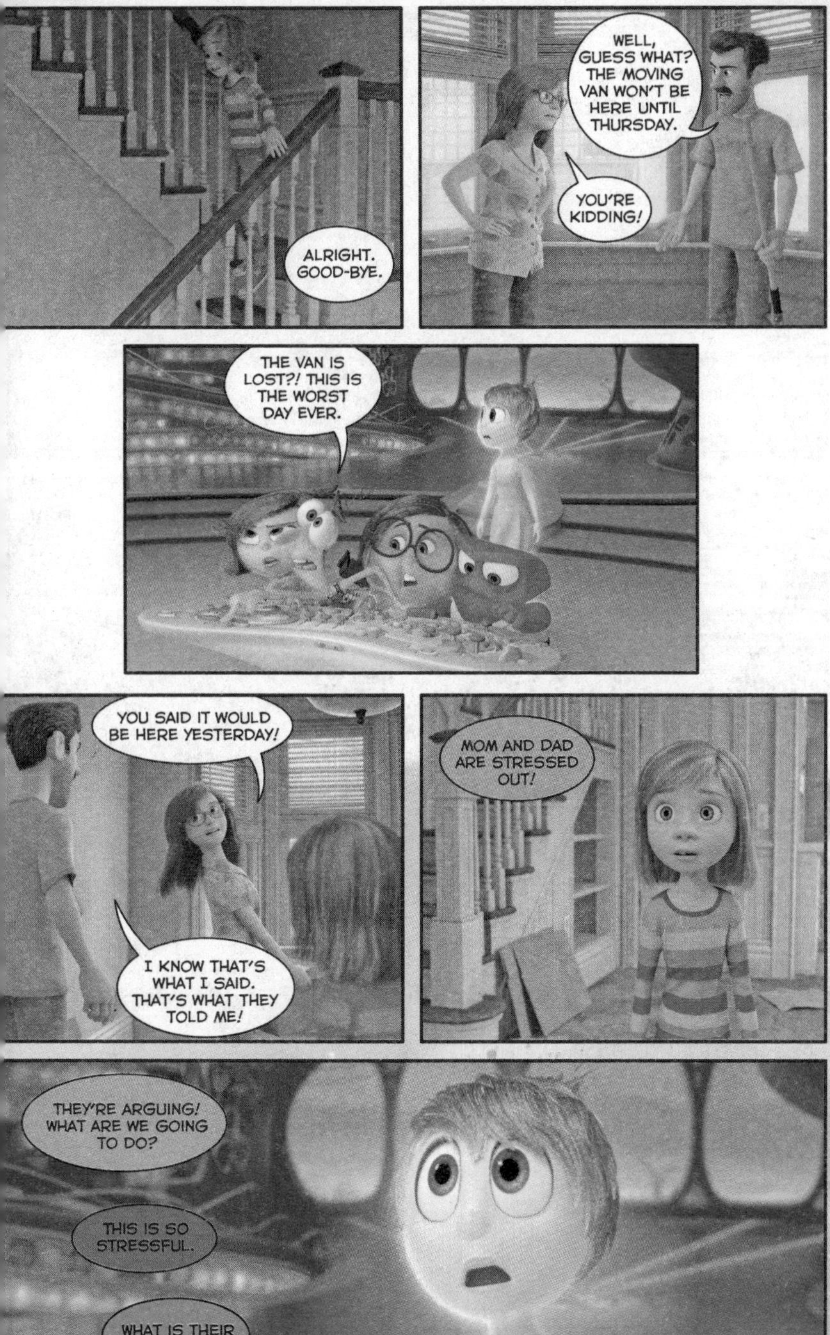
ALRIGHT. GOOD-BYE.
WELL, GUESS WHAT? THE MOVING VAN WON'T BE HERE UNTIL THURSDAY.
YOU'RE KIDDING!
THE VAN IS LOST?! THIS IS THE WORST DAY EVER.
YOU SAID IT WOULD BE HERE YESTERDAY!
I KNOW THAT'S WHAT I SAID. THAT'S WHAT THEY TOLD ME!
MOM AND DAD ARE STRESSED OUT!
THEY'RE ARGUING! WHAT ARE WE GOING TO DO?
THIS IS SO STRESSFUL.
WHAT IS THEIR PROBLEM?

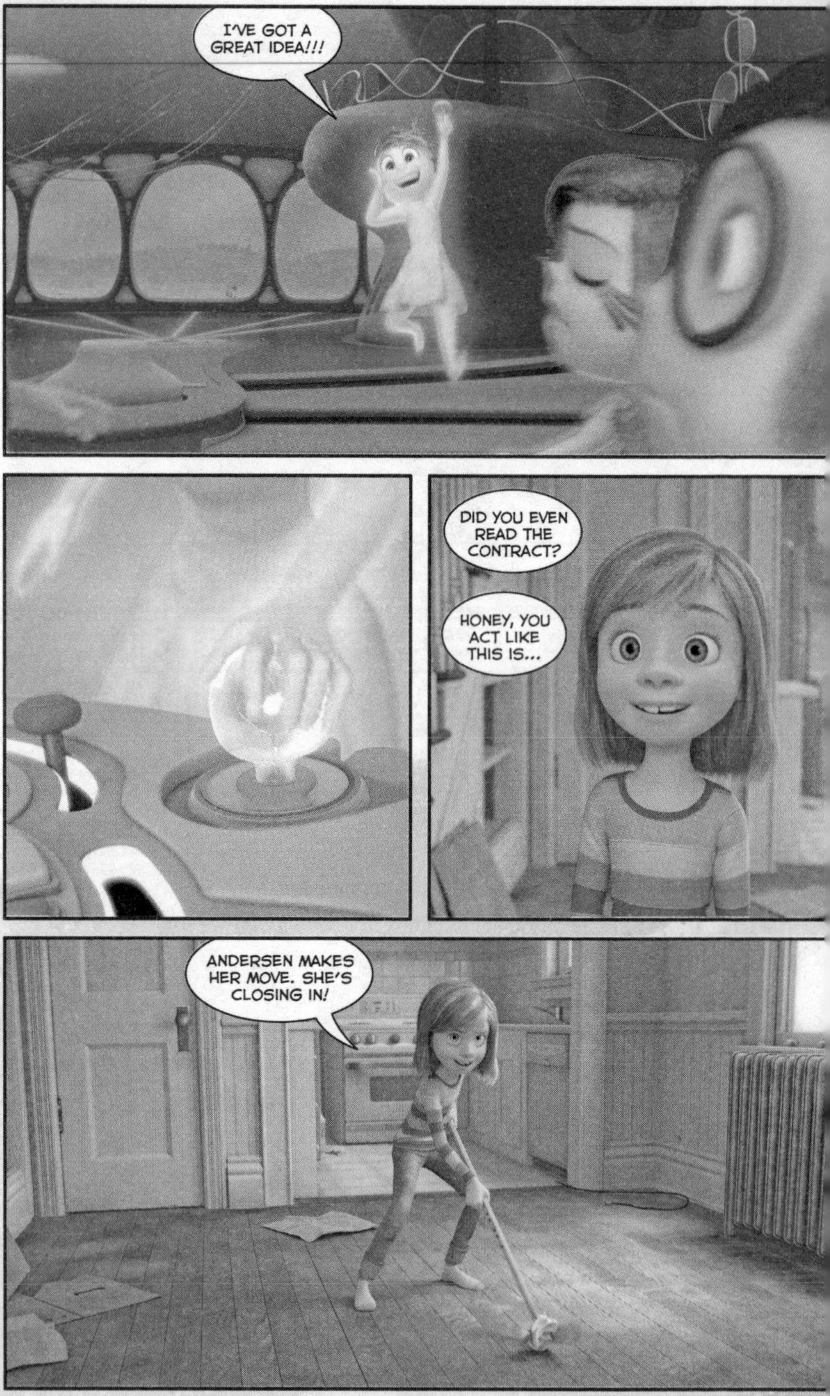
I'VE GOT A GREAT IDEA!!!
DID YOU EVEN READ THE CONTRACT?
HONEY, YOU ACT LIKE THIS IS...
ANDERSEN MAKES HER MOVE. SHE'S CLOSING IN!

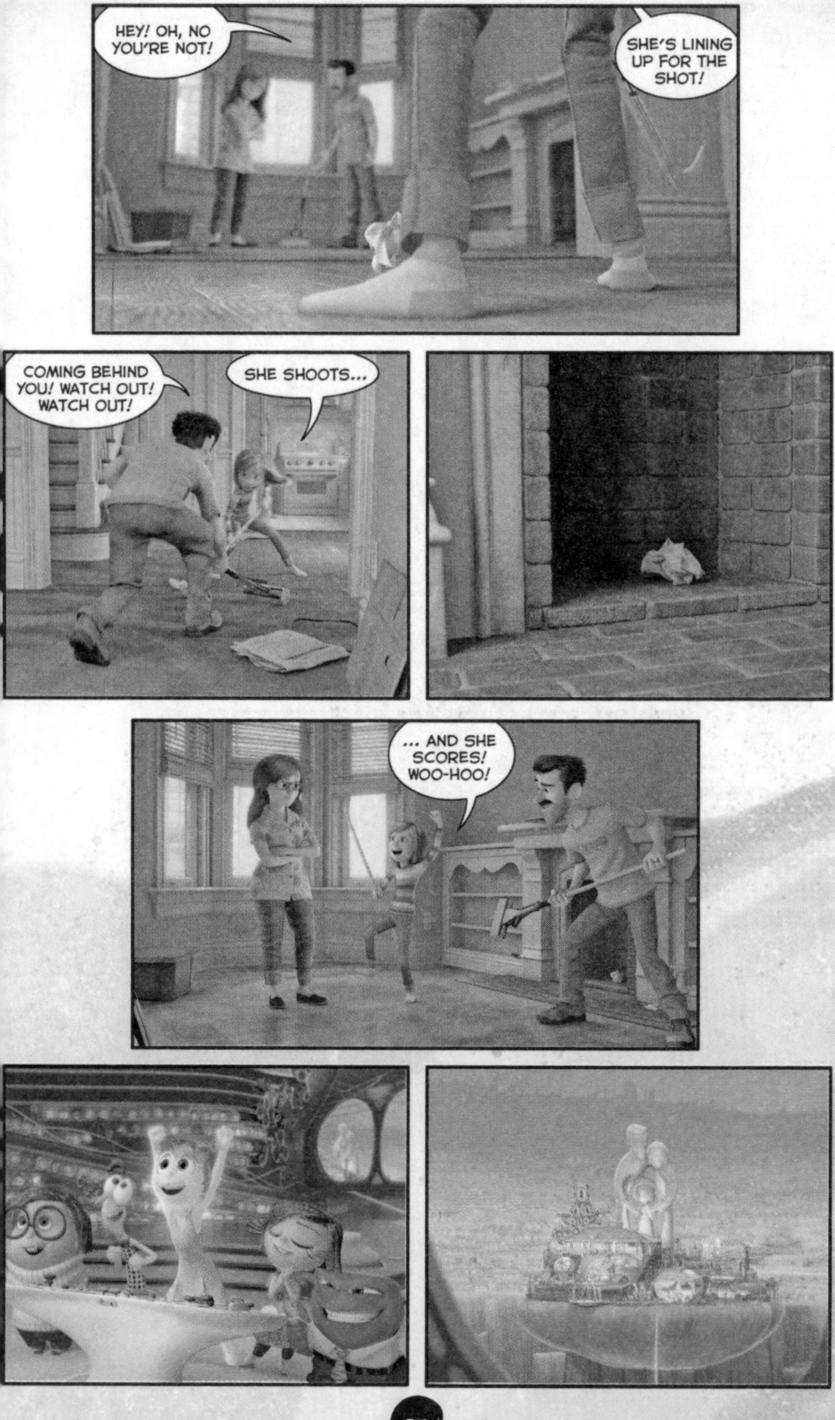
HEY! OH, NO YOU'RE NOT!
SHE'S LINING UP FOR THE SHOT!
COMING BEHIND YOU! WATCH OUT! WATCH OUT!
SHE SHOOTS...
... AND SHE SCORES! WOO-HOO!

COME ON, GRANDMA!

HA! "GRANDMA?"

UH-OH, SHE PUT HER HAIR UP, WE'RE IN FOR IT!

WOO! HEY, PUT ME DOWN!

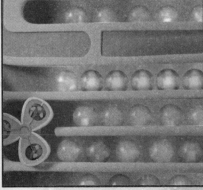

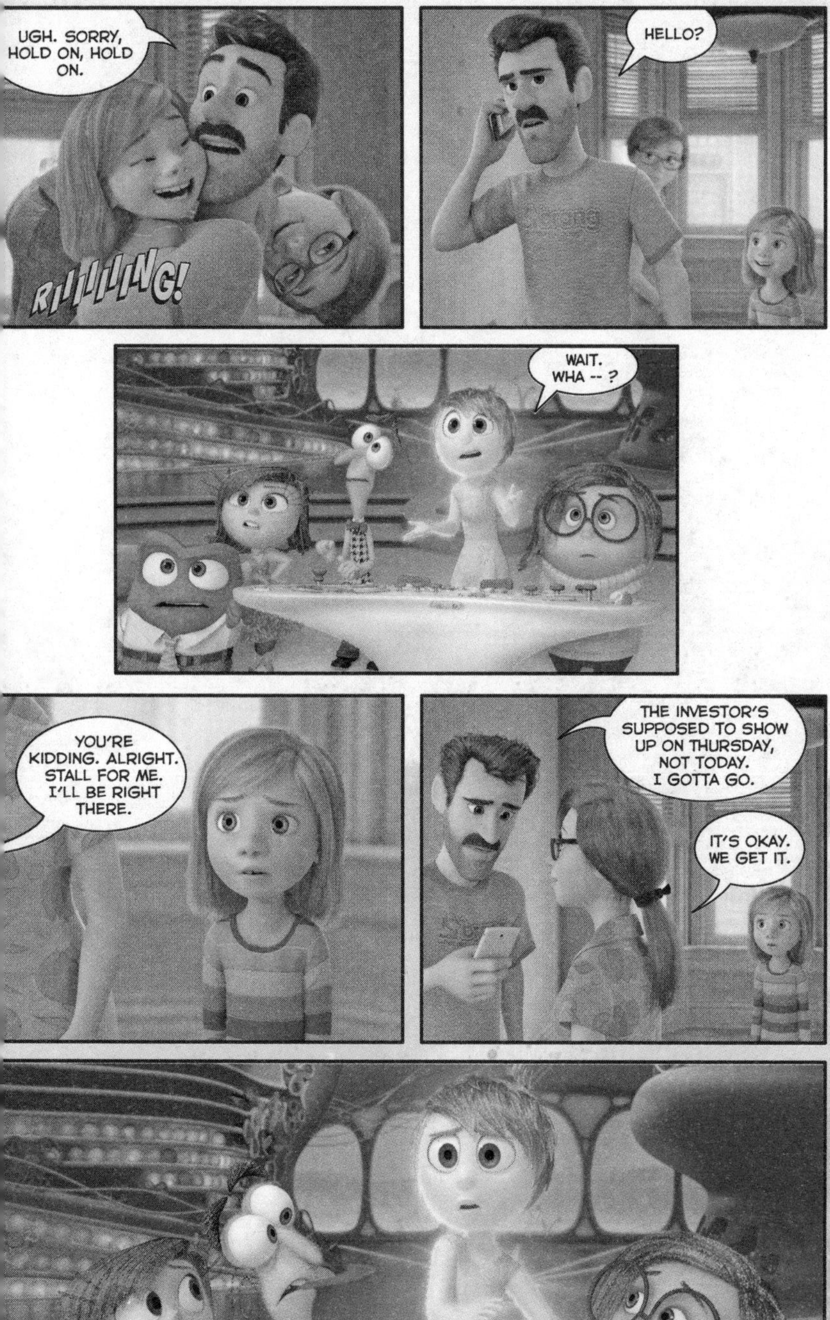
UGH. SORRY, HOLD ON, HOLD ON.
RIIIIIIING!
HELLO?
WAIT. WHA -- ?
YOU'RE KIDDING. ALRIGHT. STALL FOR ME. I'LL BE RIGHT THERE.
THE INVESTOR'S SUPPOSED TO SHOW UP ON THURSDAY, NOT TODAY. I GOTTA GO.
IT'S OKAY. WE GET IT.

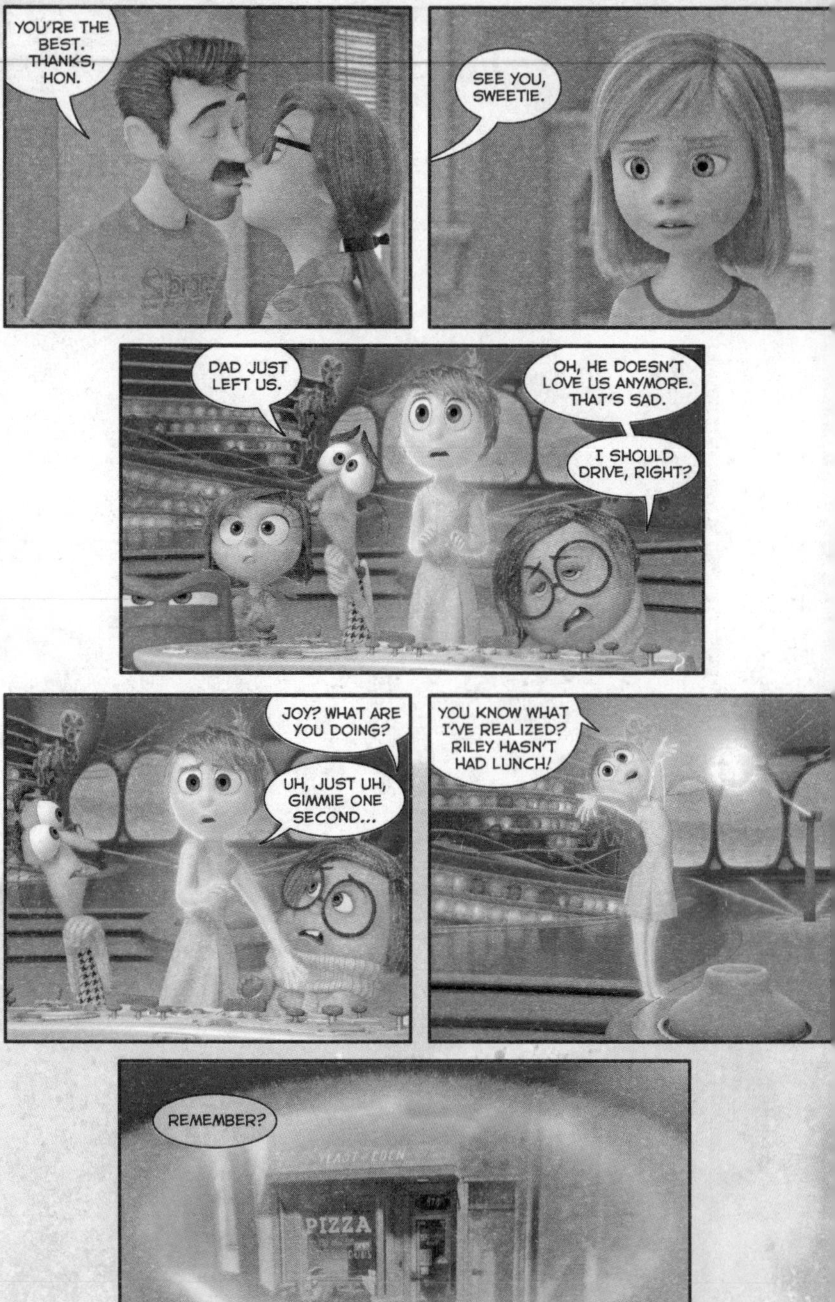

YOU'RE THE BEST. THANKS, HON.
SEE YOU, SWEETIE.
DAD JUST LEFT US.
OH, HE DOESN'T LOVE US ANYMORE. THAT'S SAD.
I SHOULD DRIVE, RIGHT?
JOY? WHAT ARE YOU DOING?
UH, JUST UH, GIMMIE ONE SECOND...
YOU KNOW WHAT I'VE REALIZED? RILEY HASN'T HAD LUNCH!
REMEMBER?
PIZZA

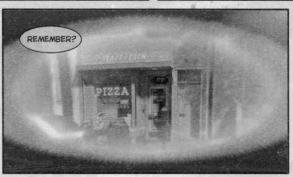

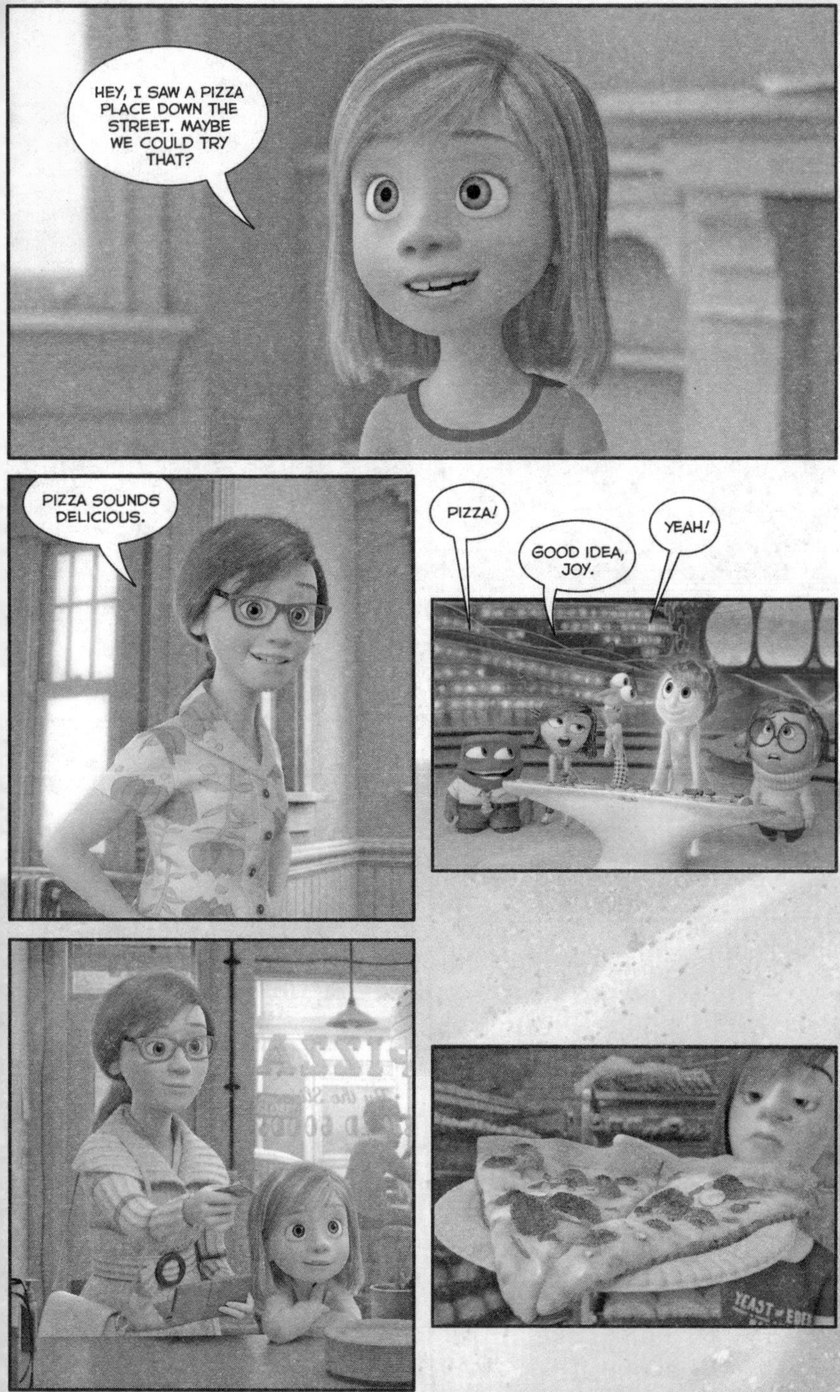
HEY, I SAW A PIZZA PLACE DOWN THE STREET. MAYBE WE COULD TRY THAT?
PIZZA SOUNDS DELICIOUS.
PIZZA!
GOOD IDEA, JOY.
YEAH!

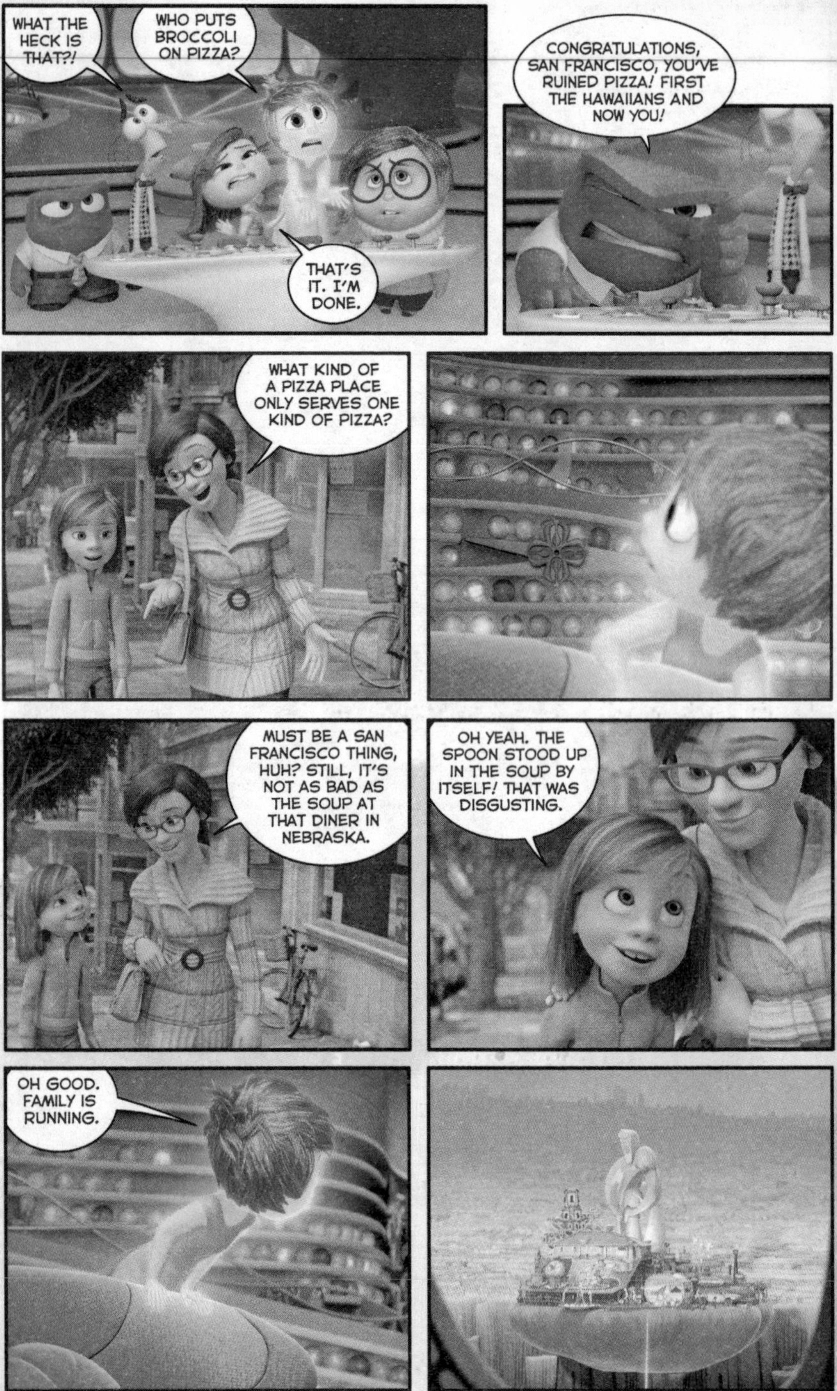
WHAT THE HECK IS THAT?!
WHO PUTS BROCCOLI ON PIZZA?
THAT'S IT. I'M DONE.
CONGRATULATIONS, SAN FRANCISCO, YOU'VE RUINED PIZZA! FIRST THE HAWAIIANS AND NOW YOU!
WHAT KIND OF A PIZZA PLACE ONLY SERVES ONE KIND OF PIZZA?
MUST BE A SAN FRANCISCO THING, HUH? STILL, IT'S NOT AS BAD AS THE SOUP AT THAT DINER IN NEBRASKA.
OH YEAH. THE SPOON STOOD UP IN THE SOUP BY ITSELF! THAT WAS DISGUSTING.
OH GOOD. FAMILY IS RUNNING.

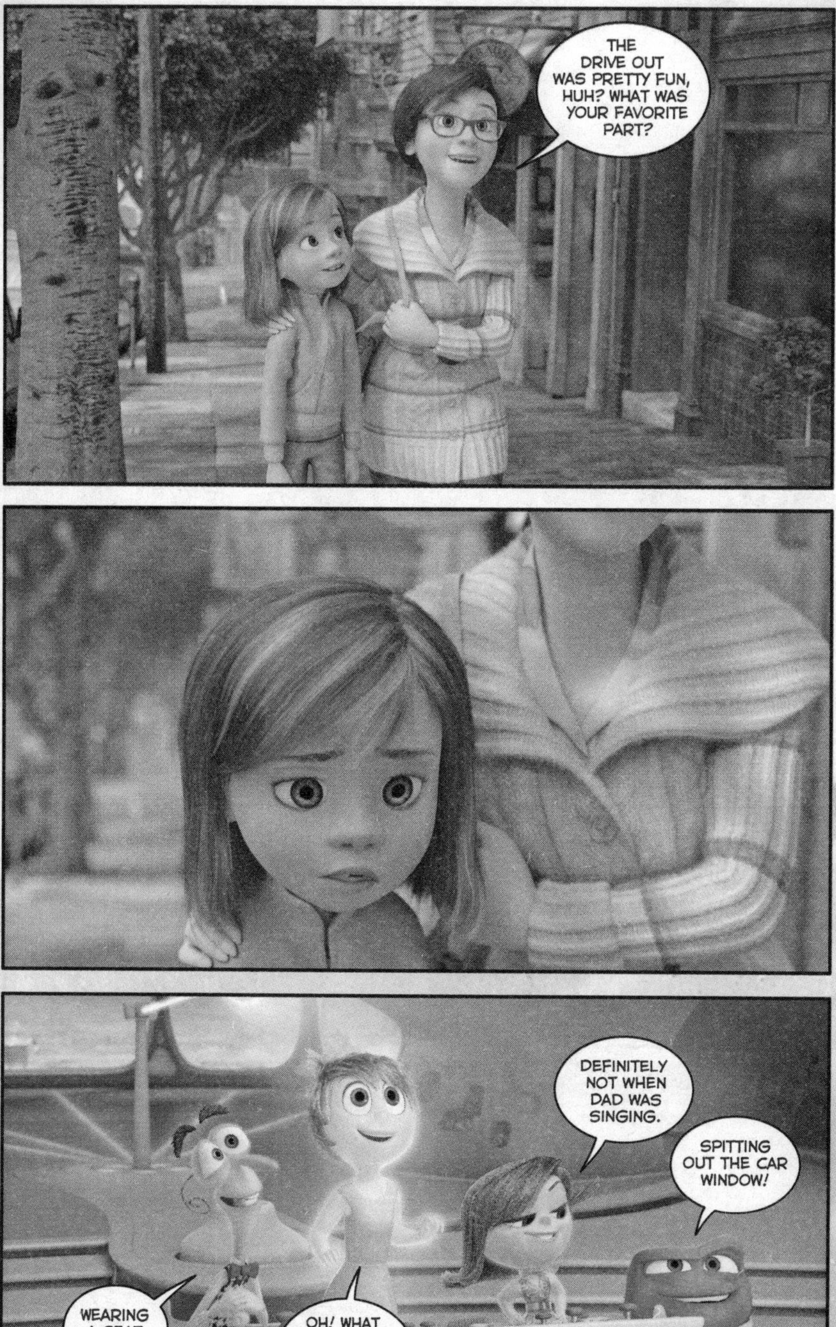
THE DRIVE OUT WAS PRETTY FUN, HUH? WHAT WAS YOUR FAVORITE PART?
DEFINITELY NOT WHEN DAD WAS SINGING.
SPITTING OUT THE CAR WINDOW!
WEARING A SEAT BELT!
OH! WHAT ABOUT THE TIME WITH THE DINOSAUR?

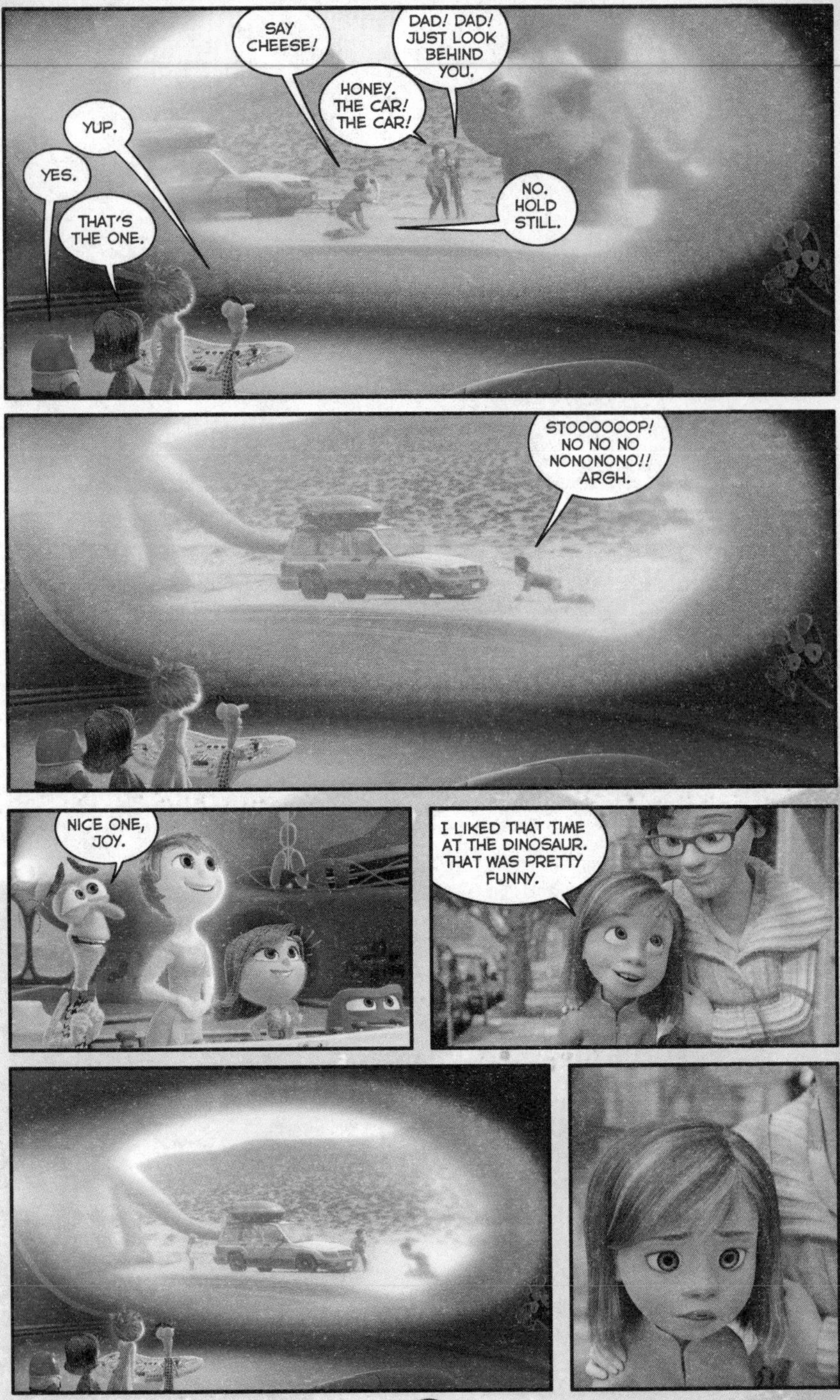

YES.
YUP.
THAT'S THE ONE.
SAY CHEESE!
HONEY. THE CAR! THE CAR!
DAD! DAD! JUST LOOK BEHIND YOU.
NO. HOLD STILL.
STOOOOOOP! NO NO NO NONONONO!! ARGH.
NICE ONE, JOY.
I LIKED THAT TIME AT THE DINOSAUR. THAT WAS PRETTY FUNNY.

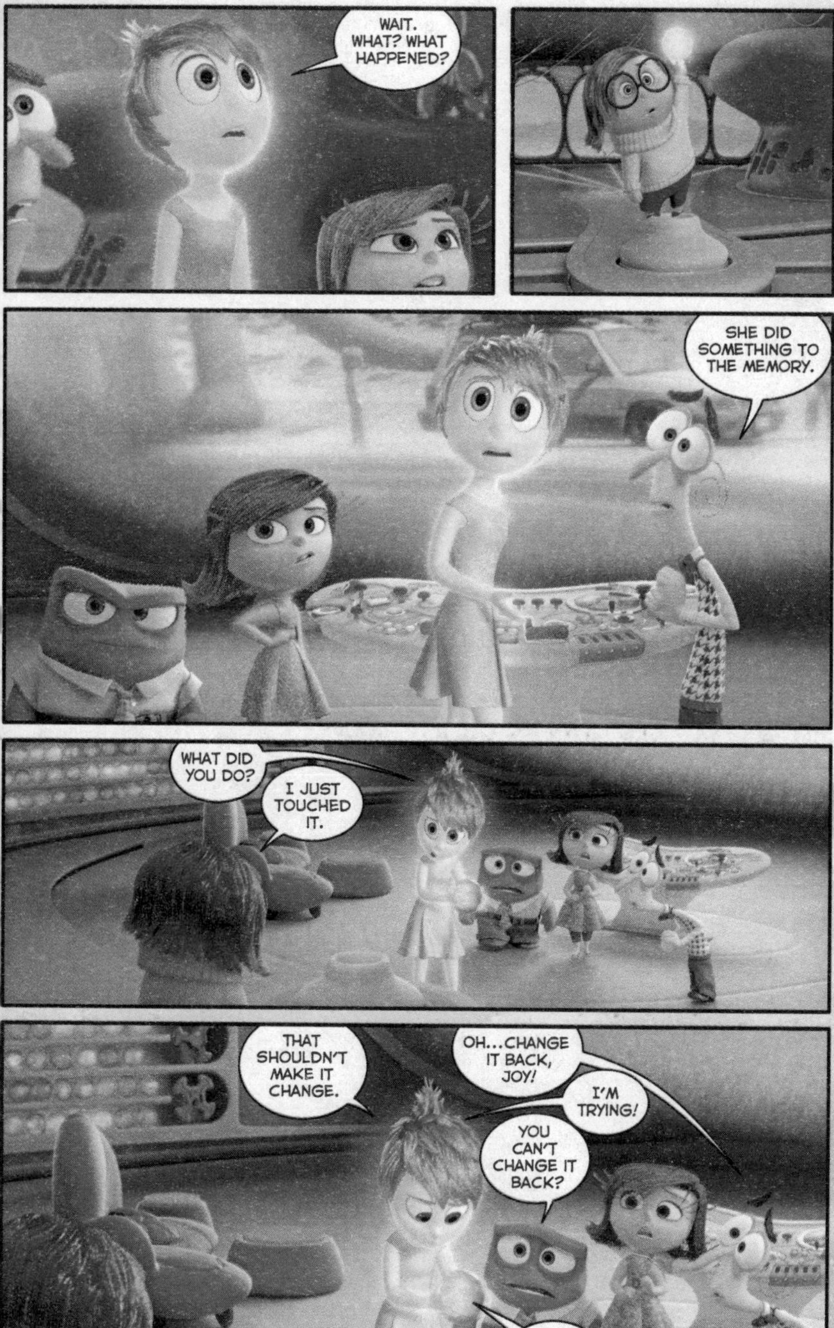
WAIT. WHAT? WHAT HAPPENED?
SHE DID SOMETHING TO THE MEMORY.
WHAT DID YOU DO?
I JUST TOUCHED IT.
THAT SHOULDN'T MAKE IT CHANGE.
OH...CHANGE IT BACK, JOY!
I'M TRYING!
YOU CAN'T CHANGE IT BACK?
NO, I GUESS I CAN'T.

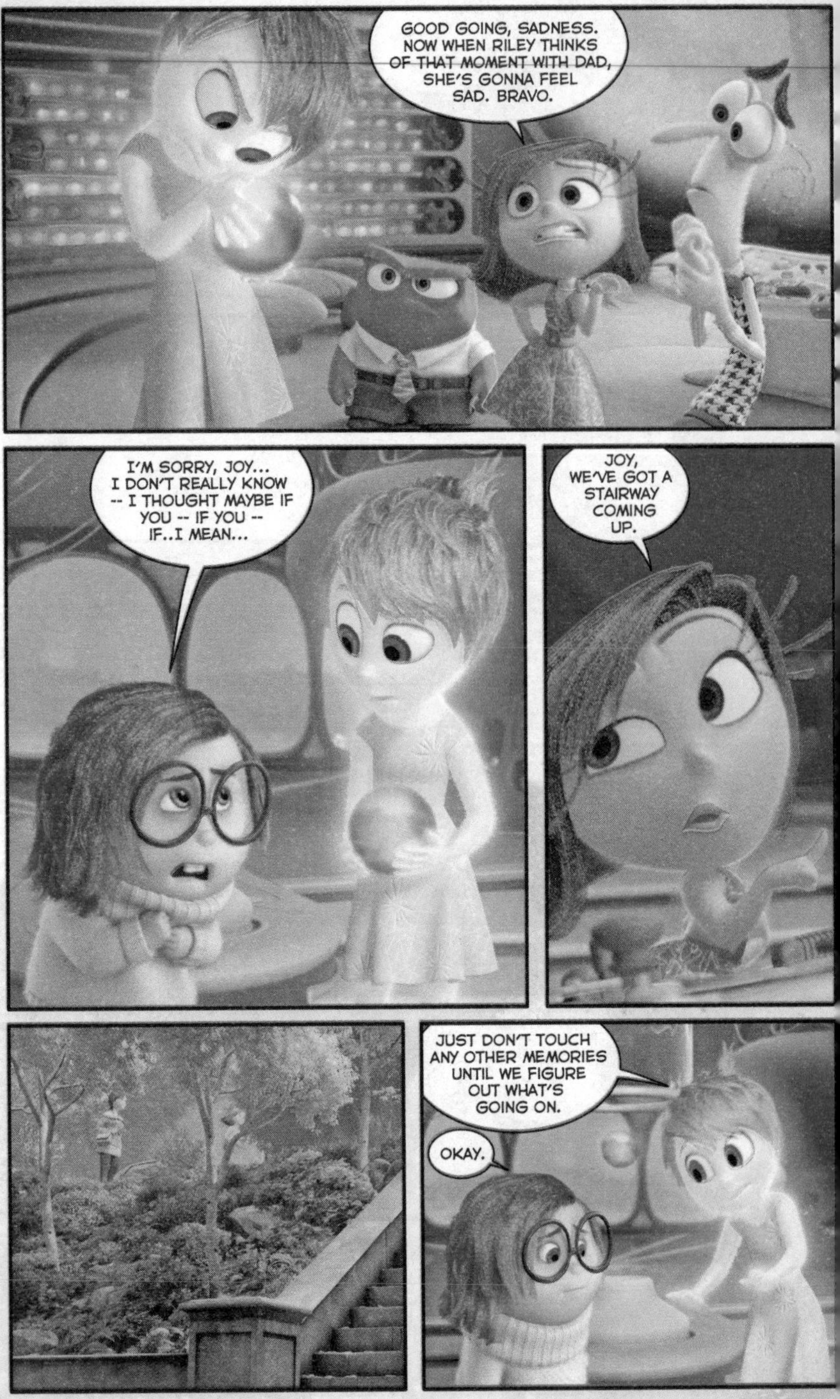
GOOD GOING, SADNESS. NOW WHEN RILEY THINKS OF THAT MOMENT WITH DAD, SHE'S GONNA FEEL SAD. BRAVO.
I'M SORRY, JOY... I DON'T REALLY KNOW -- I THOUGHT MAYBE IF YOU -- IF YOU -- IF..I MEAN...
JOY, WE'VE GOT A STAIRWAY COMING UP.
JUST DON'T TOUCH ANY OTHER MEMORIES UNTIL WE FIGURE OUT WHAT'S GOING ON.
OKAY.

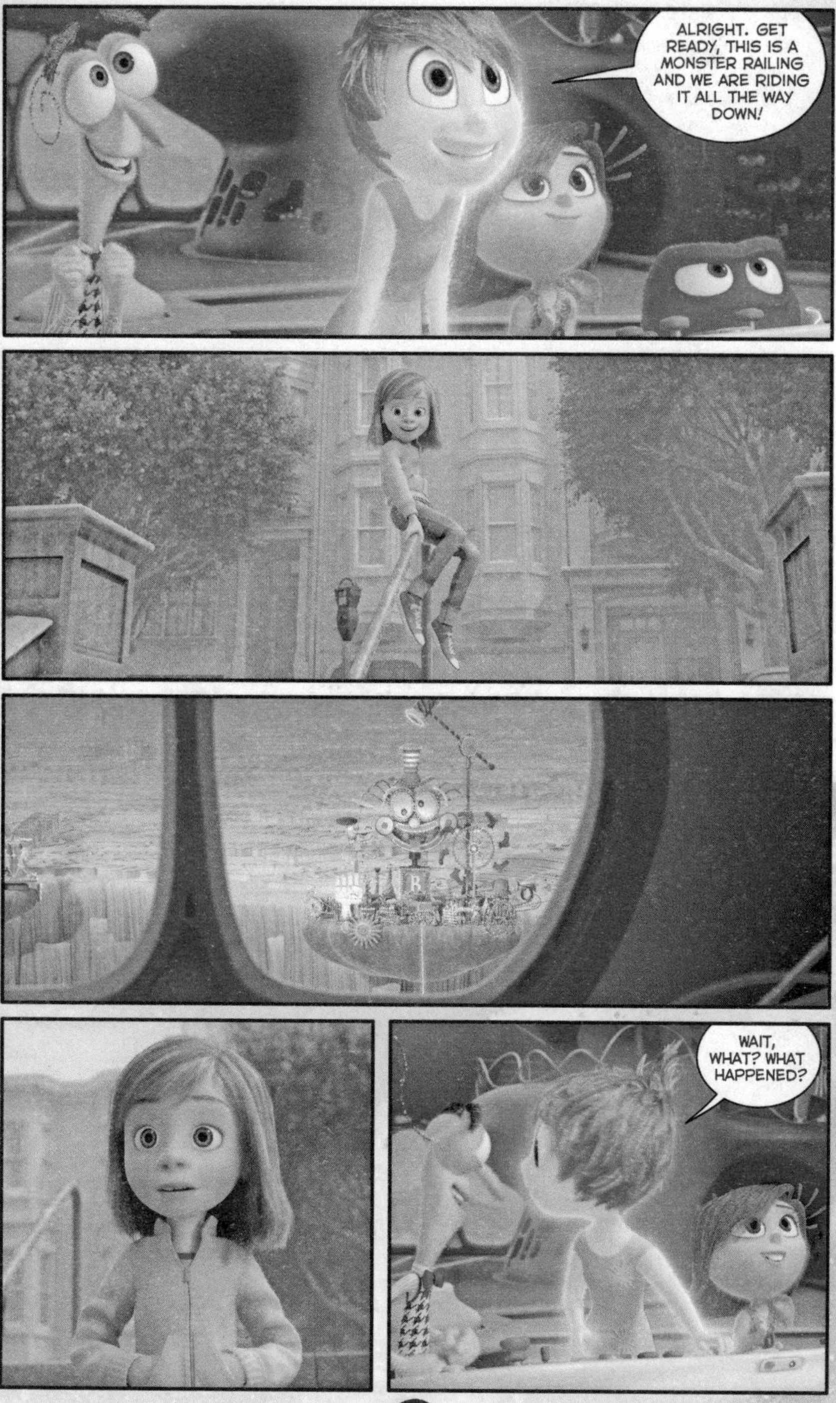
ALRIGHT. GET READY, THIS IS A MONSTER RAILING AND WE ARE RIDING IT ALL THE WAY DOWN!
WAIT, WHAT? WHAT HAPPENED?

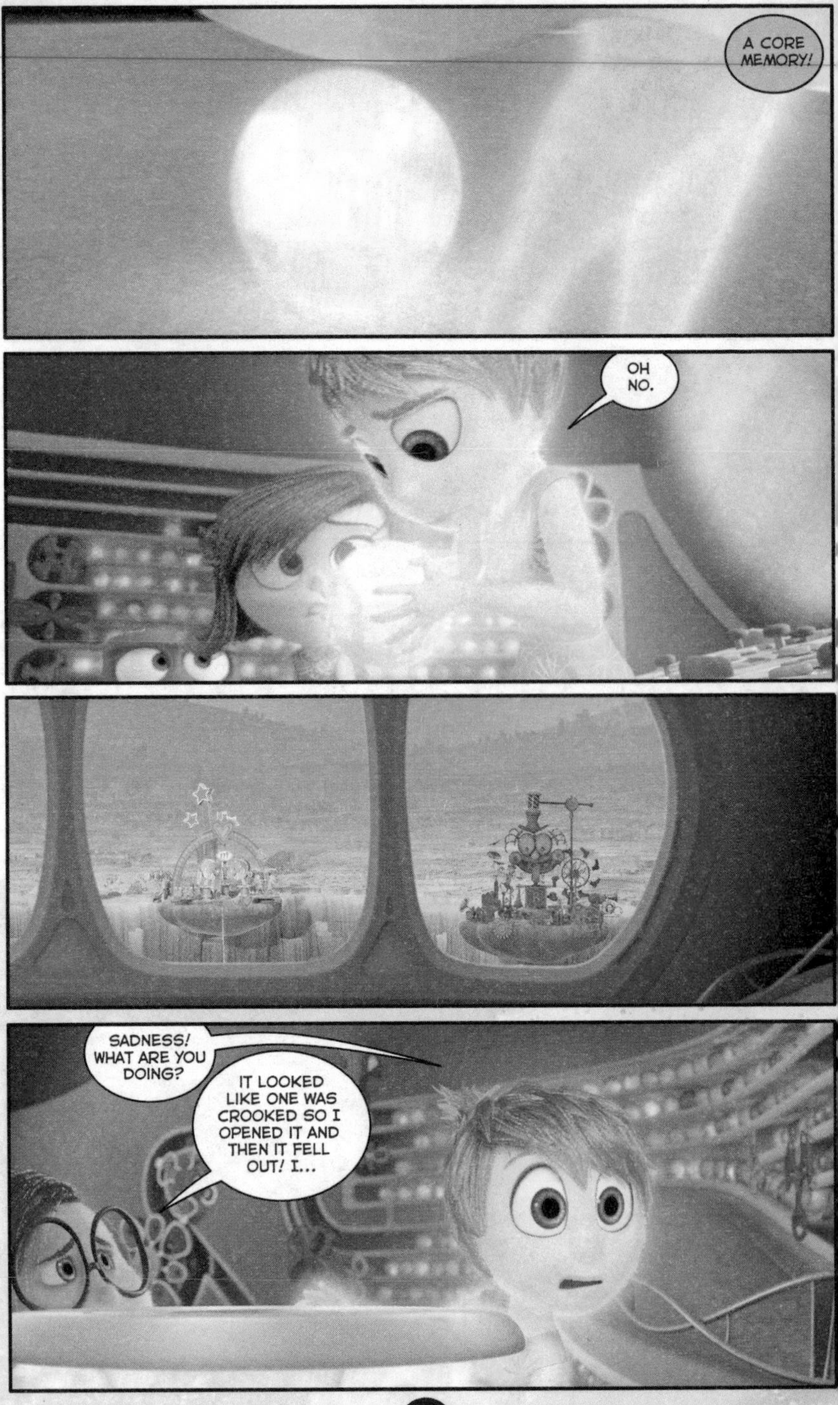
A CORE MEMORY!
OH NO.
SADNESS! WHAT ARE YOU DOING?
IT LOOKED LIKE ONE WAS CROOKED SO I OPENED IT AND THEN IT FELL OUT! I...

WOO-HOO!

IT'S JUST THAT... I WANTED TO MAYBE HOLD ONE.

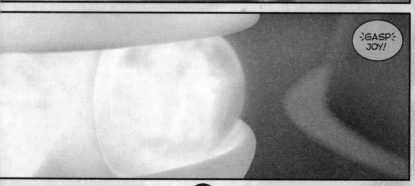

:GASP: JOY!

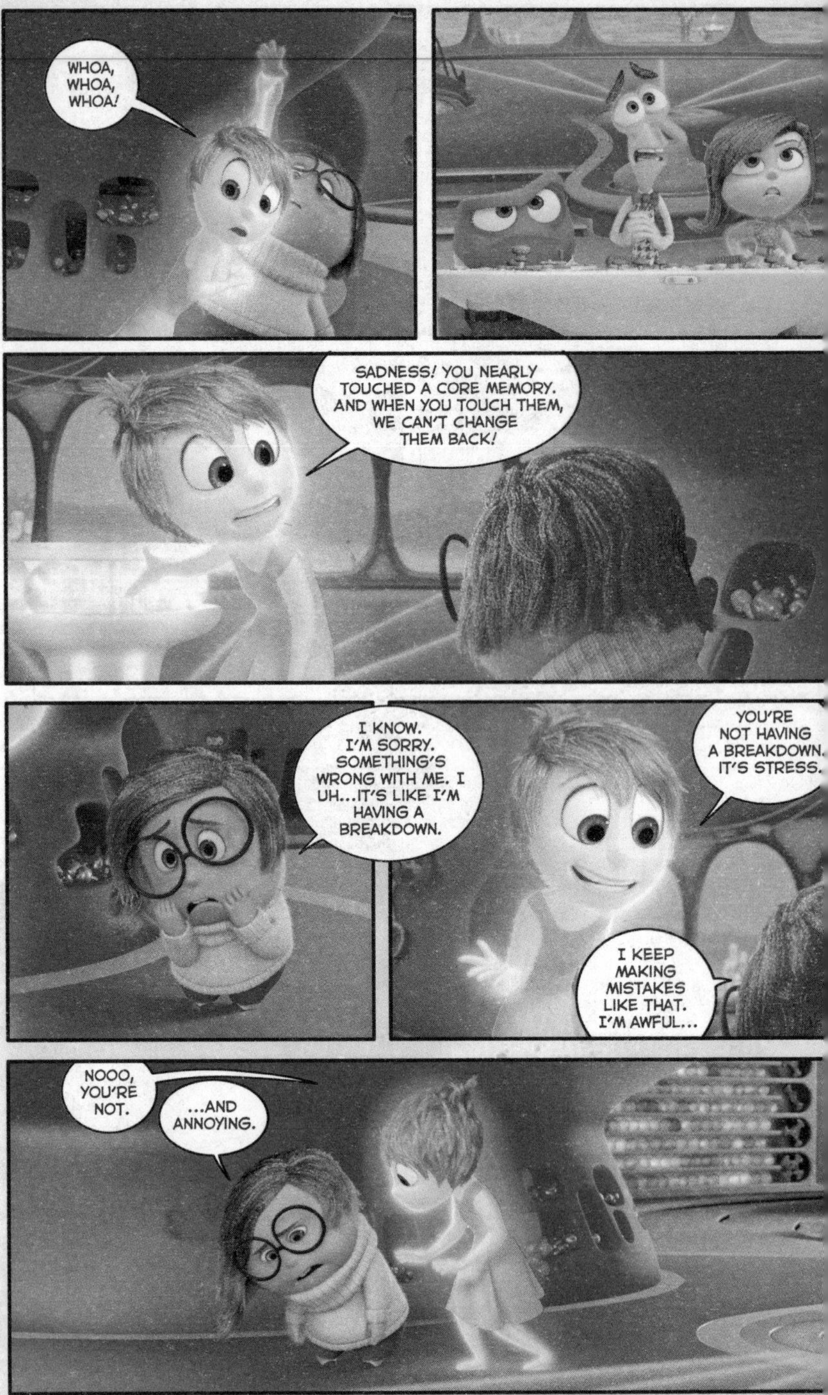
WHOA, WHOA, WHOA!
SADNESS! YOU NEARLY TOUCHED A CORE MEMORY. AND WHEN YOU TOUCH THEM, WE CAN'T CHANGE THEM BACK!
I KNOW. I'M SORRY. SOMETHING'S WRONG WITH ME. I UH...IT'S LIKE I'M HAVING A BREAKDOWN.
YOU'RE NOT HAVING A BREAKDOWN. IT'S STRESS.
I KEEP MAKING MISTAKES LIKE THAT. I'M AWFUL...
NOOO, YOU'RE NOT.
...AND ANNOYING.

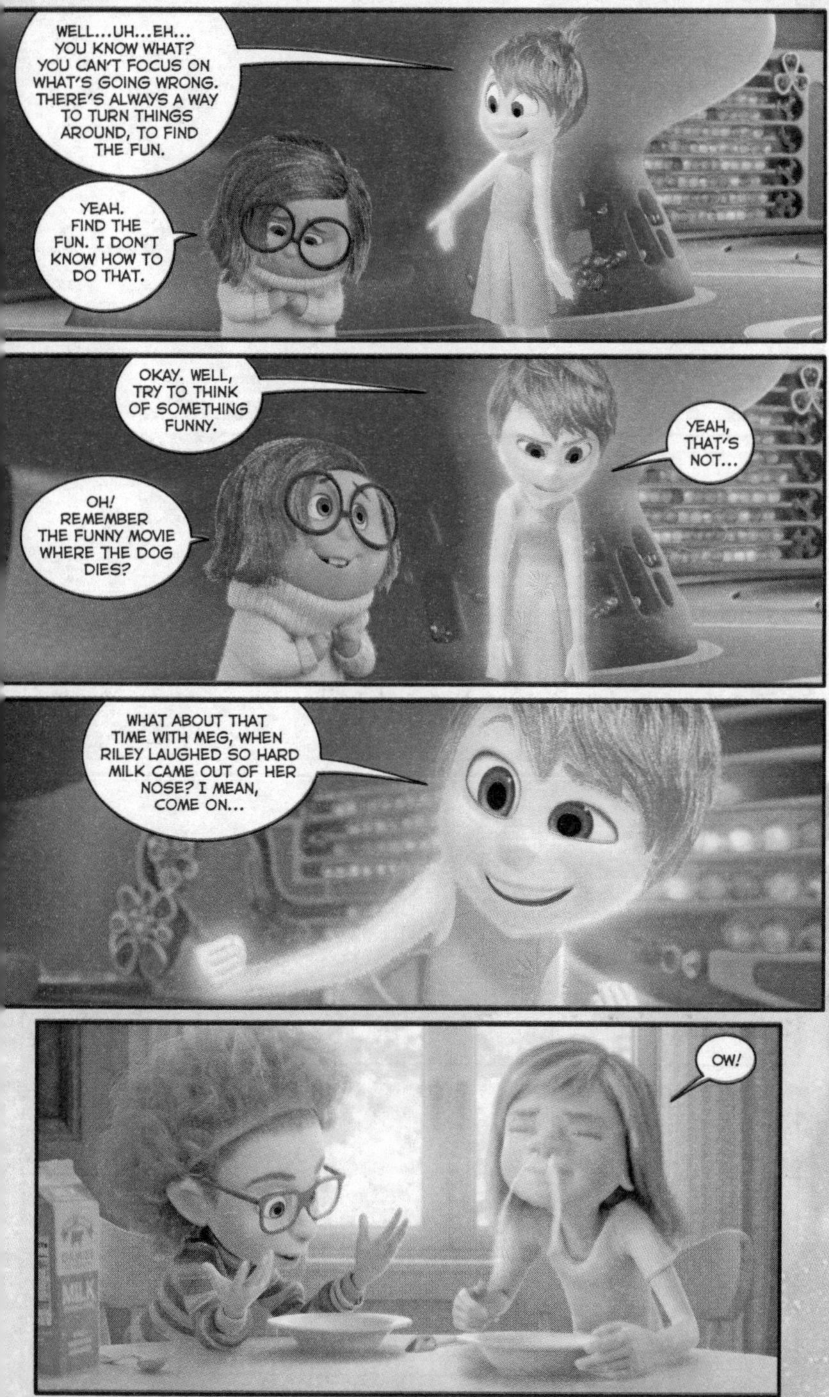
WELL...UH...EH... YOU KNOW WHAT? YOU CAN'T FOCUS ON WHAT'S GOING WRONG. THERE'S ALWAYS A WAY TO TURN THINGS AROUND, TO FIND THE FUN.
YEAH. FIND THE FUN. I DON'T KNOW HOW TO DO THAT.
OKAY. WELL, TRY TO THINK OF SOMETHING FUNNY.
OH! REMEMBER THE FUNNY MOVIE WHERE THE DOG DIES?
YEAH, THAT'S NOT...
WHAT ABOUT THAT TIME WITH MEG, WHEN RILEY LAUGHED SO HARD MILK CAME OUT OF HER NOSE? I MEAN, COME ON...
OW!
MILK

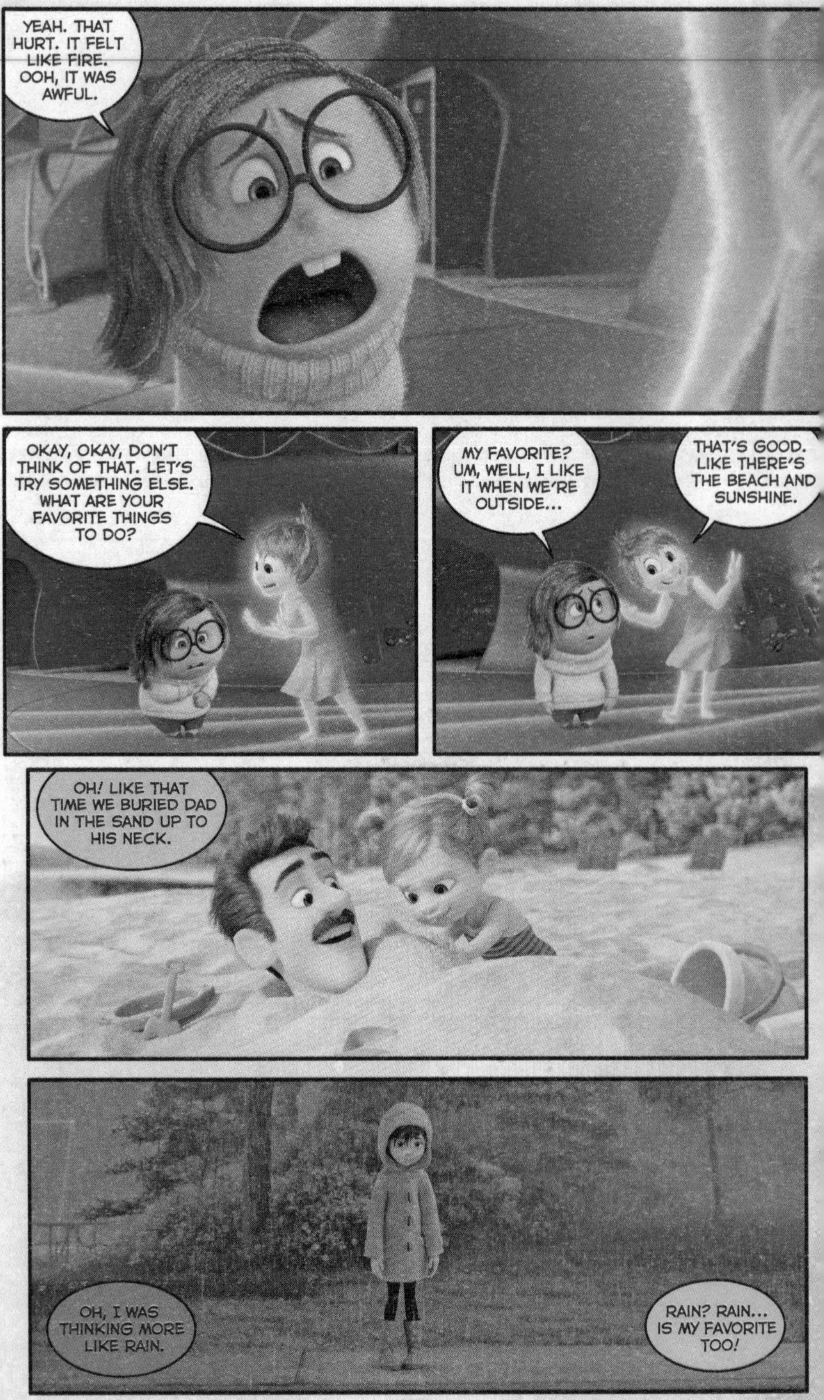

YEAH. THAT HURT. IT FELT LIKE FIRE. OOH, IT WAS AWFUL.
OKAY, OKAY, DON'T THINK OF THAT. LET'S TRY SOMETHING ELSE. WHAT ARE YOUR FAVORITE THINGS TO DO?
MY FAVORITE? UM, WELL, I LIKE IT WHEN WE'RE OUTSIDE...
THAT'S GOOD. LIKE THERE'S THE BEACH AND SUNSHINE.
OH! LIKE THAT TIME WE BURIED DAD IN THE SAND UP TO HIS NECK.
OH, I WAS THINKING MORE LIKE RAIN.
RAIN? RAIN... IS MY FAVORITE TOO!

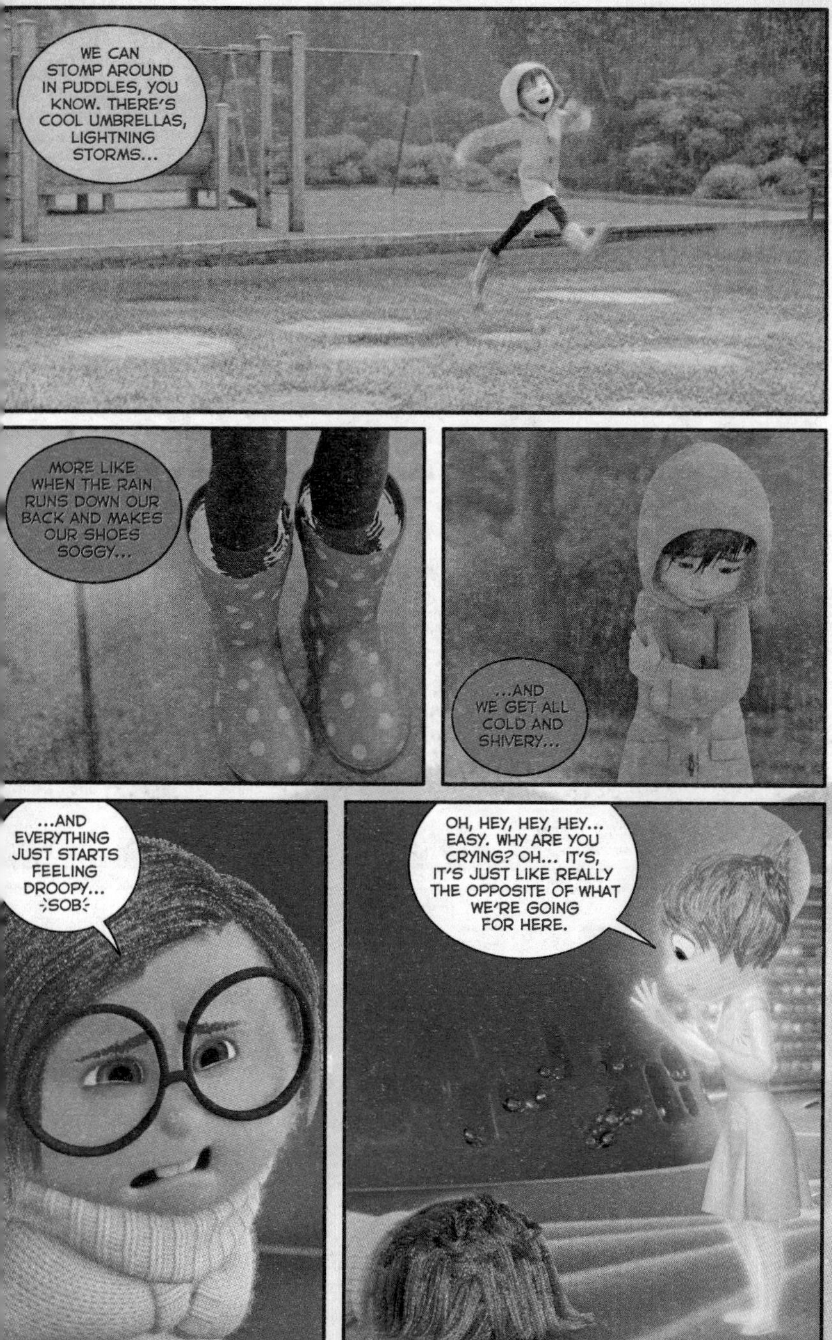
WE CAN STOMP AROUND IN PUDDLES, YOU KNOW. THERE'S COOL UMBRELLAS, LIGHTNING STORMS...
MORE LIKE WHEN THE RAIN RUNS DOWN OUR BACK AND MAKES OUR SHOES SOGGY...
...AND WE GET ALL COLD AND SHIVERY...
...AND EVERYTHING JUST STARTS FEELING DROOPY... SOB
OH, HEY, HEY, HEY... EASY. WHY ARE YOU CRYING? OH... IT'S, IT'S JUST LIKE REALLY THE OPPOSITE OF WHAT WE'RE GOING FOR HERE.

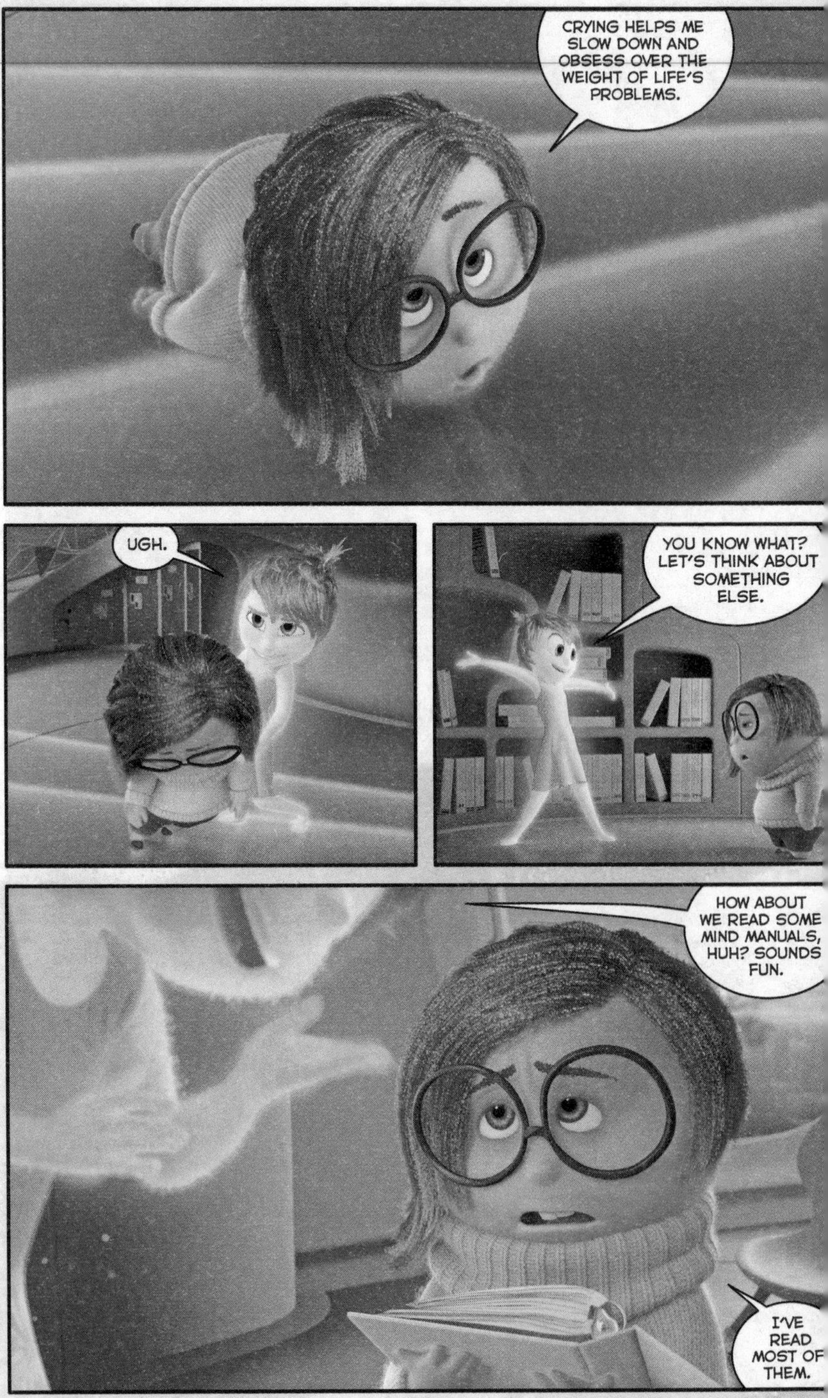
CRYING HELPS ME SLOW DOWN AND OBSESS OVER THE WEIGHT OF LIFE'S PROBLEMS.
UGH.
YOU KNOW WHAT? LET'S THINK ABOUT SOMETHING ELSE.
HOW ABOUT WE READ SOME MIND MANUALS, HUH? SOUNDS FUN.
I'VE READ MOST OF THEM.

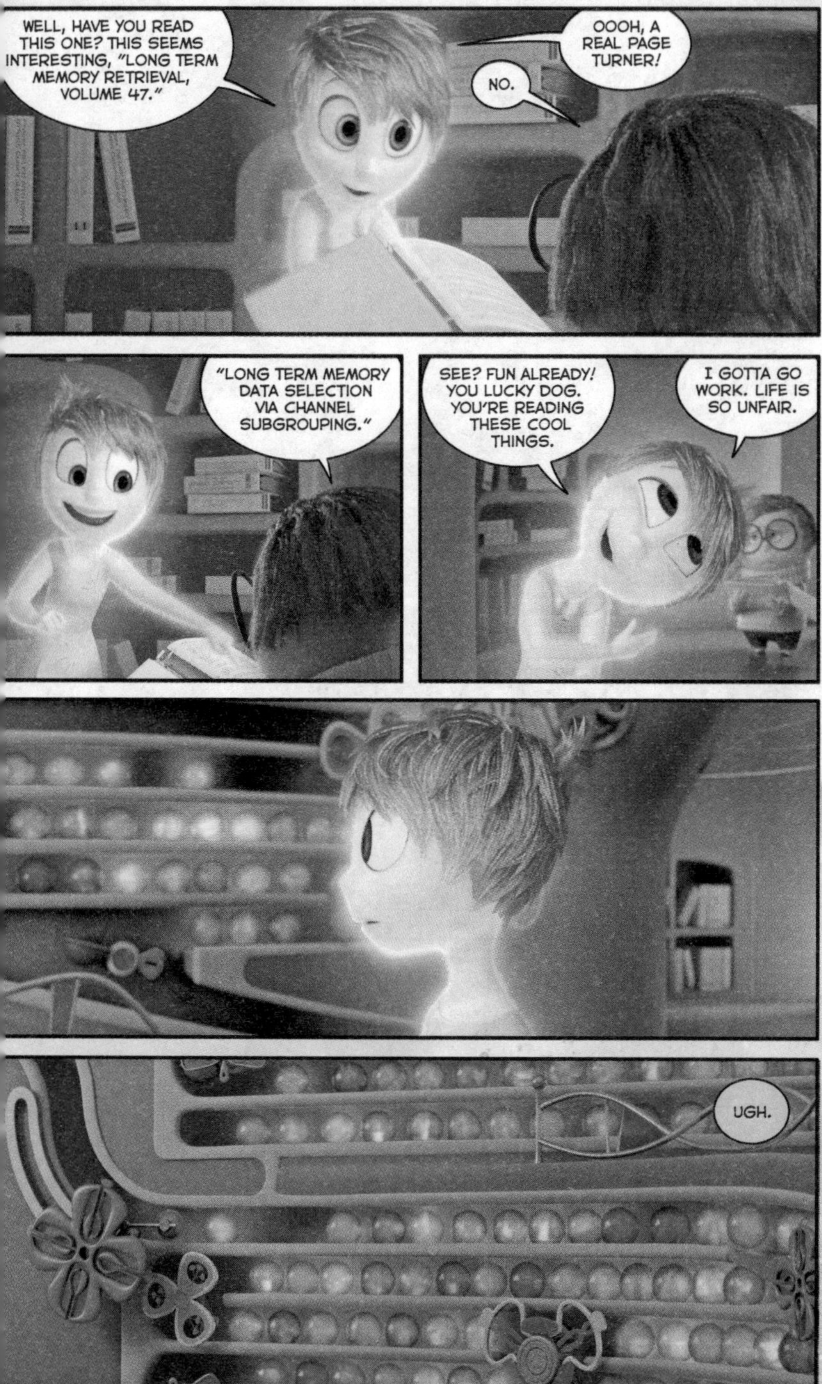
WELL, HAVE YOU READ THIS ONE? THIS SEEMS INTERESTING, "LONG TERM MEMORY RETRIEVAL, VOLUME 47."
NO.
OOOH, A REAL PAGE TURNER!
"LONG TERM MEMORY DATA SELECTION VIA CHANNEL SUBGROUPING."
SEE? FUN ALREADY! YOU LUCKY DOG. YOU'RE READING THESE COOL THINGS.
I GOTTA GO WORK. LIFE IS SO UNFAIR.
UGH.

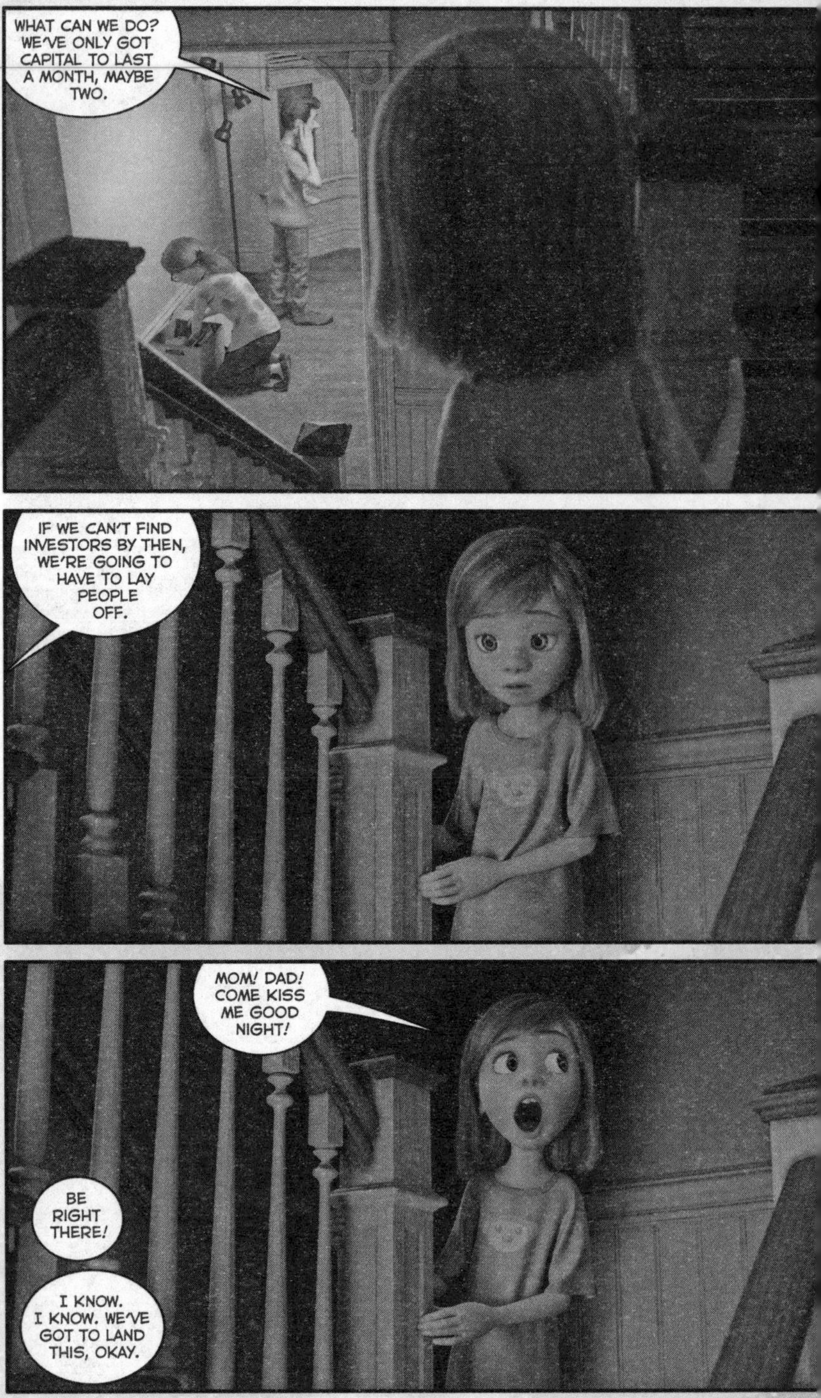
WHAT CAN WE DO? WE'VE ONLY GOT CAPITAL TO LAST A MONTH, MAYBE TWO.
IF WE CAN'T FIND INVESTORS BY THEN, WE'RE GOING TO HAVE TO LAY PEOPLE OFF.
MOM! DAD! COME KISS ME GOOD NIGHT!
BE RIGHT THERE!
I KNOW. I KNOW. WE'VE GOT TO LAND THIS, OKAY.

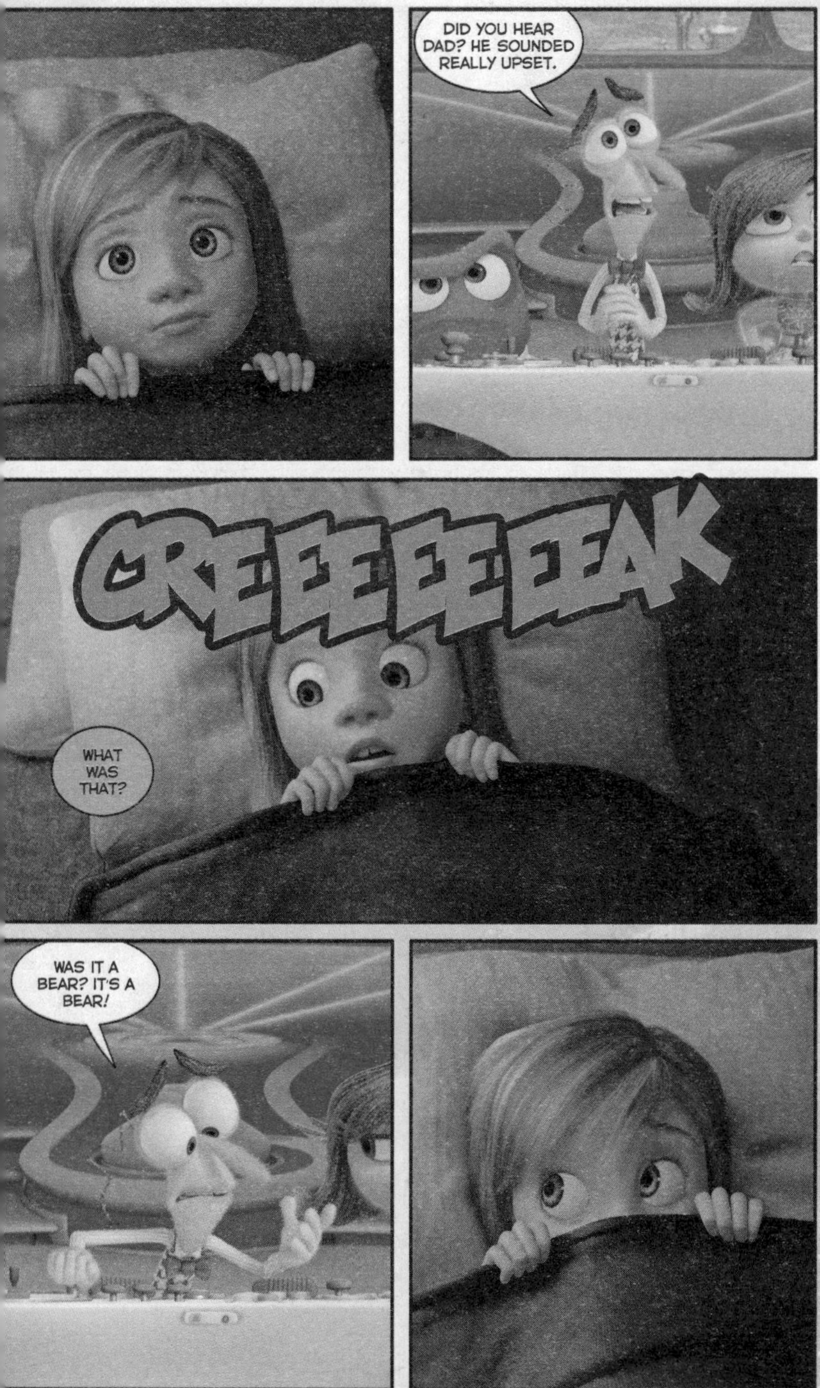
DID YOU HEAR DAD? HE SOUNDED REALLY UPSET.
CREEEEEEEAK
WHAT WAS THAT?
WAS IT A BEAR? IT'S A BEAR!

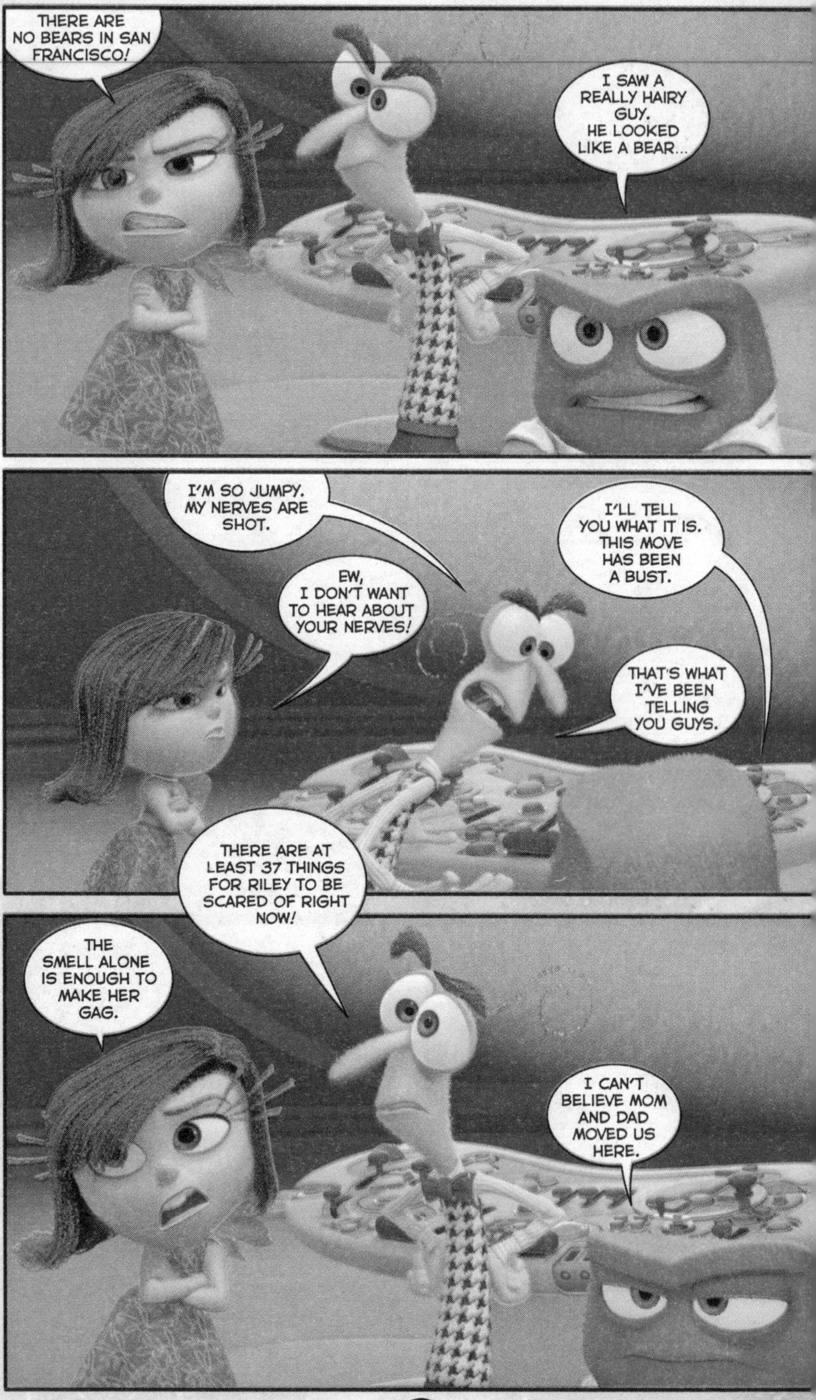
THERE ARE NO BEARS IN SAN FRANCISCO!
I SAW A REALLY HAIRY GUY. HE LOOKED LIKE A BEAR...
I'M SO JUMPY. MY NERVES ARE SHOT.
EW, I DON'T WANT TO HEAR ABOUT YOUR NERVES!
I'LL TELL YOU WHAT IT IS. THIS MOVE HAS BEEN A BUST.
THAT'S WHAT I'VE BEEN TELLING YOU GUYS.
THERE ARE AT LEAST 37 THINGS FOR RILEY TO BE SCARED OF RIGHT NOW!
THE SMELL ALONE IS ENOUGH TO MAKE HER GAG.
I CAN'T BELIEVE MOM AND DAD MOVED US HERE.

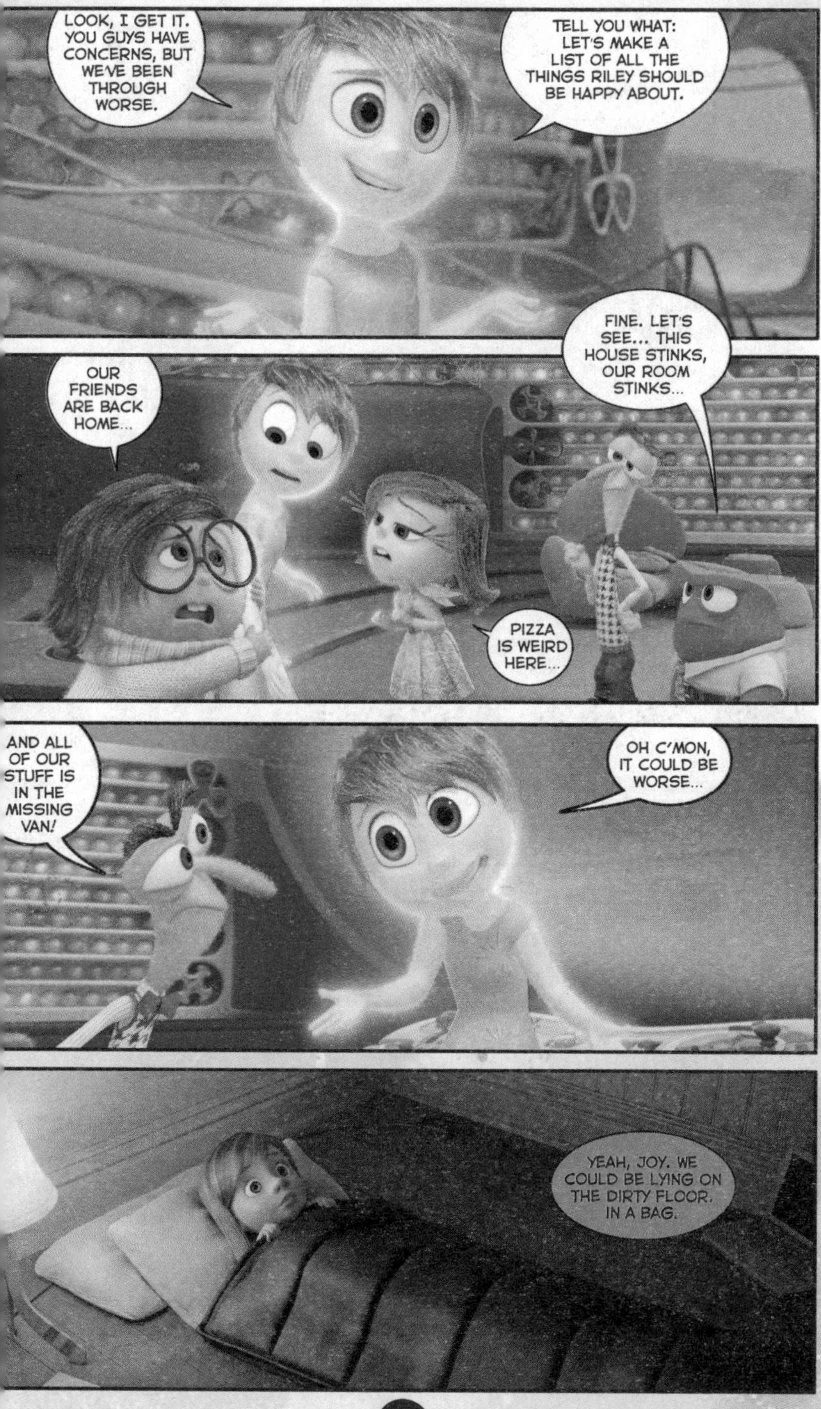
LOOK, I GET IT. YOU GUYS HAVE CONCERNS, BUT WE'VE BEEN THROUGH WORSE.
TELL YOU WHAT: LET'S MAKE A LIST OF ALL THE THINGS RILEY SHOULD BE HAPPY ABOUT.
OUR FRIENDS ARE BACK HOME...
FINE. LET'S SEE... THIS HOUSE STINKS, OUR ROOM STINKS...
PIZZA IS WEIRD HERE...
AND ALL OF OUR STUFF IS IN THE MISSING VAN!
OH C'MON, IT COULD BE WORSE...
YEAH, JOY. WE COULD BE LYING ON THE DIRTY FLOOR. IN A BAG.

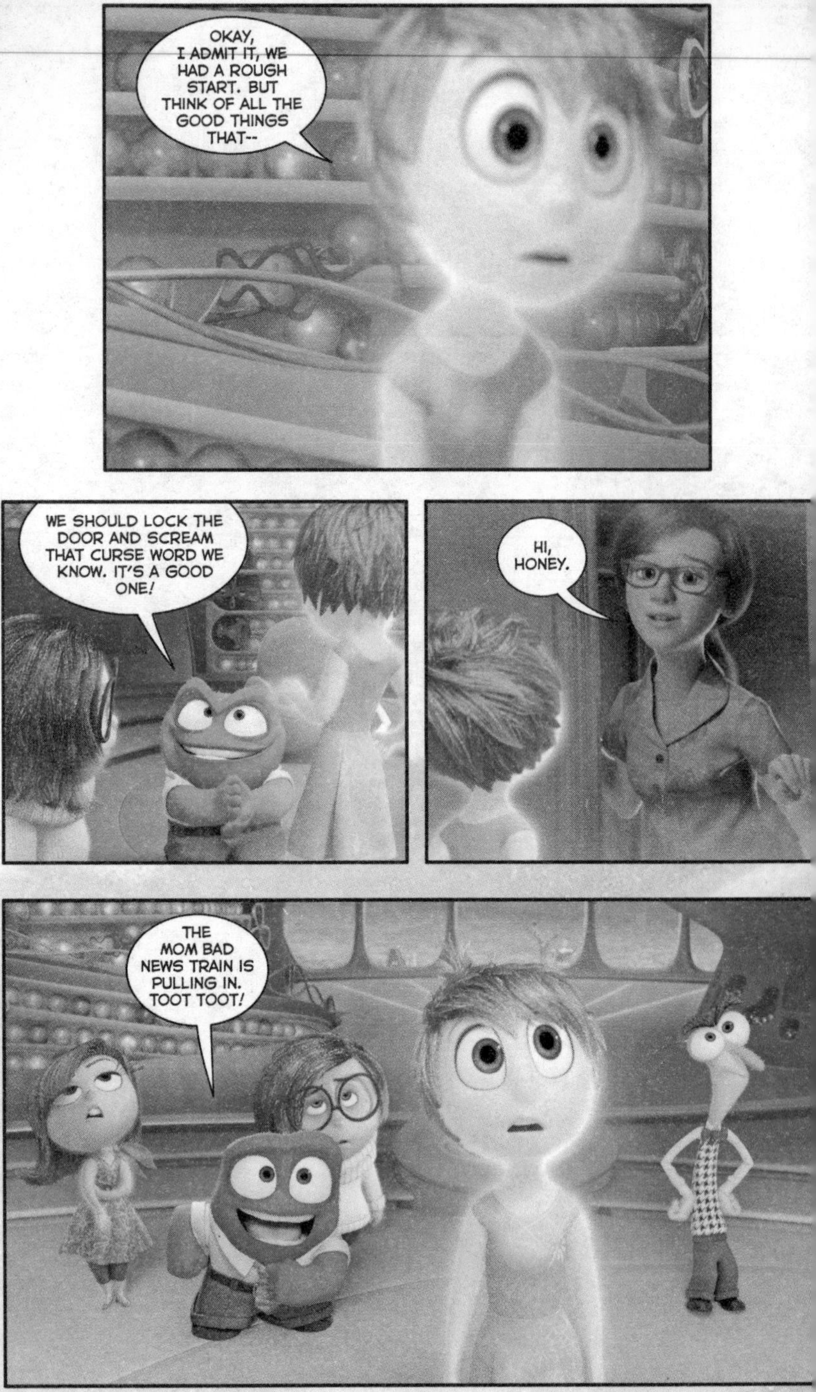
OKAY, I ADMIT IT, WE HAD A ROUGH START. BUT THINK OF ALL THE GOOD THINGS THAT--
WE SHOULD LOCK THE DOOR AND SCREAM THAT CURSE WORD WE KNOW. IT'S A GOOD ONE!
HI, HONEY.
THE MOM BAD NEWS TRAIN IS PULLING IN. TOOT TOOT!

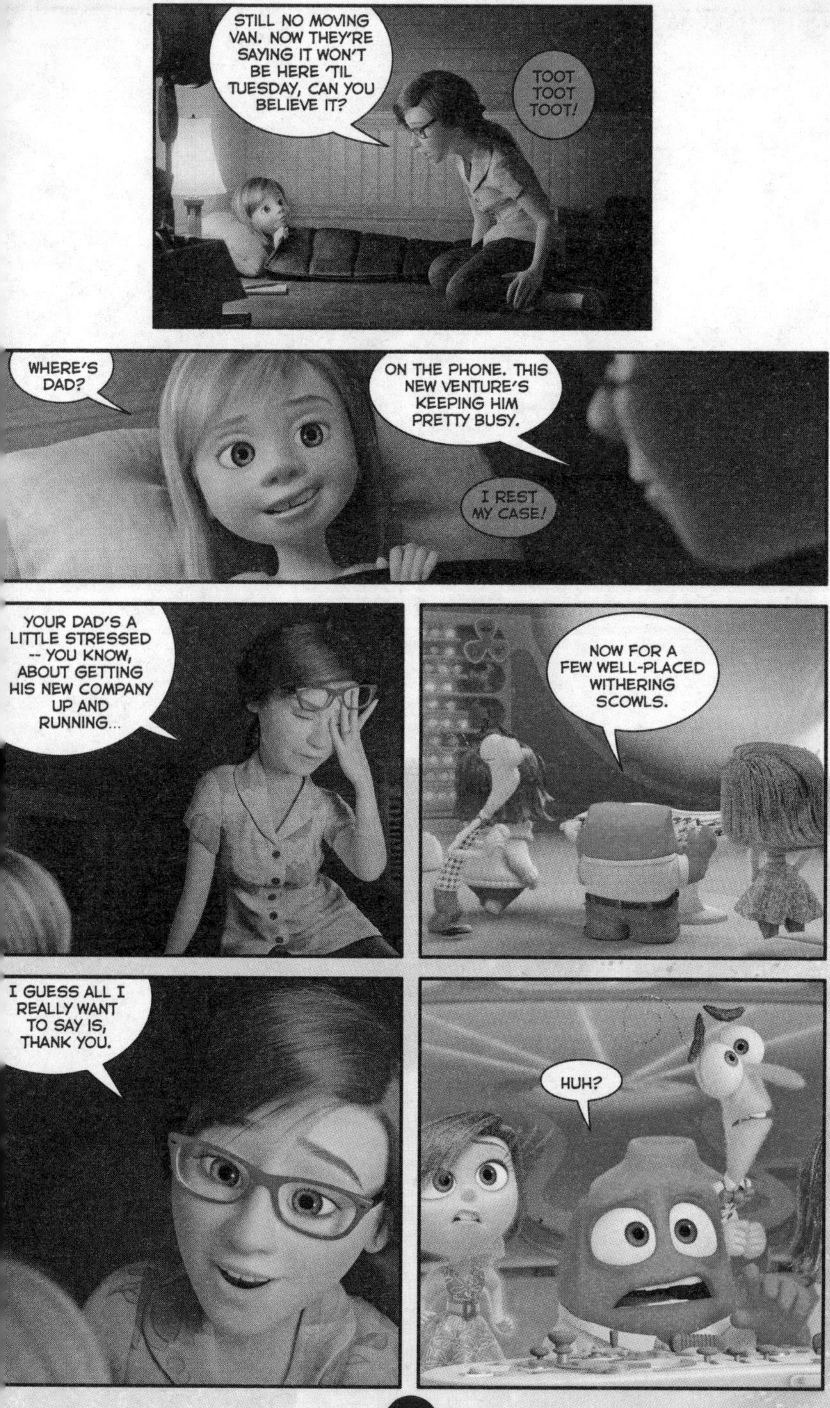
STILL NO MOVING VAN. NOW THEY'RE SAYING IT WON'T BE HERE 'TIL TUESDAY, CAN YOU BELIEVE IT?
TOOT TOOT TOOT!
WHERE'S DAD?
ON THE PHONE. THIS NEW VENTURE'S KEEPING HIM PRETTY BUSY.
I REST MY CASE!
YOUR DAD'S A LITTLE STRESSED -- YOU KNOW, ABOUT GETTING HIS NEW COMPANY UP AND RUNNING...
NOW FOR A FEW WELL-PLACED WITHERING SCOWLS.
I GUESS ALL I REALLY WANT TO SAY IS, THANK YOU.
HUH?

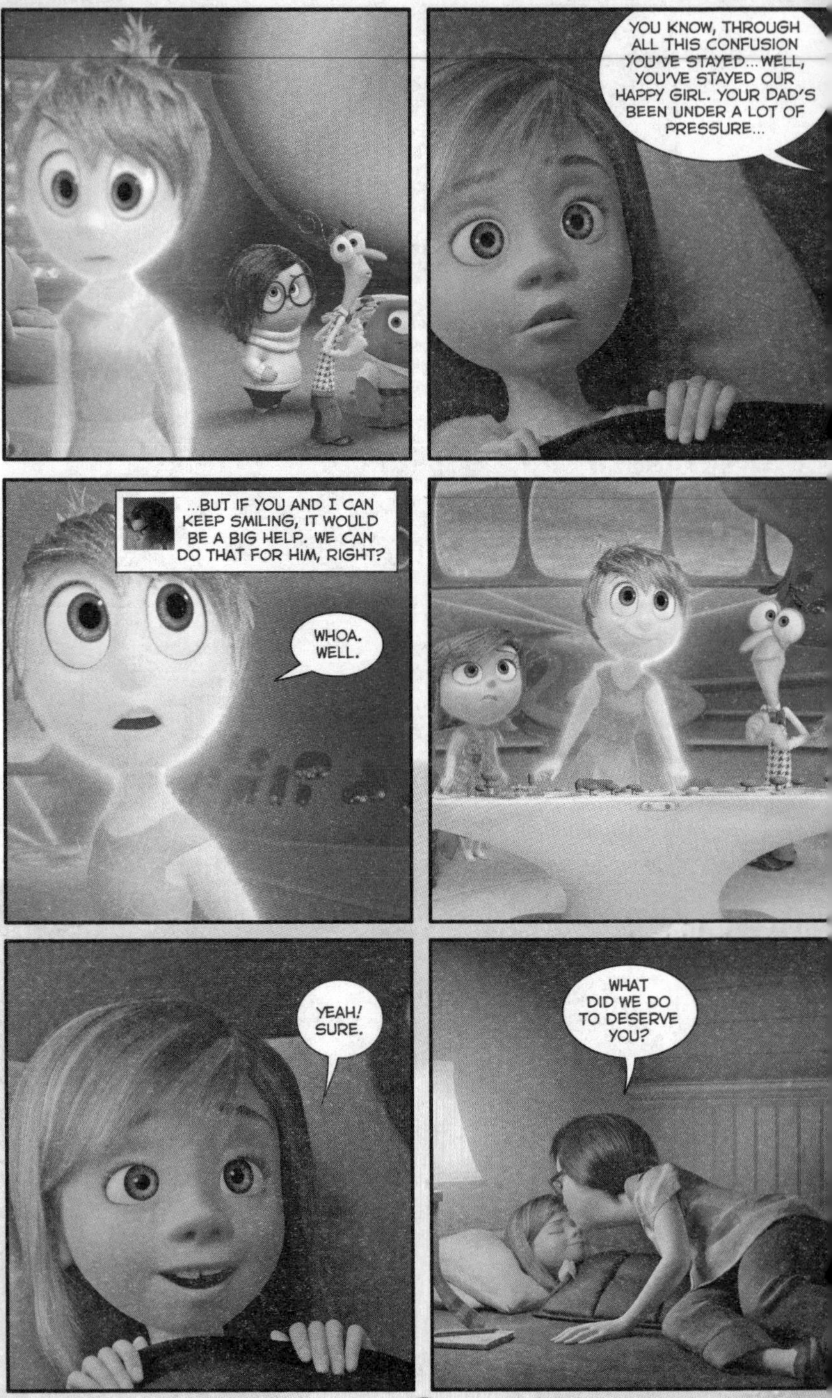
YOU KNOW, THROUGH ALL THIS CONFUSION YOU'VE STAYED...WELL, YOU'VE STAYED OUR HAPPY GIRL. YOUR DAD'S BEEN UNDER A LOT OF PRESSURE...
...BUT IF YOU AND I CAN KEEP SMILING, IT WOULD BE A BIG HELP. WE CAN DO THAT FOR HIM, RIGHT?
WHOA. WELL.
YEAH! SURE.
WHAT DID WE DO TO DESERVE YOU?

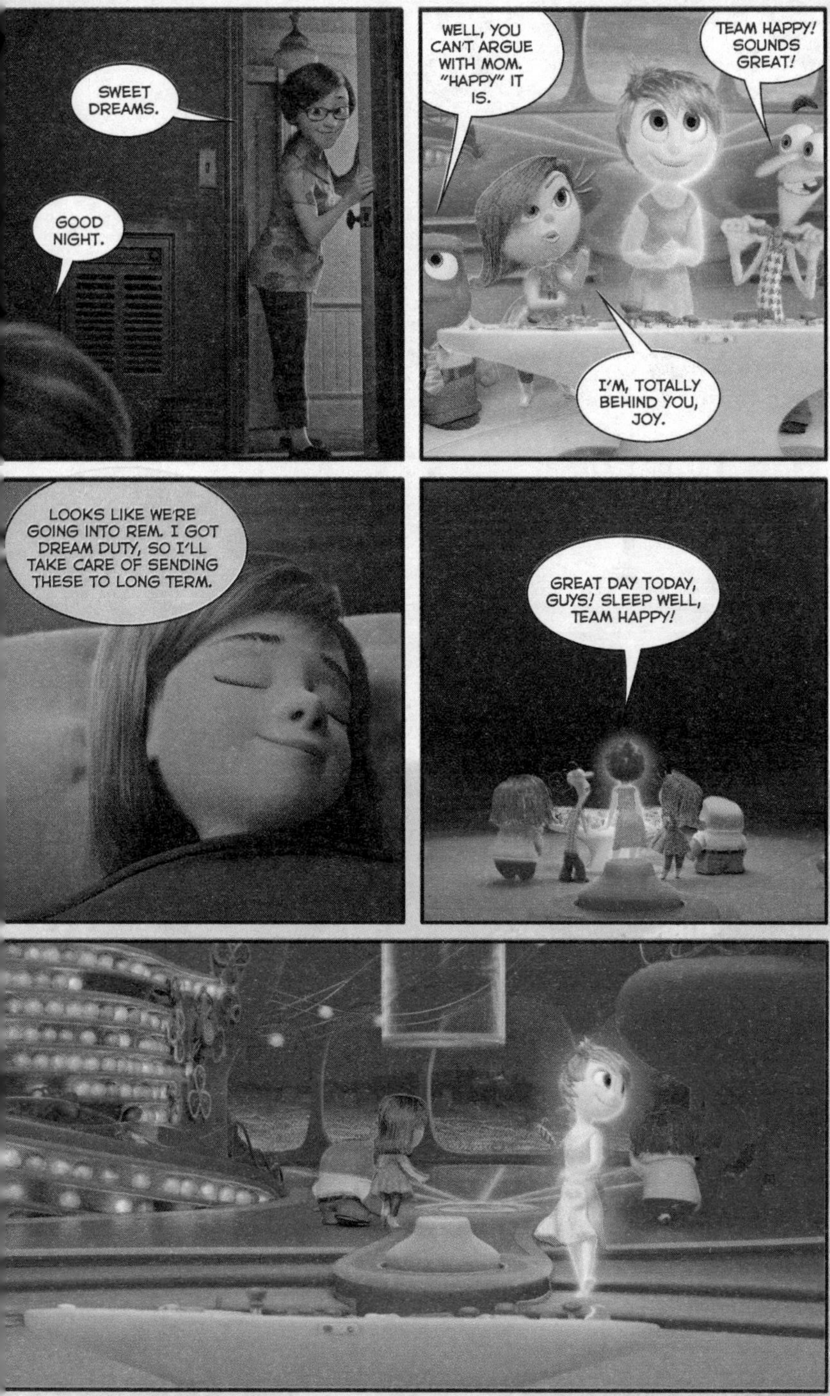
SWEET DREAMS.
GOOD NIGHT.
WELL, YOU CAN'T ARGUE WITH MOM. "HAPPY" IT IS.
TEAM HAPPY! SOUNDS GREAT!
I'M, TOTALLY BEHIND YOU, JOY.
LOOKS LIKE WE'RE GOING INTO REM. I GOT DREAM DUTY, SO I'LL TAKE CARE OF SENDING THESE TO LONG TERM.
GREAT DAY TODAY, GUYS! SLEEP WELL, TEAM HAPPY!

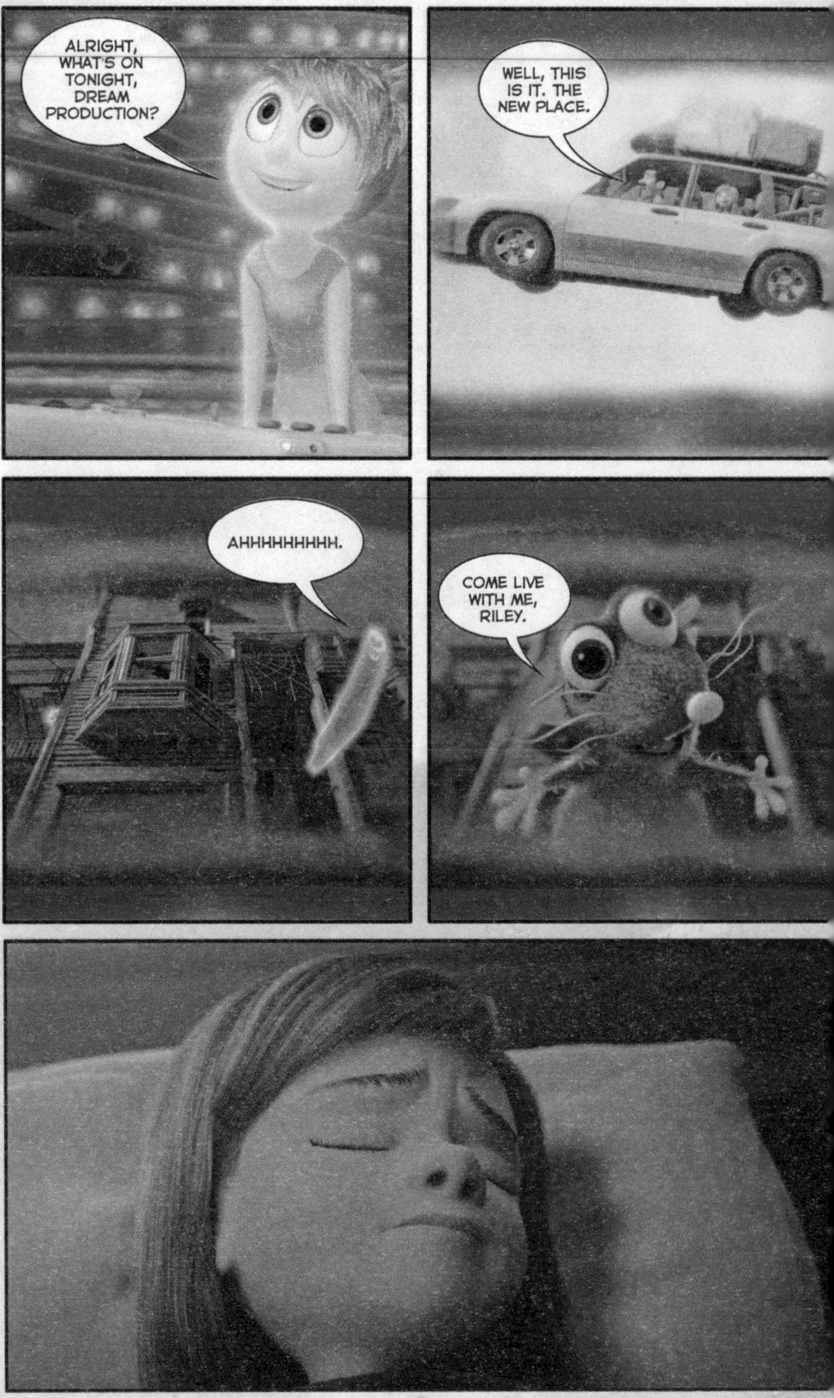
ALRIGHT, WHAT'S ON TONIGHT, DREAM PRODUCTION?
WELL, THIS IS IT. THE NEW PLACE.
AHHHHHHHHH.
COME LIVE WITH ME, RILEY.

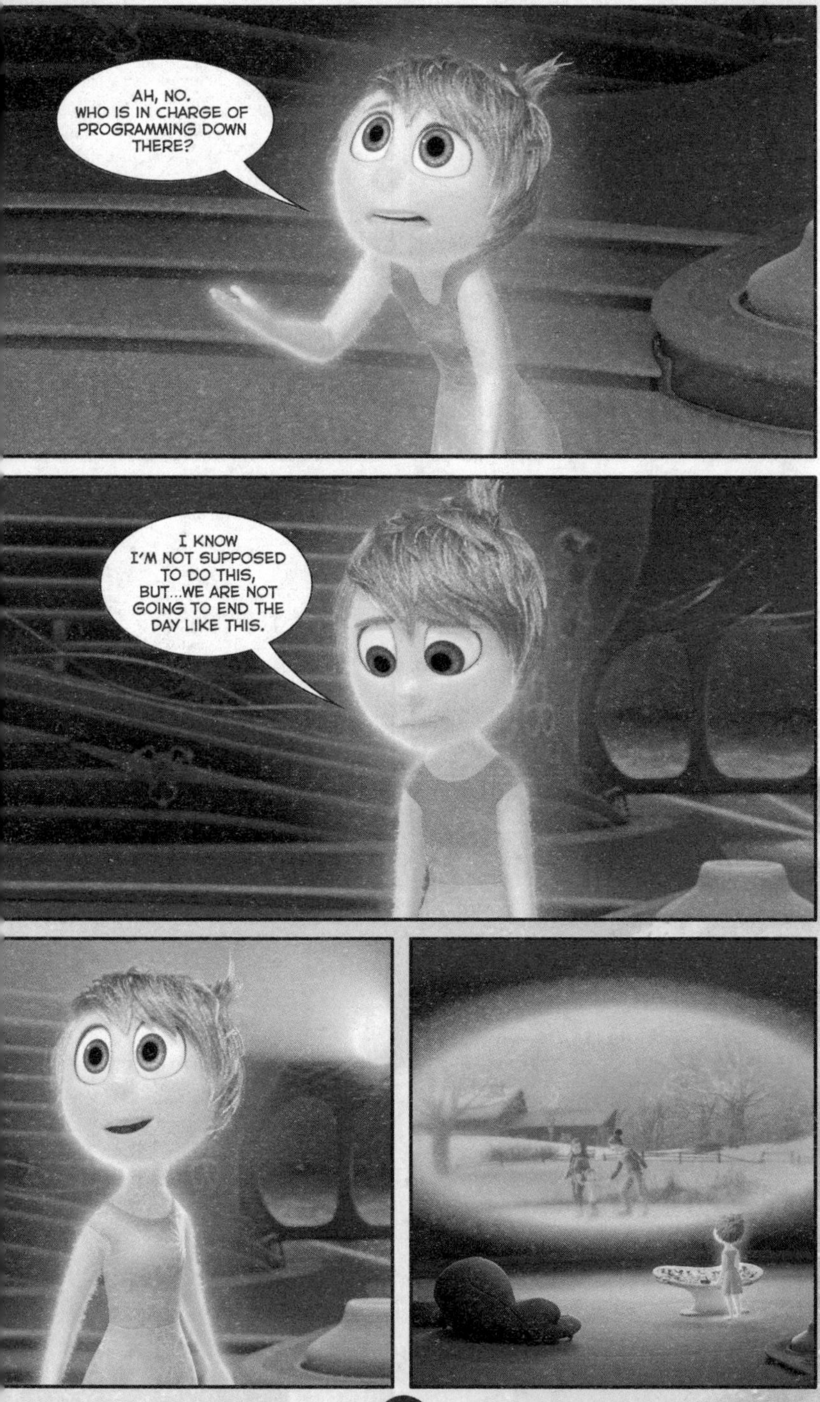
AH, NO. WHO IS IN CHARGE OF PROGRAMMING DOWN THERE?
I KNOW I'M NOT SUPPOSED TO DO THIS, BUT...WE ARE NOT GOING TO END THE DAY LIKE THIS.

DON'T YOU WORRY. I'M GONNA MAKE SURE THAT TOMORROW IS ANOTHER GREAT DAY.

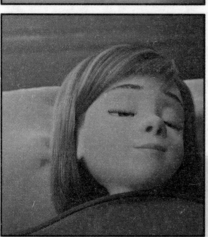

THE NEXT MORNING...

CARAMEL CORN CURLS

HELLO! DID I WAKE YOU?

DO YOU HAVE TO PLAY THAT?

WELL, I HAVE TO PRACTICE. AND I DON'T THINK OF IT AS PLAYING SO MUCH AS HUGGING.

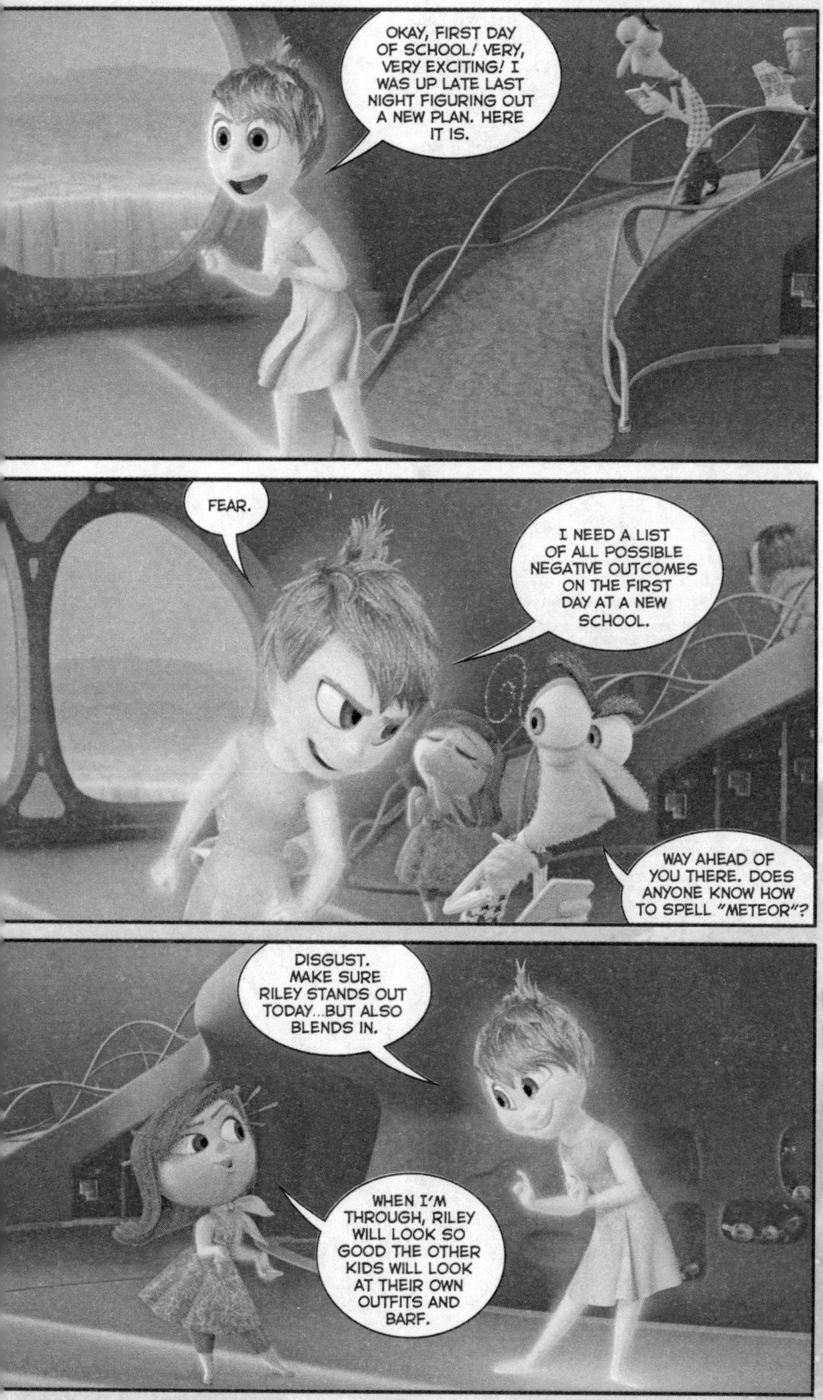
OKAY, FIRST DAY OF SCHOOL! VERY, VERY EXCITING! I WAS UP LATE LAST NIGHT FIGURING OUT A NEW PLAN. HERE IT IS.
FEAR.
I NEED A LIST OF ALL POSSIBLE NEGATIVE OUTCOMES ON THE FIRST DAY AT A NEW SCHOOL.
WAY AHEAD OF YOU THERE. DOES ANYONE KNOW HOW TO SPELL "METEOR"?
DISGUST. MAKE SURE RILEY STANDS OUT TODAY...BUT ALSO BLENDS IN.
WHEN I'M THROUGH, RILEY WILL LOOK SO GOOD THE OTHER KIDS WILL LOOK AT THEIR OWN OUTFITS AND BARF.

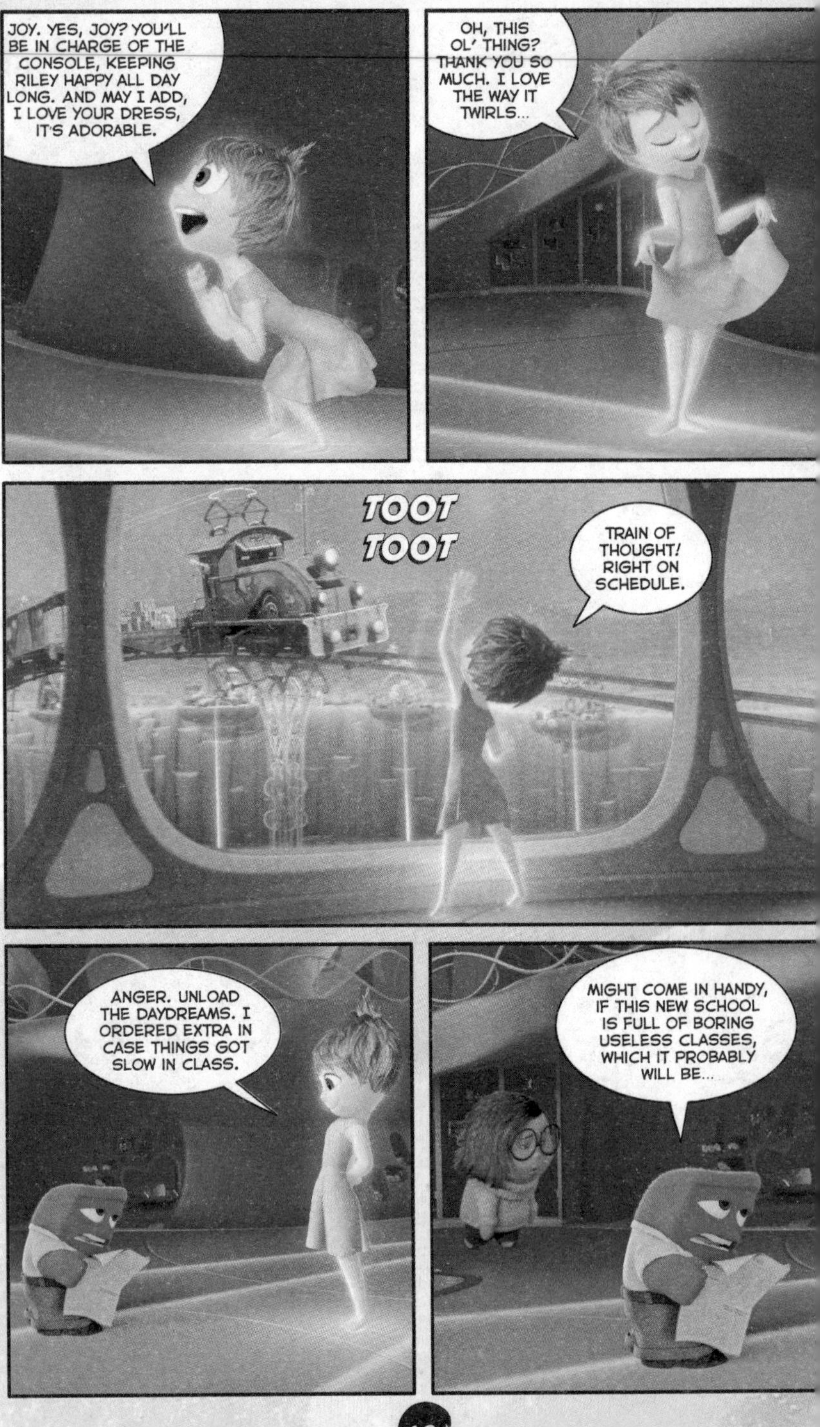
JOY. YES, JOY? YOU'LL BE IN CHARGE OF THE CONSOLE, KEEPING RILEY HAPPY ALL DAY LONG. AND MAY I ADD, I LOVE YOUR DRESS, IT'S ADORABLE.
OH, THIS OL' THING? THANK YOU SO MUCH. I LOVE THE WAY IT TWIRLS...
TOOT TOOT
TRAIN OF THOUGHT! RIGHT ON SCHEDULE.
ANGER. UNLOAD THE DAYDREAMS. I ORDERED EXTRA IN CASE THINGS GOT SLOW IN CLASS.
MIGHT COME IN HANDY, IF THIS NEW SCHOOL IS FULL OF BORING USELESS CLASSES, WHICH IT PROBABLY WILL BE...

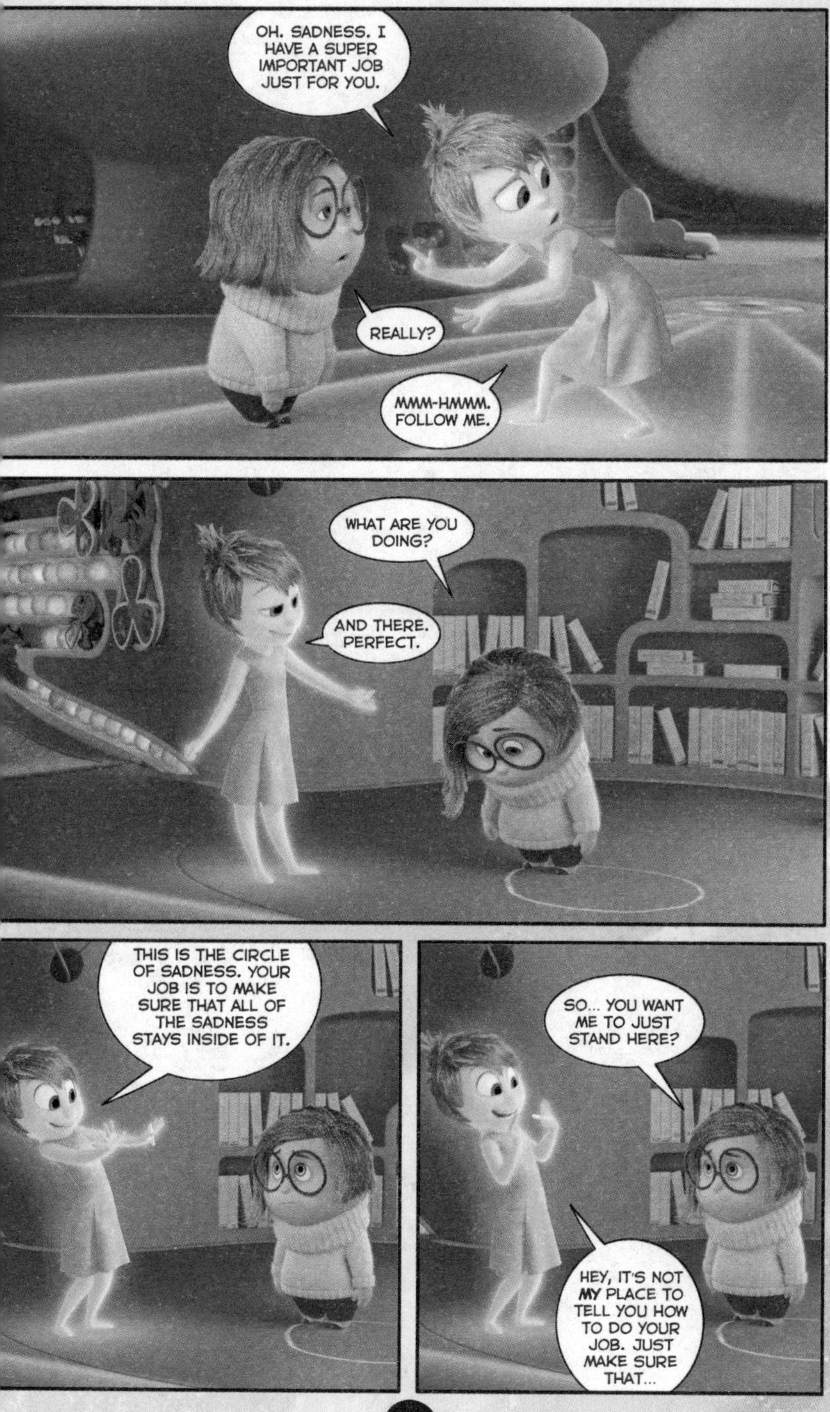

OH. SADNESS. I HAVE A SUPER IMPORTANT JOB JUST FOR YOU.
REALLY?
MMM-HMMM. FOLLOW ME.
WHAT ARE YOU DOING?
AND THERE. PERFECT.
THIS IS THE CIRCLE OF SADNESS. YOUR JOB IS TO MAKE SURE THAT ALL OF THE SADNESS STAYS INSIDE OF IT.
SO... YOU WANT ME TO JUST STAND HERE?
HEY, IT'S NOT **MY** PLACE TO TELL YOU HOW TO DO YOUR JOB. JUST MAKE SURE THAT...

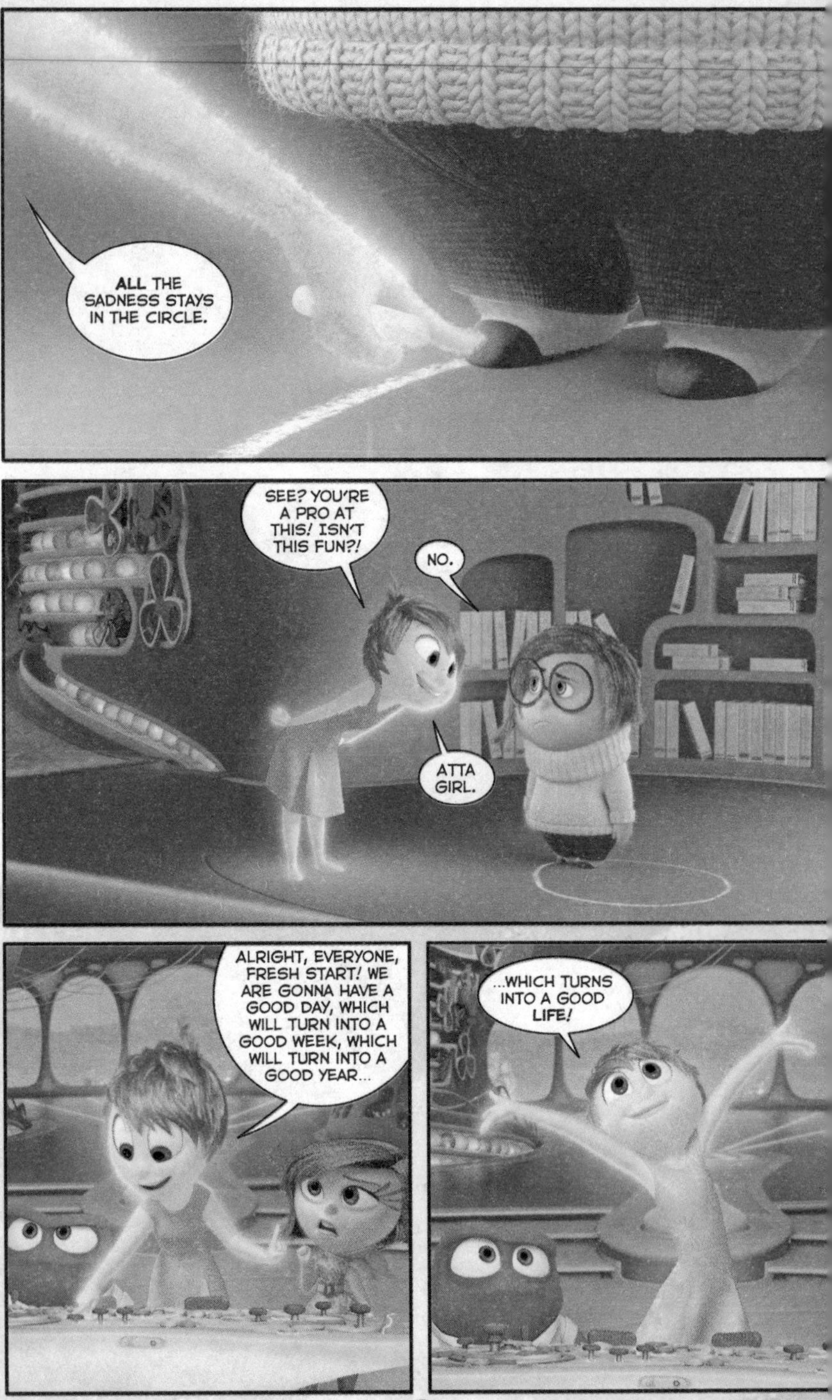
ALL THE SADNESS STAYS IN THE CIRCLE.
SEE? YOU'RE A PRO AT THIS! ISN'T THIS FUN?!
NO.
ATTA GIRL.
ALRIGHT, EVERYONE, FRESH START! WE ARE GONNA HAVE A GOOD DAY, WHICH WILL TURN INTO A GOOD WEEK, WHICH WILL TURN INTO A GOOD YEAR...
...WHICH TURNS INTO A GOOD LIFE!

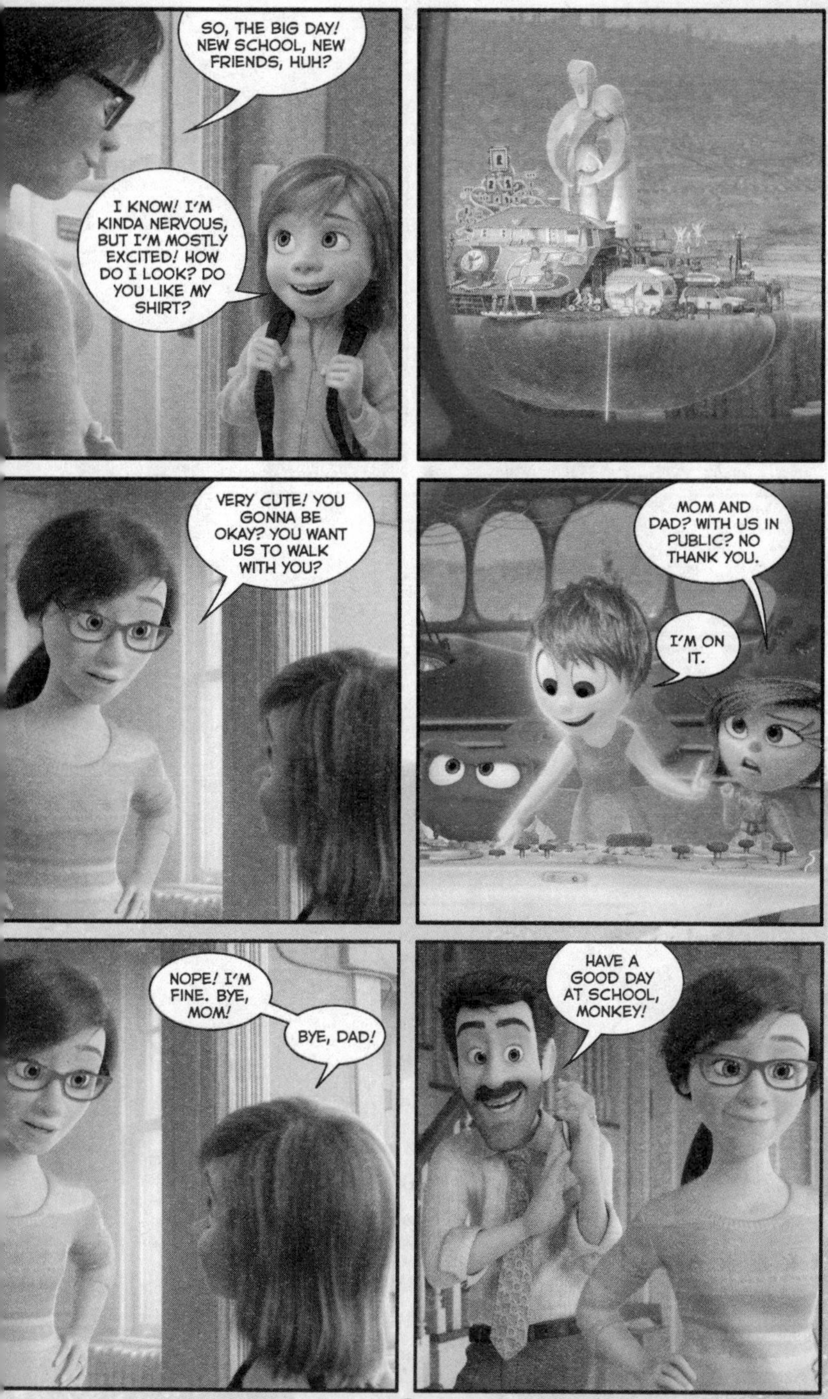
SO, THE BIG DAY! NEW SCHOOL, NEW FRIENDS, HUH?
I KNOW! I'M KINDA NERVOUS, BUT I'M MOSTLY EXCITED! HOW DO I LOOK? DO YOU LIKE MY SHIRT?
VERY CUTE! YOU GONNA BE OKAY? YOU WANT US TO WALK WITH YOU?
MOM AND DAD? WITH US IN PUBLIC? NO THANK YOU.
I'M ON IT.
NOPE! I'M FINE. BYE, MOM!
BYE, DAD!
HAVE A GOOD DAY AT SCHOOL, MONKEY!

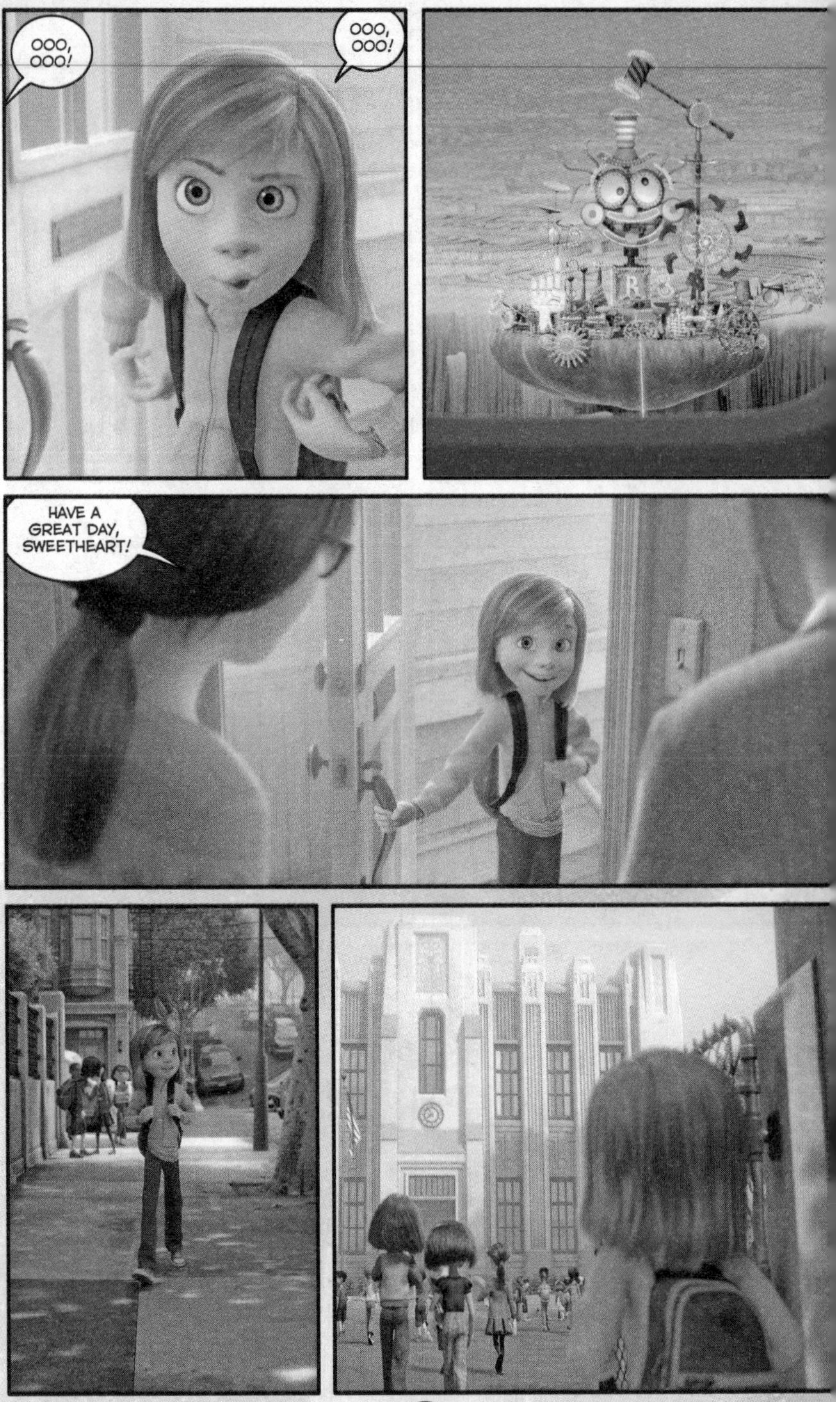
OOO,
OOO!
OOO,
OOO!
HAVE A
GREAT DAY,
SWEETHEART!

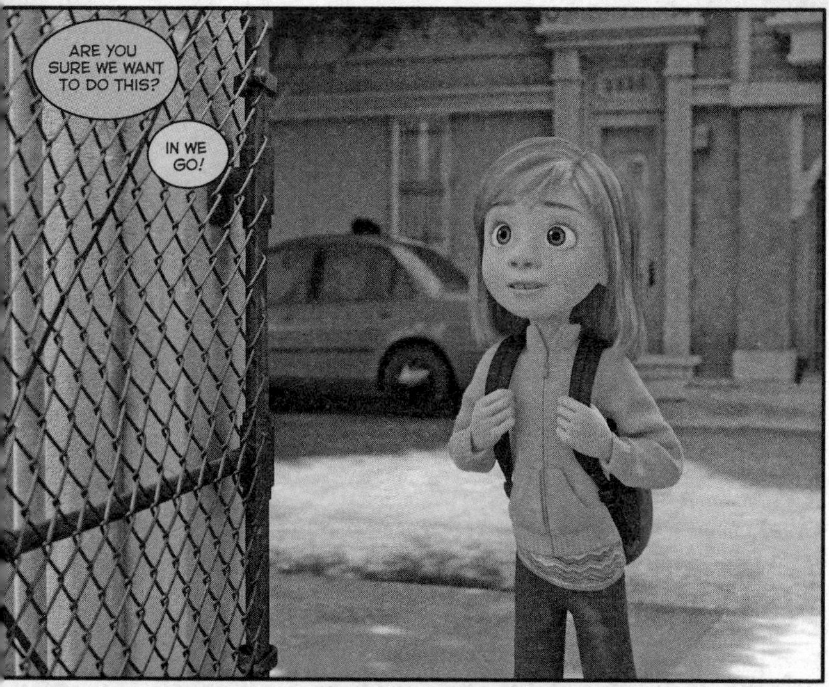
ARE YOU SURE WE WANT TO DO THIS?
IN WE GO!

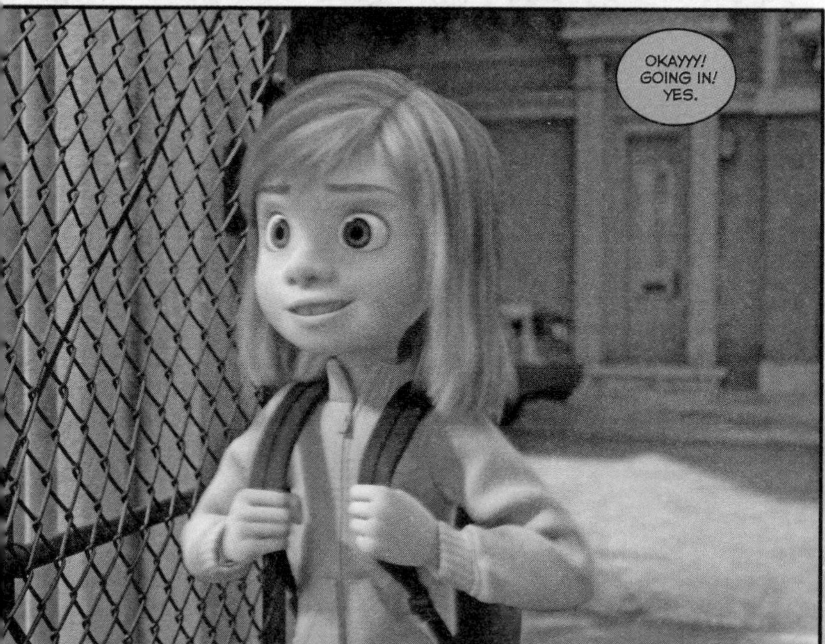
OKAYYY! GOING IN! YES.

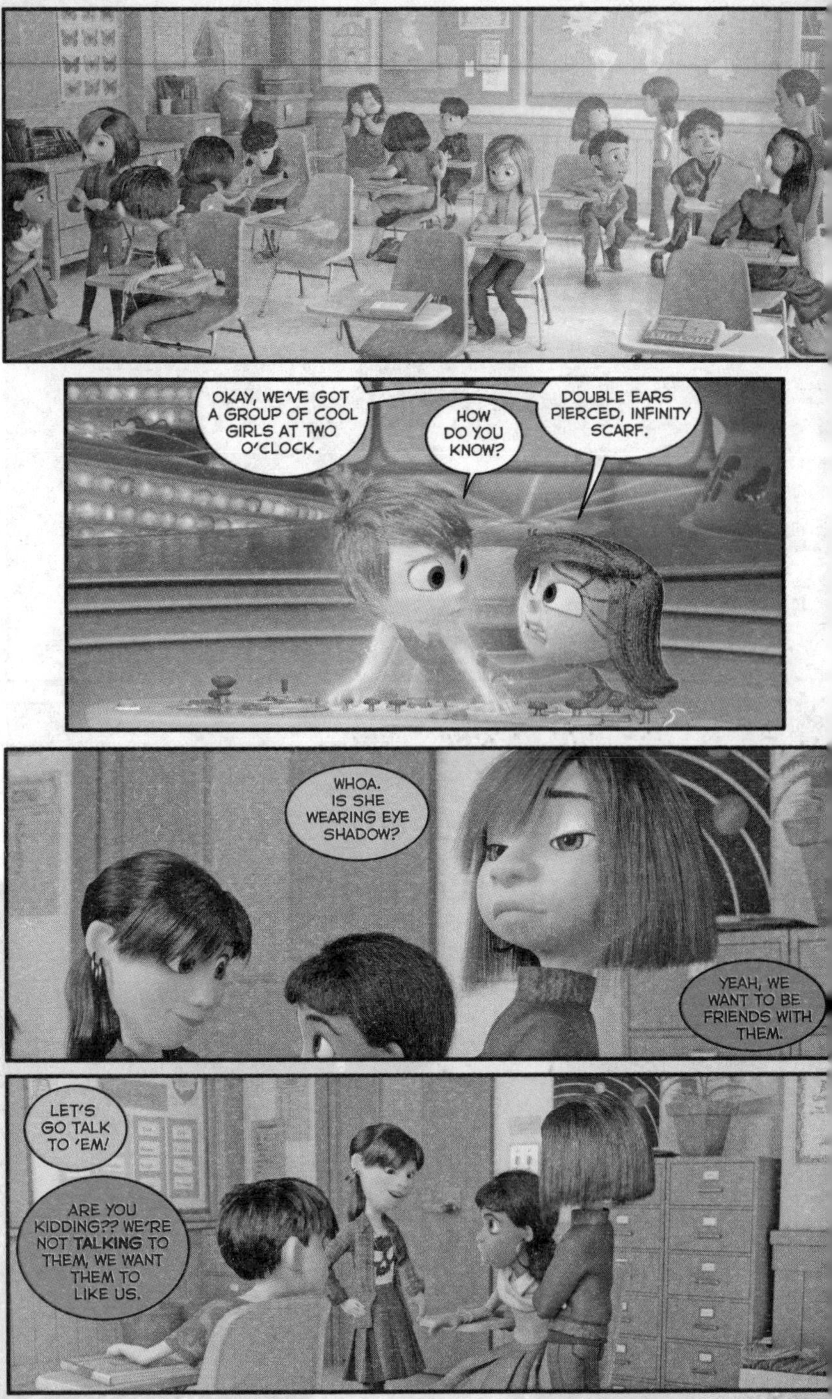
OKAY, WE'VE GOT A GROUP OF COOL GIRLS AT TWO O'CLOCK.
HOW DO YOU KNOW?
DOUBLE EARS PIERCED, INFINITY SCARF.
WHOA. IS SHE WEARING EYE SHADOW?
YEAH, WE WANT TO BE FRIENDS WITH THEM.
LET'S GO TALK TO 'EM!
ARE YOU KIDDING?? WE'RE NOT **TALKING** TO THEM, WE WANT THEM TO LIKE US.

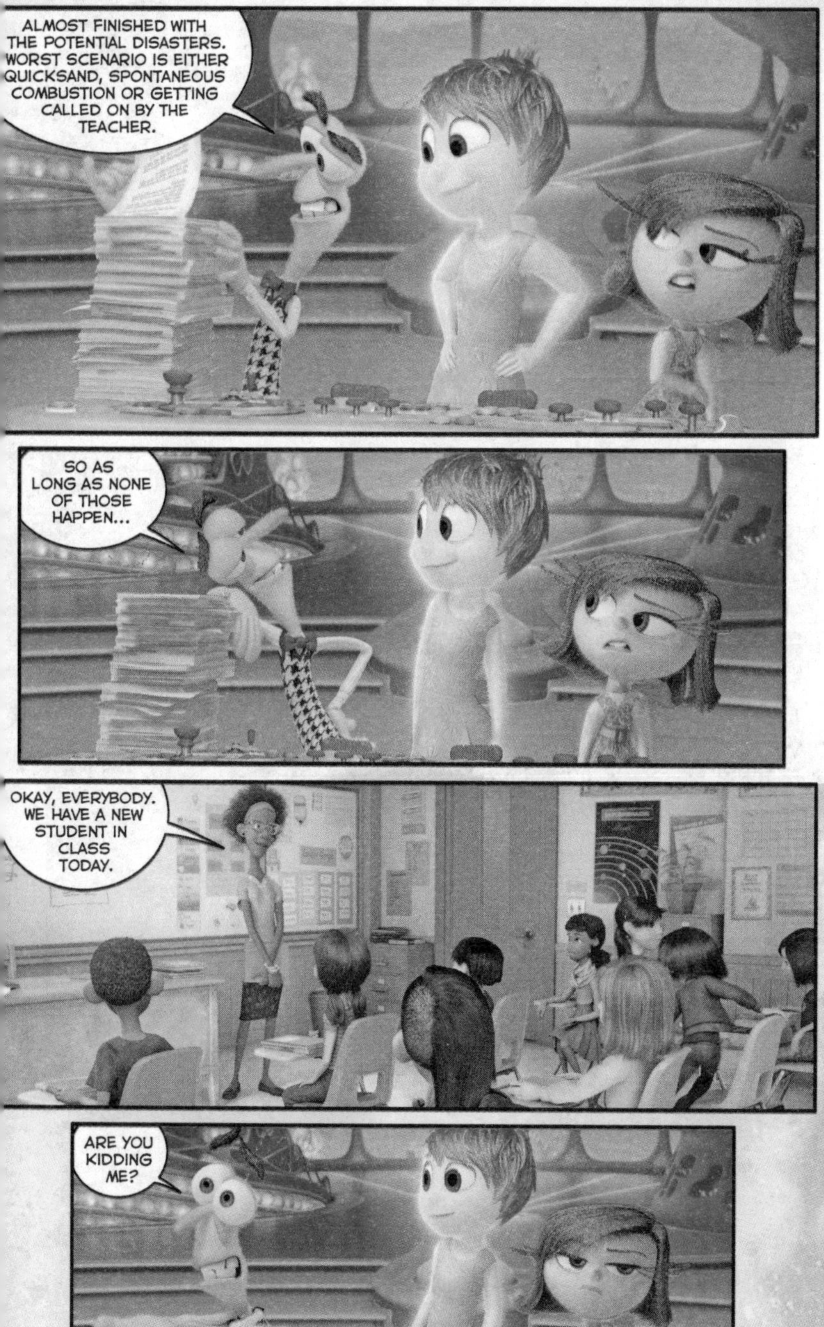
ALMOST FINISHED WITH THE POTENTIAL DISASTERS. WORST SCENARIO IS EITHER QUICKSAND, SPONTANEOUS COMBUSTION OR GETTING CALLED ON BY THE TEACHER.
SO AS LONG AS NONE OF THOSE HAPPEN...
OKAY, EVERYBODY. WE HAVE A NEW STUDENT IN CLASS TODAY.
ARE YOU KIDDING ME?

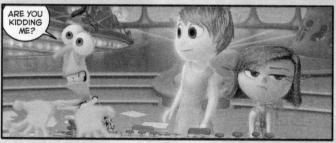

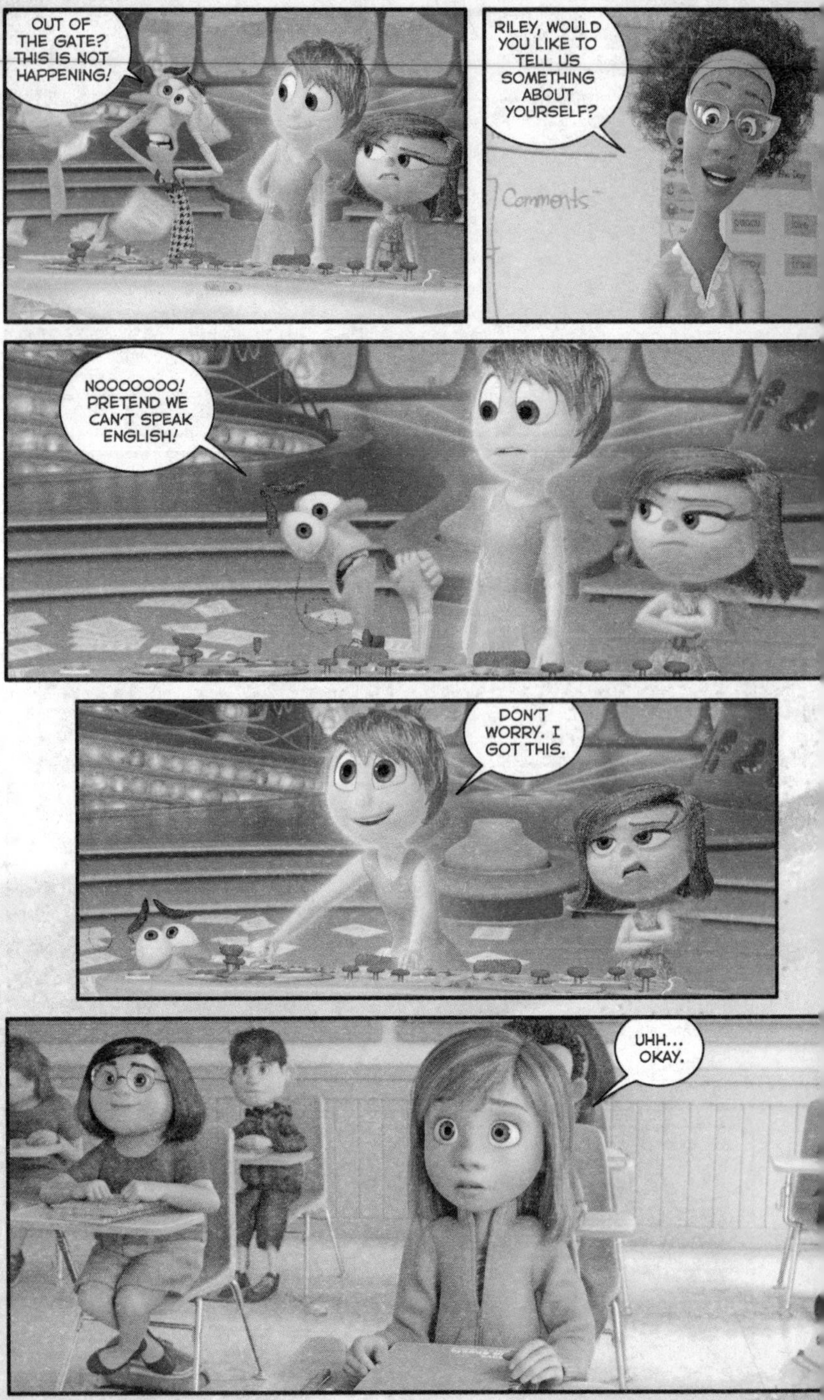
OUT OF THE GATE? THIS IS NOT HAPPENING!
RILEY, WOULD YOU LIKE TO TELL US SOMETHING ABOUT YOURSELF?
Comments
NOOOOOOO! PRETEND WE CAN'T SPEAK ENGLISH!
DON'T WORRY. I GOT THIS.
UHH... OKAY.

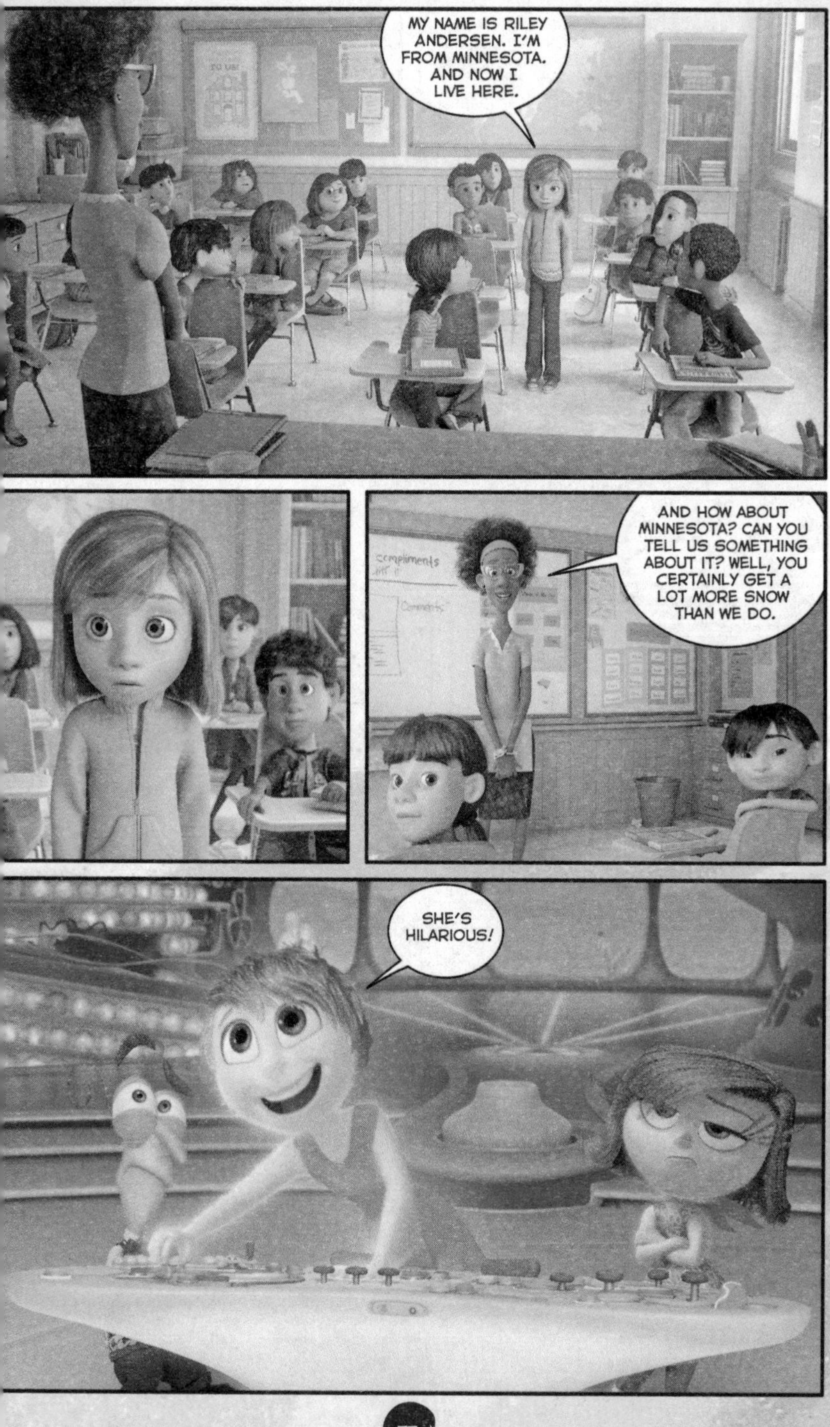
MY NAME IS RILEY ANDERSEN. I'M FROM MINNESOTA. AND NOW I LIVE HERE.
AND HOW ABOUT MINNESOTA? CAN YOU TELL US SOMETHING ABOUT IT? WELL, YOU CERTAINLY GET A LOT MORE SNOW THAN WE DO.
SHE'S HILARIOUS!

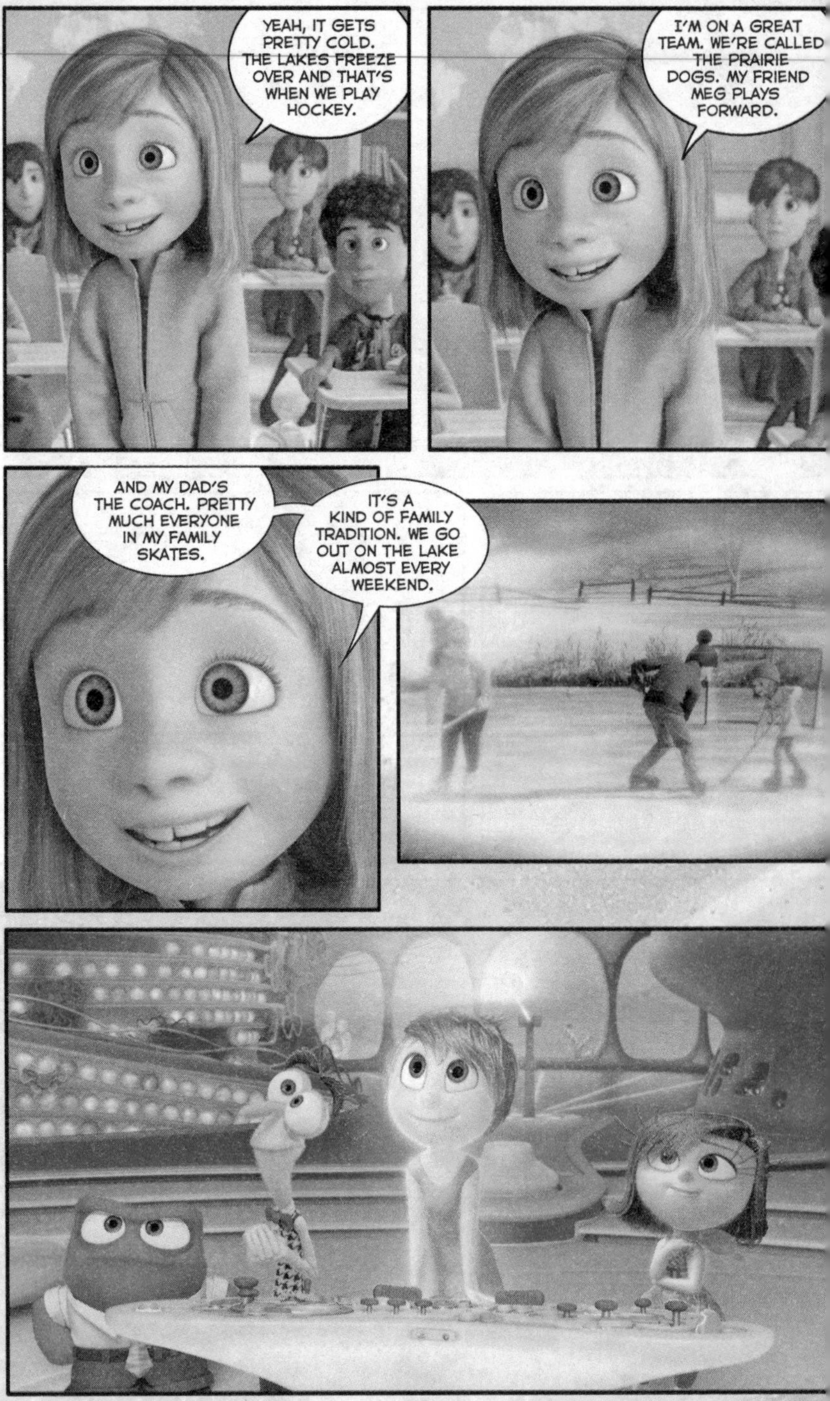

YEAH, IT GETS PRETTY COLD. THE LAKES FREEZE OVER AND THAT'S WHEN WE PLAY HOCKEY.
I'M ON A GREAT TEAM. WE'RE CALLED THE PRAIRIE DOGS. MY FRIEND MEG PLAYS FORWARD.
AND MY DAD'S THE COACH. PRETTY MUCH EVERYONE IN MY FAMILY SKATES.
IT'S A KIND OF FAMILY TRADITION. WE GO OUT ON THE LAKE ALMOST EVERY WEEKEND.

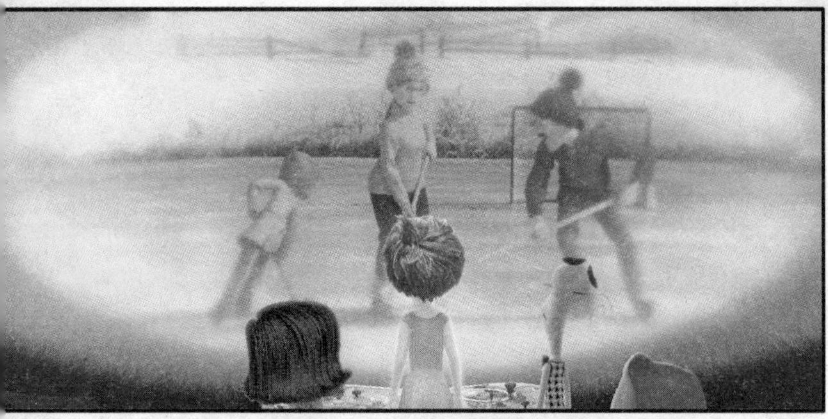
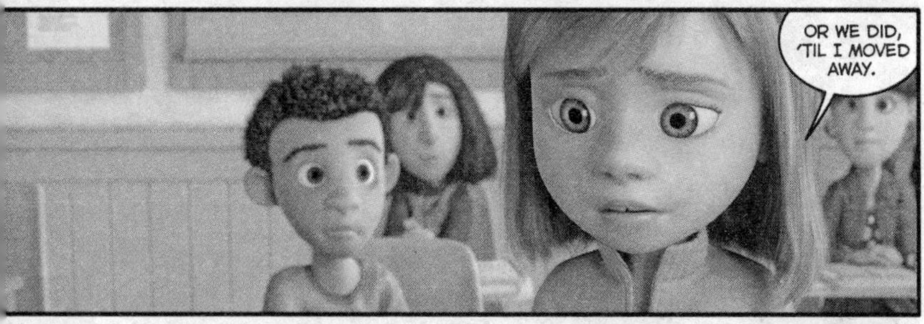
OR WE DID, 'TIL I MOVED AWAY.
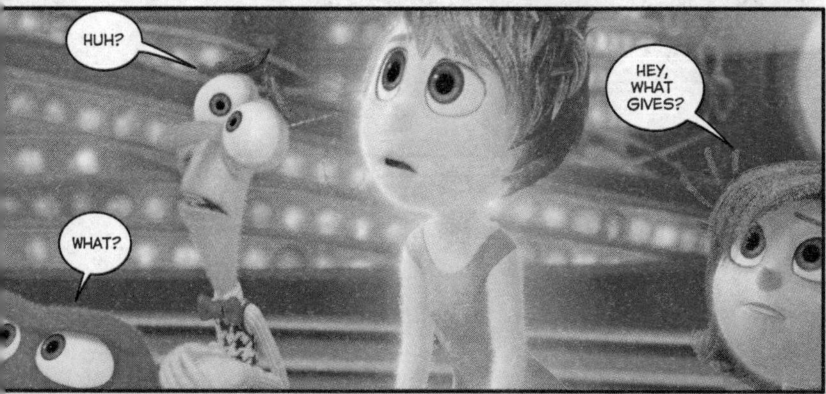
HUH?
HEY, WHAT GIVES?
WHAT?
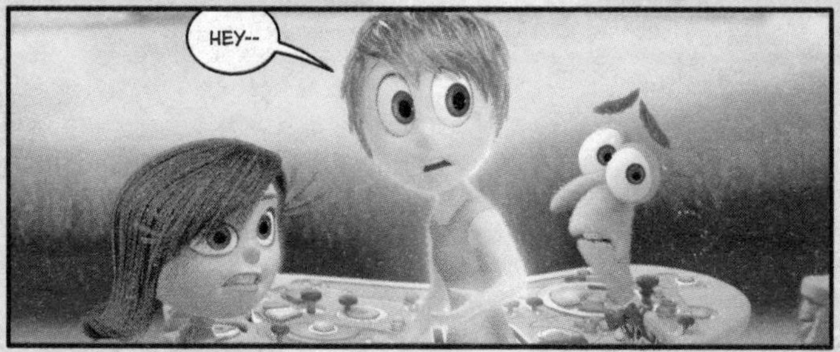
HEY--

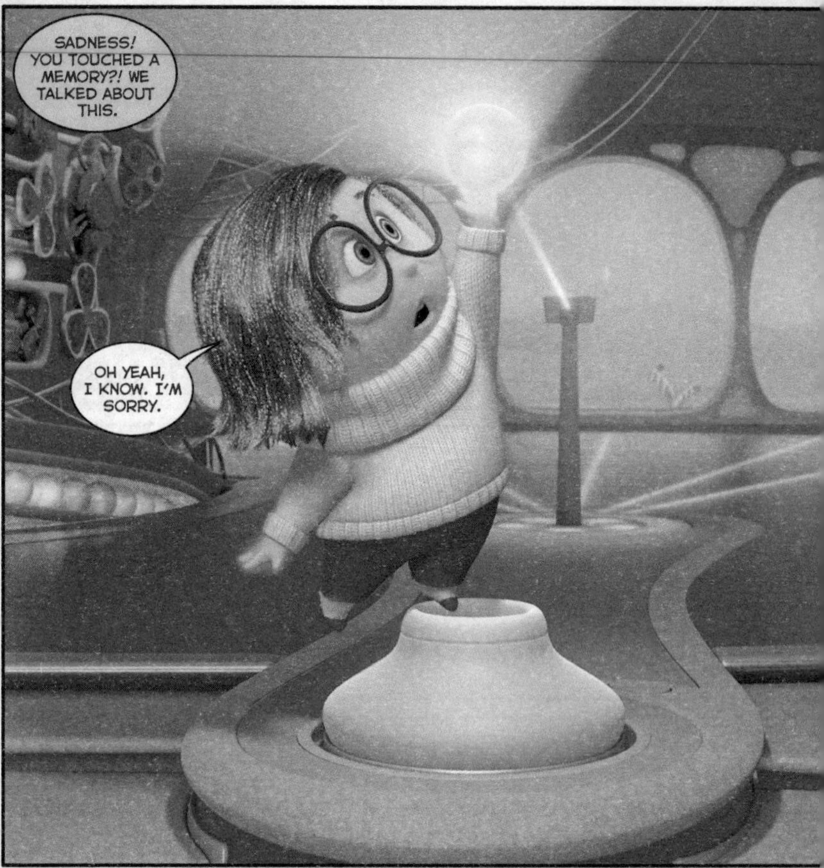
SADNESS! YOU TOUCHED A MEMORY?! WE TALKED ABOUT THIS.
OH YEAH, I KNOW. I'M SORRY.

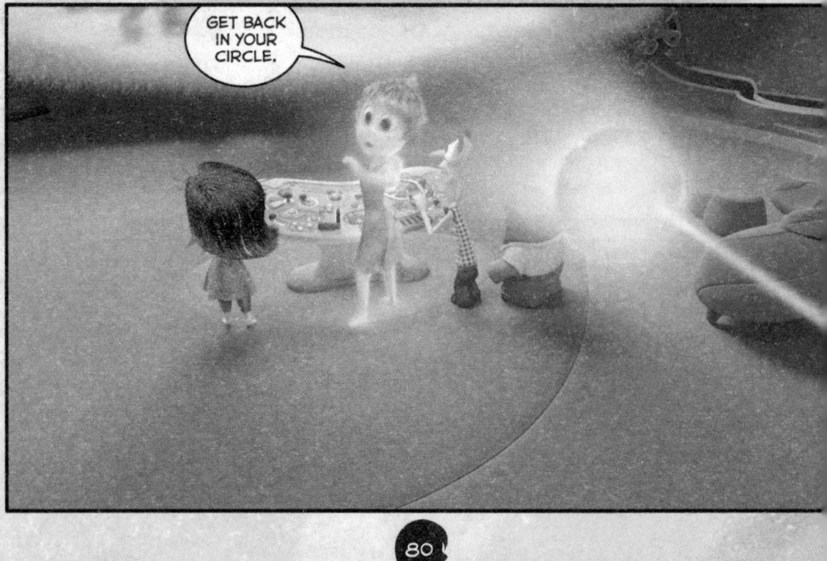
GET BACK IN YOUR CIRCLE.

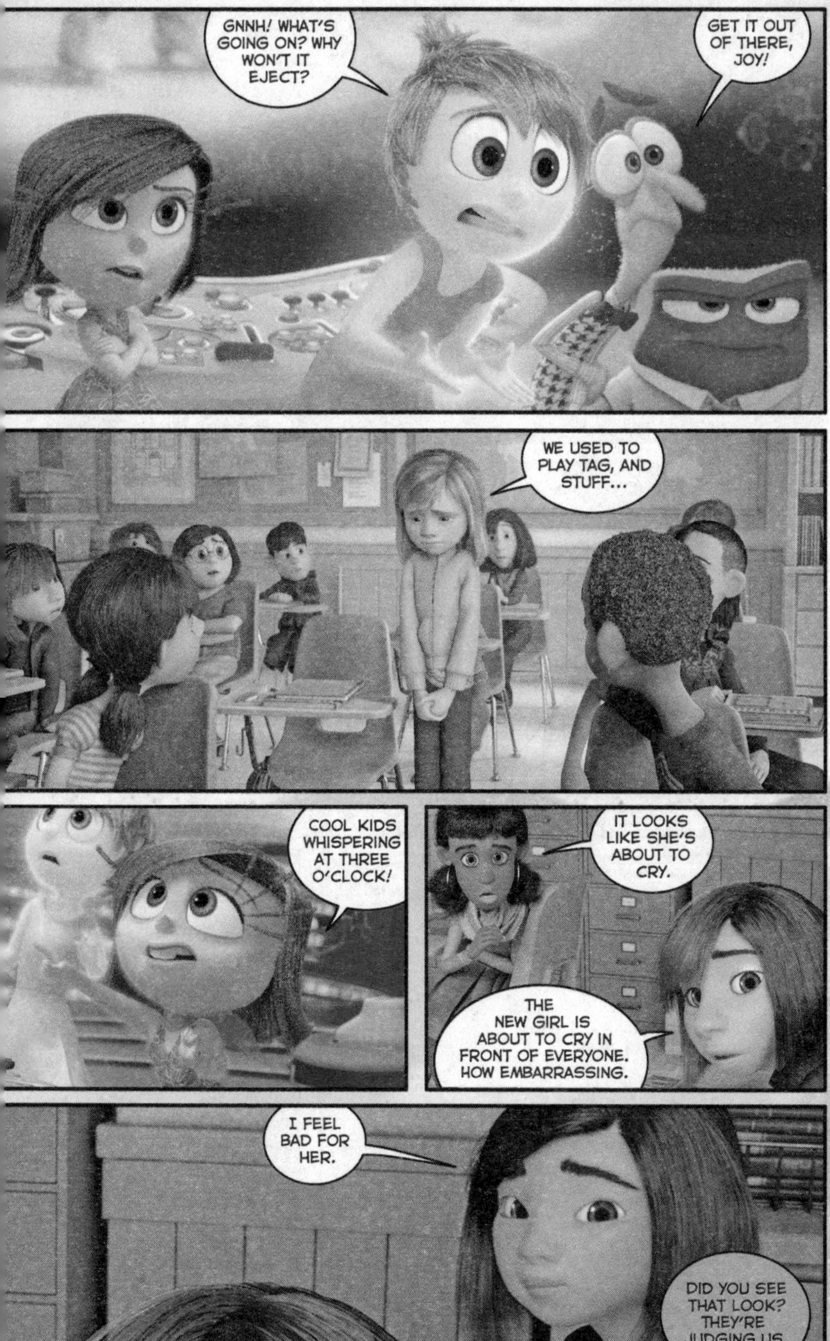
GNNH! WHAT'S GOING ON? WHY WON'T IT EJECT?
GET IT OUT OF THERE, JOY!
WE USED TO PLAY TAG, AND STUFF...
COOL KIDS WHISPERING AT THREE O'CLOCK!
IT LOOKS LIKE SHE'S ABOUT TO CRY.
THE NEW GIRL IS ABOUT TO CRY IN FRONT OF EVERYONE. HOW EMBARRASSING.
I FEEL BAD FOR HER.
DID YOU SEE THAT LOOK? THEY'RE JUDGING US.

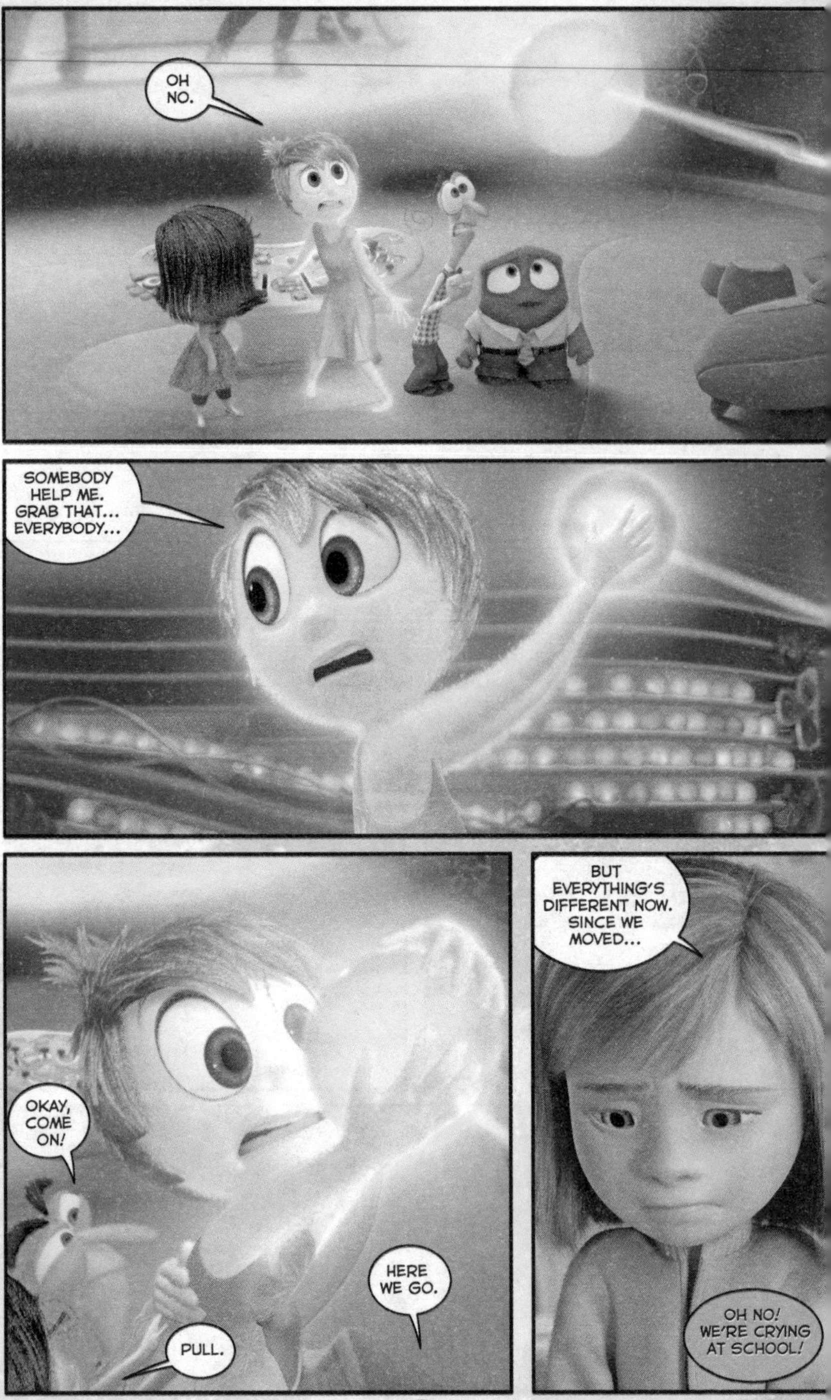
OH NO.
SOMEBODY HELP ME. GRAB THAT... EVERYBODY...
OKAY, COME ON!
HERE WE GO.
PULL.
BUT EVERYTHING'S DIFFERENT NOW. SINCE WE MOVED...
OH NO! WE'RE CRYING AT SCHOOL!

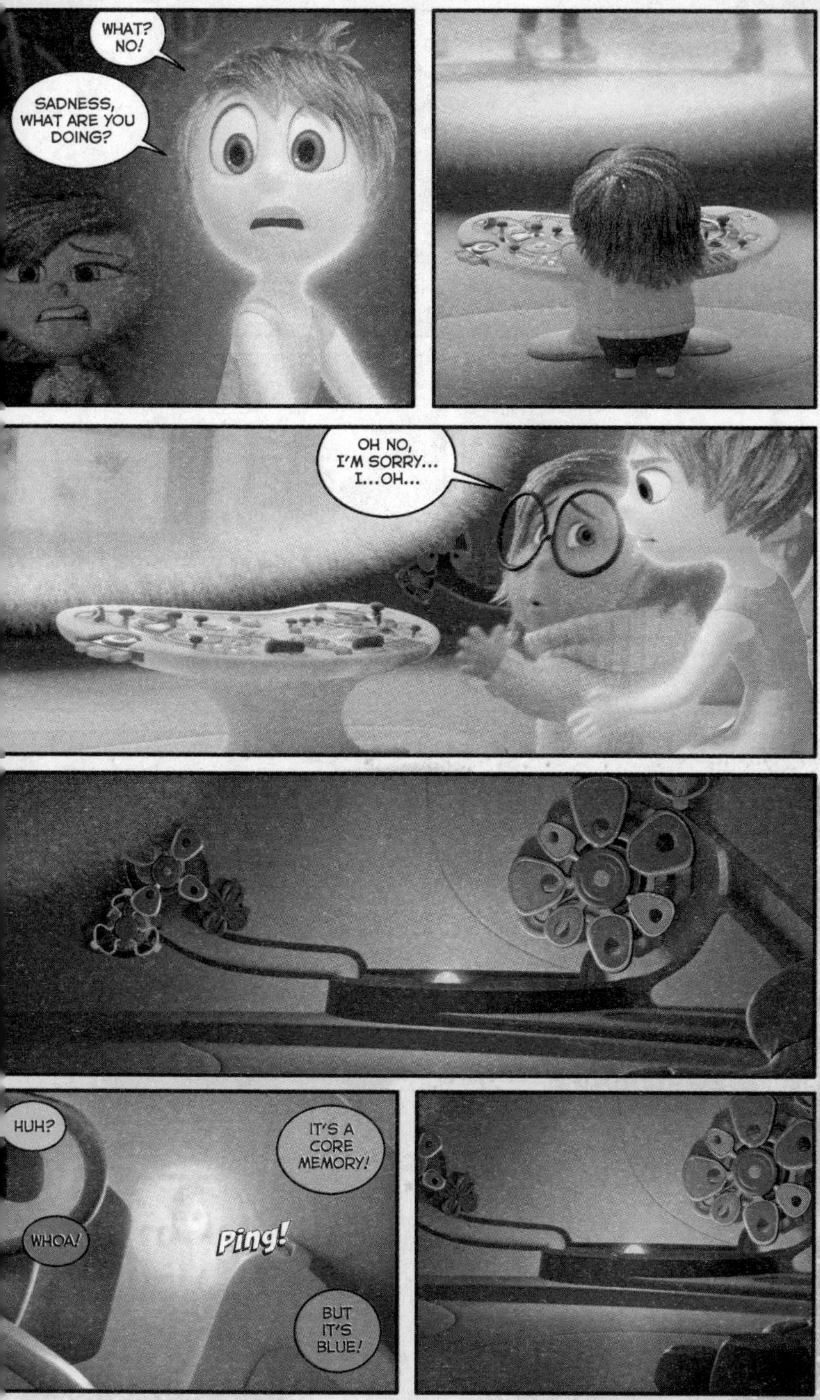
WHAT? NO!
SADNESS, WHAT ARE YOU DOING?
OH NO, I'M SORRY... I...OH...
HUH?
IT'S A CORE MEMORY!
WHOA!
Ping!
BUT IT'S BLUE!

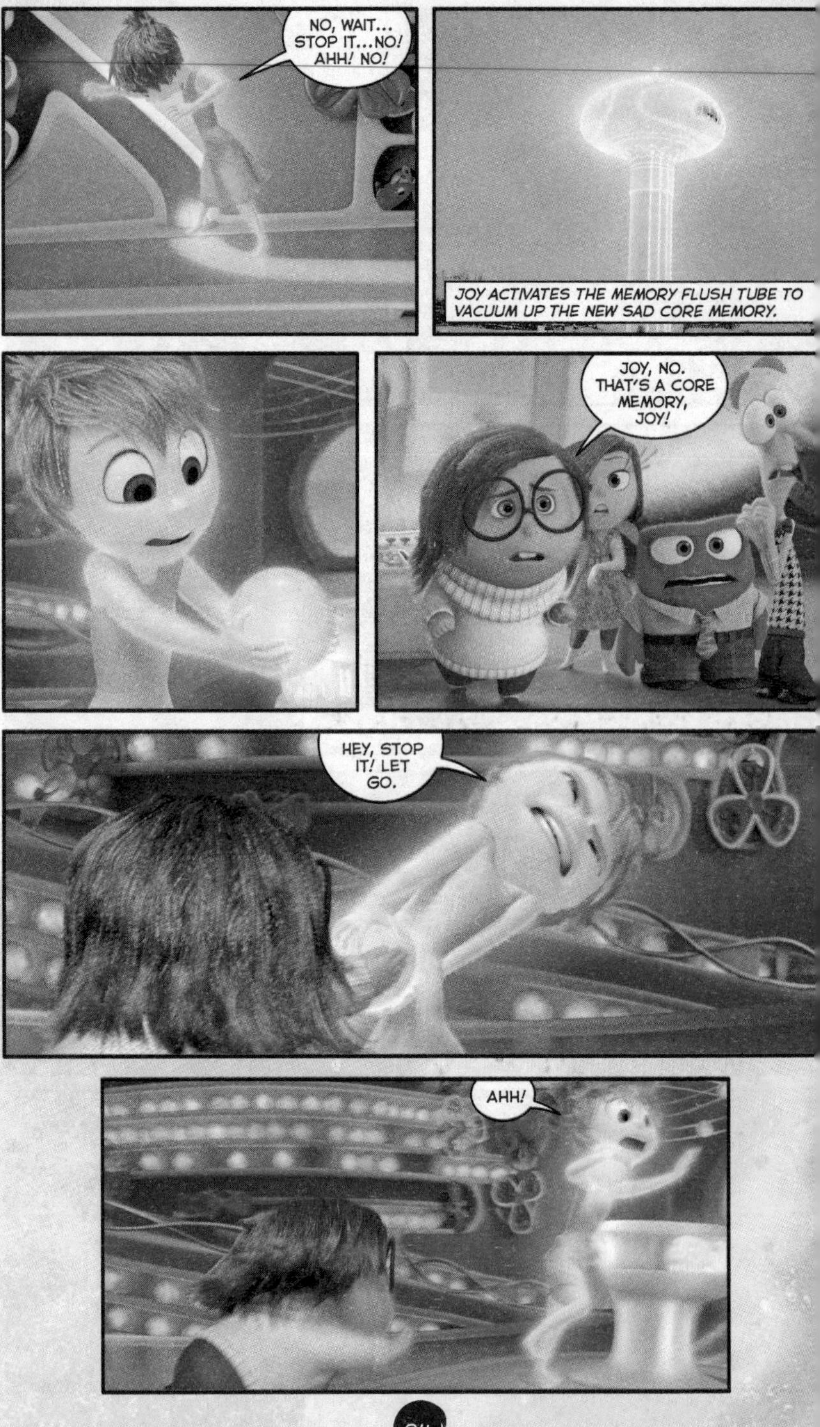
NO, WAIT... STOP IT...NO! AHH! NO!
JOY ACTIVATES THE MEMORY FLUSH TUBE TO VACUUM UP THE NEW SAD CORE MEMORY.
JOY, NO. THAT'S A CORE MEMORY, JOY!
HEY, STOP IT! LET GO.
AHH!

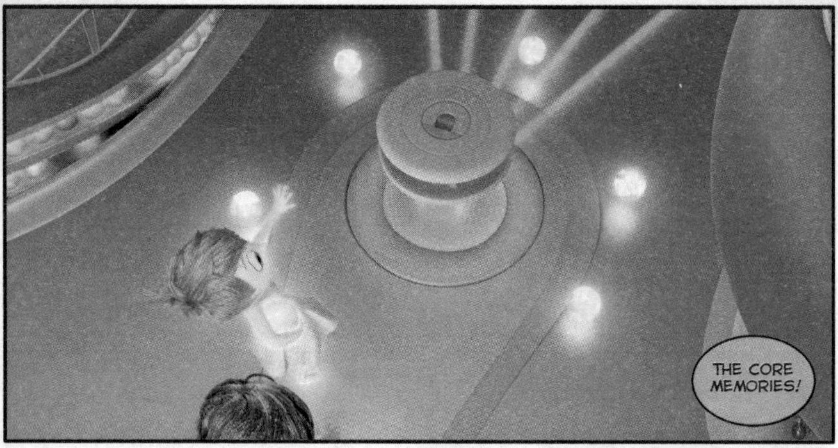
THE CORE
MEMORIES!

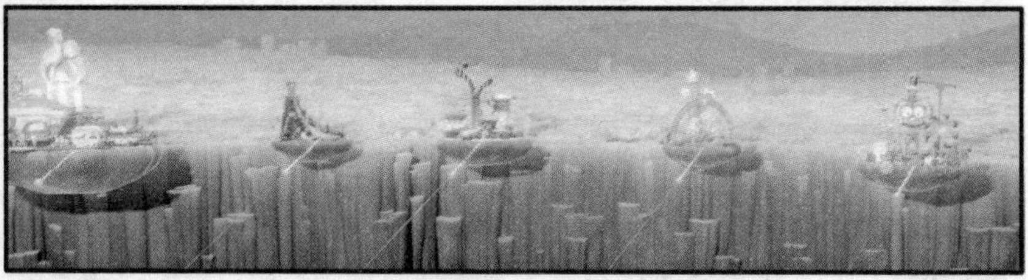

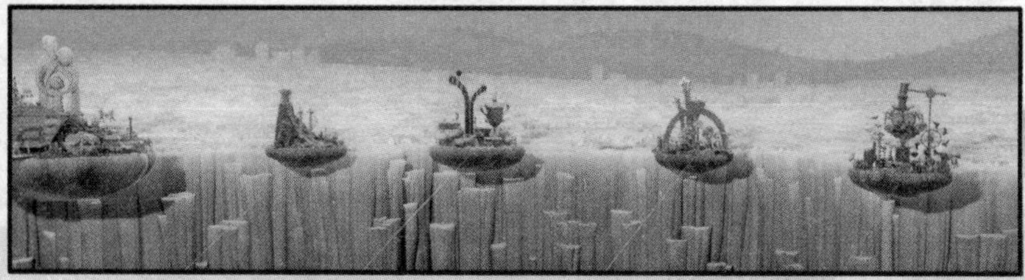

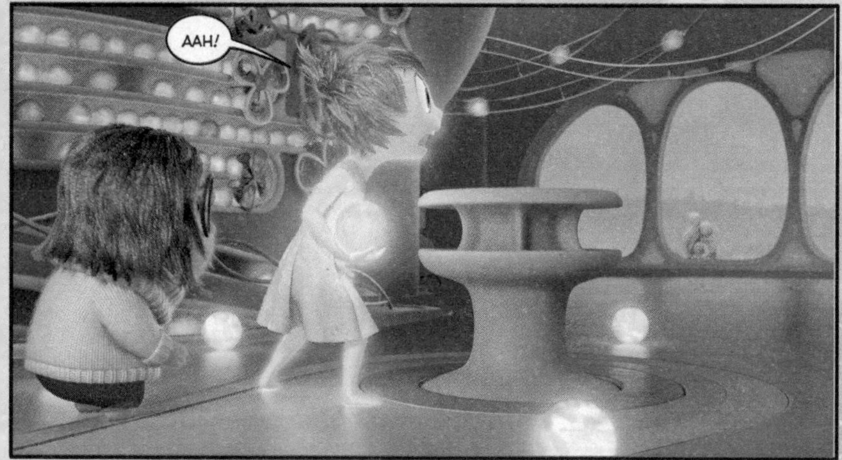
AAH!

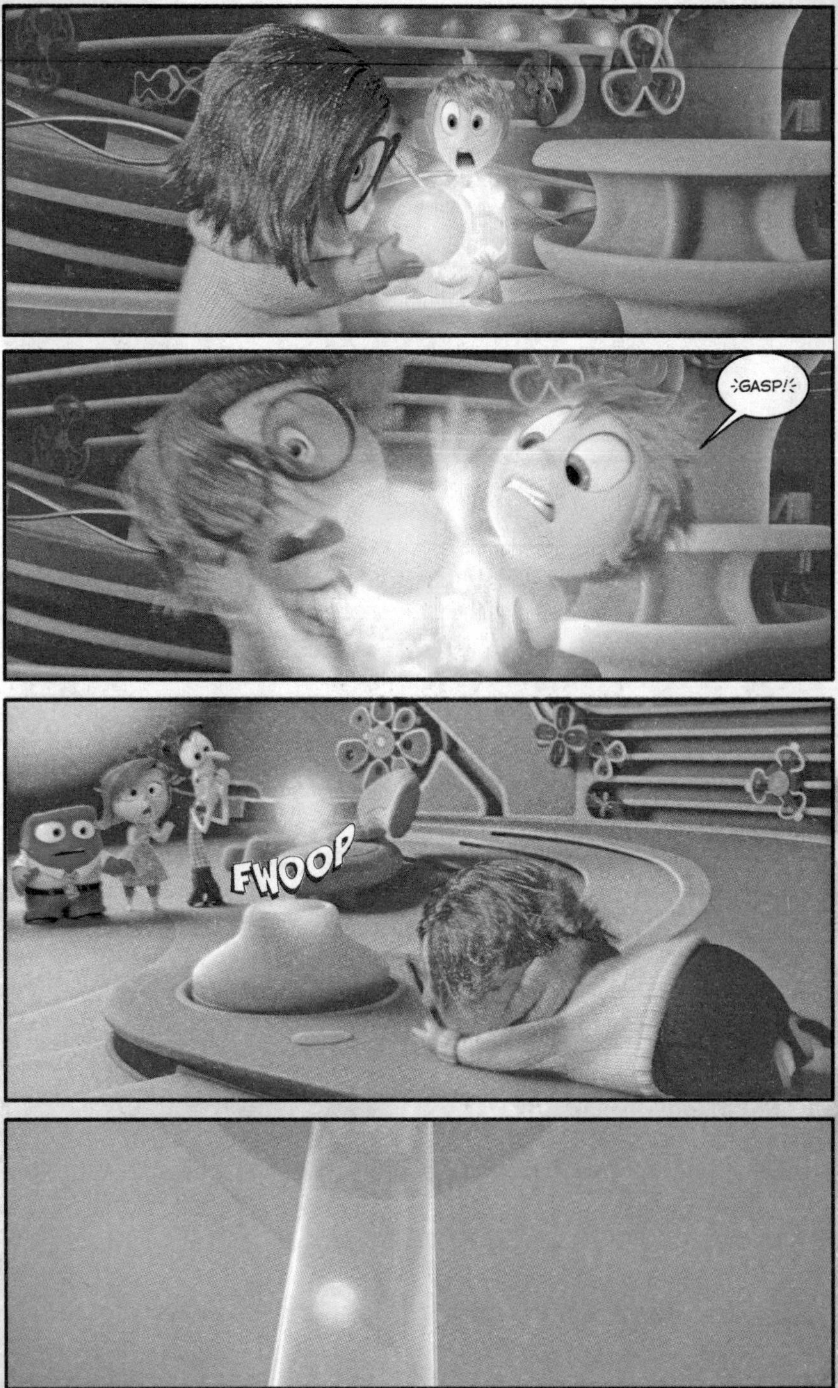
GASP!
FWOOP

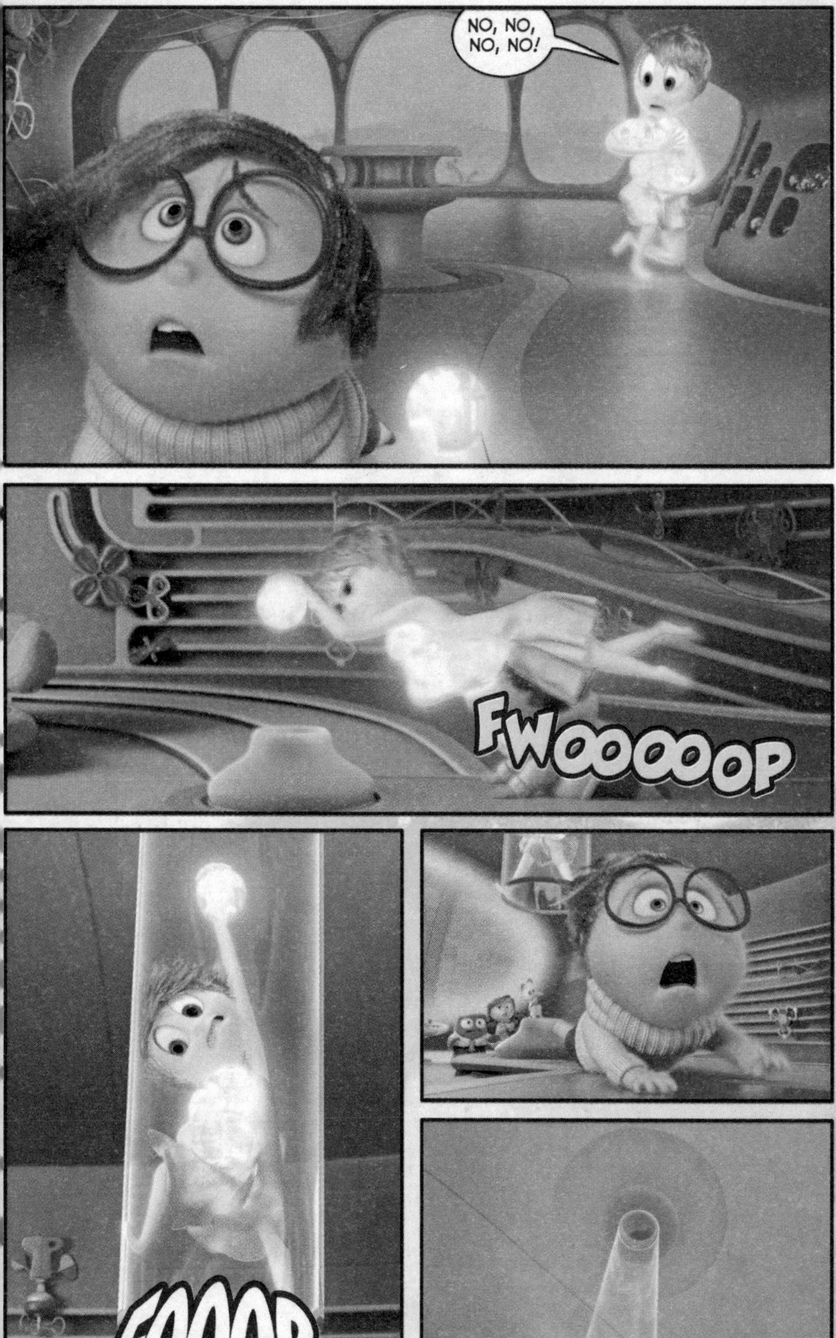
NO, NO,
NO, NO!
FWOOOOOP
FOOOP

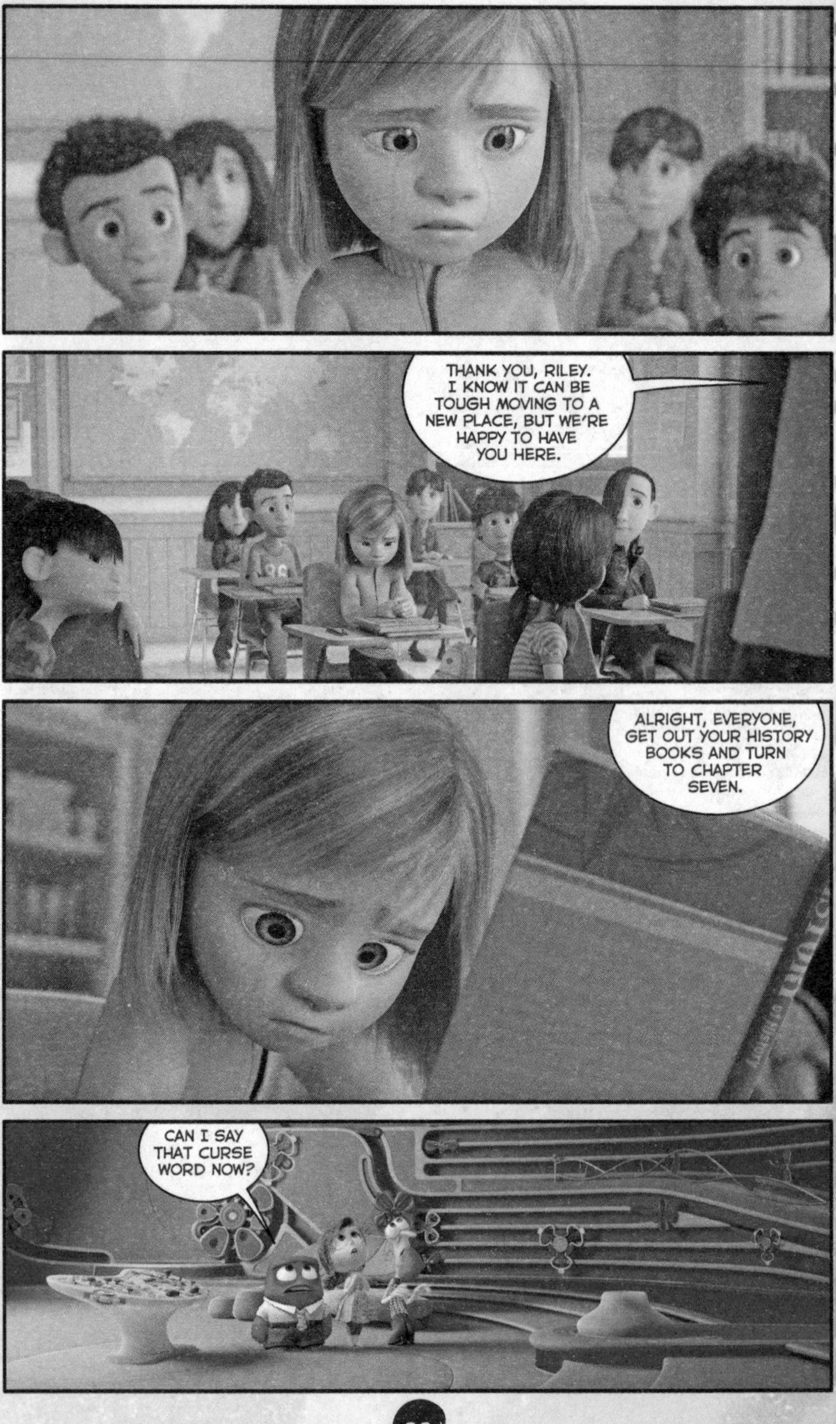
THANK YOU, RILEY. I KNOW IT CAN BE TOUGH MOVING TO A NEW PLACE, BUT WE'RE HAPPY TO HAVE YOU HERE.
ALRIGHT, EVERYONE, GET OUT YOUR HISTORY BOOKS AND TURN TO CHAPTER SEVEN.
CAN I SAY THAT CURSE WORD NOW?

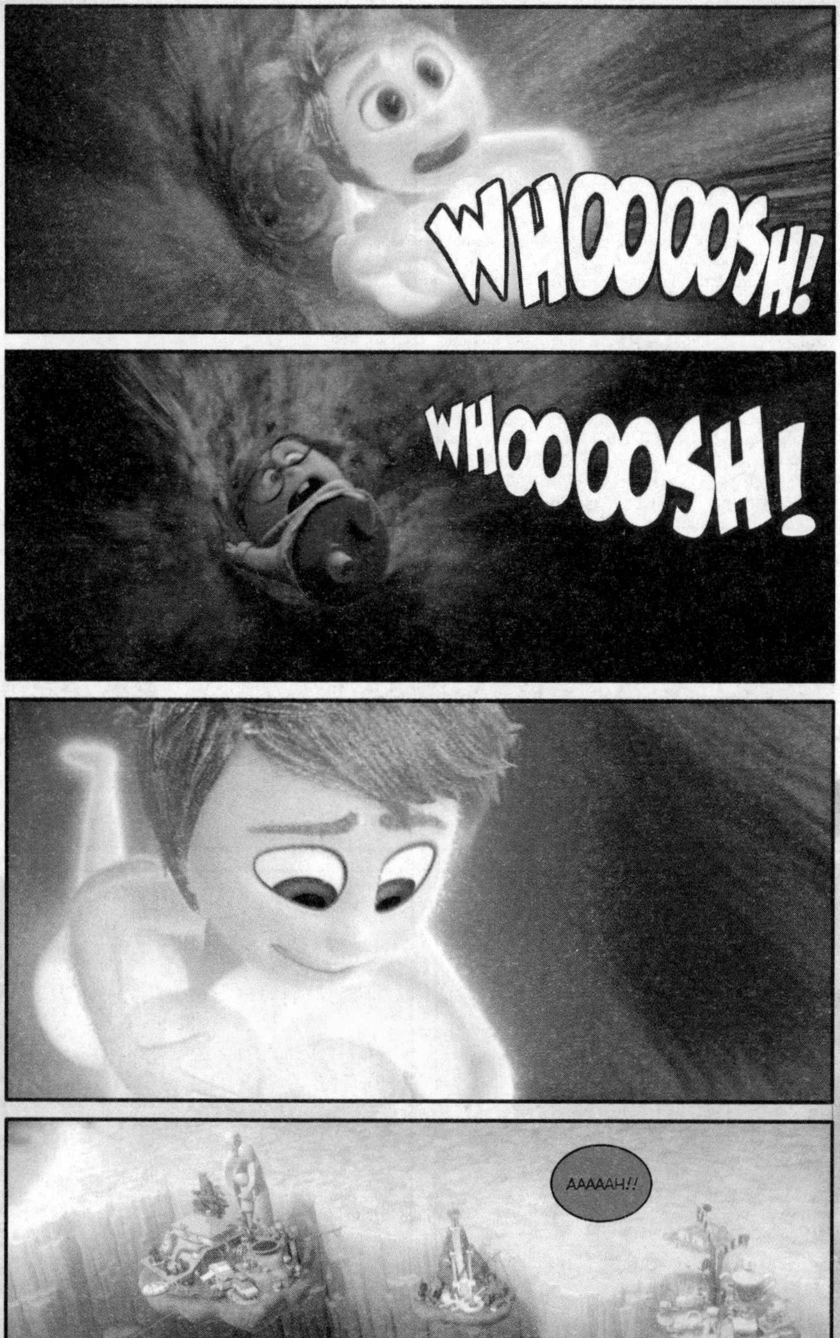
WHOOOOSH!
WHOOOOSH!
AAAAAH!!

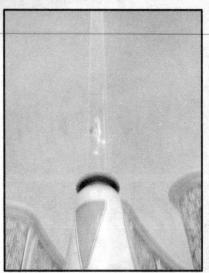

WAAAAA
AAAAAAA
OOHFPH!

OH NO...ONE,
TWO, THREE...
OKAY, GOT 'EM.
WHA -- WHERE
ARE WE?

LONG
TERM
MEMORY...!

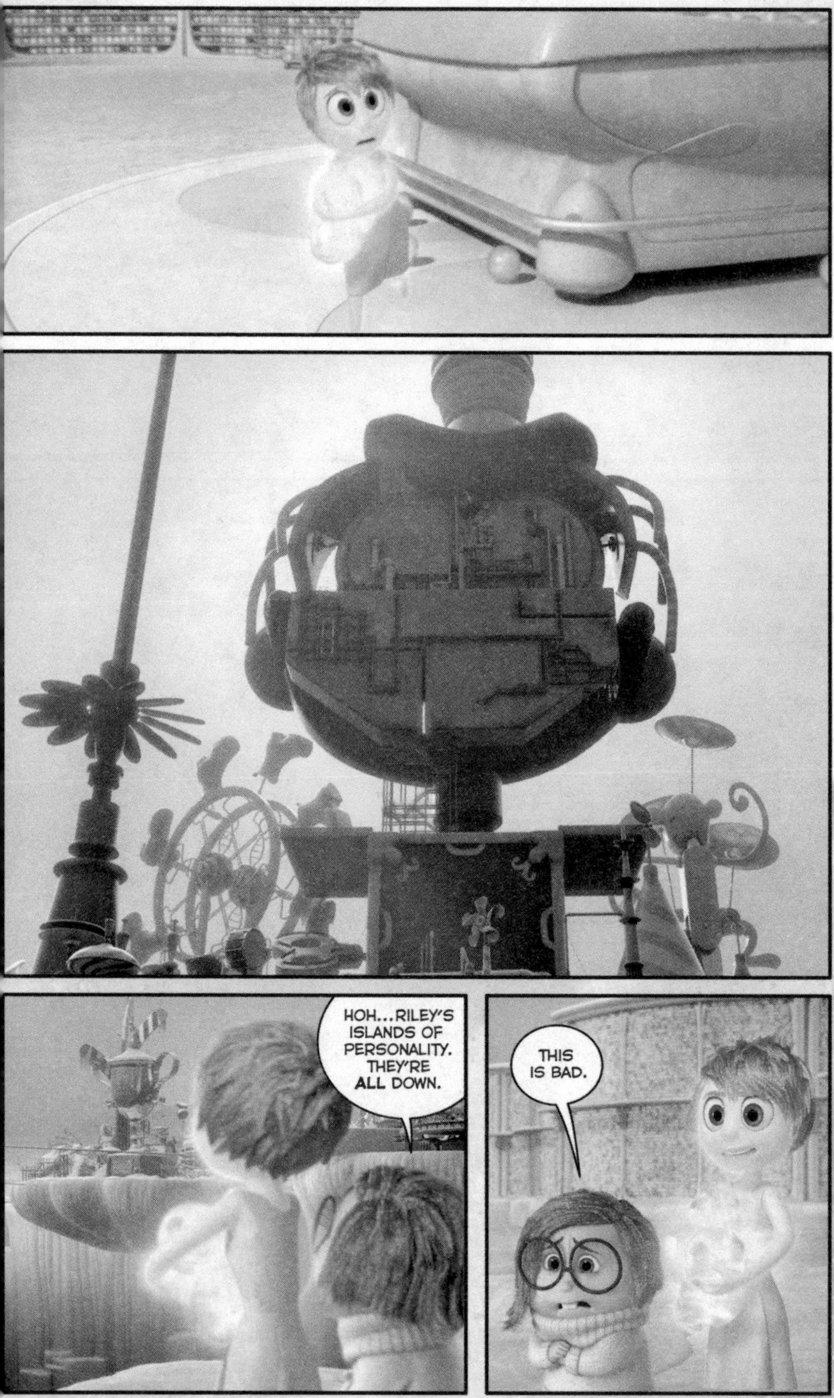
HOH...RILEY'S ISLANDS OF PERSONALITY. THEY'RE ALL DOWN.
THIS IS BAD.

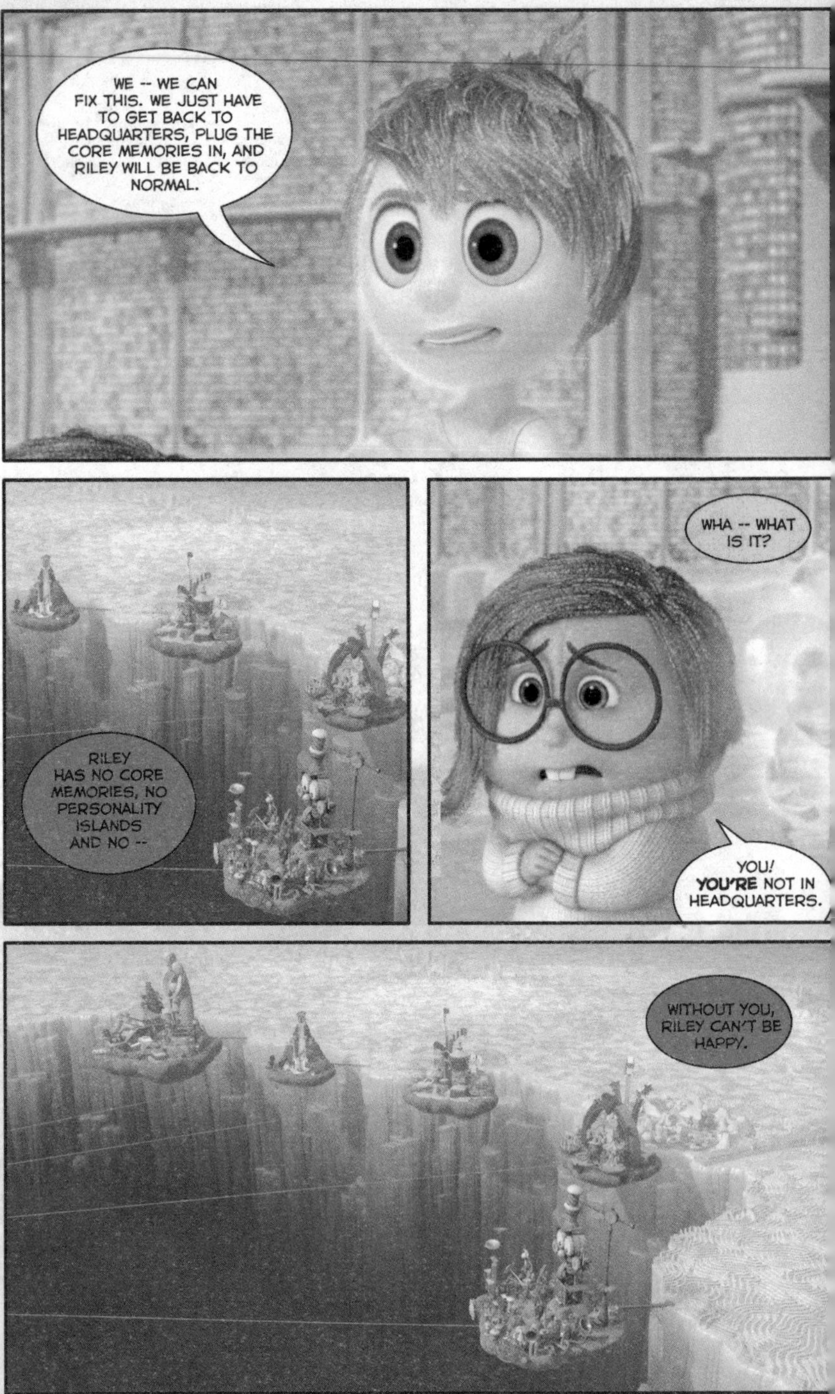
WE -- WE CAN FIX THIS. WE JUST HAVE TO GET BACK TO HEADQUARTERS, PLUG THE CORE MEMORIES IN, AND RILEY WILL BE BACK TO NORMAL.
RILEY HAS NO CORE MEMORIES, NO PERSONALITY ISLANDS AND NO --
WHA -- WHAT IS IT?
YOU! **YOU'RE** NOT IN HEADQUARTERS.
WITHOUT YOU, RILEY CAN'T BE HAPPY.

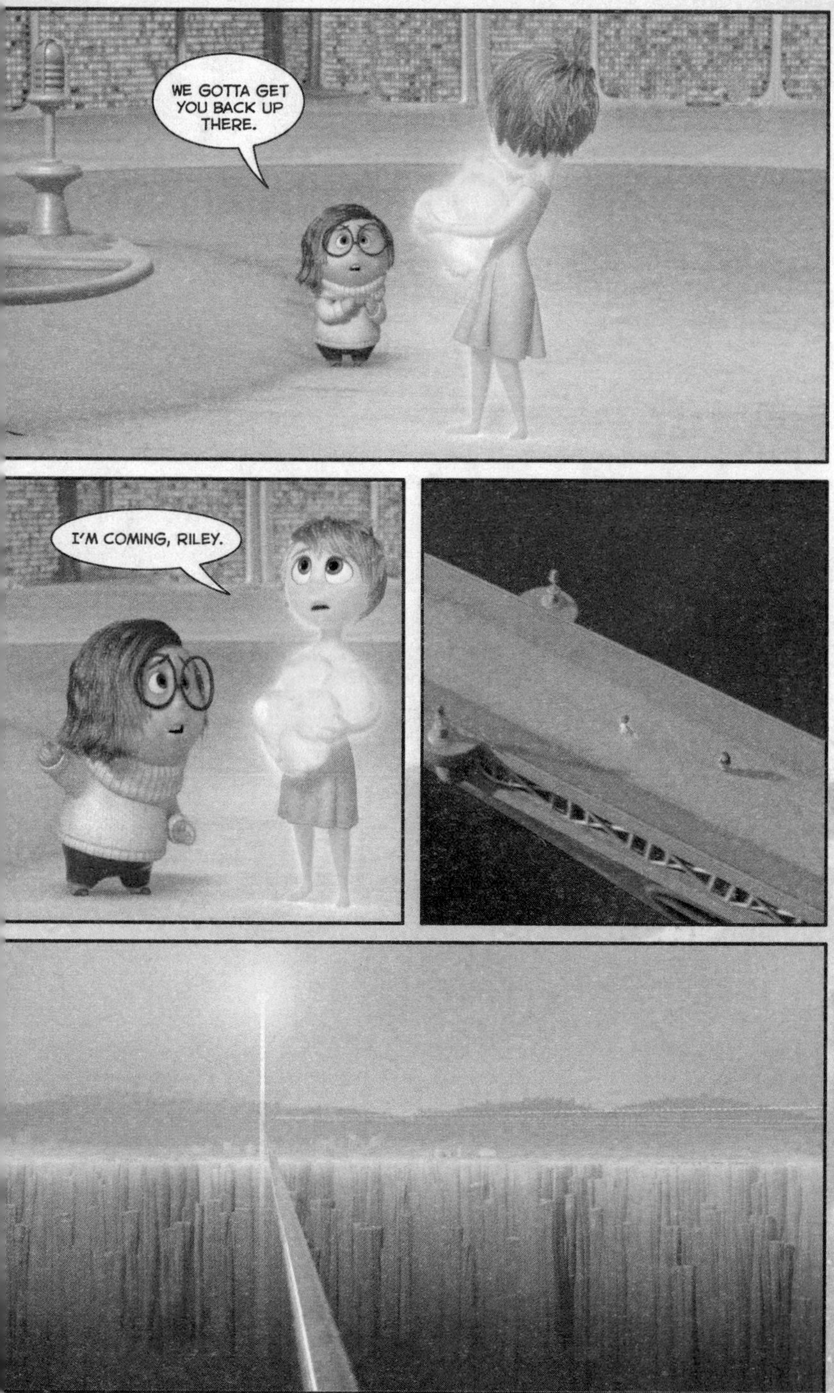
WE GOTTA GET YOU BACK UP THERE.
I'M COMING, RILEY.

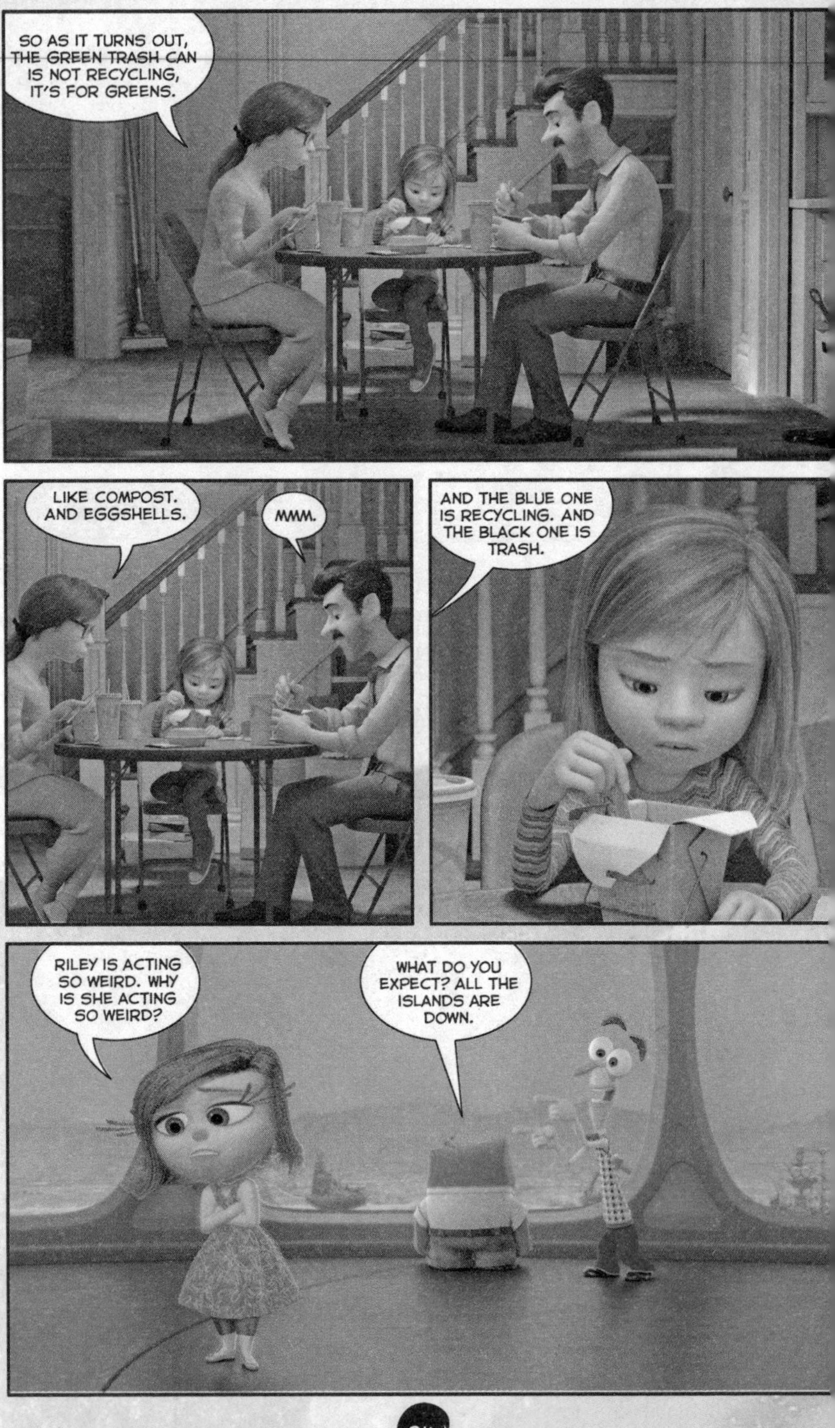
SO AS IT TURNS OUT, THE GREEN TRASH CAN IS NOT RECYCLING, IT'S FOR GREENS.
LIKE COMPOST. AND EGGSHELLS.
MMM.
AND THE BLUE ONE IS RECYCLING. AND THE BLACK ONE IS TRASH.
RILEY IS ACTING SO WEIRD. WHY IS SHE ACTING SO WEIRD?
WHAT DO YOU EXPECT? ALL THE ISLANDS ARE DOWN.

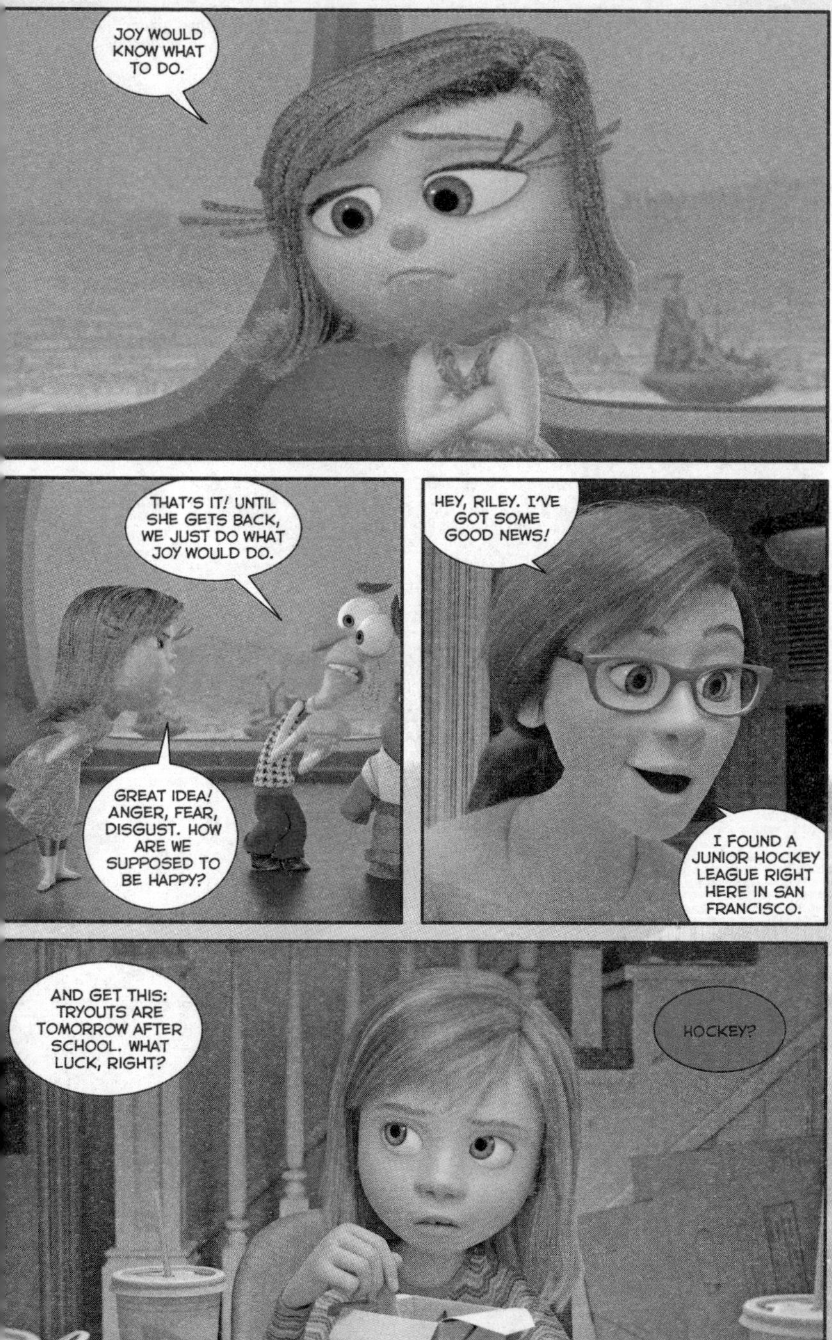
JOY WOULD KNOW WHAT TO DO.
THAT'S IT! UNTIL SHE GETS BACK, WE JUST DO WHAT JOY WOULD DO.
GREAT IDEA! ANGER, FEAR, DISGUST. HOW ARE WE SUPPOSED TO BE HAPPY?
HEY, RILEY. I'VE GOT SOME GOOD NEWS!
I FOUND A JUNIOR HOCKEY LEAGUE RIGHT HERE IN SAN FRANCISCO.
AND GET THIS: TRYOUTS ARE TOMORROW AFTER SCHOOL. WHAT LUCK, RIGHT?
HOCKEY?

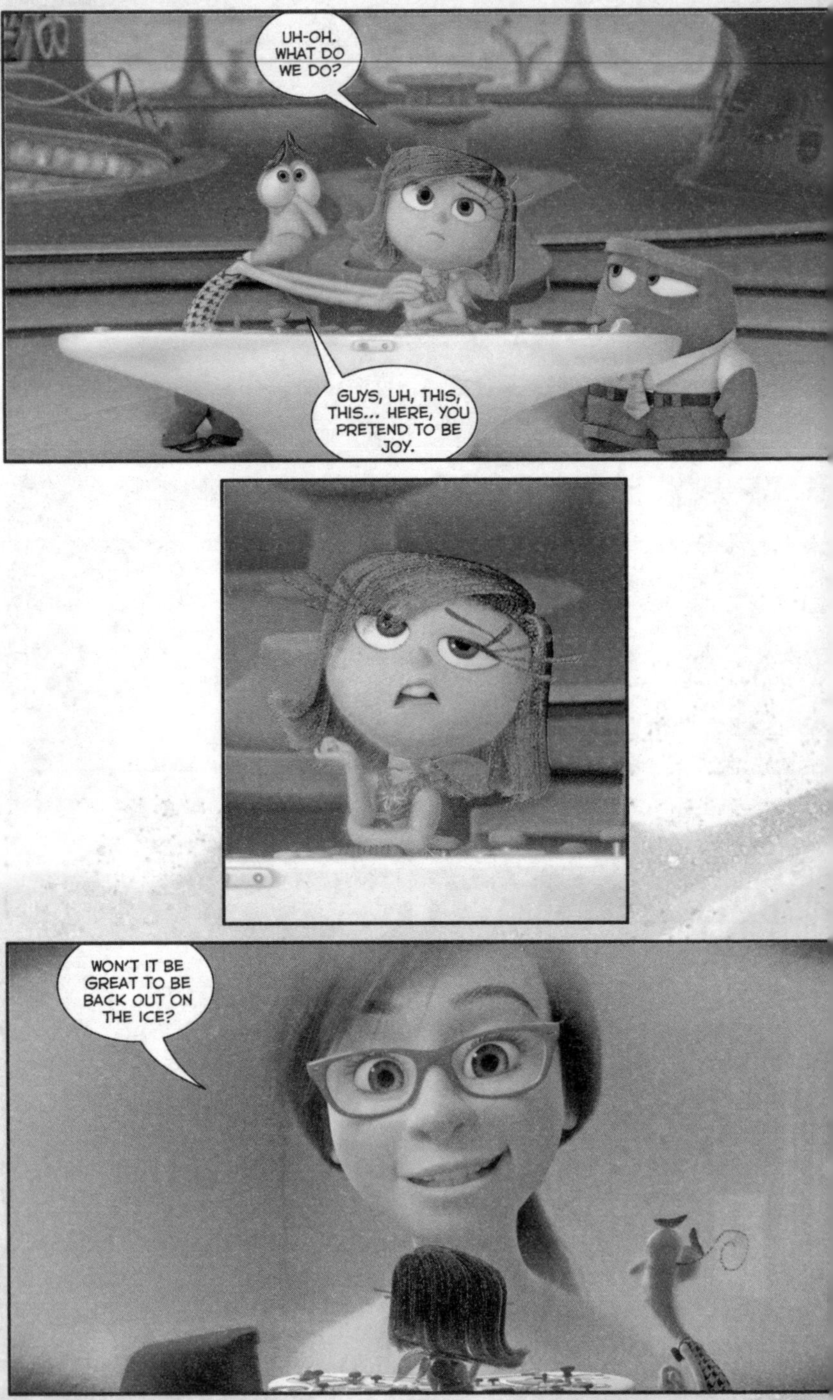
UH-OH. WHAT DO WE DO?
GUYS, UH, THIS, THIS... HERE, YOU PRETEND TO BE JOY.
WON'T IT BE GREAT TO BE BACK OUT ON THE ICE?

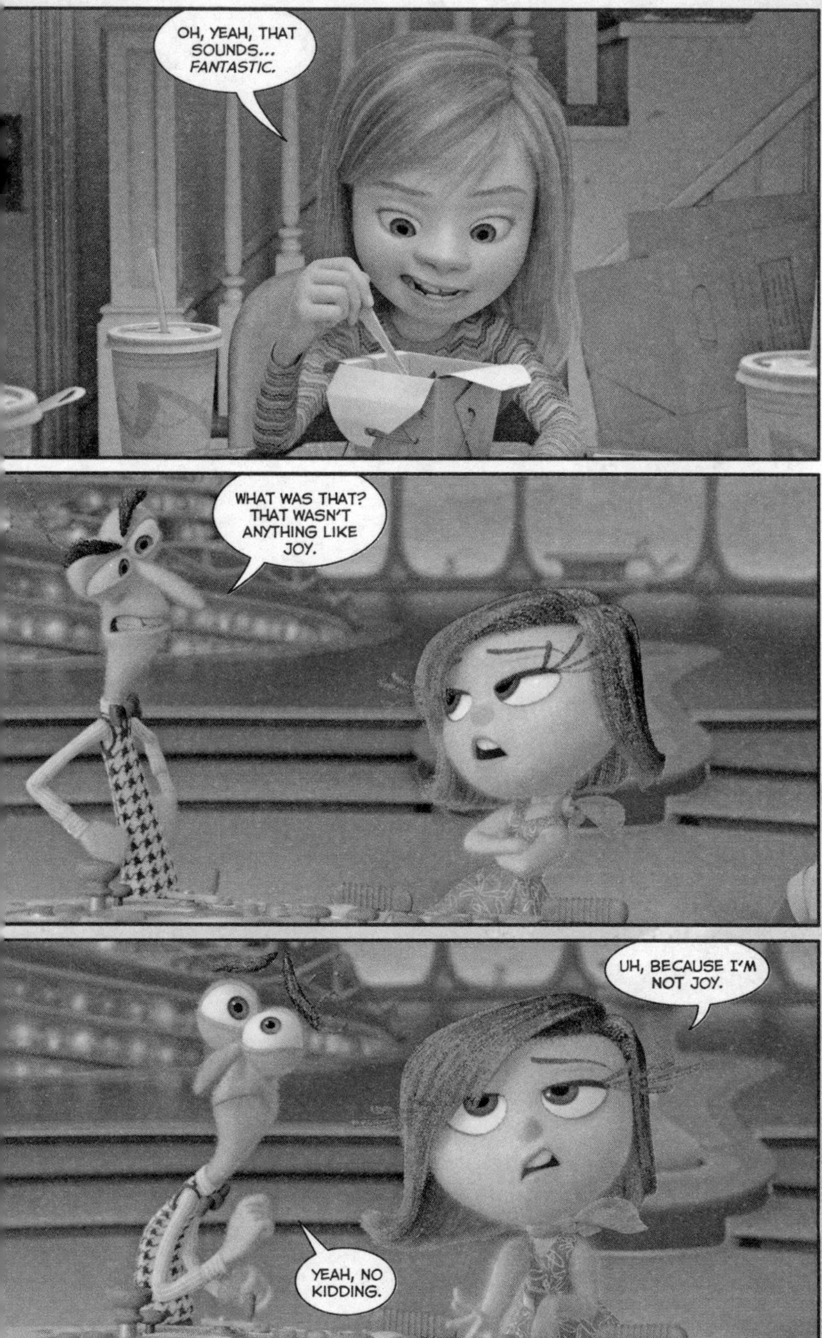
OH, YEAH, THAT SOUNDS... *FANTASTIC.*
WHAT WAS THAT? THAT WASN'T ANYTHING LIKE JOY.
UH, BECAUSE I'M NOT JOY.
YEAH, NO KIDDING.

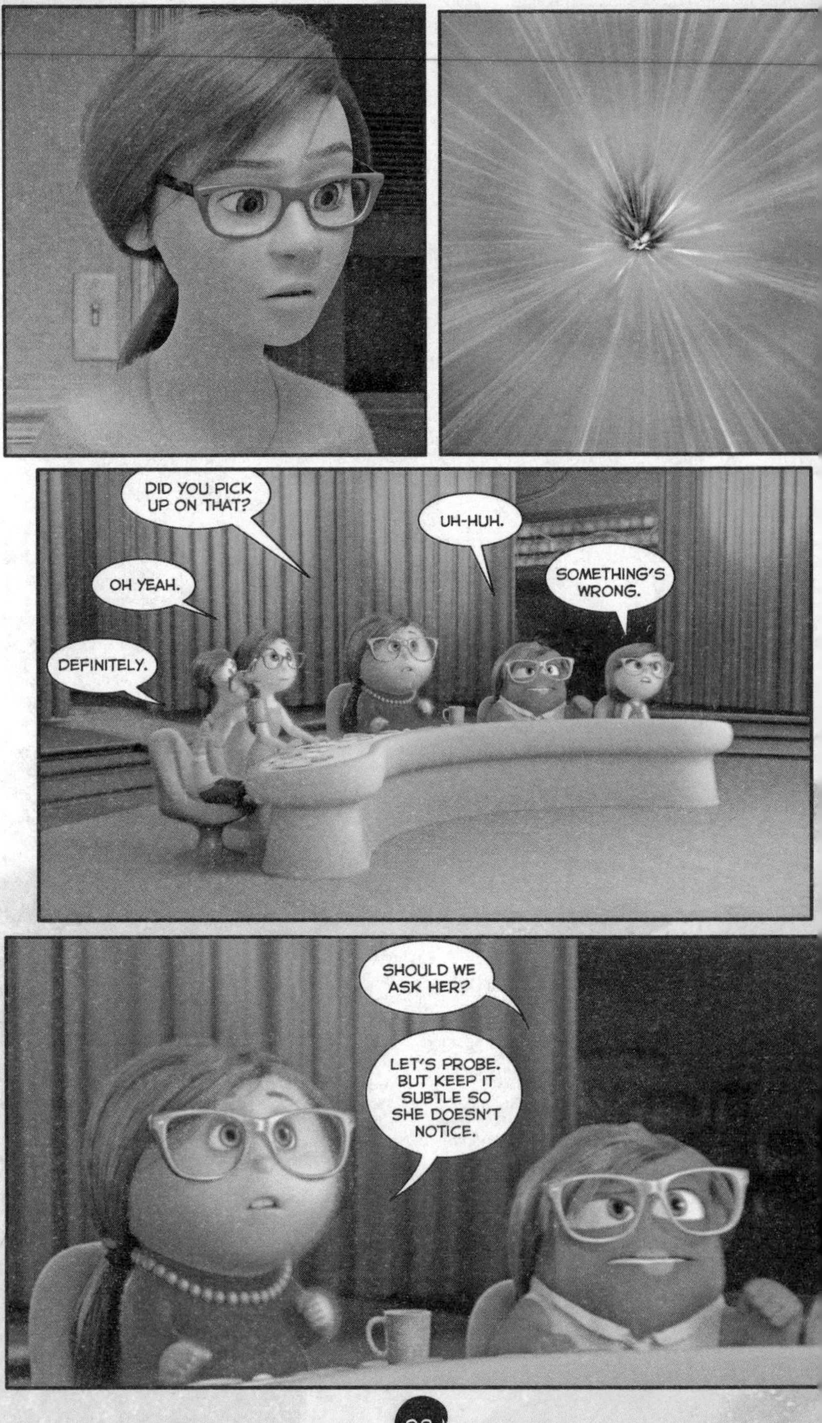
DID YOU PICK UP ON THAT?
OH YEAH.
DEFINITELY.
UH-HUH.
SOMETHING'S WRONG.
SHOULD WE ASK HER?
LET'S PROBE. BUT KEEP IT SUBTLE SO SHE DOESN'T NOTICE.

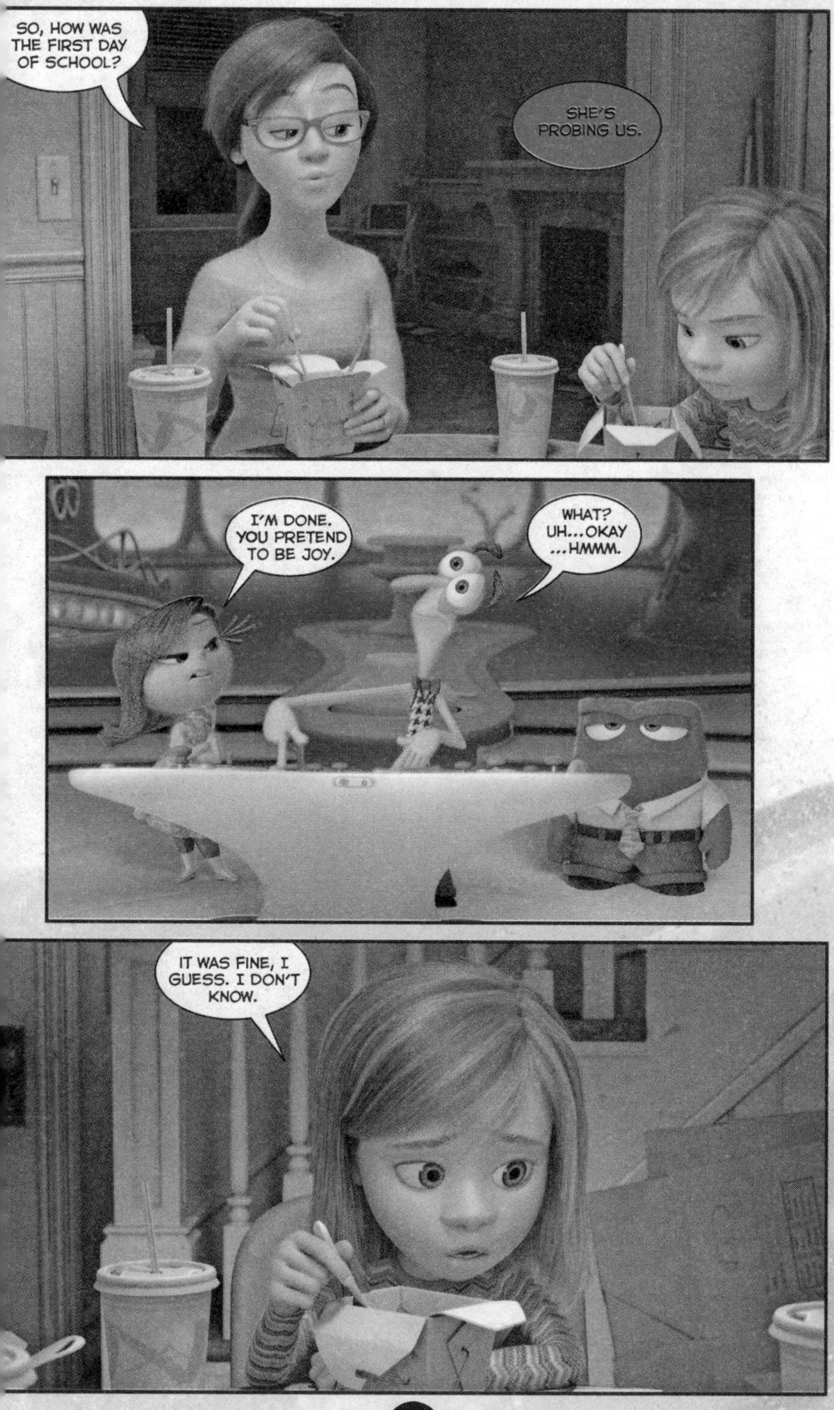
SO, HOW WAS THE FIRST DAY OF SCHOOL?
SHE'S PROBING US.
I'M DONE. YOU PRETEND TO BE JOY.
WHAT? UH...OKAY ...HMMM.
IT WAS FINE, I GUESS. I DON'T KNOW.

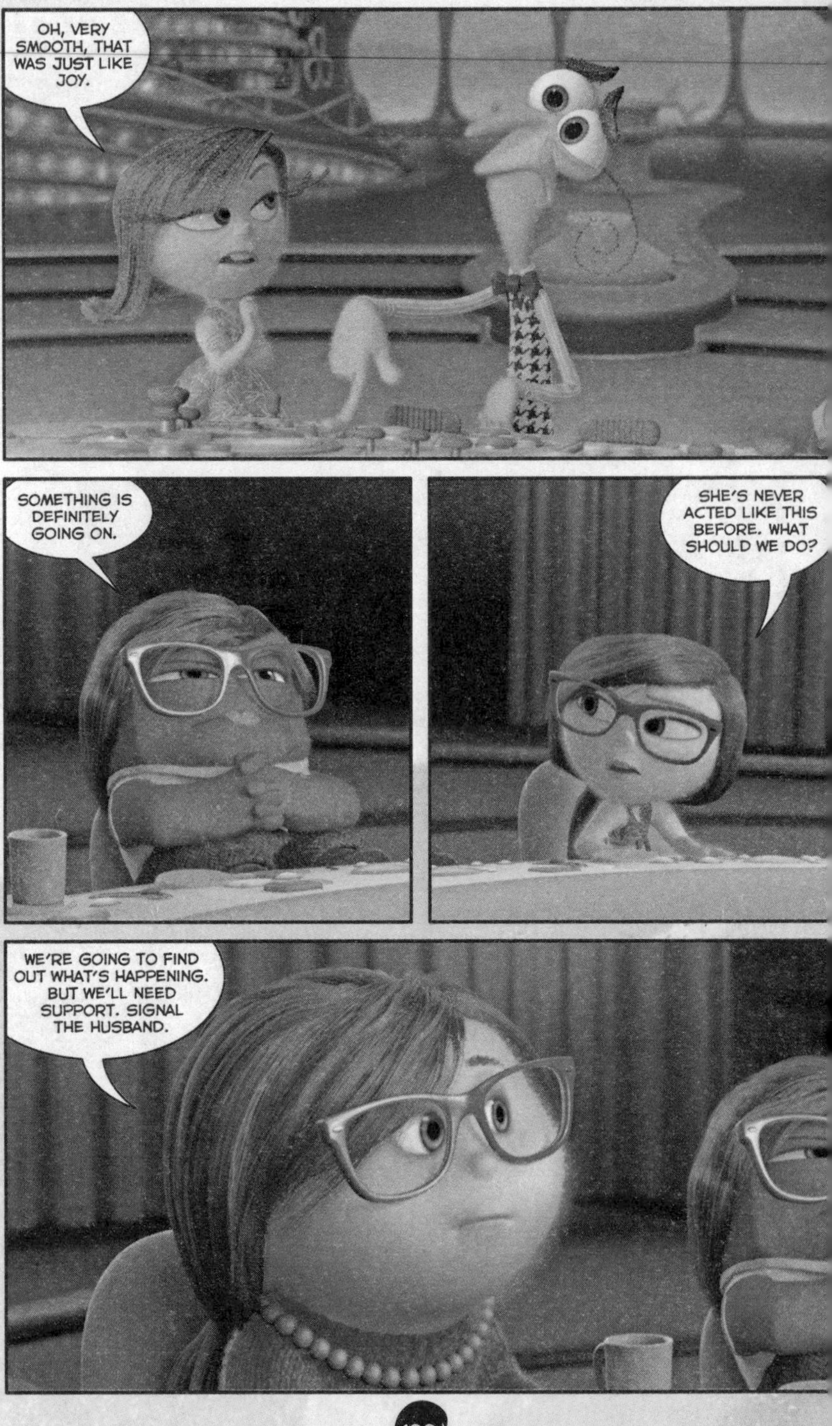
OH, VERY SMOOTH, THAT WAS JUST LIKE JOY.
SOMETHING IS DEFINITELY GOING ON.
SHE'S NEVER ACTED LIKE THIS BEFORE. WHAT SHOULD WE DO?
WE'RE GOING TO FIND OUT WHAT'S HAPPENING. BUT WE'LL NEED SUPPORT. SIGNAL THE HUSBAND.

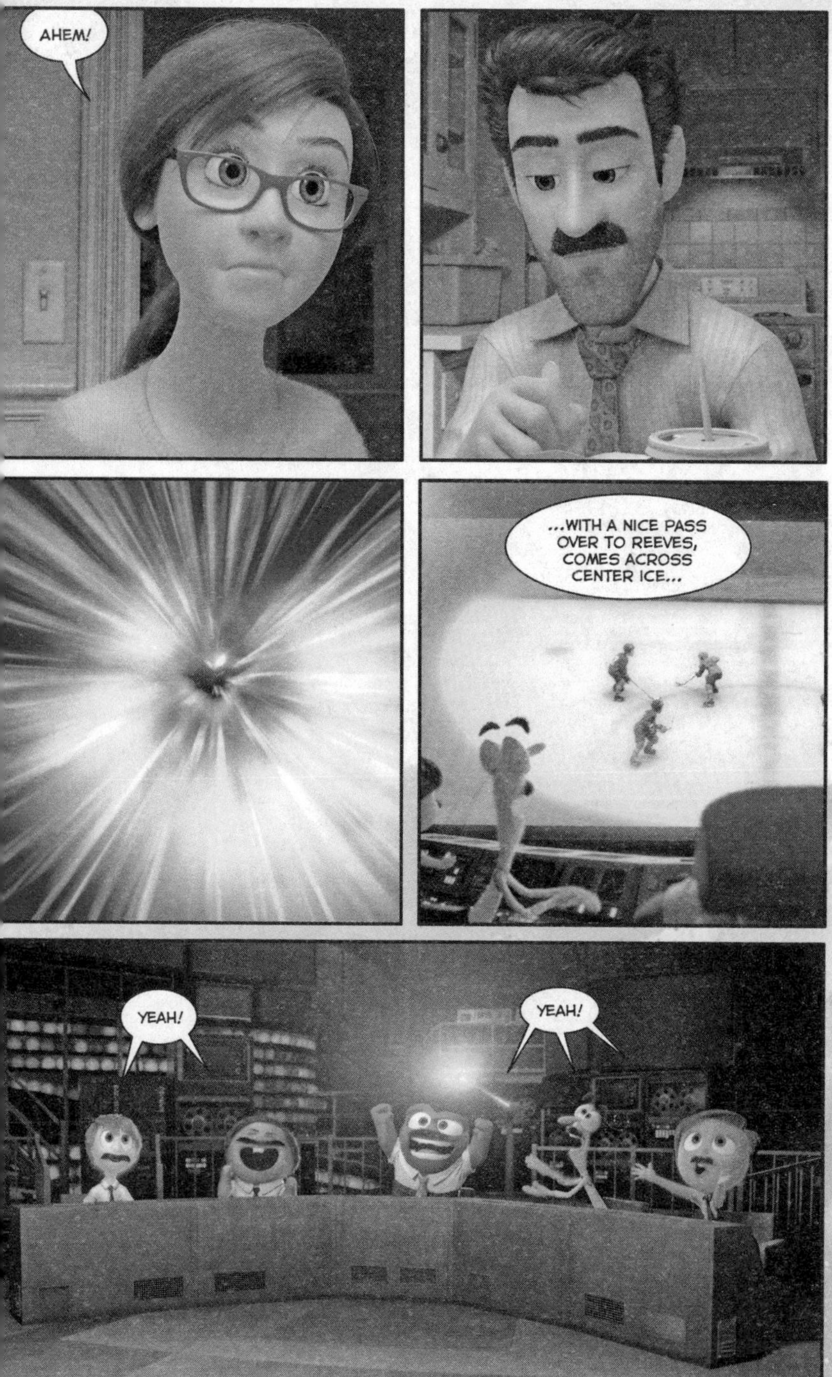
AHEM!
...WITH A NICE PASS OVER TO REEVES, COMES ACROSS CENTER ICE...
YEAH!
YEAH!

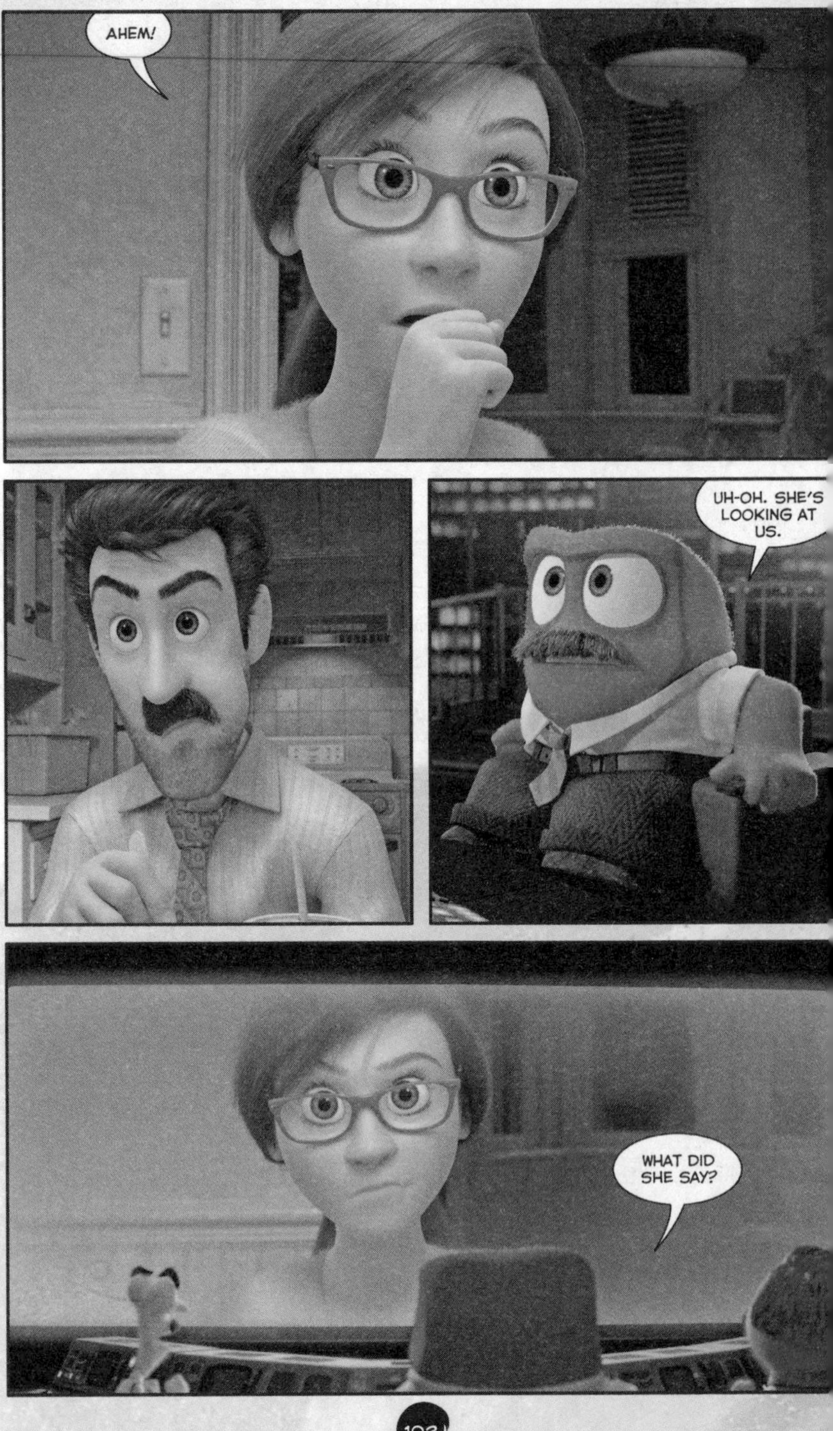
AHEM!
UH-OH. SHE'S LOOKING AT US.
WHAT DID SHE SAY?

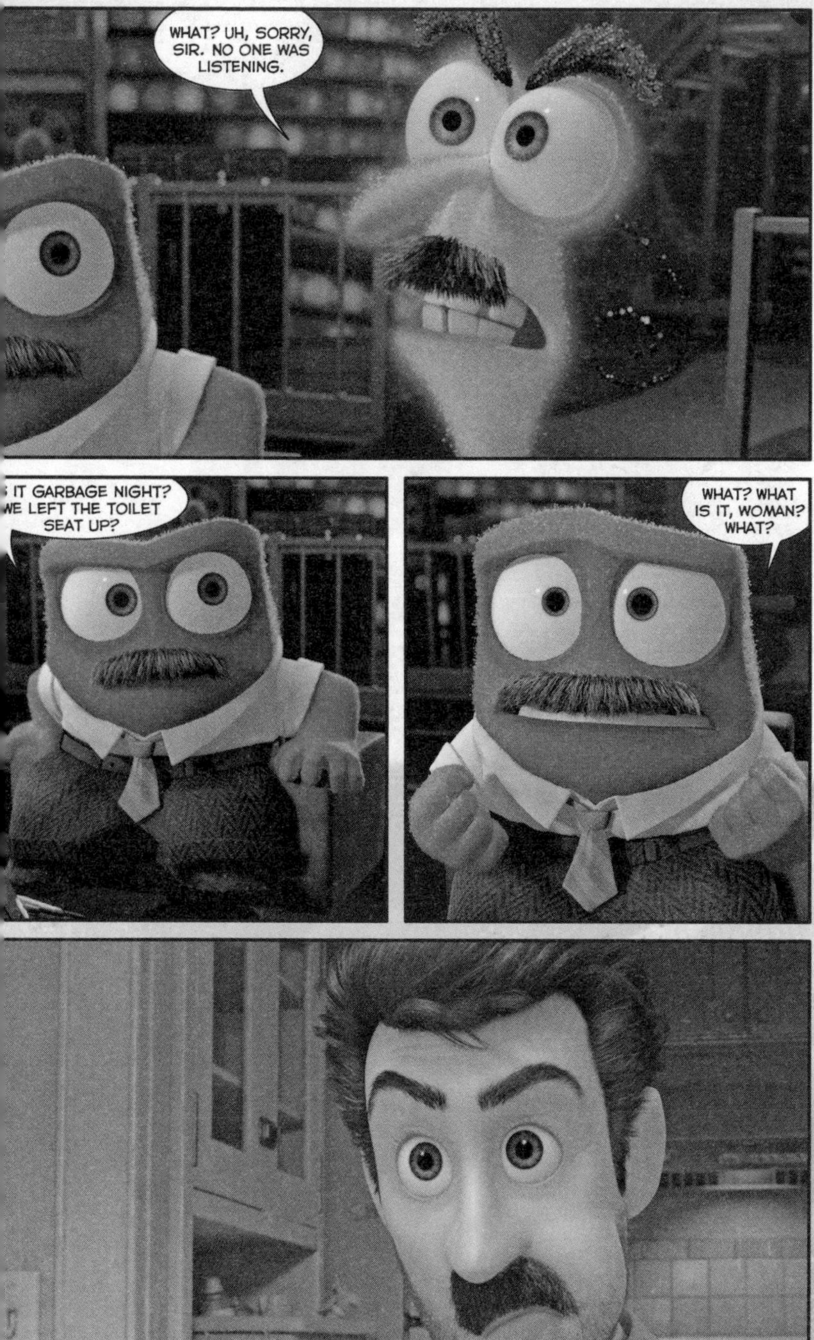
WHAT? UH, SORRY, SIR. NO ONE WAS LISTENING.
IT GARBAGE NIGHT? LEFT THE TOILET SEAT UP?
WHAT? WHAT IS IT, WOMAN? WHAT?

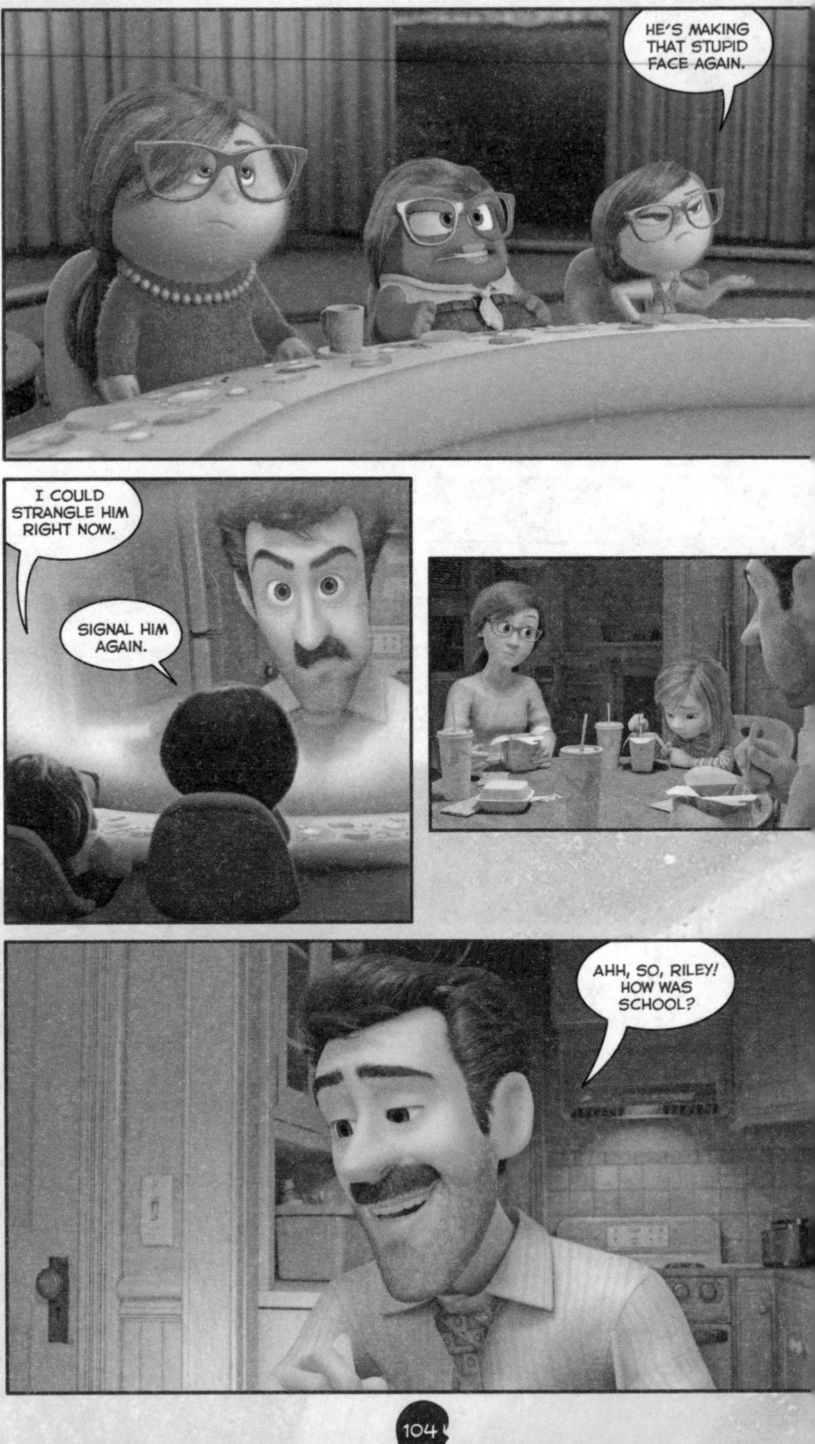
HE'S MAKING THAT STUPID FACE AGAIN.
I COULD STRANGLE HIM RIGHT NOW.
SIGNAL HIM AGAIN.
AHH, SO, RILEY! HOW WAS SCHOOL?

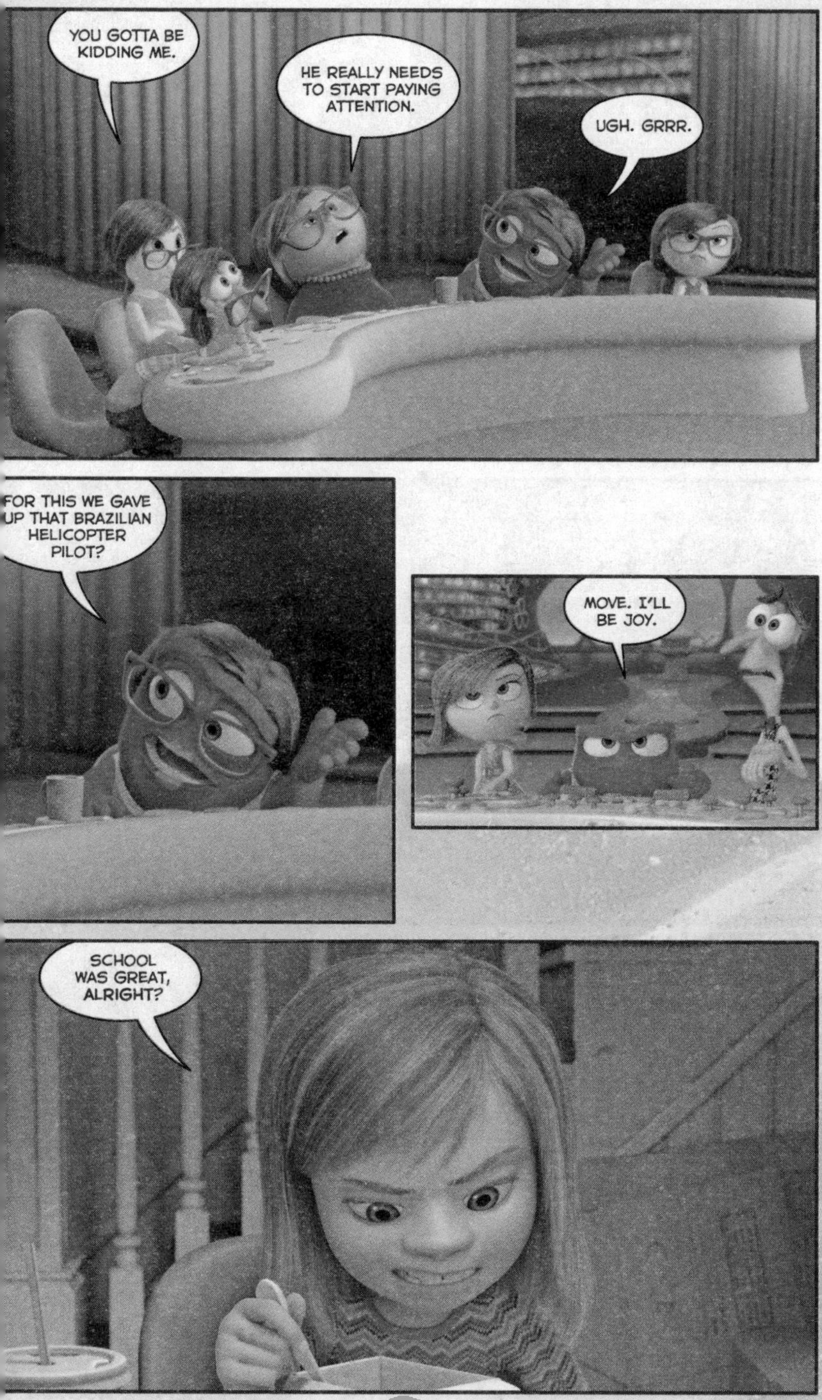
YOU GOTTA BE KIDDING ME.
HE REALLY NEEDS TO START PAYING ATTENTION.
UGH. GRRR.
FOR THIS WE GAVE UP THAT BRAZILIAN HELICOPTER PILOT?
MOVE. I'LL BE JOY.
SCHOOL WAS GREAT, ALRIGHT?

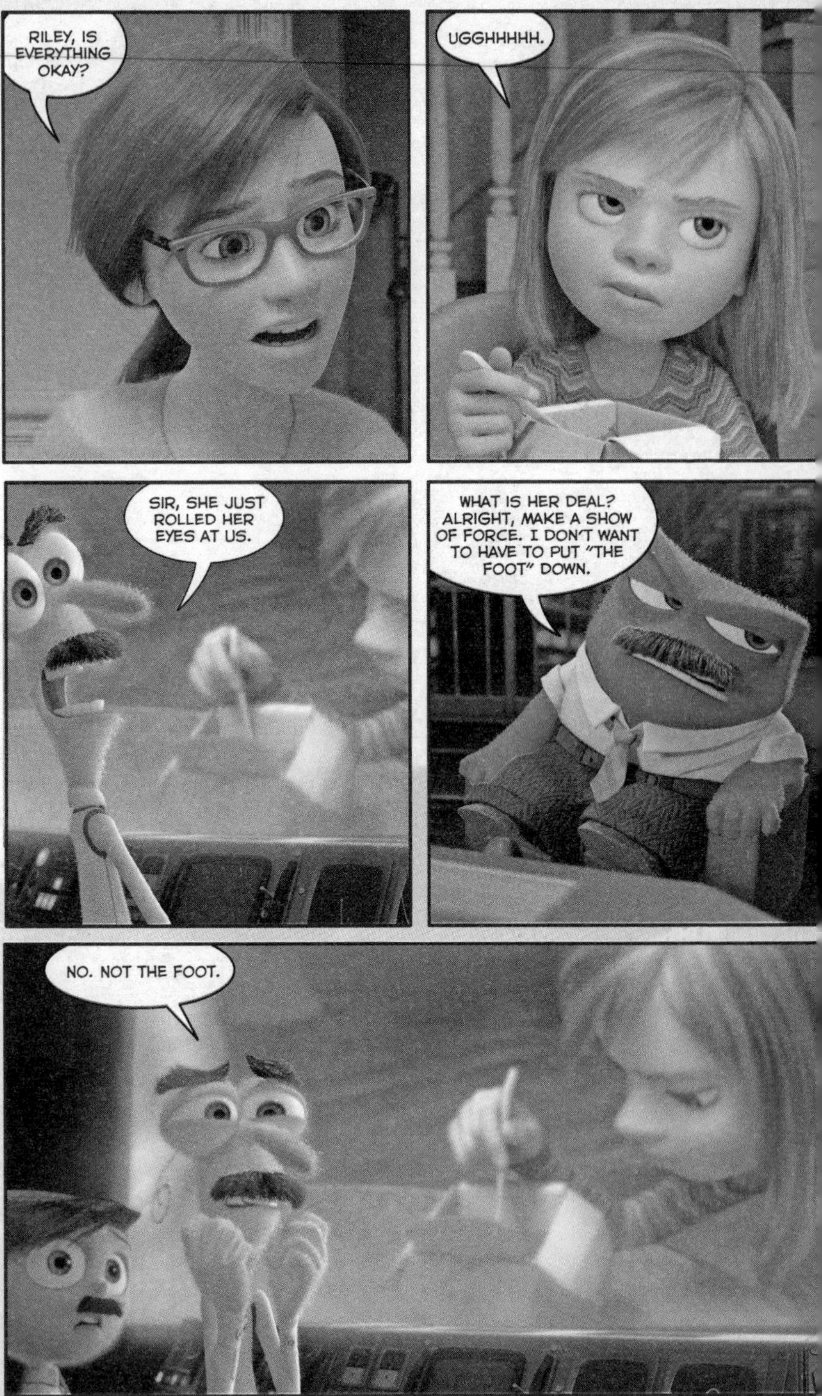
RILEY, IS EVERYTHING OKAY?
UGGHHHHH.
SIR, SHE JUST ROLLED HER EYES AT US.
WHAT IS HER DEAL? ALRIGHT, MAKE A SHOW OF FORCE. I DON'T WANT TO HAVE TO PUT "THE FOOT" DOWN.
NO. NOT THE FOOT.

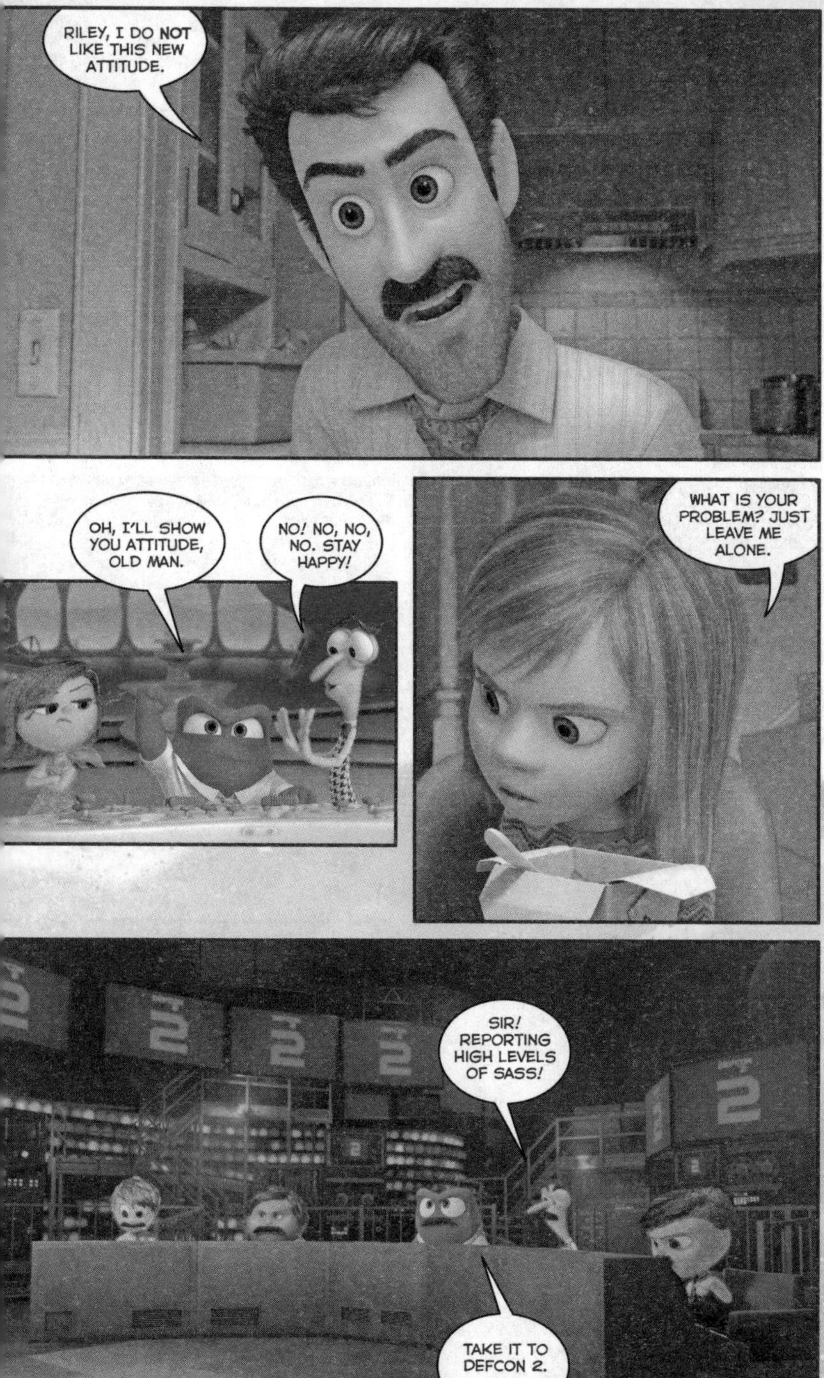
RILEY, I DO NOT LIKE THIS NEW ATTITUDE.
OH, I'LL SHOW YOU ATTITUDE, OLD MAN.
NO! NO, NO, NO. STAY HAPPY!
WHAT IS YOUR PROBLEM? JUST LEAVE ME ALONE.
SIR! REPORTING HIGH LEVELS OF SASS!
TAKE IT TO DEFCON 2.

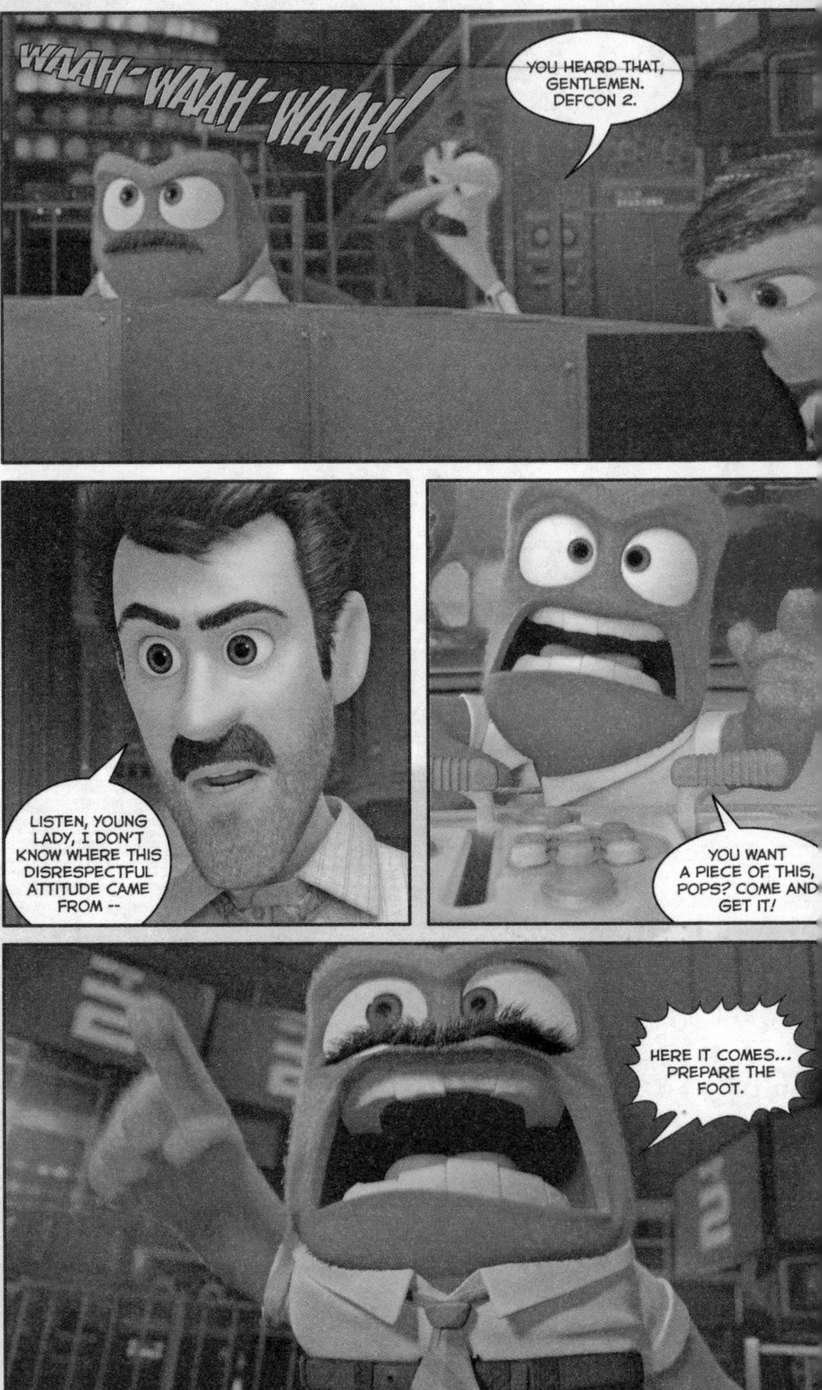
WAAH-WAAH-WAAH!
YOU HEARD THAT, GENTLEMEN. DEFCON 2.
LISTEN, YOUNG LADY, I DON'T KNOW WHERE THIS DISRESPECTFUL ATTITUDE CAME FROM --
YOU WANT A PIECE OF THIS, POPS? COME AND GET IT!
HERE IT COMES... PREPARE THE FOOT.

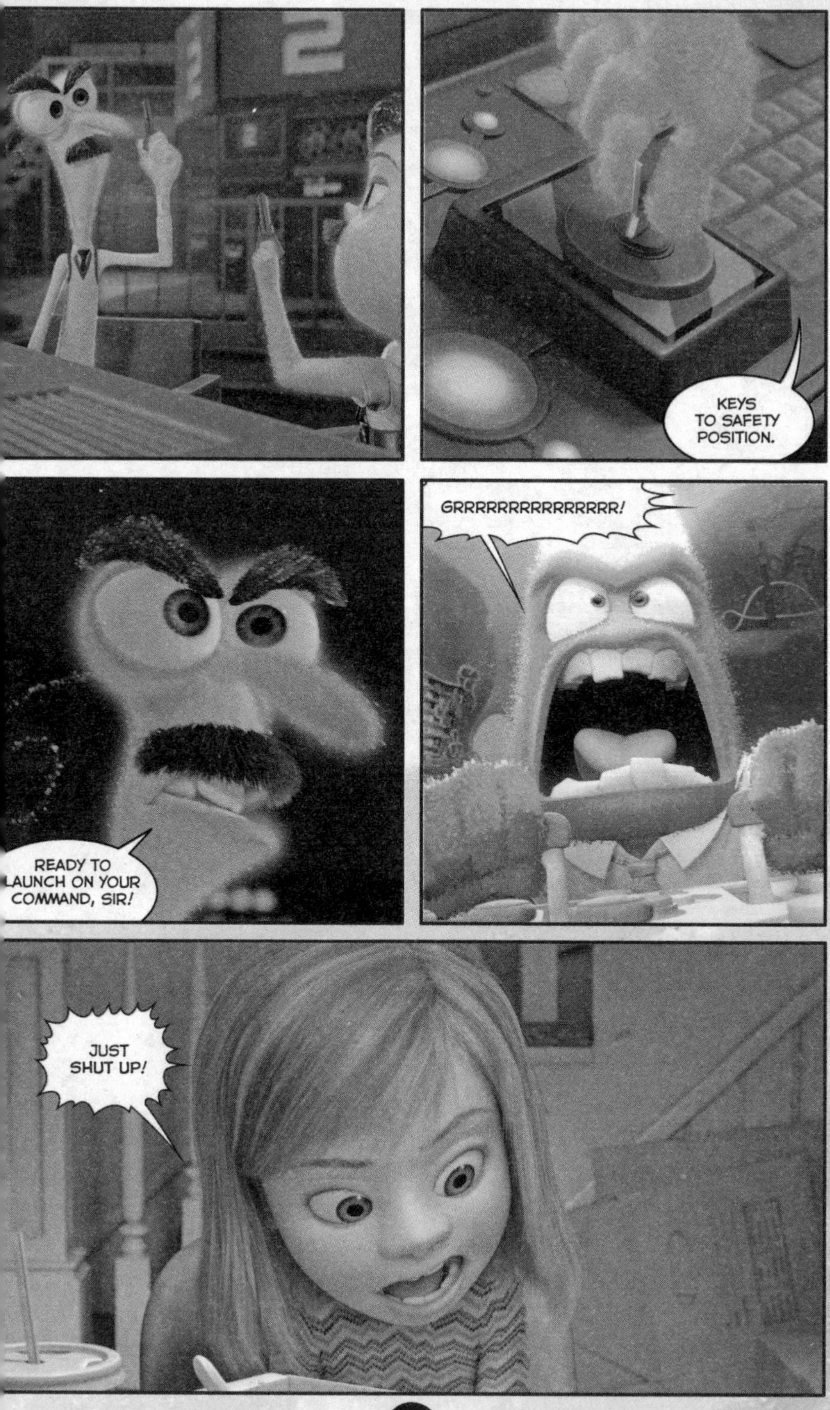
KEYS TO SAFETY POSITION.
READY TO LAUNCH ON YOUR COMMAND, SIR!
GRRRRRRRRRRRRRR!
JUST SHUT UP!

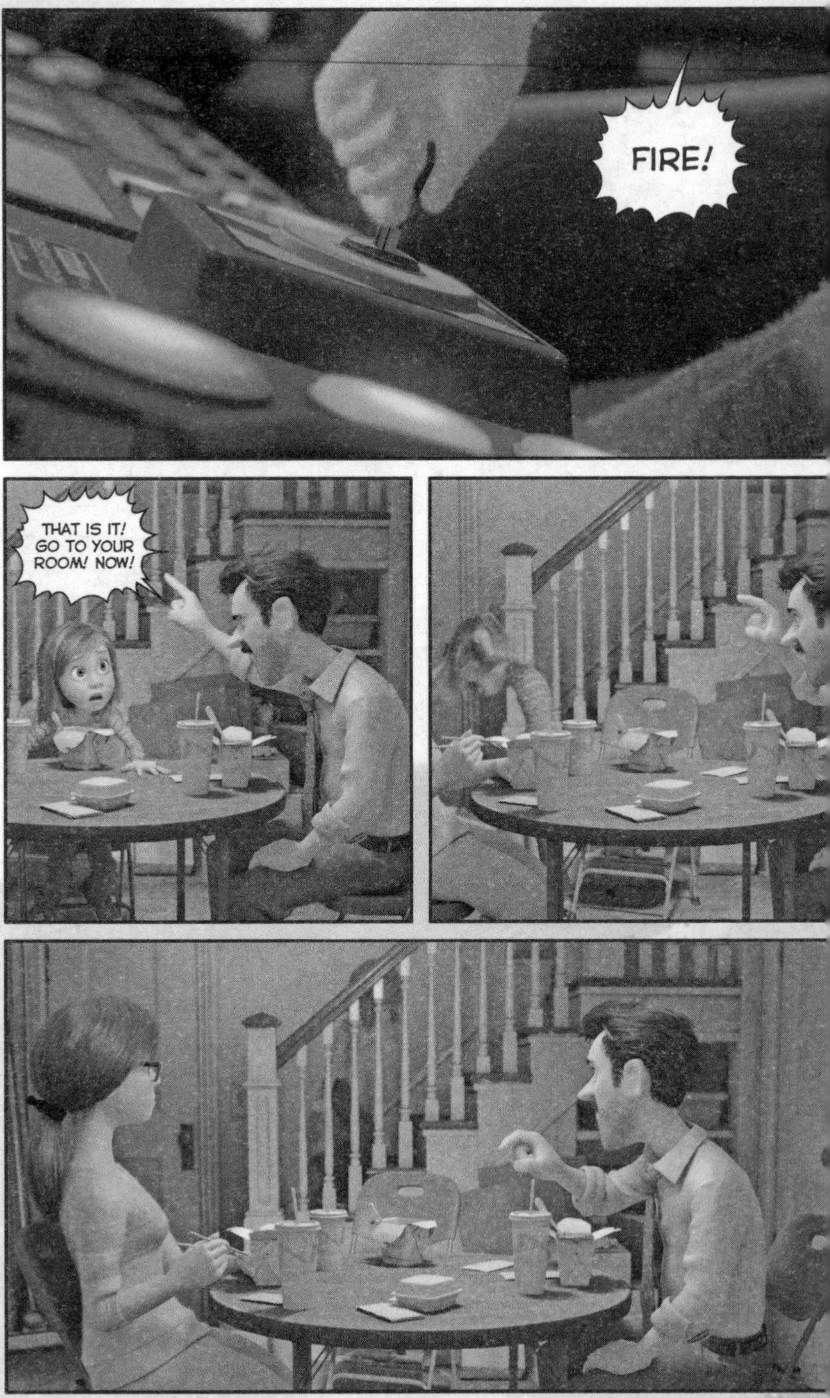
FIRE!
THAT IS IT! GO TO YOUR ROOM! NOW!

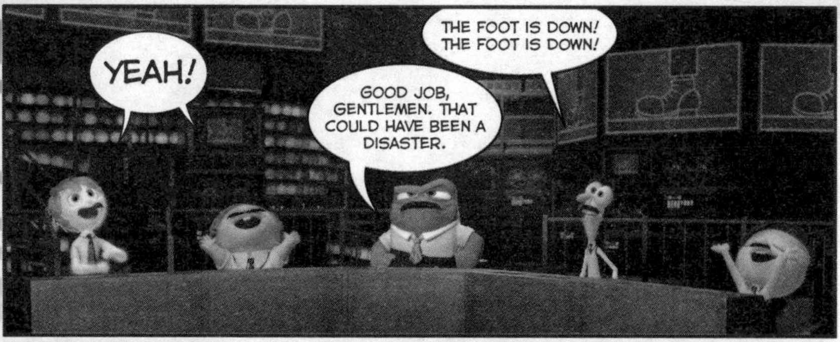
YEAH!
GOOD JOB, GENTLEMEN. THAT COULD HAVE BEEN A DISASTER.
THE FOOT IS DOWN! THE FOOT IS DOWN!

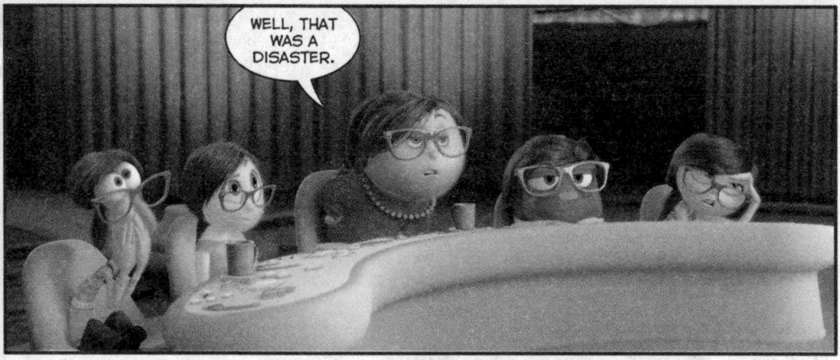
WELL, THAT WAS A DISASTER.

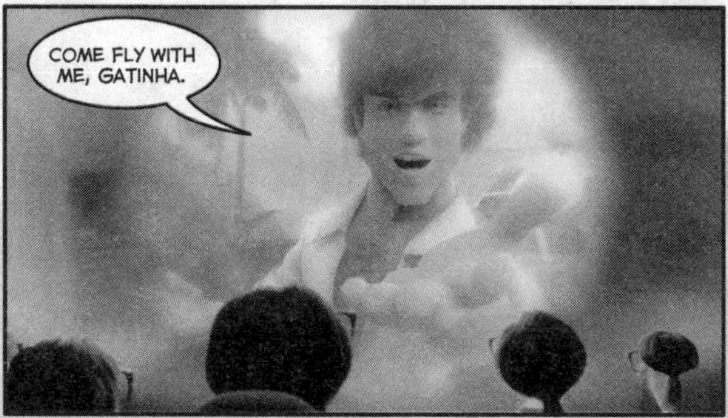
COME FLY WITH ME, GATINHA.

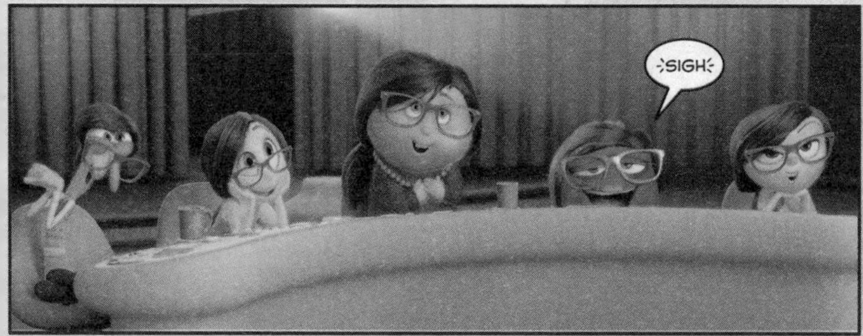
SIGH

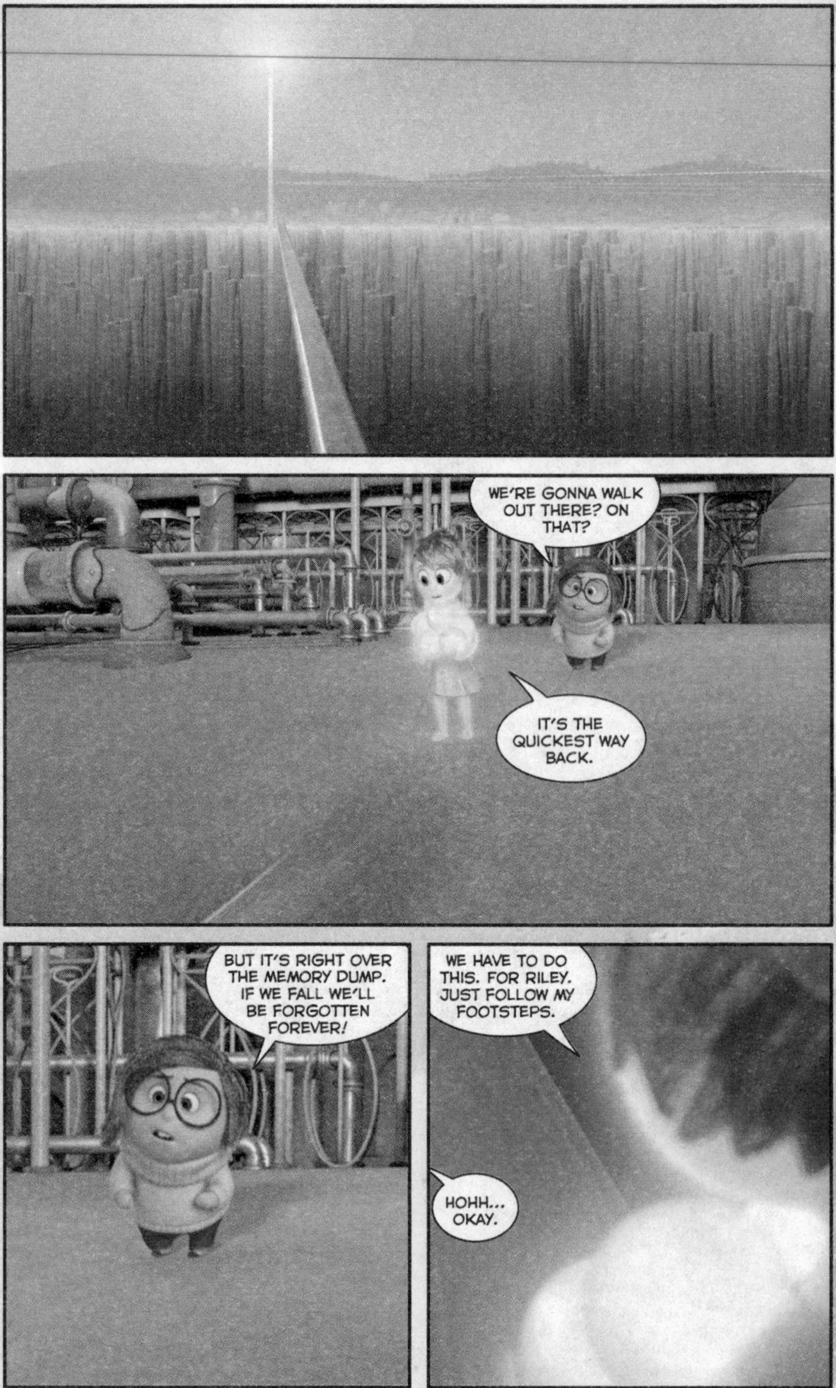
WE'RE GONNA WALK OUT THERE? ON THAT?
IT'S THE QUICKEST WAY BACK.
BUT IT'S RIGHT OVER THE MEMORY DUMP. IF WE FALL WE'LL BE FORGOTTEN FOREVER!
WE HAVE TO DO THIS. FOR RILEY. JUST FOLLOW MY FOOTSTEPS.
HOHH... OKAY.

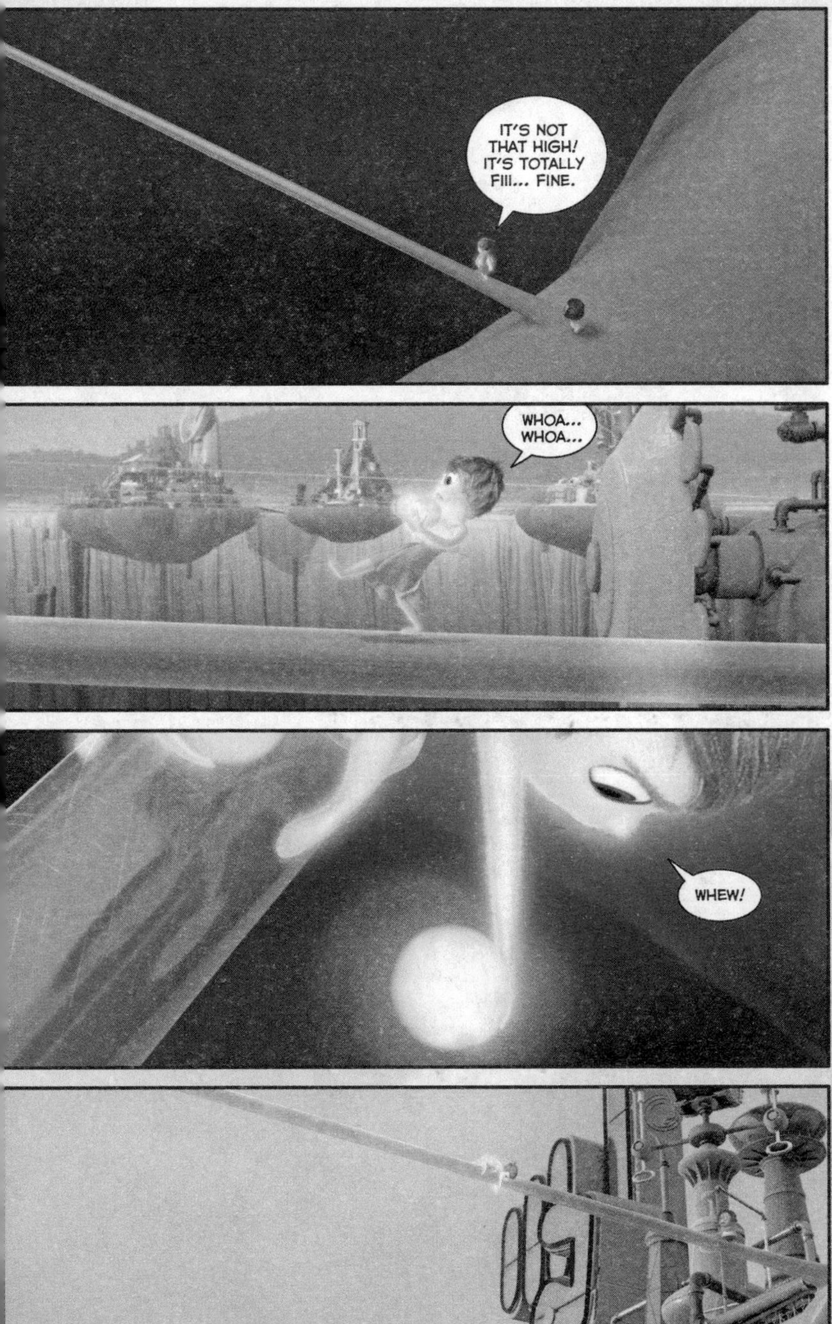
IT'S NOT
THAT HIGH!
IT'S TOTALLY
FIII... FINE.
WHOA...
WHOA...
WHEW!

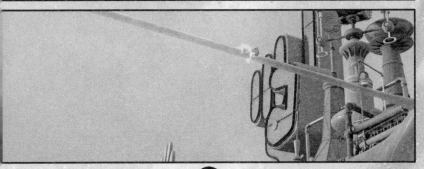

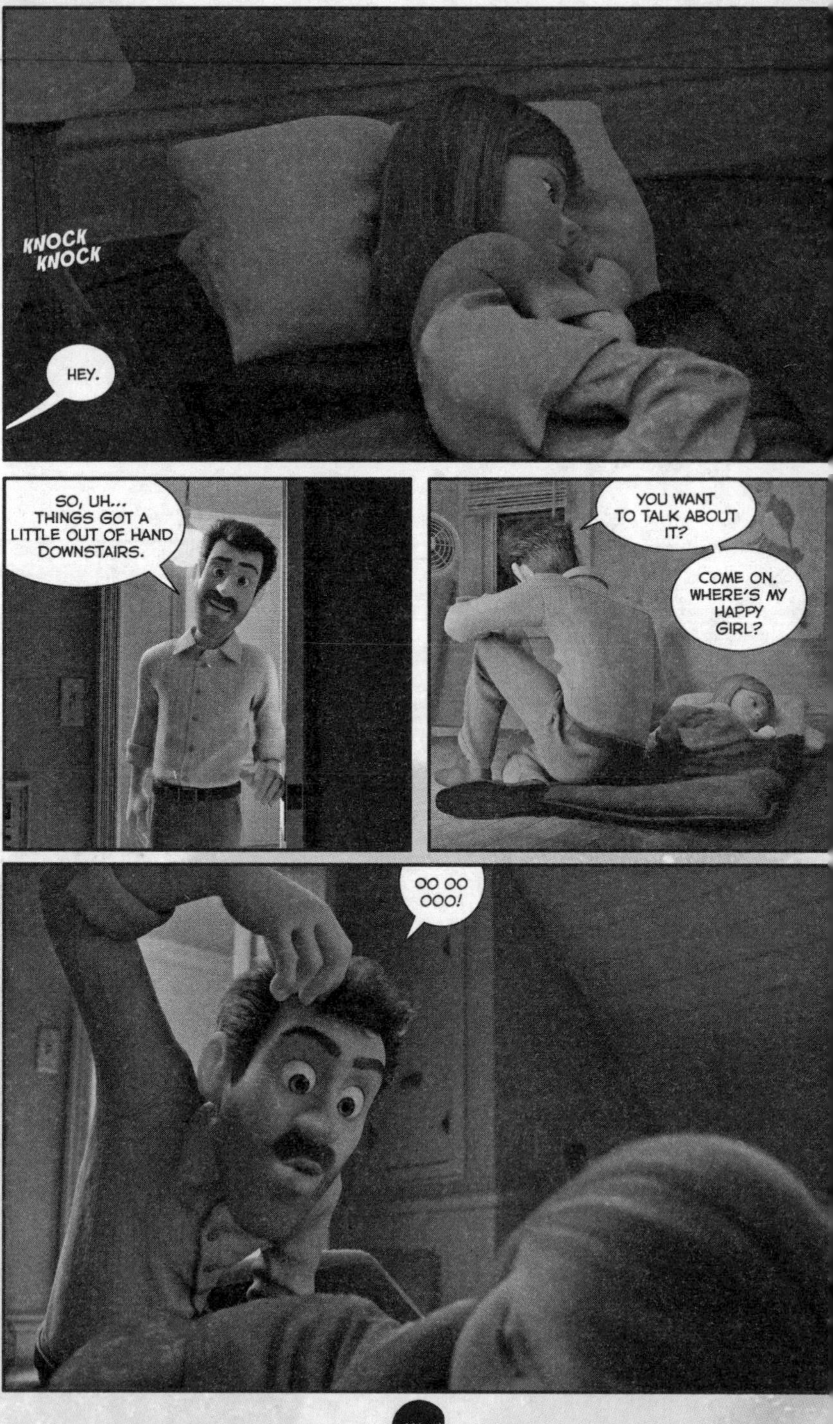
KNOCK KNOCK
HEY.
SO, UH... THINGS GOT A LITTLE OUT OF HAND DOWNSTAIRS.
YOU WANT TO TALK ABOUT IT?
COME ON. WHERE'S MY HAPPY GIRL?
OO OO OOO!

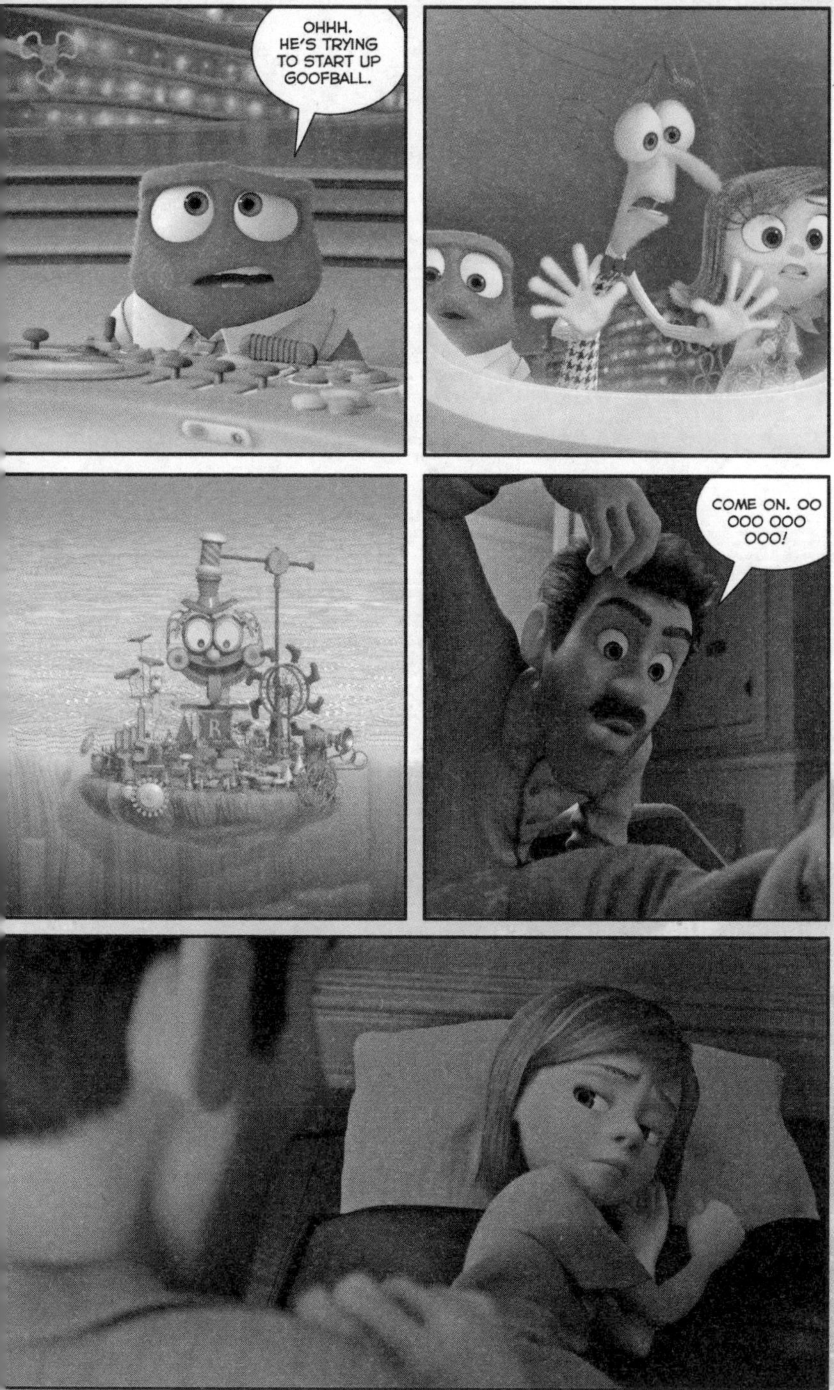
OHHH. HE'S TRYING TO START UP GOOFBALL.
COME ON. OO OOO OOO OOO!

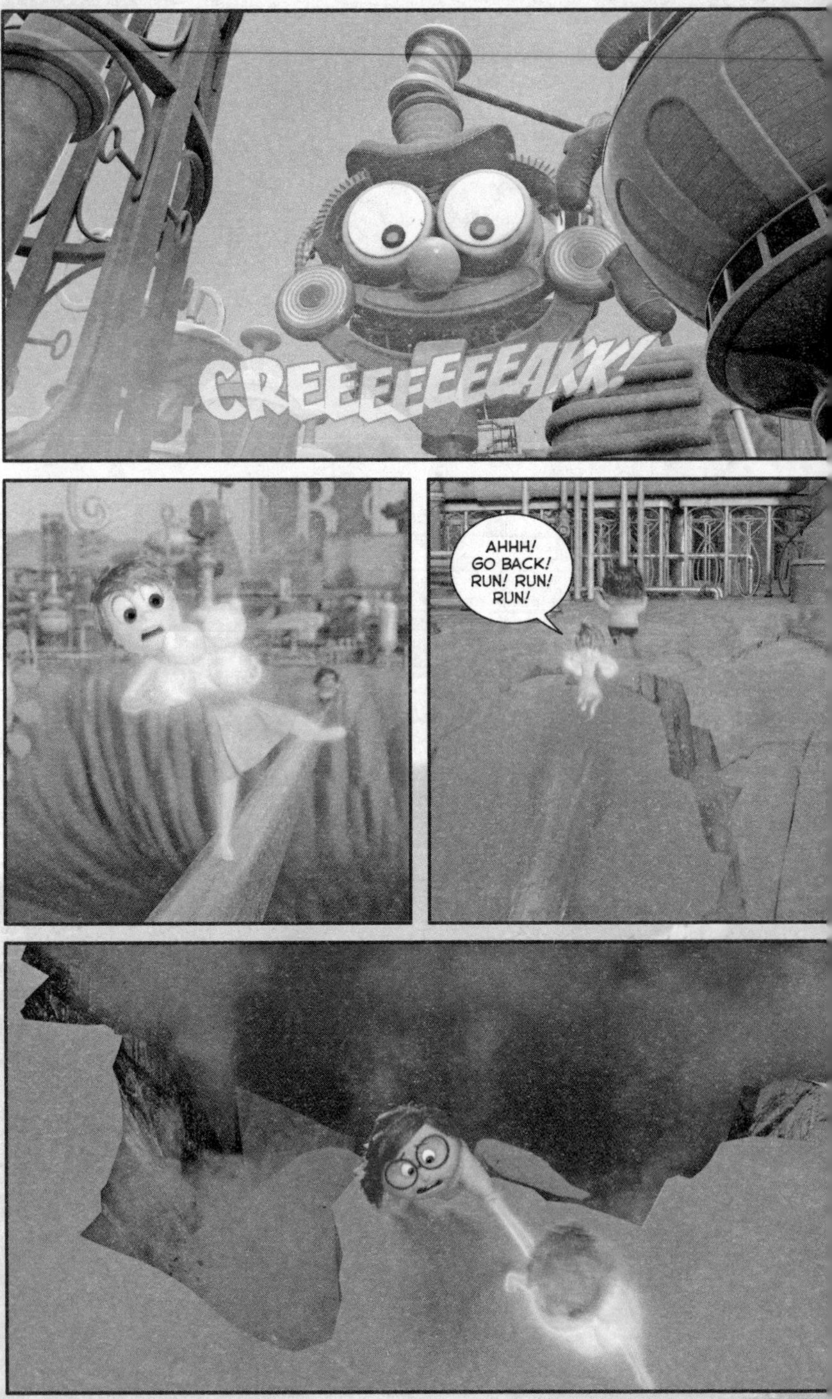
CREEEEEEEEAKK!
AHHH! GO BACK! RUN! RUN! RUN!

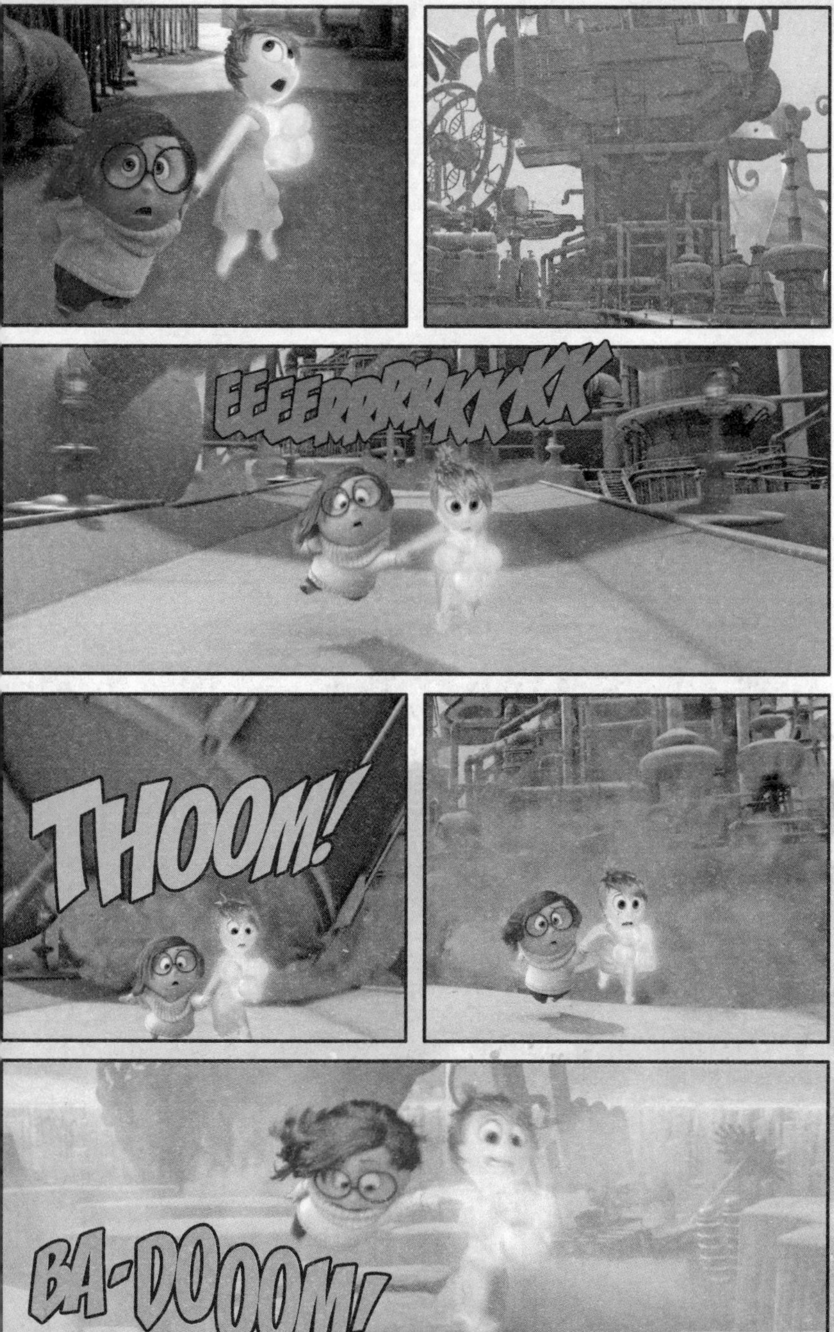
EEEERRRRRKKKKK
THOOM!
BA-DOOOM!

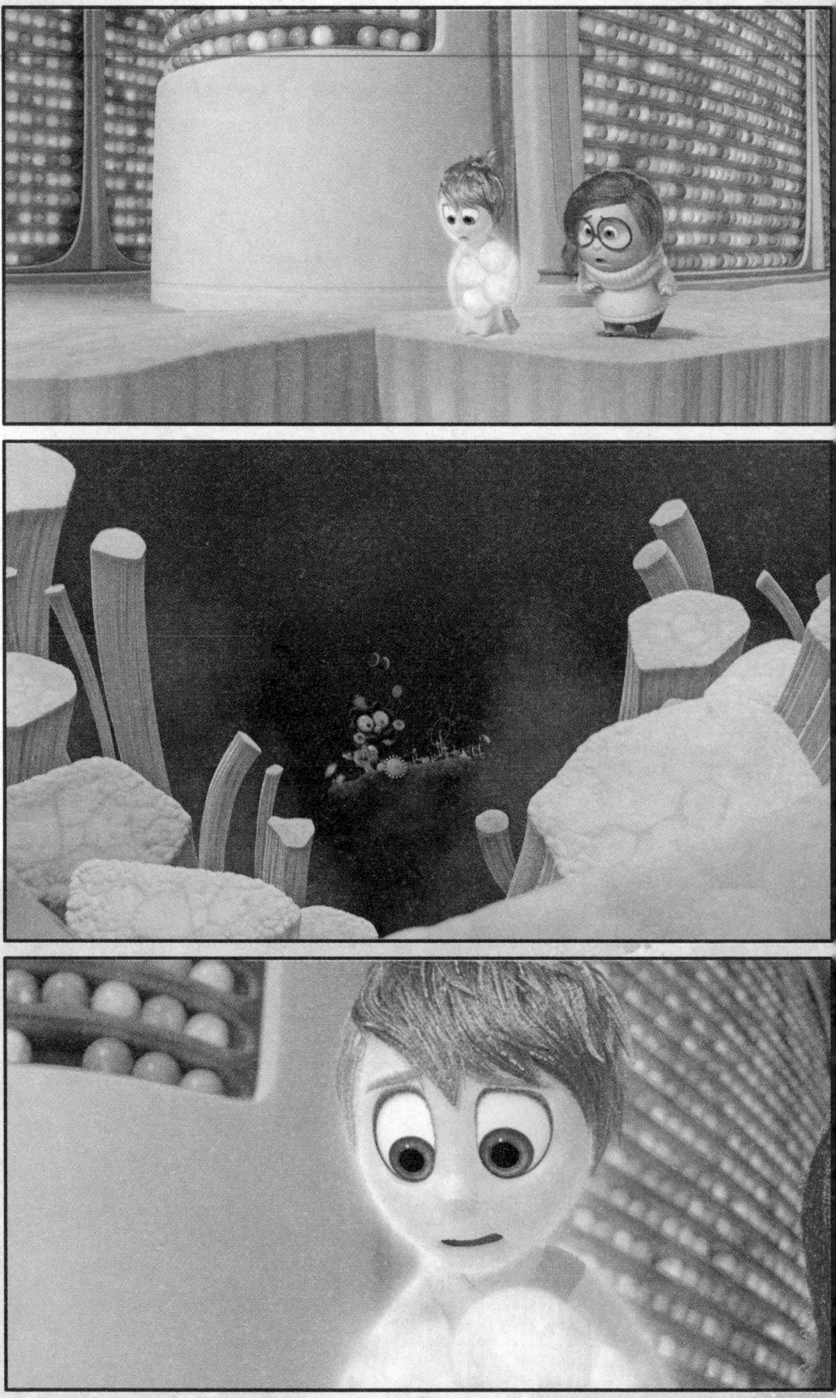

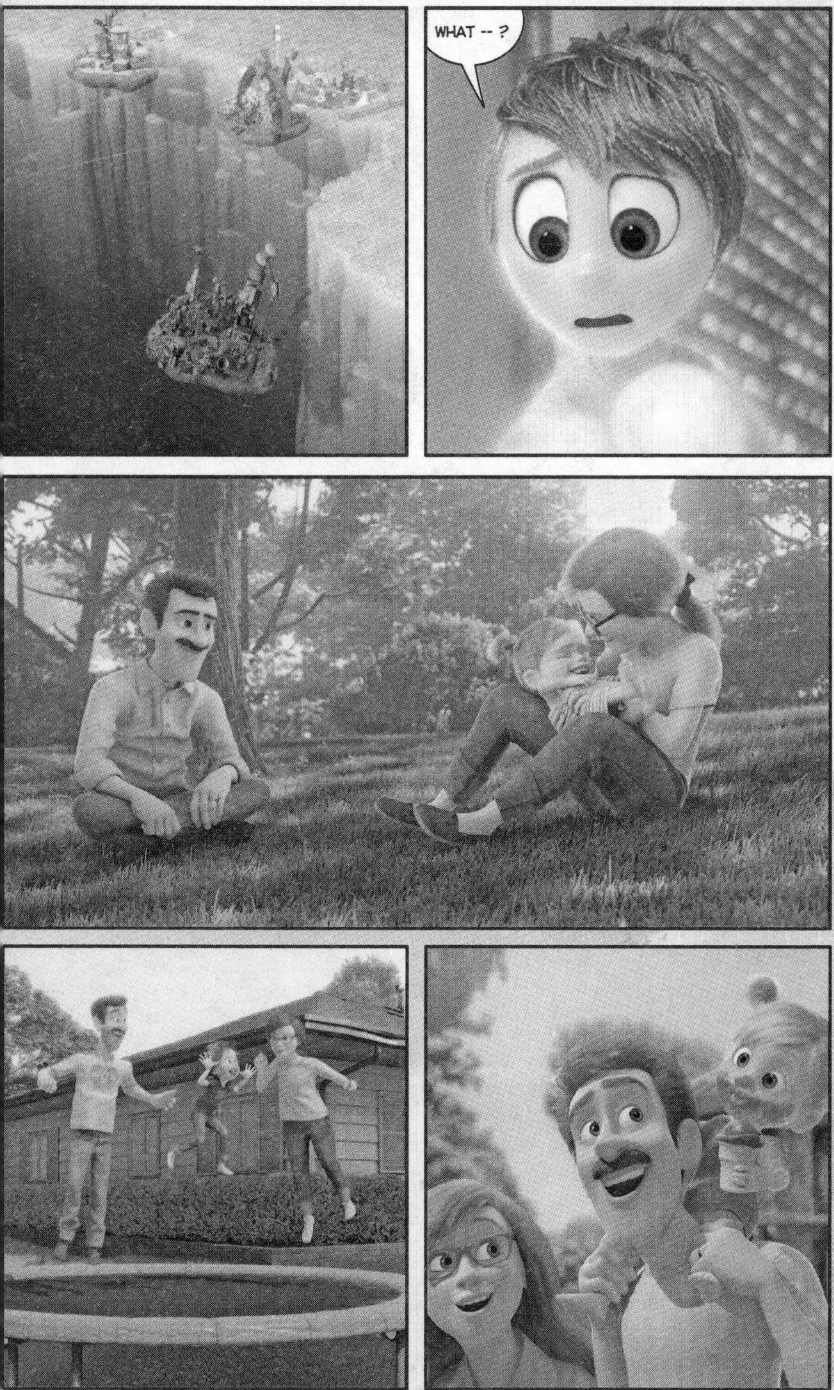
WHAT -- ?

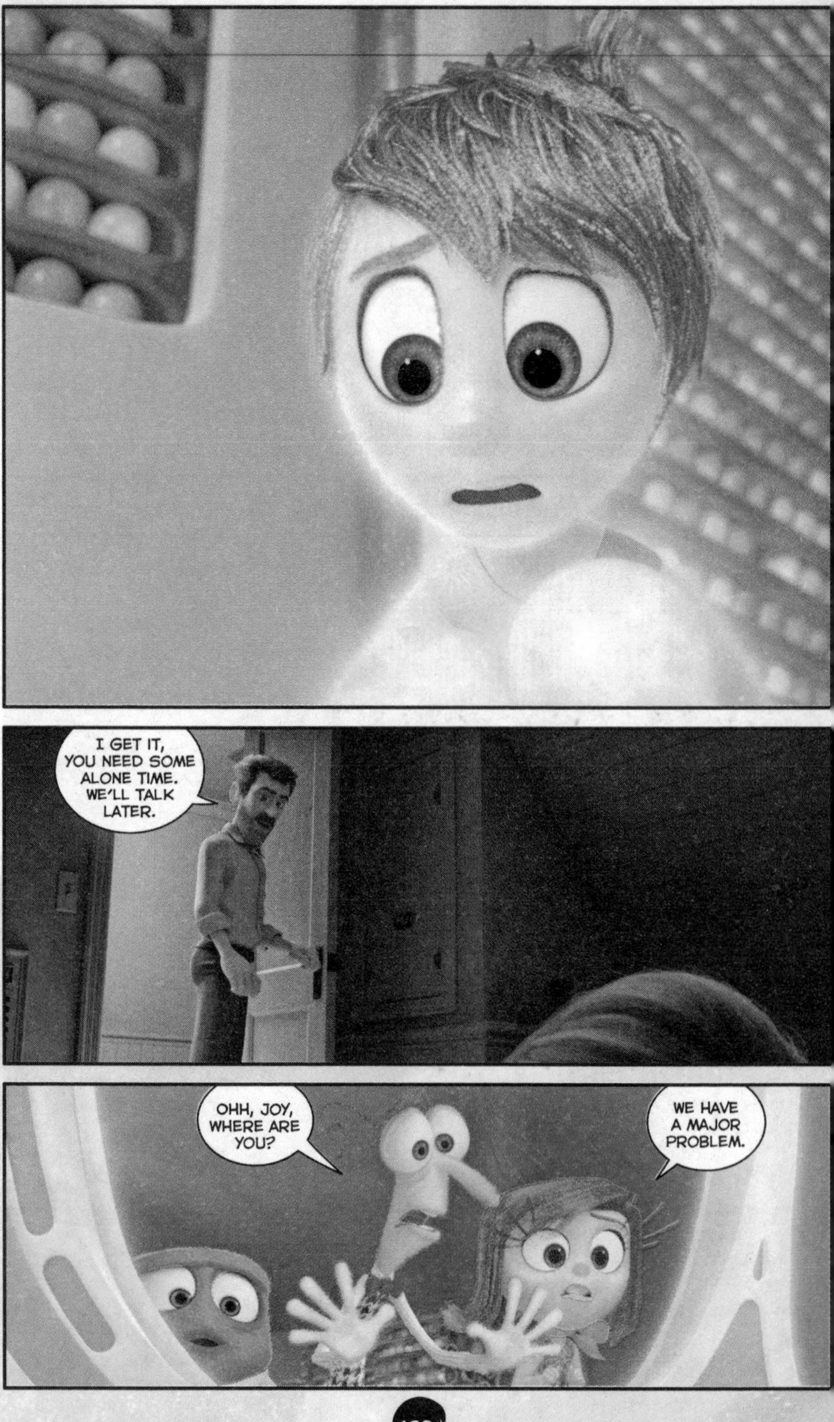
I GET IT, YOU NEED SOME ALONE TIME. WE'LL TALK LATER.
OHH, JOY, WHERE ARE YOU?
WE HAVE A MAJOR PROBLEM.

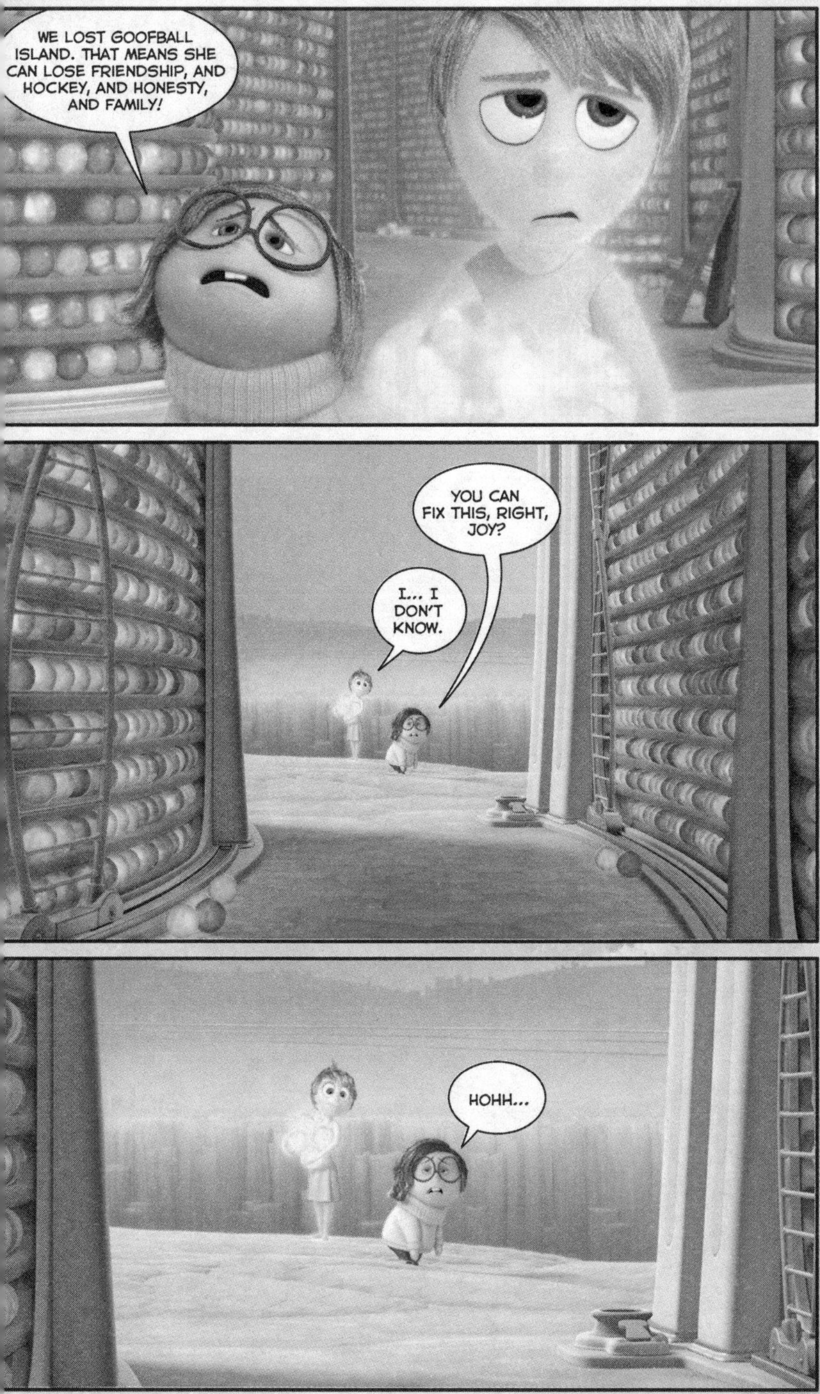
WE LOST GOOFBALL ISLAND. THAT MEANS SHE CAN LOSE FRIENDSHIP, AND HOCKEY, AND HONESTY, AND FAMILY!
YOU CAN FIX THIS, RIGHT, JOY?
I... I DON'T KNOW.
HOHH...

BUT WE HAVE TO TRY. OKAY, C'MON.

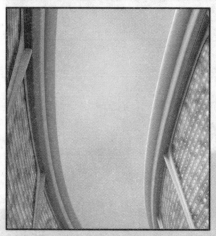

RILEY'S GONE TO SLEEP...WHICH IS A GOOD THING WHEN YOU THINK ABOUT IT...

...NOTHING ELSE BAD CAN HAPPEN WHILE SHE'S ASLEEP AND WE'LL BE BACK TO HEADQUARTERS BEFORE SHE WAKES UP.

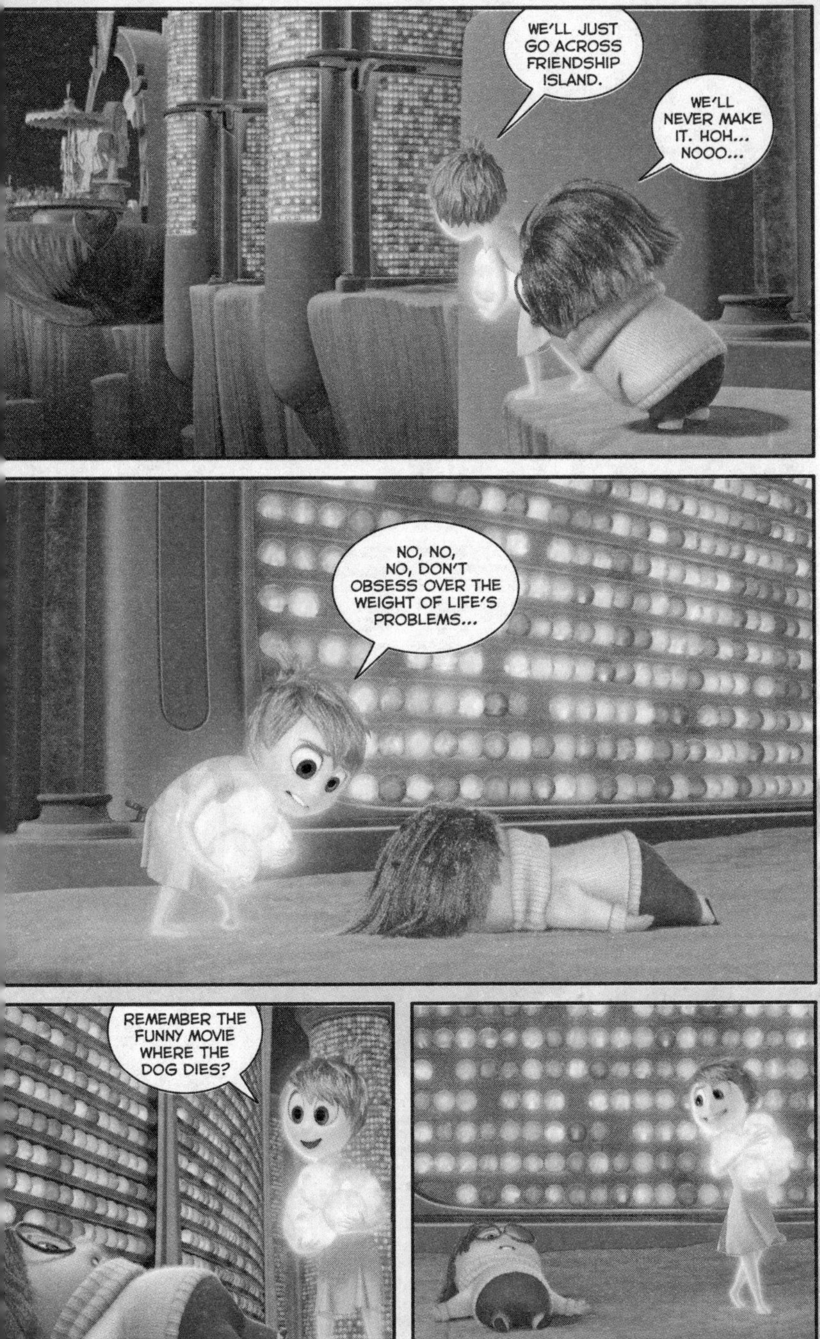
WE'LL JUST GO ACROSS FRIENDSHIP ISLAND.
WE'LL NEVER MAKE IT. HOH... NOOO...
NO, NO, NO, DON'T OBSESS OVER THE WEIGHT OF LIFE'S PROBLEMS...
REMEMBER THE FUNNY MOVIE WHERE THE DOG DIES?

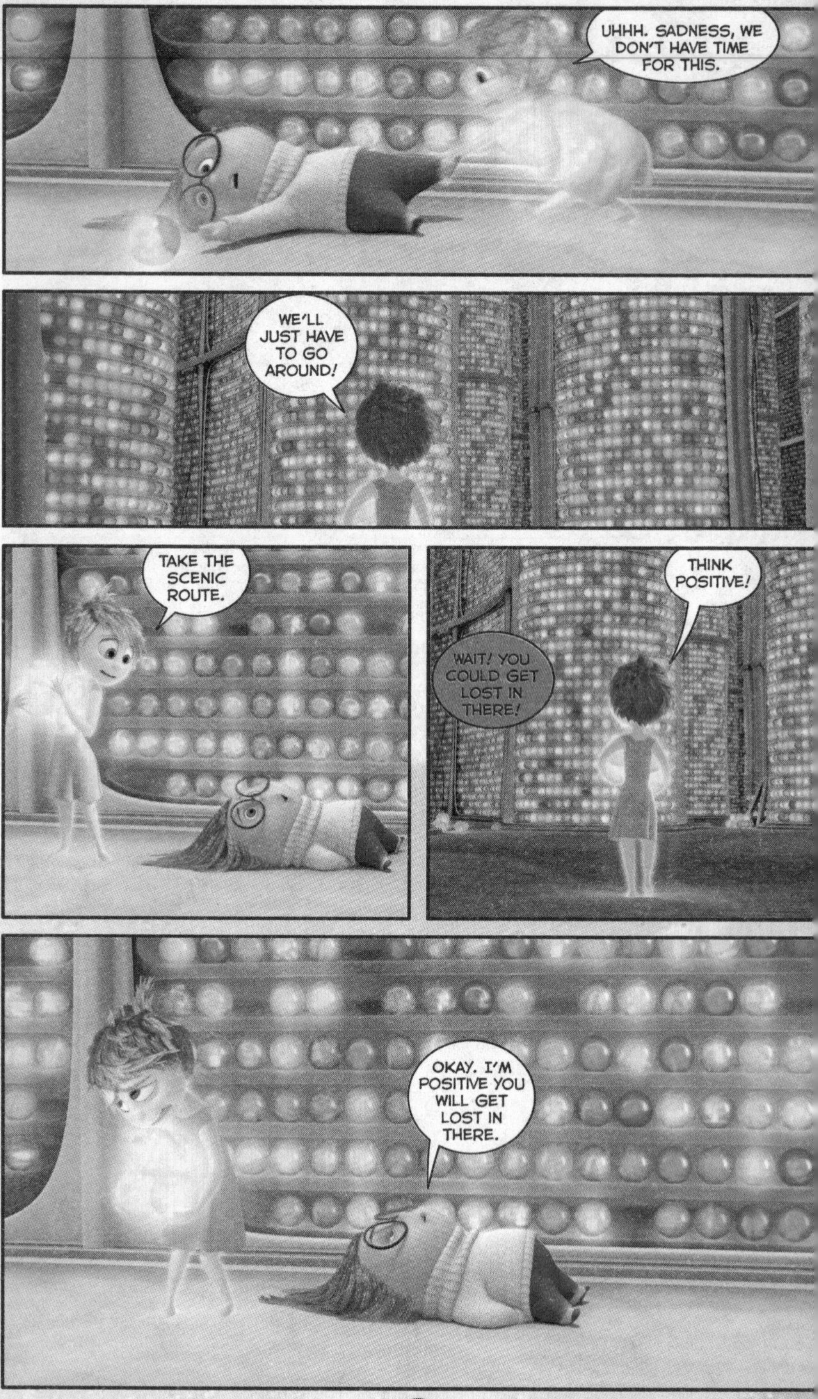
UHHH. SADNESS, WE DON'T HAVE TIME FOR THIS.
WE'LL JUST HAVE TO GO AROUND!
TAKE THE SCENIC ROUTE.
THINK POSITIVE!
WAIT! YOU COULD GET LOST IN THERE!
OKAY. I'M POSITIVE YOU WILL GET LOST IN THERE.

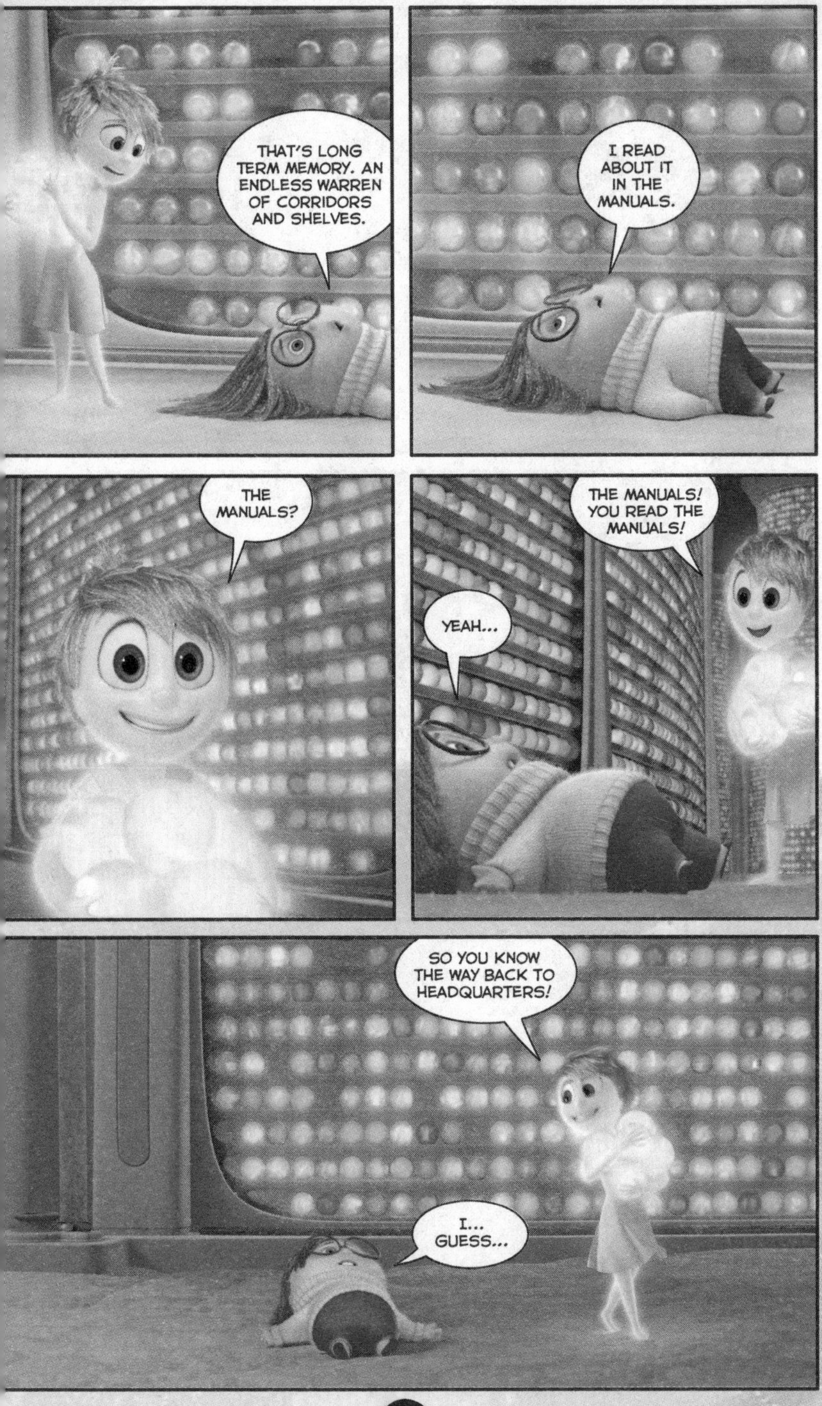
THAT'S LONG TERM MEMORY. AN ENDLESS WARREN OF CORRIDORS AND SHELVES.
I READ ABOUT IT IN THE MANUALS.
THE MANUALS?
THE MANUALS! YOU READ THE MANUALS!
YEAH...
SO YOU KNOW THE WAY BACK TO HEADQUARTERS!
I... GUESS...

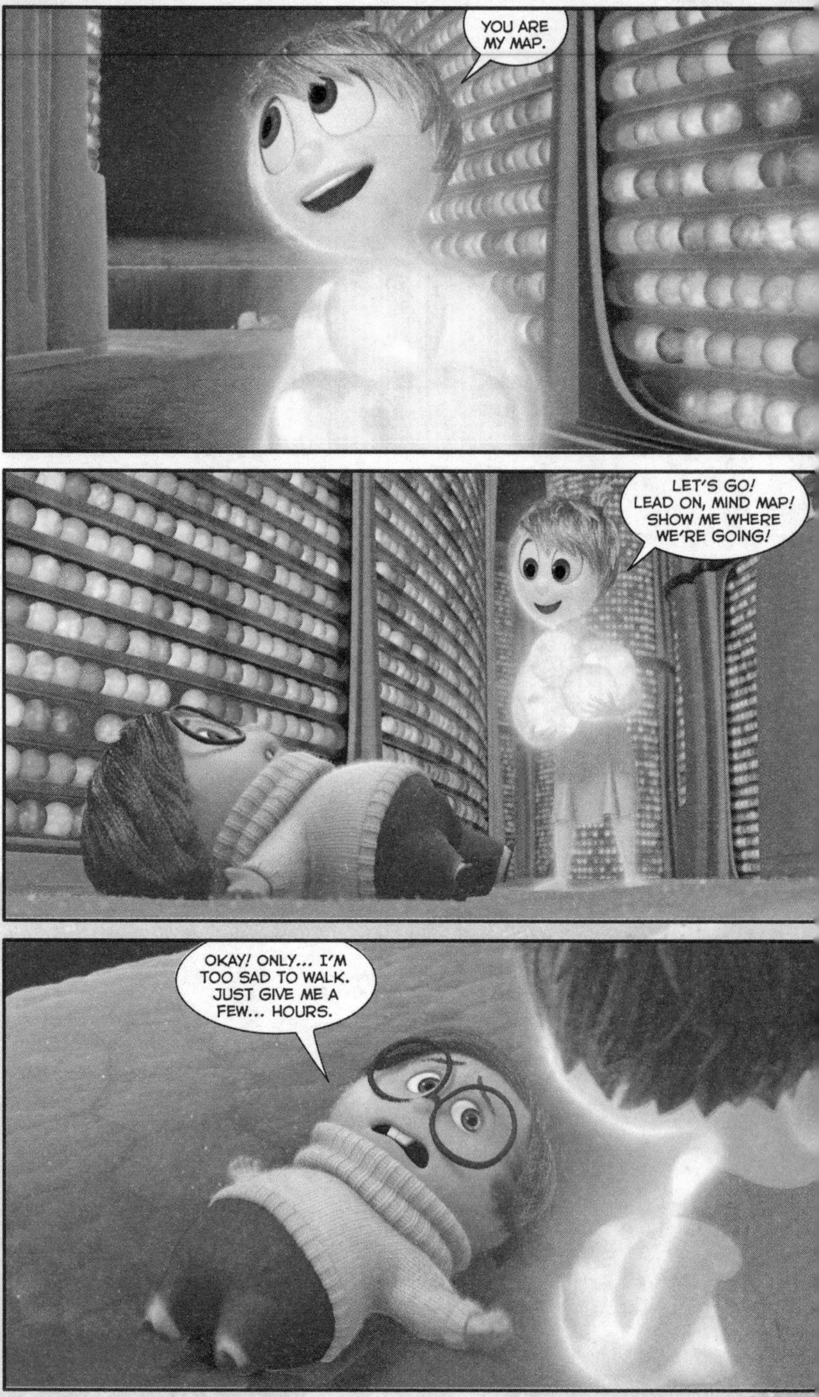
YOU ARE MY MAP.
LET'S GO! LEAD ON, MIND MAP! SHOW ME WHERE WE'RE GOING!
OKAY! ONLY... I'M TOO SAD TO WALK. JUST GIVE ME A FEW... HOURS.

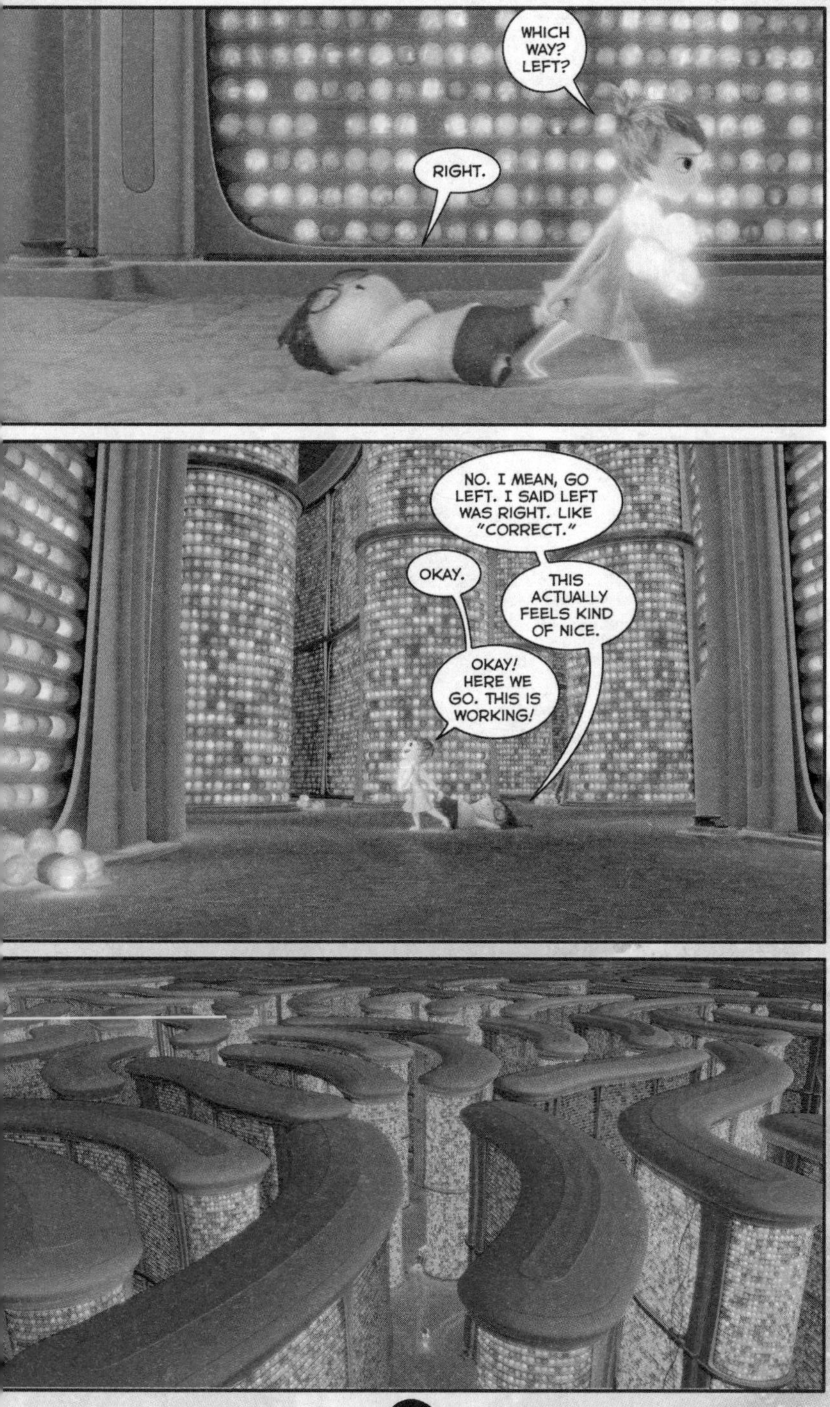
WHICH WAY? LEFT?
RIGHT.
NO. I MEAN, GO LEFT. I SAID LEFT WAS RIGHT. LIKE "CORRECT."
OKAY.
THIS ACTUALLY FEELS KIND OF NICE.
OKAY! HERE WE GO. THIS IS WORKING!

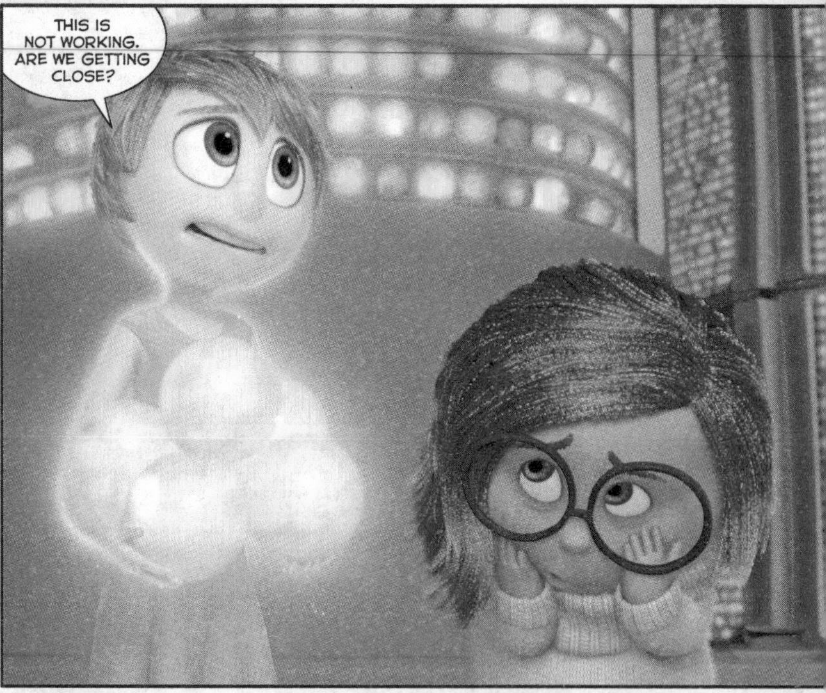
THIS IS NOT WORKING. ARE WE GETTING CLOSE?

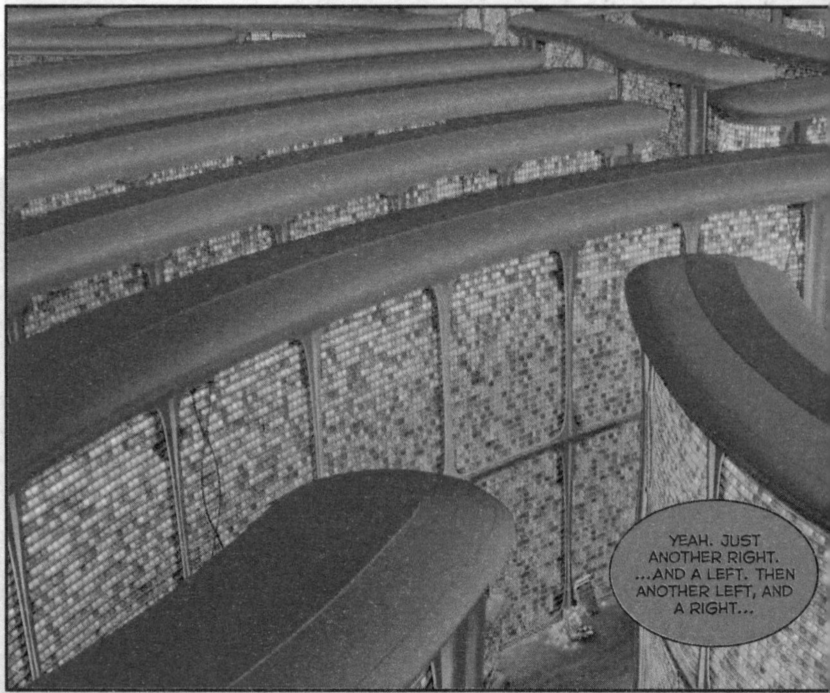
YEAH. JUST ANOTHER RIGHT. ...AND A LEFT. THEN ANOTHER LEFT, AND A RIGHT...

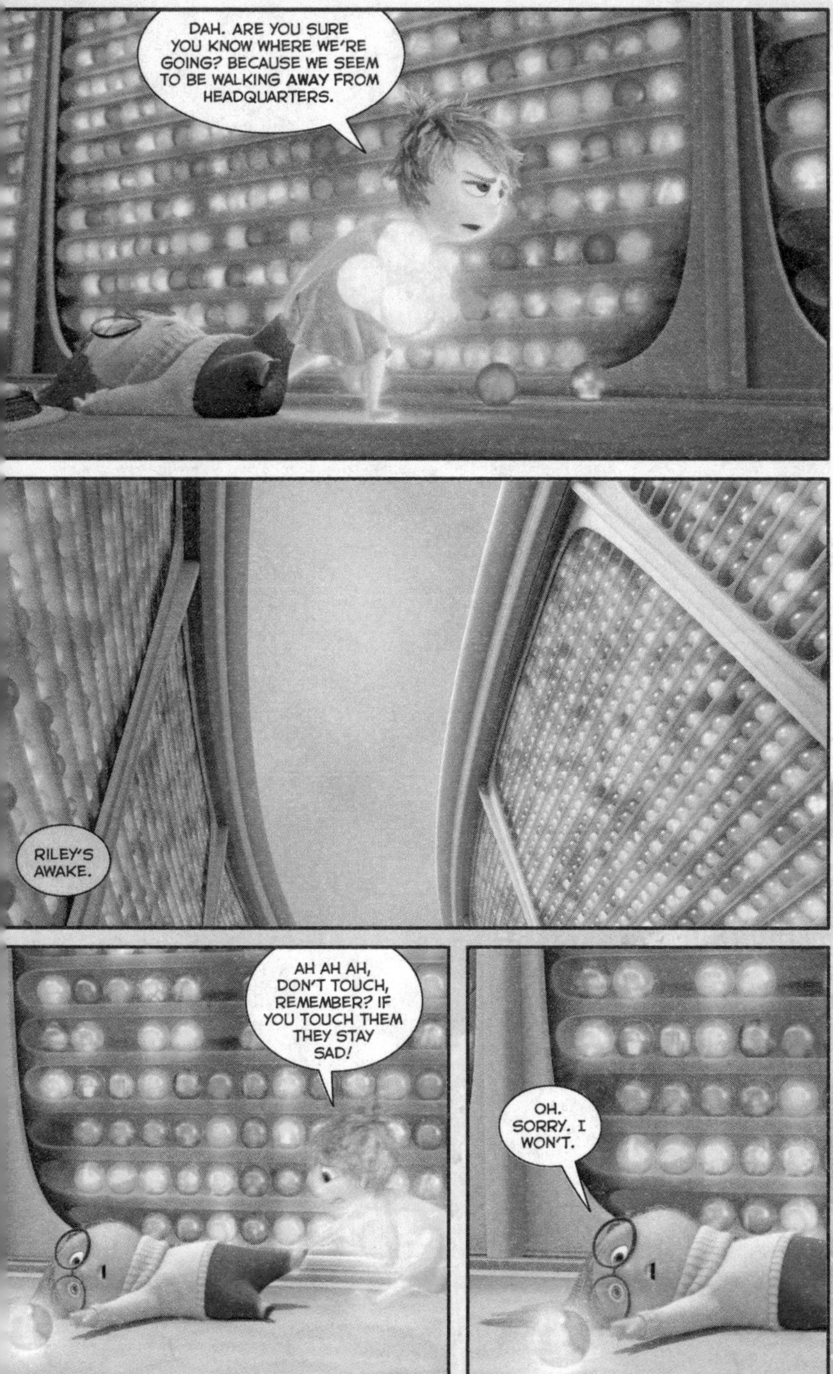
DAH. ARE YOU SURE YOU KNOW WHERE WE'RE GOING? BECAUSE WE SEEM TO BE WALKING AWAY FROM HEADQUARTERS.
RILEY'S AWAKE.
AH AH AH, DON'T TOUCH, REMEMBER? IF YOU TOUCH THEM THEY STAY SAD!
OH. SORRY. I WON'T.

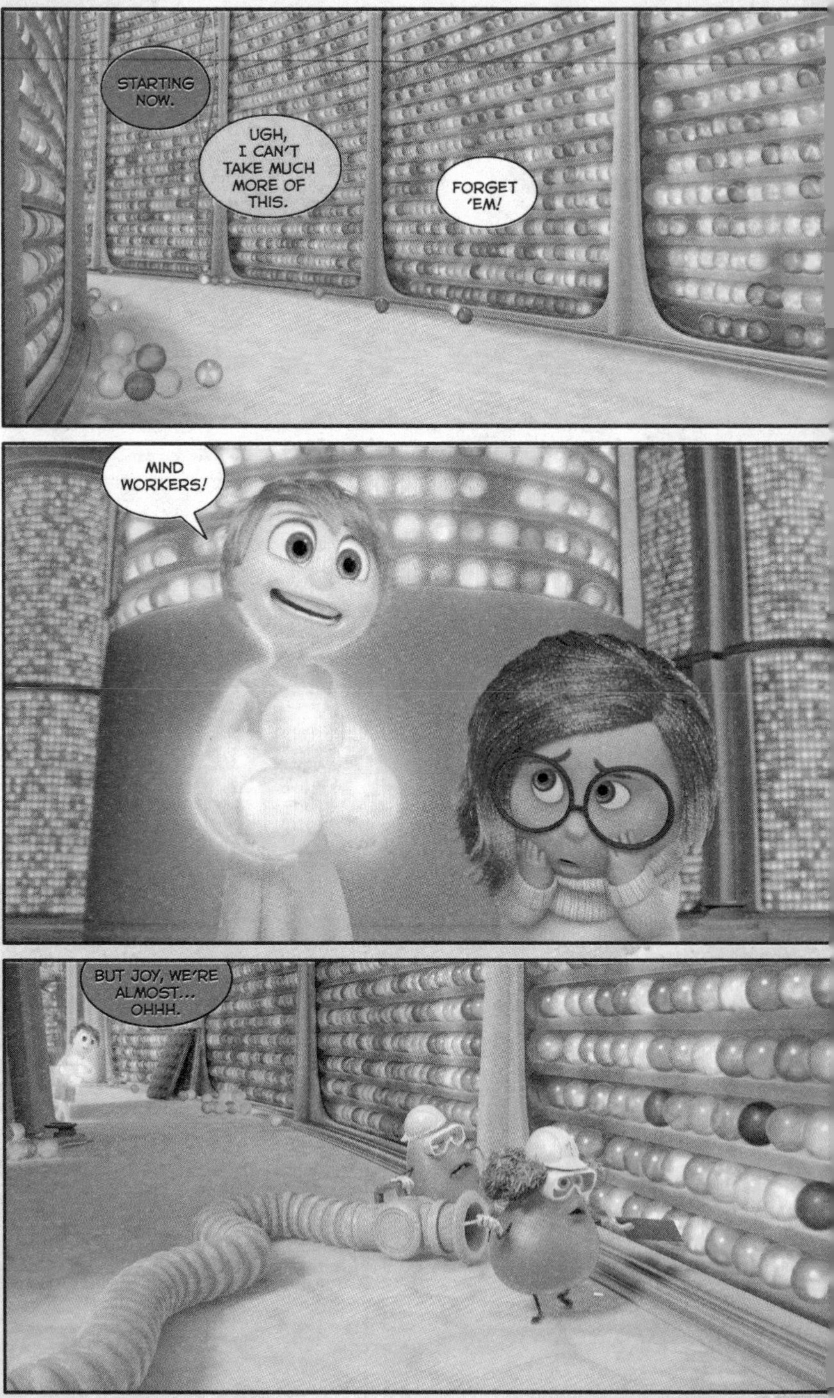
STARTING NOW.
UGH, I CAN'T TAKE MUCH MORE OF THIS.
FORGET 'EM!
MIND WORKERS!
BUT JOY, WE'RE ALMOST... OHHH.

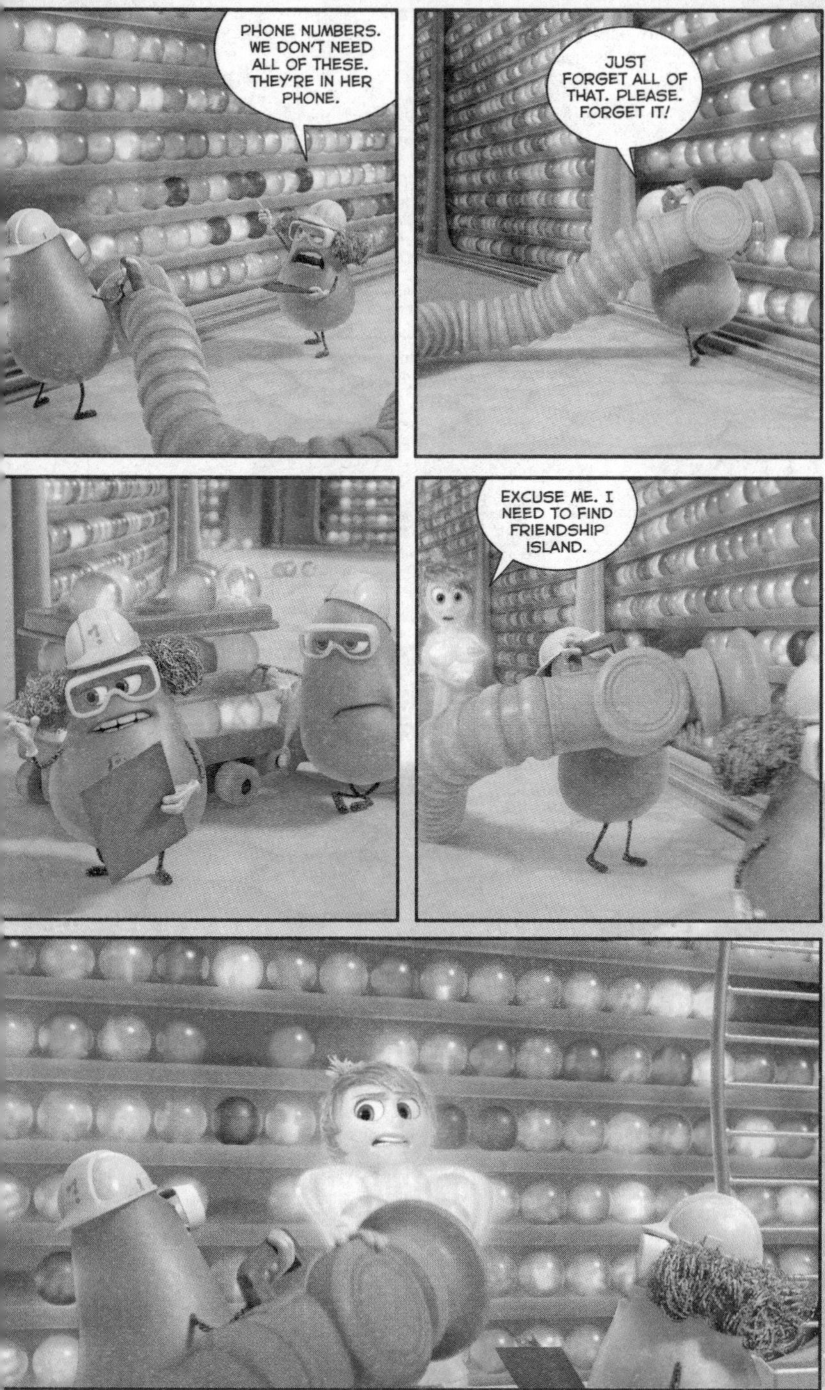
PHONE NUMBERS. WE DON'T NEED ALL OF THESE. THEY'RE IN HER PHONE.
JUST FORGET ALL OF THAT. PLEASE. FORGET IT!
EXCUSE ME. I NEED TO FIND FRIENDSHIP ISLAND.

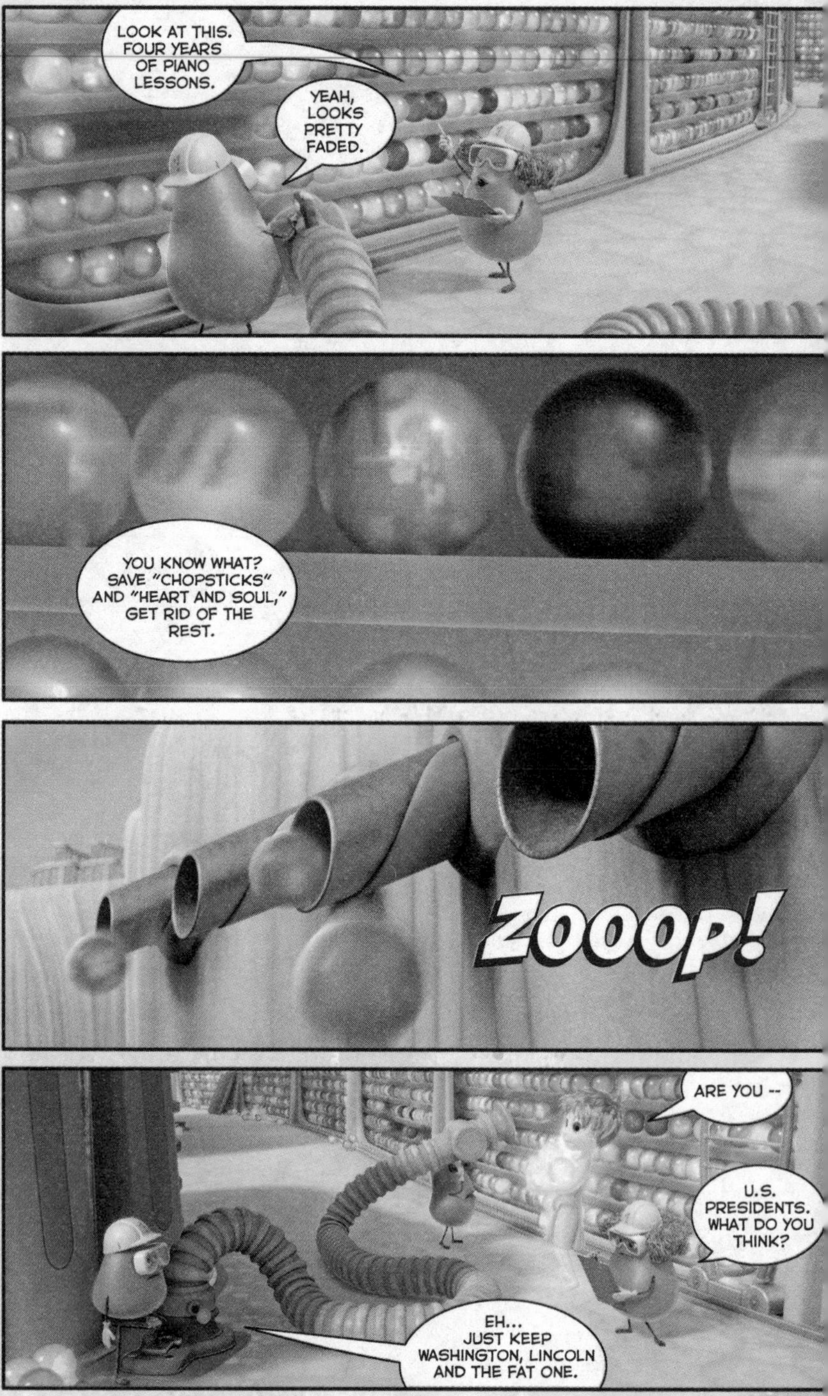
LOOK AT THIS. FOUR YEARS OF PIANO LESSONS.
YEAH, LOOKS PRETTY FADED.
YOU KNOW WHAT? SAVE "CHOPSTICKS" AND "HEART AND SOUL," GET RID OF THE REST.
ZOOOP!
ARE YOU --
U.S. PRESIDENTS. WHAT DO YOU THINK?
EH... JUST KEEP WASHINGTON, LINCOLN AND THE FAT ONE.

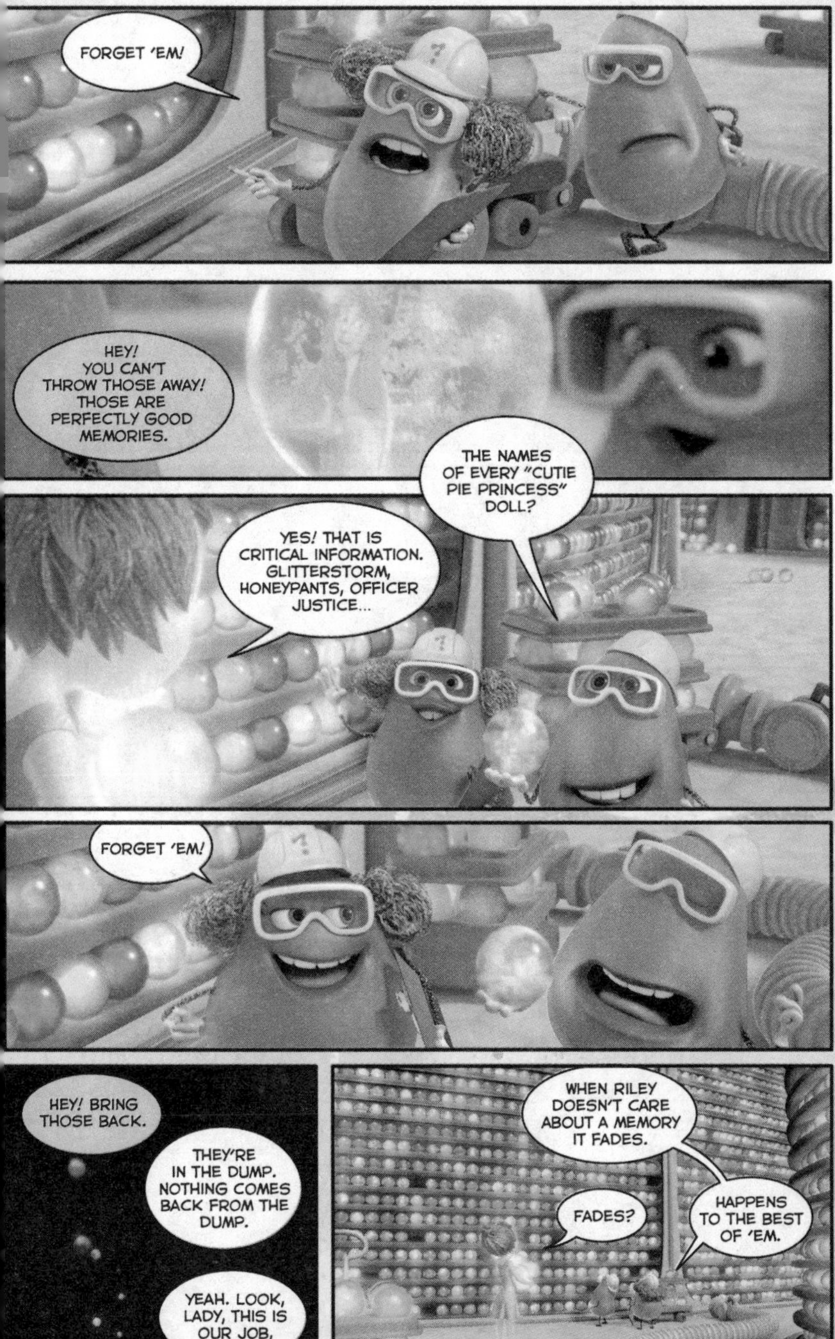
FORGET 'EM!
HEY! YOU CAN'T THROW THOSE AWAY! THOSE ARE PERFECTLY GOOD MEMORIES.
THE NAMES OF EVERY "CUTIE PIE PRINCESS" DOLL?
YES! THAT IS CRITICAL INFORMATION. GLITTERSTORM, HONEYPANTS, OFFICER JUSTICE...
FORGET 'EM!
HEY! BRING THOSE BACK.
THEY'RE IN THE DUMP. NOTHING COMES BACK FROM THE DUMP.
YEAH. LOOK, LADY, THIS IS OUR JOB, OKAY?
WHEN RILEY DOESN'T CARE ABOUT A MEMORY IT FADES.
FADES?
HAPPENS TO THE BEST OF 'EM.

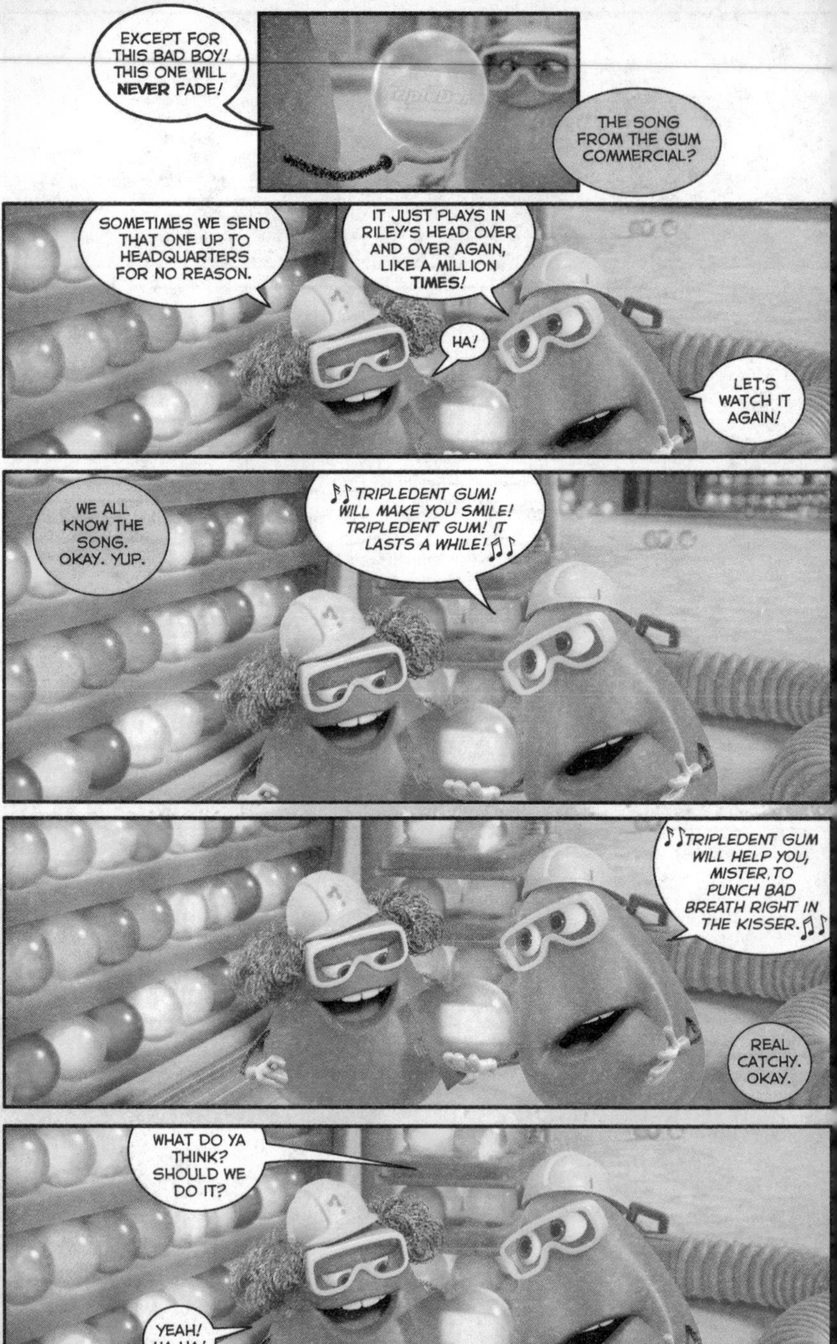
EXCEPT FOR THIS BAD BOY! THIS ONE WILL NEVER FADE!
THE SONG FROM THE GUM COMMERCIAL?
SOMETIMES WE SEND THAT ONE UP TO HEADQUARTERS FOR NO REASON.
IT JUST PLAYS IN RILEY'S HEAD OVER AND OVER AGAIN, LIKE A MILLION TIMES!
HA!
LET'S WATCH IT AGAIN!
WE ALL KNOW THE SONG. OKAY. YUP.
♫ TRIPLEDENT GUM! WILL MAKE YOU SMILE! TRIPLEDENT GUM! IT LASTS A WHILE! ♫
♫ TRIPLEDENT GUM WILL HELP YOU, MISTER, TO PUNCH BAD BREATH RIGHT IN THE KISSER. ♫
REAL CATCHY. OKAY.
WHAT DO YA THINK? SHOULD WE DO IT?
YEAH! HA-HA!

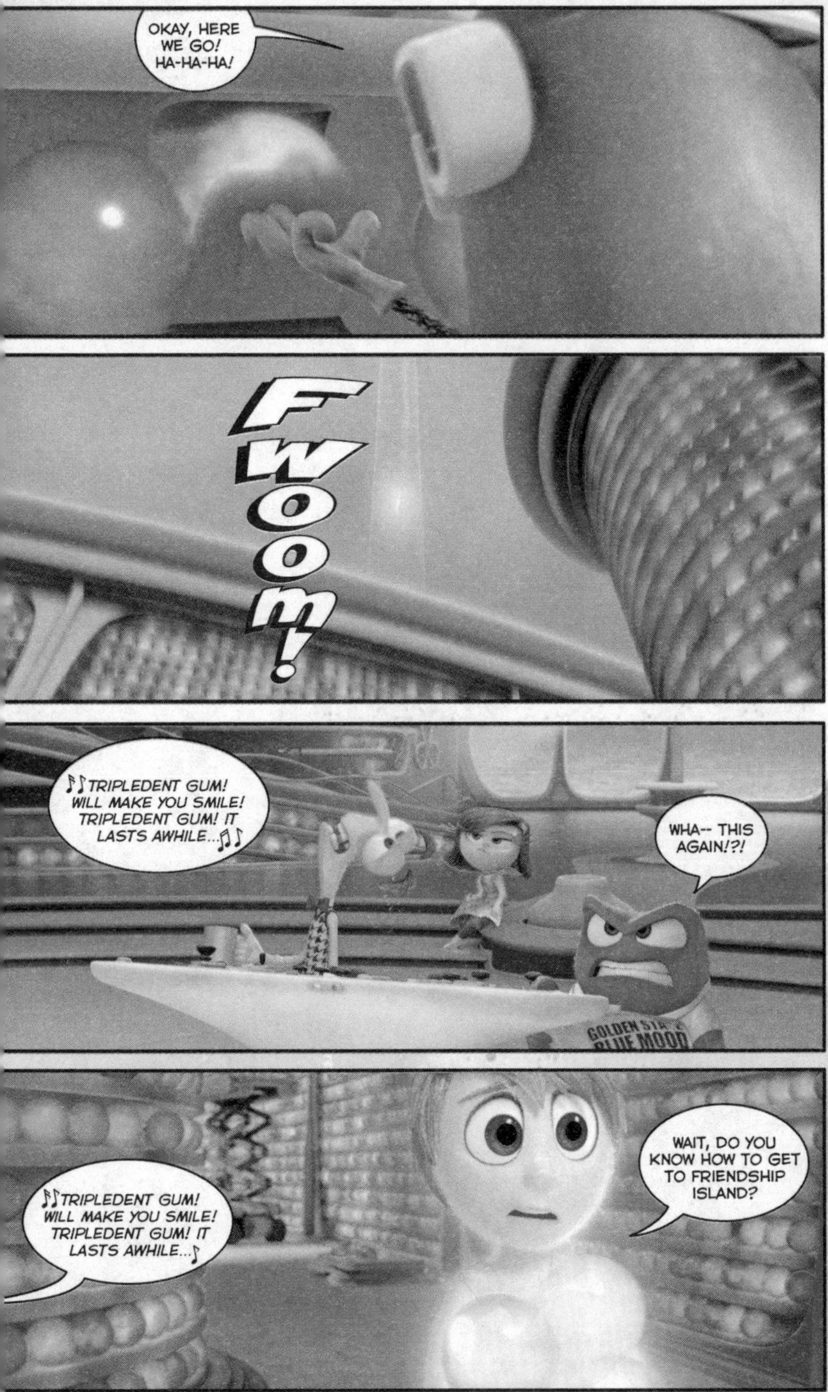
OKAY, HERE WE GO! HA-HA-HA!
FWOOM!
TRIPLEDENT GUM! WILL MAKE YOU SMILE! TRIPLEDENT GUM! IT LASTS AWHILE...
WHA-- THIS AGAIN!?!
GOLDEN STATE BLUE MOOD
TRIPLEDENT GUM! WILL MAKE YOU SMILE! TRIPLEDENT GUM! IT LASTS AWHILE...
WAIT, DO YOU KNOW HOW TO GET TO FRIENDSHIP ISLAND?

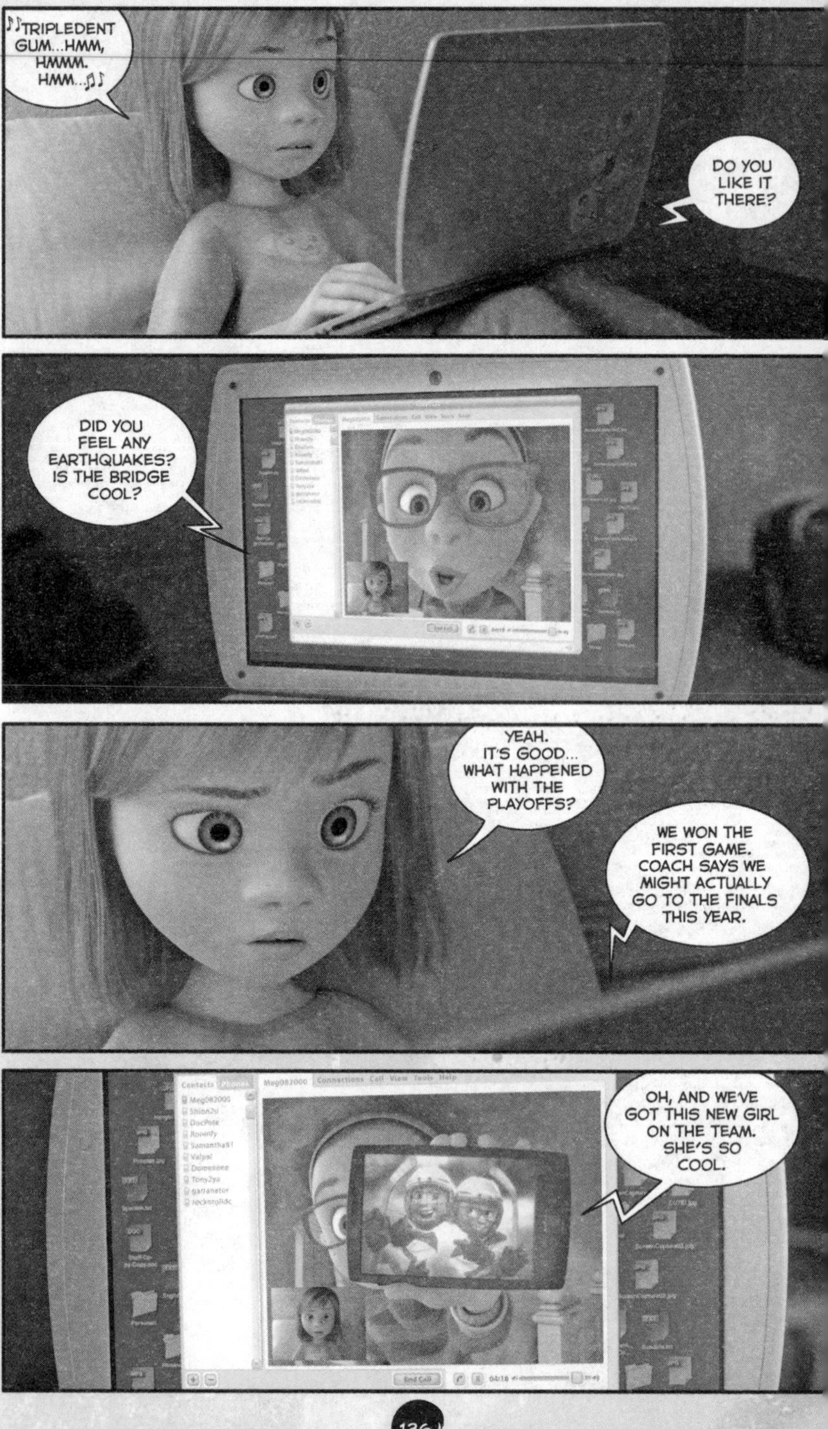
♪♪TRIPLEDENT GUM...HMM, HMMM. HMM...♫♪
DO YOU LIKE IT THERE?
DID YOU FEEL ANY EARTHQUAKES? IS THE BRIDGE COOL?
YEAH. IT'S GOOD... WHAT HAPPENED WITH THE PLAYOFFS?
WE WON THE FIRST GAME. COACH SAYS WE MIGHT ACTUALLY GO TO THE FINALS THIS YEAR.
OH, AND WE'VE GOT THIS NEW GIRL ON THE TEAM. SHE'S SO COOL.

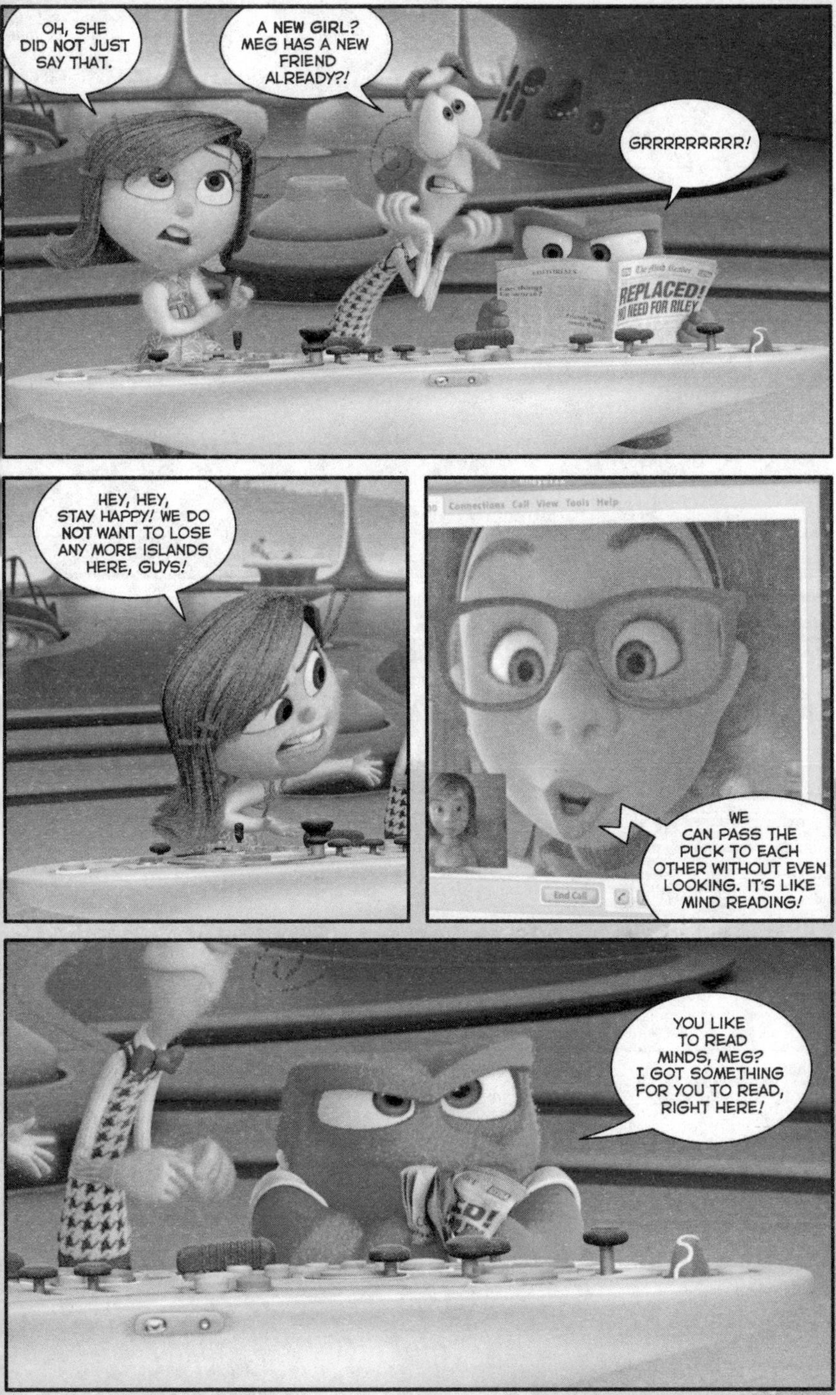
OH, SHE DID NOT JUST SAY THAT.
A NEW GIRL? MEG HAS A NEW FRIEND ALREADY?!
GRRRRRRRRR!
REPLACED!
HEY, HEY, STAY HAPPY! WE DO NOT WANT TO LOSE ANY MORE ISLANDS HERE, GUYS!
Connections Call View Tools Help
End Call
WE CAN PASS THE PUCK TO EACH OTHER WITHOUT EVEN LOOKING. IT'S LIKE MIND READING!
YOU LIKE TO READ MINDS, MEG? I GOT SOMETHING FOR YOU TO READ, RIGHT HERE!

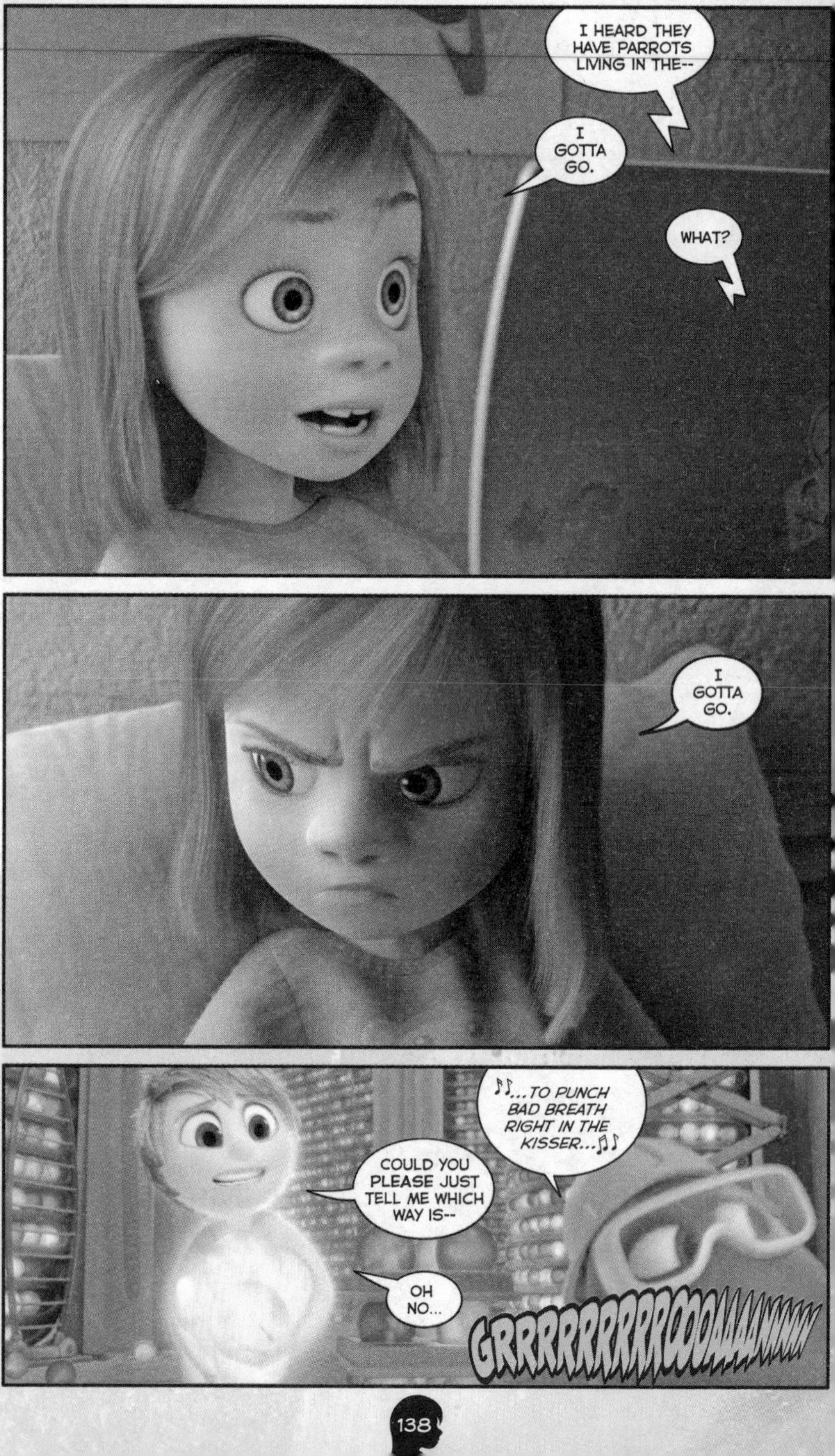
I HEARD THEY HAVE PARROTS LIVING IN THE--
I GOTTA GO.
WHAT?
I GOTTA GO.
COULD YOU PLEASE JUST TELL ME WHICH WAY IS--
♪♪...TO PUNCH BAD BREATH RIGHT IN THE KISSER...♫♪
OH NO...
GRRRRRRRRROOOAAAANNNN

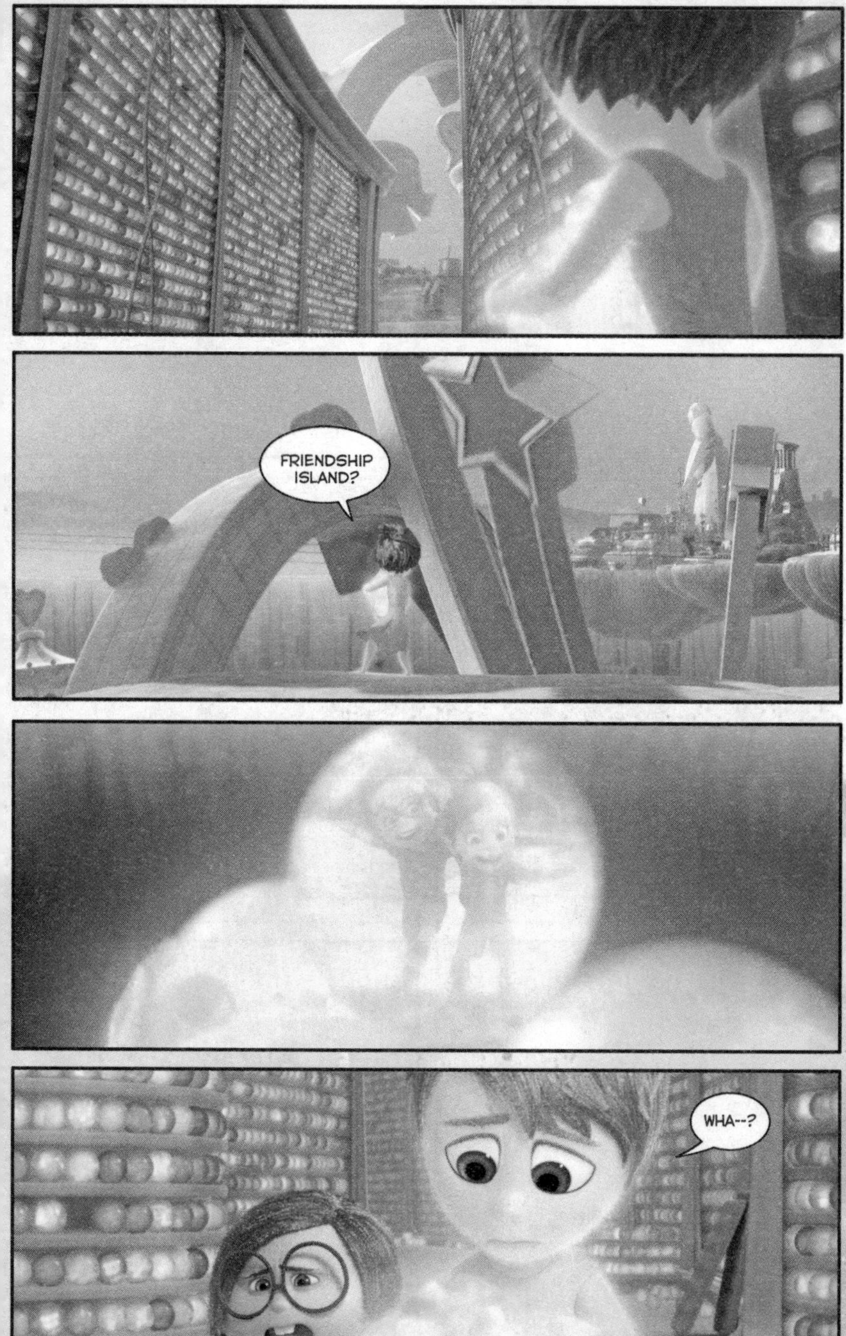
FRIENDSHIP ISLAND?
WHA--?

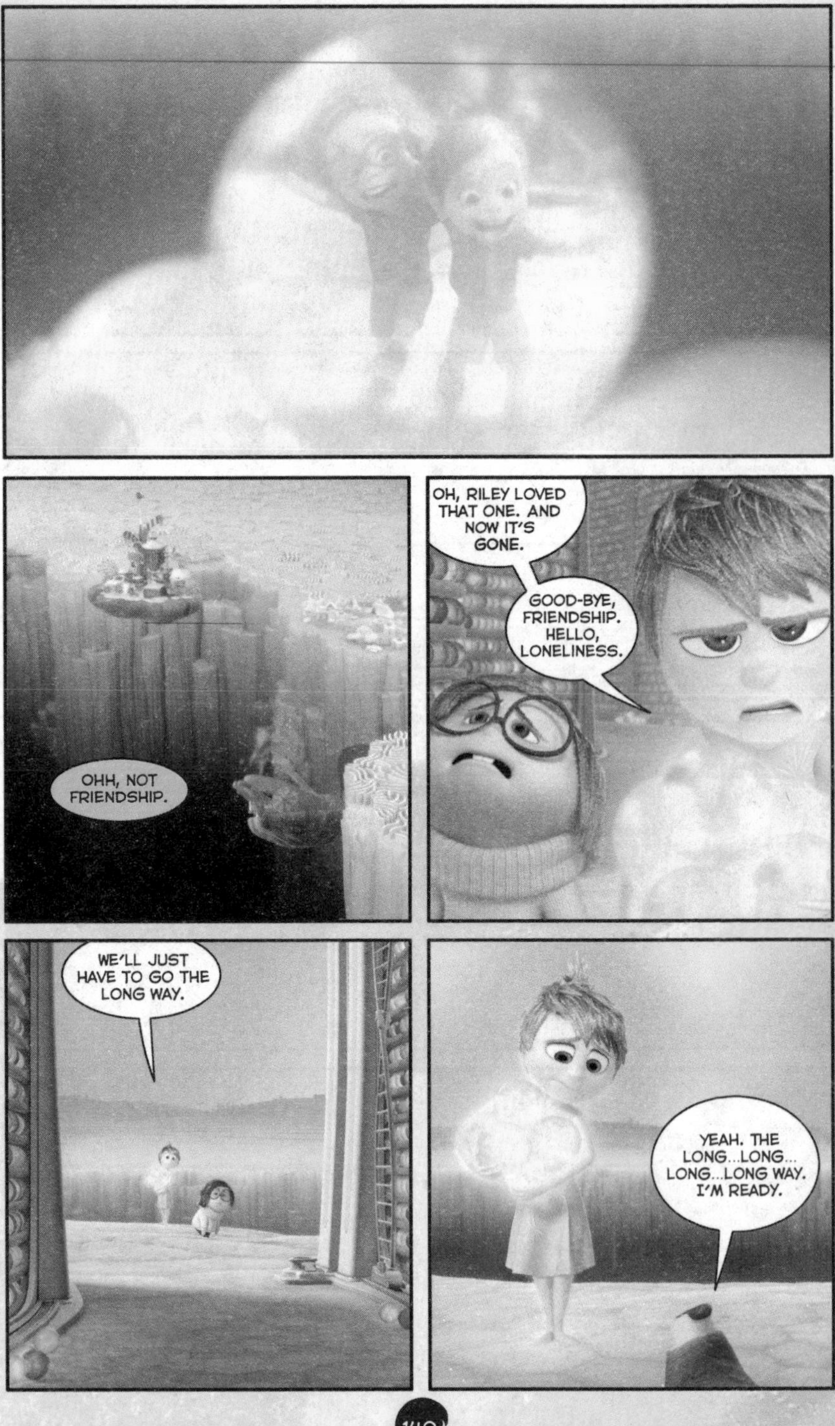
OHH, NOT FRIENDSHIP.
OH, RILEY LOVED THAT ONE. AND NOW IT'S GONE.
GOOD-BYE, FRIENDSHIP. HELLO, LONELINESS.
WE'LL JUST HAVE TO GO THE LONG WAY.
YEAH. THE LONG...LONG... LONG...LONG WAY. I'M READY.

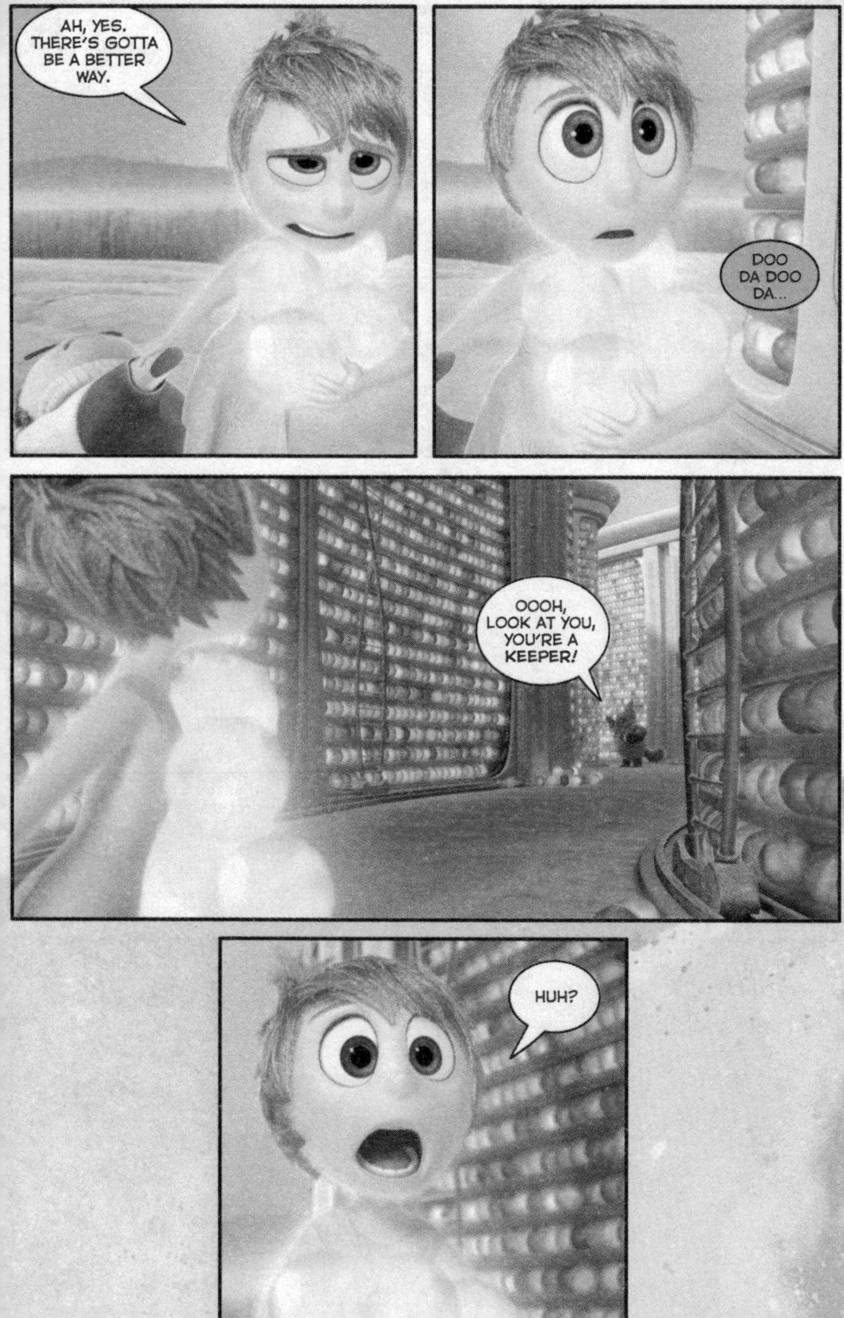
AH, YES. THERE'S GOTTA BE A BETTER WAY.
DOO DA DOO DA...
OOOH, LOOK AT YOU, YOU'RE A KEEPER!
HUH?

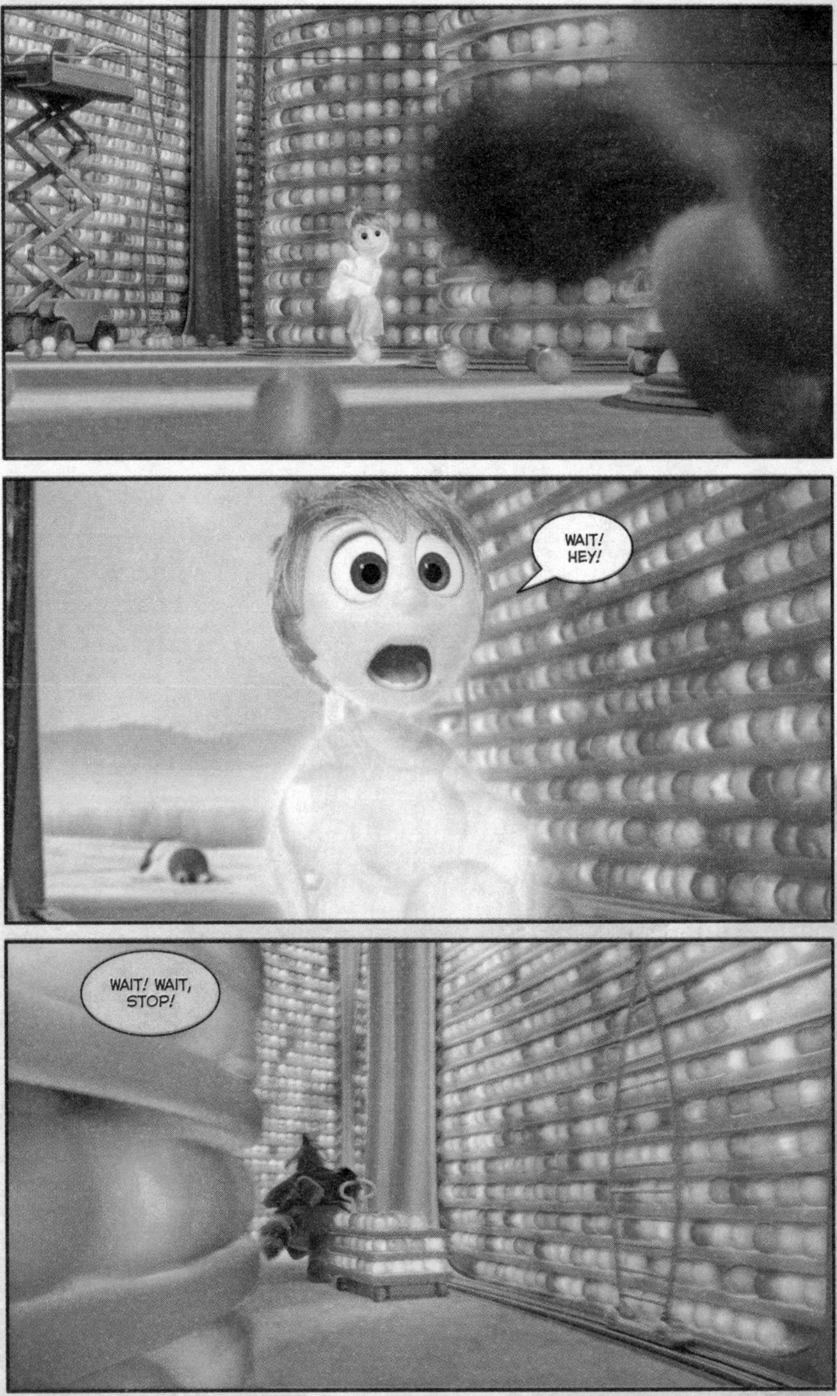
WAIT! HEY!
WAIT! WAIT, STOP!

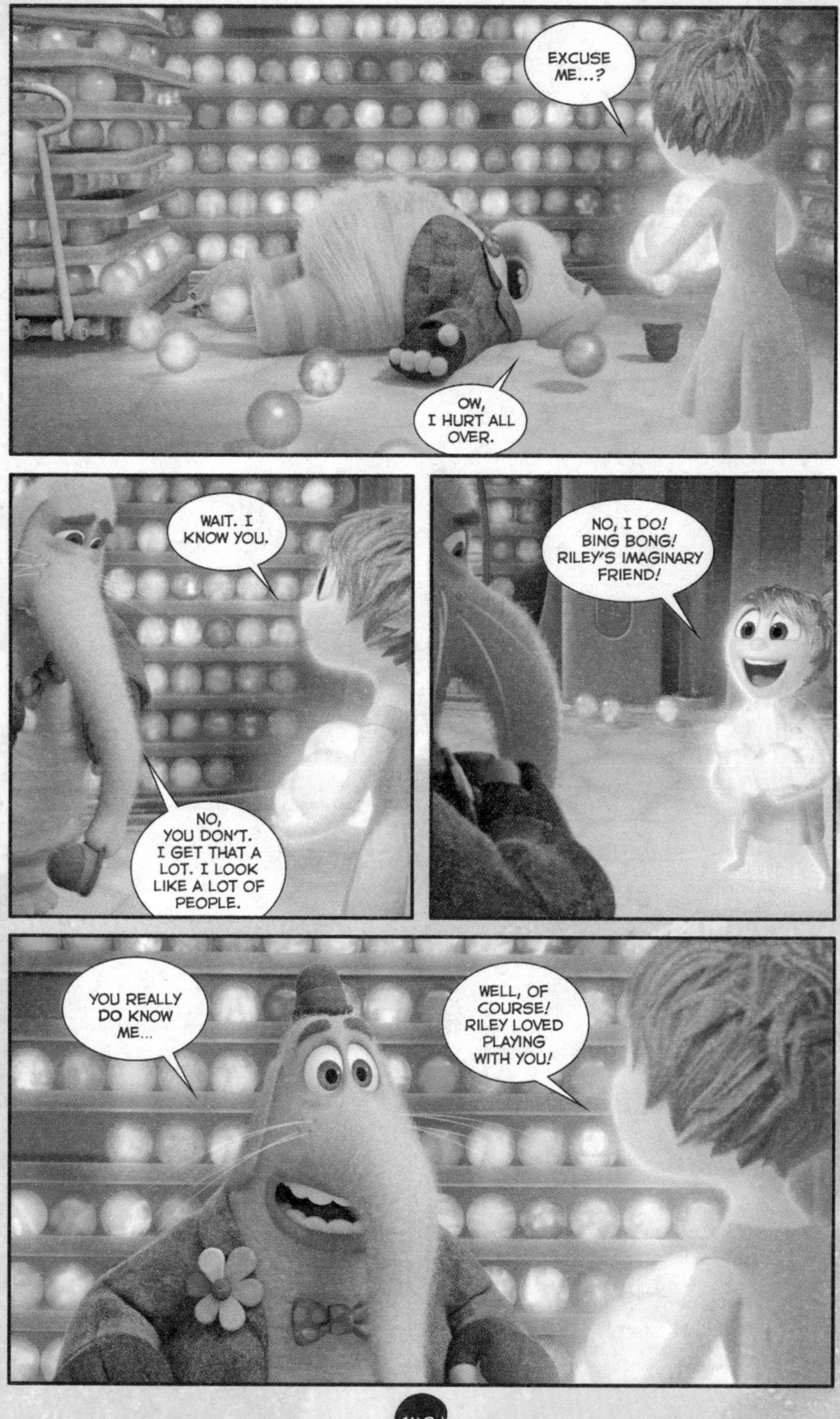
EXCUSE ME...?
OW, I HURT ALL OVER.
WAIT. I KNOW YOU.
NO, YOU DON'T. I GET THAT A LOT. I LOOK LIKE A LOT OF PEOPLE.
NO, I DO! BING BONG! RILEY'S IMAGINARY FRIEND!
YOU REALLY DO KNOW ME...
WELL, OF COURSE! RILEY LOVED PLAYING WITH YOU!

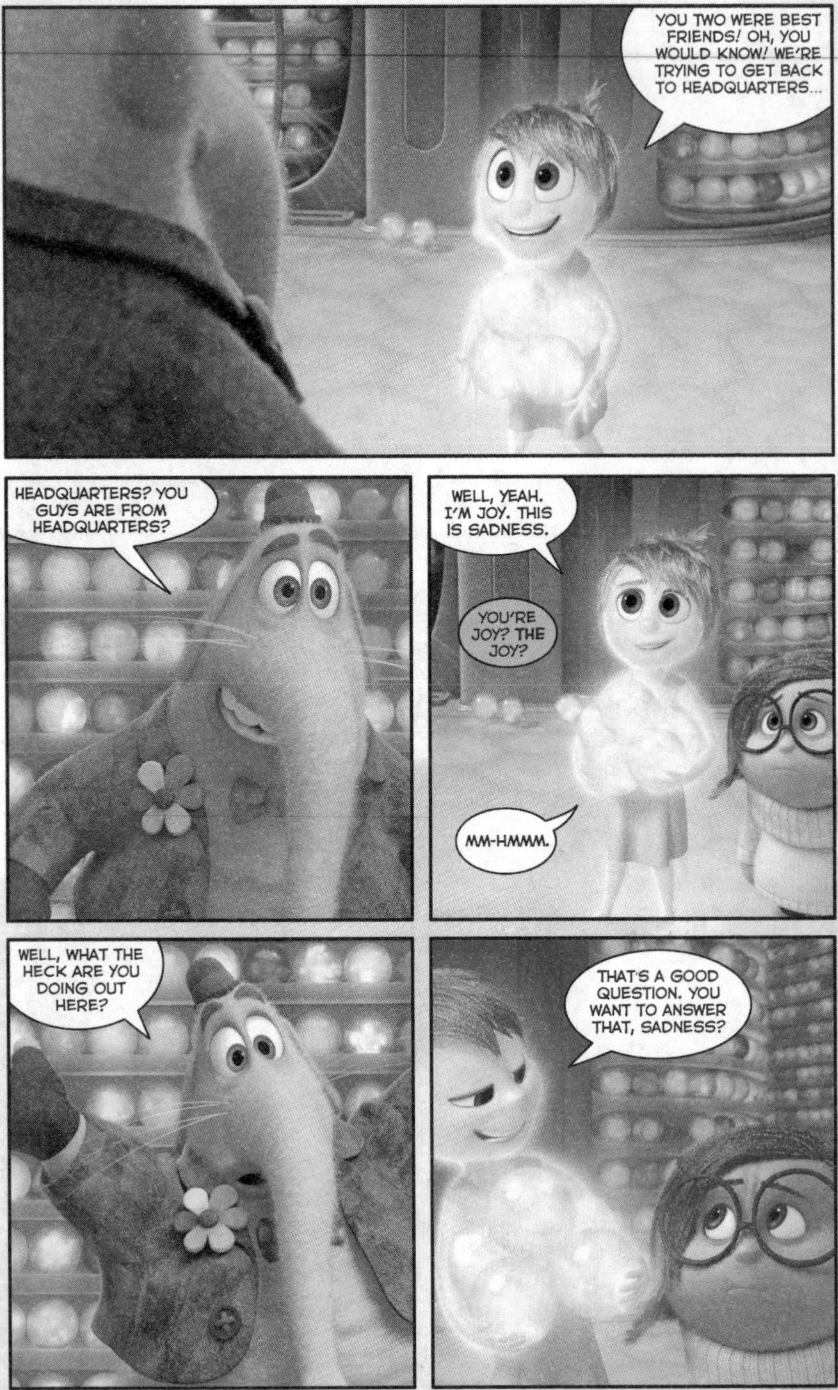
YOU TWO WERE BEST FRIENDS! OH, YOU WOULD KNOW! WE'RE TRYING TO GET BACK TO HEADQUARTERS...
HEADQUARTERS? YOU GUYS ARE FROM HEADQUARTERS?
WELL, YEAH. I'M JOY. THIS IS SADNESS.
YOU'RE JOY? THE JOY?
MM-HMMM.
WELL, WHAT THE HECK ARE YOU DOING OUT HERE?
THAT'S A GOOD QUESTION. YOU WANT TO ANSWER THAT, SADNESS?

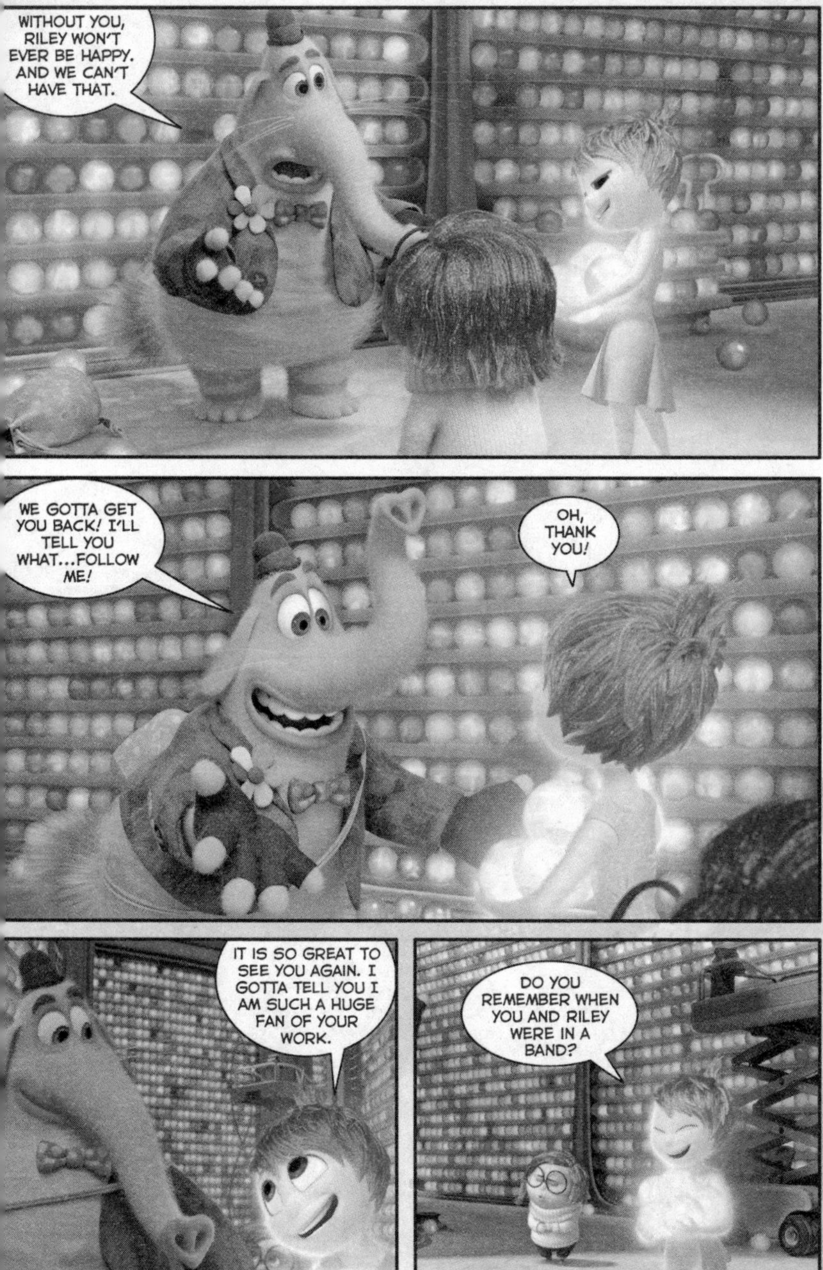
WITHOUT YOU, RILEY WON'T EVER BE HAPPY. AND WE CAN'T HAVE THAT.
WE GOTTA GET YOU BACK! I'LL TELL YOU WHAT...FOLLOW ME!
OH, THANK YOU!
IT IS SO GREAT TO SEE YOU AGAIN. I GOTTA TELL YOU I AM SUCH A HUGE FAN OF YOUR WORK.
DO YOU REMEMBER WHEN YOU AND RILEY WERE IN A BAND?

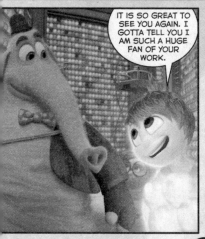

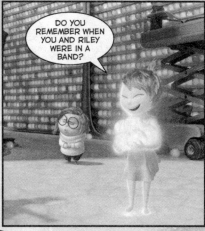

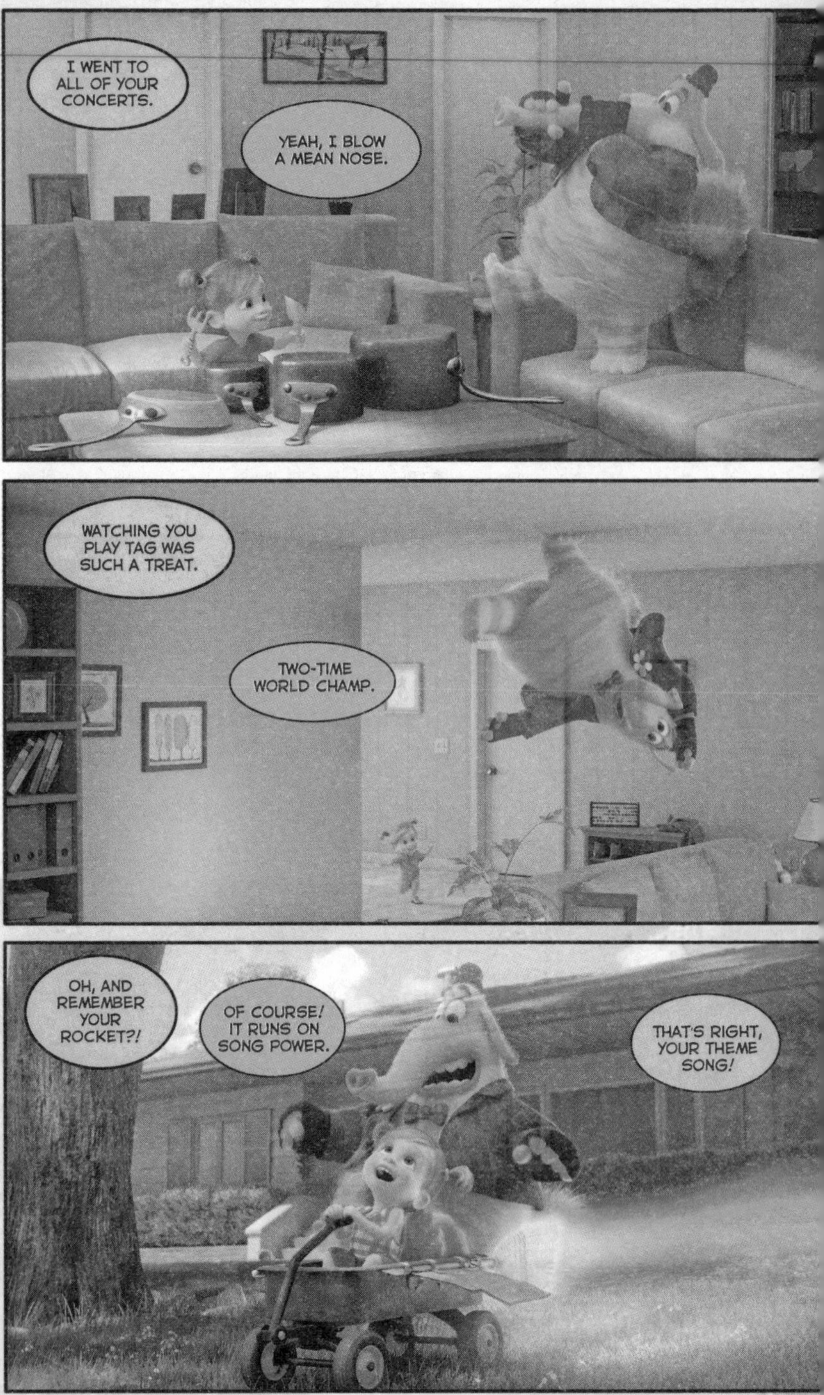
I WENT TO ALL OF YOUR CONCERTS.
YEAH, I BLOW A MEAN NOSE.
WATCHING YOU PLAY TAG WAS SUCH A TREAT.
TWO-TIME WORLD CHAMP.
OH, AND REMEMBER YOUR ROCKET?!
OF COURSE! IT RUNS ON SONG POWER.
THAT'S RIGHT, YOUR THEME SONG!

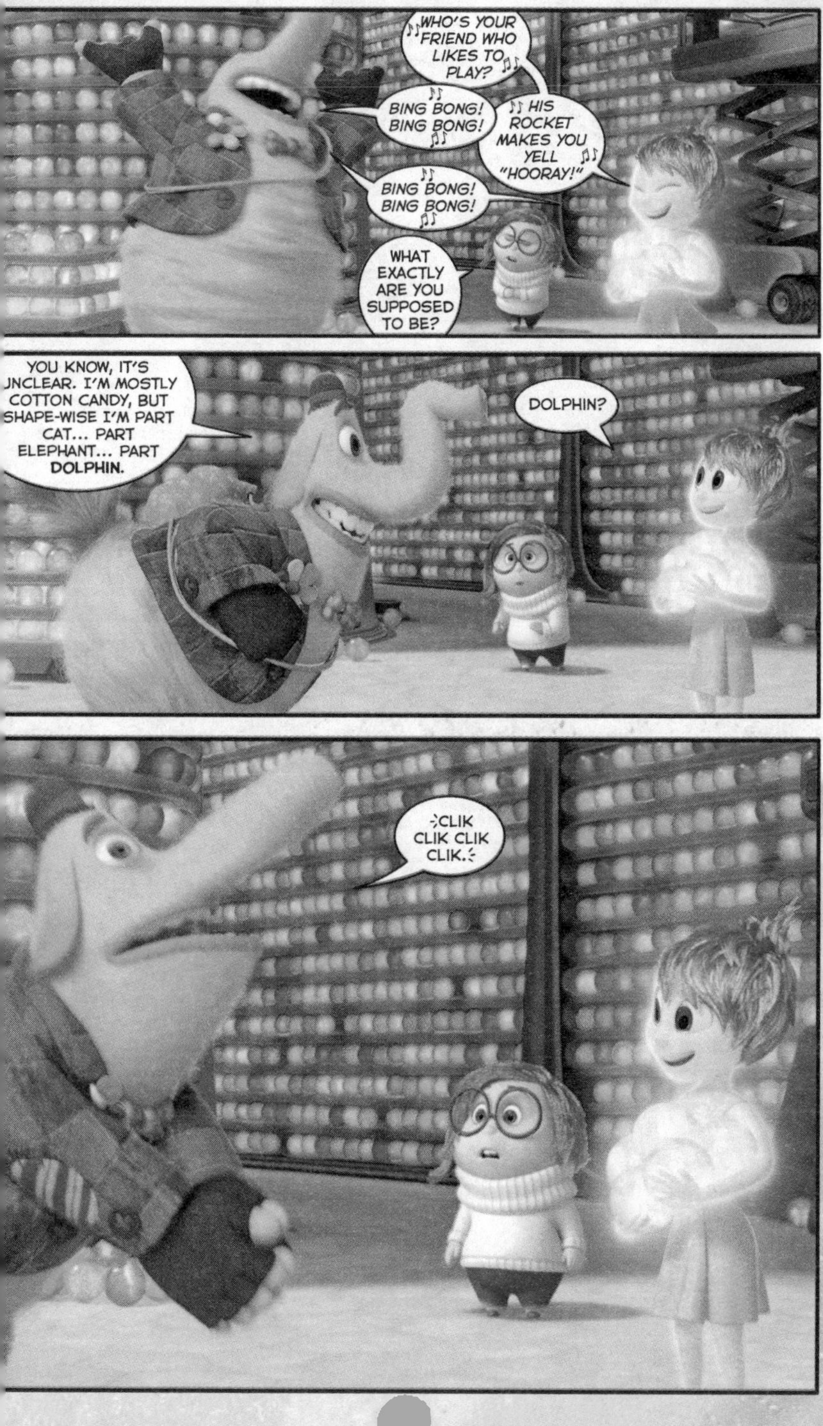
WHO'S YOUR FRIEND WHO LIKES TO PLAY?
BING BONG! BING BONG!
HIS ROCKET MAKES YOU YELL "HOORAY!"
BING BONG! BING BONG!
WHAT EXACTLY ARE YOU SUPPOSED TO BE?
YOU KNOW, IT'S UNCLEAR. I'M MOSTLY COTTON CANDY, BUT SHAPE-WISE I'M PART CAT... PART ELEPHANT... PART DOLPHIN.
DOLPHIN?
CLIK CLIK CLIK CLIK.

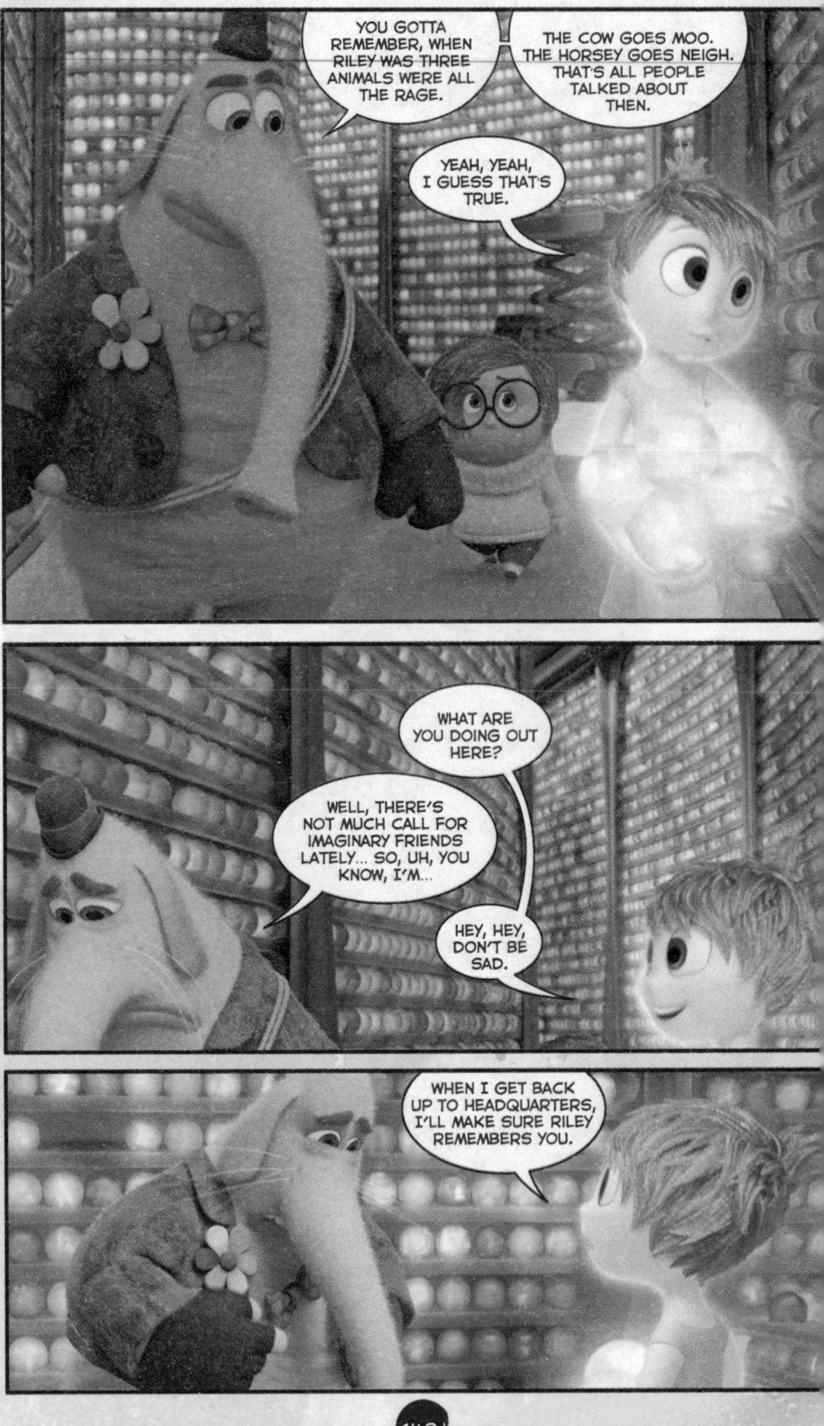
YOU GOTTA REMEMBER, WHEN RILEY WAS THREE ANIMALS WERE ALL THE RAGE.
THE COW GOES MOO. THE HORSEY GOES NEIGH. THAT'S ALL PEOPLE TALKED ABOUT THEN.
YEAH, YEAH, I GUESS THAT'S TRUE.
WHAT ARE YOU DOING OUT HERE?
WELL, THERE'S NOT MUCH CALL FOR IMAGINARY FRIENDS LATELY... SO, UH, YOU KNOW, I'M...
HEY, HEY, DON'T BE SAD.
WHEN I GET BACK UP TO HEADQUARTERS, I'LL MAKE SURE RILEY REMEMBERS YOU.

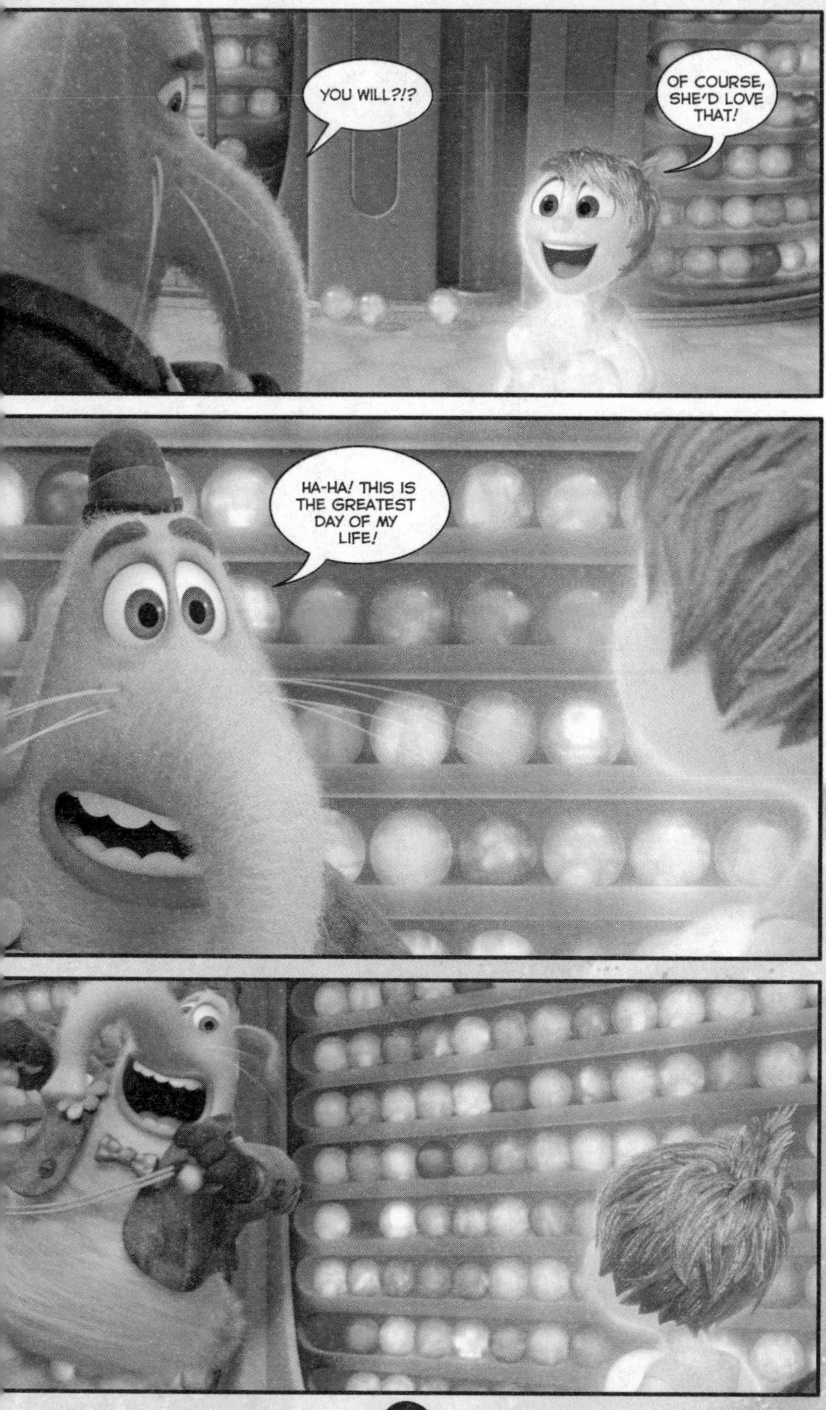
YOU WILL?!?
OF COURSE, SHE'D LOVE THAT!
HA-HA! THIS IS THE GREATEST DAY OF MY LIFE!

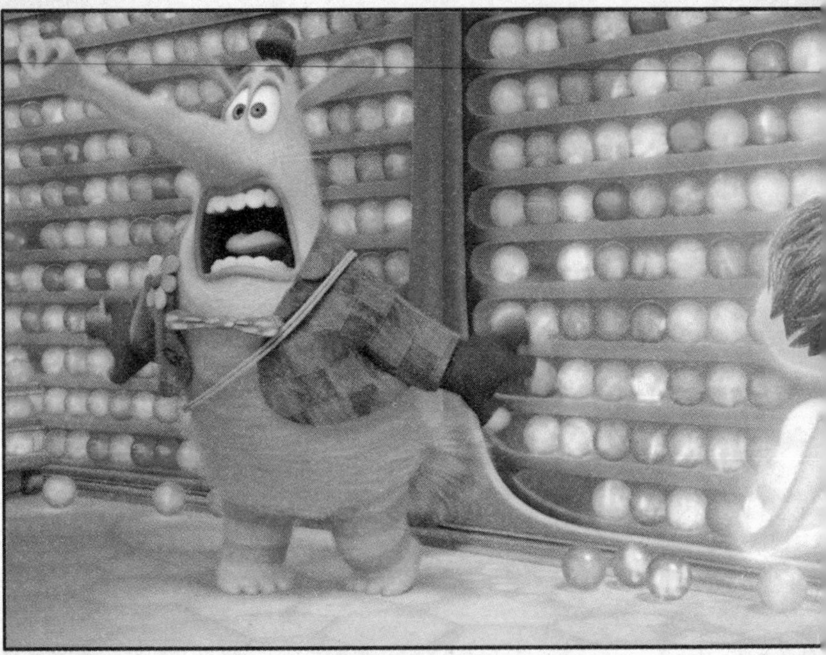

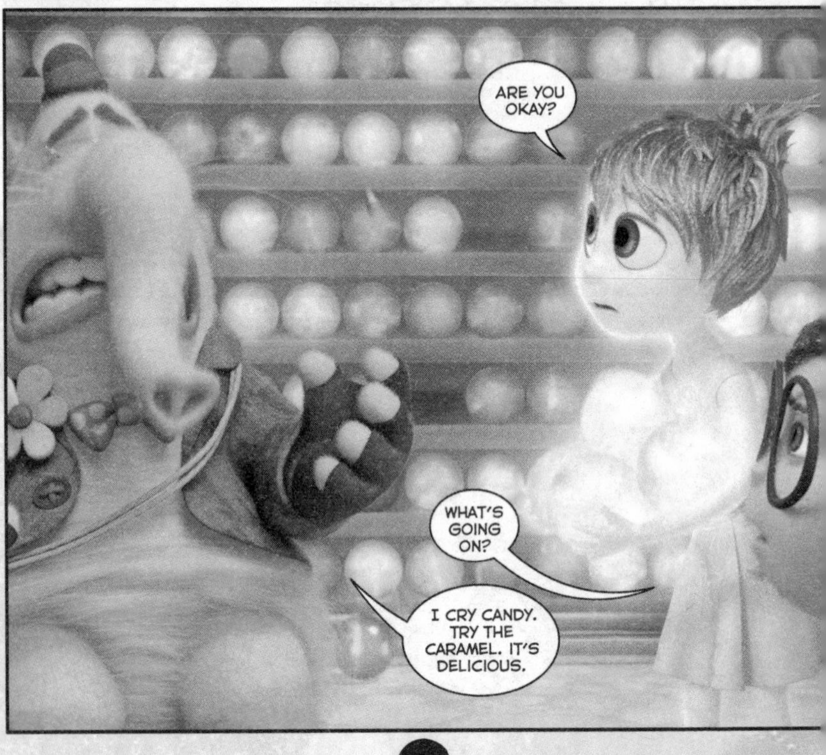
ARE YOU OKAY?
WHAT'S GOING ON?
I CRY CANDY. TRY THE CARAMEL. IT'S DELICIOUS.

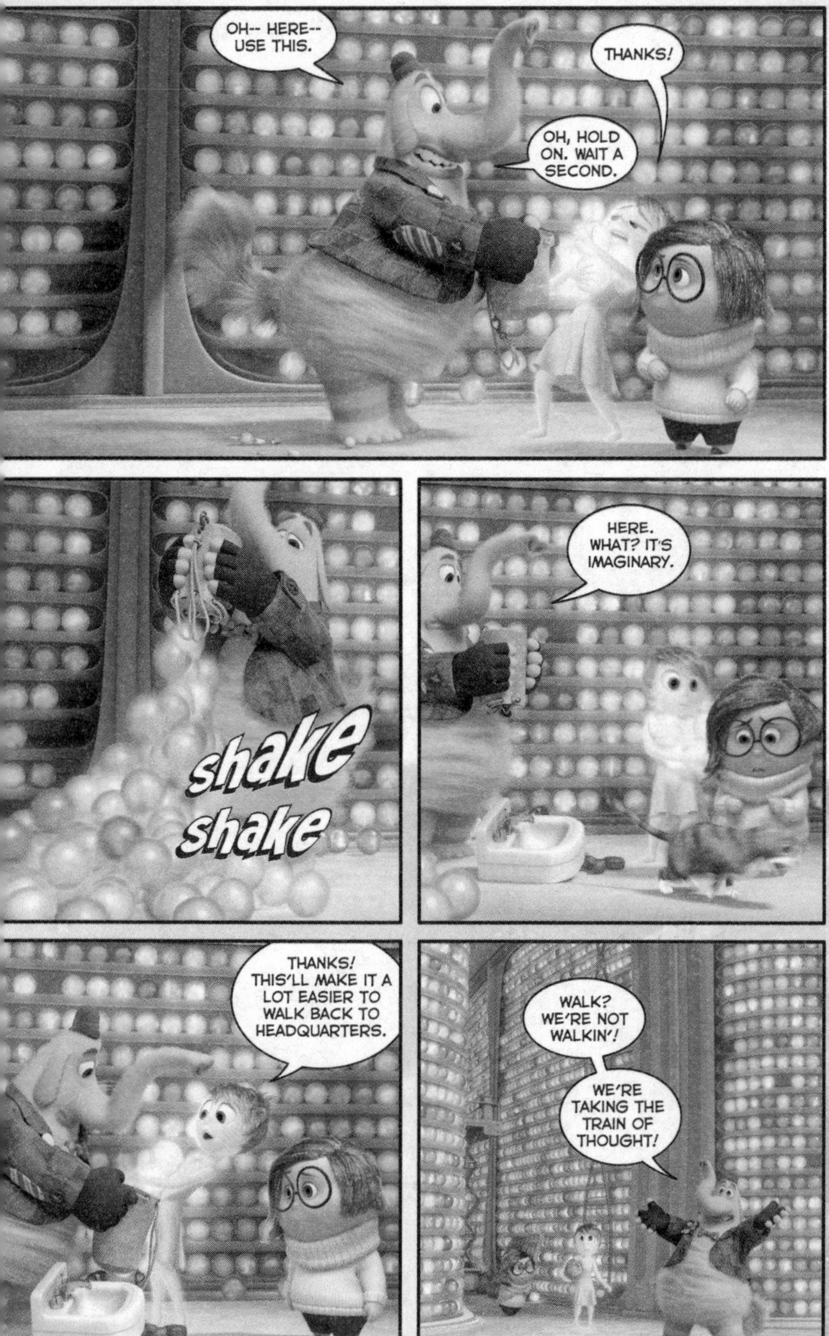
OH-- HERE-- USE THIS.
OH, HOLD ON. WAIT A SECOND.
THANKS!
shake shake
HERE. WHAT? IT'S IMAGINARY.
THANKS! THIS'LL MAKE IT A LOT EASIER TO WALK BACK TO HEADQUARTERS.
WALK? WE'RE NOT WALKIN'!
WE'RE TAKING THE TRAIN OF THOUGHT!

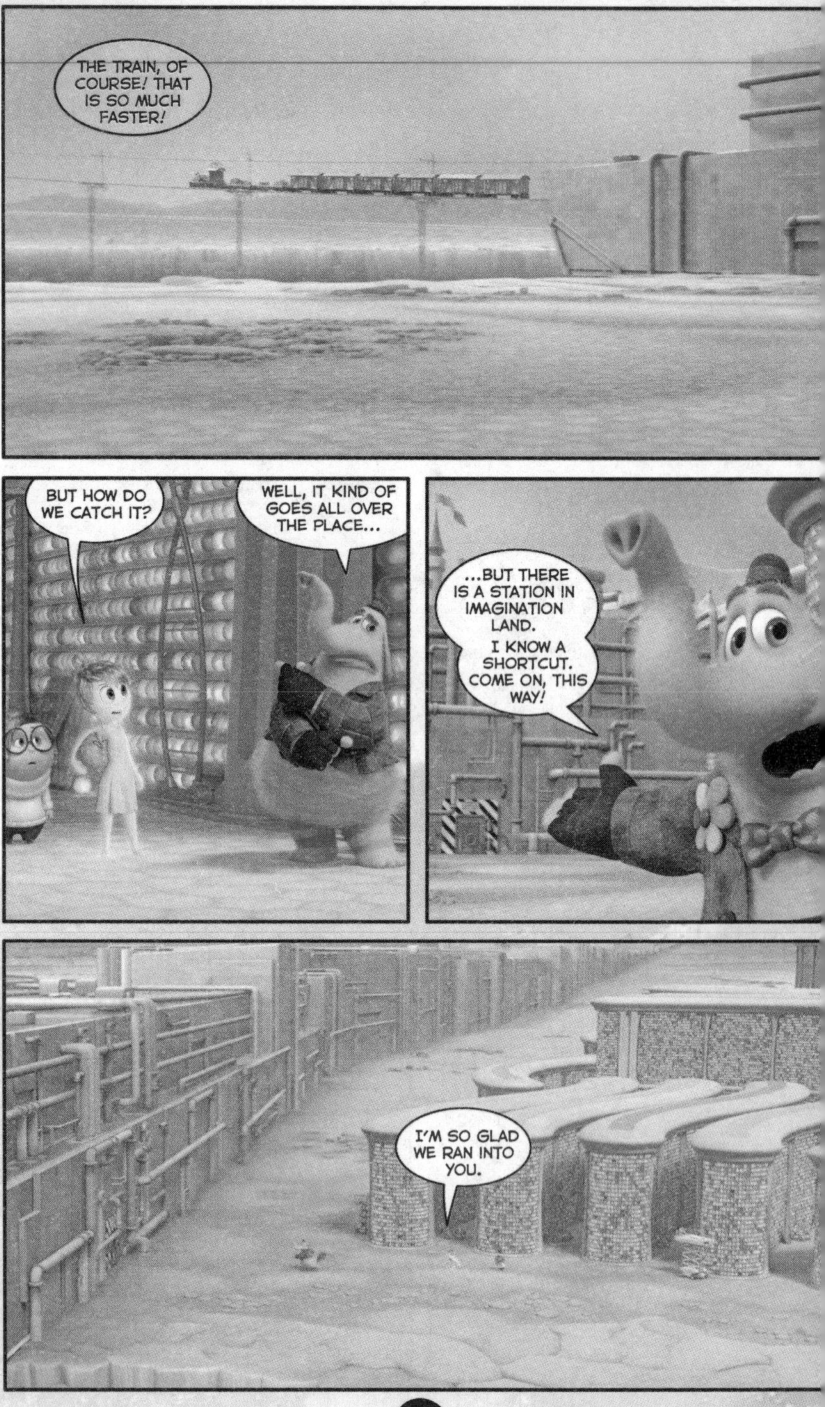
THE TRAIN, OF COURSE! THAT IS SO MUCH FASTER!
BUT HOW DO WE CATCH IT?
WELL, IT KIND OF GOES ALL OVER THE PLACE...
...BUT THERE IS A STATION IN IMAGINATION LAND.
I KNOW A SHORTCUT. COME ON, THIS WAY!
I'M SO GLAD WE RAN INTO YOU.

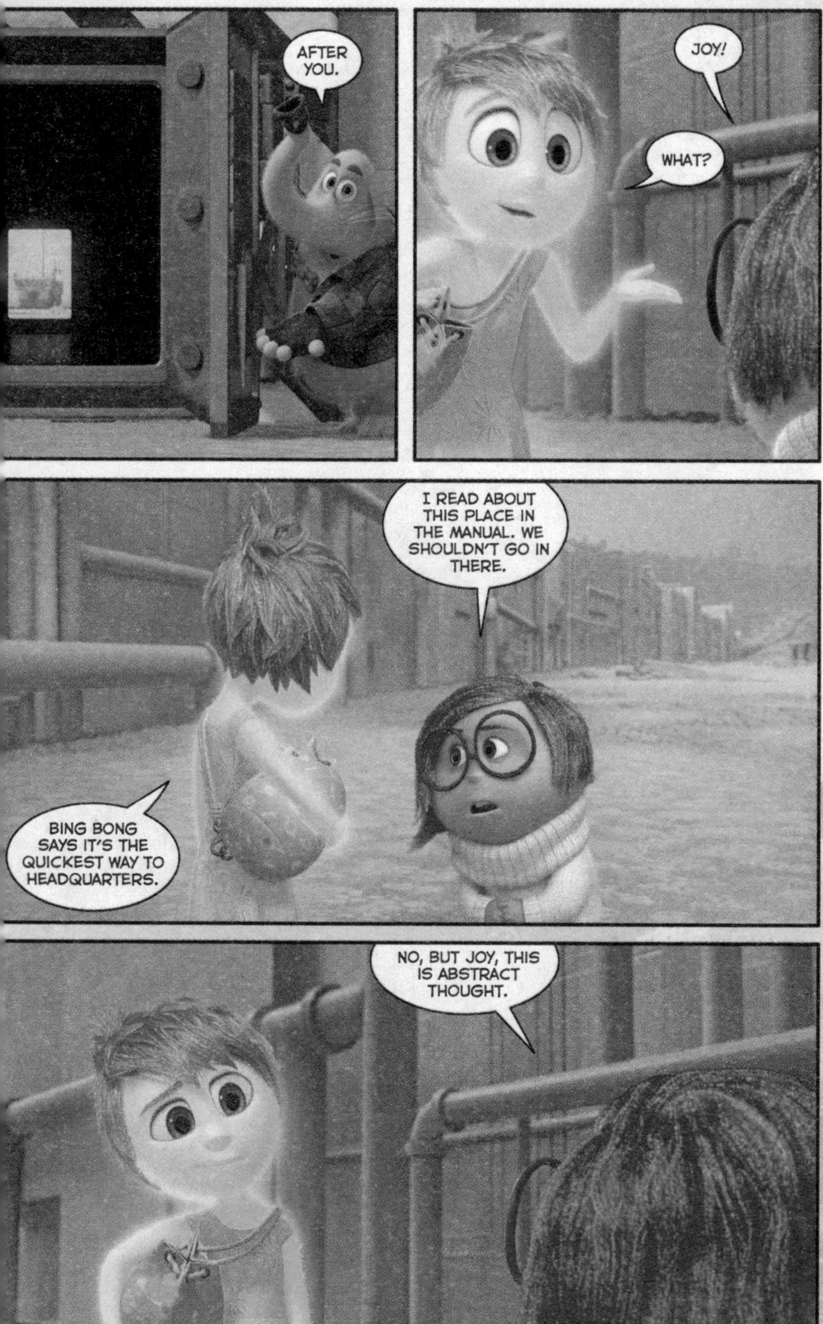
AFTER YOU.
JOY!
WHAT?
I READ ABOUT THIS PLACE IN THE MANUAL. WE SHOULDN'T GO IN THERE.
BING BONG SAYS IT'S THE QUICKEST WAY TO HEADQUARTERS.
NO, BUT JOY, THIS IS ABSTRACT THOUGHT.

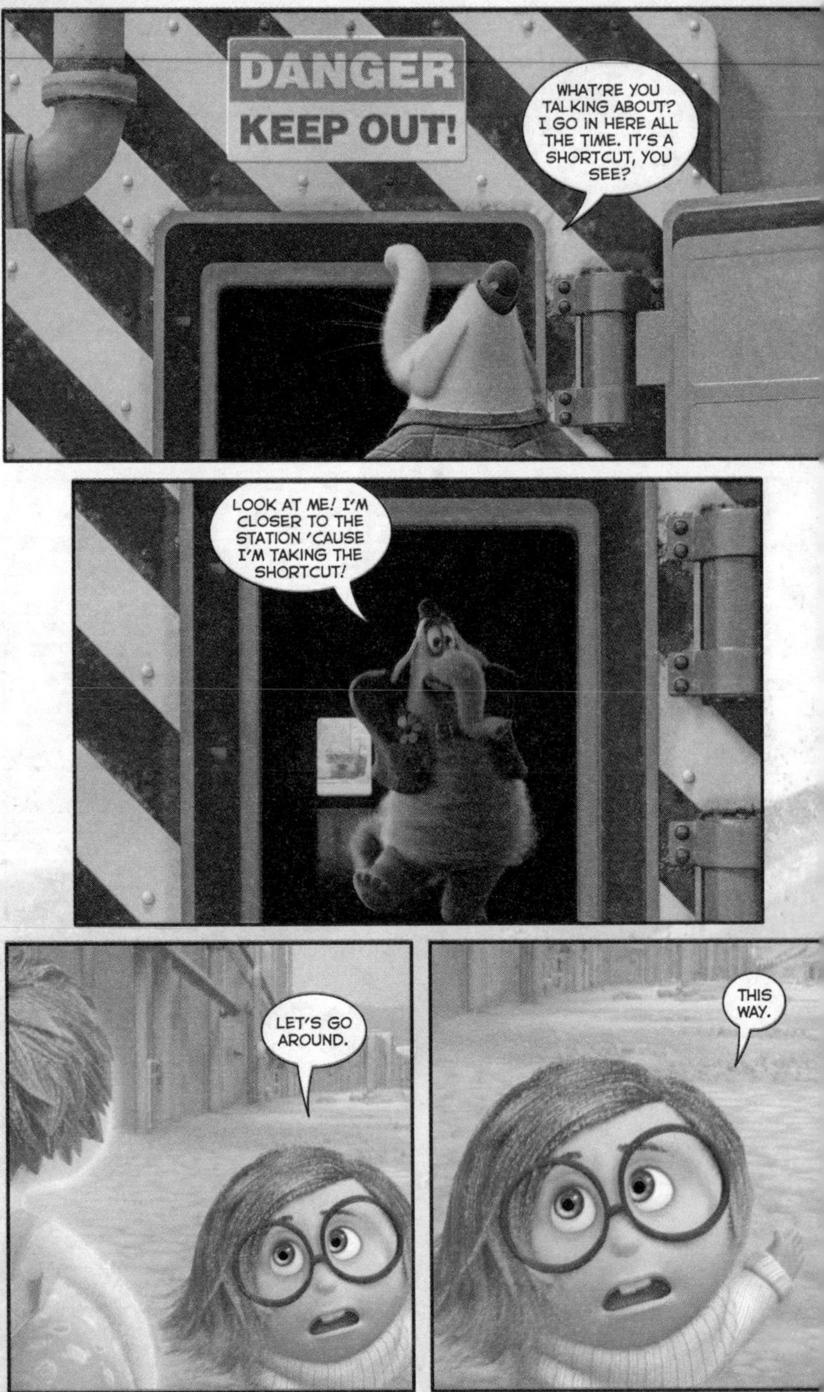
DANGER
KEEP OUT!
WHAT'RE YOU TALKING ABOUT? I GO IN HERE ALL THE TIME. IT'S A SHORTCUT, YOU SEE?
LOOK AT ME! I'M CLOSER TO THE STATION 'CAUSE I'M TAKING THE SHORTCUT!
LET'S GO AROUND.
THIS WAY.

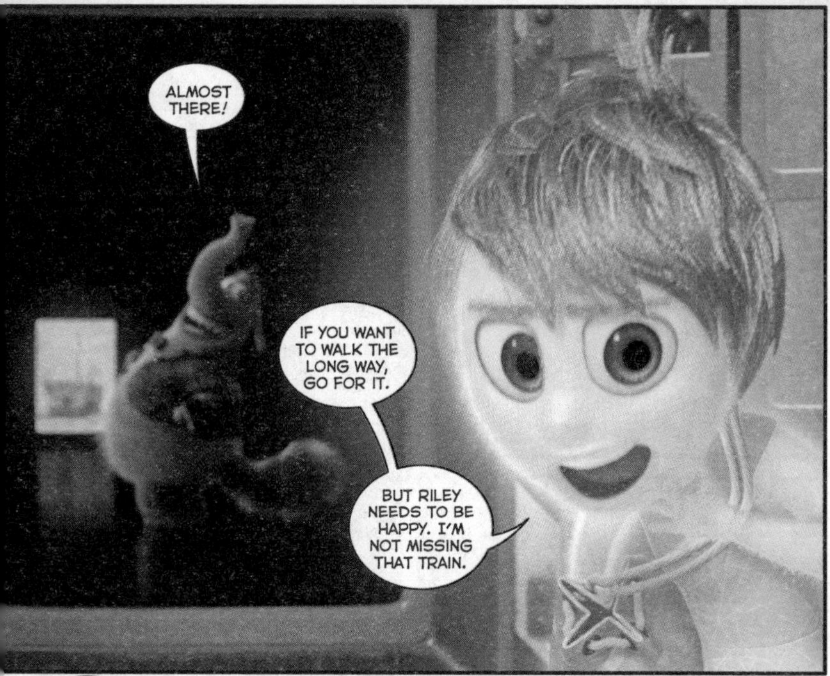
ALMOST THERE!
IF YOU WANT TO WALK THE LONG WAY, GO FOR IT.
BUT RILEY NEEDS TO BE HAPPY. I'M NOT MISSING THAT TRAIN.

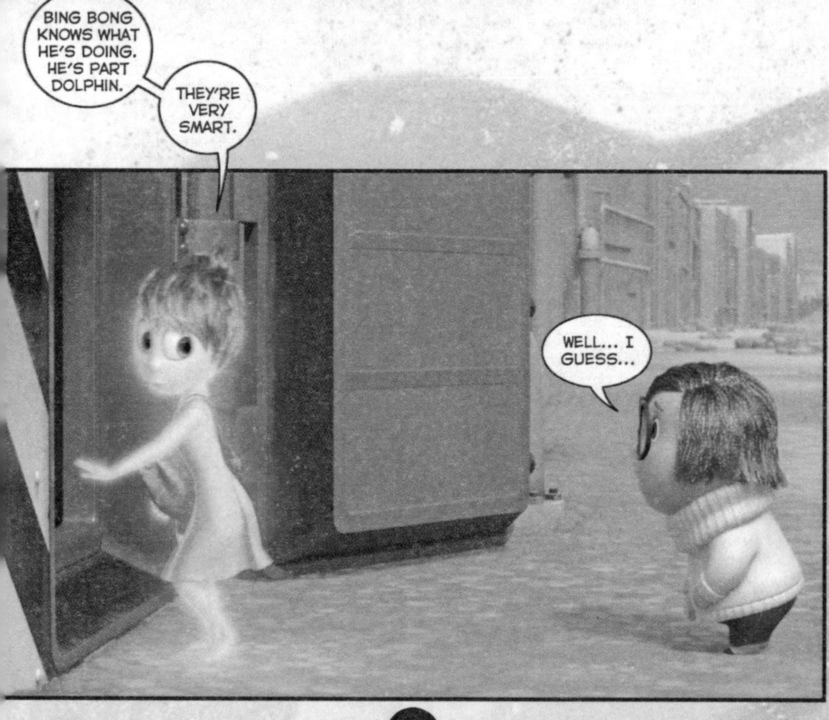
BING BONG KNOWS WHAT HE'S DOING. HE'S PART DOLPHIN.
THEY'RE VERY SMART.
WELL... I GUESS...

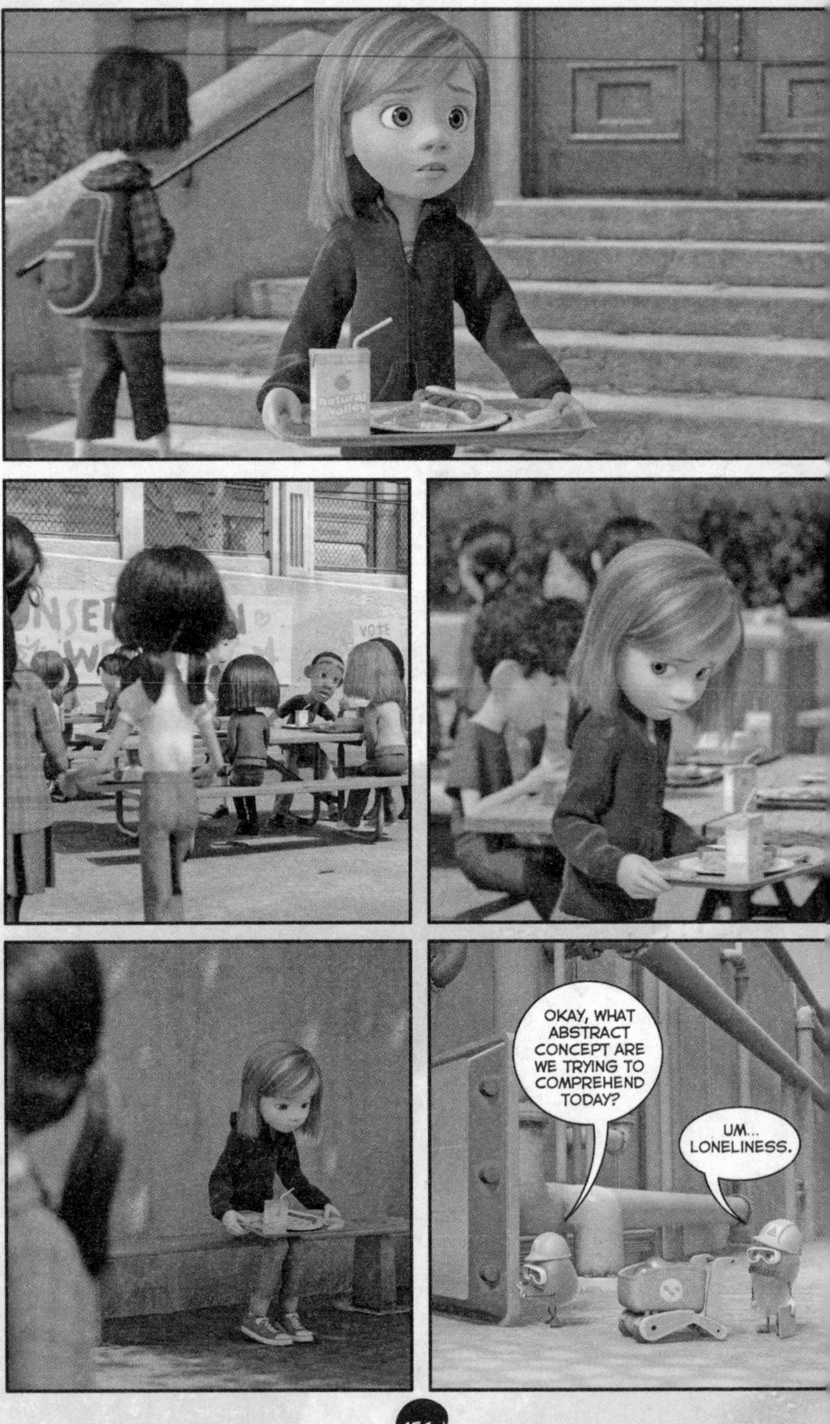
Natural Valley
VOTE
OKAY, WHAT ABSTRACT CONCEPT ARE WE TRYING TO COMPREHEND TODAY?
UM... LONELINESS.

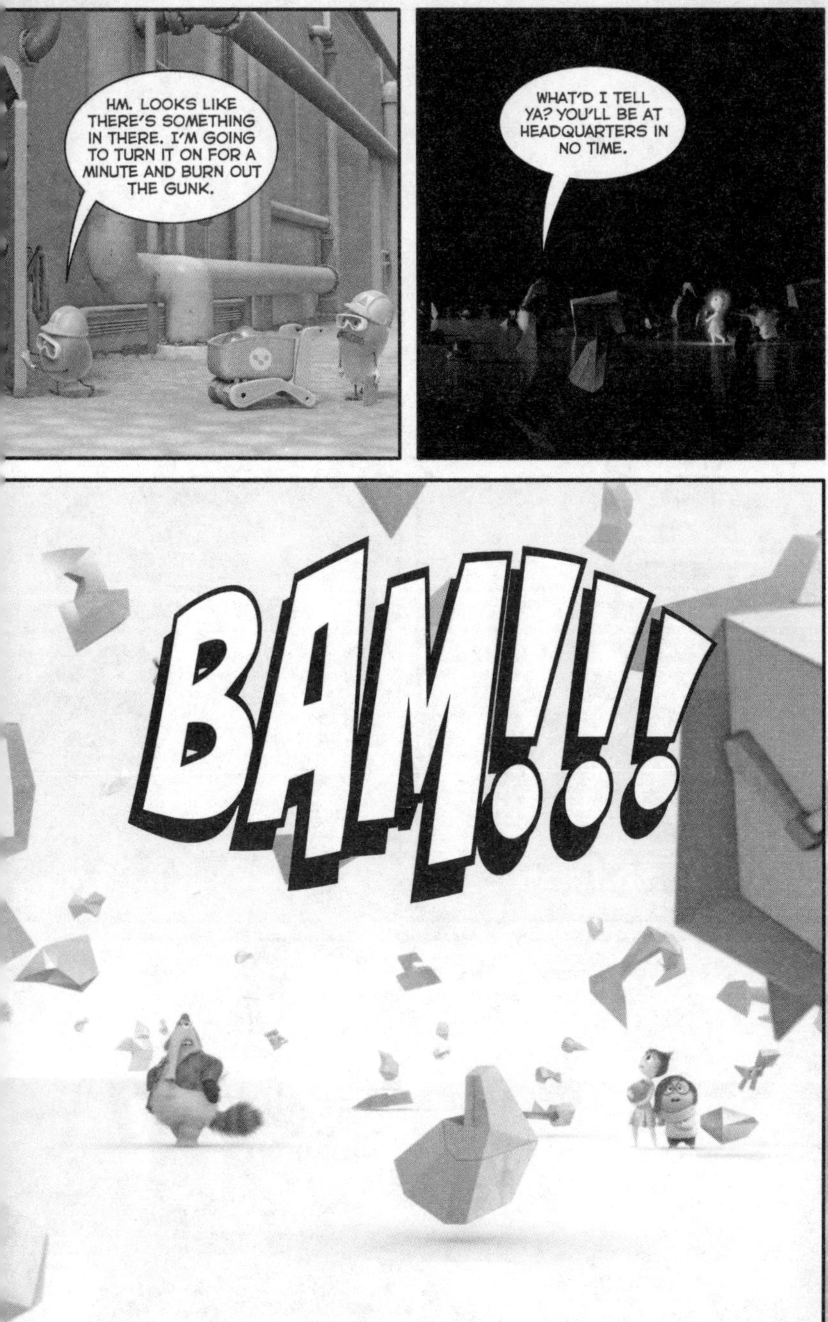
HM. LOOKS LIKE THERE'S SOMETHING IN THERE. I'M GOING TO TURN IT ON FOR A MINUTE AND BURN OUT THE GUNK.
WHAT'D I TELL YA? YOU'LL BE AT HEADQUARTERS IN NO TIME.
BAM!!!

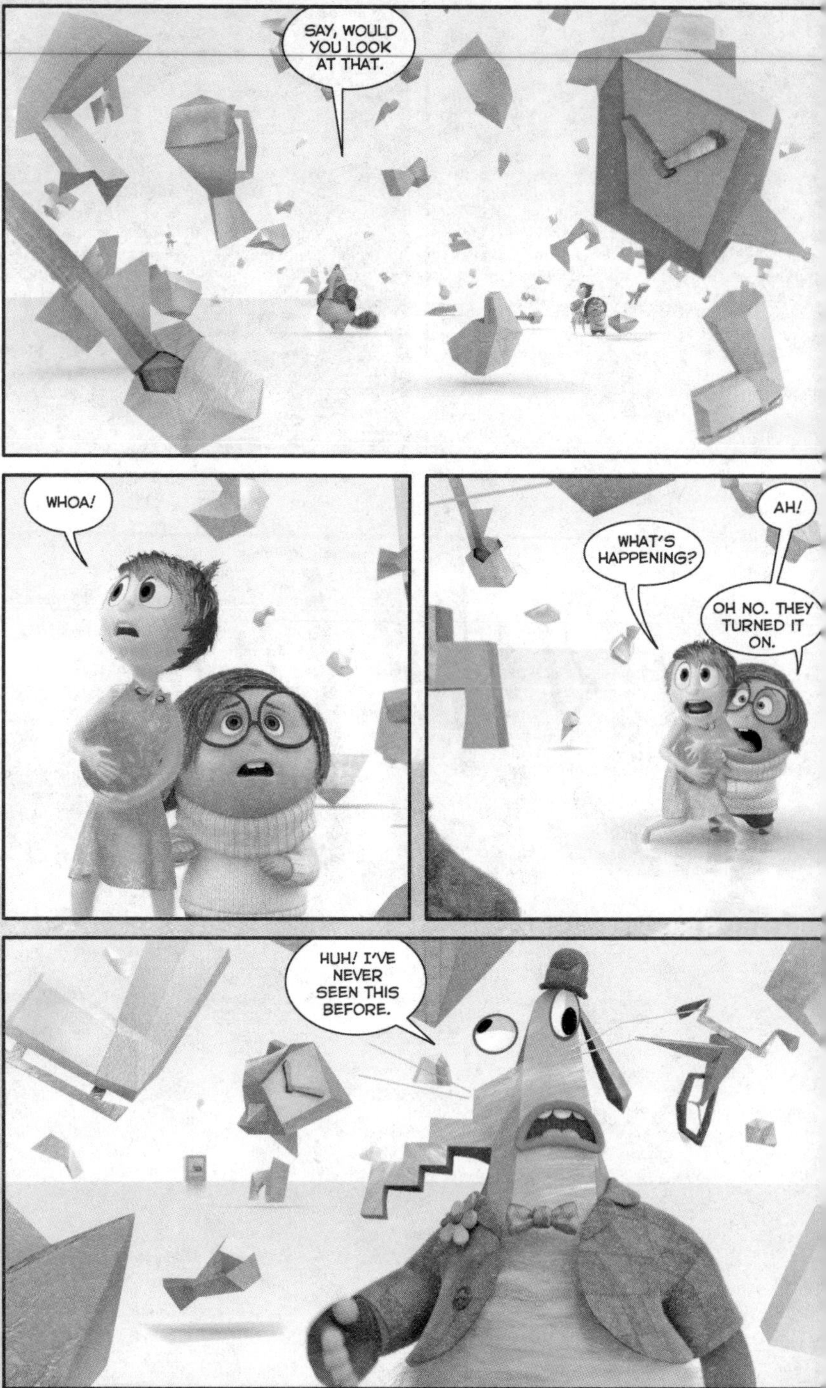
SAY, WOULD YOU LOOK AT THAT.
WHOA!
WHAT'S HAPPENING?
AH!
OH NO. THEY TURNED IT ON.
HUH! I'VE NEVER SEEN THIS BEFORE.

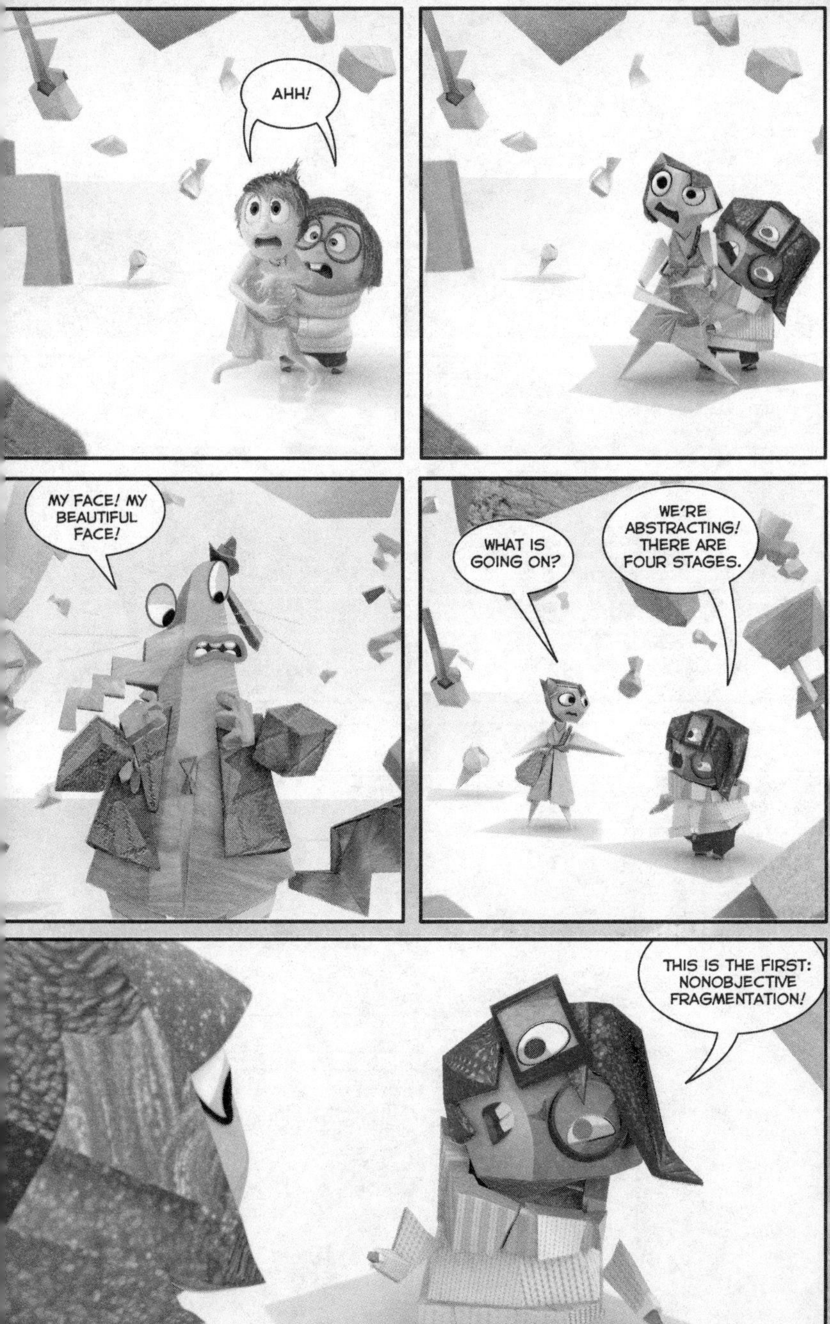
AHH!
MY FACE! MY BEAUTIFUL FACE!
WHAT IS GOING ON?
WE'RE ABSTRACTING! THERE ARE FOUR STAGES.
THIS IS THE FIRST: NONOBJECTIVE FRAGMENTATION!

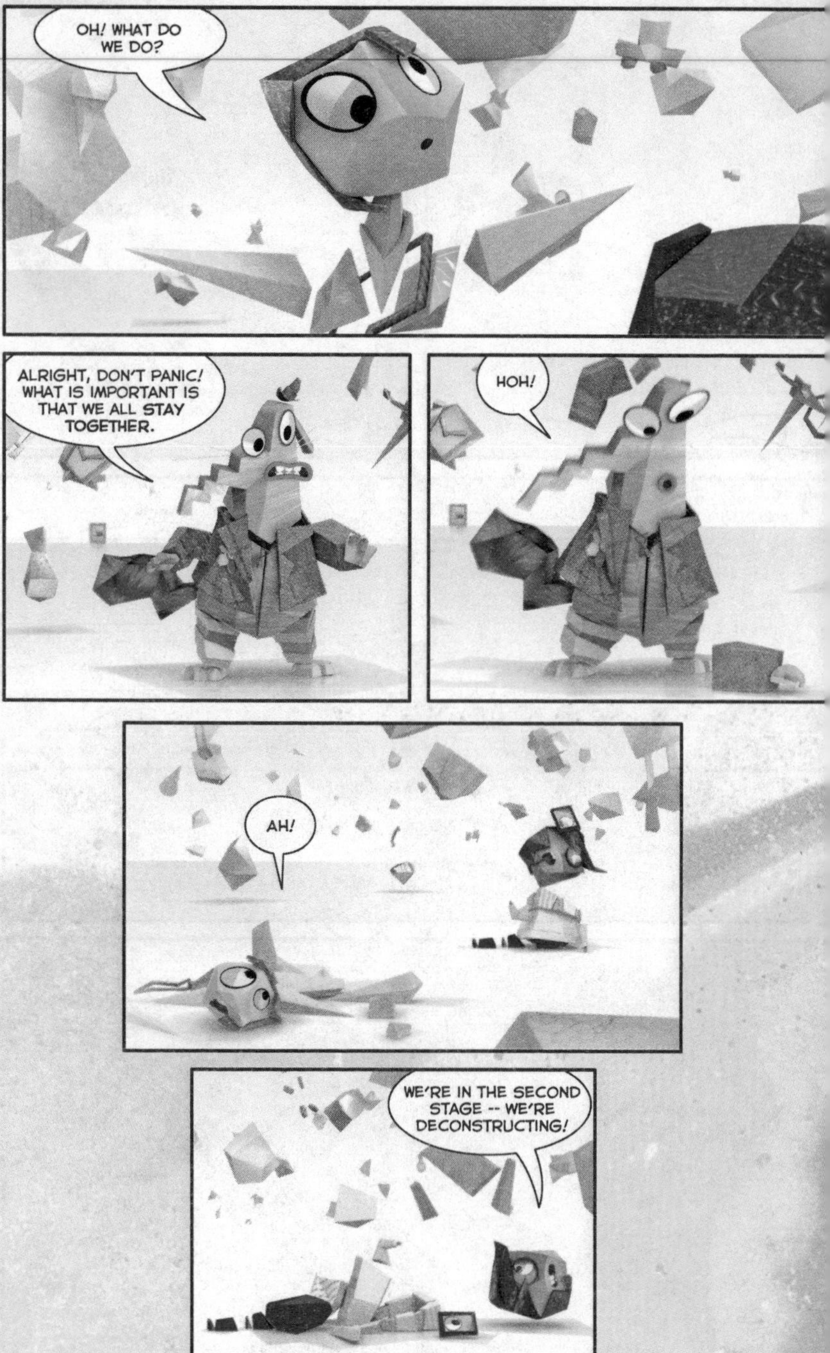
OH! WHAT DO WE DO?
ALRIGHT, DON'T PANIC! WHAT IS IMPORTANT IS THAT WE ALL STAY TOGETHER.
HOH!
AH!
WE'RE IN THE SECOND STAGE -- WE'RE DECONSTRUCTING!

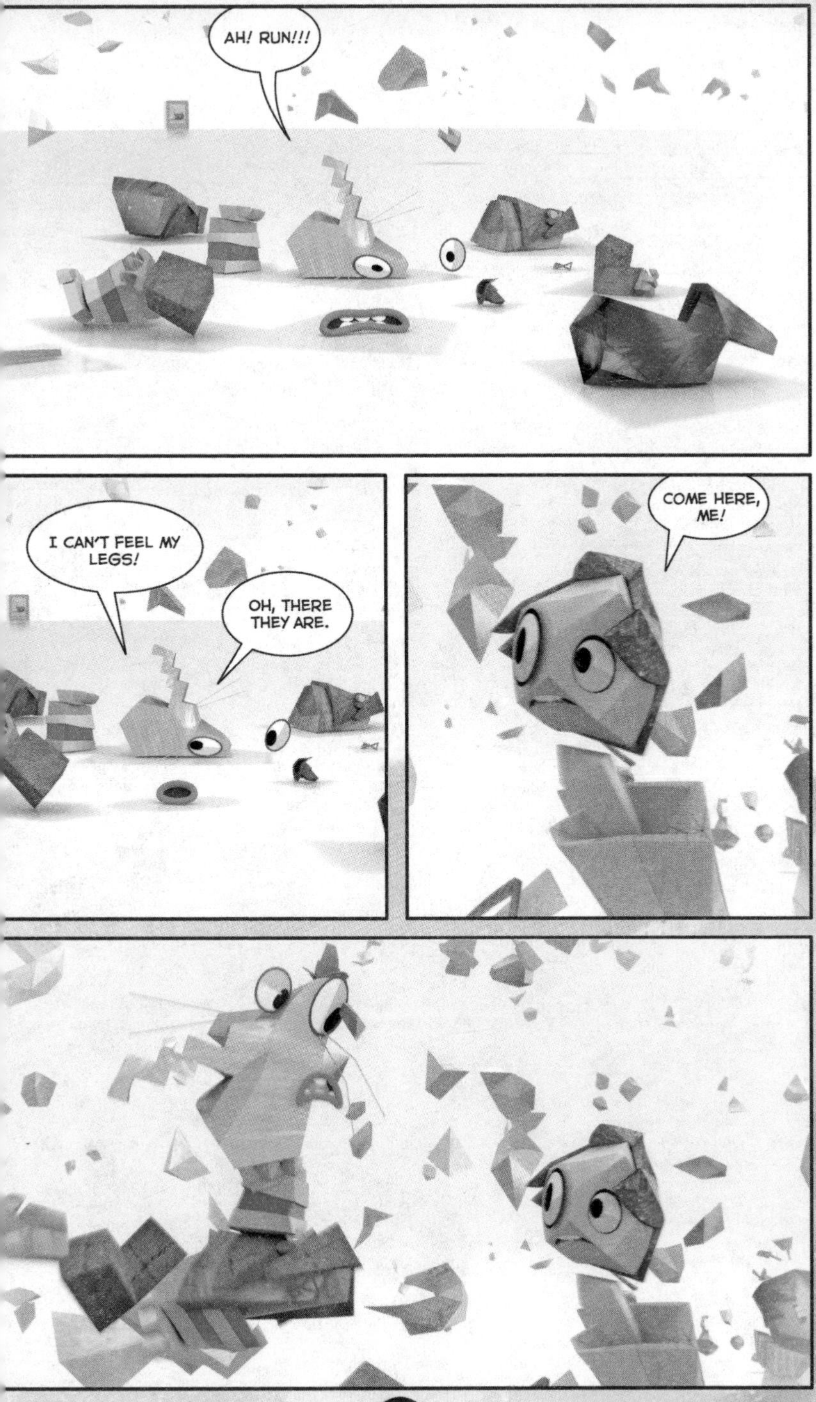
AH! RUN!!!
I CAN'T FEEL MY LEGS!
OH, THERE THEY ARE.
COME HERE, ME!

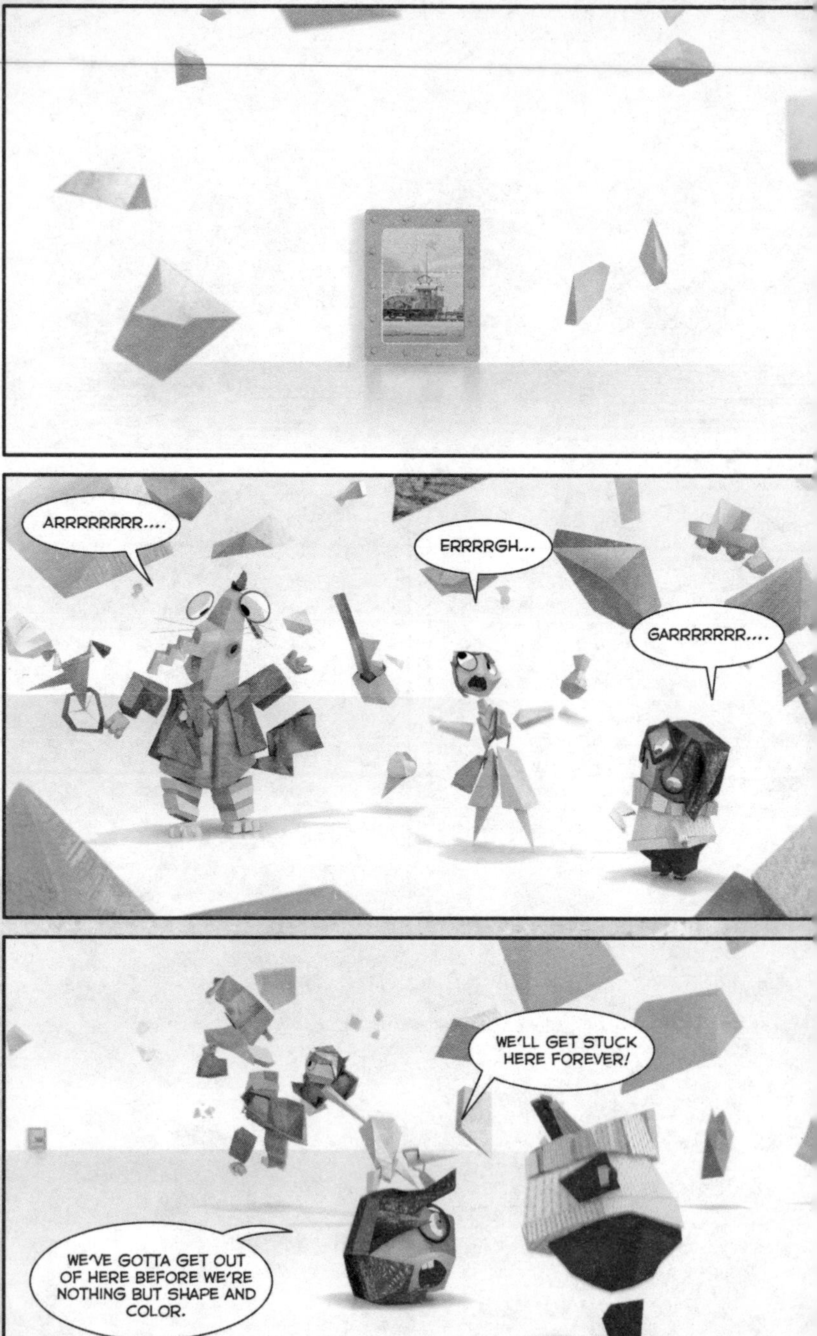
ARRRRRRRR....
ERRRRGH...
GARRRRRRR....
WE'LL GET STUCK HERE FOREVER!
WE'VE GOTTA GET OUT OF HERE BEFORE WE'RE NOTHING BUT SHAPE AND COLOR.

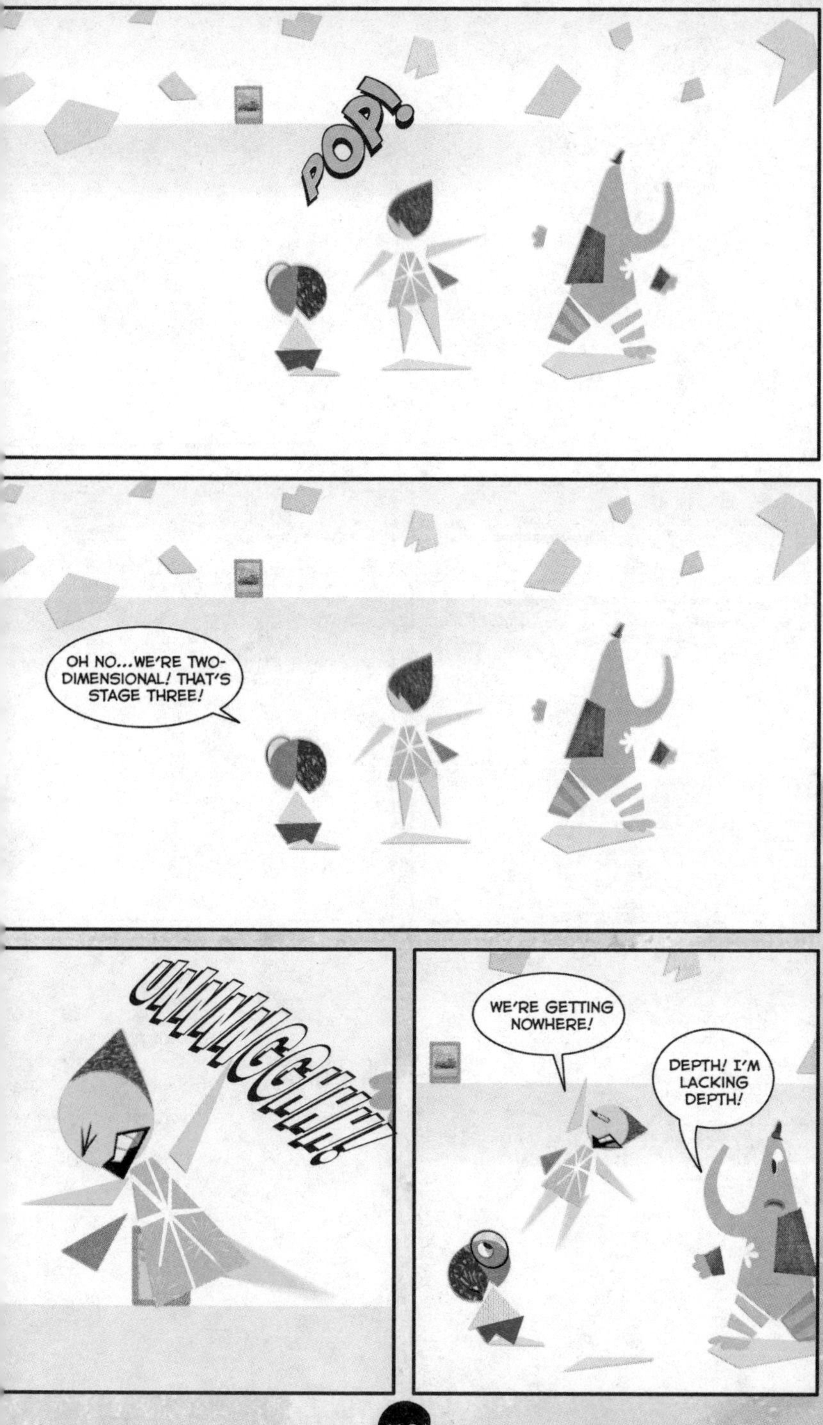
POP!
OH NO...WE'RE TWO-DIMENSIONAL! THAT'S STAGE THREE!
UNNNGGHH!
WE'RE GETTING NOWHERE!
DEPTH! I'M LACKING DEPTH!

COME ON!
POP!
AUGH! WE CAN'T FIT!
OH NO, WE'RE NON-FIGURATIVE.
THIS IS THE LAST STAGE!
WE'RE NOT GOING TO MAKE IT.
HOOOHHHH...
WAIT! WE'RE TWO-DIMENSIONAL.
FALL ON YOUR FACE!

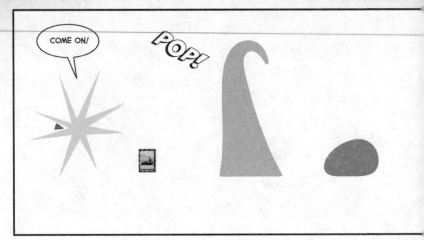

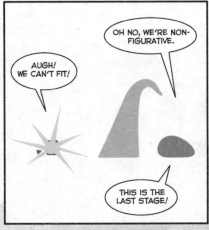

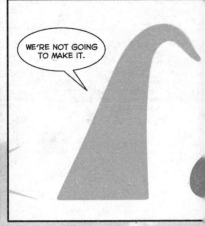

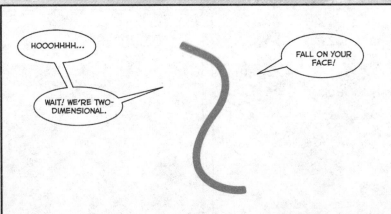

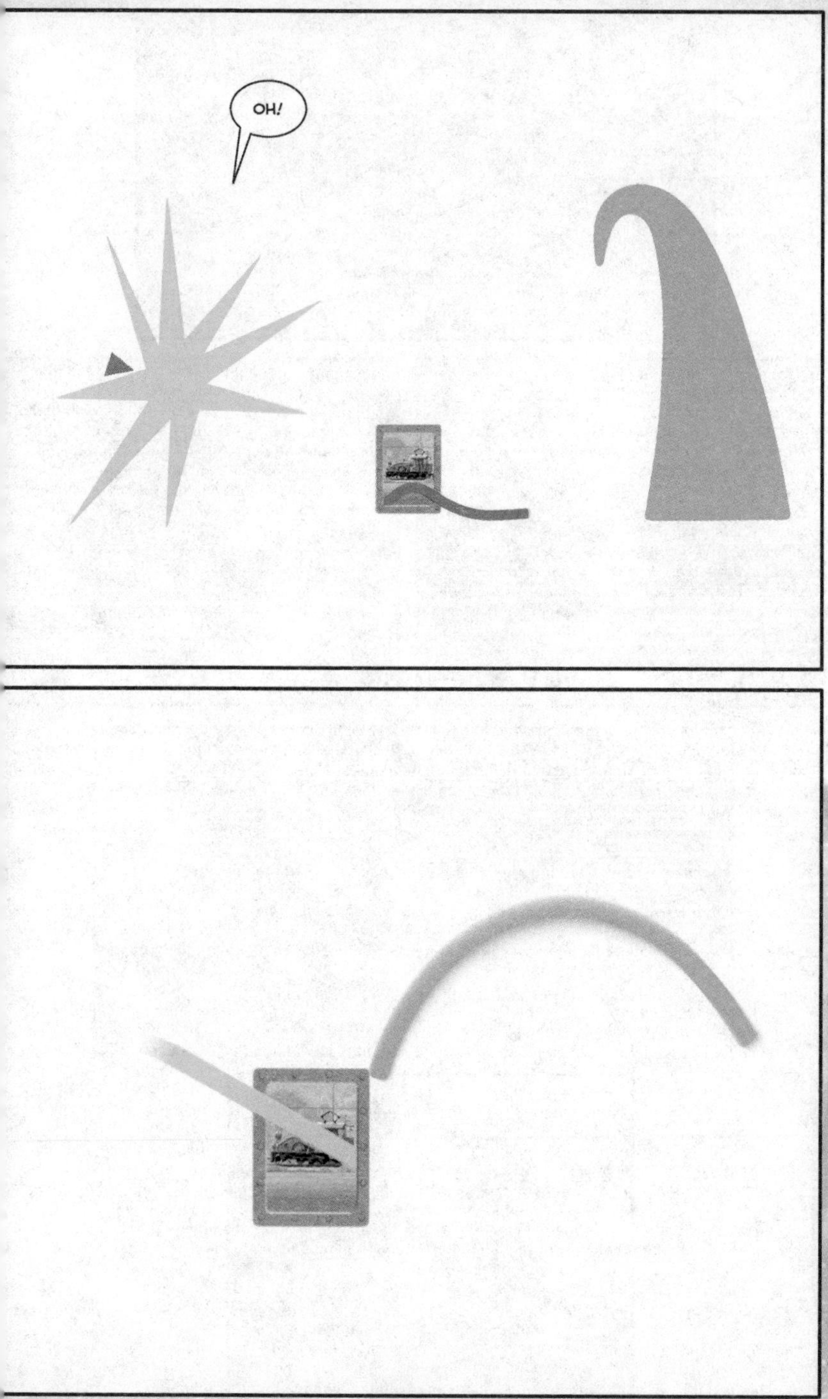
OH!

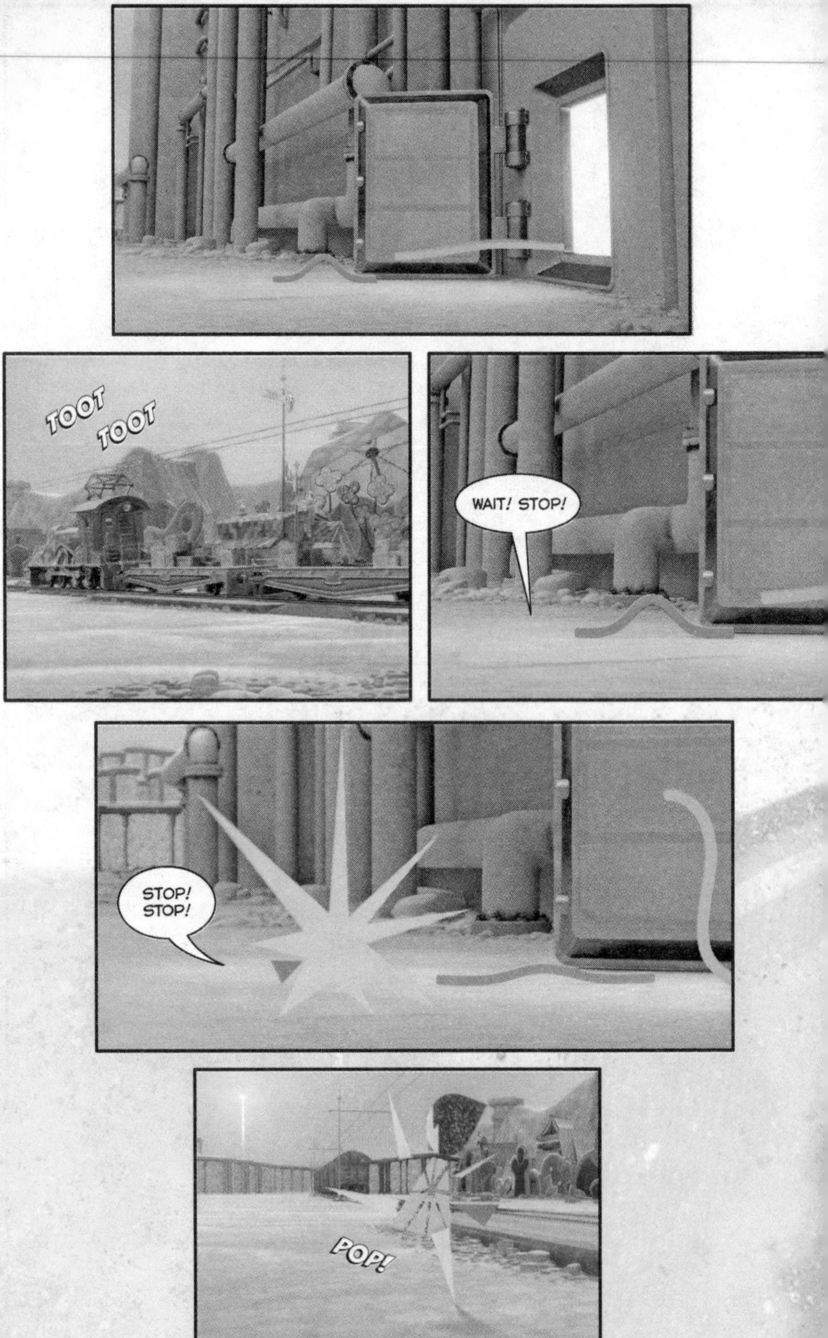
TOOT
TOOT
WAIT! STOP!
STOP!
STOP!
POP!

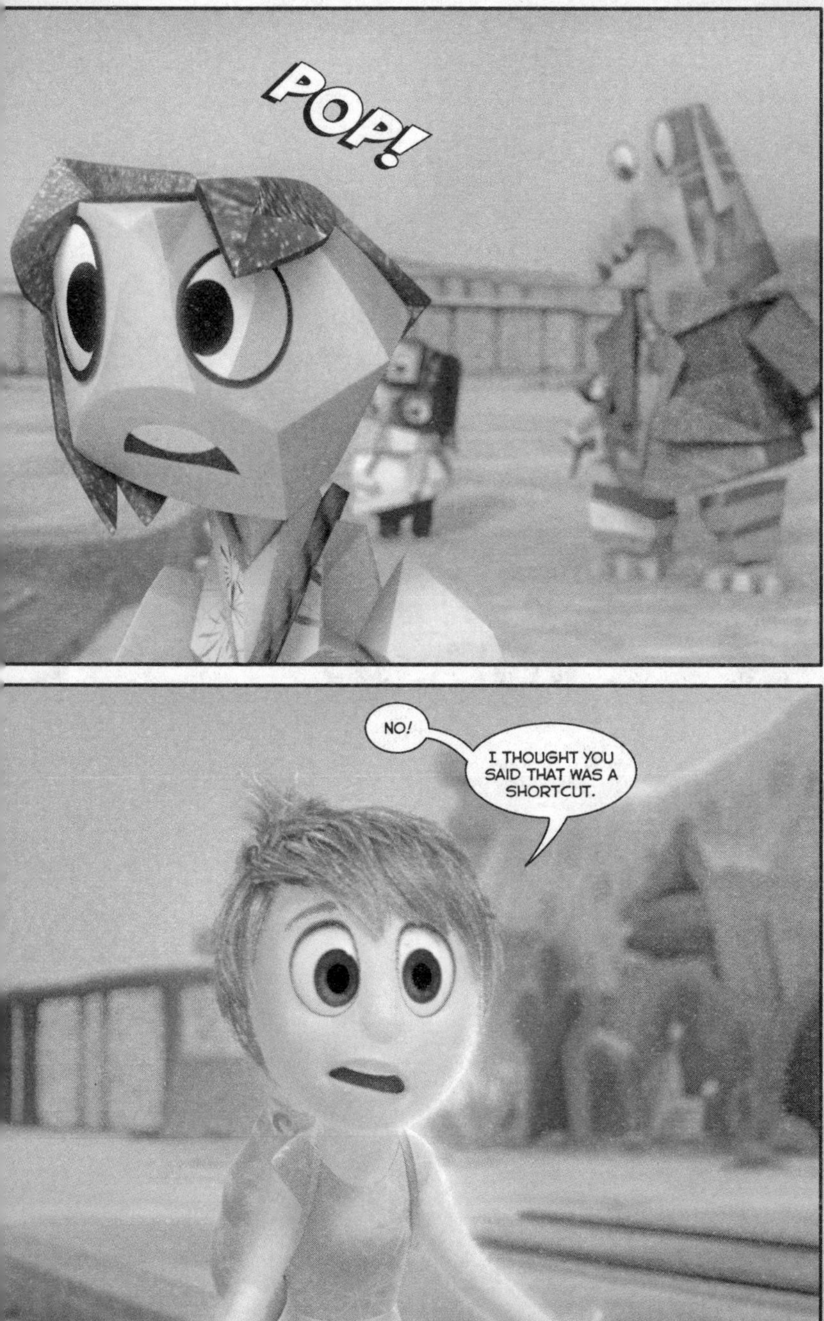
POP!
NO!
I THOUGHT YOU SAID THAT WAS A SHORTCUT.

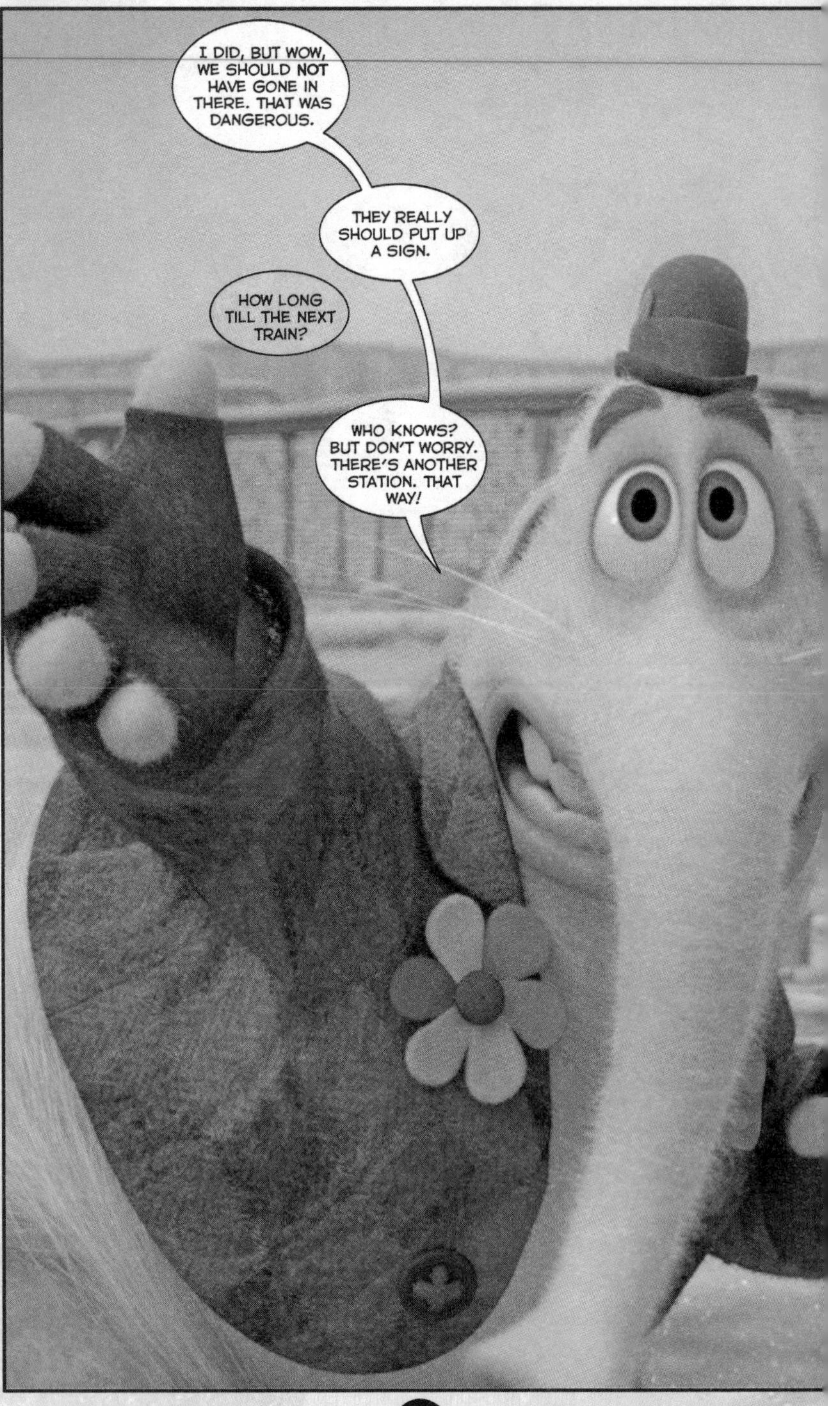
I DID, BUT WOW, WE SHOULD NOT HAVE GONE IN THERE. THAT WAS DANGEROUS.
THEY REALLY SHOULD PUT UP A SIGN.
HOW LONG TILL THE NEXT TRAIN?
WHO KNOWS? BUT DON'T WORRY. THERE'S ANOTHER STATION. THAT WAY!

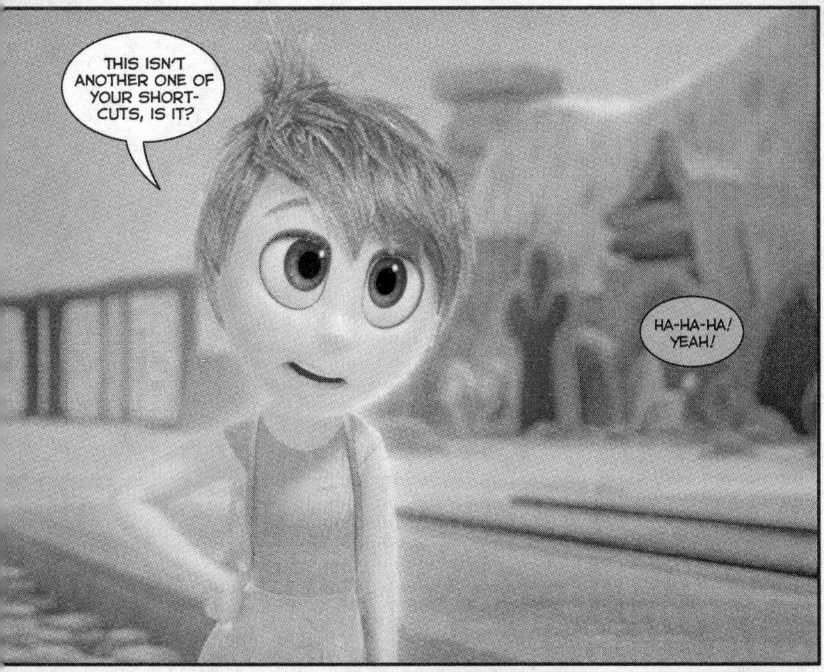
THIS ISN'T ANOTHER ONE OF YOUR SHORT-CUTS, IS IT?
HA-HA-HA! YEAH!

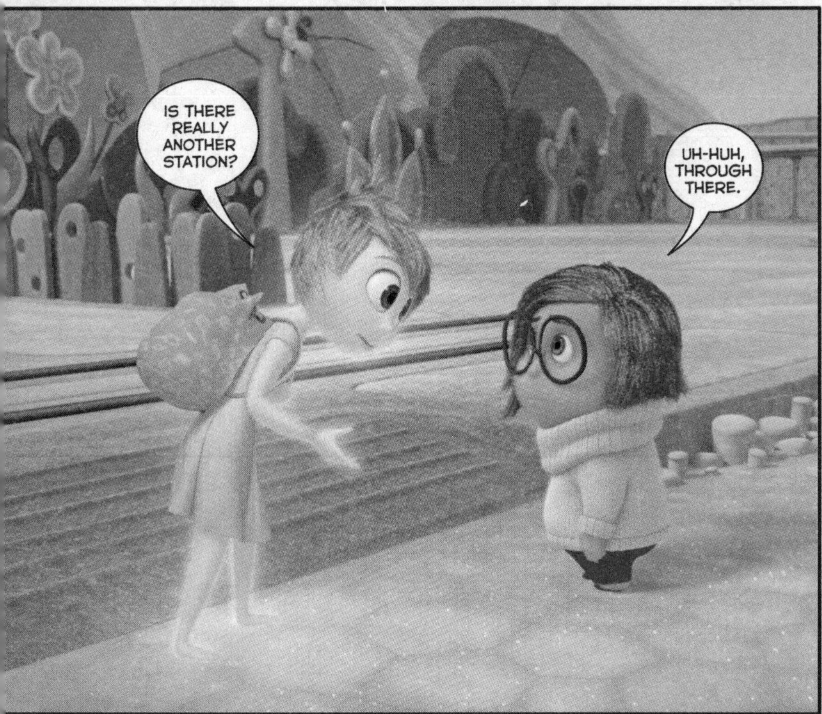
IS THERE REALLY ANOTHER STATION?
UH-HUH, THROUGH THERE.

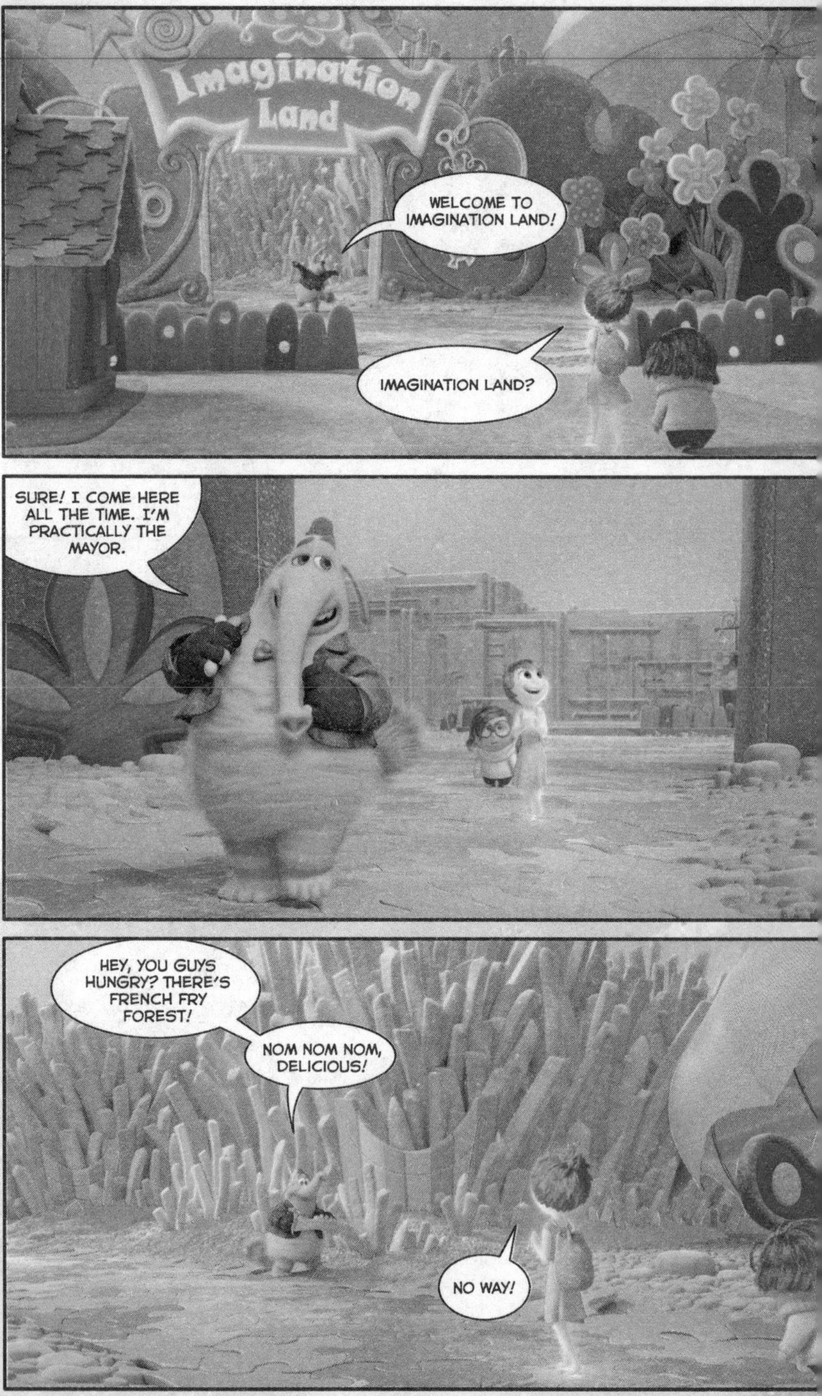
Imagination Land
WELCOME TO IMAGINATION LAND!
IMAGINATION LAND?
SURE! I COME HERE ALL THE TIME. I'M PRACTICALLY THE MAYOR.
HEY, YOU GUYS HUNGRY? THERE'S FRENCH FRY FOREST!
NOM NOM NOM, DELICIOUS!
NO WAY!

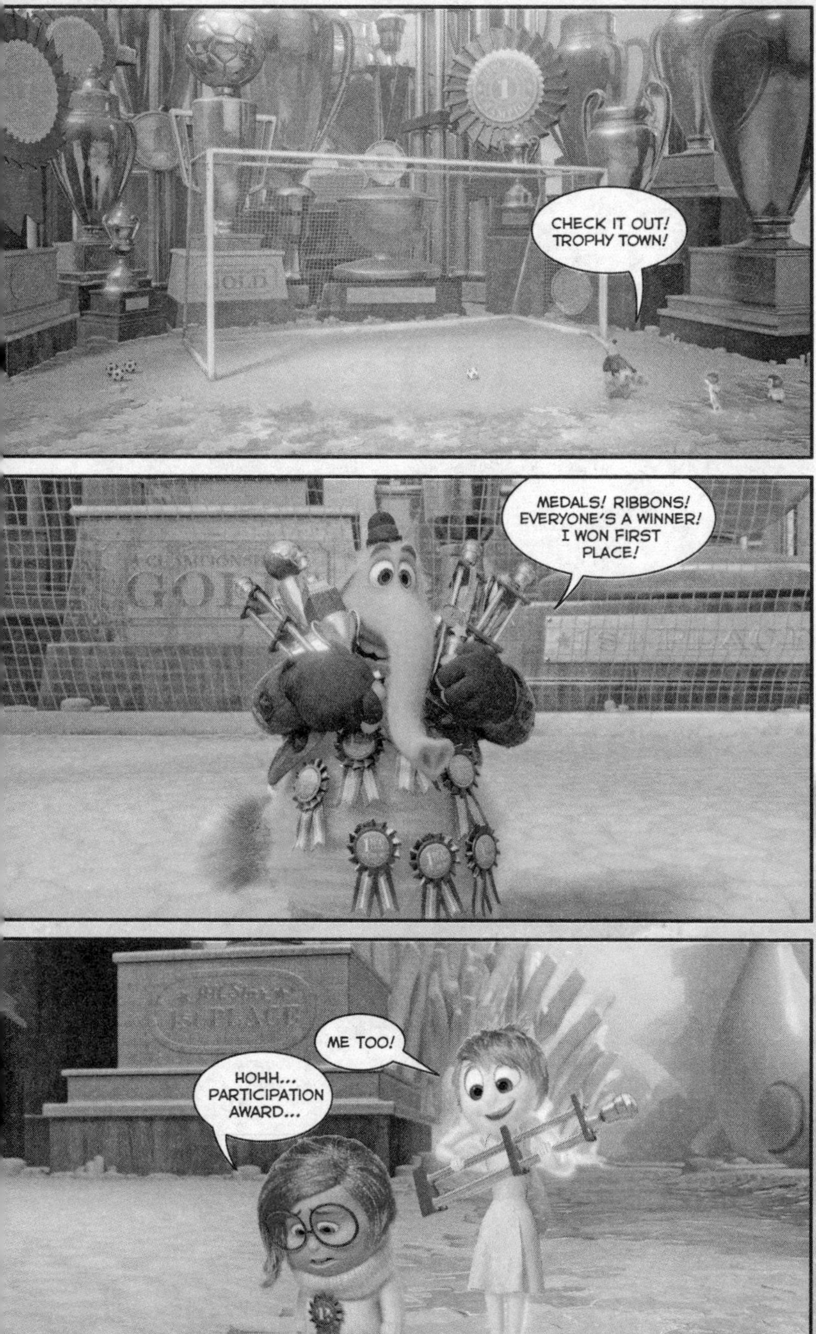
CHECK IT OUT! TROPHY TOWN!
MEDALS! RIBBONS! EVERYONE'S A WINNER! I WON FIRST PLACE!
ME TOO!
HOHH... PARTICIPATION AWARD...

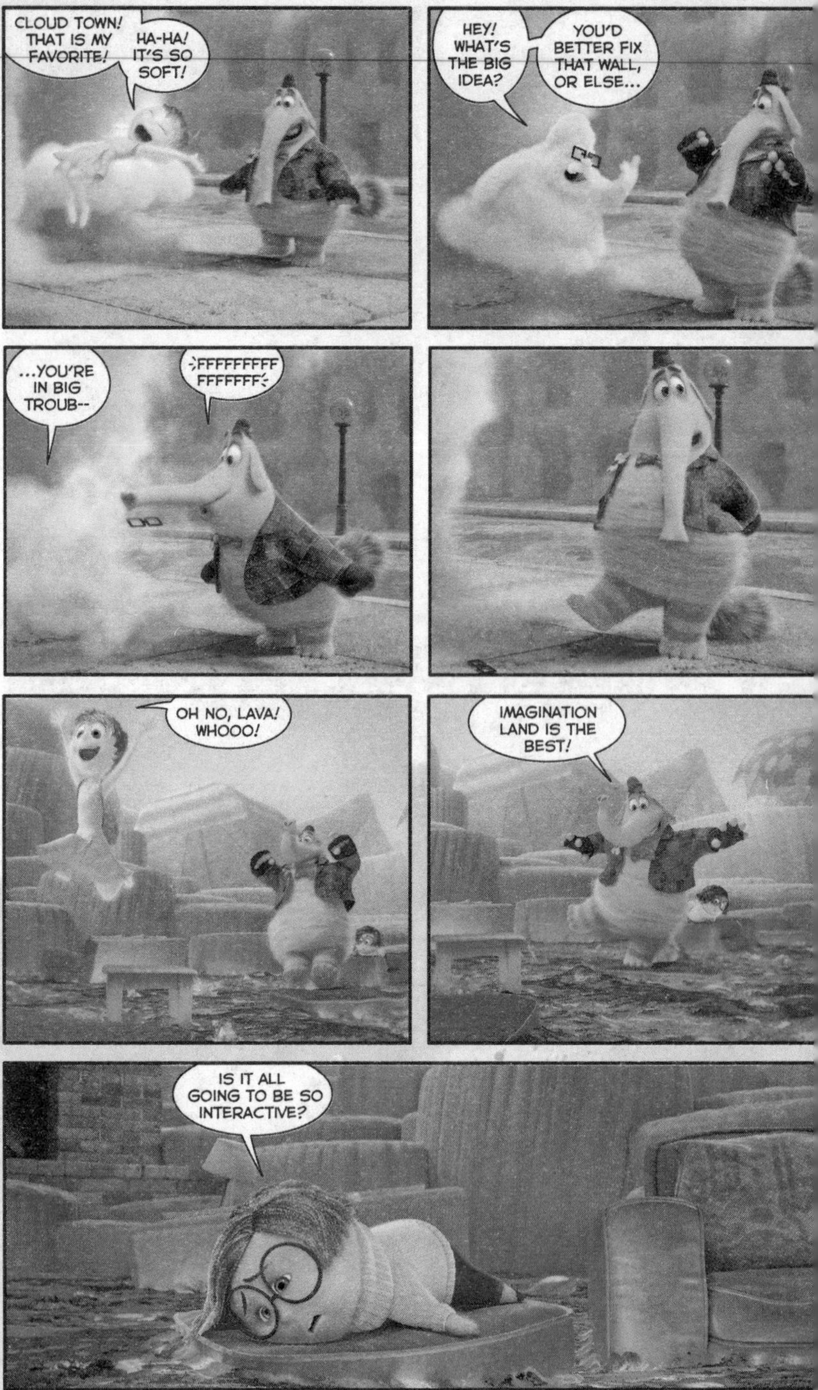
CLOUD TOWN! THAT IS MY FAVORITE!
HA-HA! IT'S SO SOFT!
HEY! WHAT'S THE BIG IDEA?
YOU'D BETTER FIX THAT WALL, OR ELSE...
...YOU'RE IN BIG TROUB--
FFFFFFFFF FFFFFFF
OH NO, LAVA! WHOOO!
IMAGINATION LAND IS THE BEST!
IS IT ALL GOING TO BE SO INTERACTIVE?

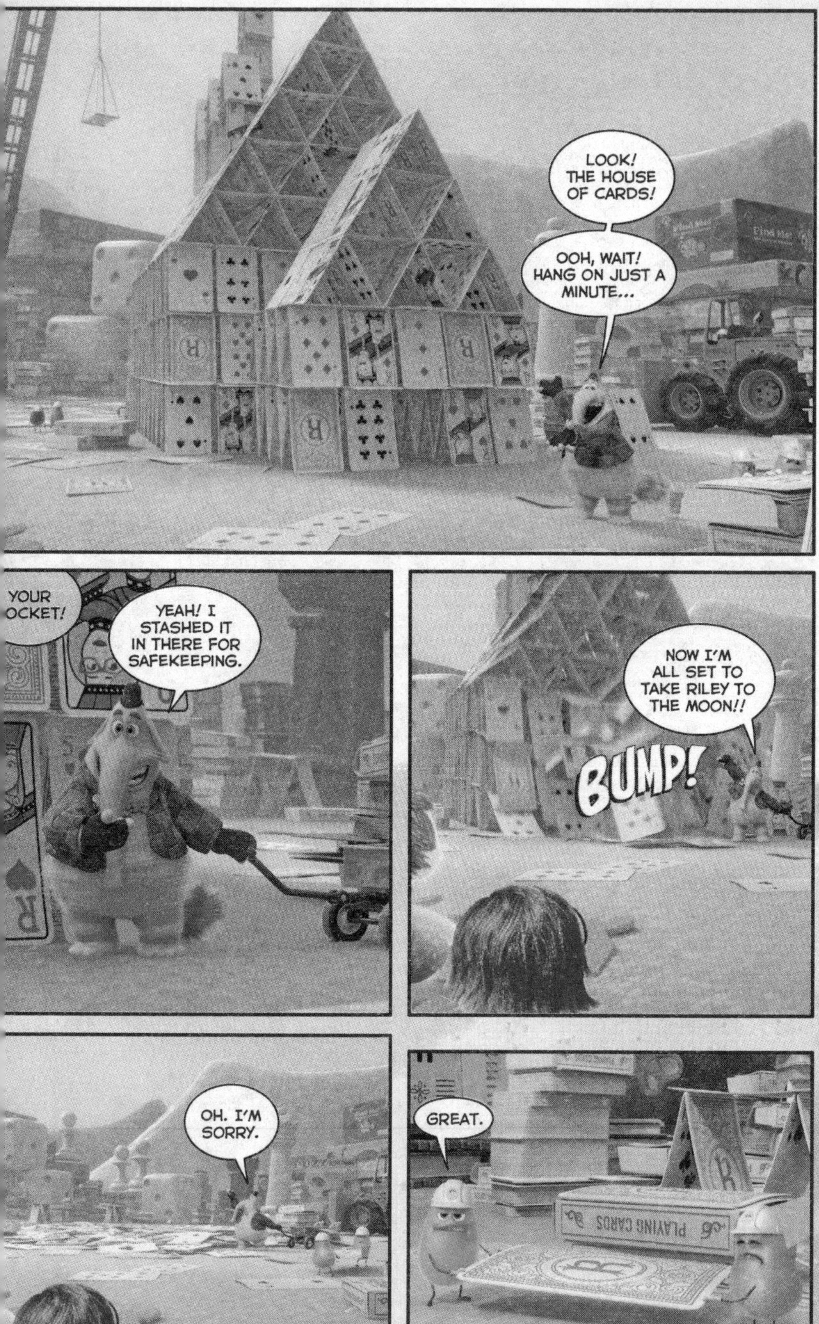
LOOK! THE HOUSE OF CARDS!
OOH, WAIT! HANG ON JUST A MINUTE...
YOUR
OCKET!
YEAH! I STASHED IT IN THERE FOR SAFEKEEPING.
NOW I'M ALL SET TO TAKE RILEY TO THE MOON!!
BUMP!
OH. I'M SORRY.
GREAT.
PLAYING CARDS

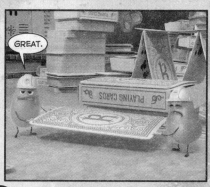

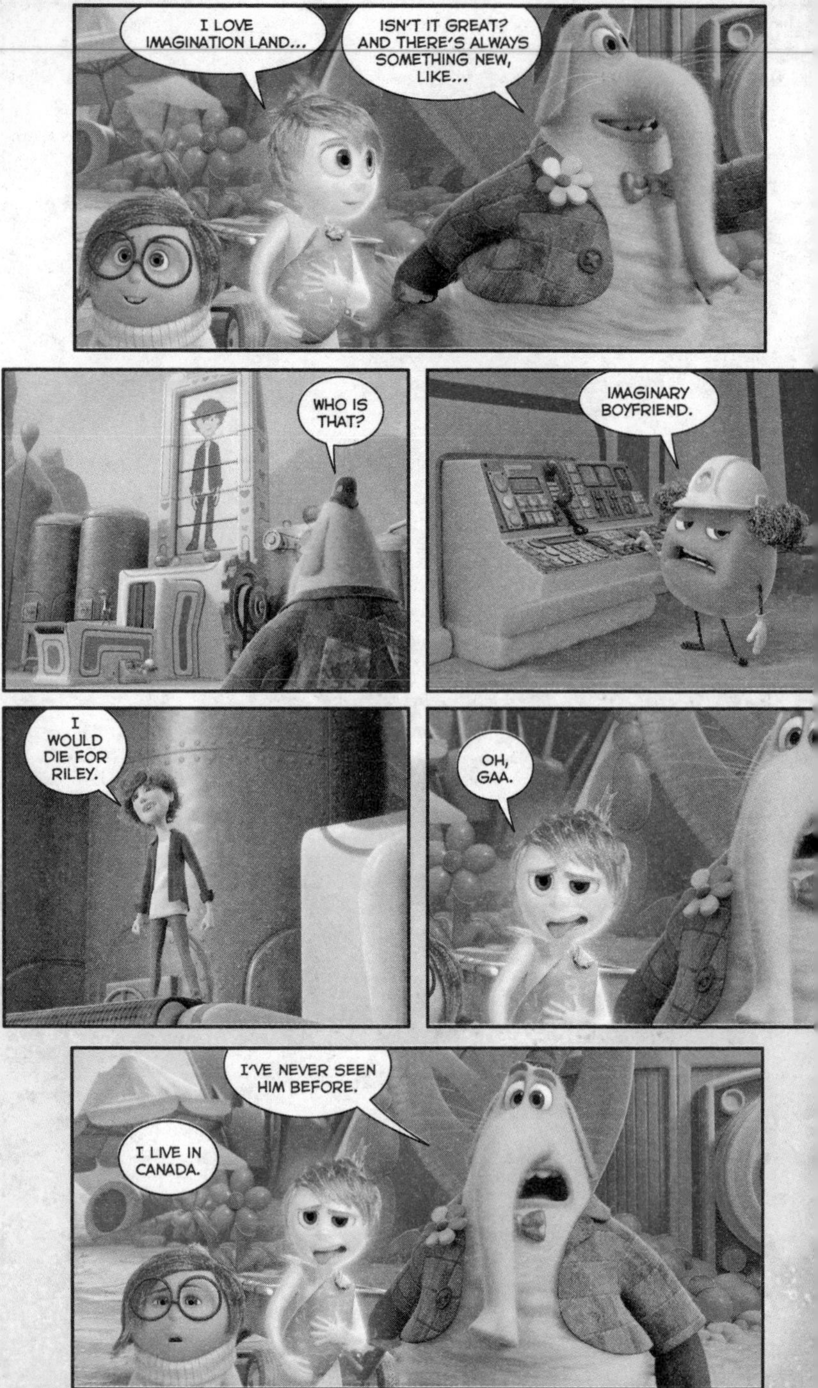
I LOVE IMAGINATION LAND...
ISN'T IT GREAT? AND THERE'S ALWAYS SOMETHING NEW, LIKE...
WHO IS THAT?
IMAGINARY BOYFRIEND.
I WOULD DIE FOR RILEY.
OH, GAA.
I'VE NEVER SEEN HIM BEFORE.
I LIVE IN CANADA.

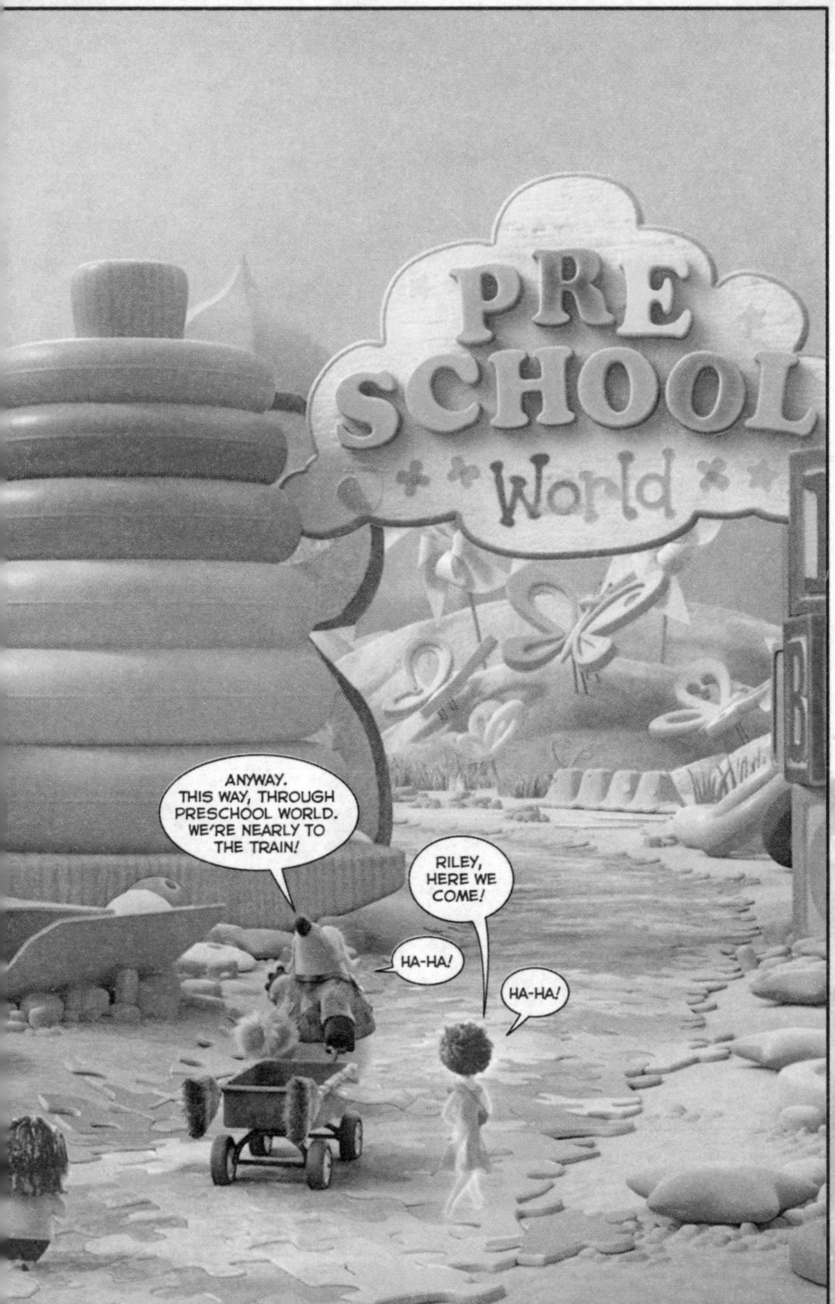
PRE SCHOOL World
ANYWAY. THIS WAY, THROUGH PRESCHOOL WORLD. WE'RE NEARLY TO THE TRAIN!
RILEY, HERE WE COME!
HA-HA!
HA-HA!

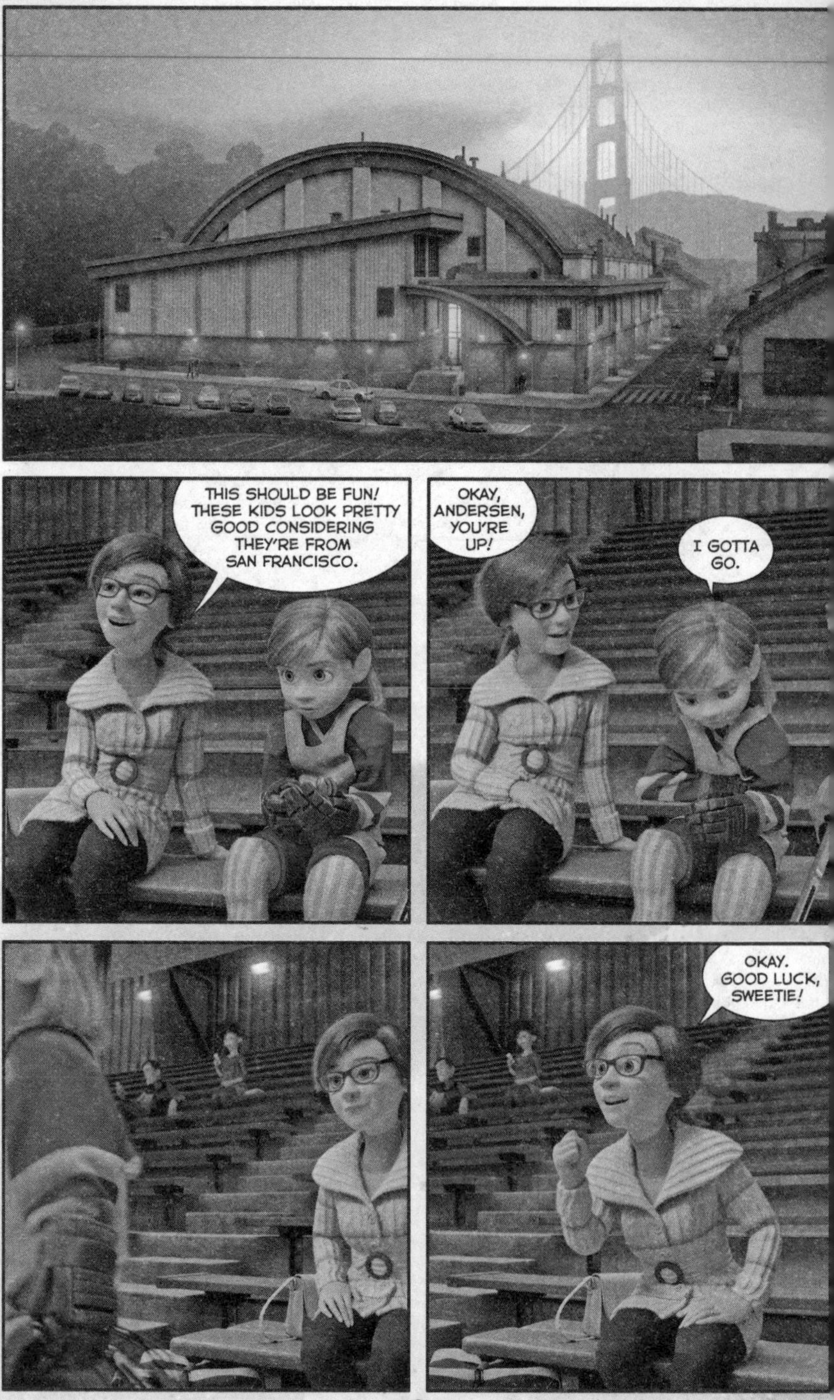
THIS SHOULD BE FUN! THESE KIDS LOOK PRETTY GOOD CONSIDERING THEY'RE FROM SAN FRANCISCO.
OKAY, ANDERSEN, YOU'RE UP!
I GOTTA GO.
OKAY. GOOD LUCK, SWEETIE!

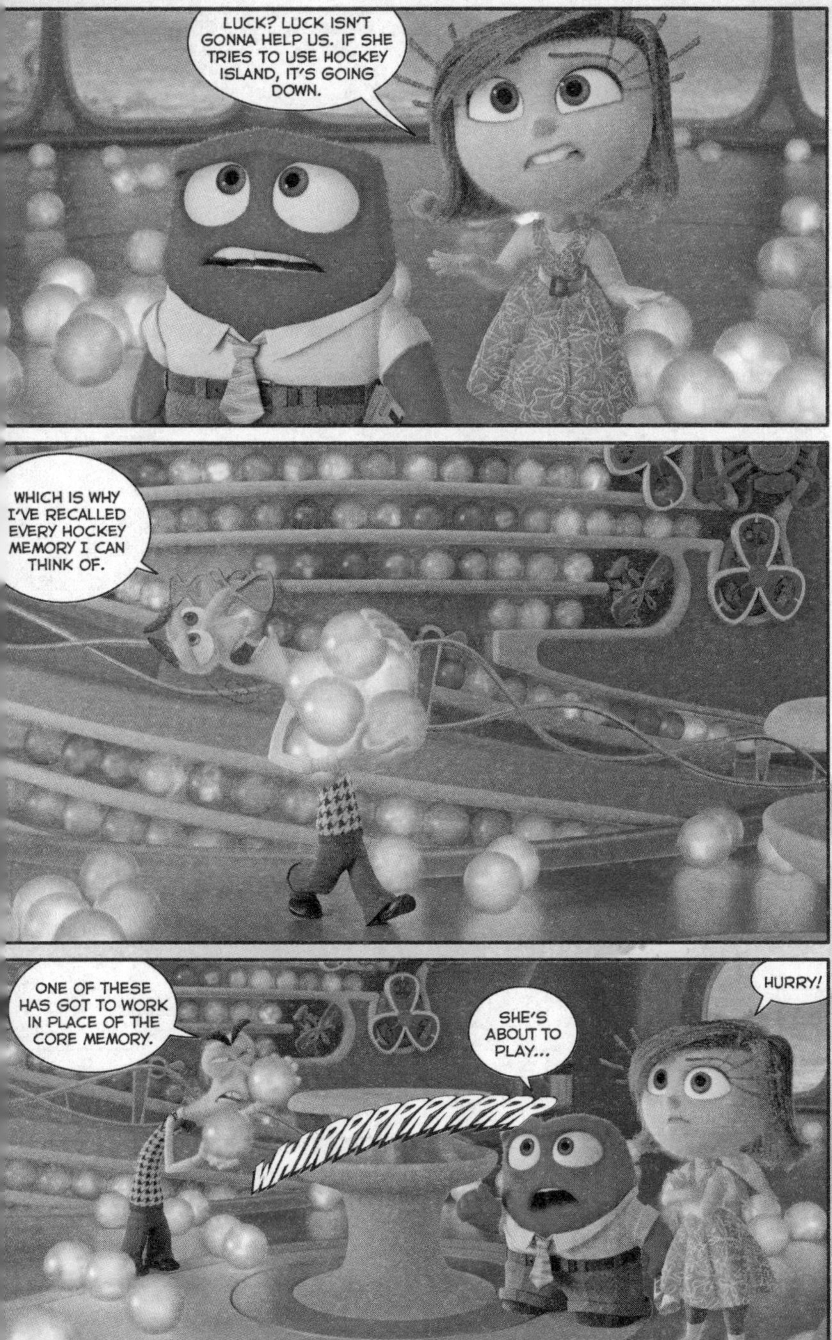
LUCK? LUCK ISN'T GONNA HELP US. IF SHE TRIES TO USE HOCKEY ISLAND, IT'S GOING DOWN.
WHICH IS WHY I'VE RECALLED EVERY HOCKEY MEMORY I CAN THINK OF.
ONE OF THESE HAS GOT TO WORK IN PLACE OF THE CORE MEMORY.
SHE'S ABOUT TO PLAY...
HURRY!
WHIRRRRRRRRRR

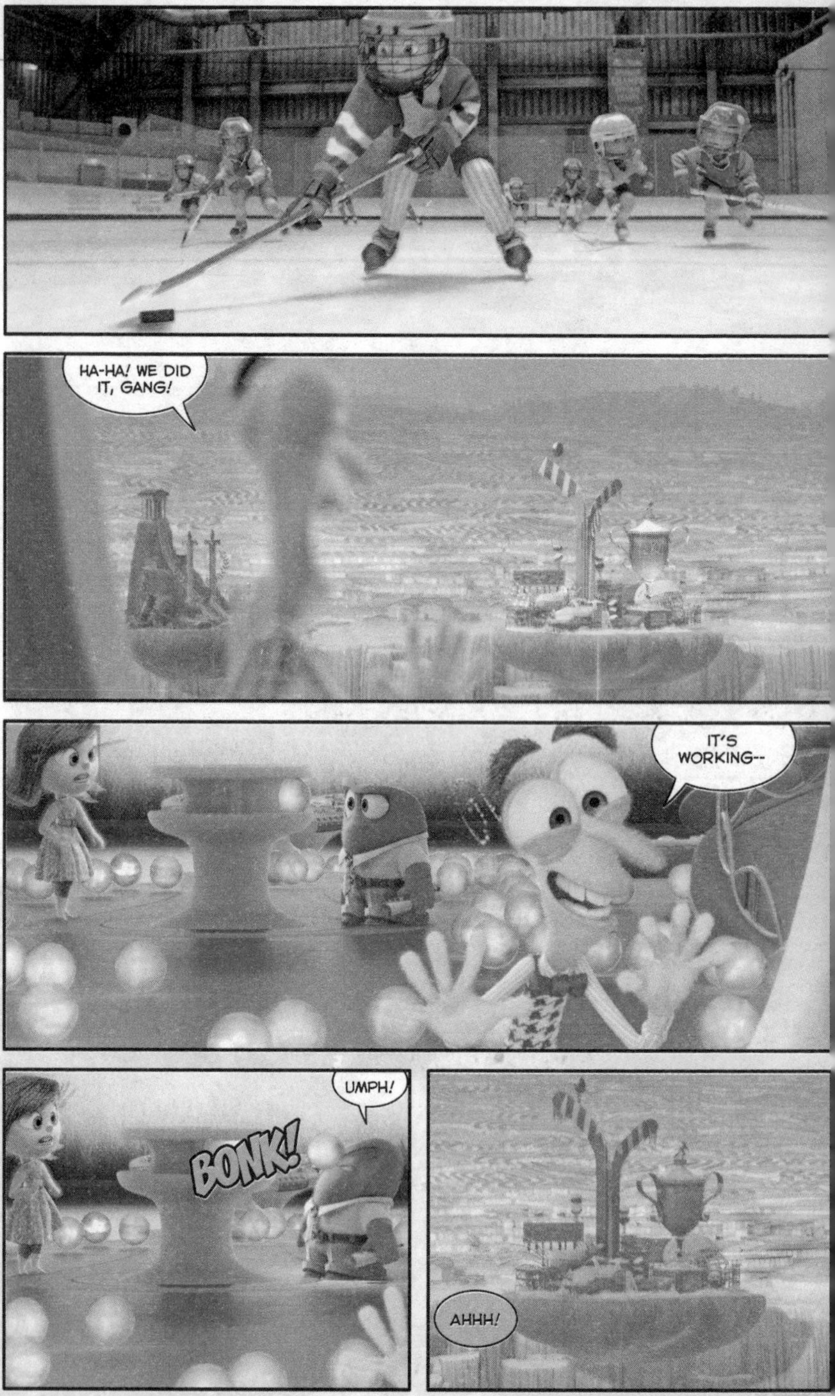
HA-HA! WE DID IT, GANG!
IT'S WORKING--
UMPH!
BONK!
AHHH!

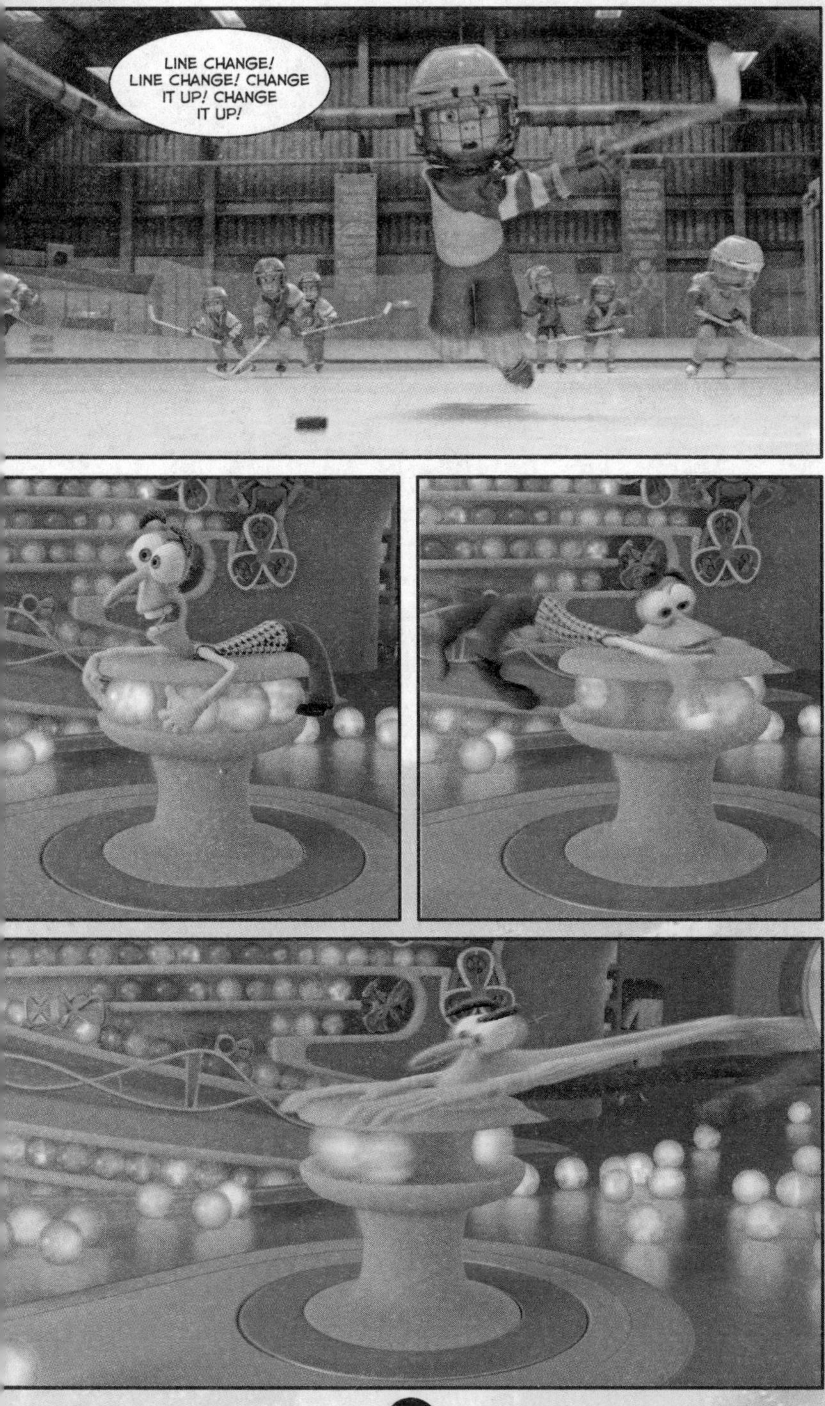
LINE CHANGE! LINE CHANGE! CHANGE IT UP! CHANGE IT UP!

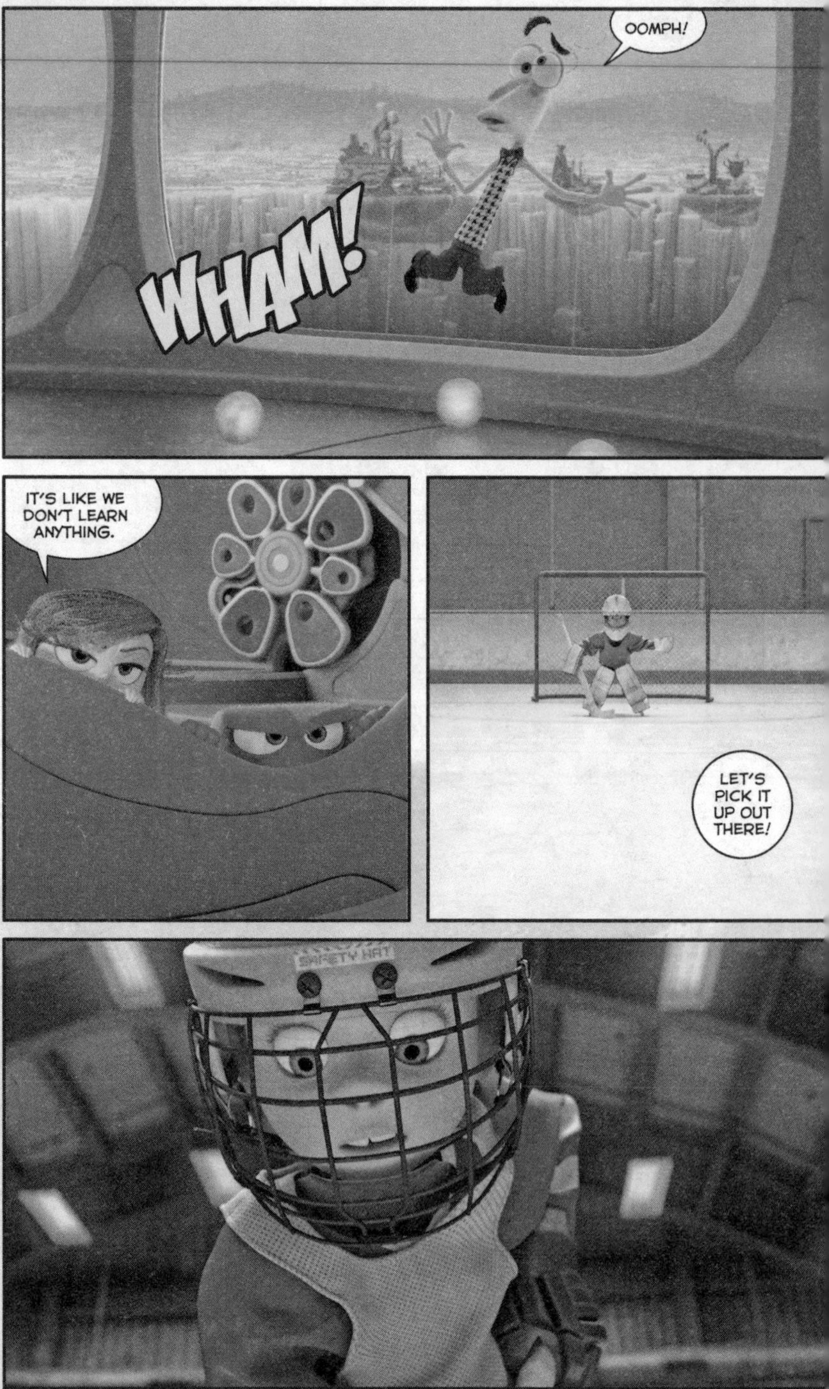
OOMPH!
WHAM!
IT'S LIKE WE DON'T LEARN ANYTHING.
LET'S PICK IT UP OUT THERE!
SAFETY HAT

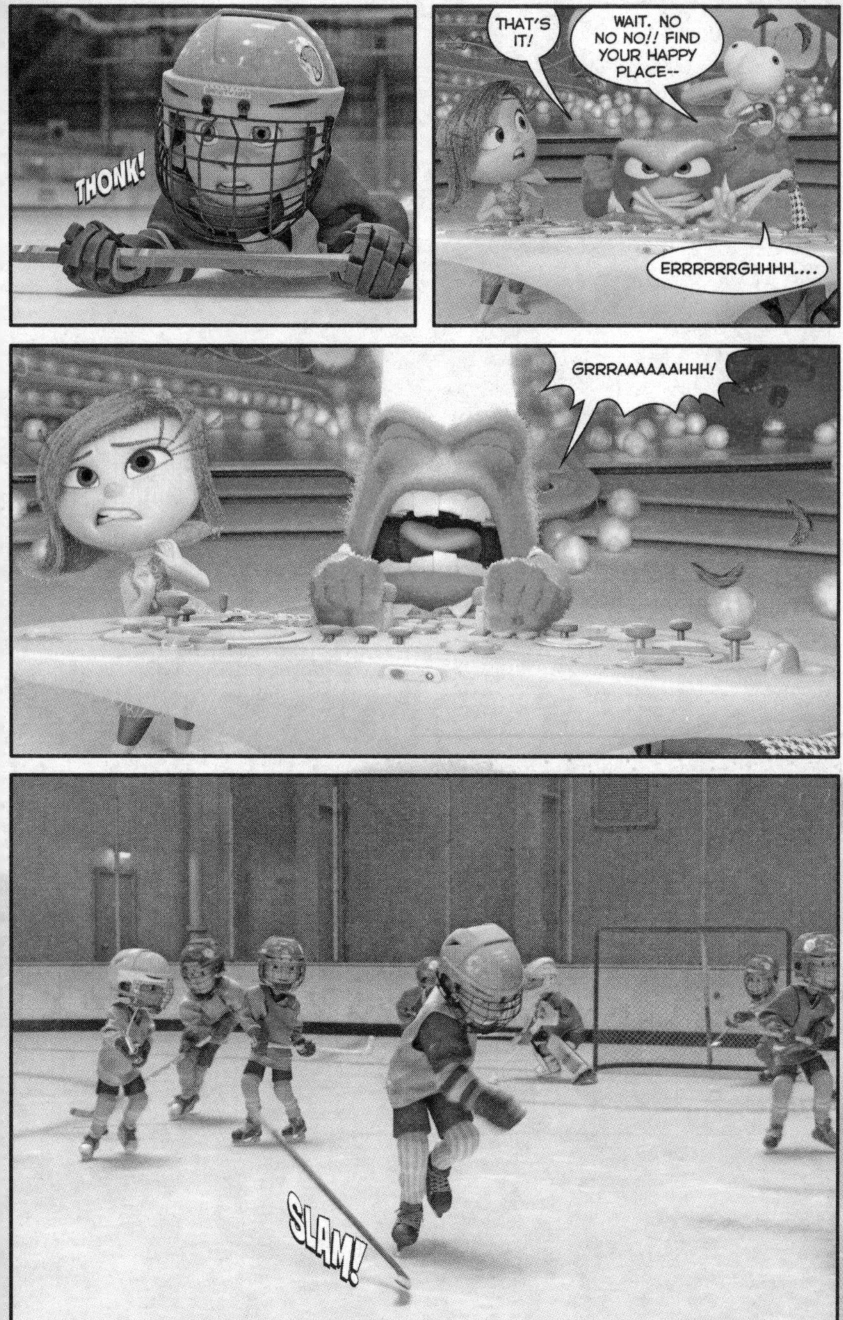
THONK!
THAT'S IT!
WAIT. NO NO NO!! FIND YOUR HAPPY PLACE--
ERRRRRRGHHHH....
GRRRAAAAAAAHHH!
SLAM!

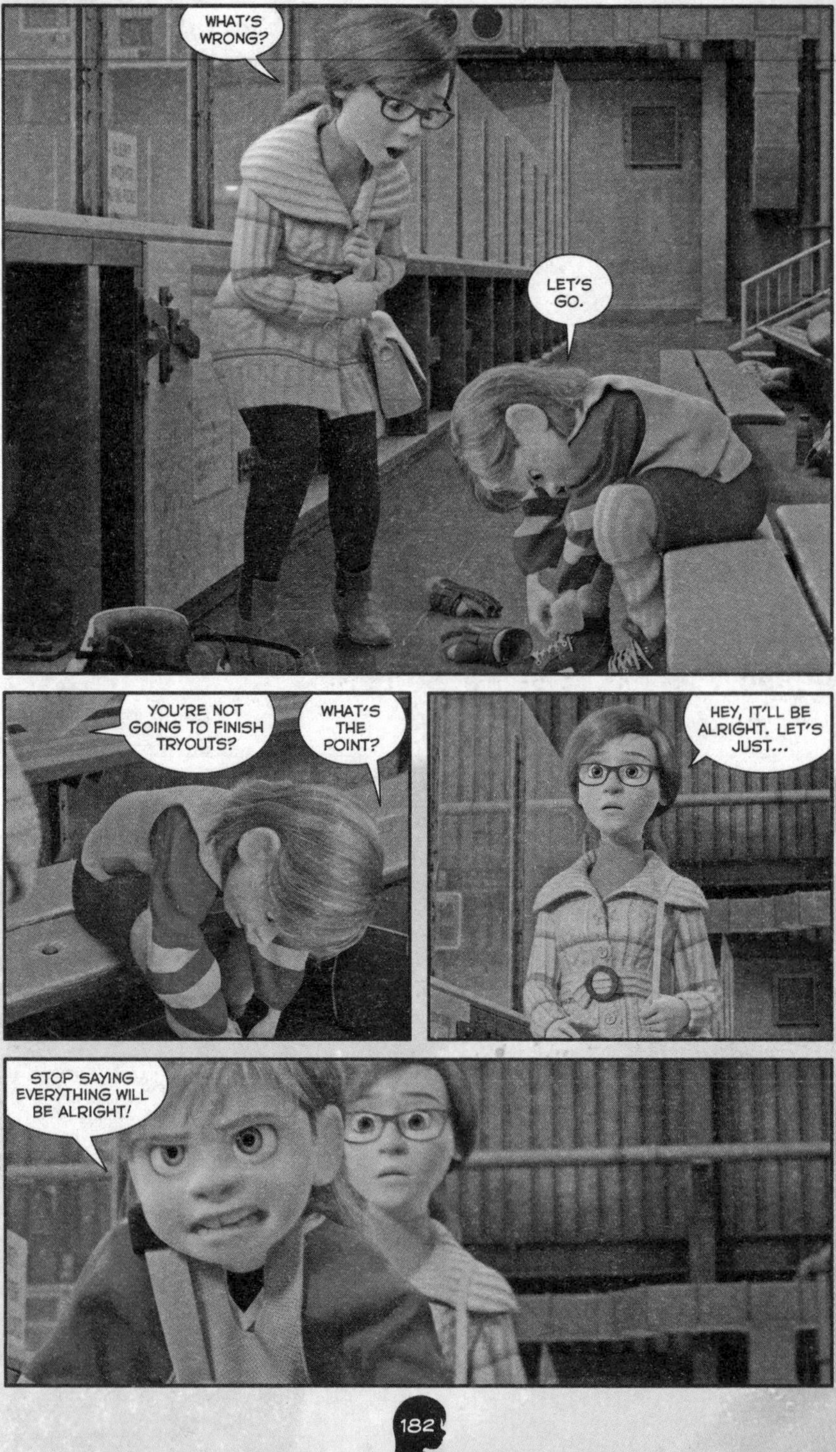
WHAT'S WRONG?
LET'S GO.
YOU'RE NOT GOING TO FINISH TRYOUTS?
WHAT'S THE POINT?
HEY, IT'LL BE ALRIGHT. LET'S JUST...
STOP SAYING EVERYTHING WILL BE ALRIGHT!

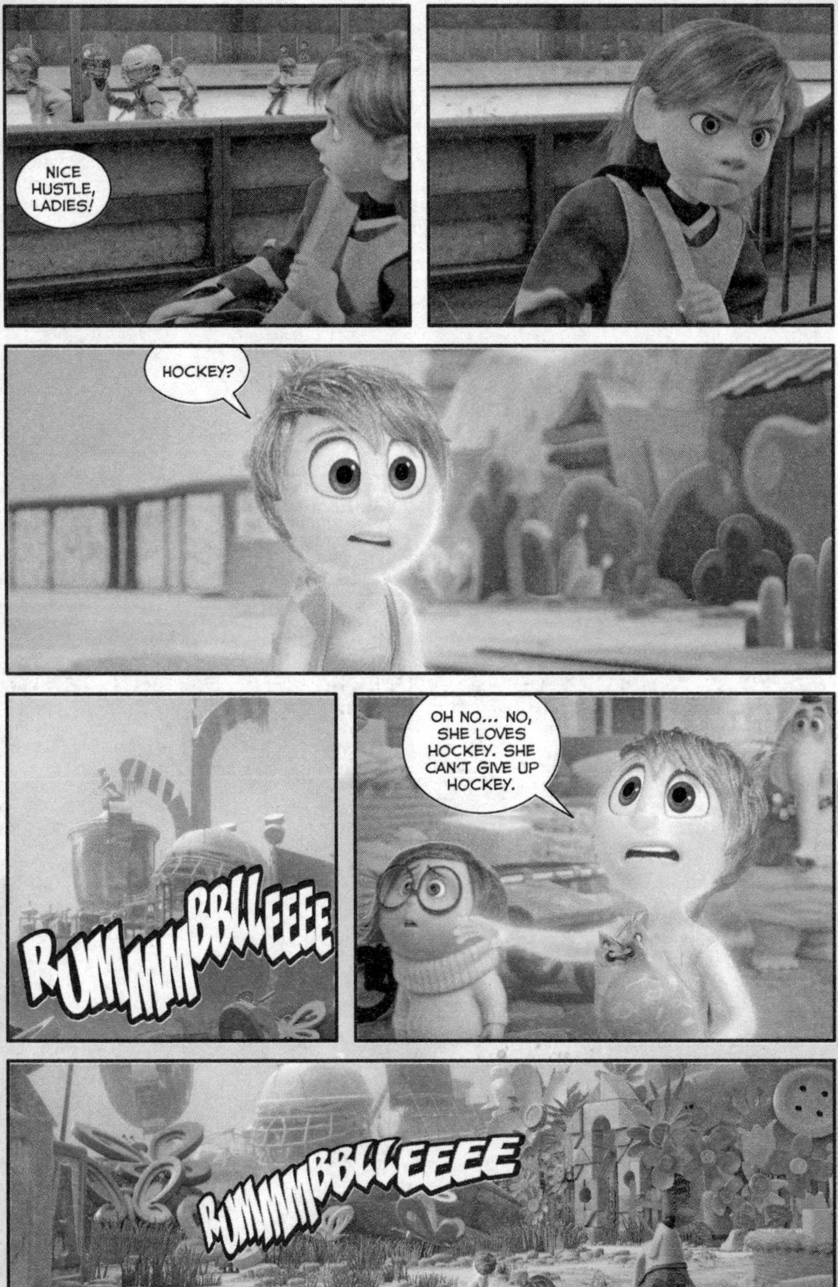
NICE HUSTLE, LADIES!
HOCKEY?
RUMMMMBBLLEEEE
OH NO... NO, SHE LOVES HOCKEY. SHE CAN'T GIVE UP HOCKEY.
RUMMMBBLLEEEE

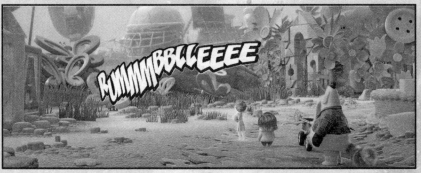

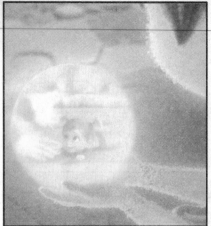

BING BONG, WE HAVE TO GET TO THAT STATION.

SURE THING. THIS WAY, JUST PAST GRAHAM CRACKER CASTLE.

HEY. THAT'S WEIRD. GRAHAM CRACKER CASTLE USED TO BE RIGHT HERE. I WONDER WHY THEY MOVED IT.

WOW, THAT'S NOT... I WOULD HAVE SWORN SPARKLE PONY MOUNTAIN WAS RIGHT HERE.

HEY, WHAT'S GOING ON?

YEAH, YEAH, I DUNNO, WE'LL HAVE TO COME BACK AND---

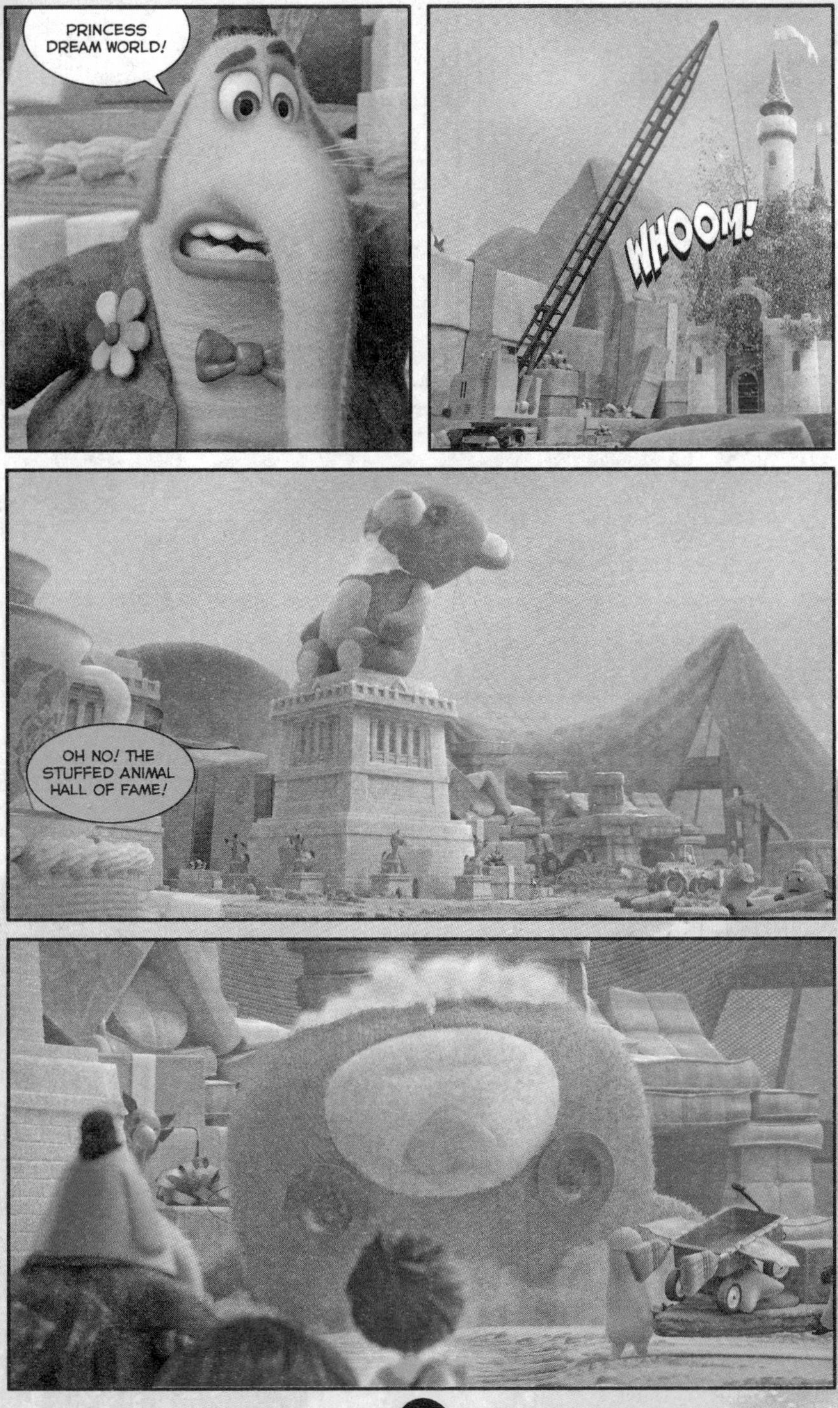
PRINCESS DREAM WORLD!
WHOOM!
OH NO! THE STUFFED ANIMAL HALL OF FAME!

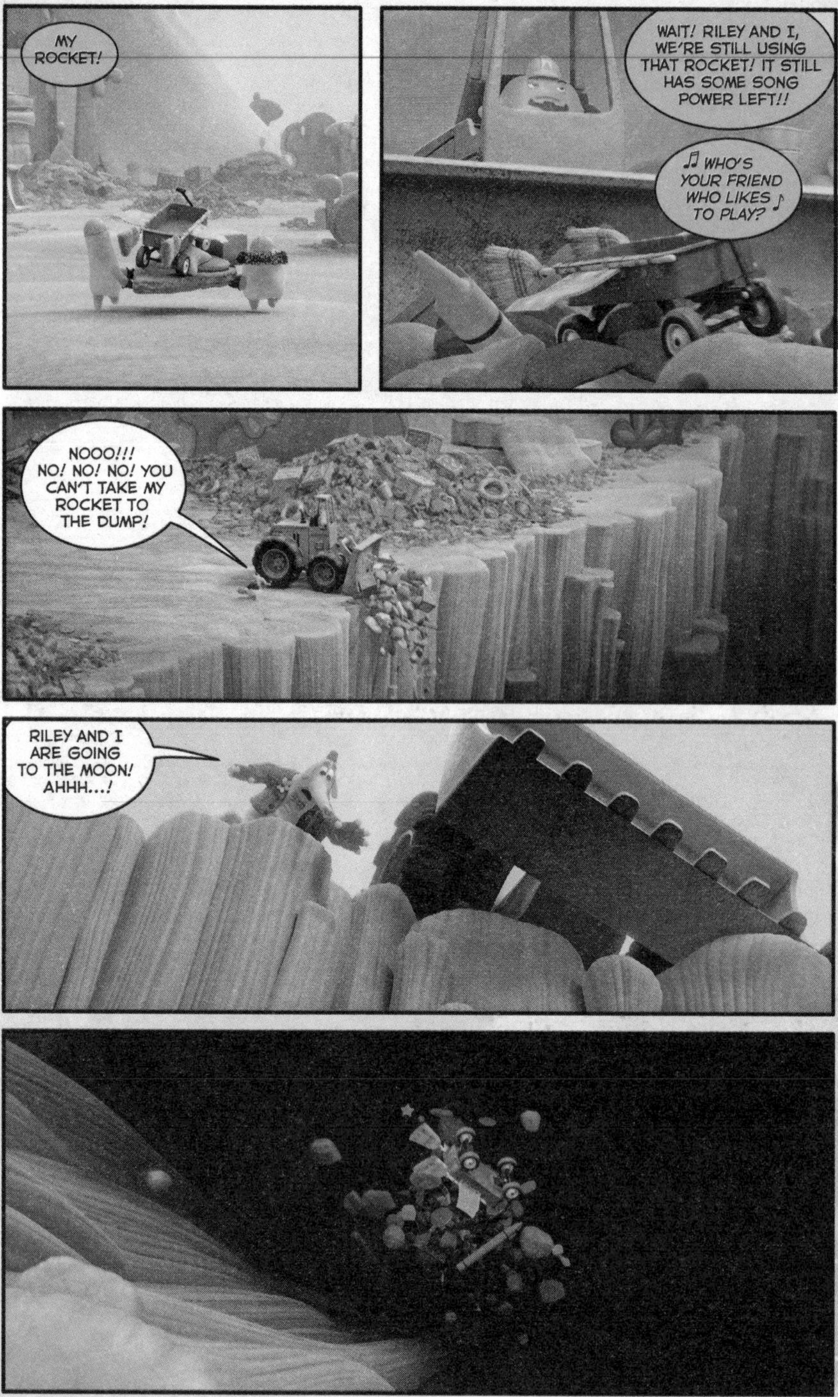
MY ROCKET!
WAIT! RILEY AND I, WE'RE STILL USING THAT ROCKET! IT STILL HAS SOME SONG POWER LEFT!!
♫ WHO'S YOUR FRIEND WHO LIKES TO PLAY? ♪
NOOO!!! NO! NO! NO! YOU CAN'T TAKE MY ROCKET TO THE DUMP!
RILEY AND I ARE GOING TO THE MOON! AHHH...!

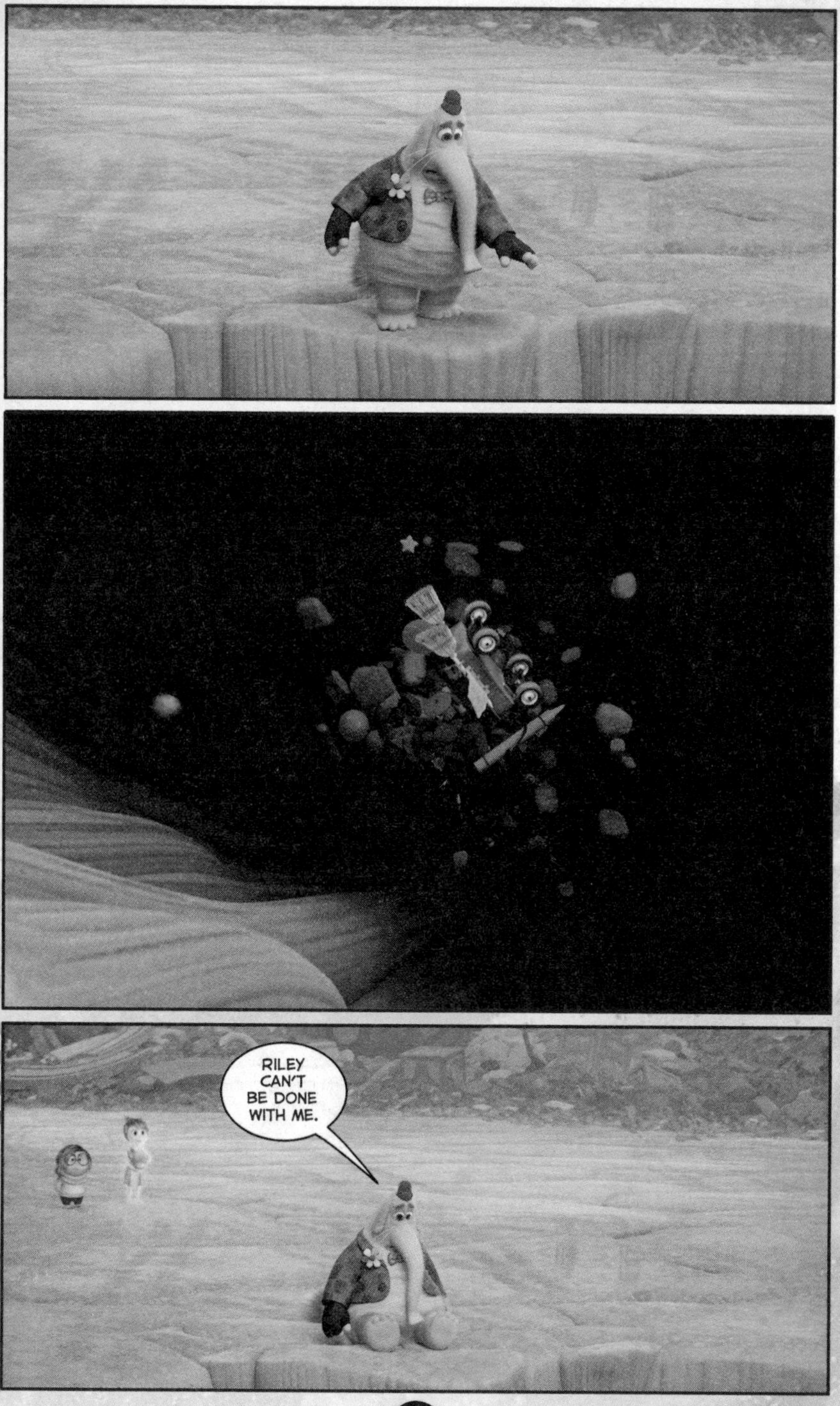
RILEY CAN'T BE DONE WITH ME.

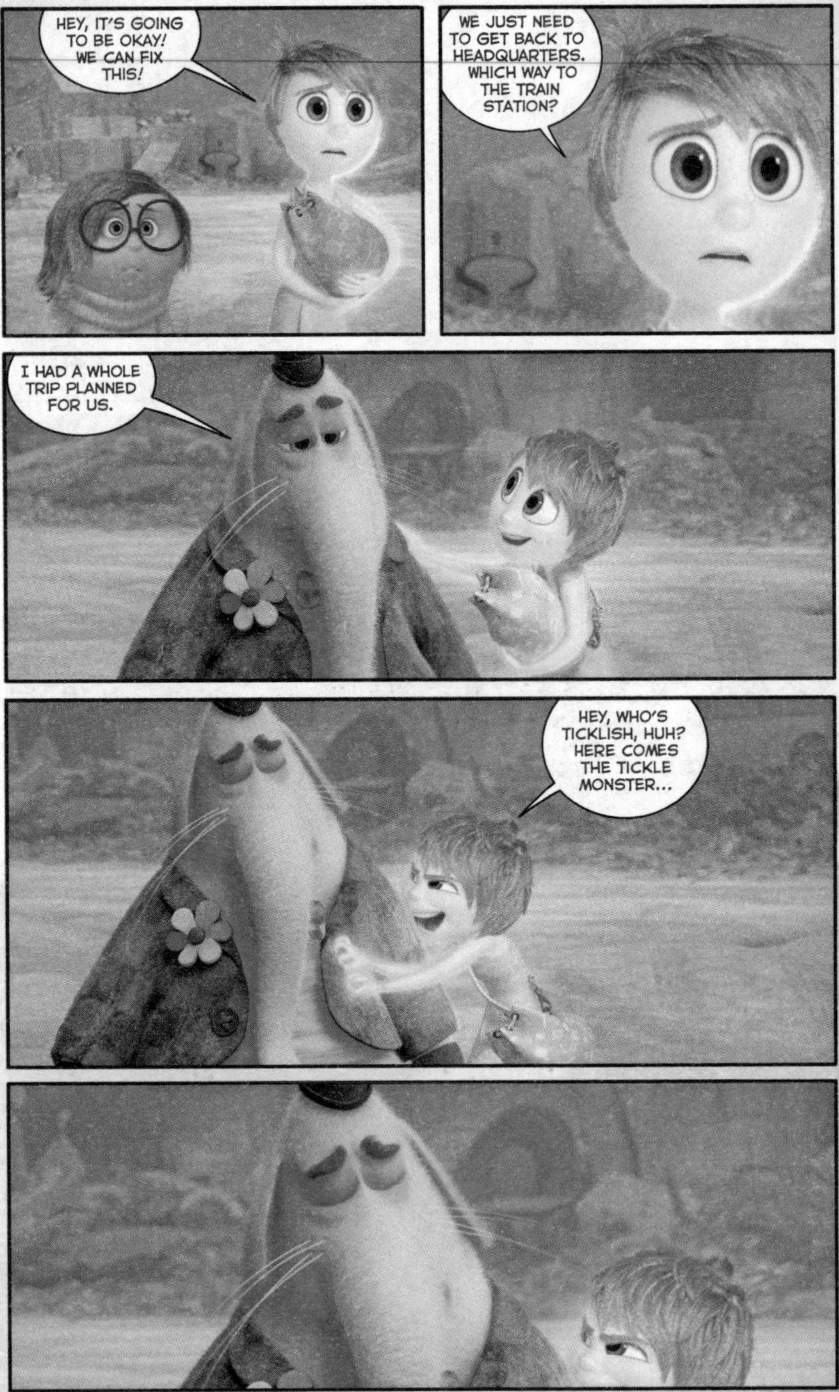
HEY, IT'S GOING TO BE OKAY! WE CAN FIX THIS!
WE JUST NEED TO GET BACK TO HEADQUARTERS. WHICH WAY TO THE TRAIN STATION?
I HAD A WHOLE TRIP PLANNED FOR US.
HEY, WHO'S TICKLISH, HUH? HERE COMES THE TICKLE MONSTER...

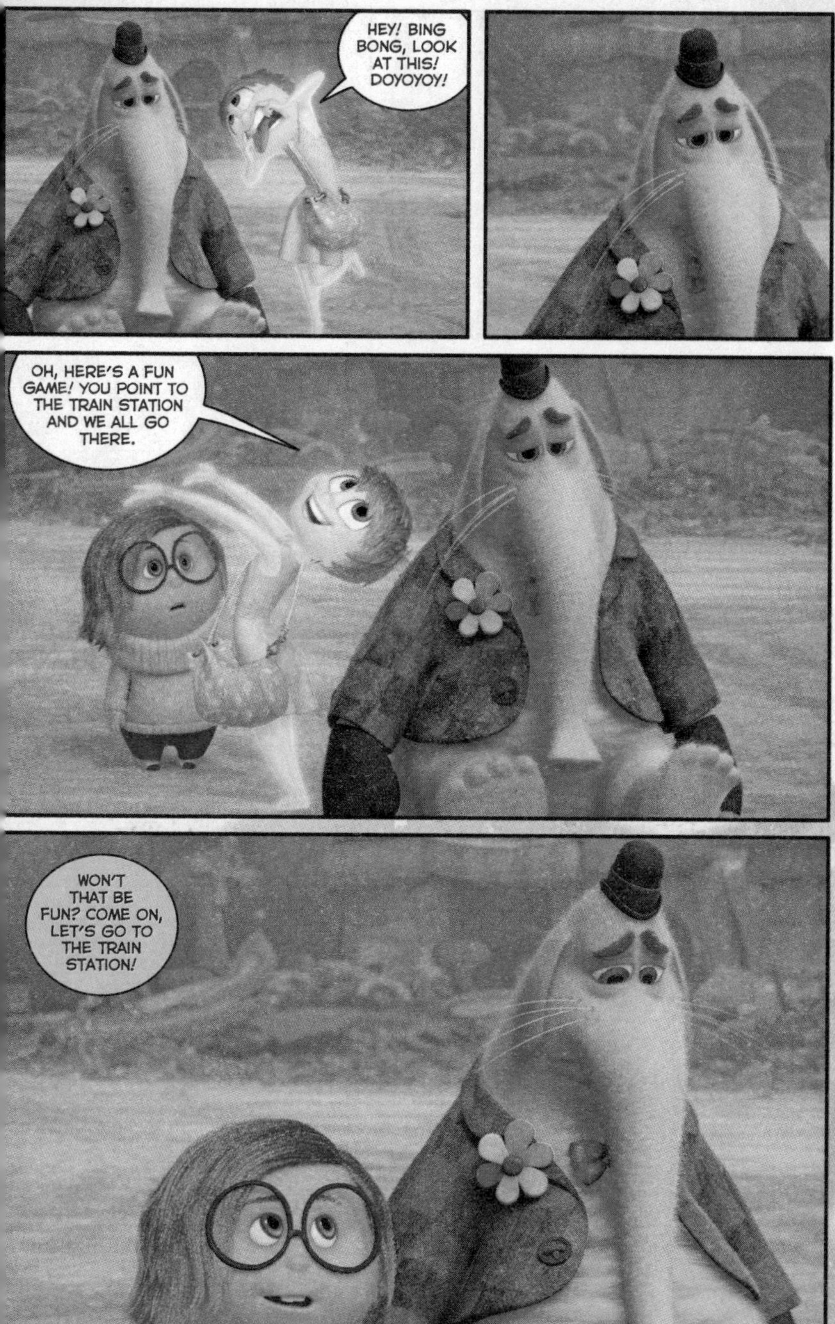
HEY! BING BONG, LOOK AT THIS! DOYOYOY!
OH, HERE'S A FUN GAME! YOU POINT TO THE TRAIN STATION AND WE ALL GO THERE.
WON'T THAT BE FUN? COME ON, LET'S GO TO THE TRAIN STATION!

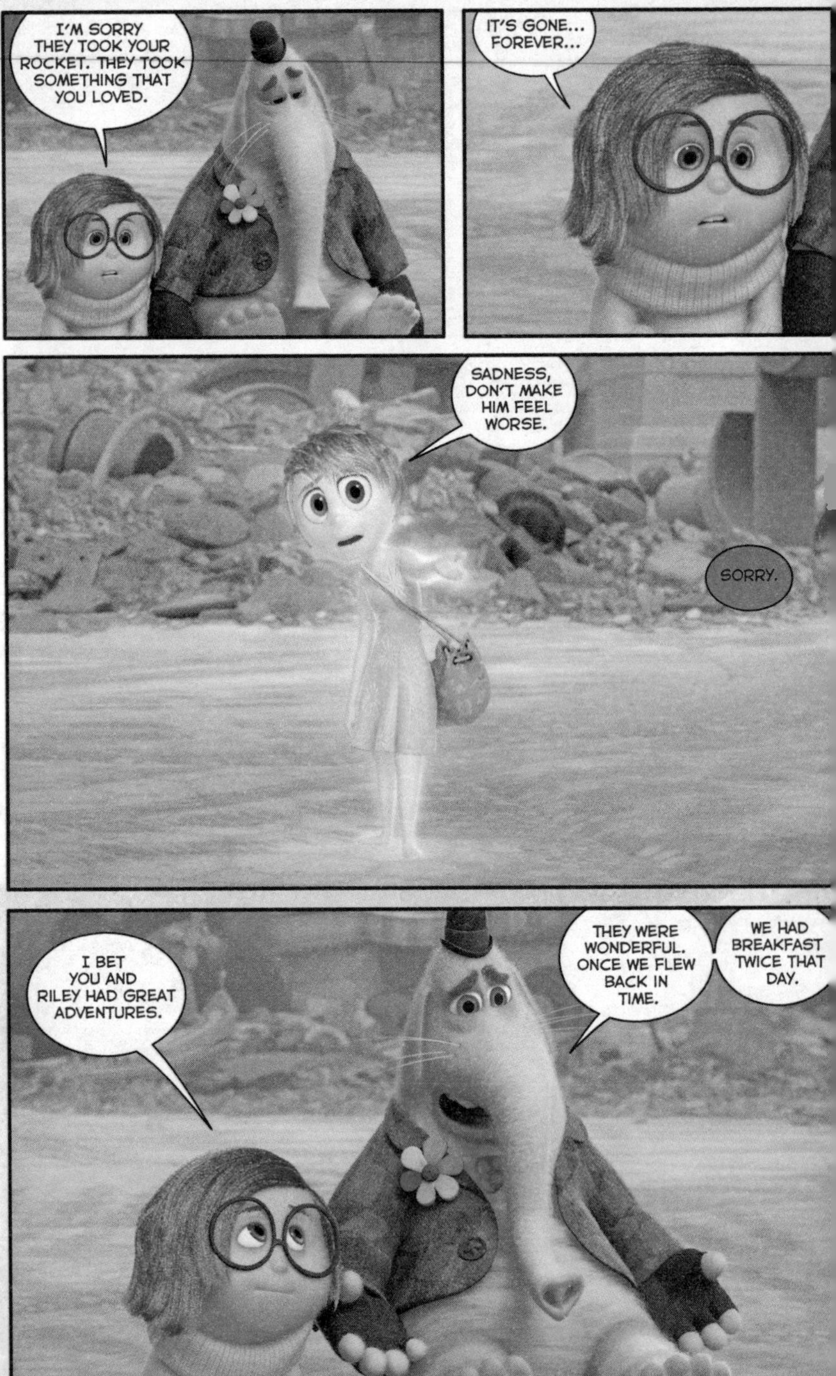
I'M SORRY THEY TOOK YOUR ROCKET. THEY TOOK SOMETHING THAT YOU LOVED.
IT'S GONE... FOREVER...
SADNESS, DON'T MAKE HIM FEEL WORSE.
SORRY.
I BET YOU AND RILEY HAD GREAT ADVENTURES.
THEY WERE WONDERFUL. ONCE WE FLEW BACK IN TIME.
WE HAD BREAKFAST TWICE THAT DAY.

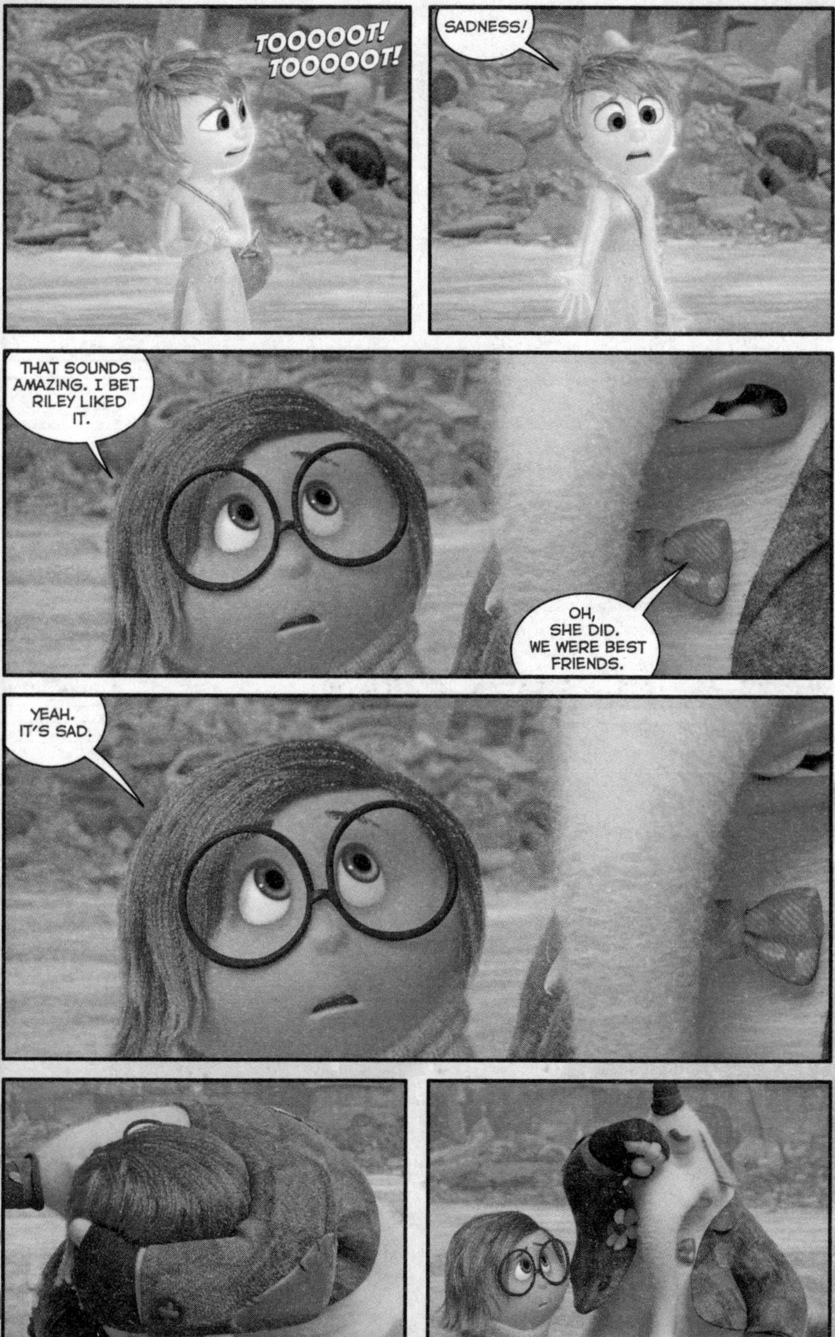
TOOOOOT! TOOOOOT!
SADNESS!
THAT SOUNDS AMAZING. I BET RILEY LIKED IT.
OH, SHE DID. WE WERE BEST FRIENDS.
YEAH. IT'S SAD.

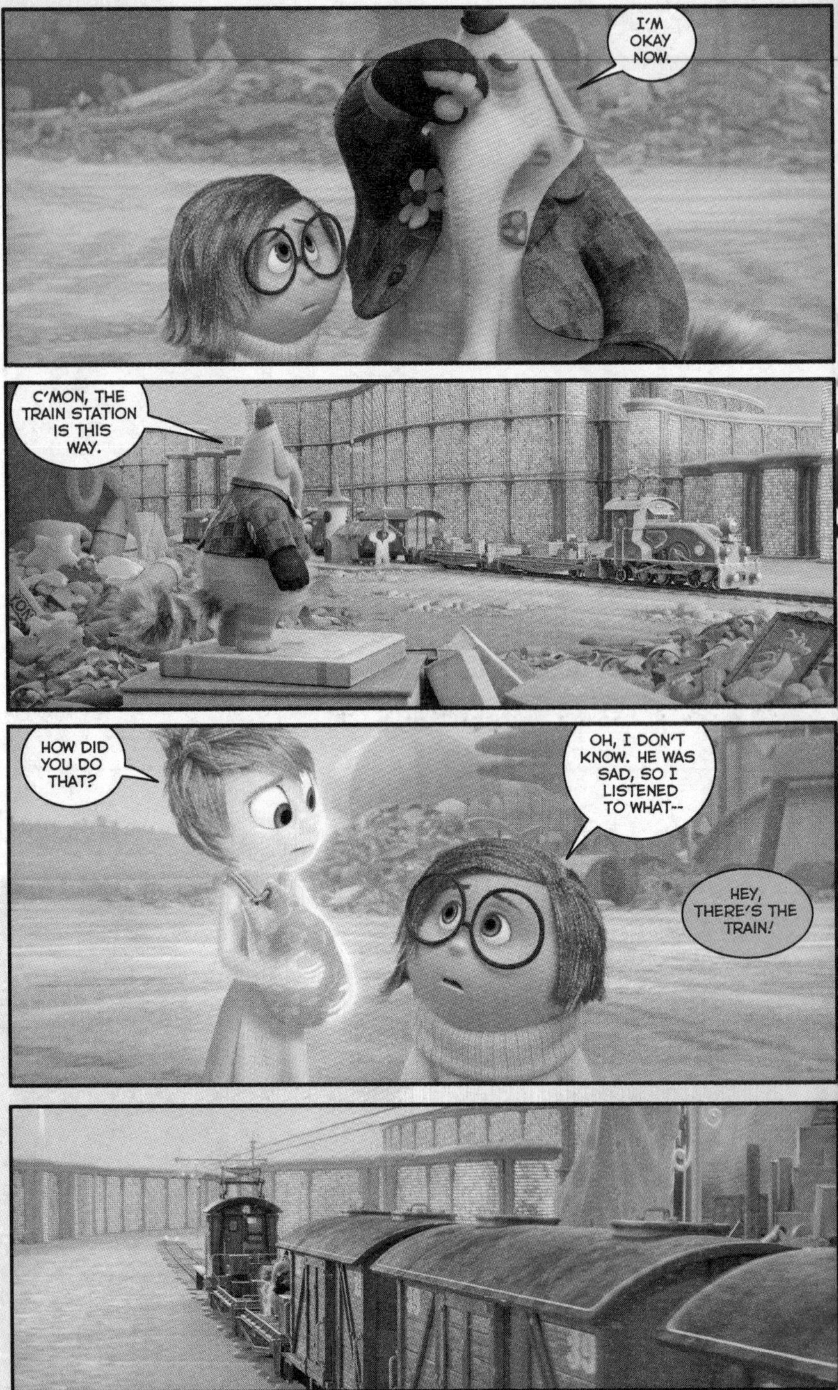
I'M OKAY NOW.
C'MON, THE TRAIN STATION IS THIS WAY.
HOW DID YOU DO THAT?
OH, I DON'T KNOW. HE WAS SAD, SO I LISTENED TO WHAT--
HEY, THERE'S THE TRAIN!

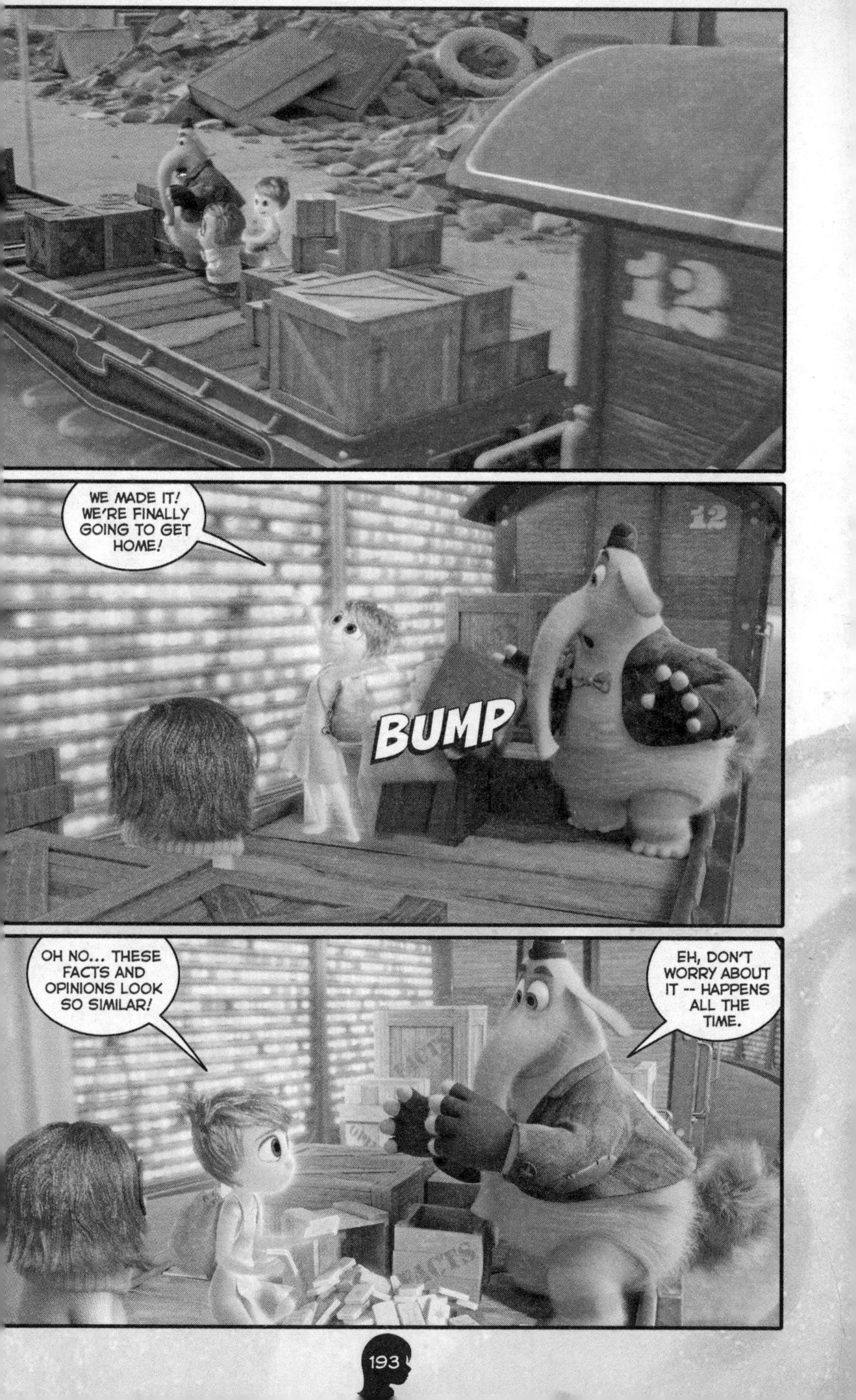
WE MADE IT! WE'RE FINALLY GOING TO GET HOME!
BUMP
OH NO... THESE FACTS AND OPINIONS LOOK SO SIMILAR!
EH, DON'T WORRY ABOUT IT -- HAPPENS ALL THE TIME.

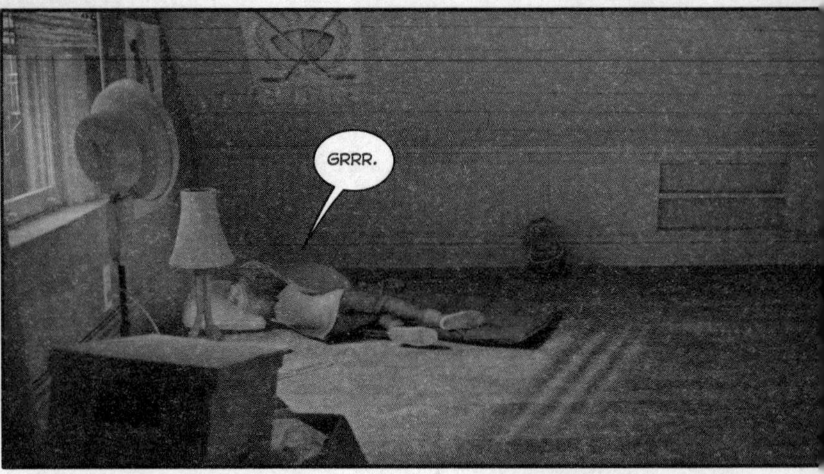
GRRR.

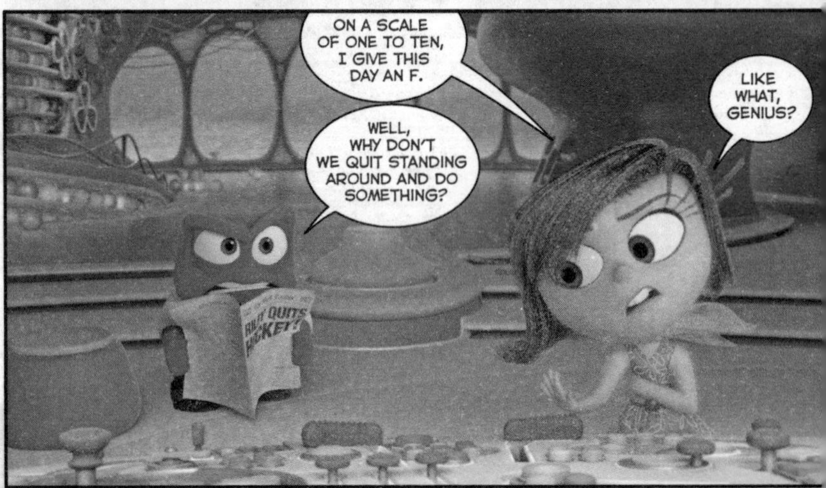
ON A SCALE OF ONE TO TEN, I GIVE THIS DAY AN F.
WELL, WHY DON'T WE QUIT STANDING AROUND AND DO SOMETHING?
LIKE WHAT, GENIUS?

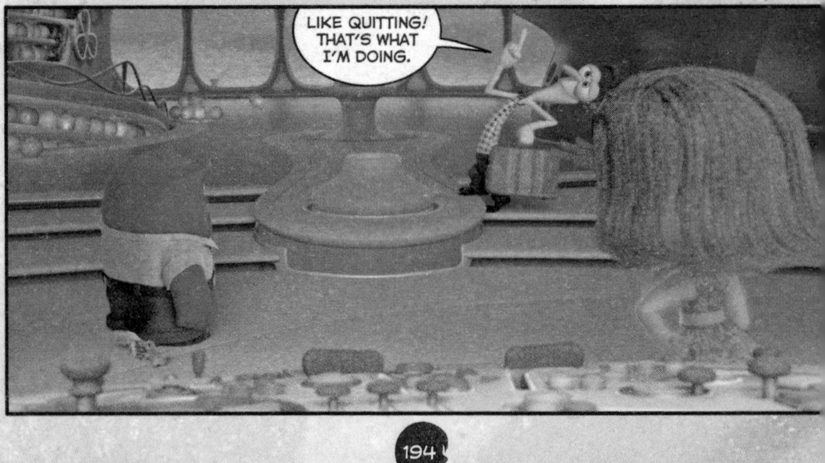
LIKE QUITTING! THAT'S WHAT I'M DOING.

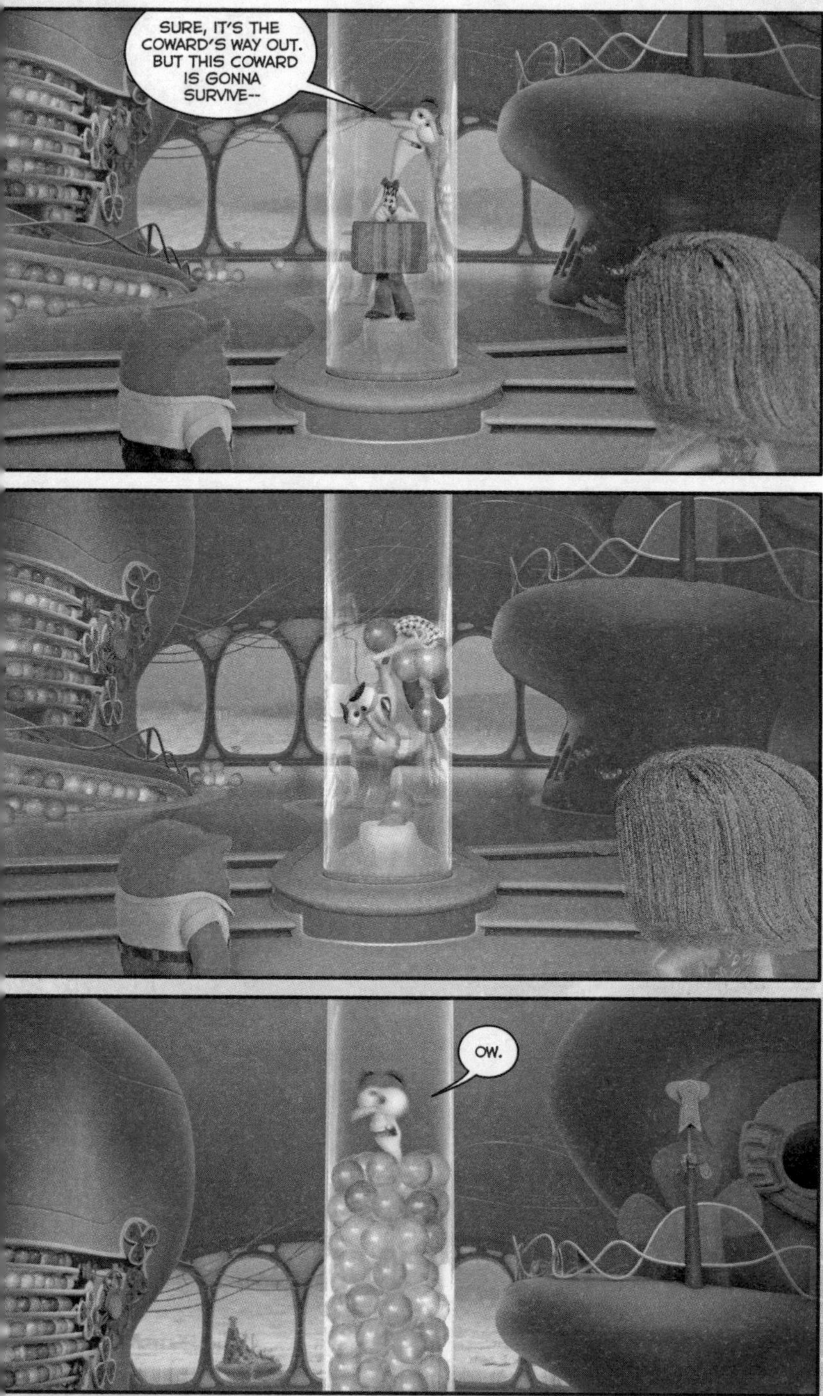
SURE, IT'S THE COWARD'S WAY OUT. BUT THIS COWARD IS GONNA SURVIVE--
OW.

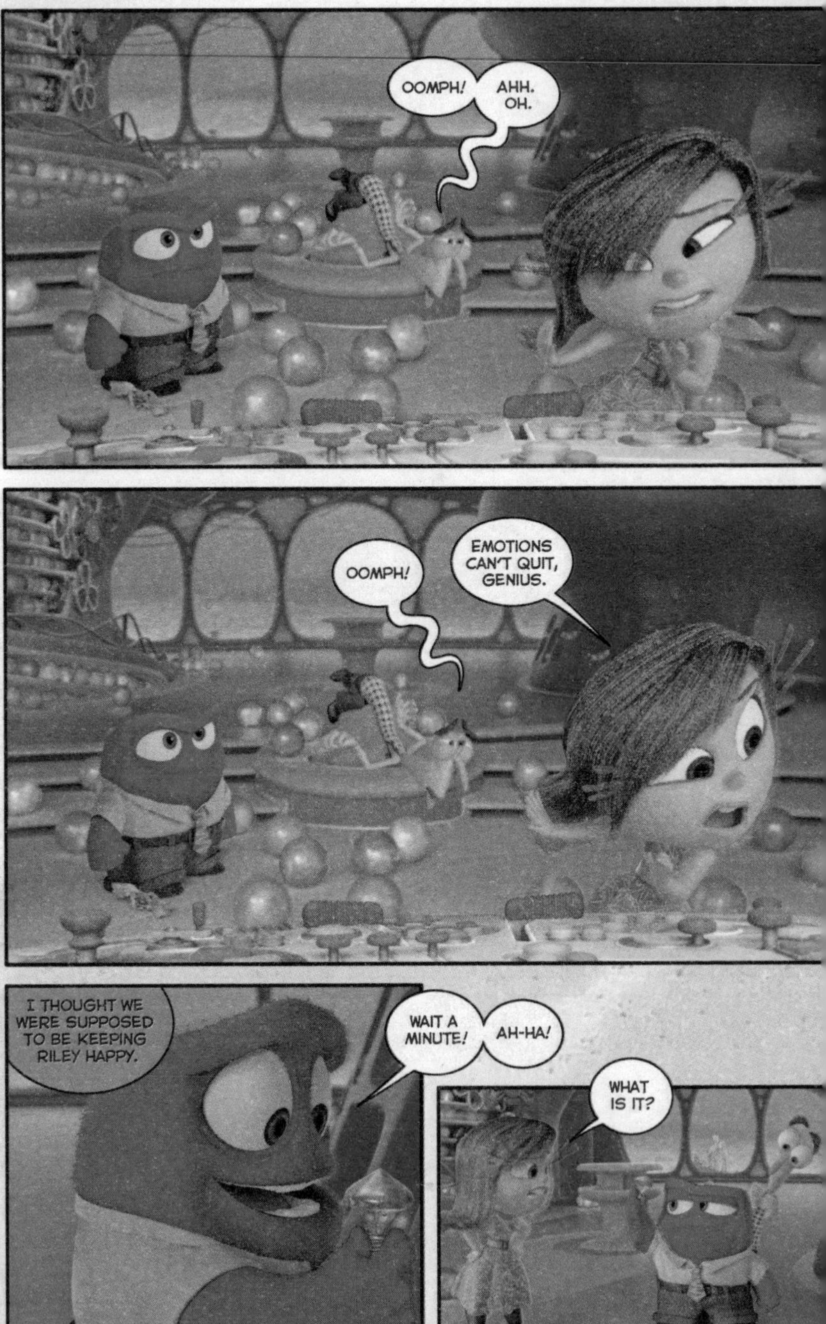
OOMPH!
AHH. OH.
OOMPH!
EMOTIONS CAN'T QUIT, GENIUS.
I THOUGHT WE WERE SUPPOSED TO BE KEEPING RILEY HAPPY.
WAIT A MINUTE!
AH-HA!
WHAT IS IT?

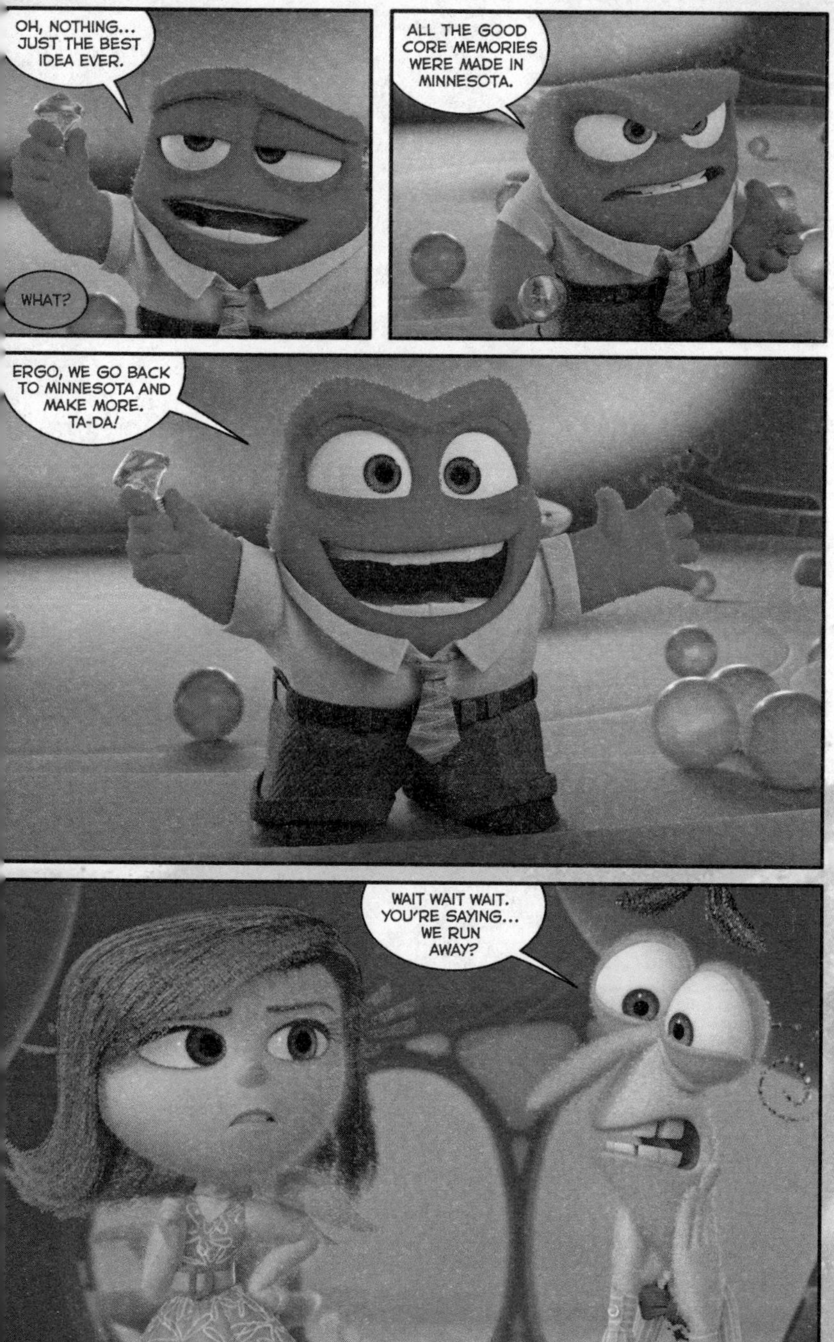
OH, NOTHING... JUST THE BEST IDEA EVER.
WHAT?
ALL THE GOOD CORE MEMORIES WERE MADE IN MINNESOTA.
ERGO, WE GO BACK TO MINNESOTA AND MAKE MORE. TA-DA!
WAIT WAIT WAIT. YOU'RE SAYING... WE RUN AWAY?

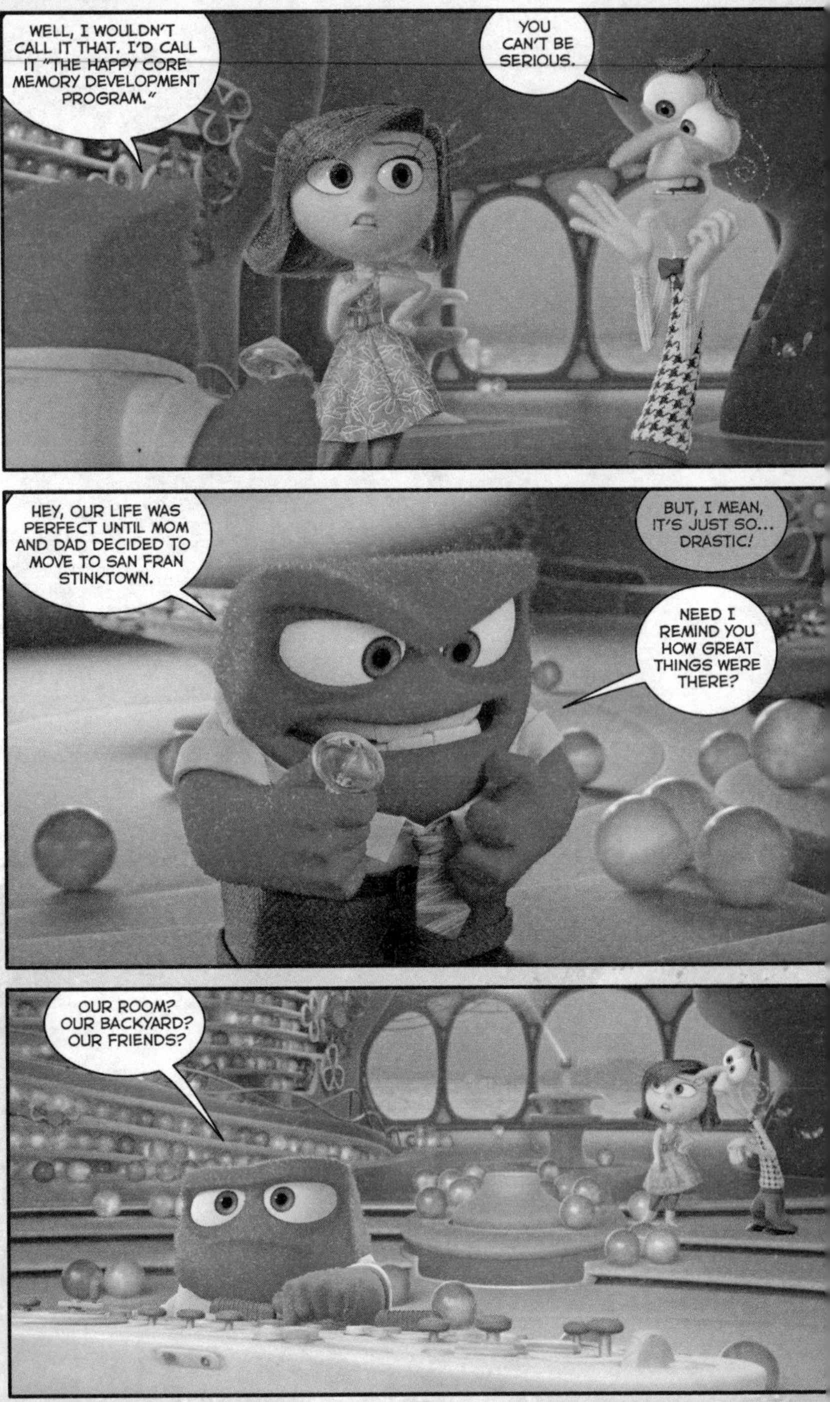
WELL, I WOULDN'T CALL IT THAT. I'D CALL IT "THE HAPPY CORE MEMORY DEVELOPMENT PROGRAM."
YOU CAN'T BE SERIOUS.
HEY, OUR LIFE WAS PERFECT UNTIL MOM AND DAD DECIDED TO MOVE TO SAN FRAN STINKTOWN.
BUT, I MEAN, IT'S JUST SO... DRASTIC!
NEED I REMIND YOU HOW GREAT THINGS WERE THERE?
OUR ROOM? OUR BACKYARD? OUR FRIENDS?

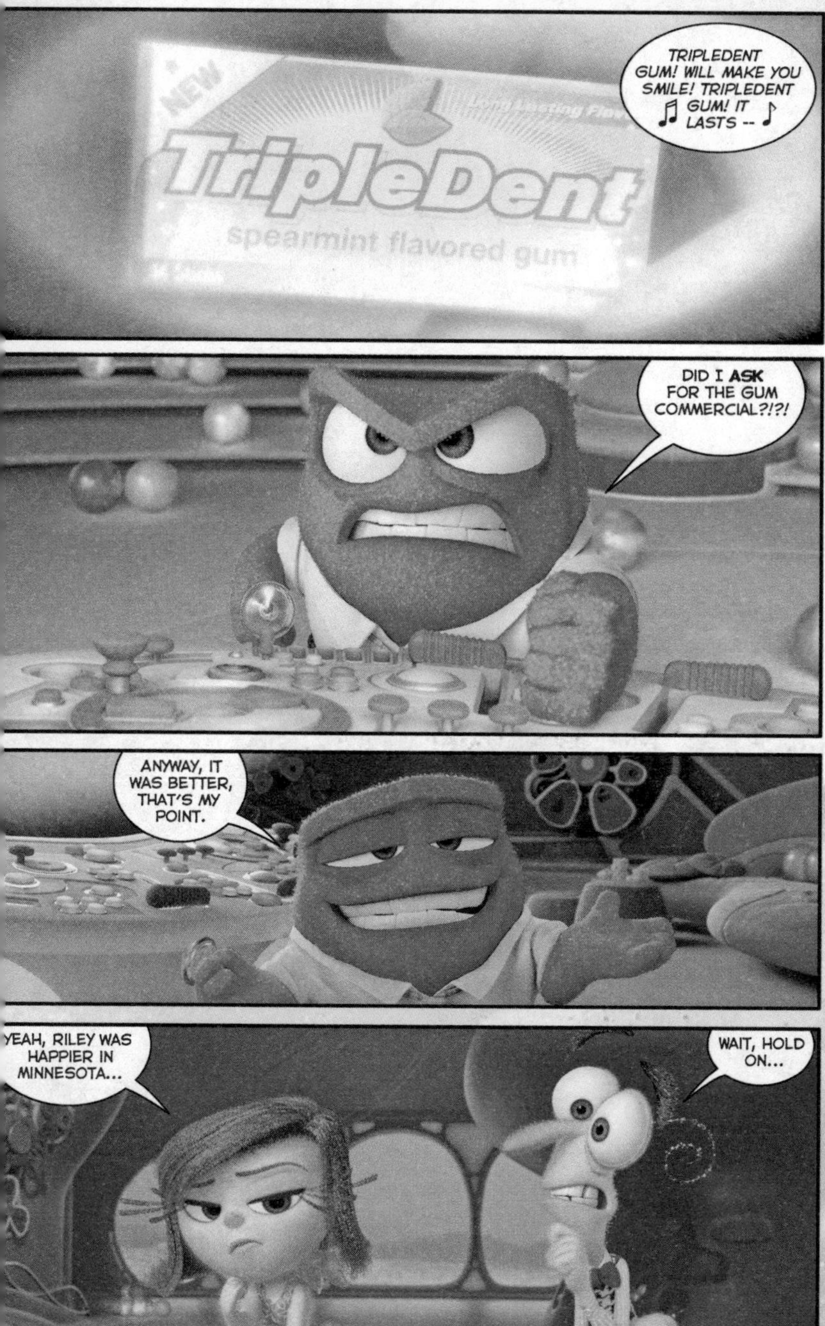
TRIPLEDENT GUM! WILL MAKE YOU SMILE! TRIPLEDENT GUM! IT LASTS --
NEW
TripleDent
spearmint flavored gum
DID I **ASK** FOR THE GUM COMMERCIAL?!?!
ANYWAY, IT WAS BETTER, THAT'S MY POINT.
YEAH, RILEY WAS HAPPIER IN MINNESOTA...
WAIT, HOLD ON...

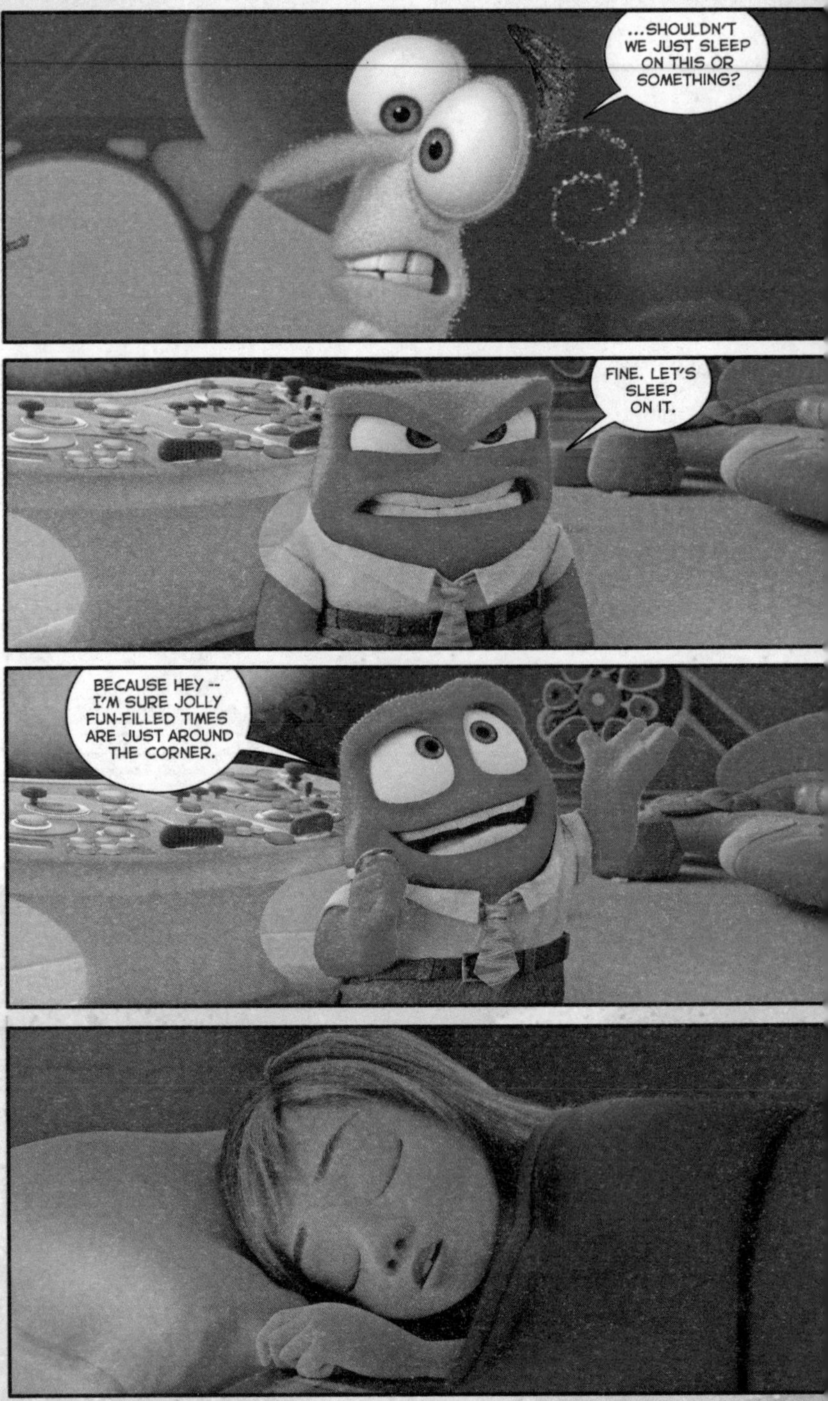
...SHOULDN'T WE JUST SLEEP ON THIS OR SOMETHING?
FINE. LET'S SLEEP ON IT.
BECAUSE HEY -- I'M SURE JOLLY FUN-FILLED TIMES ARE JUST AROUND THE CORNER.

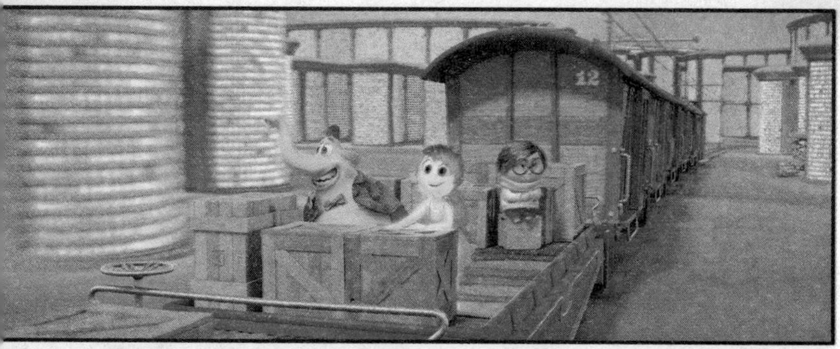

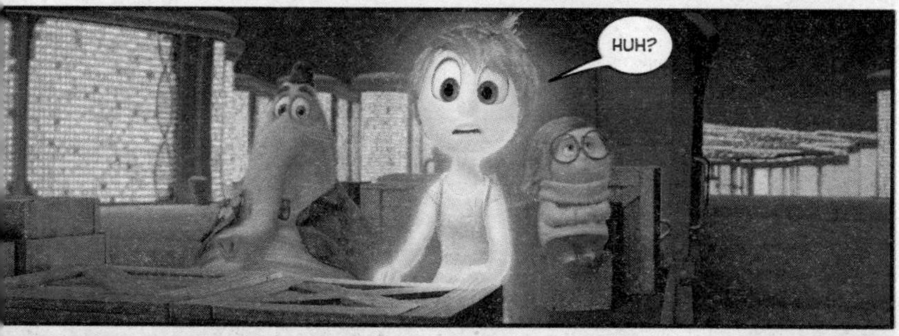
HUH?

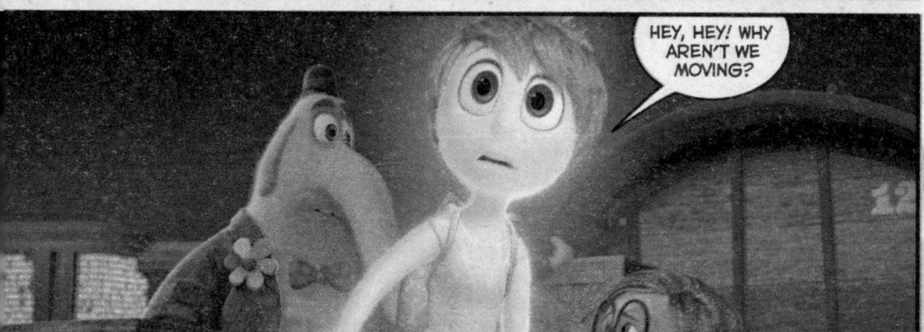
HEY, HEY! WHY AREN'T WE MOVING?

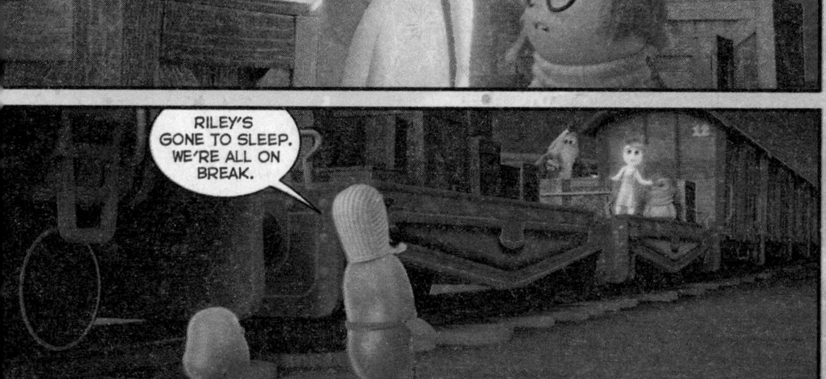
RILEY'S GONE TO SLEEP. WE'RE ALL ON BREAK.

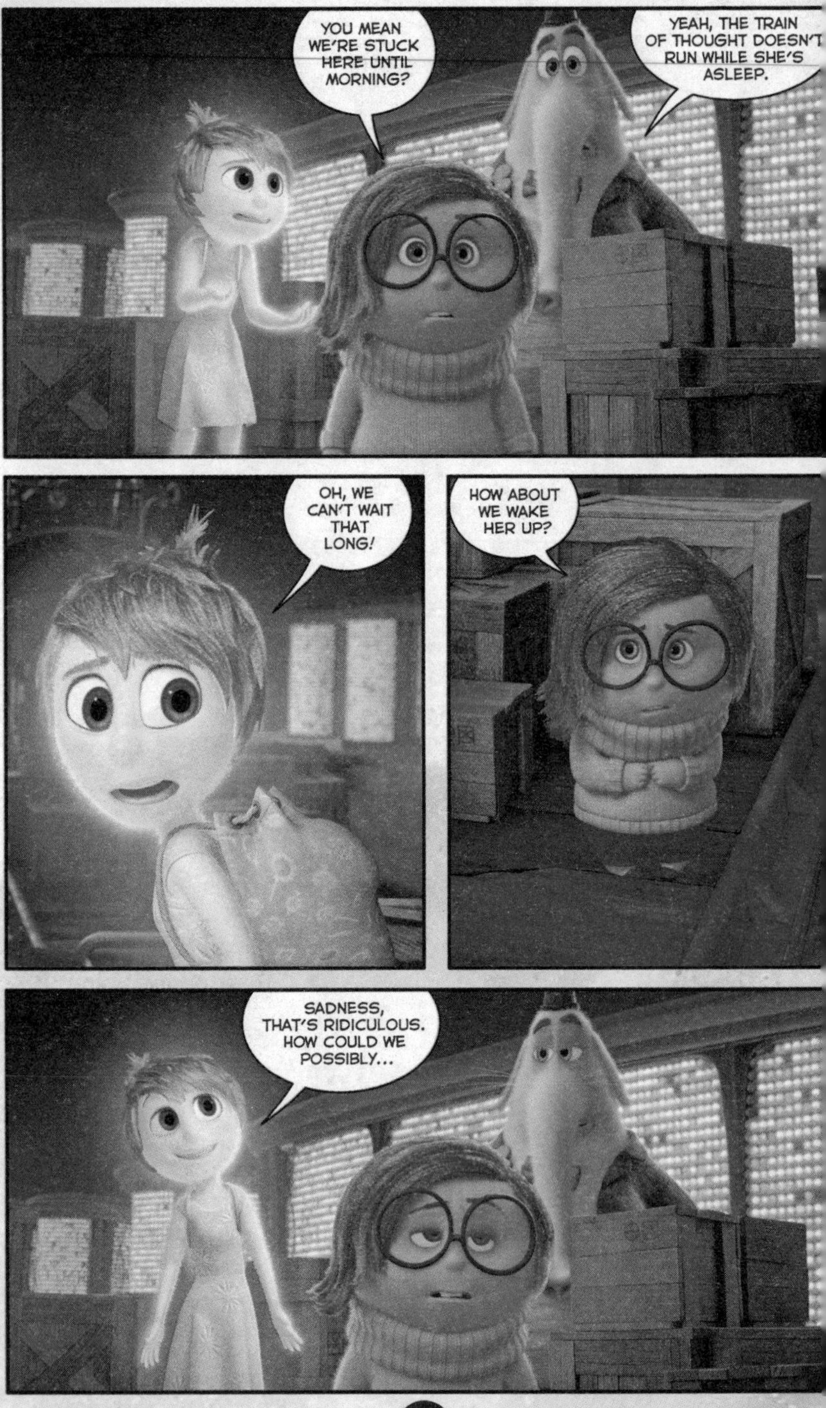
YOU MEAN WE'RE STUCK HERE UNTIL MORNING?
YEAH, THE TRAIN OF THOUGHT DOESN'T RUN WHILE SHE'S ASLEEP.
OH, WE CAN'T WAIT THAT LONG!
HOW ABOUT WE WAKE HER UP?
SADNESS, THAT'S RIDICULOUS. HOW COULD WE POSSIBLY...

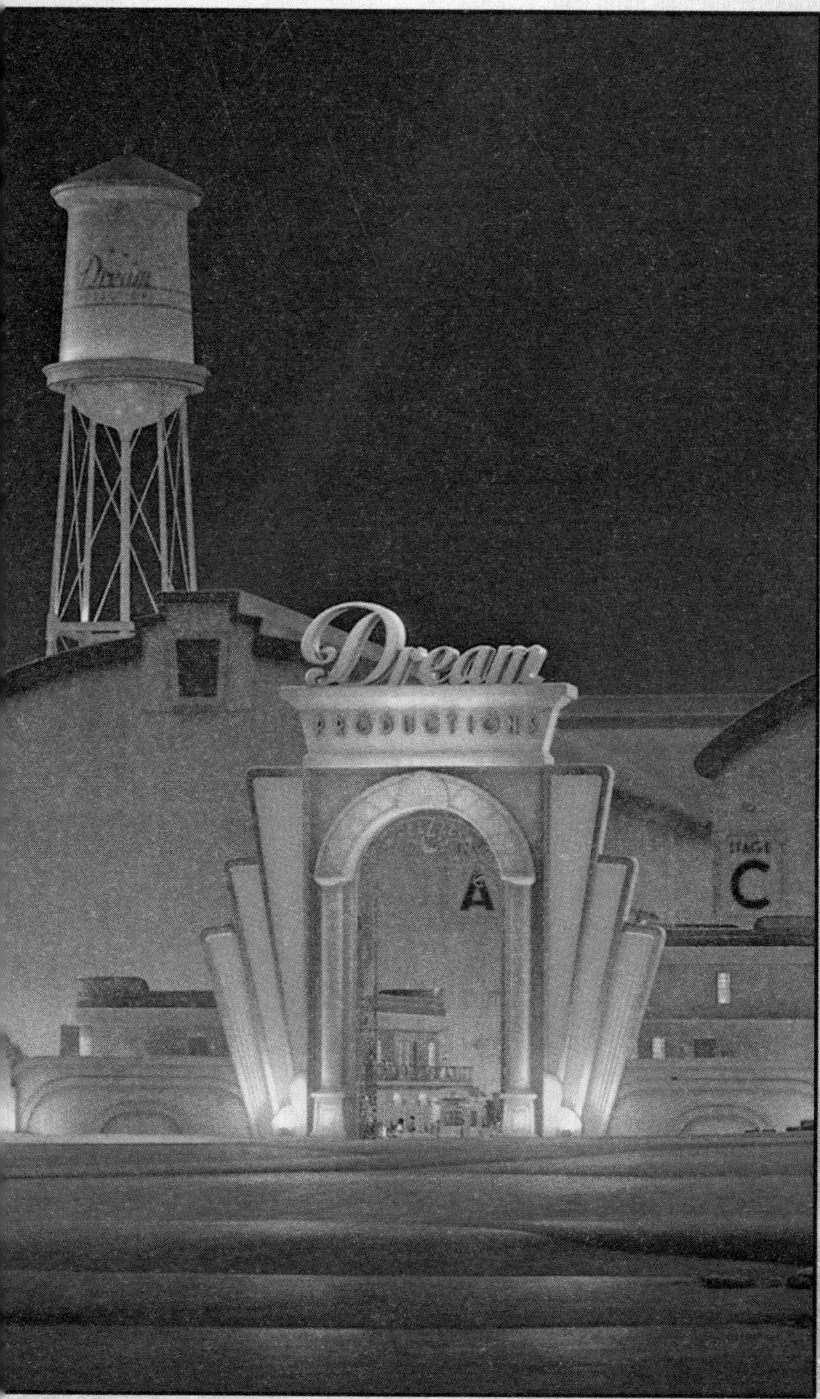
Dream
PRODUCTIONS
A
STAGE
C

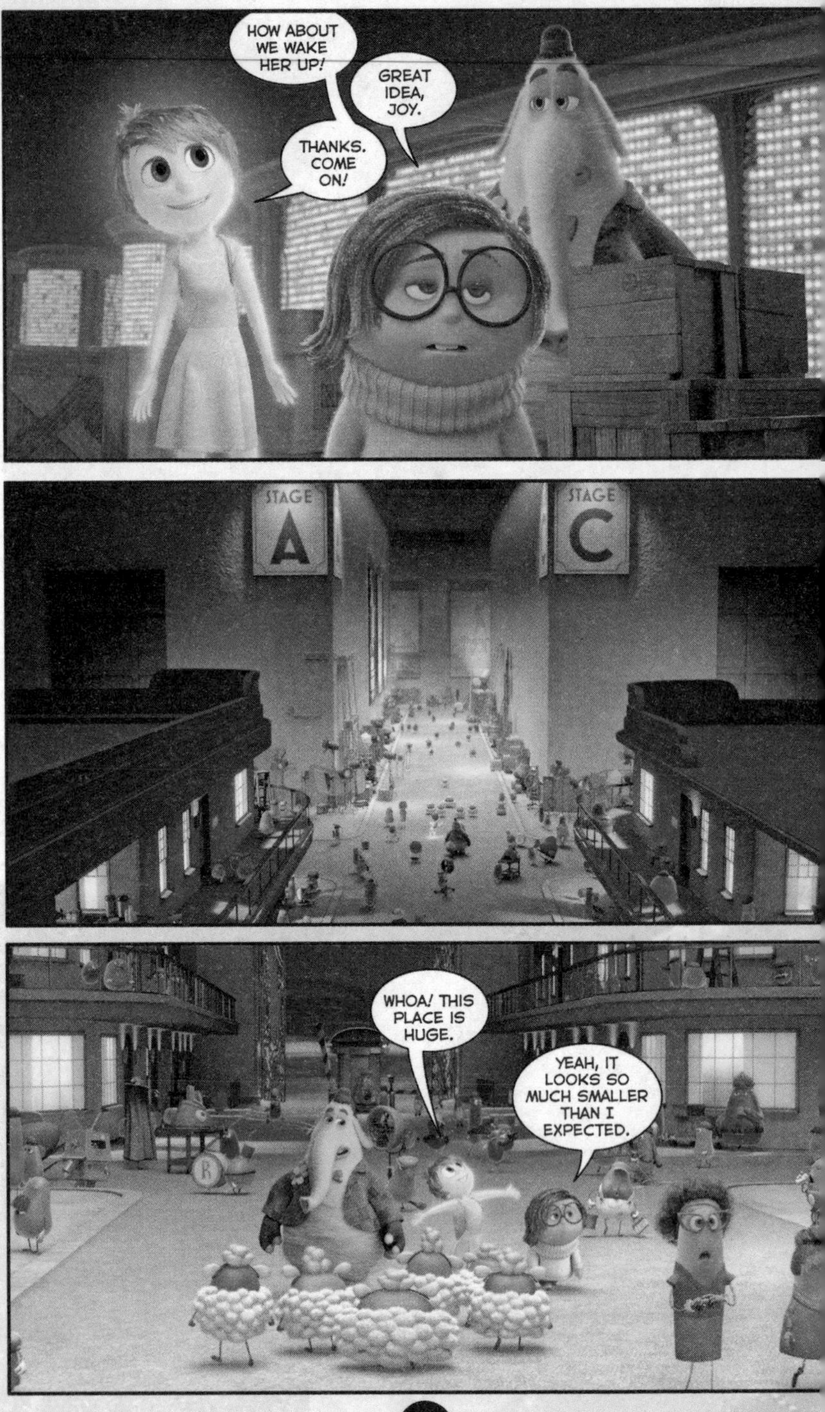
HOW ABOUT WE WAKE HER UP!
GREAT IDEA, JOY.
THANKS. COME ON!
STAGE A
STAGE C
WHOA! THIS PLACE IS HUGE.
YEAH, IT LOOKS SO MUCH SMALLER THAN I EXPECTED.

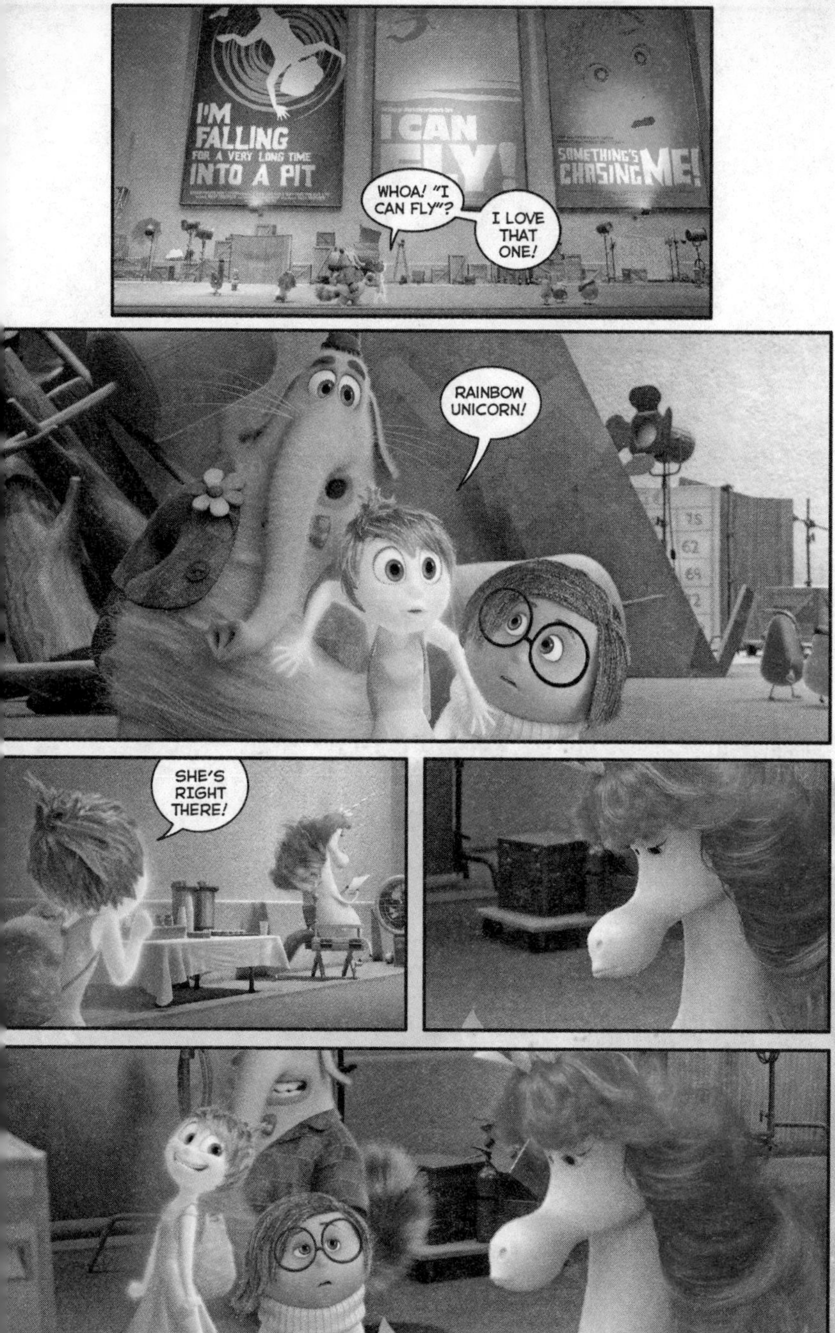
I'M FALLING
FOR A VERY LONG TIME
INTO A PIT
I CAN
SOMETHING'S CHASING ME!
WHOA! "I CAN FLY"?
I LOVE THAT ONE!
RAINBOW UNICORN!
SHE'S RIGHT THERE!

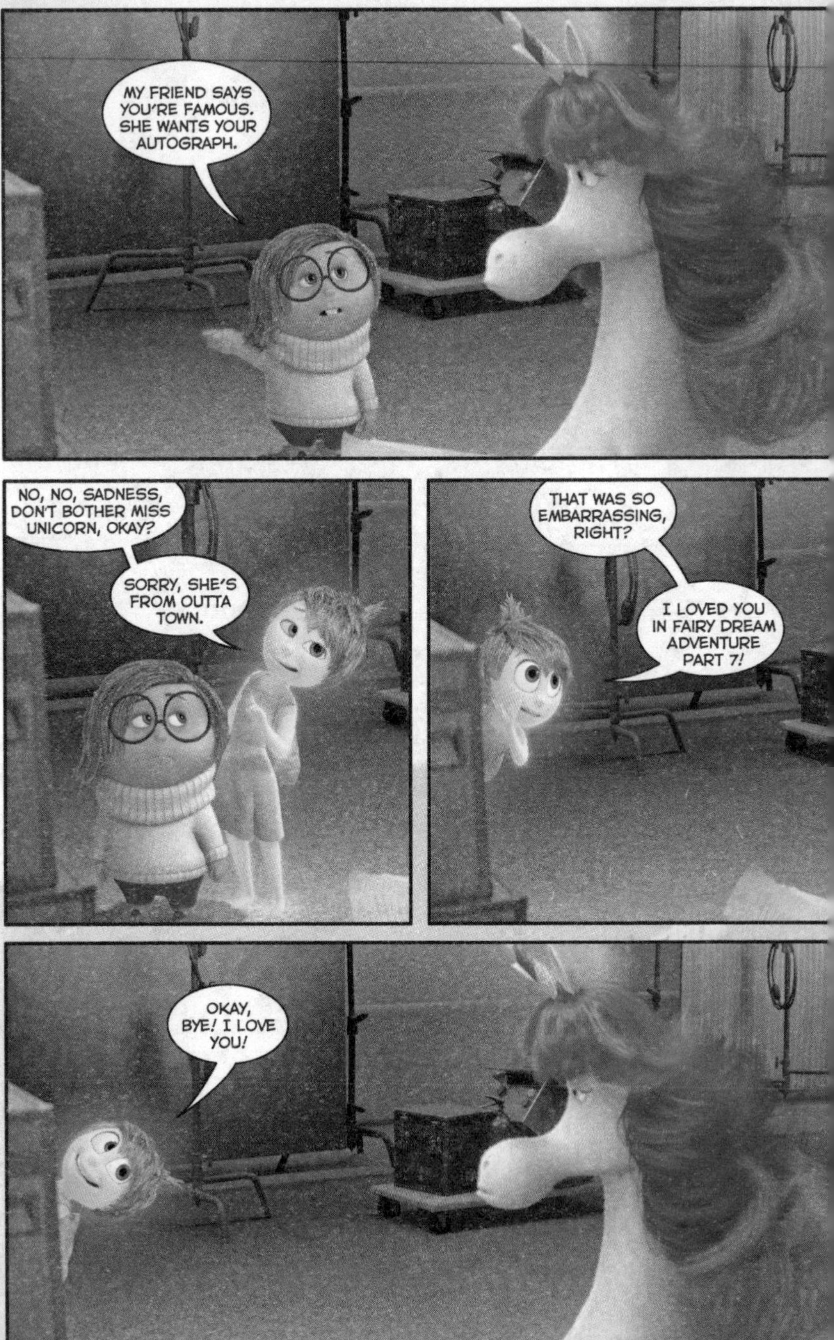
MY FRIEND SAYS YOU'RE FAMOUS. SHE WANTS YOUR AUTOGRAPH.
NO, NO, SADNESS, DON'T BOTHER MISS UNICORN, OKAY?
SORRY, SHE'S FROM OUTTA TOWN.
THAT WAS SO EMBARRASSING, RIGHT?
I LOVED YOU IN FAIRY DREAM ADVENTURE PART 7!
OKAY, BYE! I LOVE YOU!

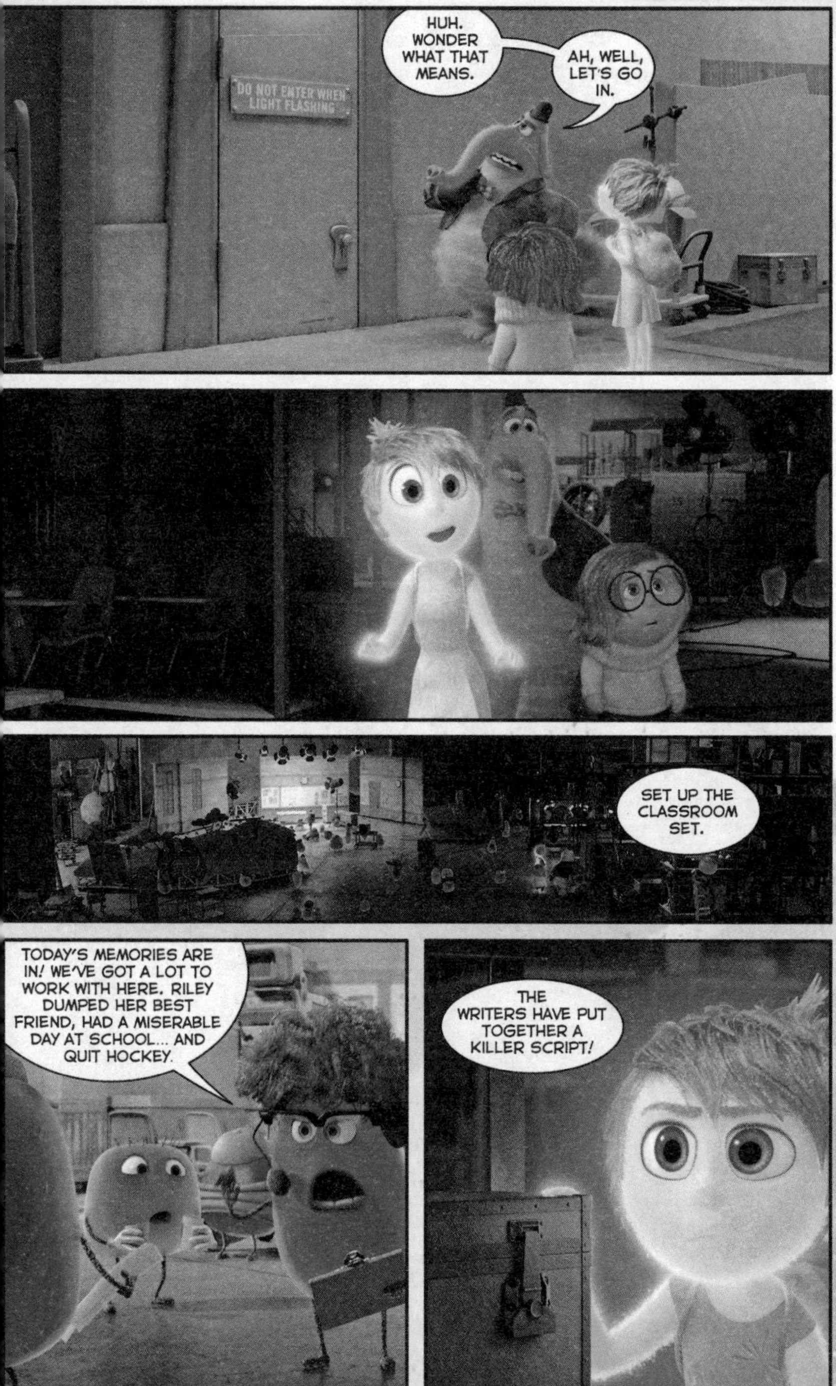
DO NOT ENTER WHEN LIGHT FLASHING
HUH. WONDER WHAT THAT MEANS.
AH, WELL, LET'S GO IN.
SET UP THE CLASSROOM SET.
TODAY'S MEMORIES ARE IN! WE'VE GOT A LOT TO WORK WITH HERE. RILEY DUMPED HER BEST FRIEND, HAD A MISERABLE DAY AT SCHOOL... AND QUIT HOCKEY.
THE WRITERS HAVE PUT TOGETHER A KILLER SCRIPT!

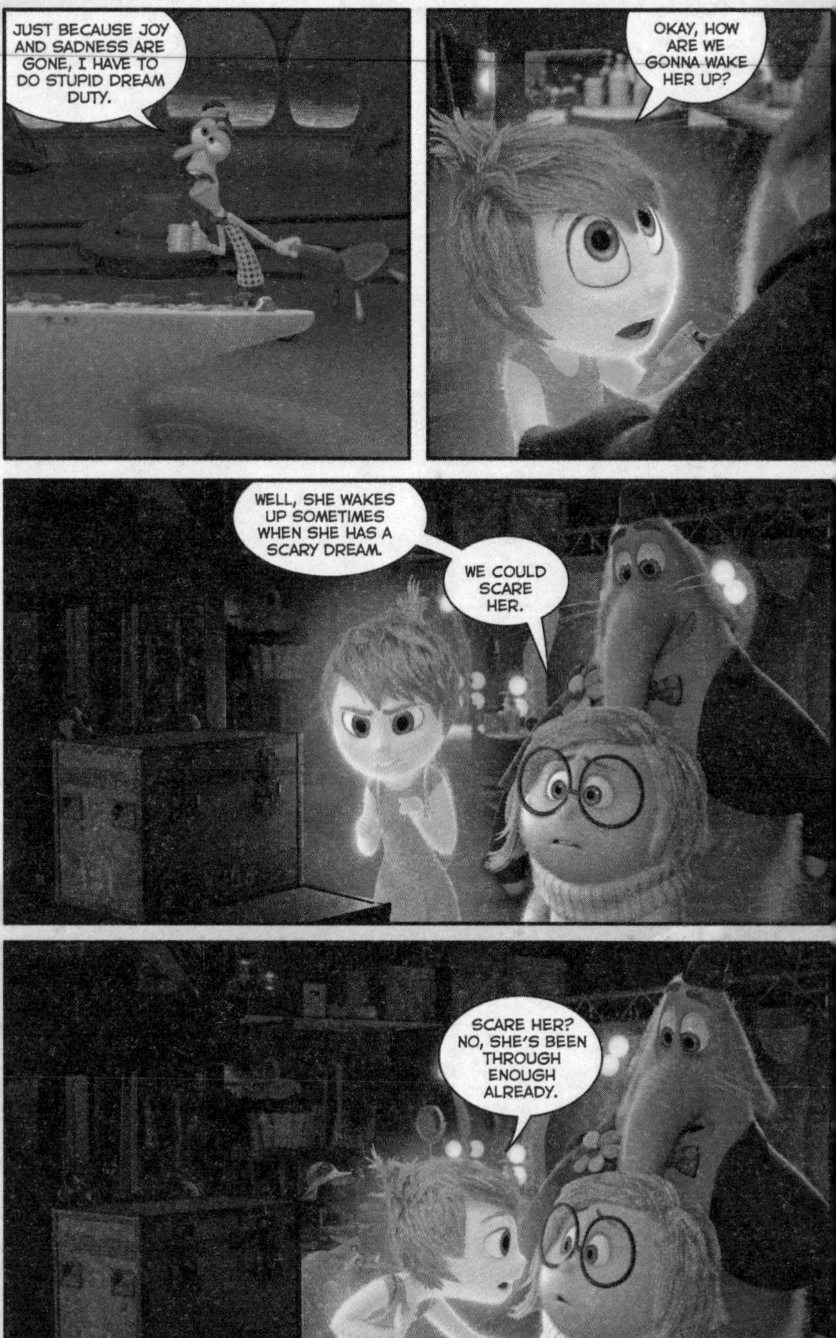
JUST BECAUSE JOY AND SADNESS ARE GONE, I HAVE TO DO STUPID DREAM DUTY.
OKAY, HOW ARE WE GONNA WAKE HER UP?
WELL, SHE WAKES UP SOMETIMES WHEN SHE HAS A SCARY DREAM.
WE COULD SCARE HER.
SCARE HER? NO, SHE'S BEEN THROUGH ENOUGH ALREADY.

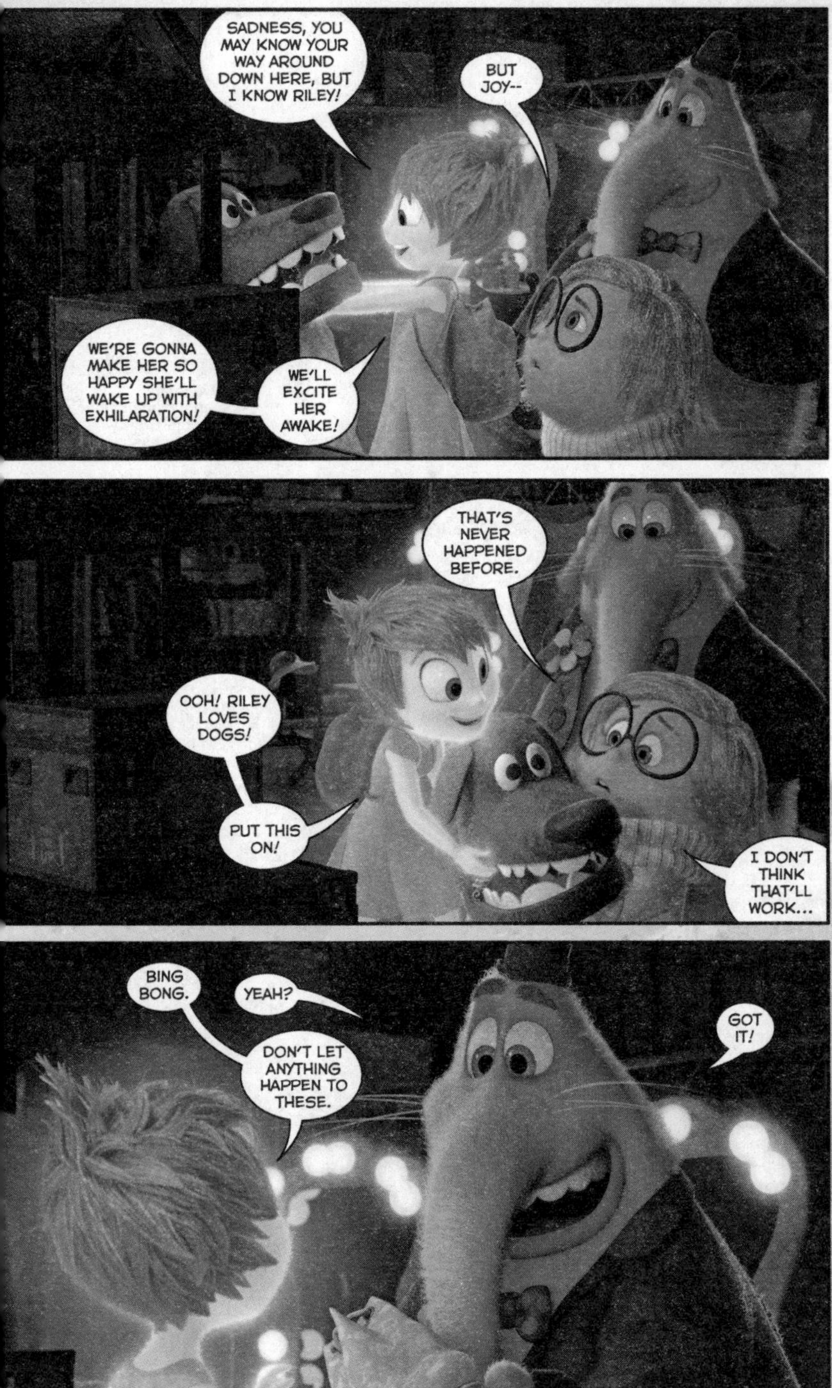
SADNESS, YOU MAY KNOW YOUR WAY AROUND DOWN HERE, BUT I KNOW RILEY!
BUT JOY--
WE'RE GONNA MAKE HER SO HAPPY SHE'LL WAKE UP WITH EXHILARATION!
WE'LL EXCITE HER AWAKE!
THAT'S NEVER HAPPENED BEFORE.
OOH! RILEY LOVES DOGS!
PUT THIS ON!
I DON'T THINK THAT'LL WORK...
BING BONG.
YEAH?
DON'T LET ANYTHING HAPPEN TO THESE.
GOT IT!

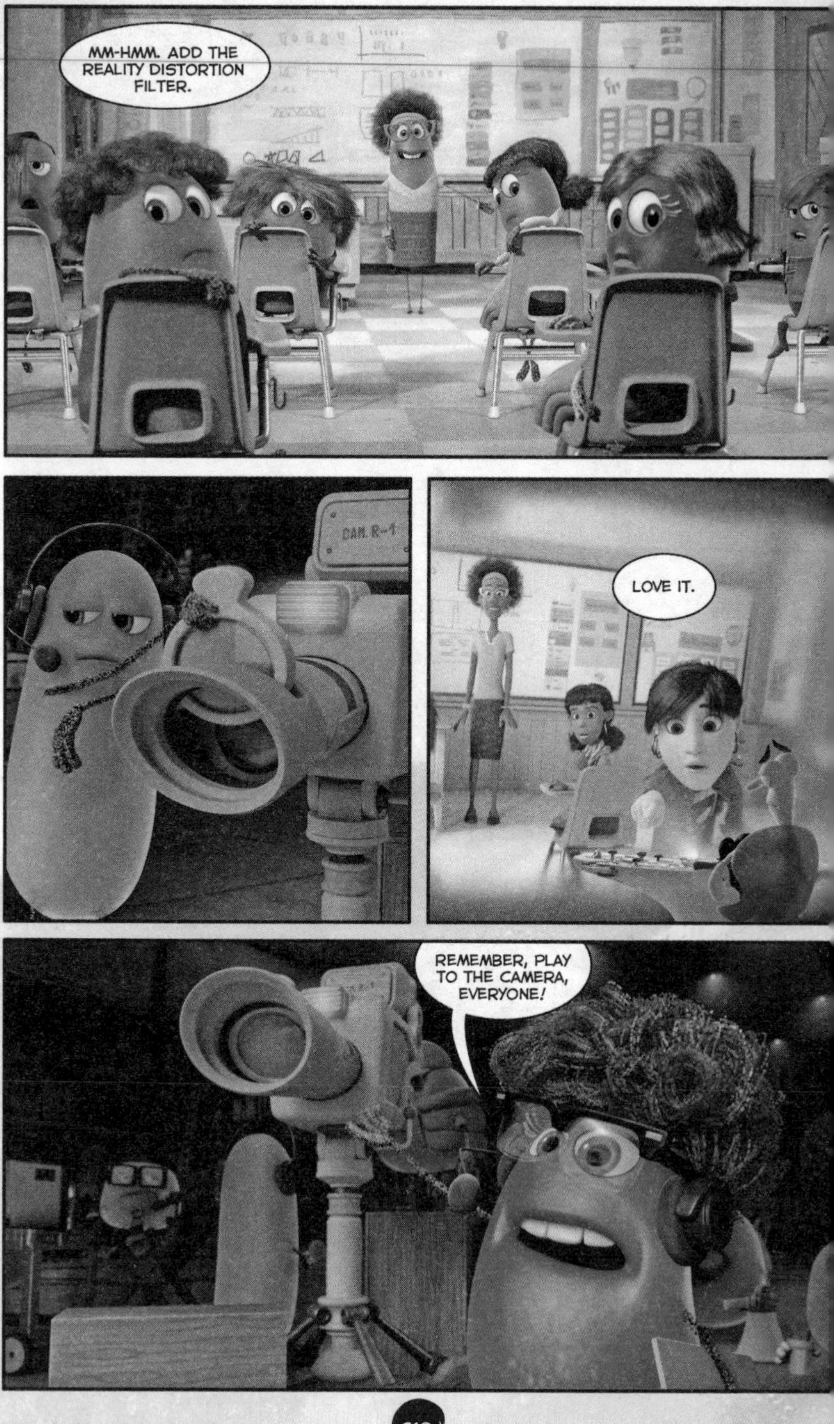
MM-HMM. ADD THE REALITY DISTORTION FILTER.
CAM. R-1
LOVE IT.
REMEMBER, PLAY TO THE CAMERA, EVERYONE!

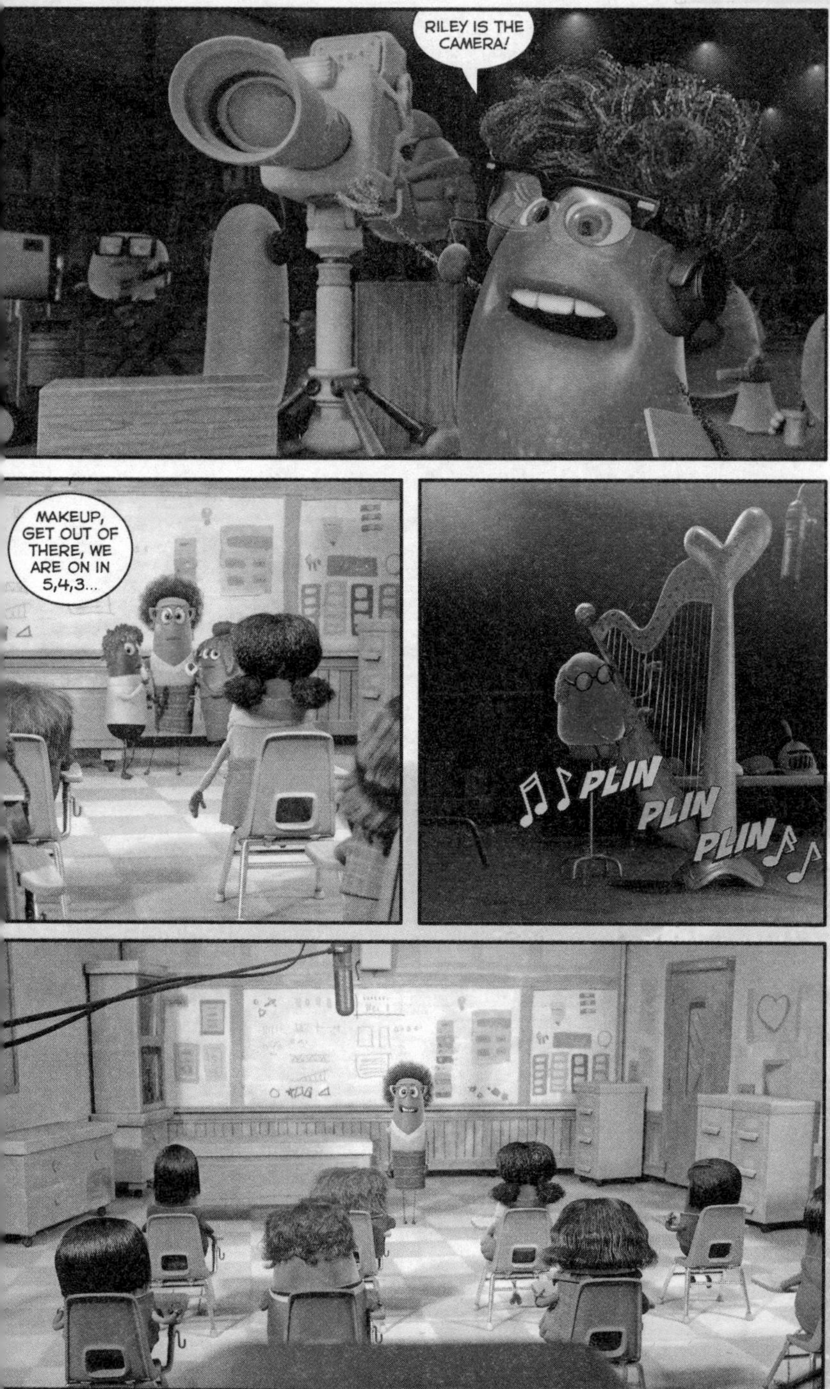
RILEY IS THE CAMERA!
MAKEUP, GET OUT OF THERE, WE ARE ON IN 5,4,3...
PLIN
PLIN
PLIN

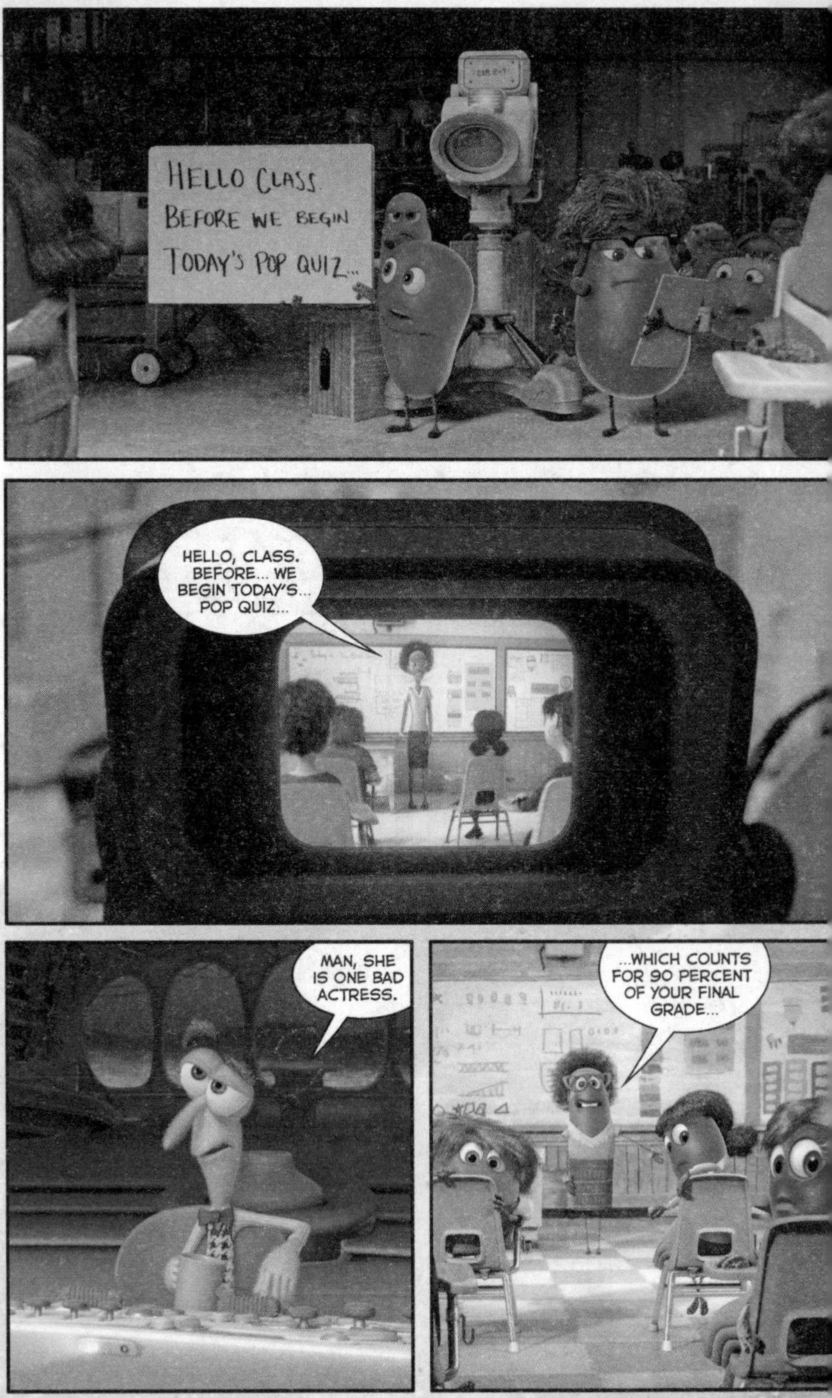
HELLO CLASS.
BEFORE WE BEGIN
TODAY'S POP QUIZ...
HELLO, CLASS. BEFORE... WE BEGIN TODAY'S... POP QUIZ...
MAN, SHE IS ONE BAD ACTRESS.
...WHICH COUNTS FOR 90 PERCENT OF YOUR FINAL GRADE...

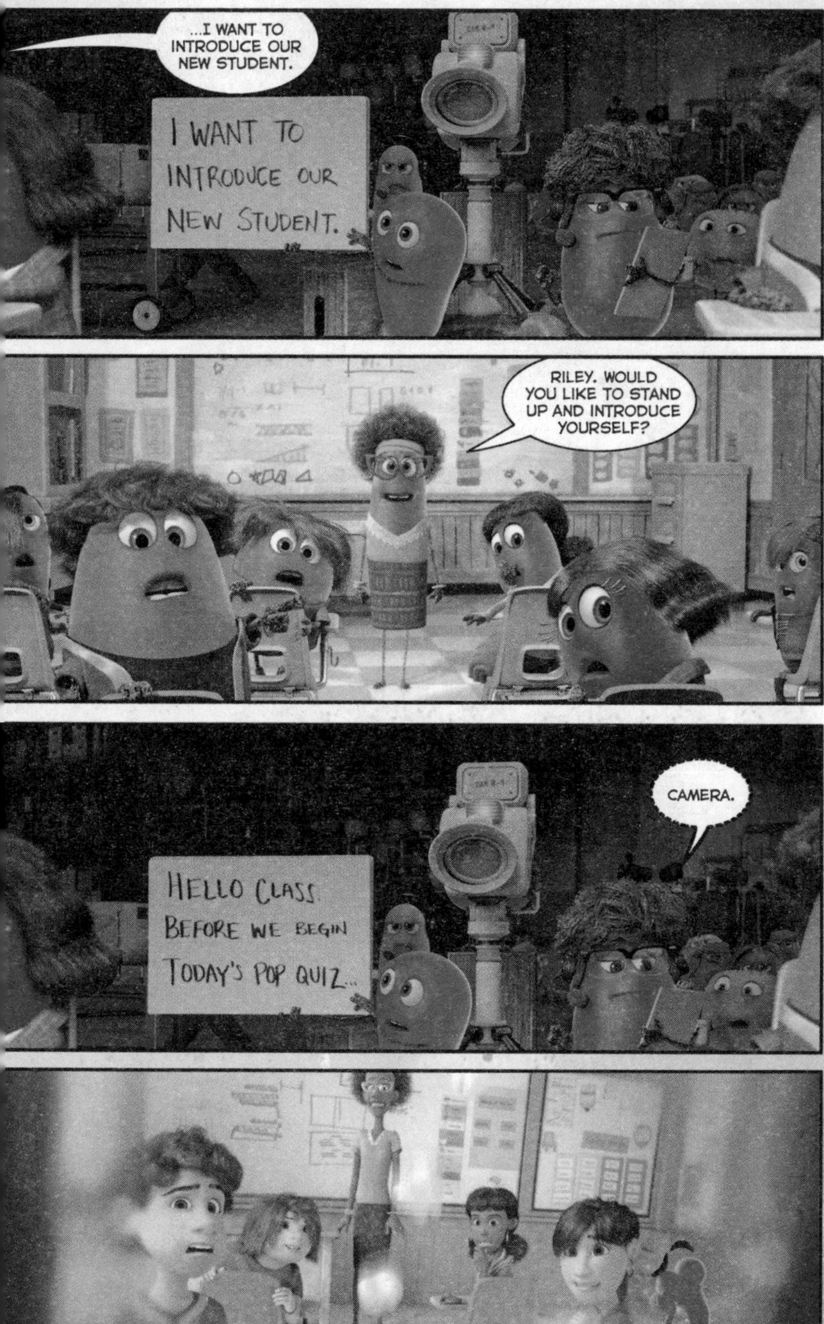
...I WANT TO INTRODUCE OUR NEW STUDENT.
I WANT TO INTRODUCE OUR NEW STUDENT.
RILEY. WOULD YOU LIKE TO STAND UP AND INTRODUCE YOURSELF?
CAMERA.
HELLO CLASS. BEFORE WE BEGIN TODAY'S POP QUIZ...

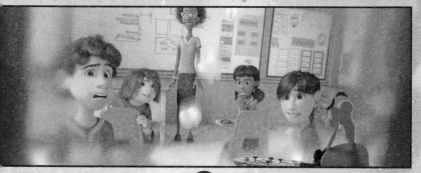

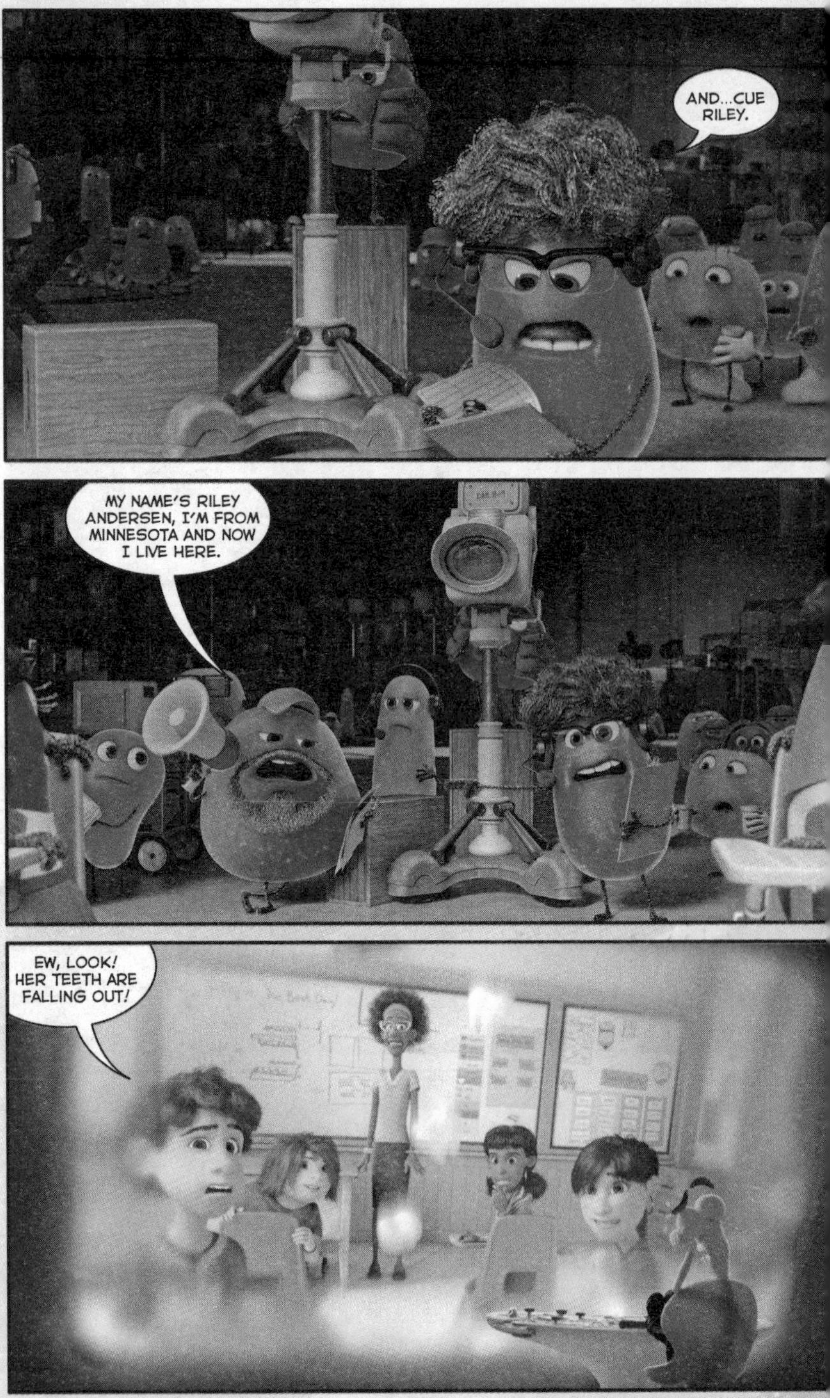
AND...CUE RILEY.
MY NAME'S RILEY ANDERSEN, I'M FROM MINNESOTA AND NOW I LIVE HERE.
EW, LOOK! HER TEETH ARE FALLING OUT!

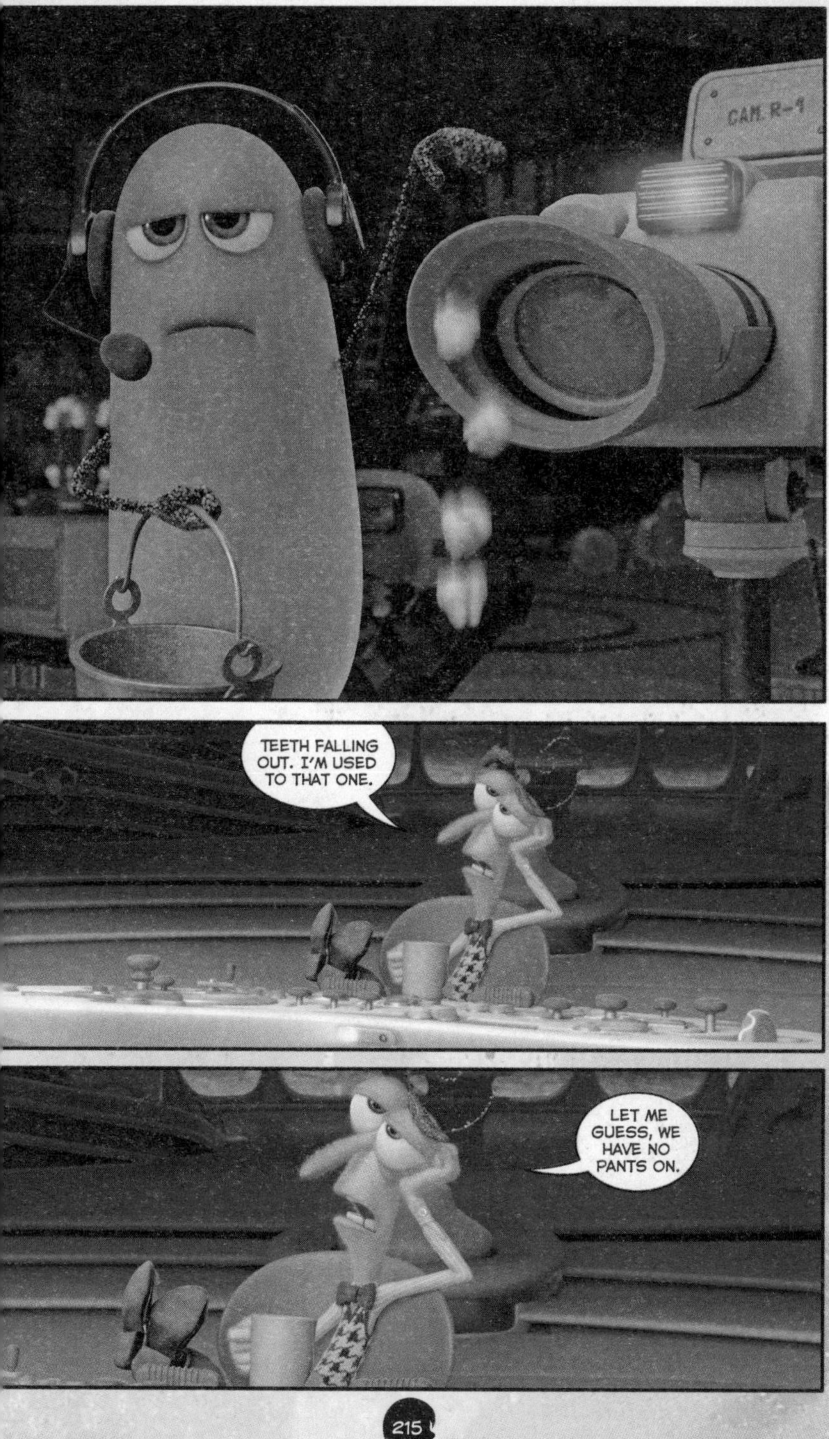
CAM. R-1
TEETH FALLING OUT. I'M USED TO THAT ONE.
LET ME GUESS, WE HAVE NO PANTS ON.

HEY, LOOK! SHECAME TO SCHOOL WITH NO PANTS ON!
CALLED IT!
NICE!

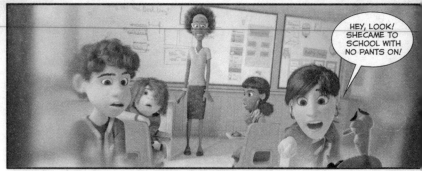

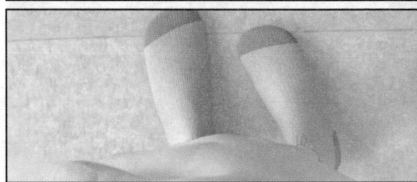

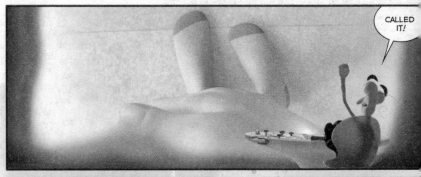

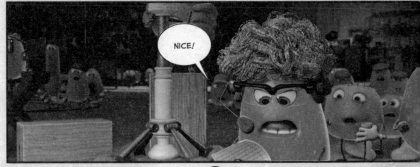

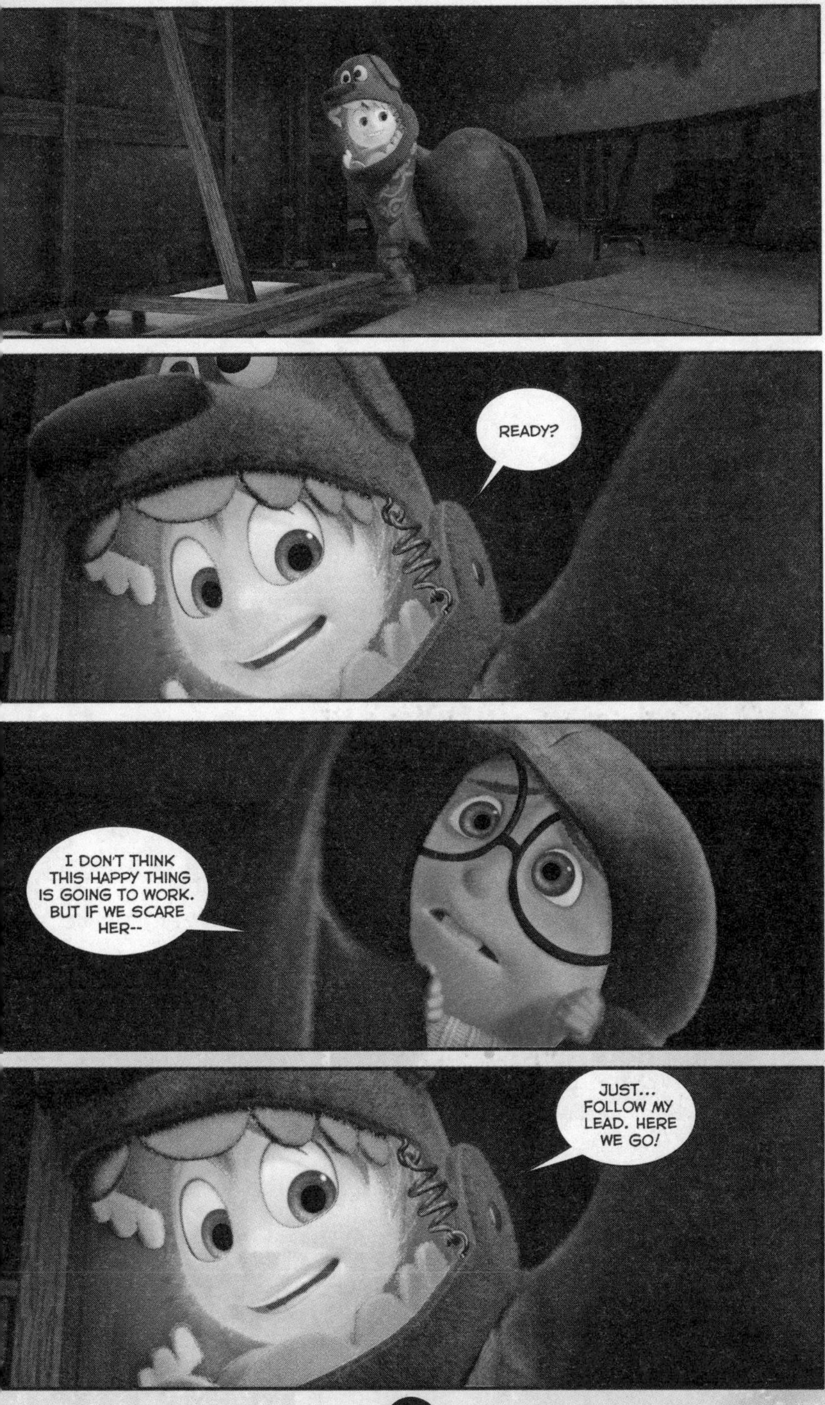
READY?
I DON'T THINK THIS HAPPY THING IS GOING TO WORK. BUT IF WE SCARE HER--
JUST... FOLLOW MY LEAD. HERE WE GO!

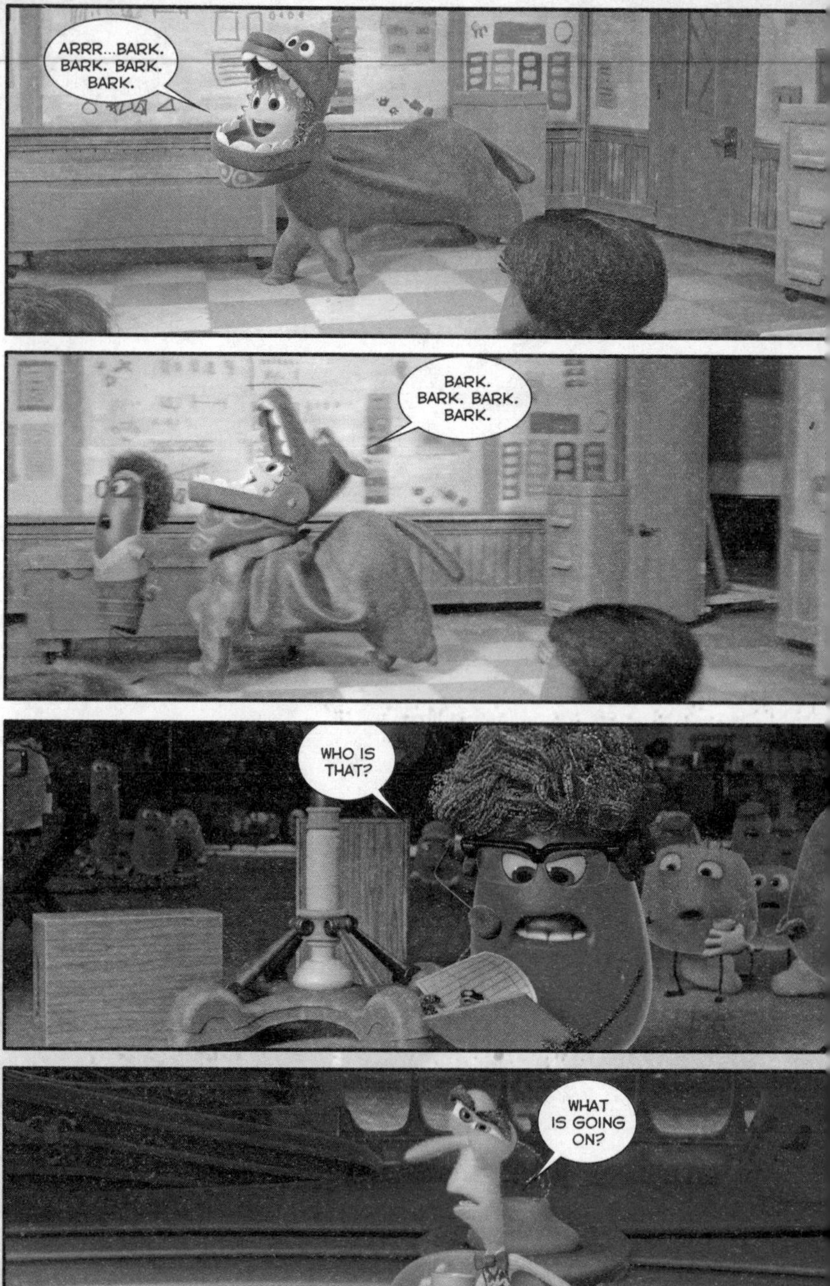
ARRR...BARK. BARK. BARK. BARK.
BARK. BARK. BARK. BARK.
WHO IS THAT?
WHAT IS GOING ON?

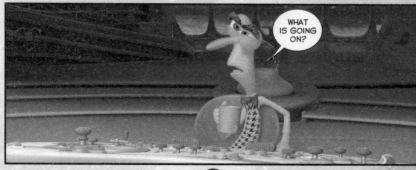

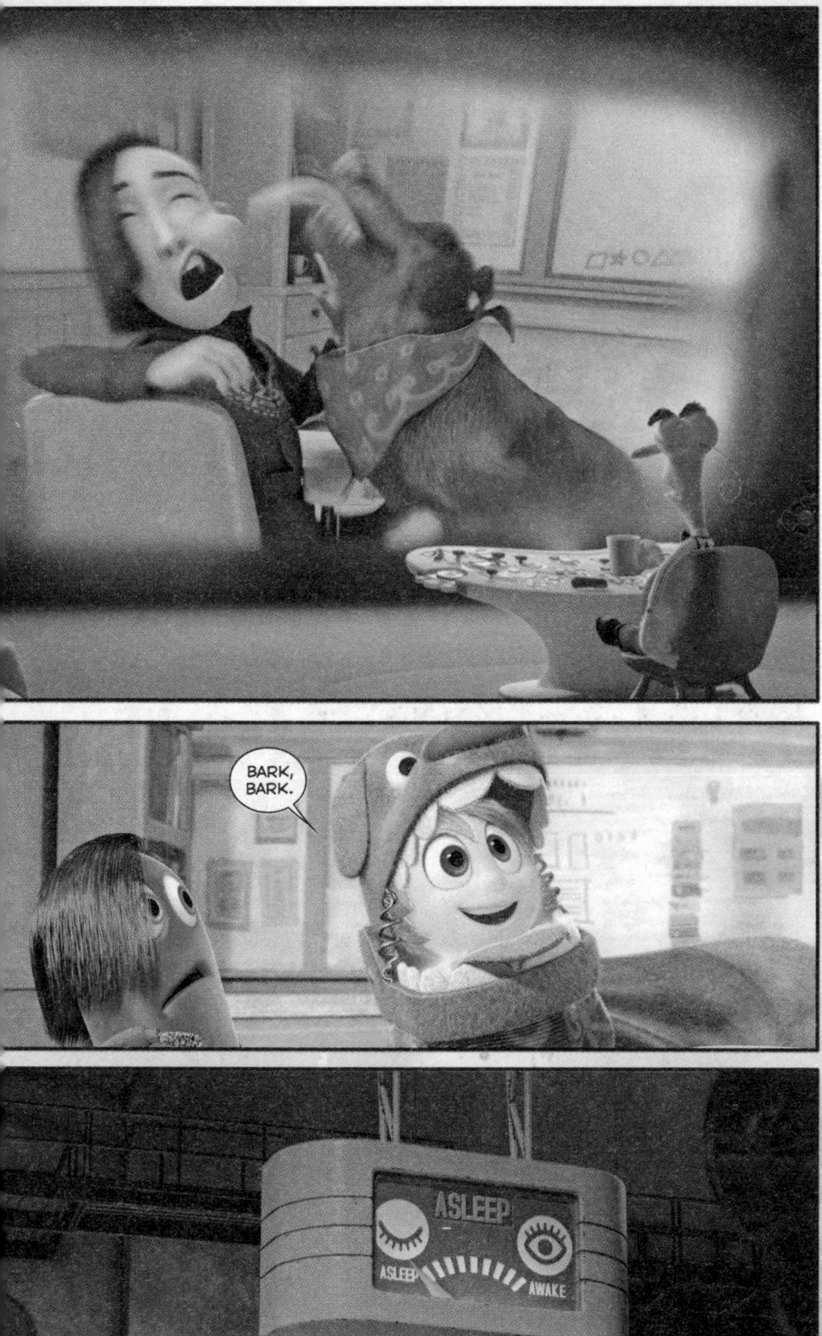
BARK, BARK.
ASLEEP
ASLEEP
AWAKE

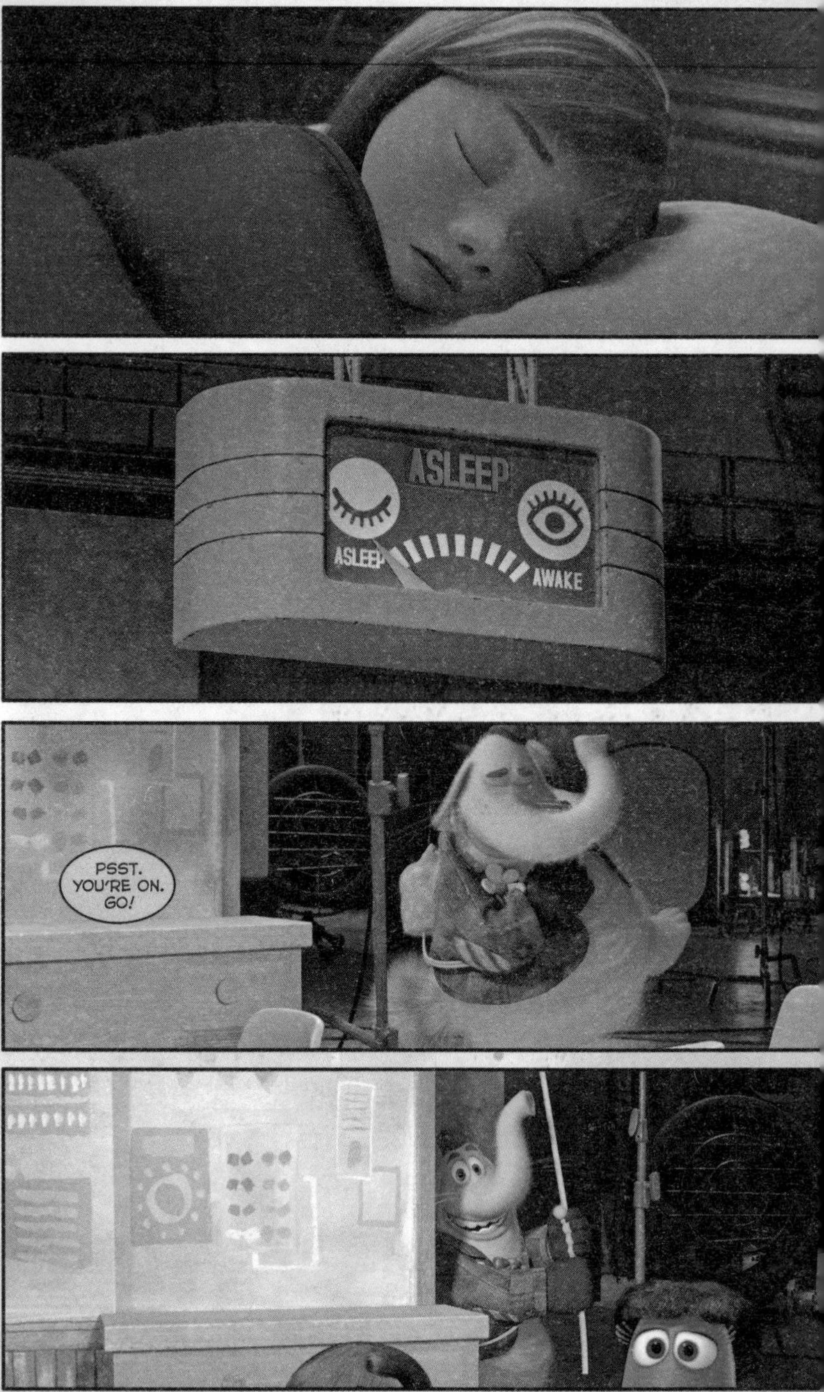
ASLEEP
ASLEEP
AWAKE
PSST. YOU'RE ON. GO!

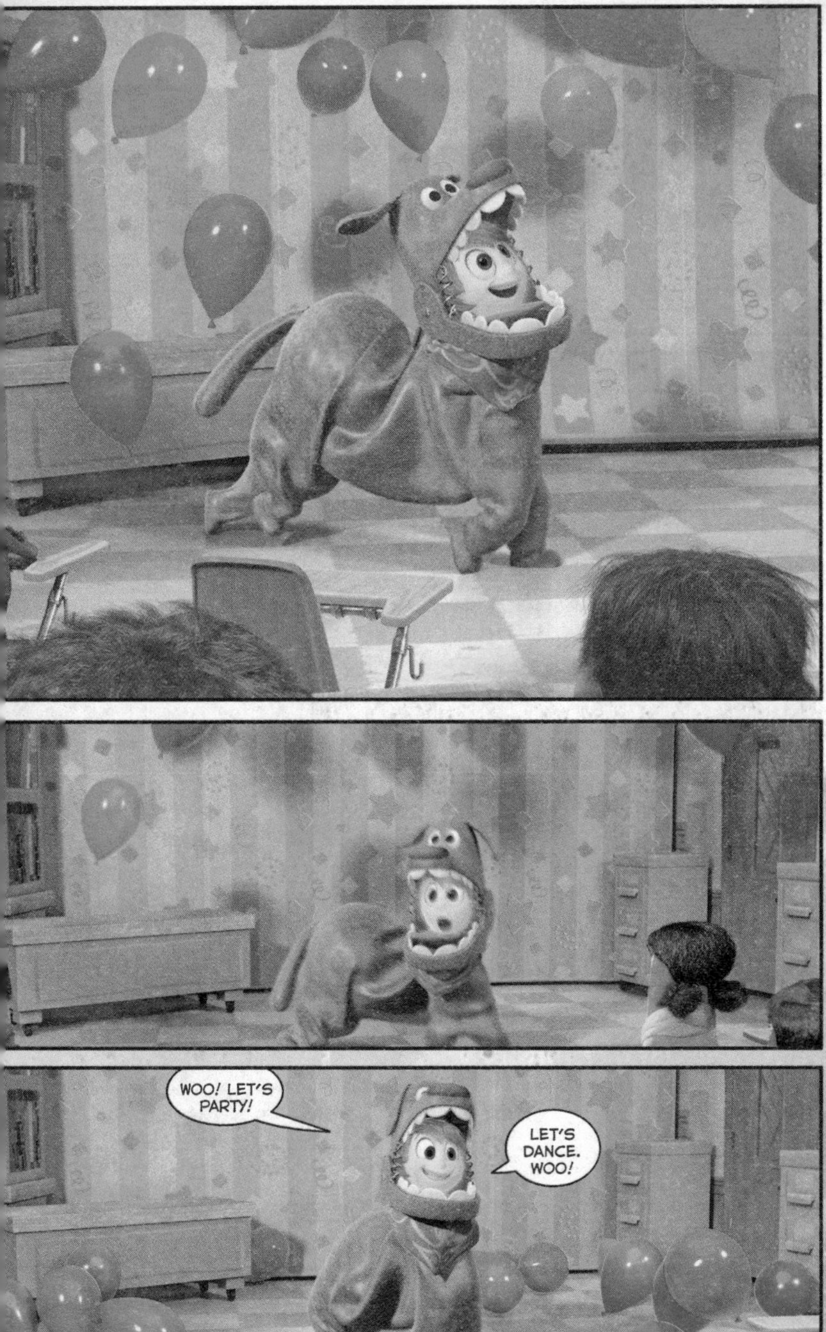
WOO! LET'S PARTY!
LET'S DANCE. WOO!

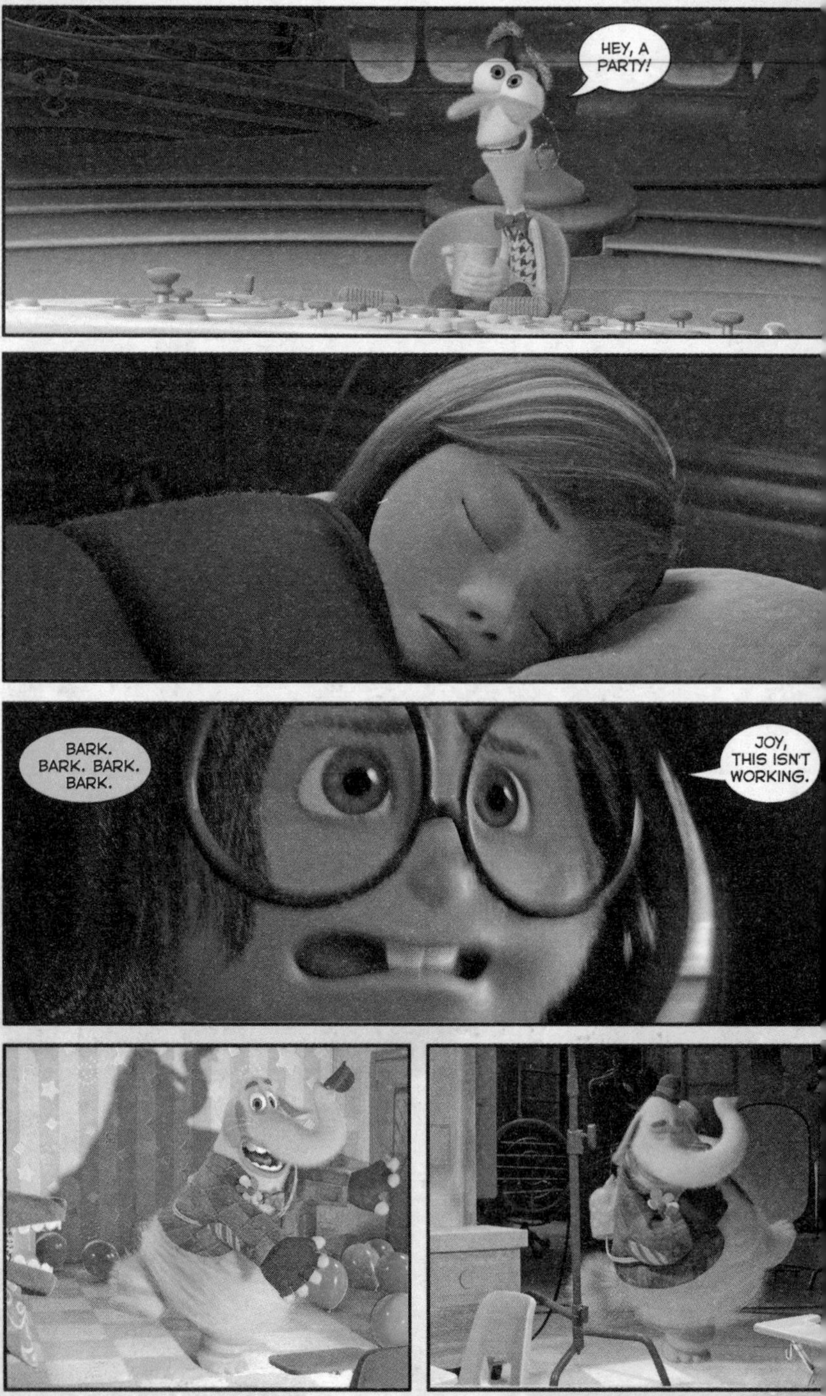
HEY, A PARTY!
BARK. BARK. BARK. BARK.
JOY, THIS ISN'T WORKING.

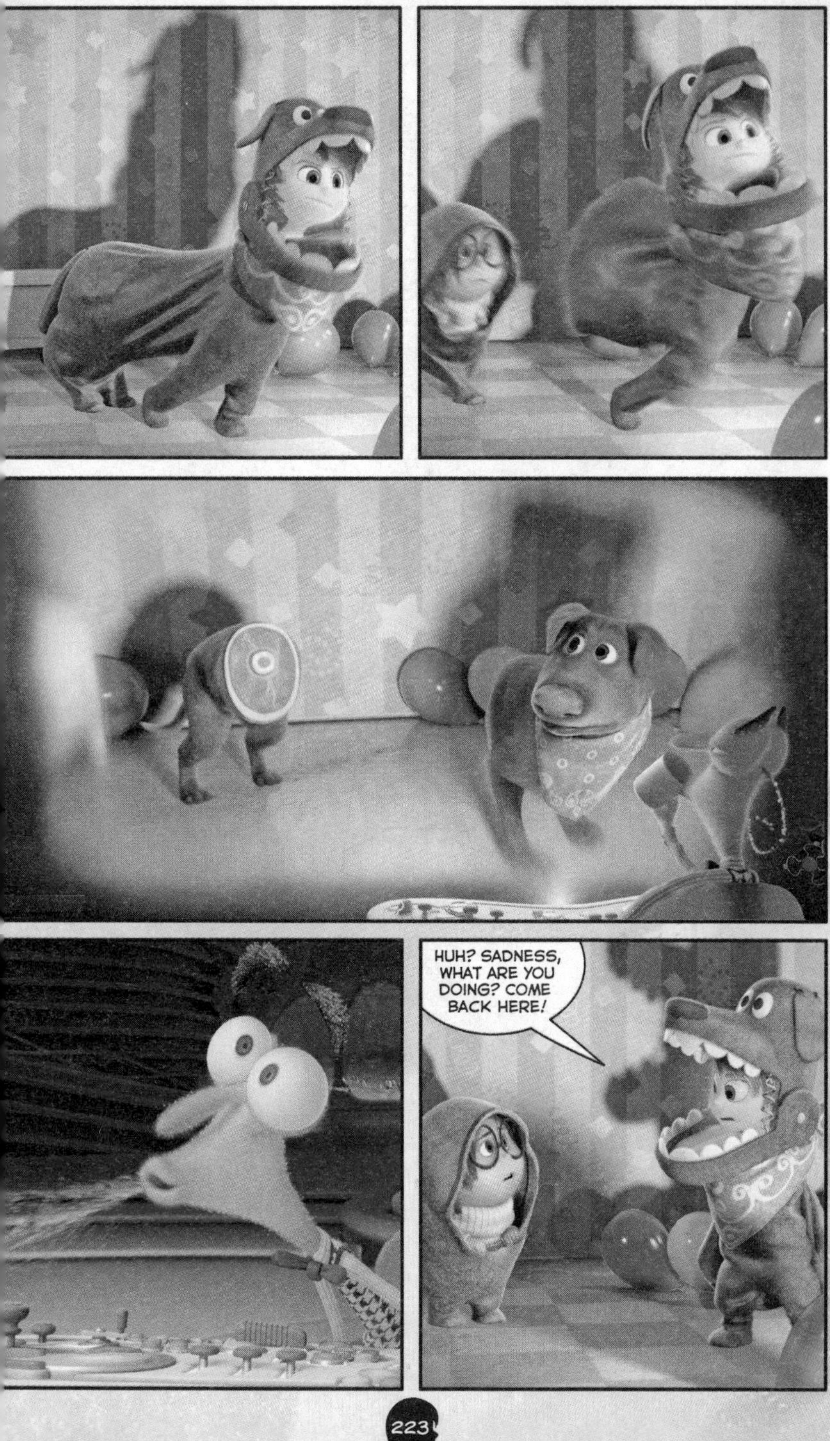
HUH? SADNESS, WHAT ARE YOU DOING? COME BACK HERE!

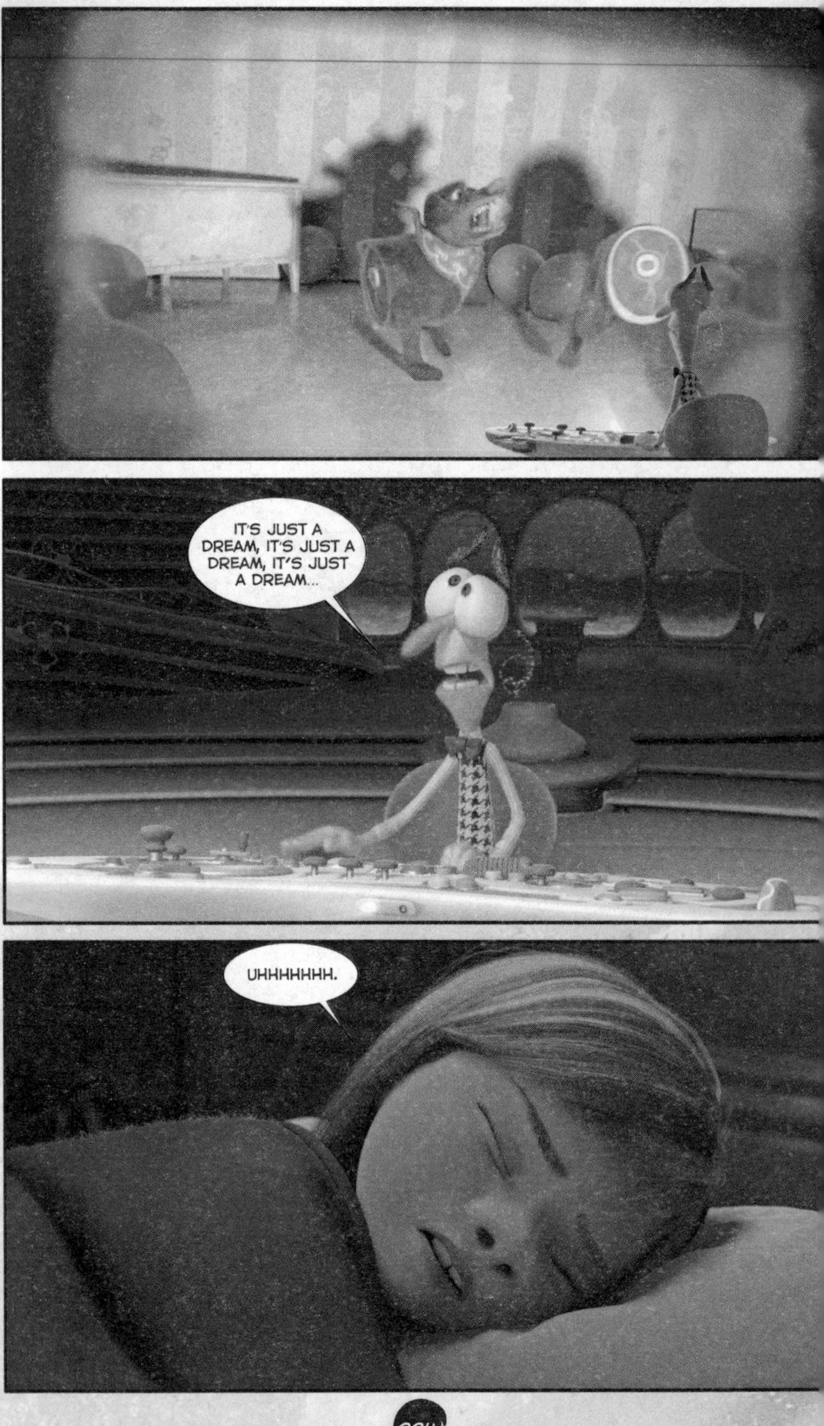
IT'S JUST A DREAM, IT'S JUST A DREAM, IT'S JUST A DREAM...
UHHHHHHH.

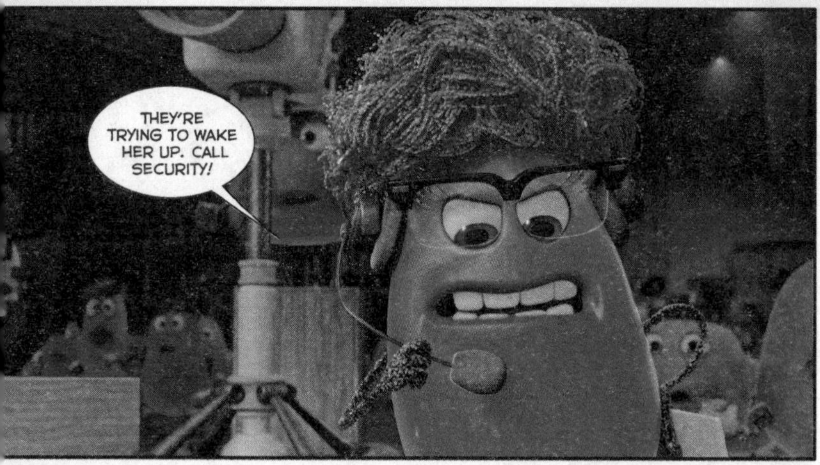
THEY'RE TRYING TO WAKE HER UP. CALL SECURITY!

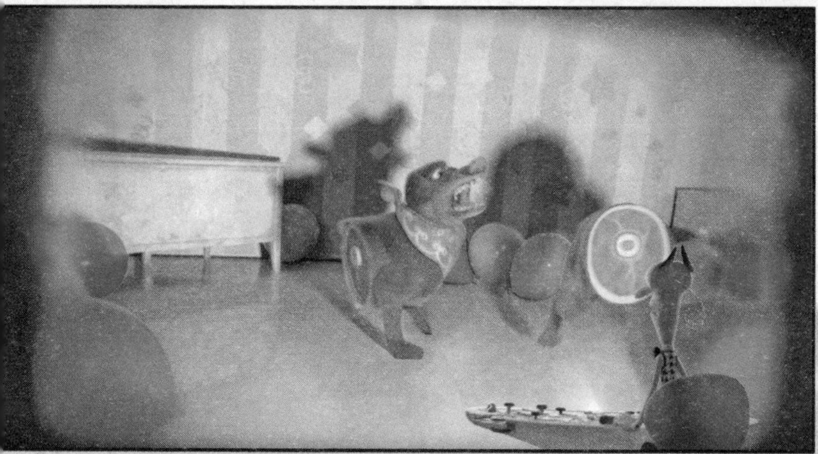

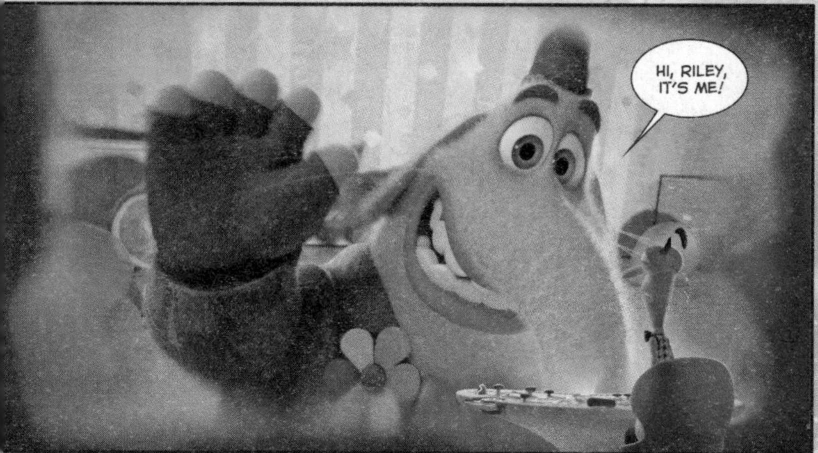
HI, RILEY, IT'S ME!

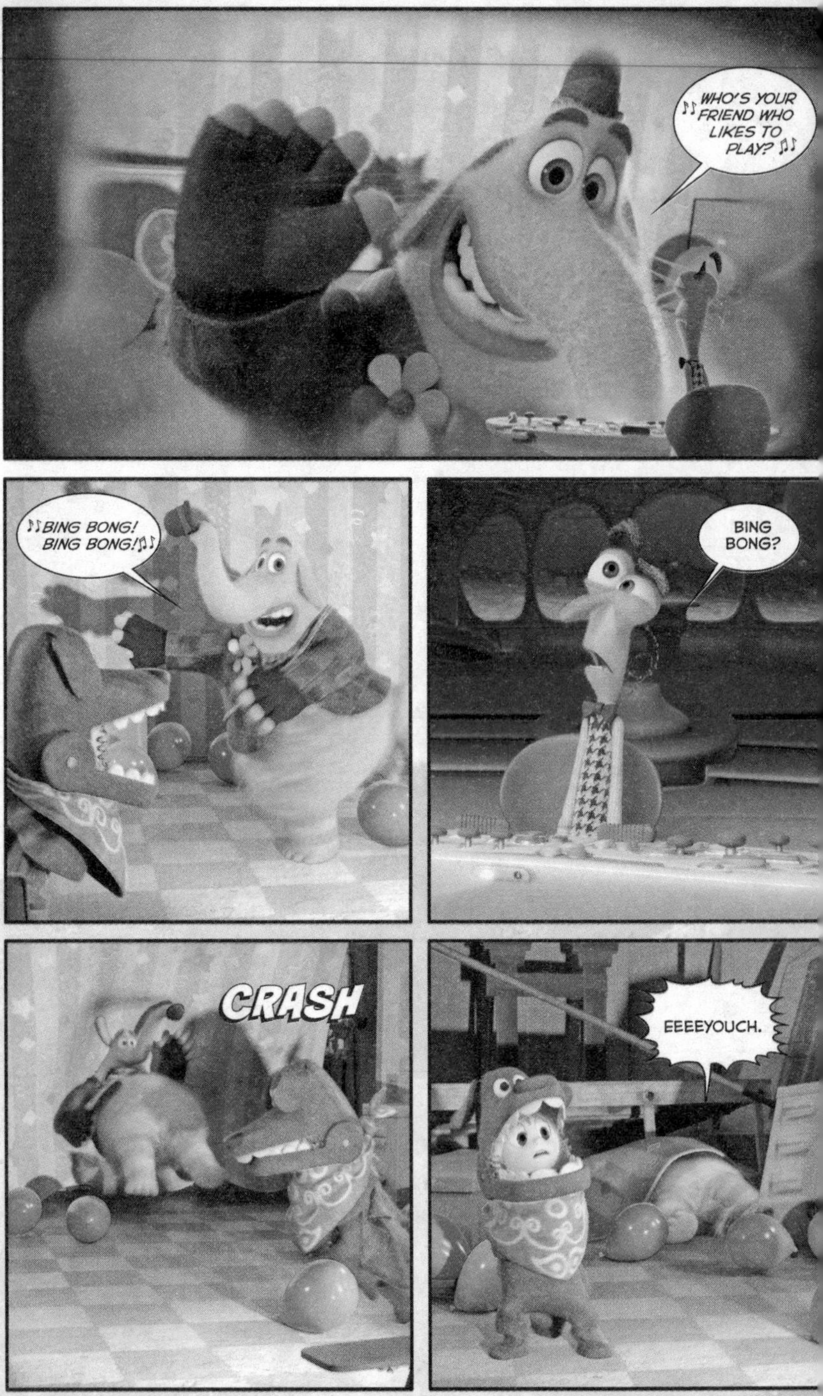
♫ WHO'S YOUR FRIEND WHO LIKES TO PLAY? ♫
♫BING BONG! BING BONG!♫
BING BONG?
CRASH
EEEEYOUCH.

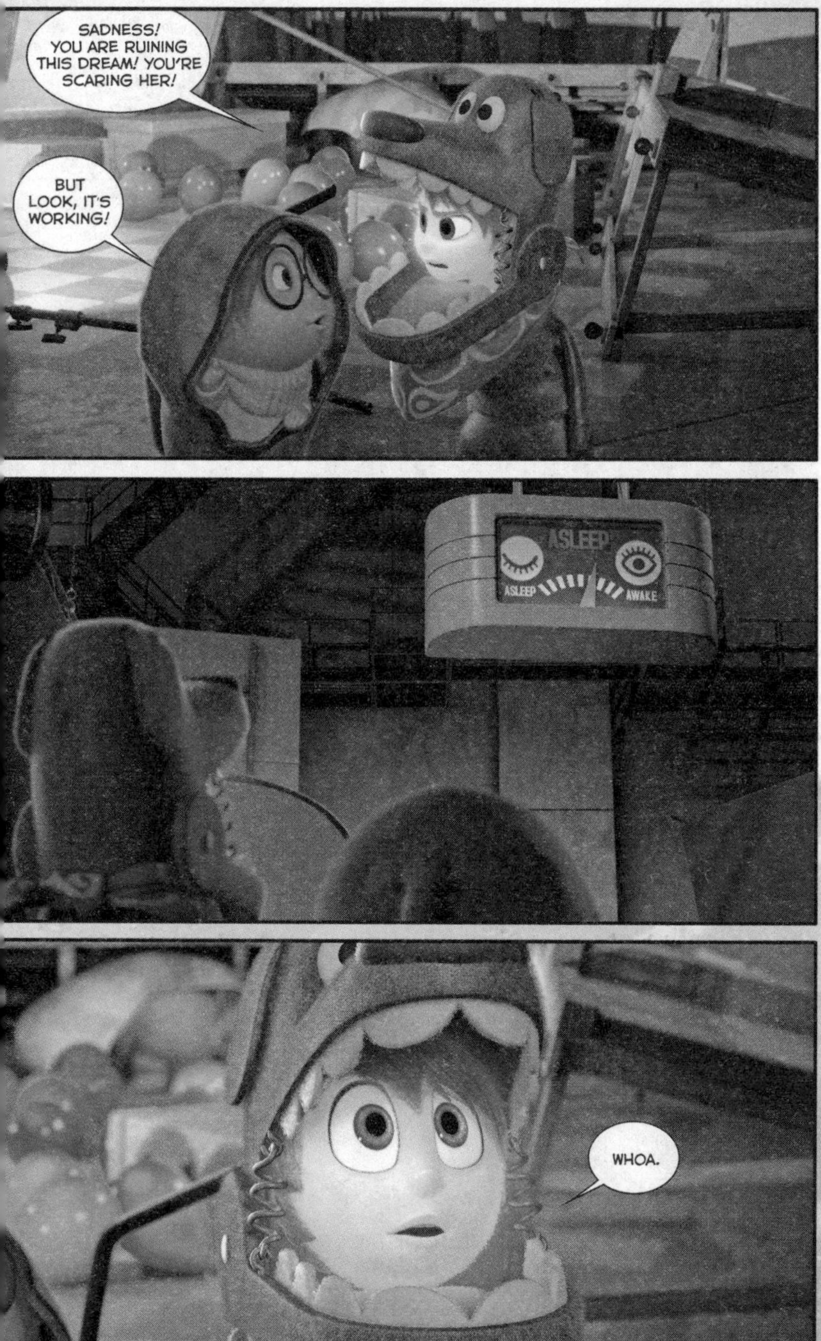
SADNESS! YOU ARE RUINING THIS DREAM! YOU'RE SCARING HER!
BUT LOOK, IT'S WORKING!
ASLEEP
ASLEEP
AWAKE
WHOA.

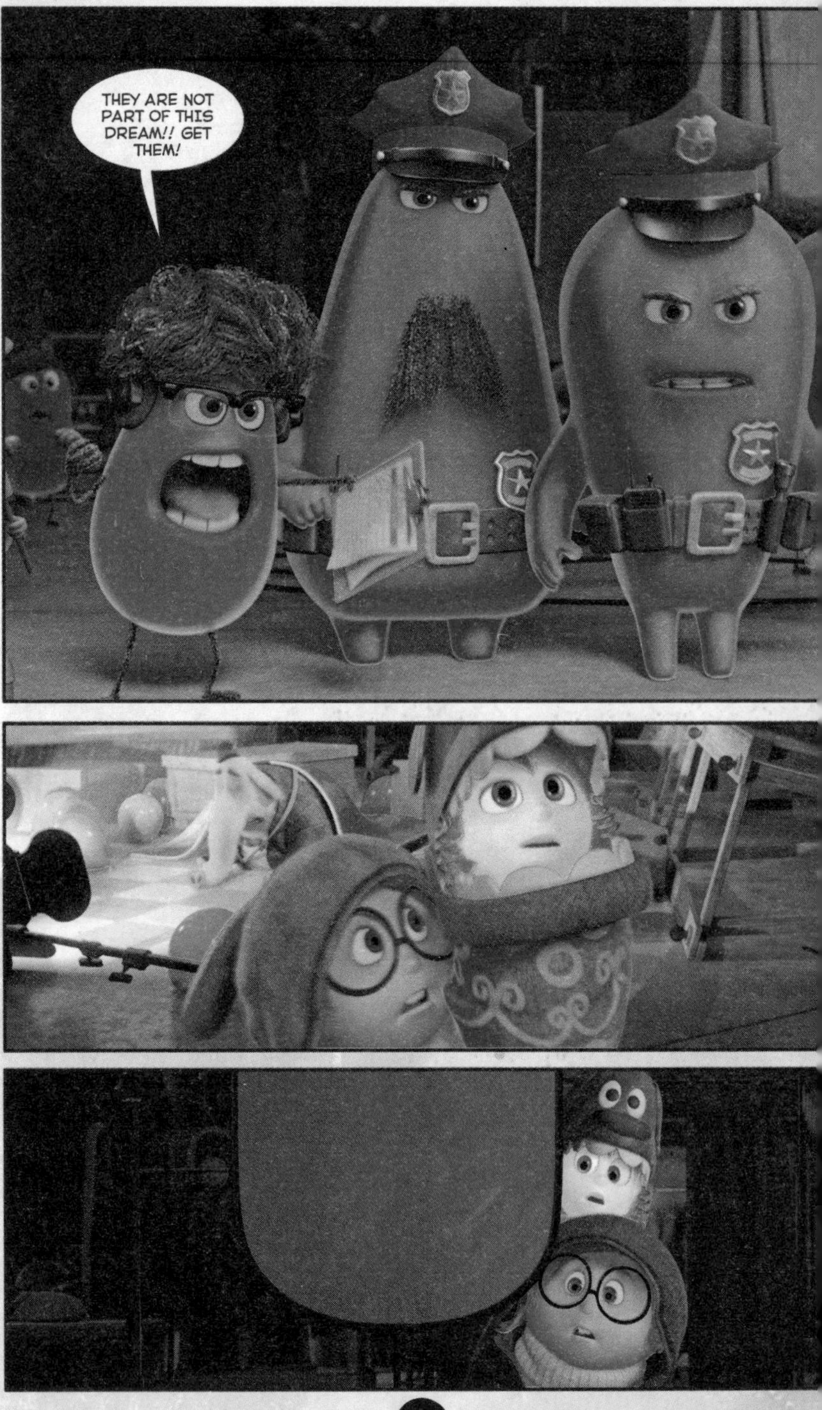
THEY ARE NOT PART OF THIS DREAM!! GET THEM!

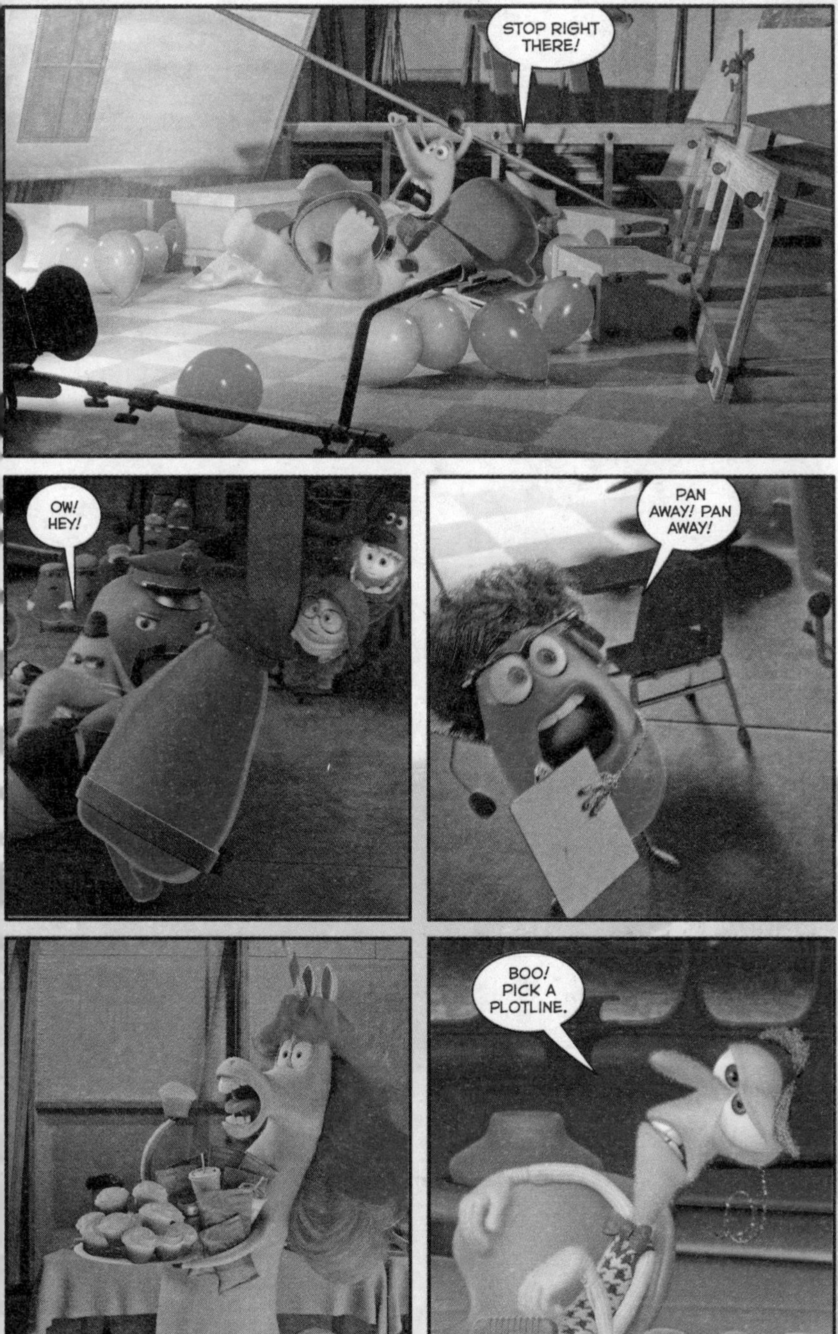
STOP RIGHT THERE!
OW! HEY!
PAN AWAY! PAN AWAY!
BOO! PICK A PLOTLINE.

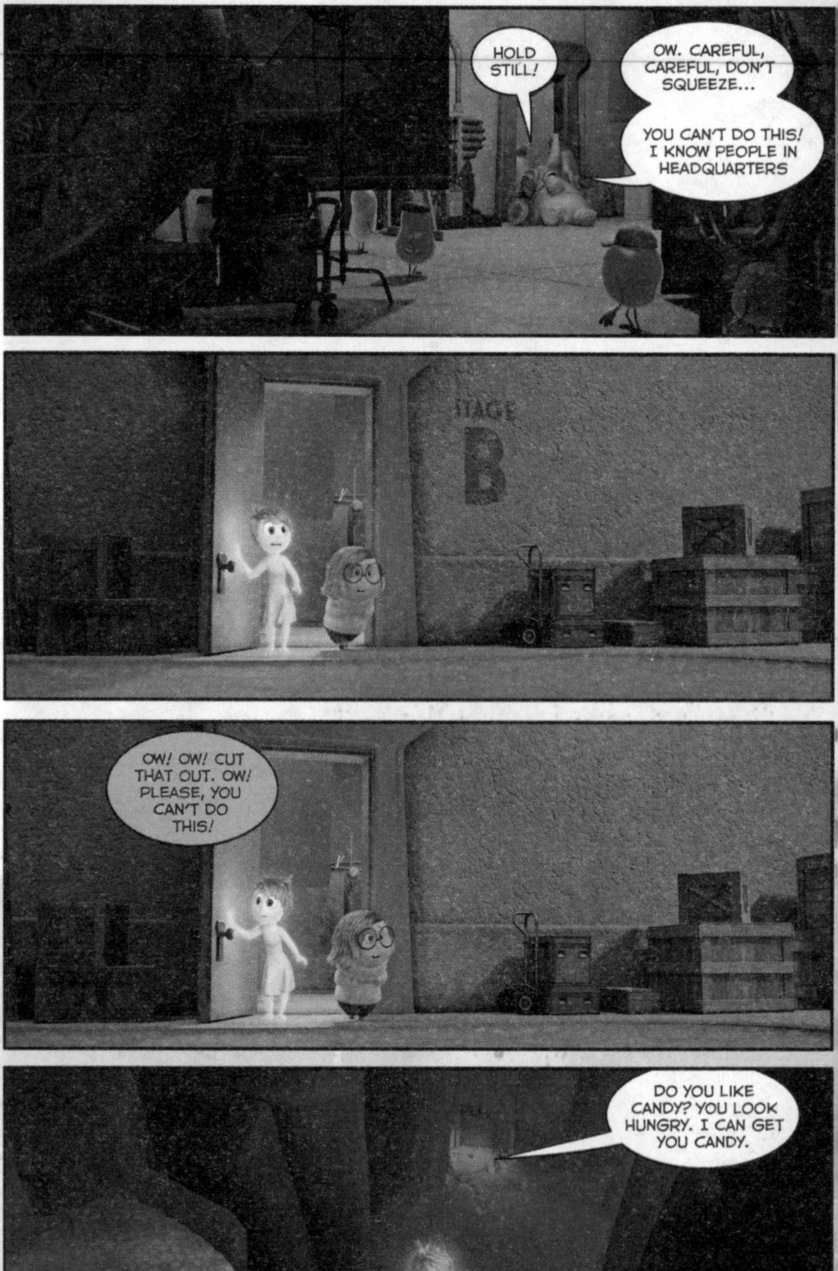
HOLD STILL!
OW. CAREFUL, CAREFUL, DON'T SQUEEZE...
YOU CAN'T DO THIS! I KNOW PEOPLE IN HEADQUARTERS
STAGE B
OW! OW! CUT THAT OUT. OW! PLEASE, YOU CAN'T DO THIS!
DO YOU LIKE CANDY? YOU LOOK HUNGRY. I CAN GET YOU CANDY.

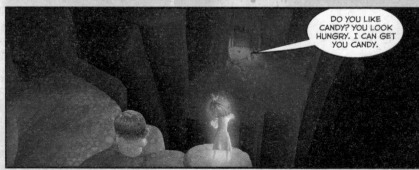

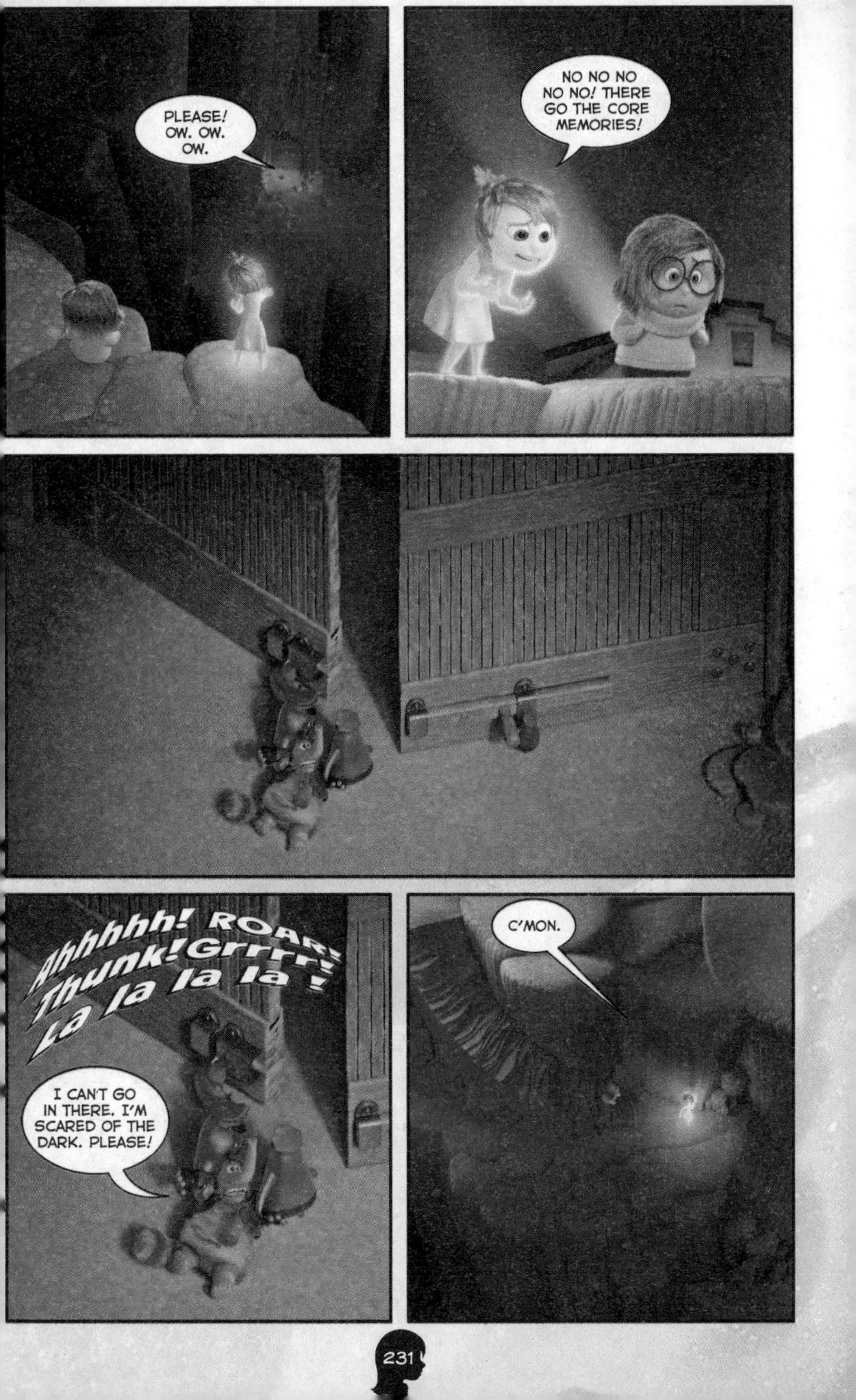
PLEASE! OW. OW. OW.
NO NO NO NO NO! THERE GO THE CORE MEMORIES!
Ahhhhh! ROAR! Thunk! Grrrrr! La la la la!
I CAN'T GO IN THERE. I'M SCARED OF THE DARK. PLEASE!
C'MON.

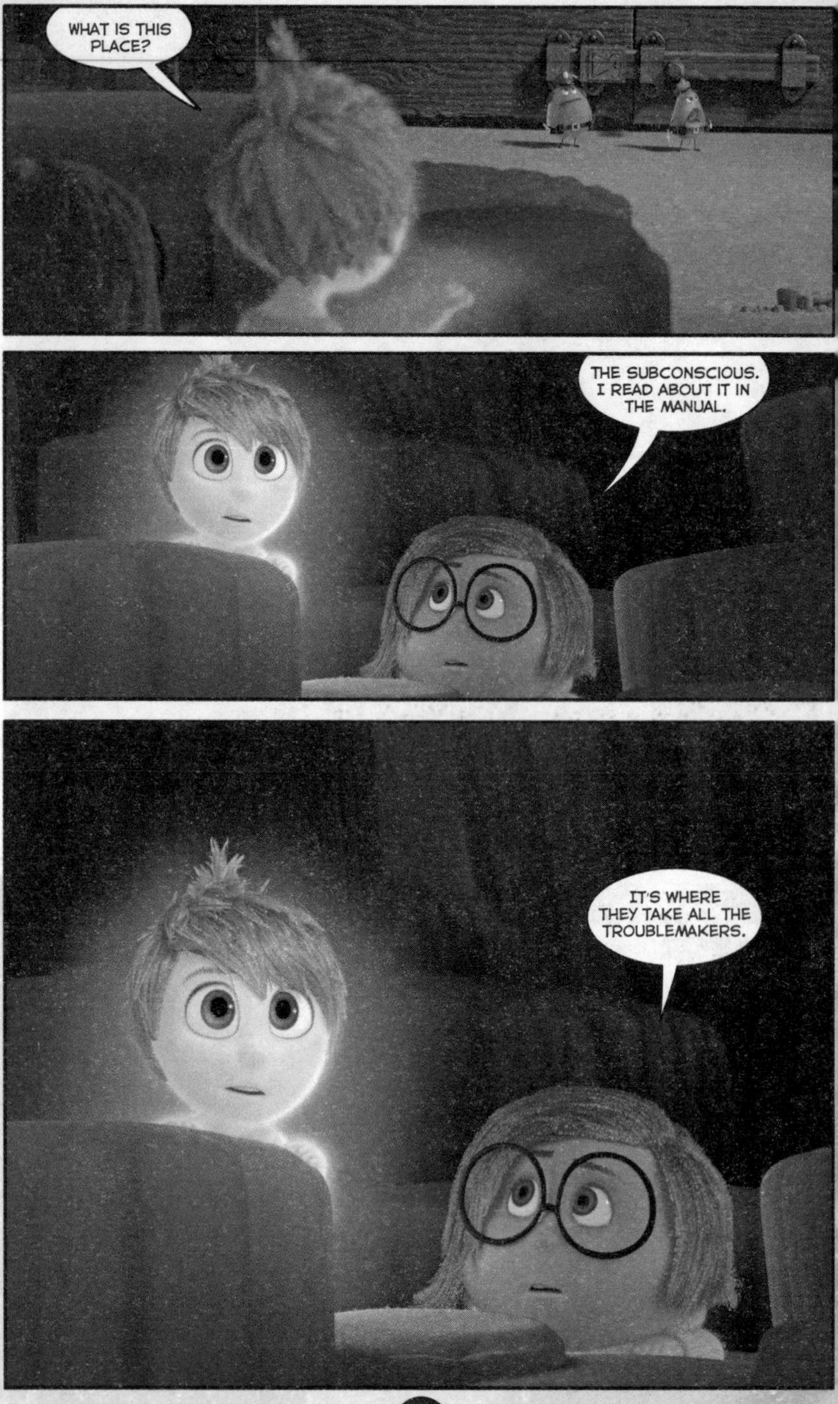
WHAT IS THIS PLACE?
THE SUBCONSCIOUS. I READ ABOUT IT IN THE MANUAL.
IT'S WHERE THEY TAKE ALL THE TROUBLEMAKERS.

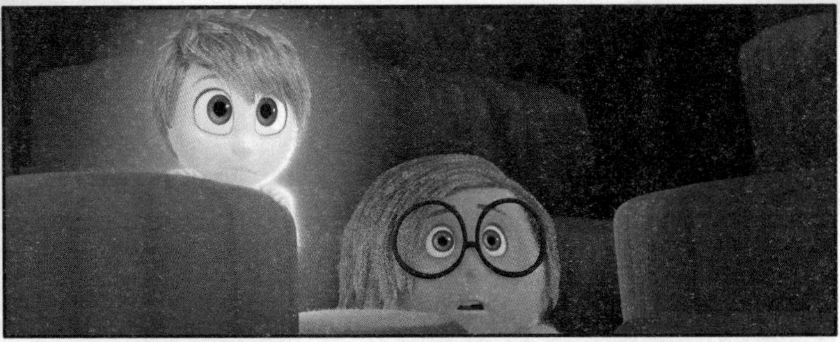

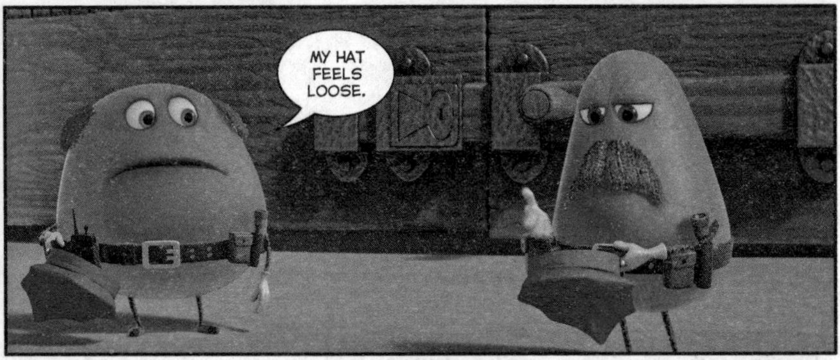
MY HAT
FEELS
LOOSE.

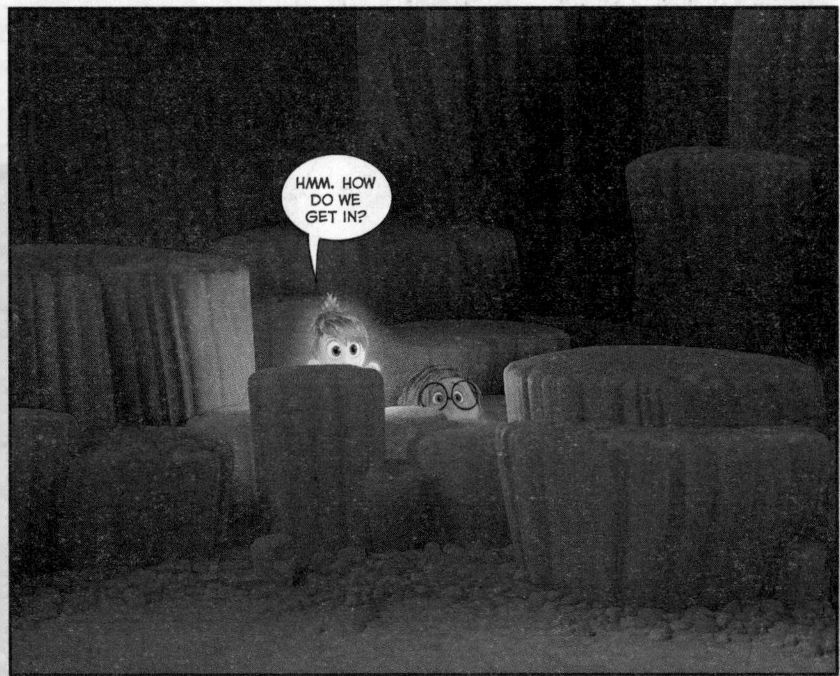
HMM. HOW
DO WE
GET IN?

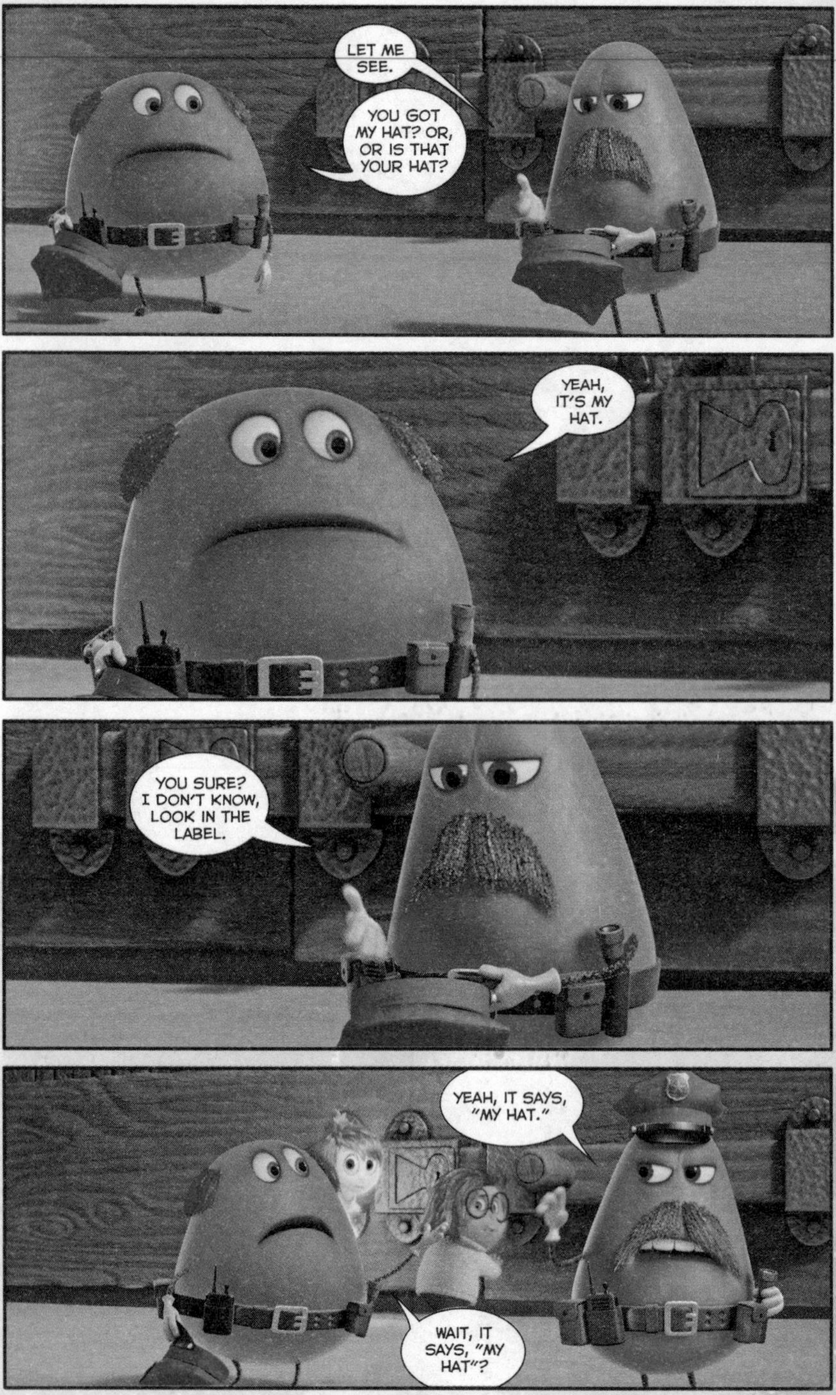
LET ME SEE.
YOU GOT MY HAT? OR, OR IS THAT YOUR HAT?
YEAH, IT'S MY HAT.
YOU SURE? I DON'T KNOW, LOOK IN THE LABEL.
YEAH, IT SAYS, "MY HAT."
WAIT, IT SAYS, "MY HAT"?

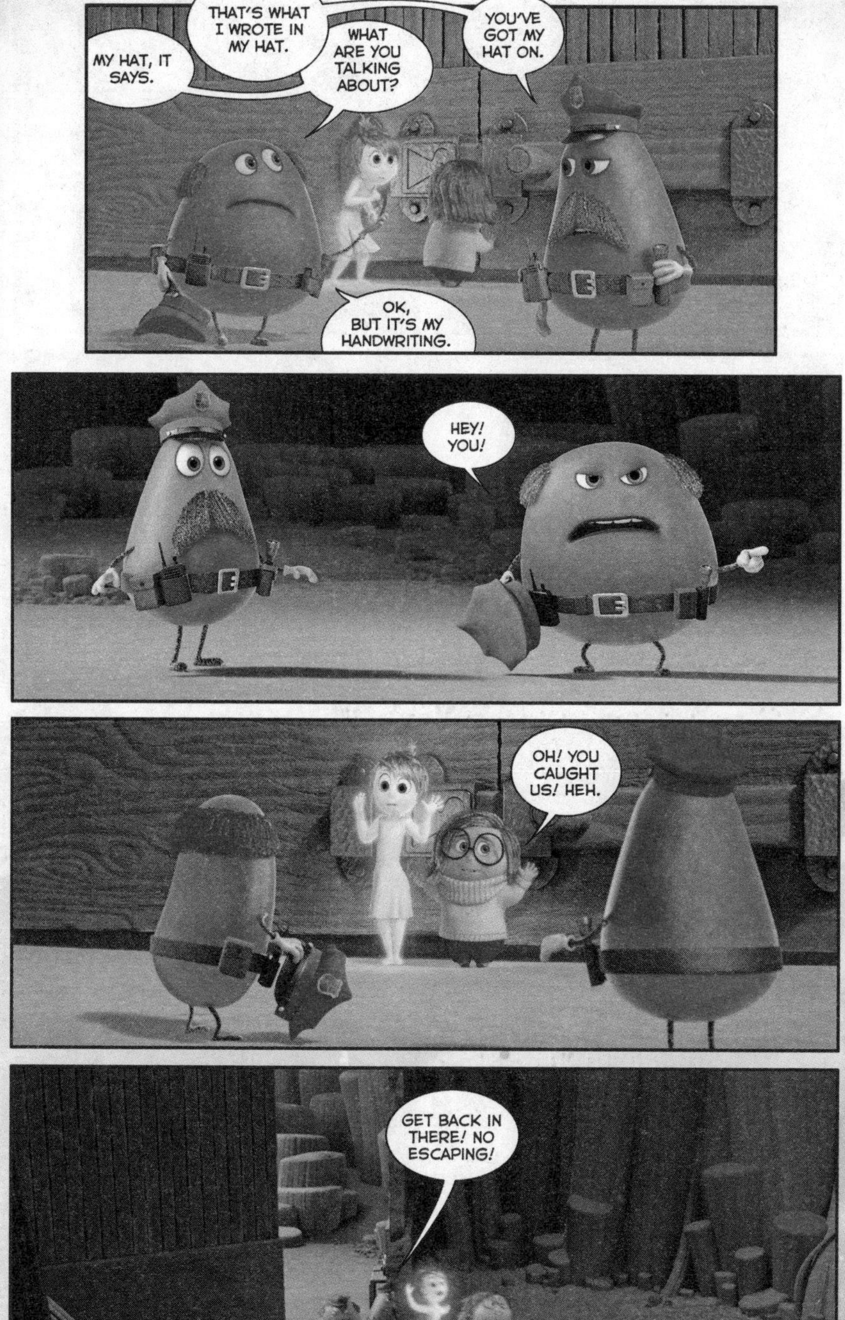
YOU'VE GOT MY HAT ON.
WHAT ARE YOU TALKING ABOUT?
MY HAT, IT SAYS.
THAT'S WHAT I WROTE IN MY HAT.
OK, BUT IT'S MY HANDWRITING.
HEY! YOU!
OH! YOU CAUGHT US! HEH.
GET BACK IN THERE! NO ESCAPING!

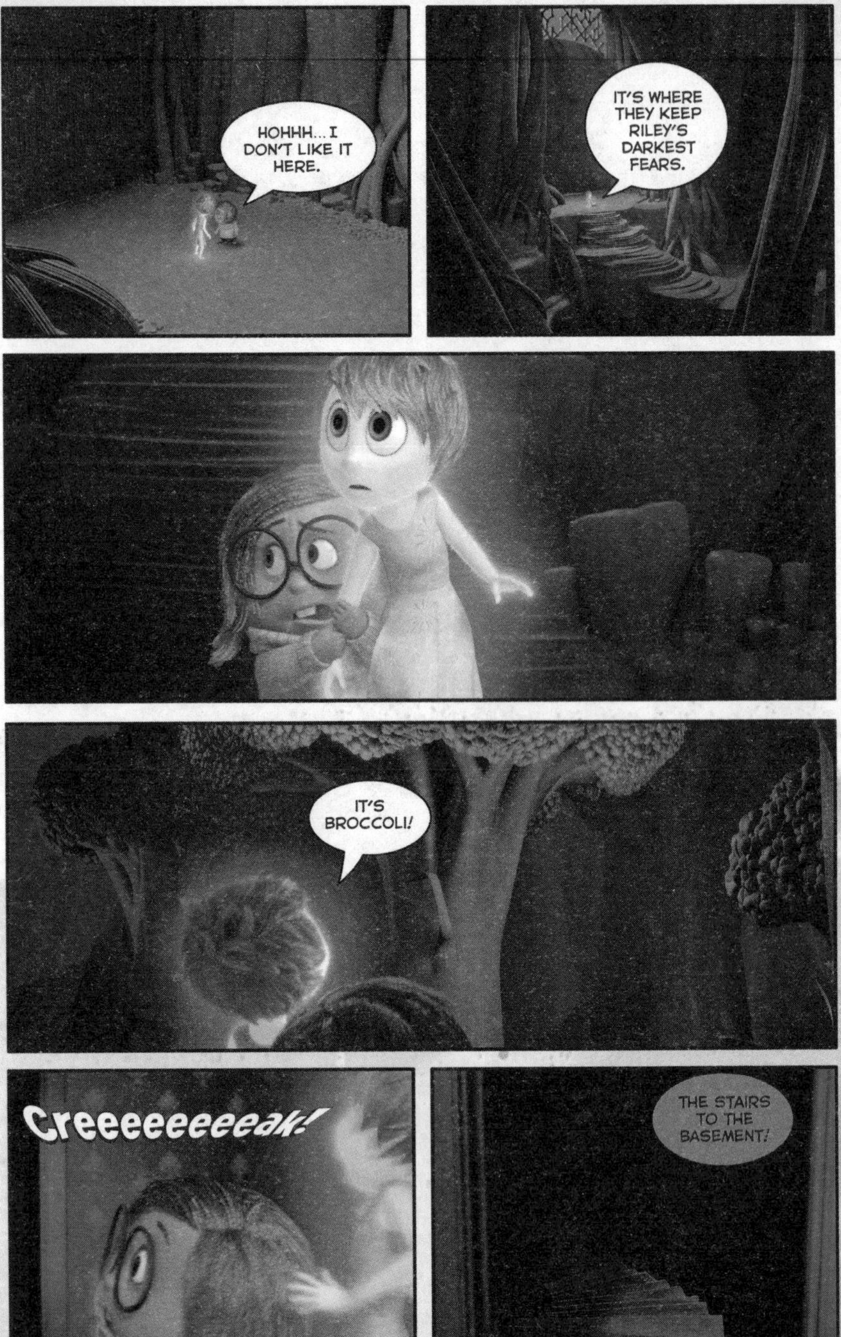
HOHHH... I DON'T LIKE IT HERE.
IT'S WHERE THEY KEEP RILEY'S DARKEST FEARS.
IT'S BROCCOLI!
Creeeeeeeeeak!
THE STAIRS TO THE BASEMENT!

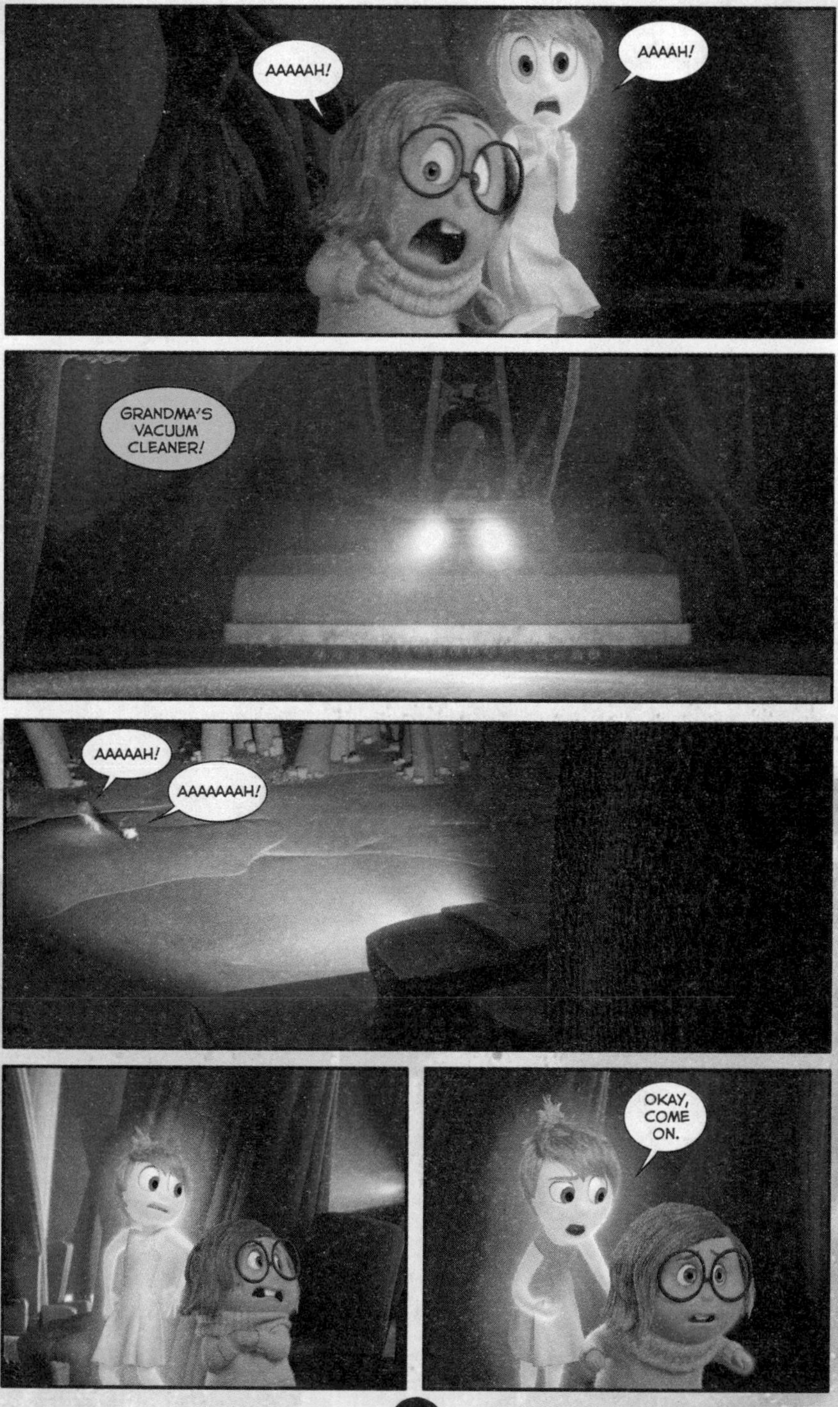
AAAAAH!
AAAAH!
GRANDMA'S VACUUM CLEANER!
AAAAAH!
AAAAAAAH!
OKAY, COME ON.

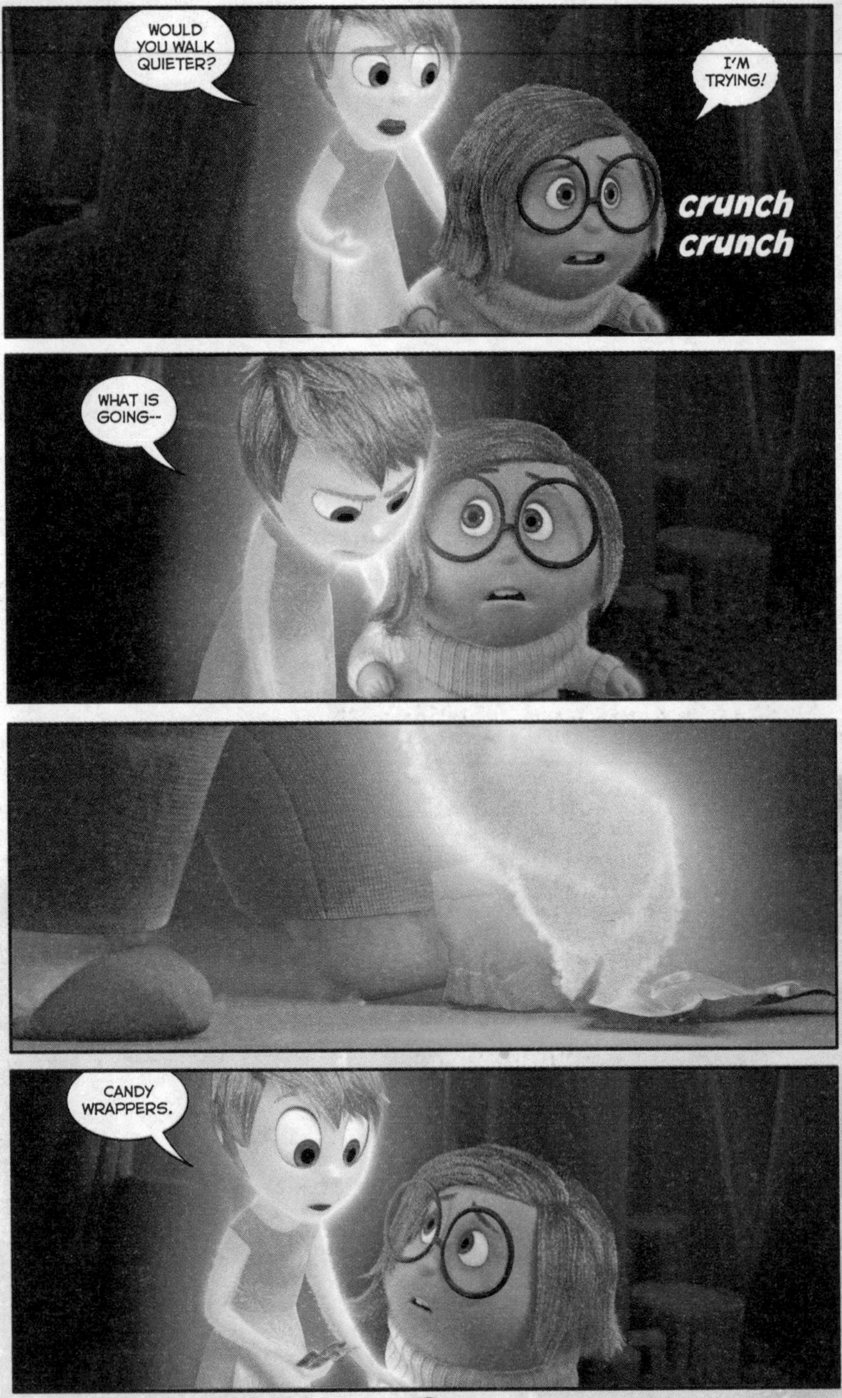
WOULD YOU WALK QUIETER?
I'M TRYING!
crunch crunch
WHAT IS GOING--
CANDY WRAPPERS.

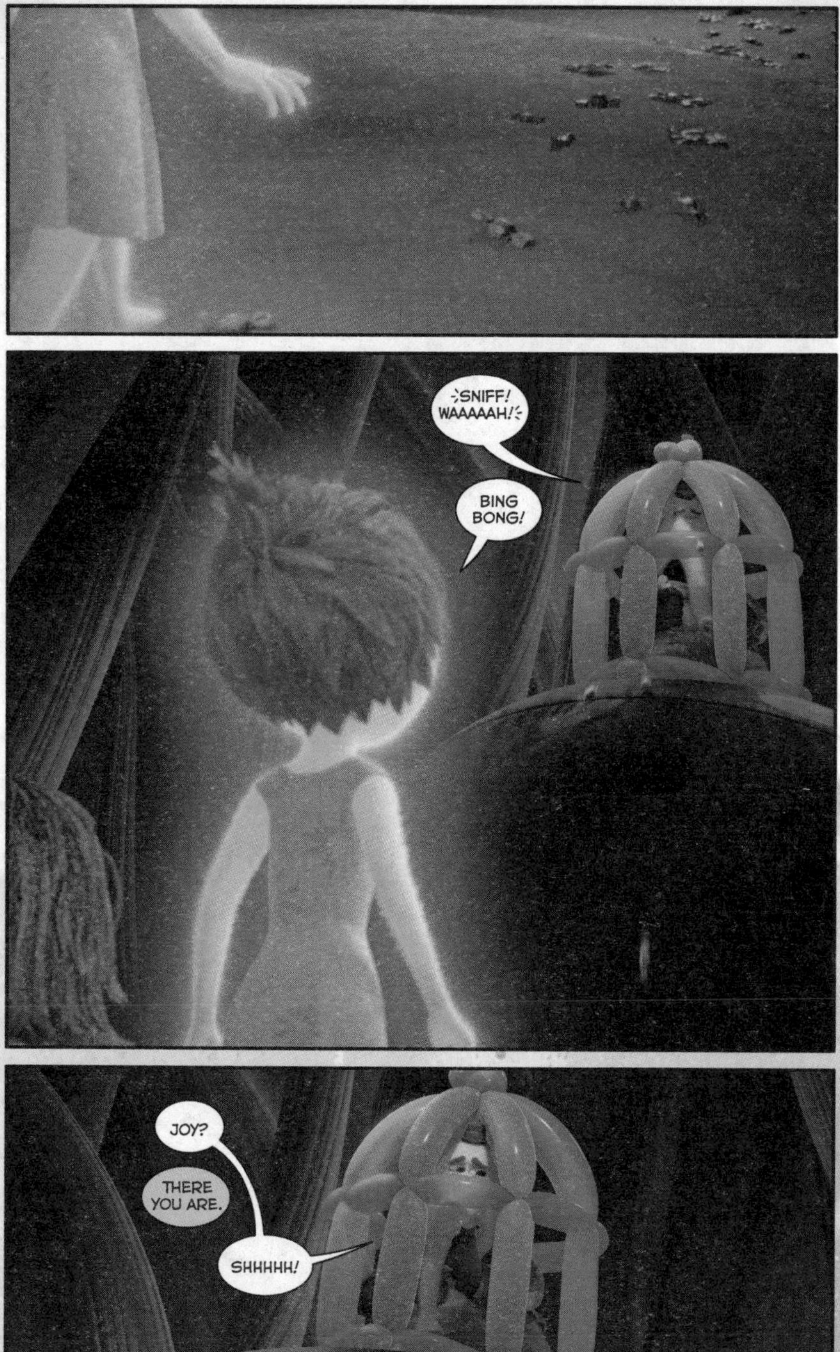
SNIFF! WAAAAAH!
BING BONG!
JOY?
THERE YOU ARE.
SHHHHH!

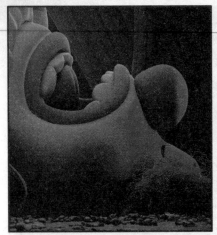

IT'S JANGLES!

WHO'S THE BIRTHDAY GIRL? WHO'S THE BIRTHDAY GIRL?

Snoooooooooore...'

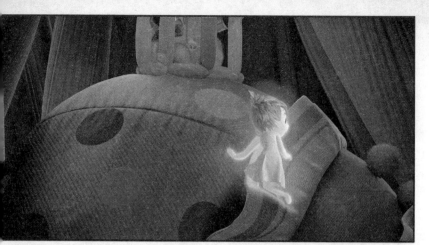

DO YOU HAVE THE CORE MEMORIES?

YEAH. ALL HE CARED ABOUT WAS THE CANDY.

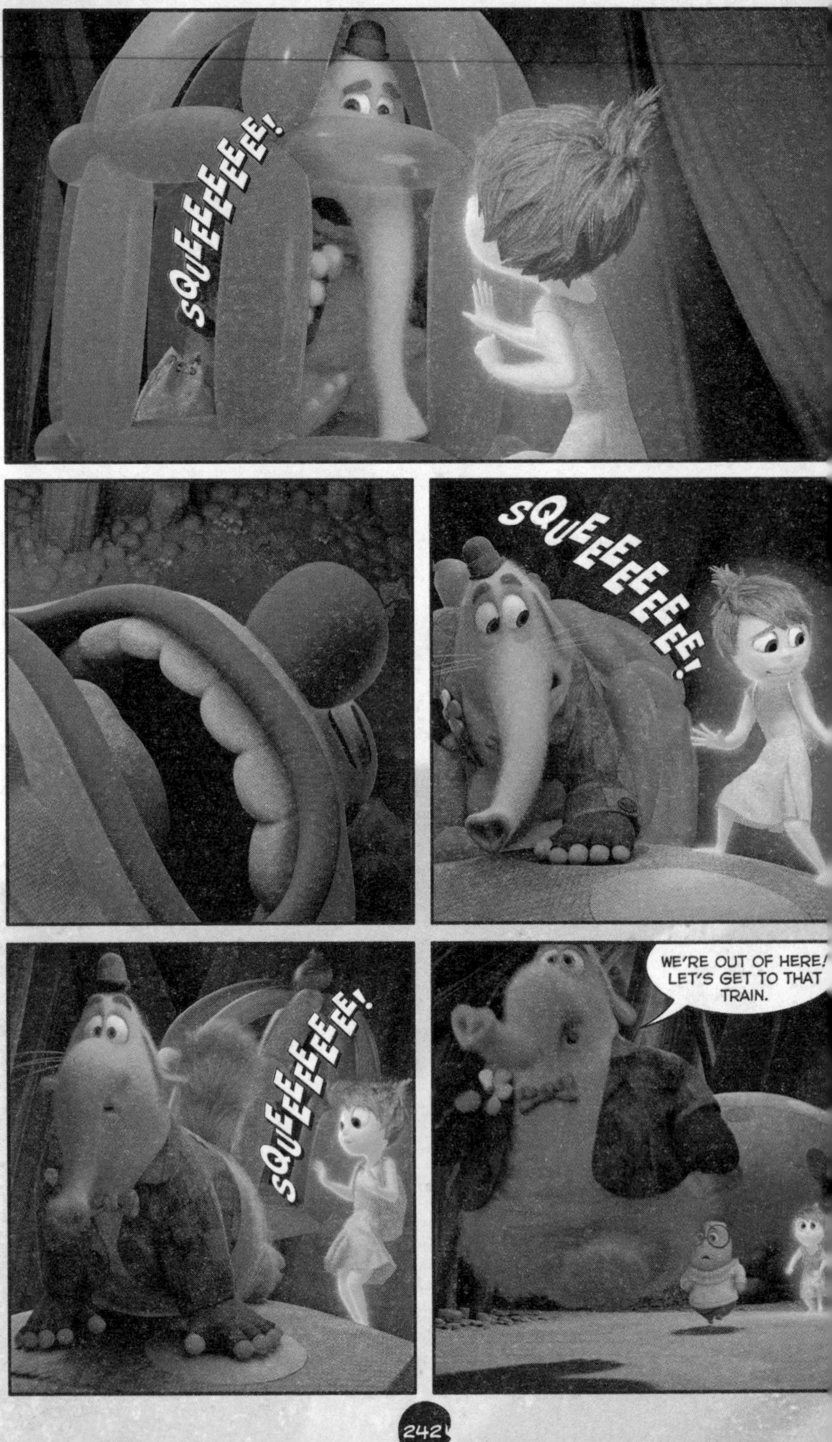
SQUEEEEEEEE!
SQUEEEEEEEE!
SQUEEEEEEEE!
WE'RE OUT OF HERE! LET'S GET TO THAT TRAIN.

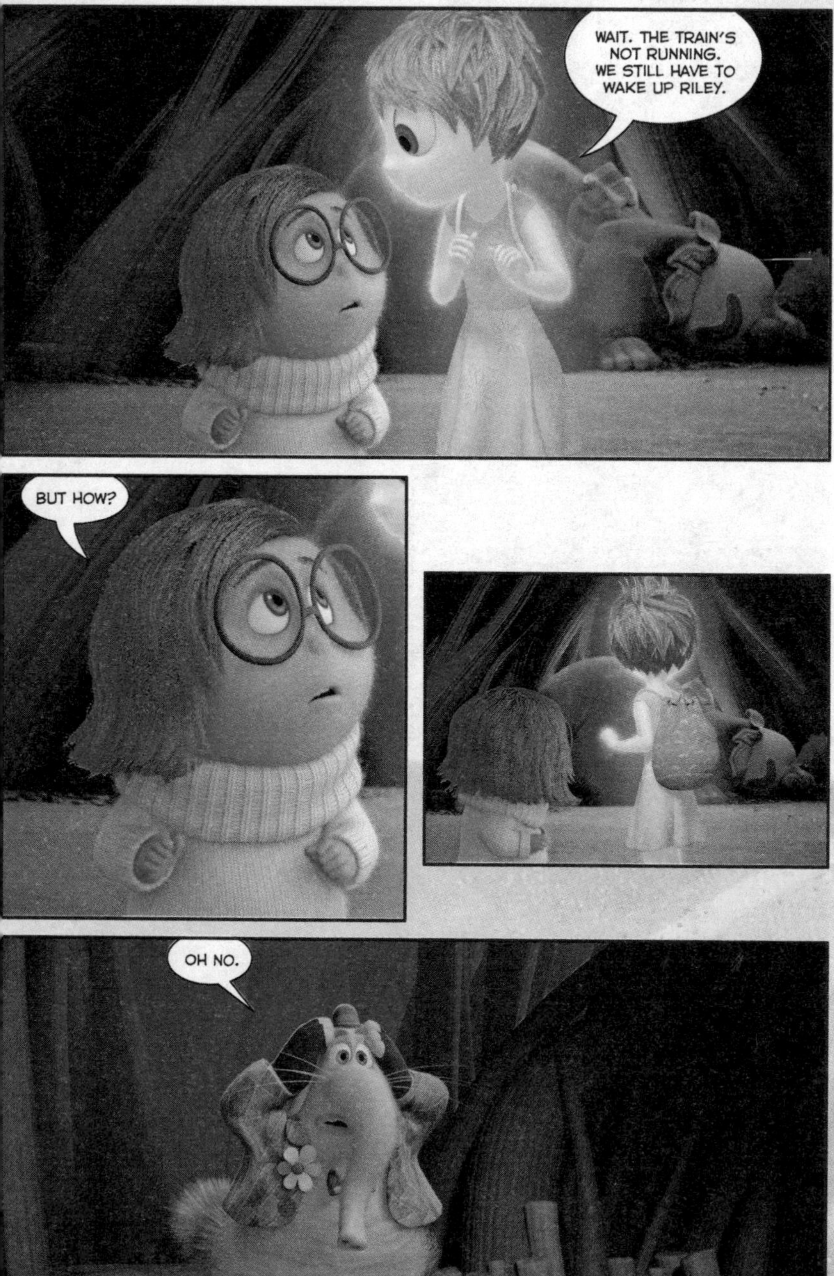
WAIT. THE TRAIN'S NOT RUNNING. WE STILL HAVE TO WAKE UP RILEY.
BUT HOW?
OH NO.

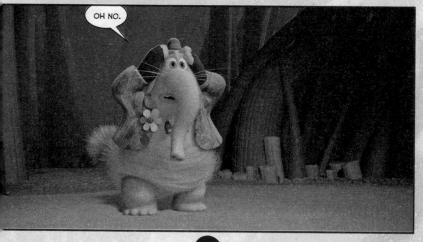

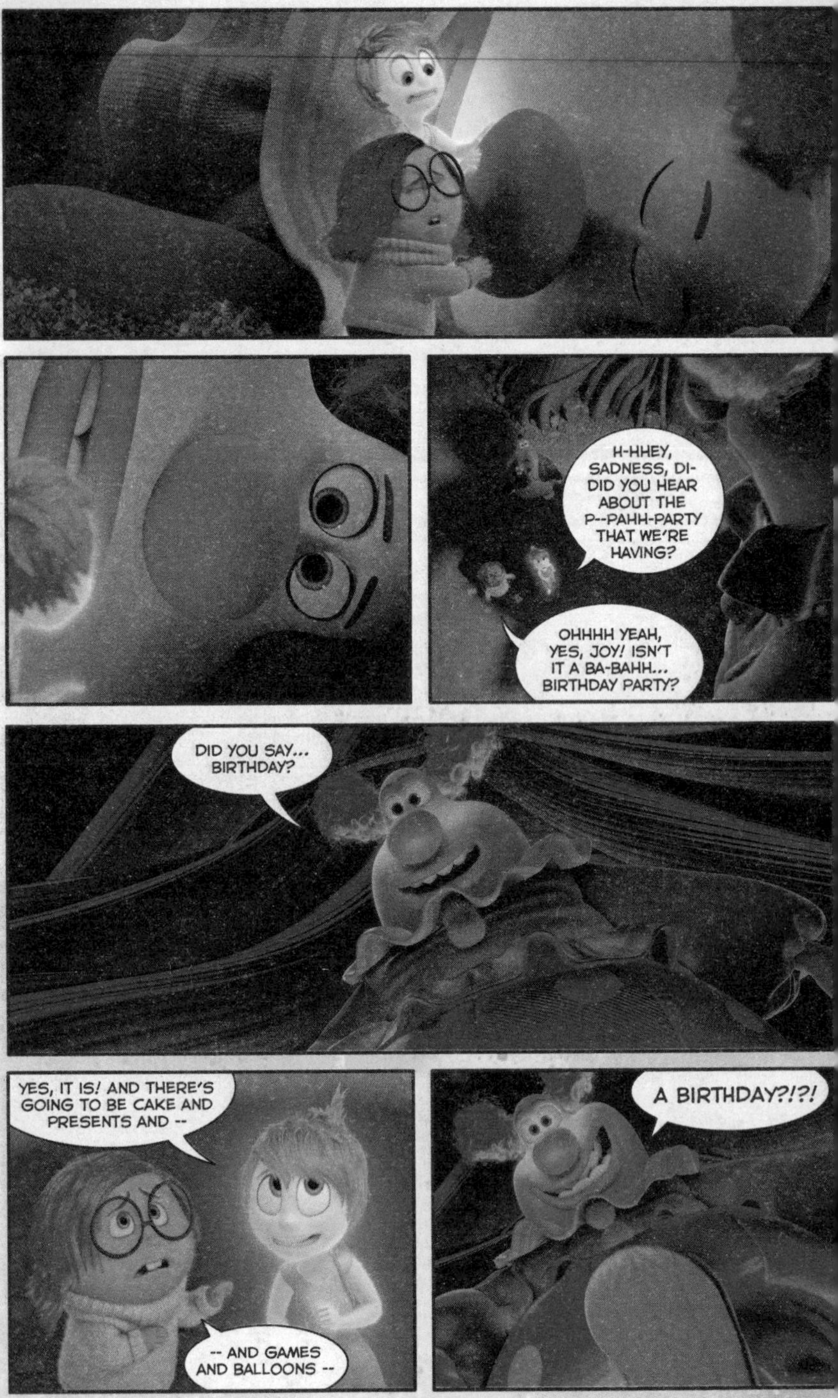
H-HHEY, SADNESS, DI-DID YOU HEAR ABOUT THE P--PAHH-PARTY THAT WE'RE HAVING?
OHHHH YEAH, YES, JOY! ISN'T IT A BA-BAHH... BIRTHDAY PARTY?
DID YOU SAY... BIRTHDAY?
YES, IT IS! AND THERE'S GOING TO BE CAKE AND PRESENTS AND --
-- AND GAMES AND BALLOONS --
A BIRTHDAY?!?!

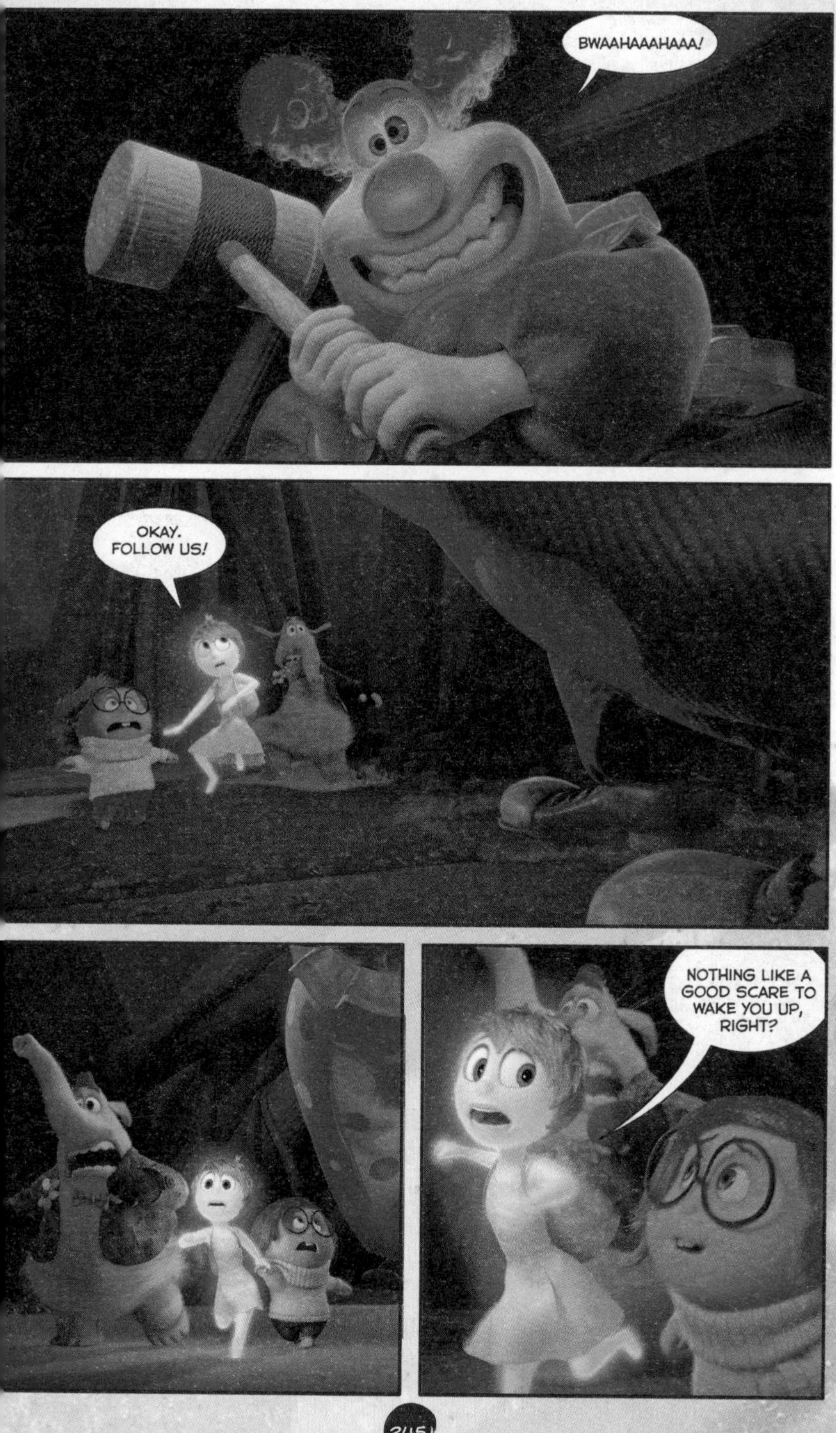
BWAAHAAAHAAA!
OKAY. FOLLOW US!
NOTHING LIKE A GOOD SCARE TO WAKE YOU UP, RIGHT?

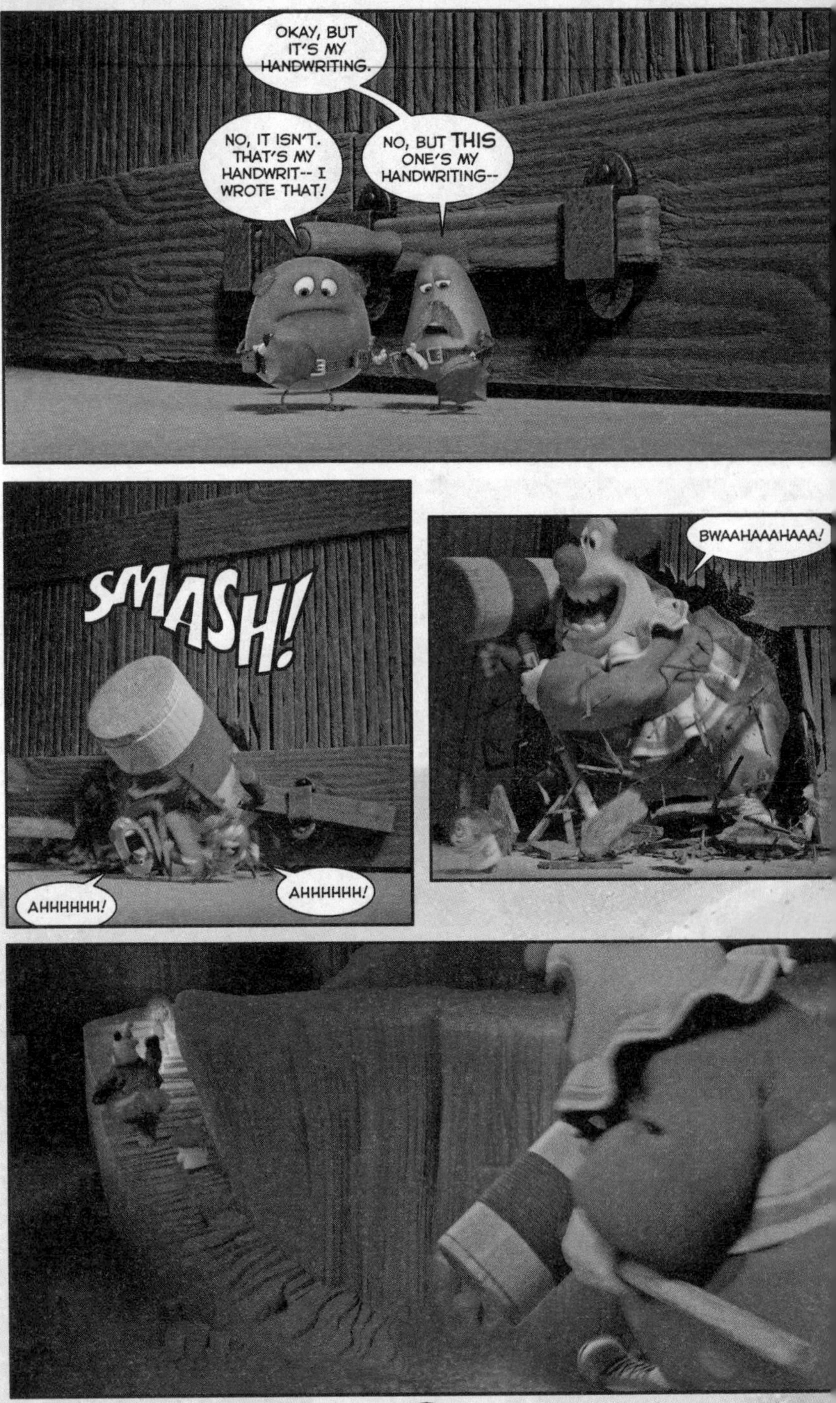
OKAY, BUT IT'S MY HANDWRITING.
NO, IT ISN'T. THAT'S MY HANDWRIT-- I WROTE THAT!
NO, BUT THIS ONE'S MY HANDWRITING--
SMASH!
AHHHHHH!
AHHHHHH!
BWAAHAAAHAAA!

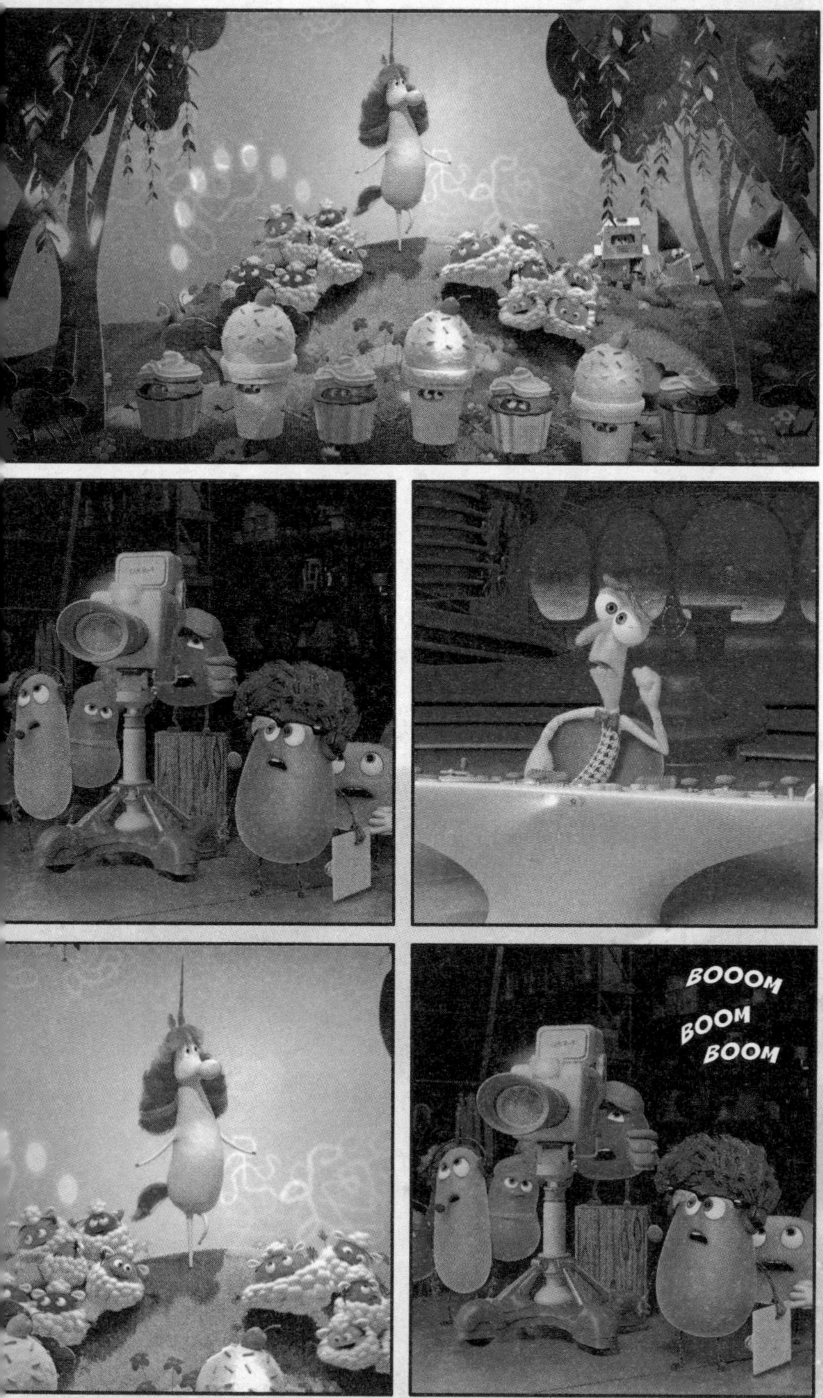
BOOOM
BOOM
BOOM

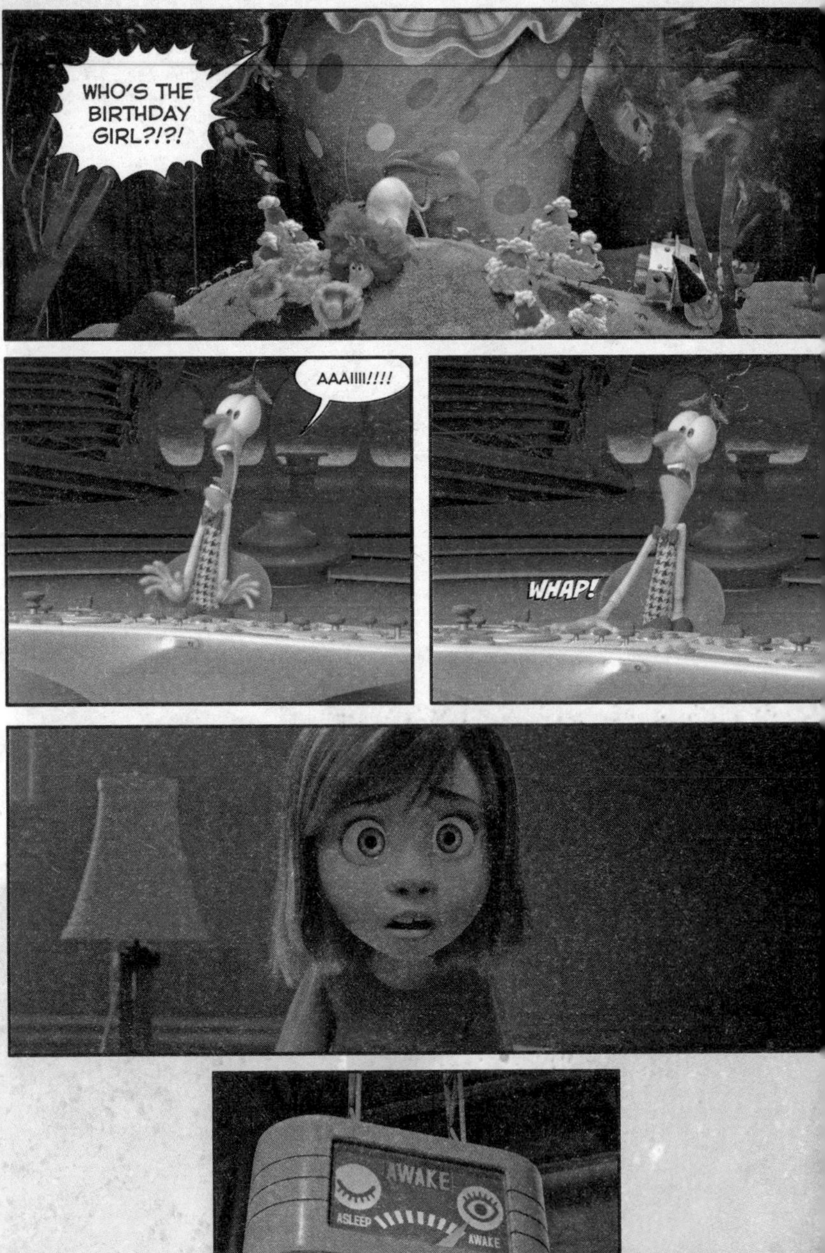
WHO'S THE BIRTHDAY GIRL?!?!
AAAIIII!!!!
WHAP!
AWAKE
ASLEEP
AWAKE

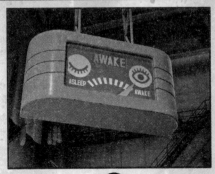

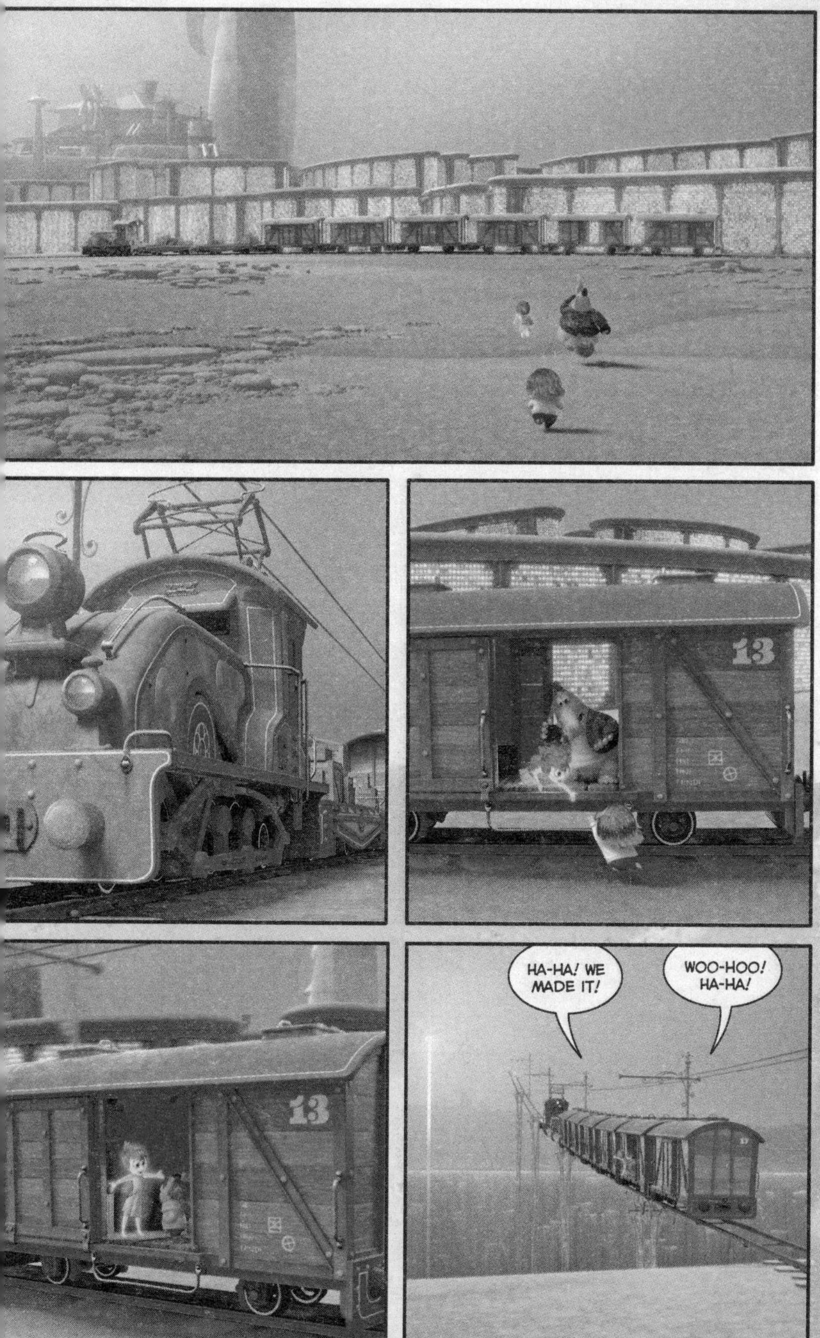
HA-HA! WE MADE IT!
WOO-HOO! HA-HA!

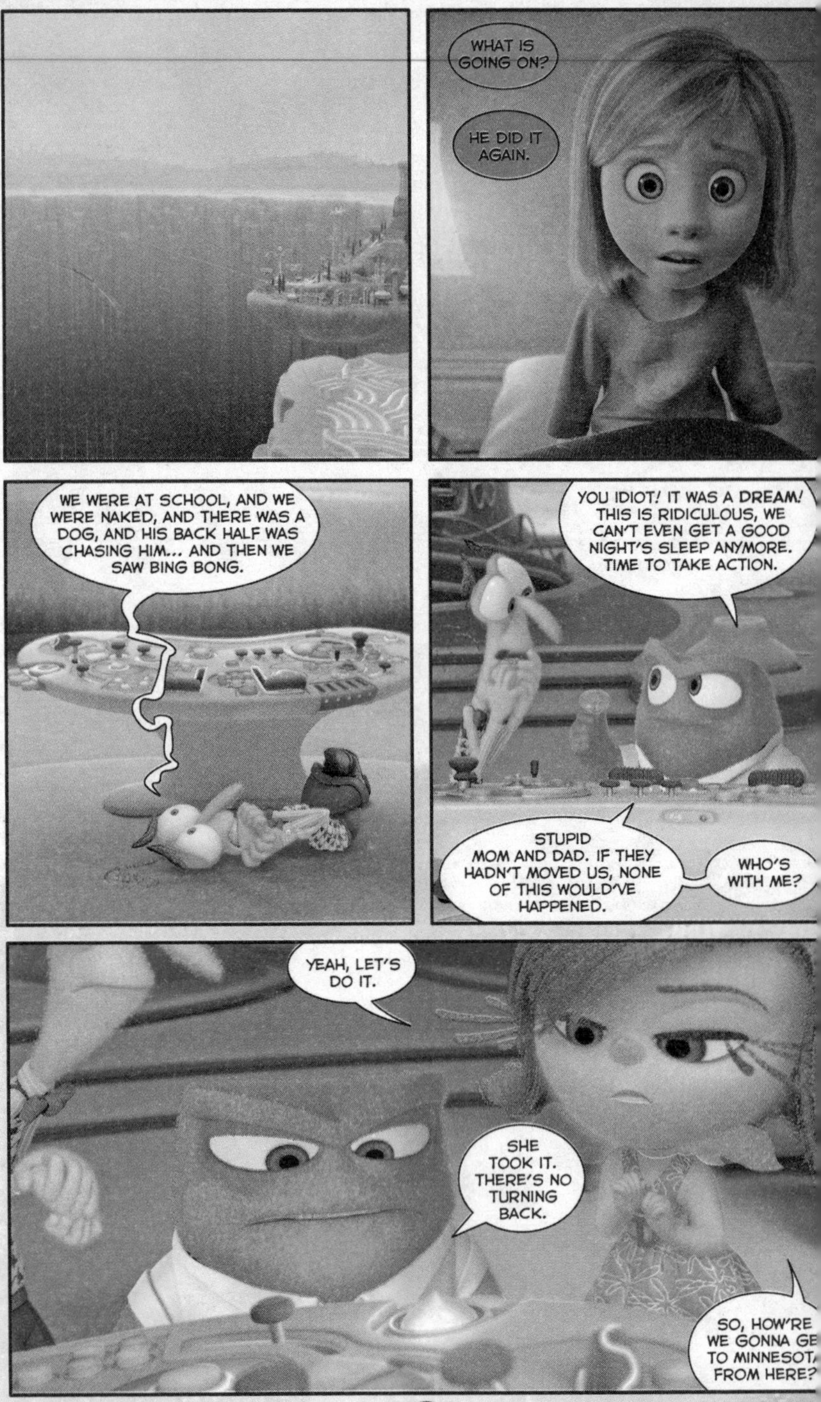
WHAT IS GOING ON?
HE DID IT AGAIN.
WE WERE AT SCHOOL, AND WE WERE NAKED, AND THERE WAS A DOG, AND HIS BACK HALF WAS CHASING HIM... AND THEN WE SAW BING BONG.
YOU IDIOT! IT WAS A DREAM! THIS IS RIDICULOUS, WE CAN'T EVEN GET A GOOD NIGHT'S SLEEP ANYMORE. TIME TO TAKE ACTION.
STUPID MOM AND DAD. IF THEY HADN'T MOVED US, NONE OF THIS WOULD'VE HAPPENED.
WHO'S WITH ME?
YEAH, LET'S DO IT.
SHE TOOK IT. THERE'S NO TURNING BACK.
SO, HOW'RE WE GONNA GE TO MINNESOT FROM HERE?

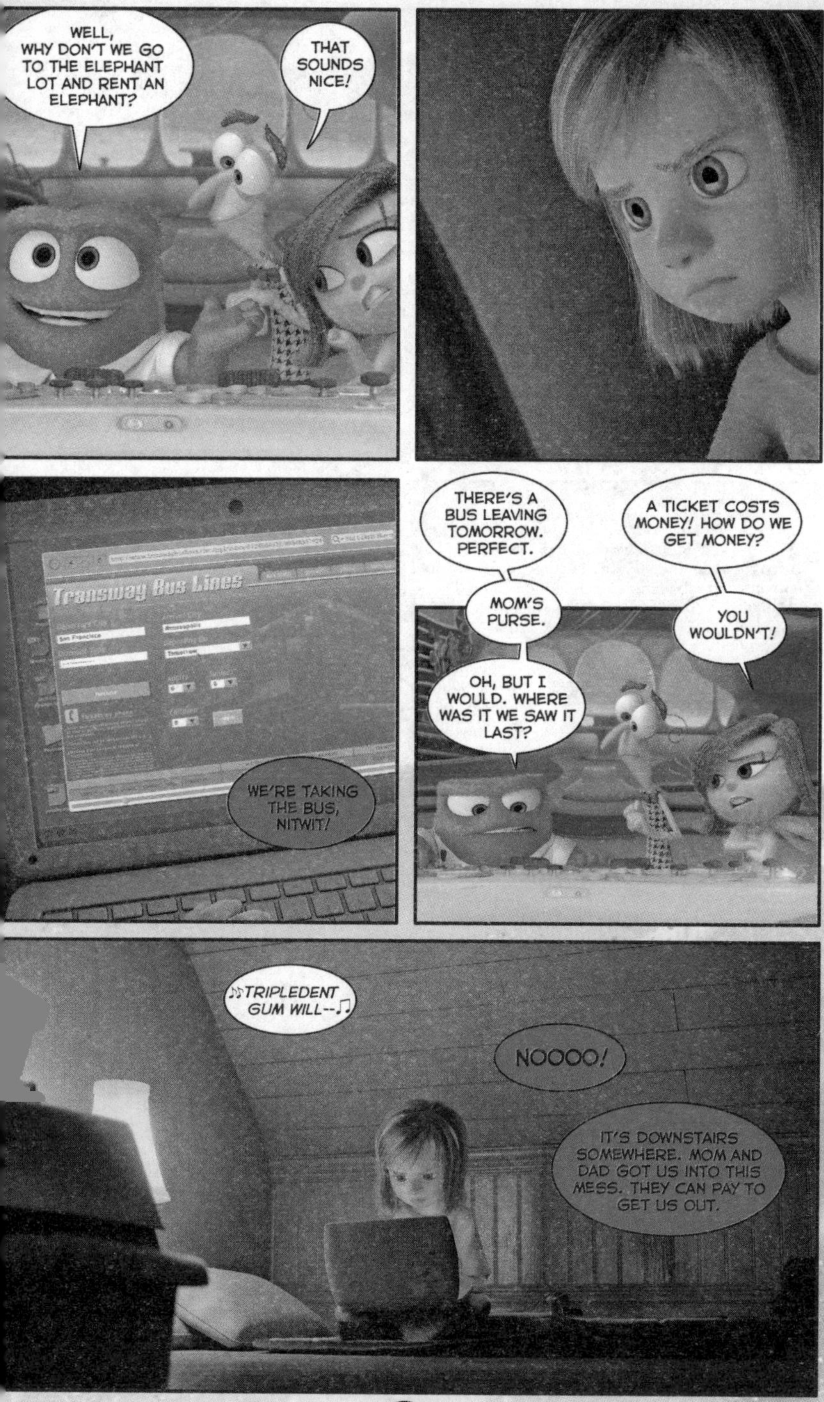
WELL, WHY DON'T WE GO TO THE ELEPHANT LOT AND RENT AN ELEPHANT?
THAT SOUNDS NICE!
Transway Bus Lines
WE'RE TAKING THE BUS, NITWIT!
THERE'S A BUS LEAVING TOMORROW. PERFECT.
A TICKET COSTS MONEY! HOW DO WE GET MONEY?
MOM'S PURSE.
YOU WOULDN'T!
OH, BUT I WOULD. WHERE WAS IT WE SAW IT LAST?
♫TRIPLEDENT GUM WILL--♫
NOOOO!
IT'S DOWNSTAIRS SOMEWHERE. MOM AND DAD GOT US INTO THIS MESS. THEY CAN PAY TO GET US OUT.

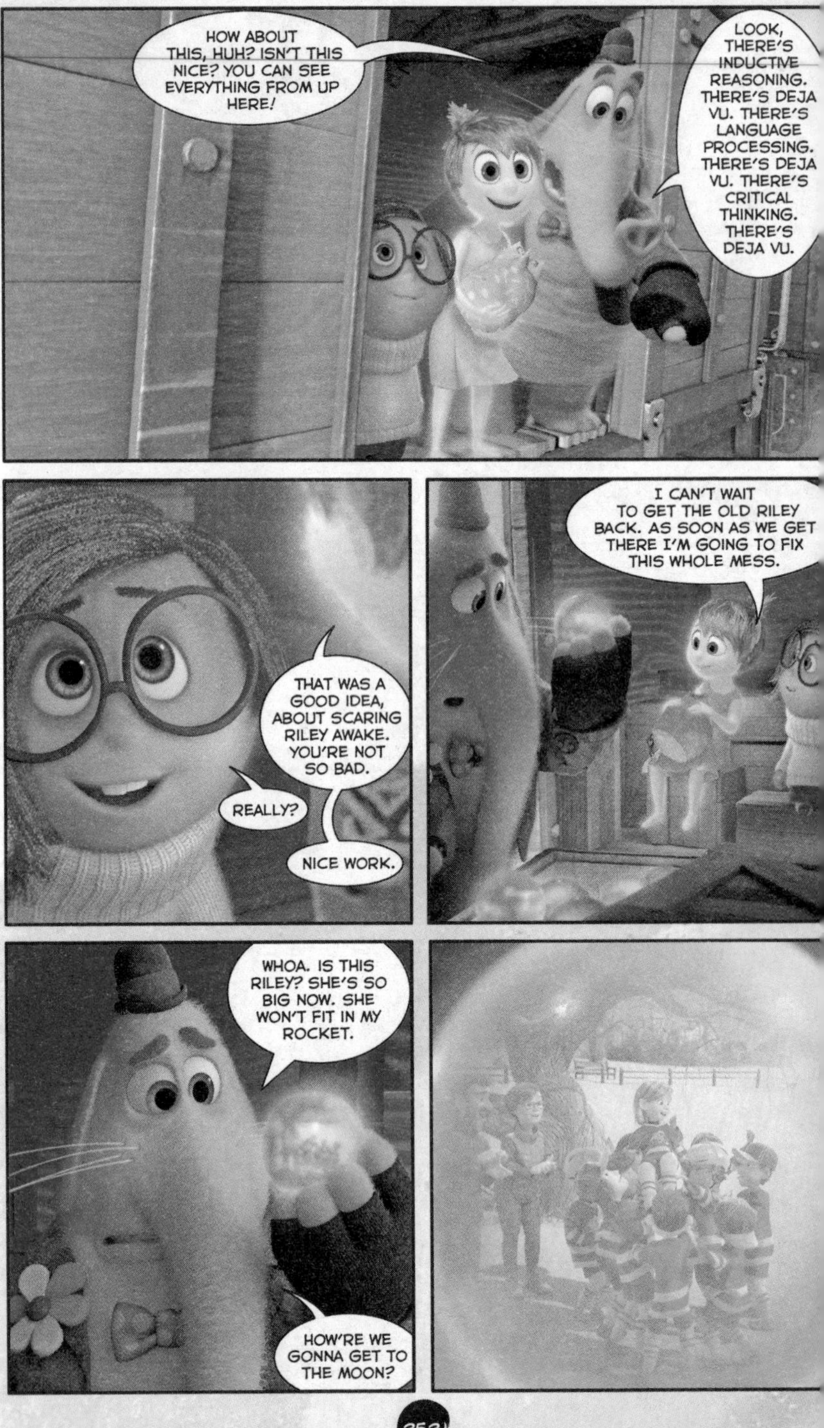
HOW ABOUT THIS, HUH? ISN'T THIS NICE? YOU CAN SEE EVERYTHING FROM UP HERE!
LOOK, THERE'S INDUCTIVE REASONING. THERE'S DEJA VU. THERE'S LANGUAGE PROCESSING. THERE'S DEJA VU. THERE'S CRITICAL THINKING. THERE'S DEJA VU.
THAT WAS A GOOD IDEA, ABOUT SCARING RILEY AWAKE. YOU'RE NOT SO BAD.
REALLY?
NICE WORK.
I CAN'T WAIT TO GET THE OLD RILEY BACK. AS SOON AS WE GET THERE I'M GOING TO FIX THIS WHOLE MESS.
WHOA. IS THIS RILEY? SHE'S SO BIG NOW. SHE WON'T FIT IN MY ROCKET.
HOW'RE WE GONNA GET TO THE MOON?

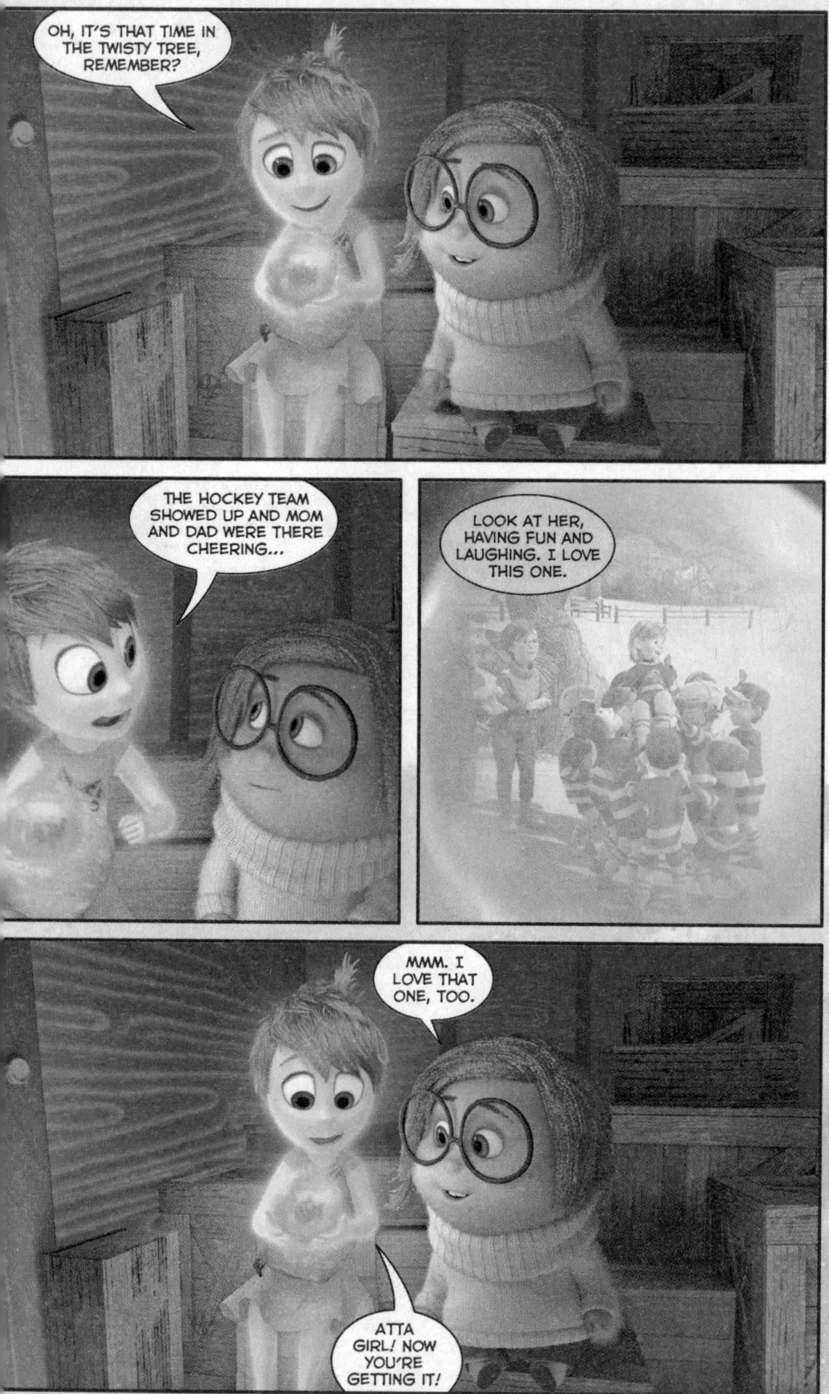
OH, IT'S THAT TIME IN THE TWISTY TREE, REMEMBER?
THE HOCKEY TEAM SHOWED UP AND MOM AND DAD WERE THERE CHEERING...
LOOK AT HER, HAVING FUN AND LAUGHING. I LOVE THIS ONE.
MMM. I LOVE THAT ONE, TOO.
ATTA GIRL! NOW YOU'RE GETTING IT!

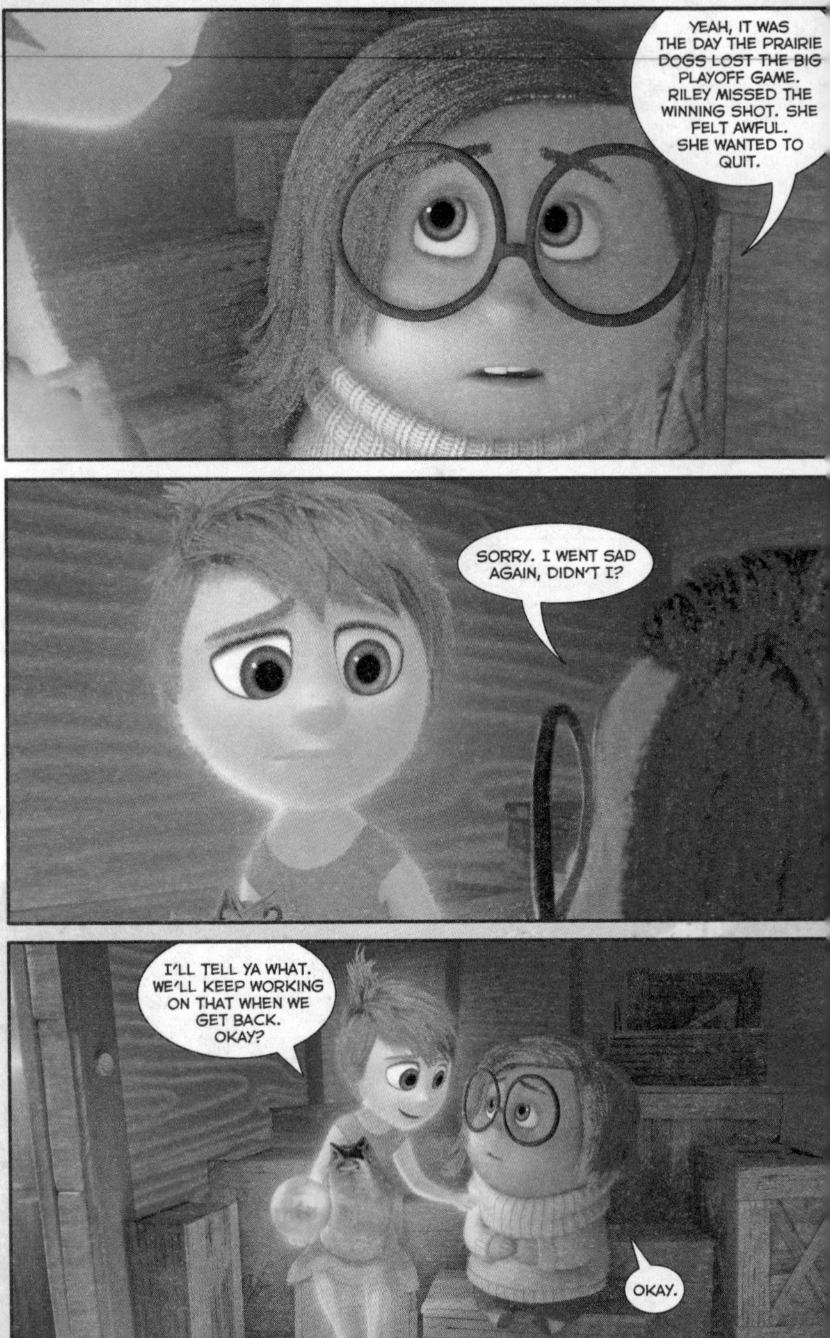
YEAH, IT WAS THE DAY THE PRAIRIE DOGS LOST THE BIG PLAYOFF GAME. RILEY MISSED THE WINNING SHOT. SHE FELT AWFUL. SHE WANTED TO QUIT.
SORRY. I WENT SAD AGAIN, DIDN'T I?
I'LL TELL YA WHAT. WE'LL KEEP WORKING ON THAT WHEN WE GET BACK. OKAY?
OKAY.

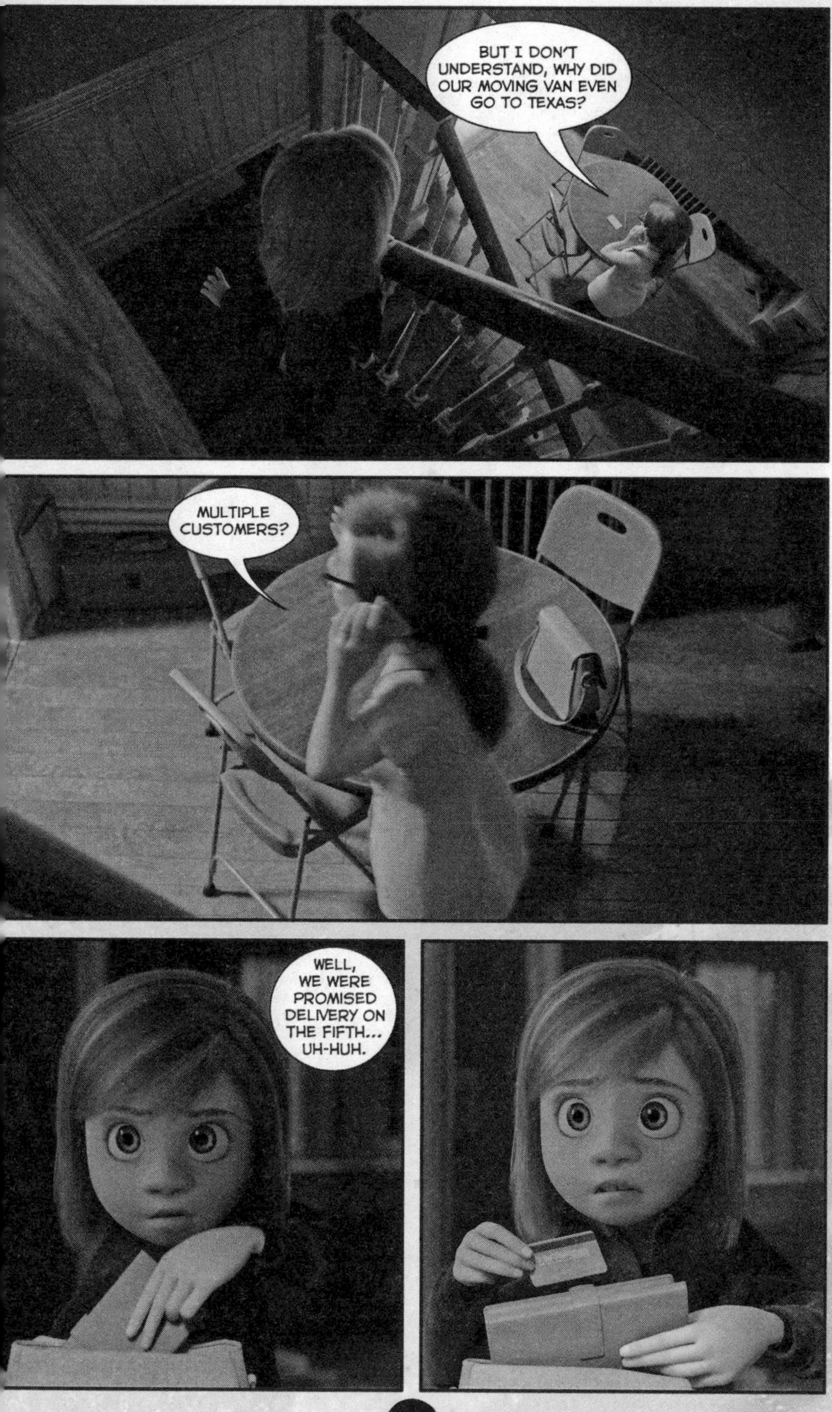
BUT I DON'T UNDERSTAND, WHY DID OUR MOVING VAN EVEN GO TO TEXAS?
MULTIPLE CUSTOMERS?
WELL, WE WERE PROMISED DELIVERY ON THE FIFTH... UH-HUH.

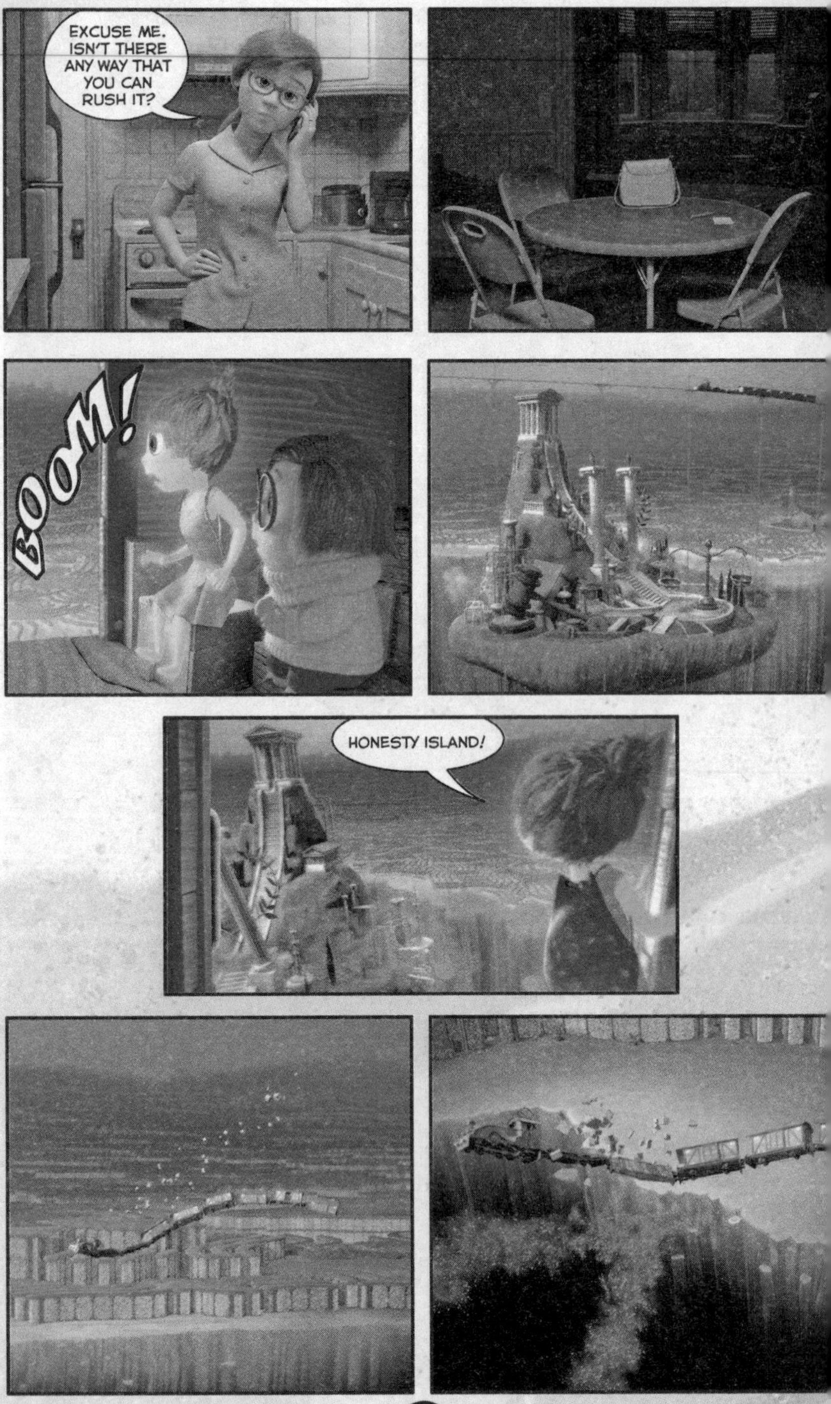
EXCUSE ME. ISN'T THERE ANY WAY THAT YOU CAN RUSH IT?
BOOM!
HONESTY ISLAND!

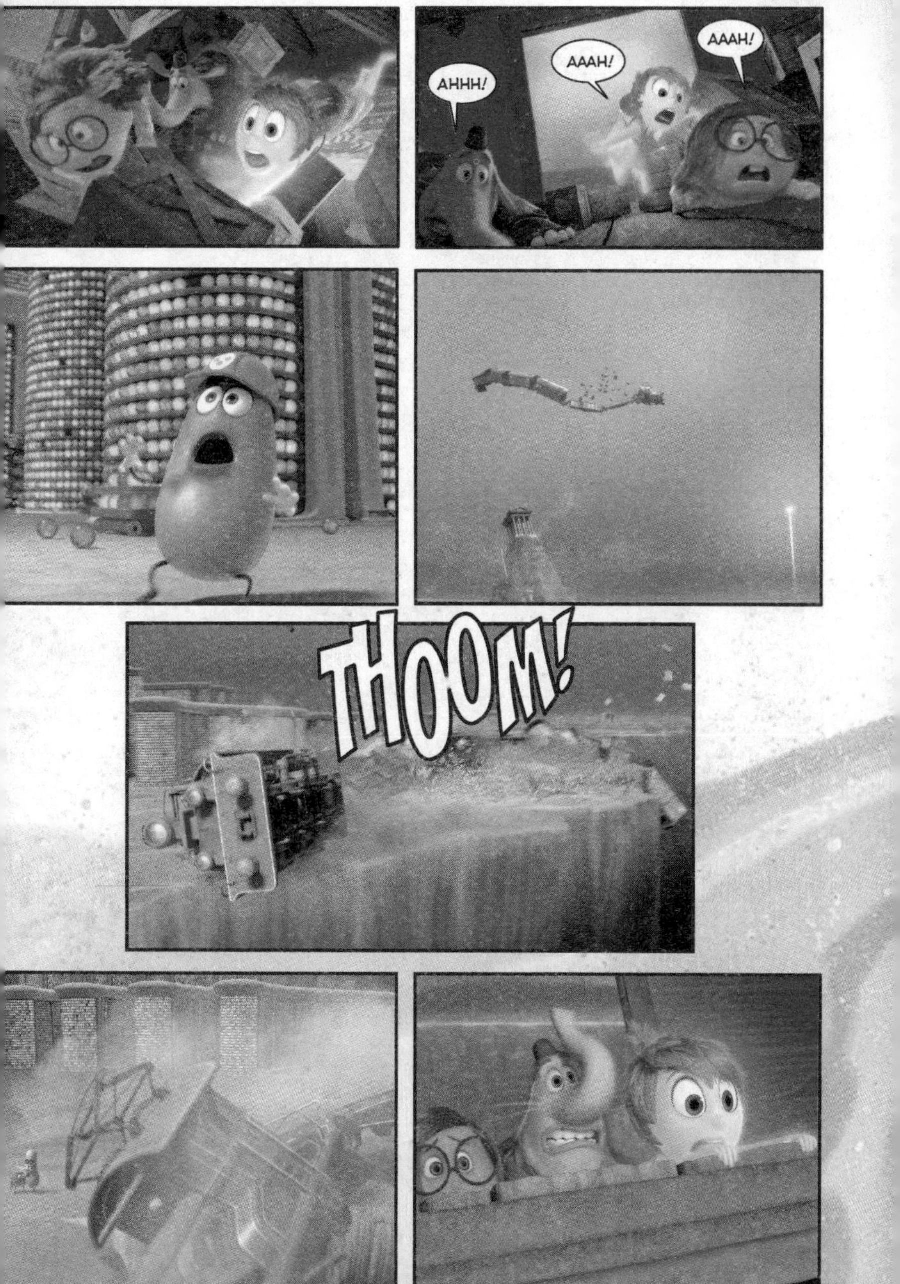
AHHH!
AAAH!
AAAH!
THOOM!

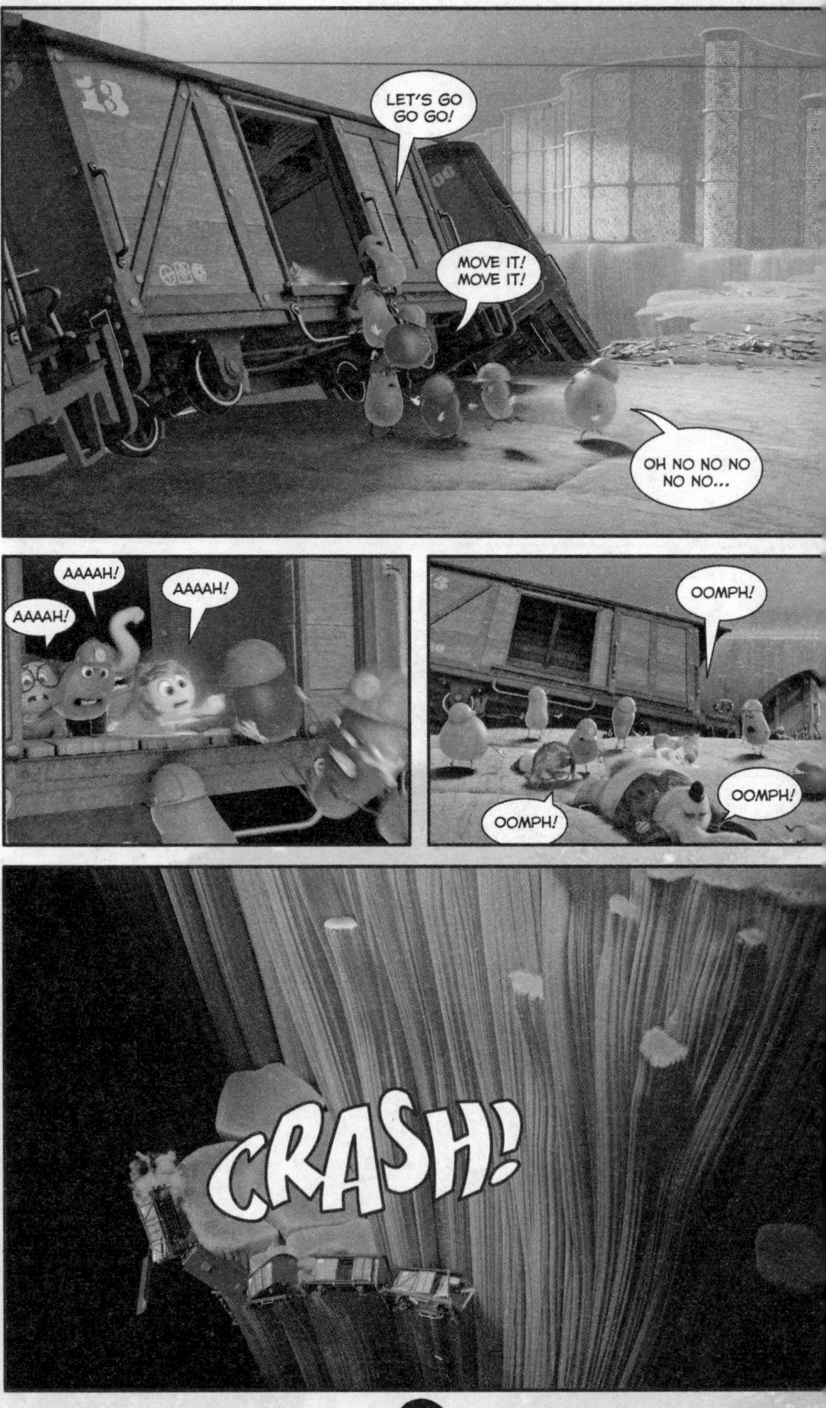
LET'S GO GO GO!
MOVE IT! MOVE IT!
OH NO NO NO NO NO...
AAAAH!
AAAAH!
AAAAH!
OOMPH!
OOMPH!
OOMPH!
CRASH!

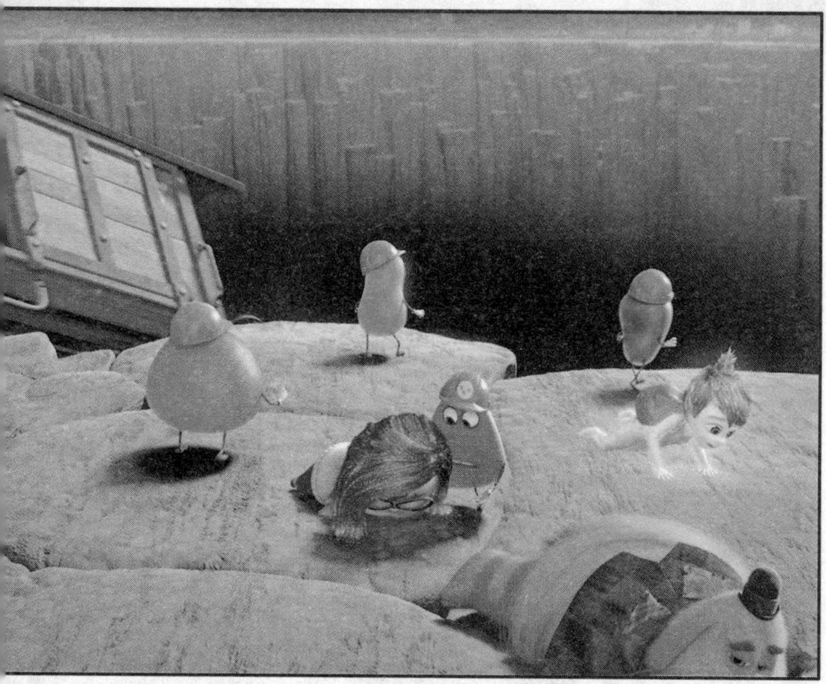

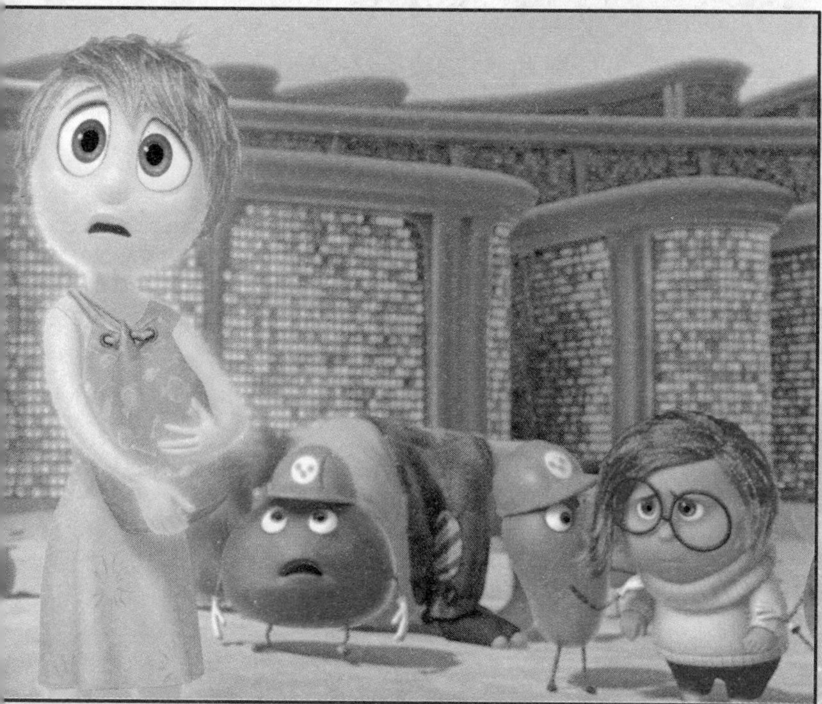

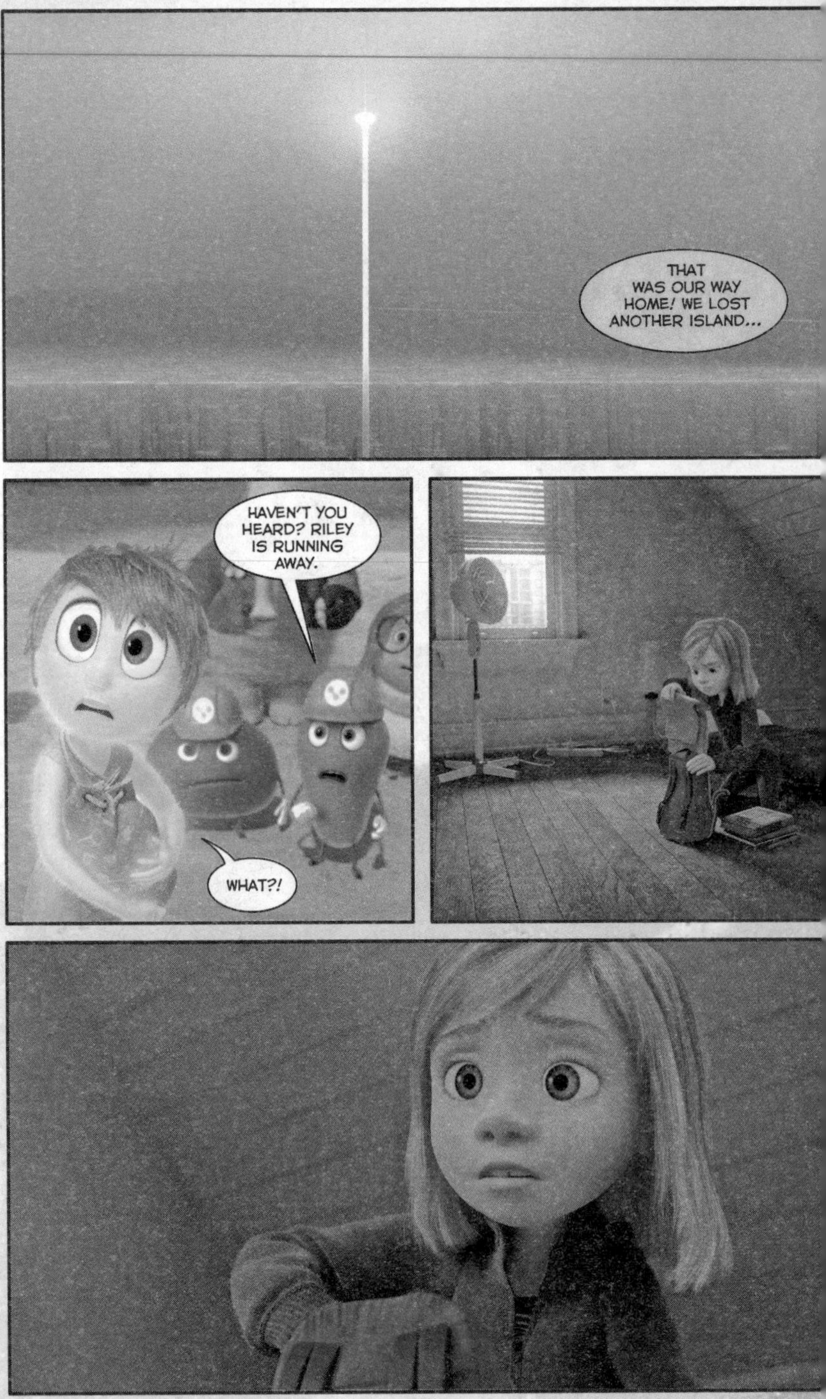
THAT WAS OUR WAY HOME! WE LOST ANOTHER ISLAND...
HAVEN'T YOU HEARD? RILEY IS RUNNING AWAY.
WHAT?!

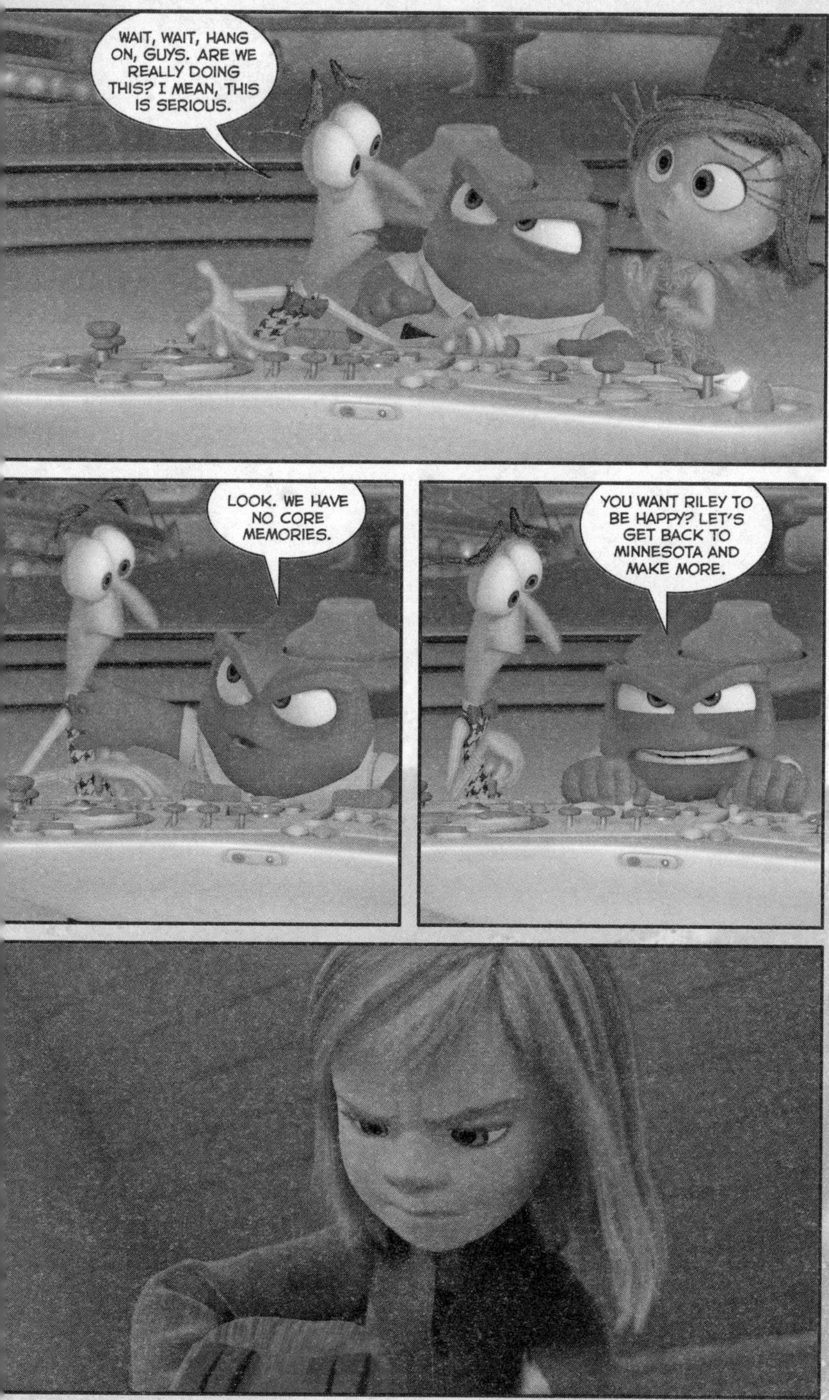
WAIT, WAIT, HANG ON, GUYS. ARE WE REALLY DOING THIS? I MEAN, THIS IS SERIOUS.
LOOK. WE HAVE NO CORE MEMORIES.
YOU WANT RILEY TO BE HAPPY? LET'S GET BACK TO MINNESOTA AND MAKE MORE.

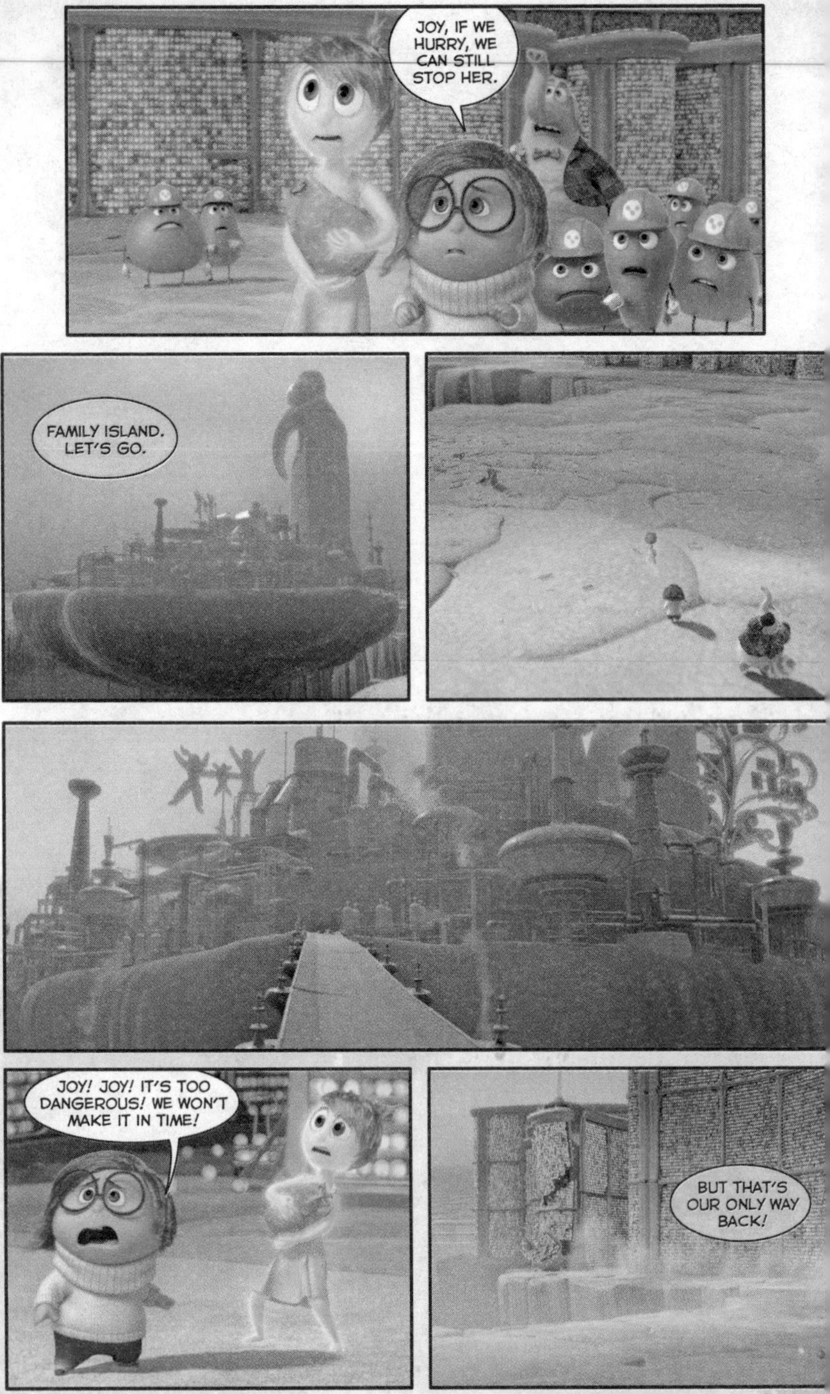
JOY, IF WE HURRY, WE CAN STILL STOP HER.
FAMILY ISLAND. LET'S GO.
JOY! JOY! IT'S TOO DANGEROUS! WE WON'T MAKE IT IN TIME!
BUT THAT'S OUR ONLY WAY BACK!

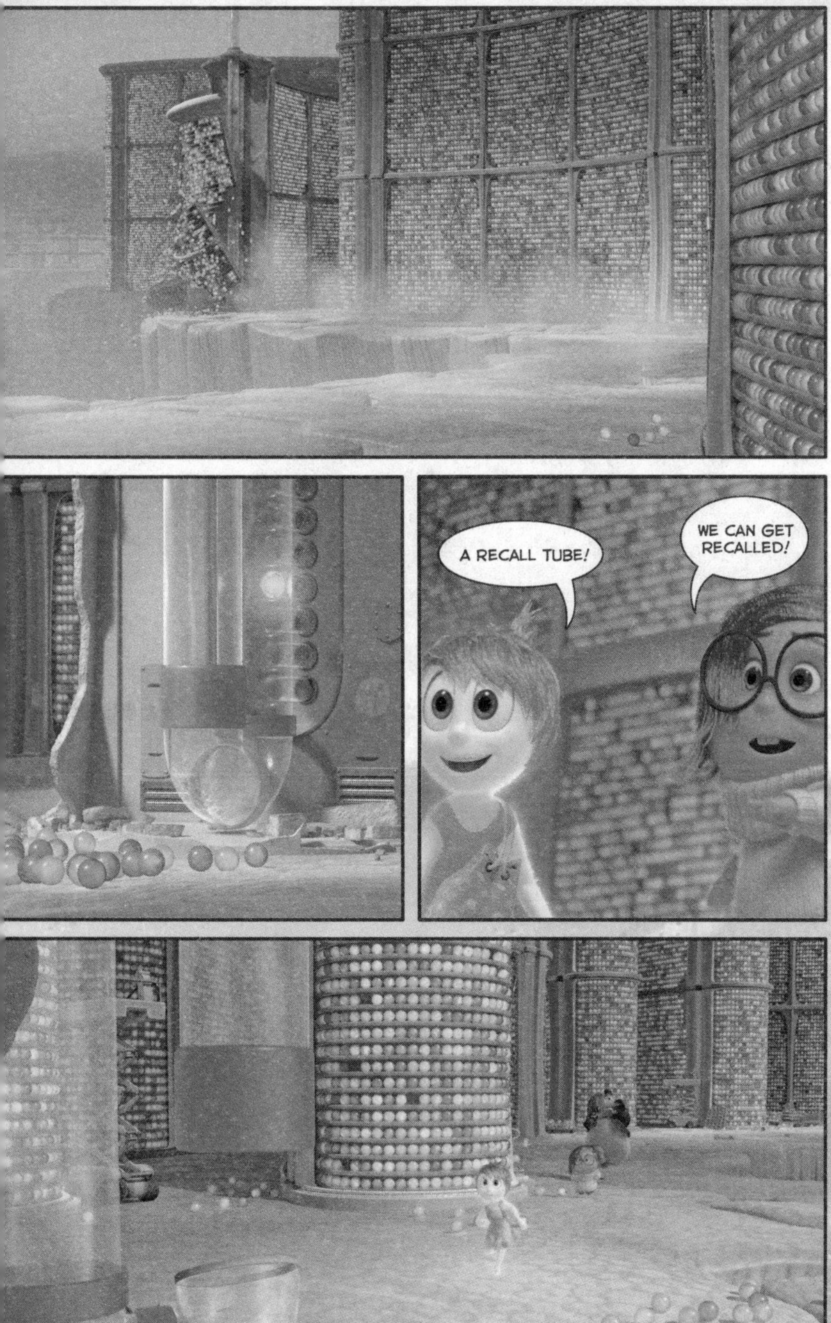
A RECALL TUBE!
WE CAN GET RECALLED!

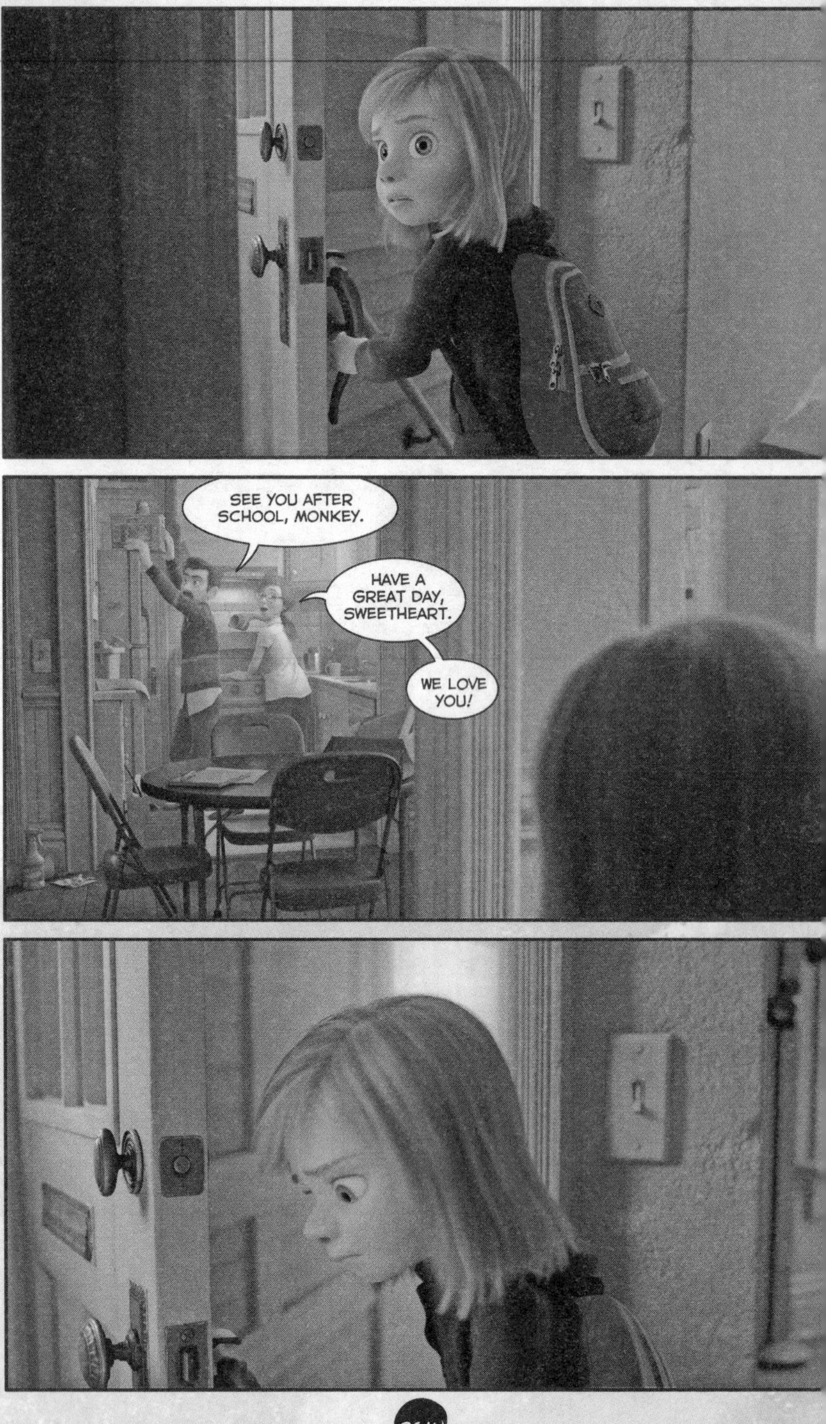
SEE YOU AFTER SCHOOL, MONKEY.
HAVE A GREAT DAY, SWEETHEART.
WE LOVE YOU!

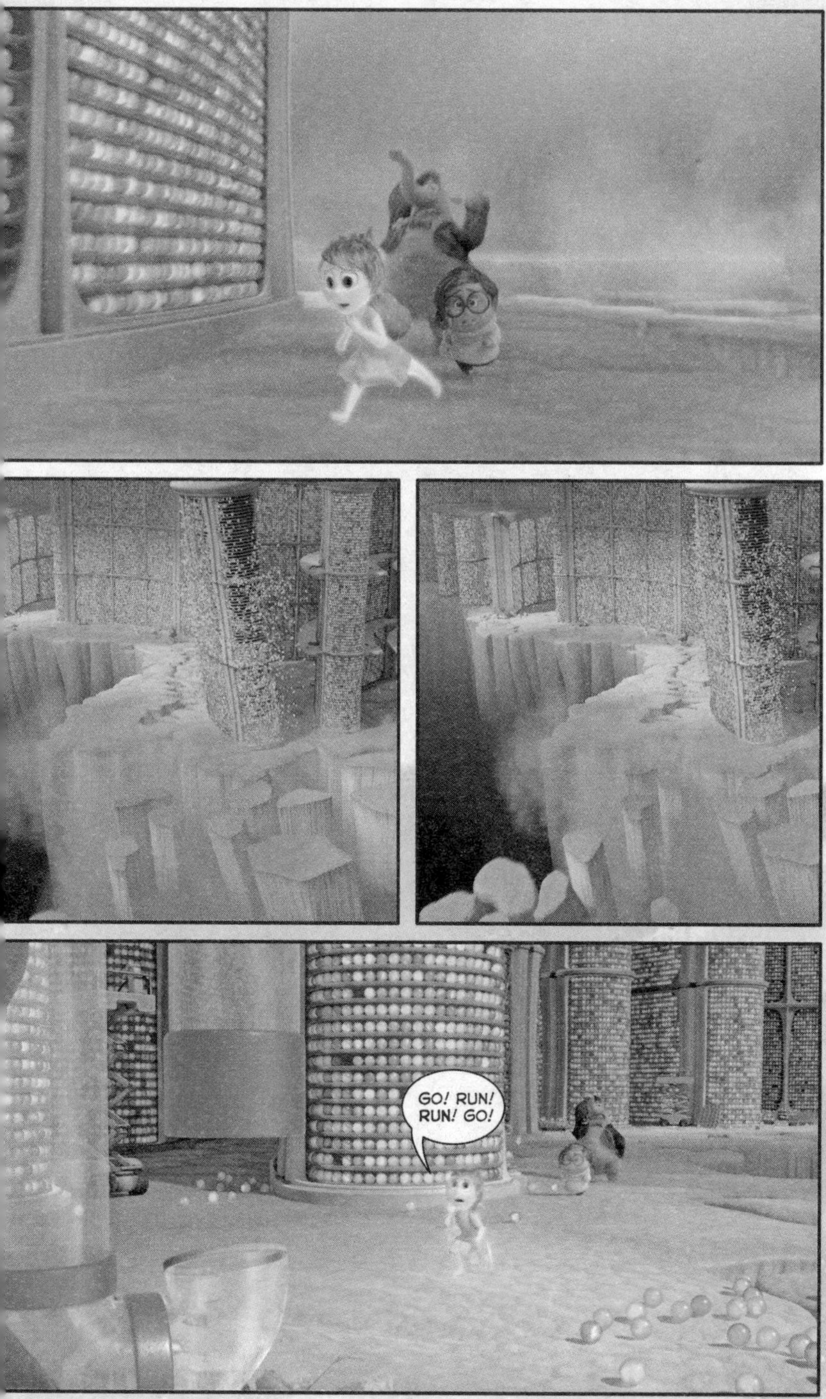
GO! RUN! RUN! GO!

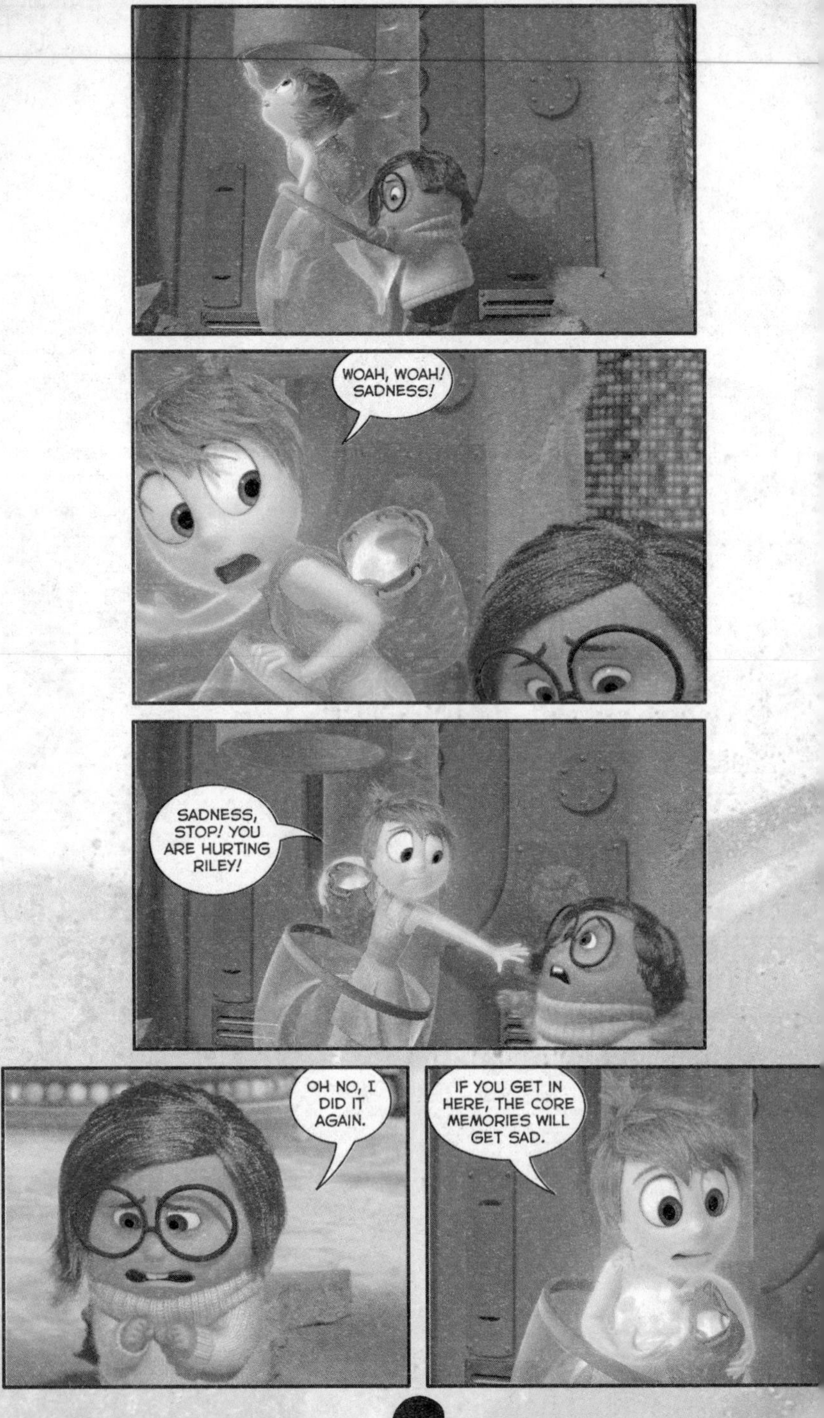
WOAH, WOAH! SADNESS!
SADNESS, STOP! YOU ARE HURTING RILEY!
OH NO, I DID IT AGAIN.
IF YOU GET IN HERE, THE CORE MEMORIES WILL GET SAD.

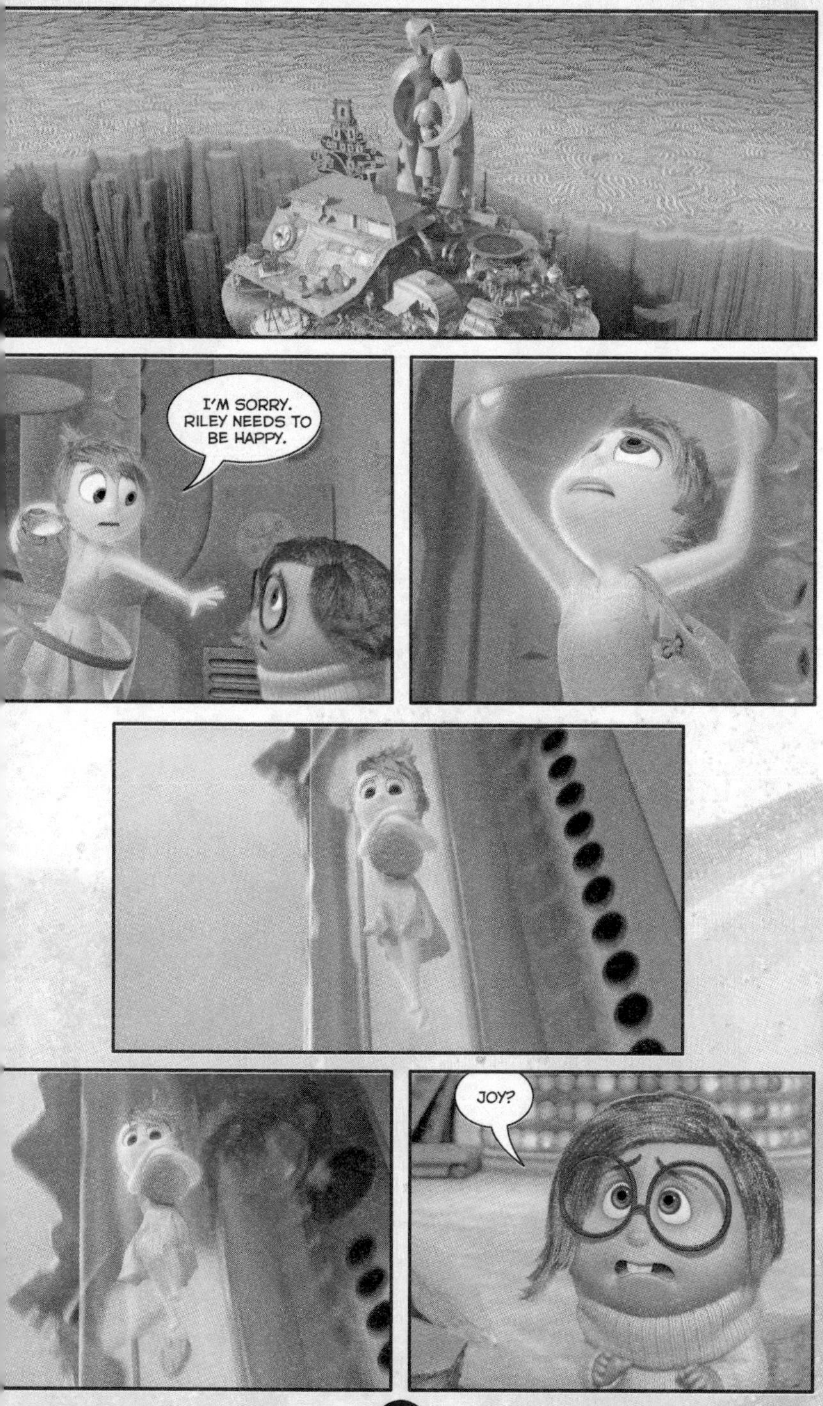
I'M SORRY. RILEY NEEDS TO BE HAPPY.
JOY?

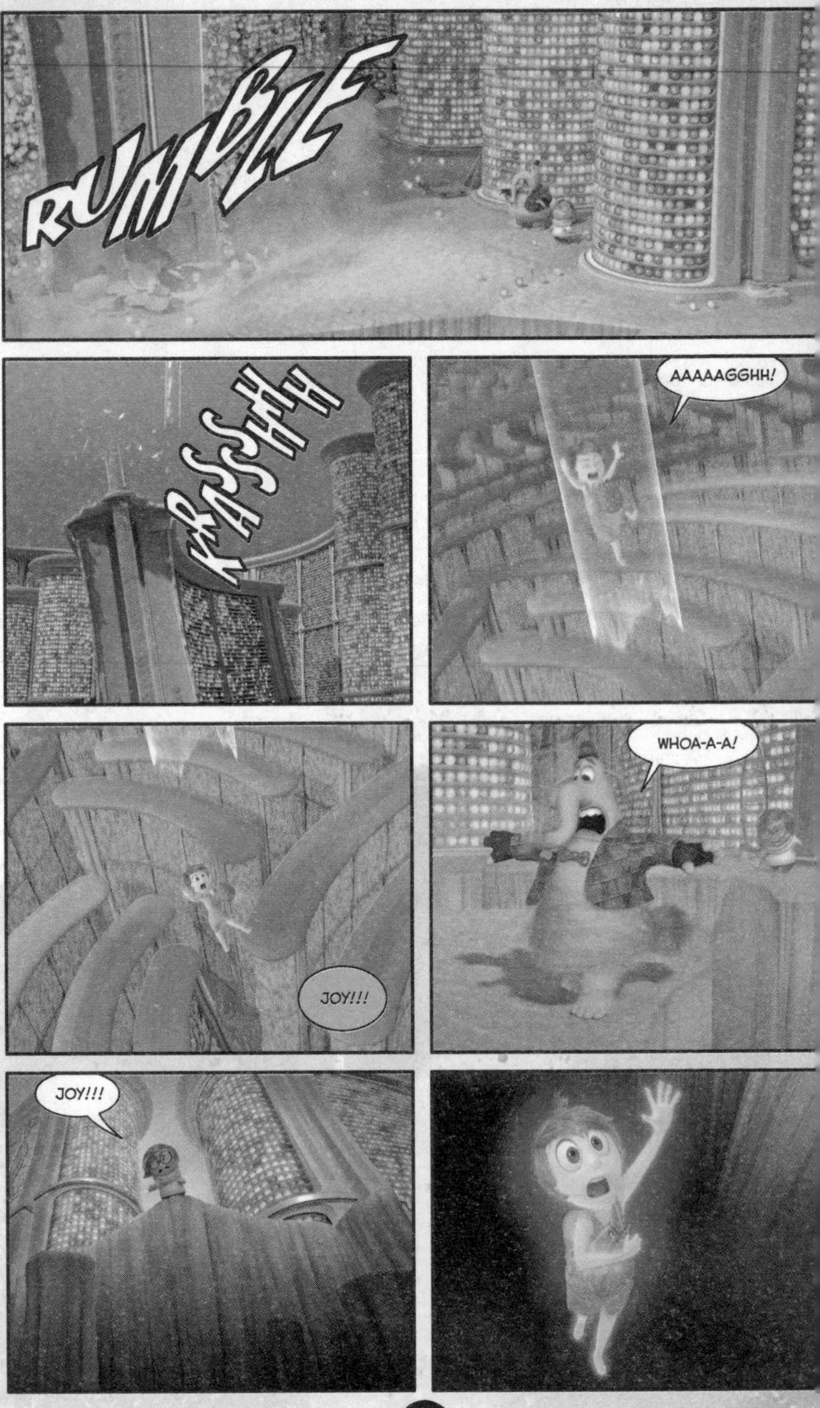
RUMBLE
KRASSHH
AAAAAGGHH!
JOY!!!
WHOA-A-A!
JOY!!!

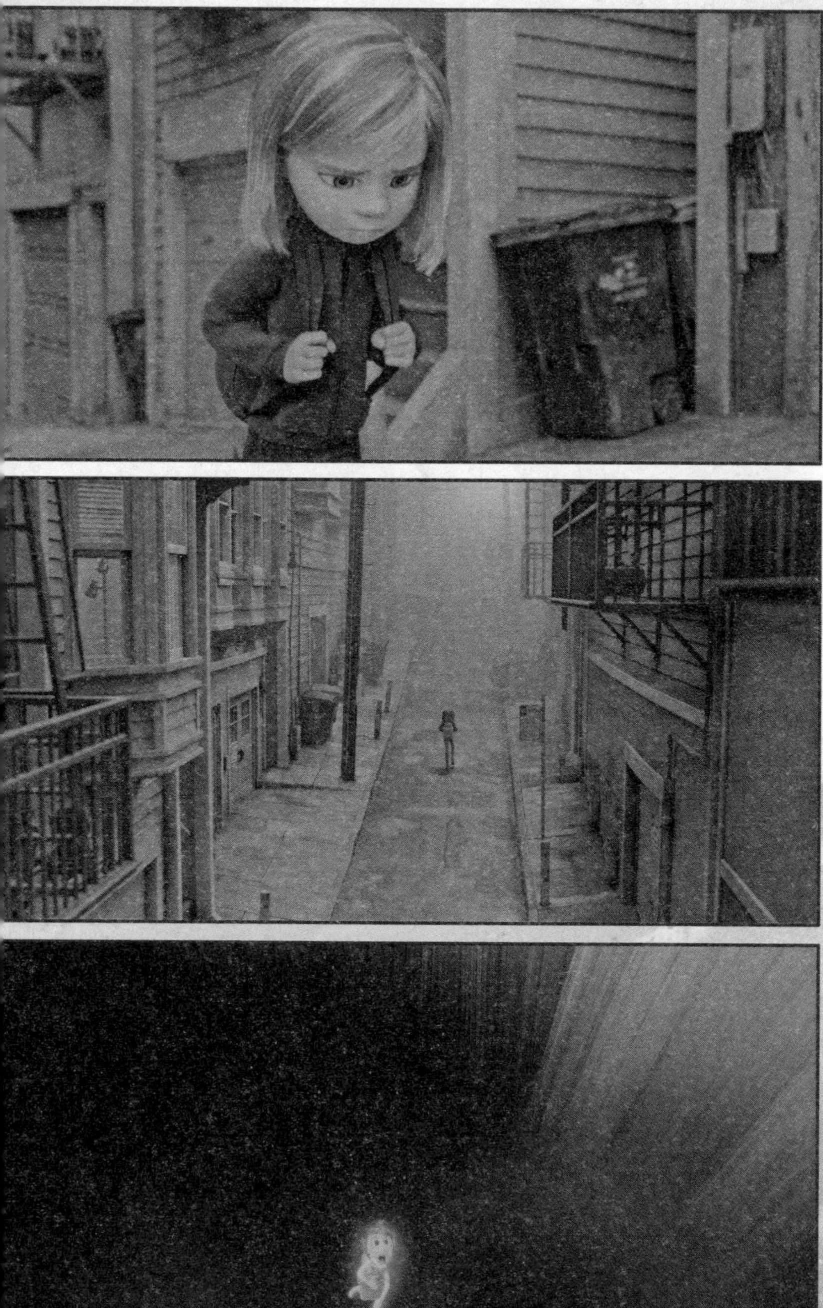

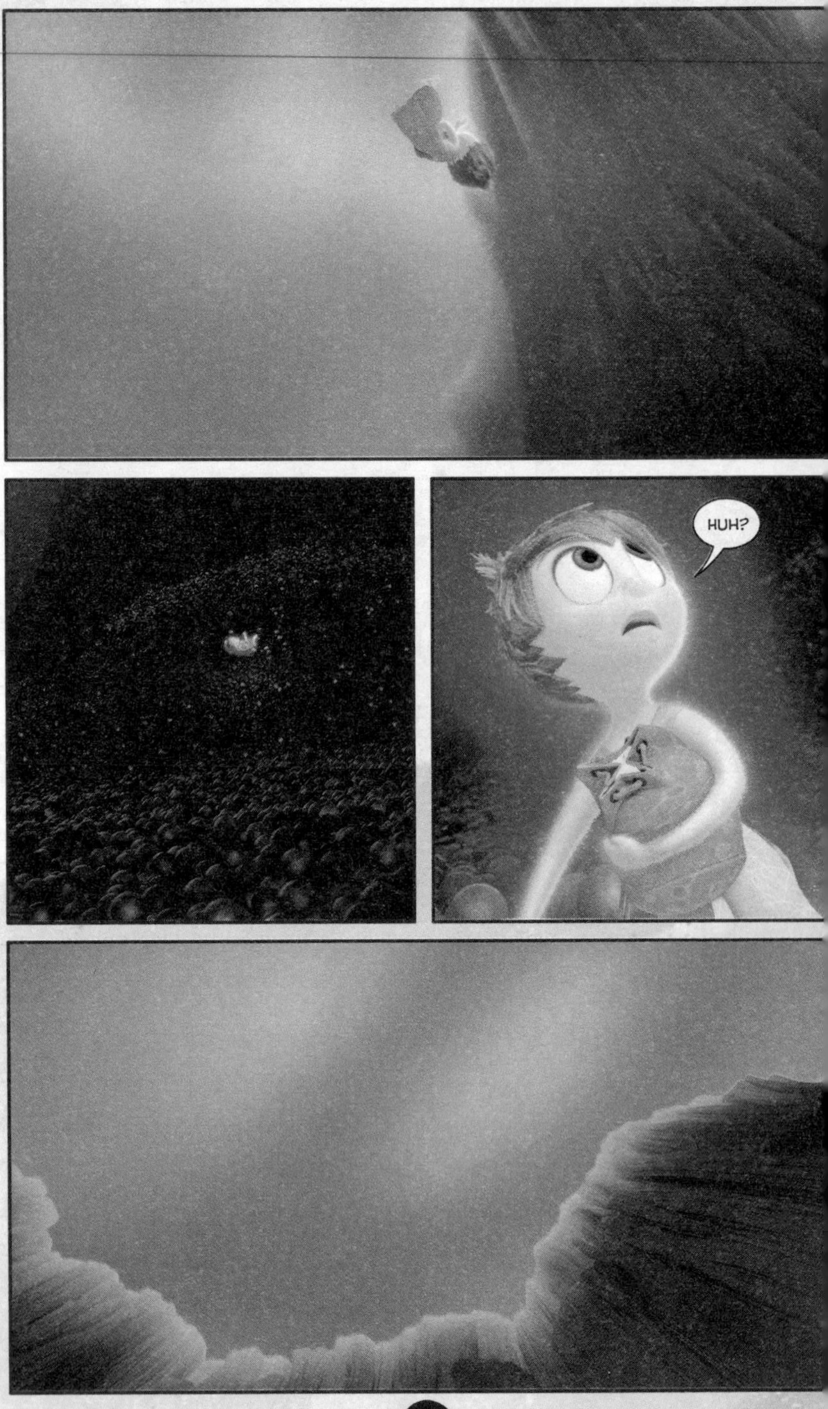
HUH?

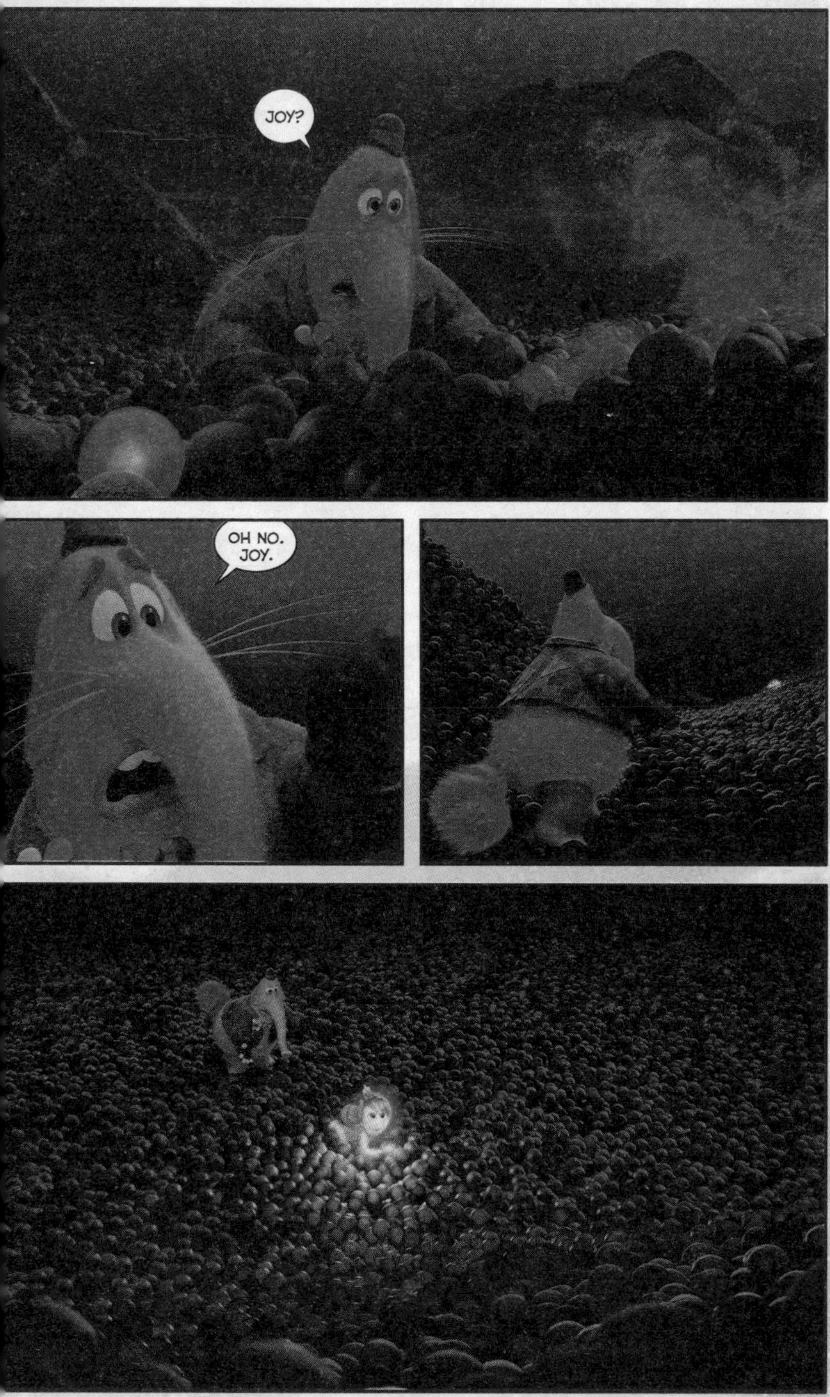
JOY?
OH NO. JOY.

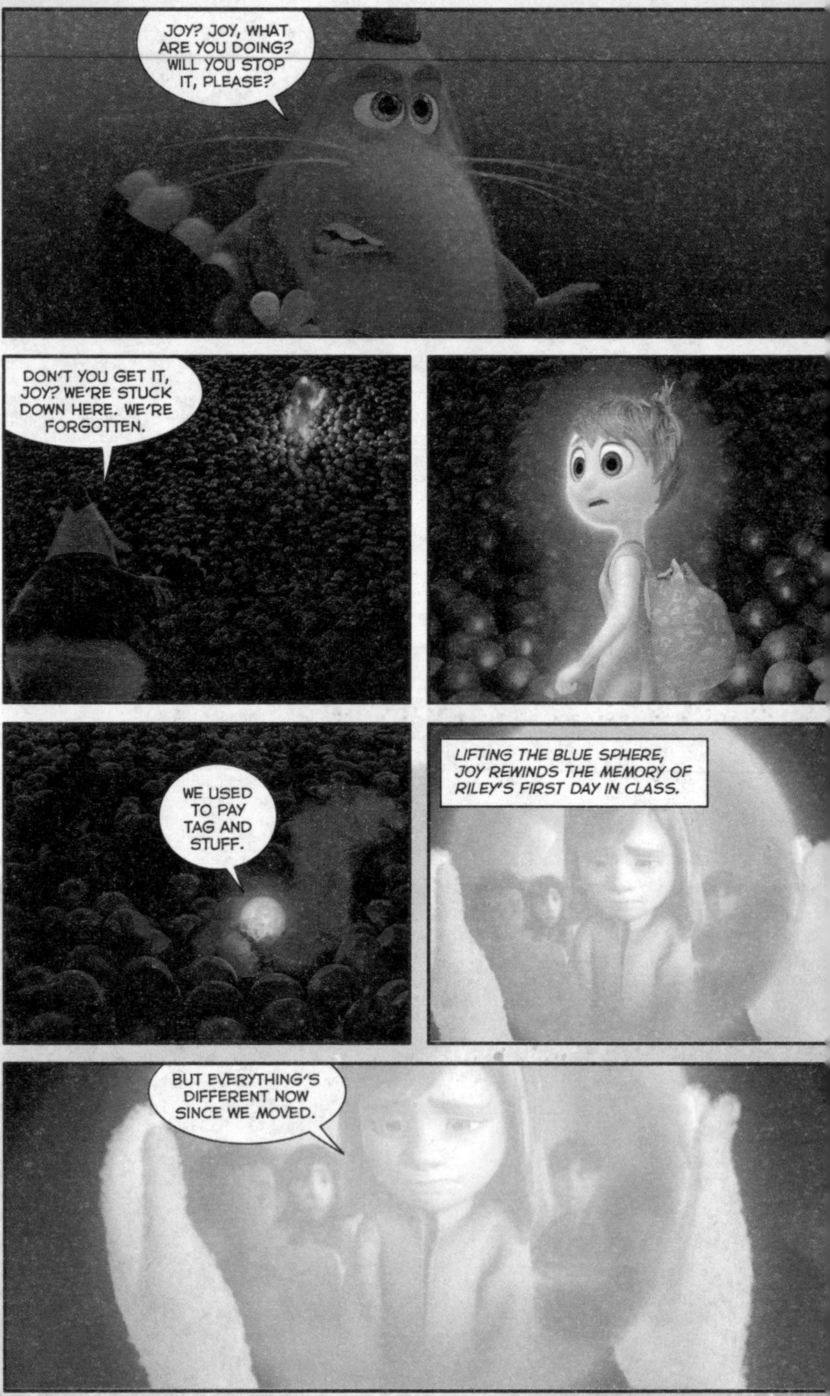
JOY? JOY, WHAT ARE YOU DOING? WILL YOU STOP IT, PLEASE?
DON'T YOU GET IT, JOY? WE'RE STUCK DOWN HERE. WE'RE FORGOTTEN.
WE USED TO PAY TAG AND STUFF.
LIFTING THE BLUE SPHERE, JOY REWINDS THE MEMORY OF RILEY'S FIRST DAY IN CLASS.
BUT EVERYTHING'S DIFFERENT NOW SINCE WE MOVED.

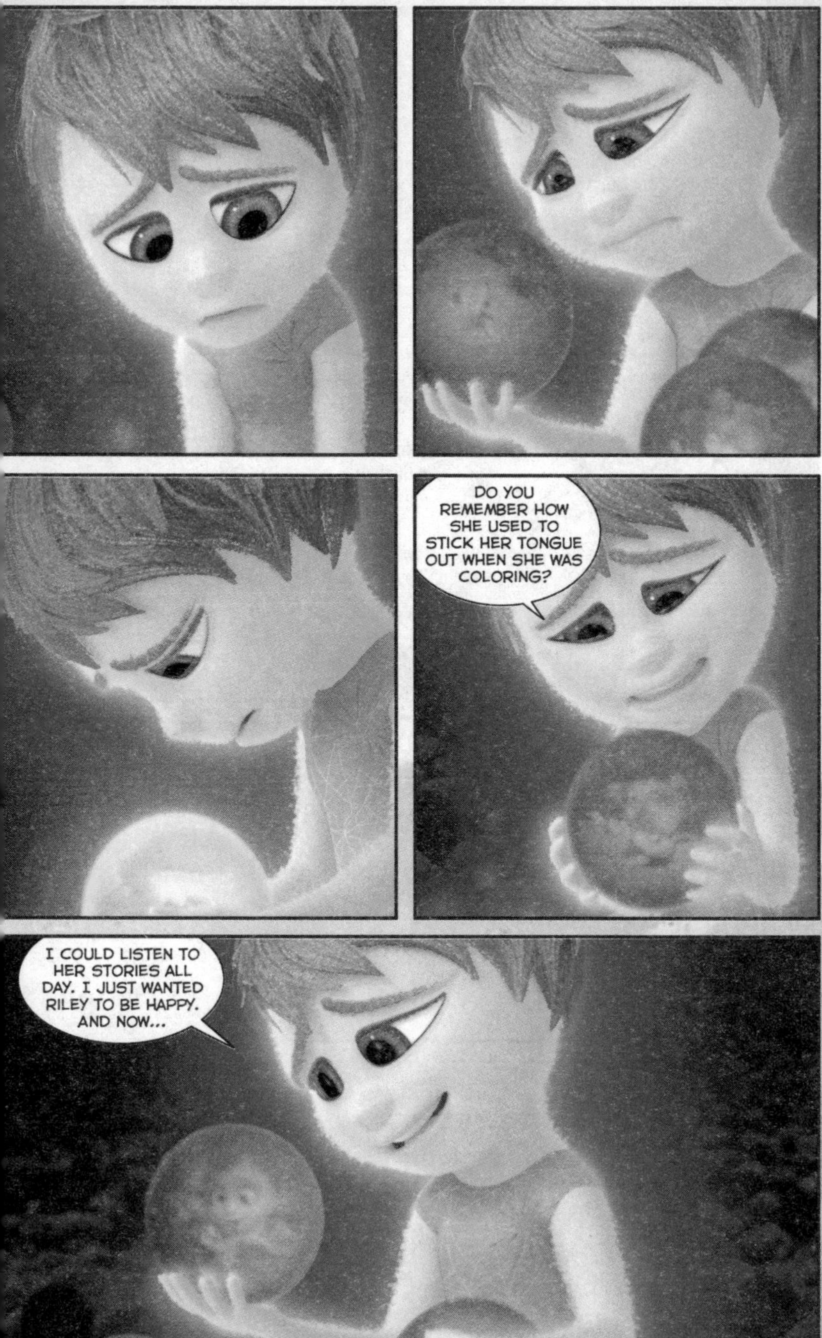
DO YOU REMEMBER HOW SHE USED TO STICK HER TONGUE OUT WHEN SHE WAS COLORING?
I COULD LISTEN TO HER STORIES ALL DAY. I JUST WANTED RILEY TO BE HAPPY. AND NOW...

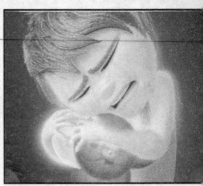

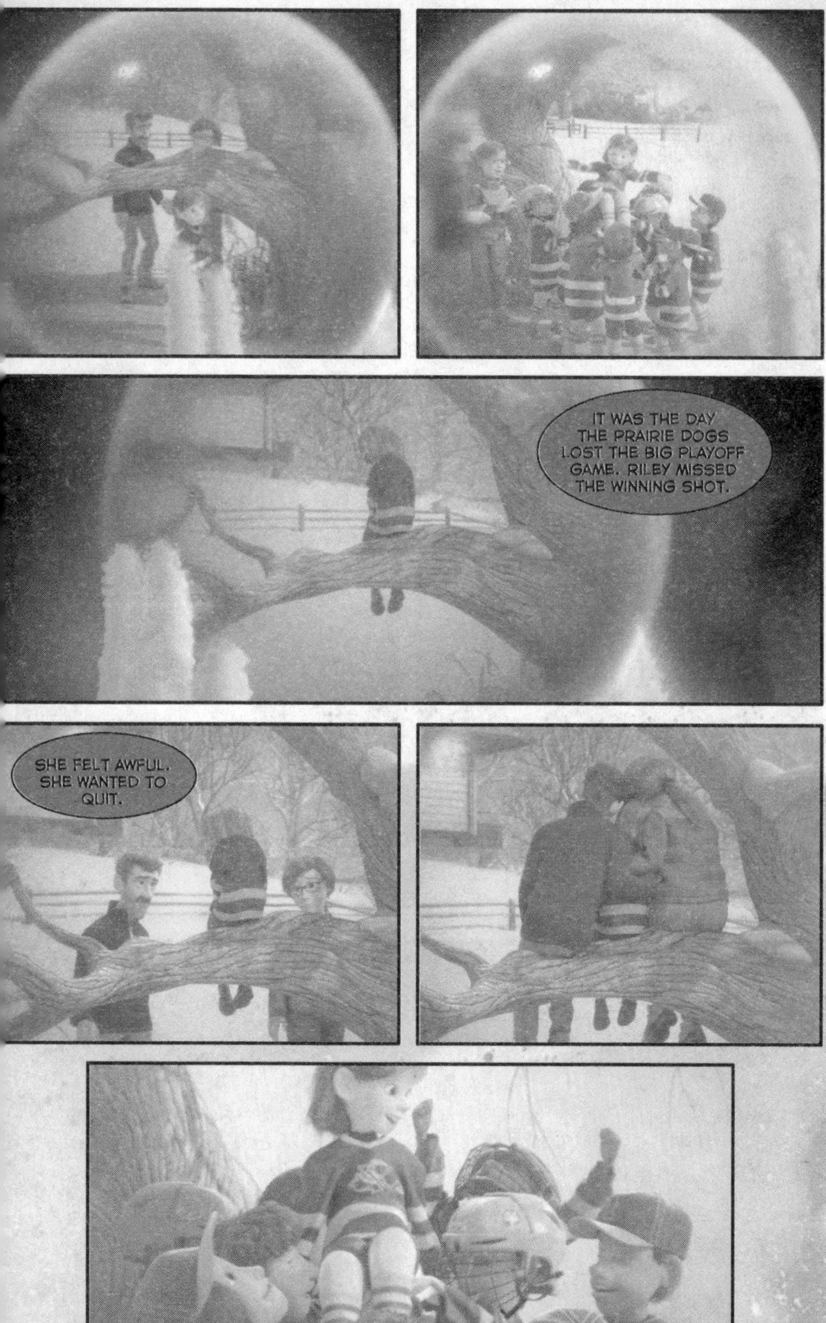
IT WAS THE DAY THE PRAIRIE DOGS LOST THE BIG PLAYOFF GAME. RILEY MISSED THE WINNING SHOT.
SHE FELT AWFUL. SHE WANTED TO QUIT.

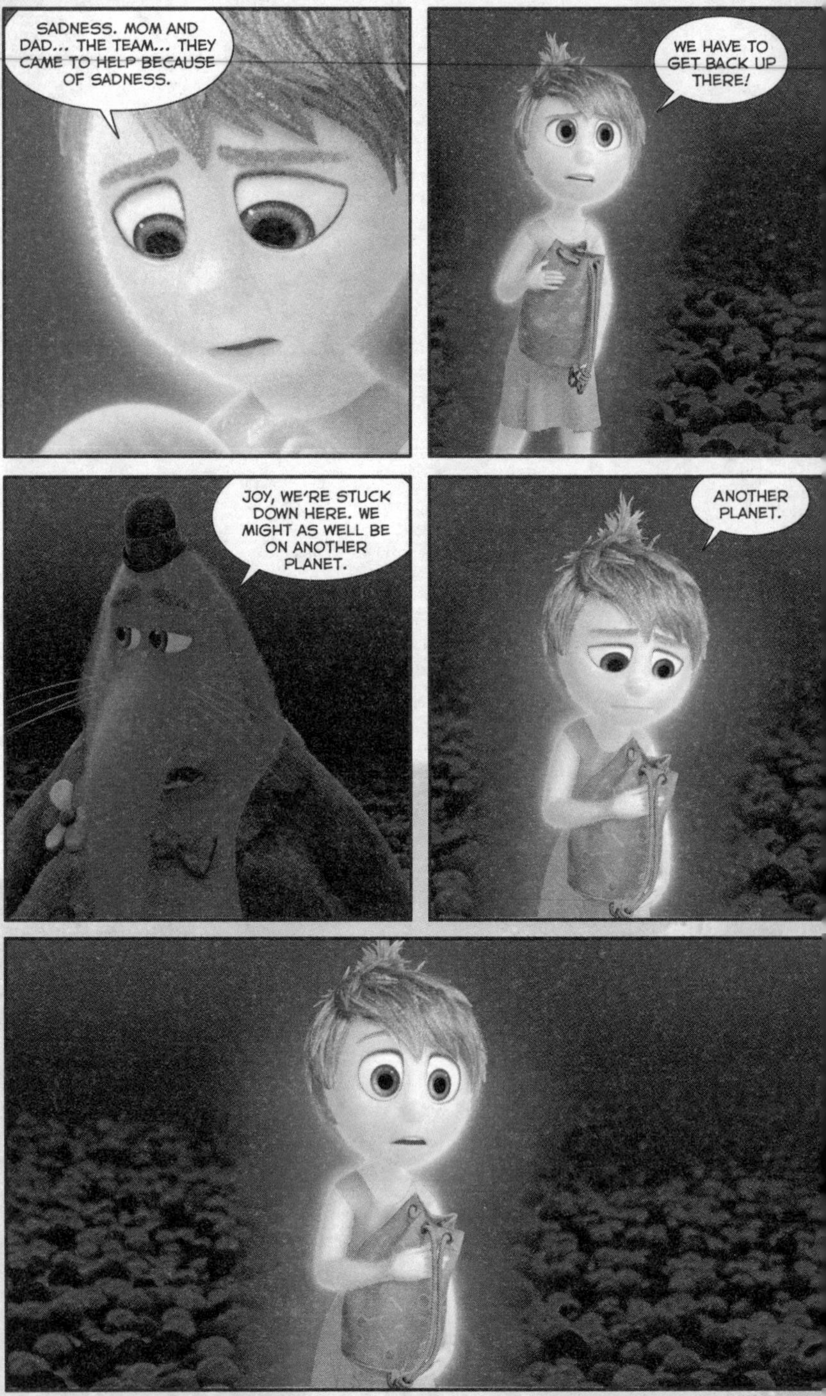
SADNESS. MOM AND DAD... THE TEAM... THEY CAME TO HELP BECAUSE OF SADNESS.
WE HAVE TO GET BACK UP THERE!
JOY, WE'RE STUCK DOWN HERE. WE MIGHT AS WELL BE ON ANOTHER PLANET.
ANOTHER PLANET.

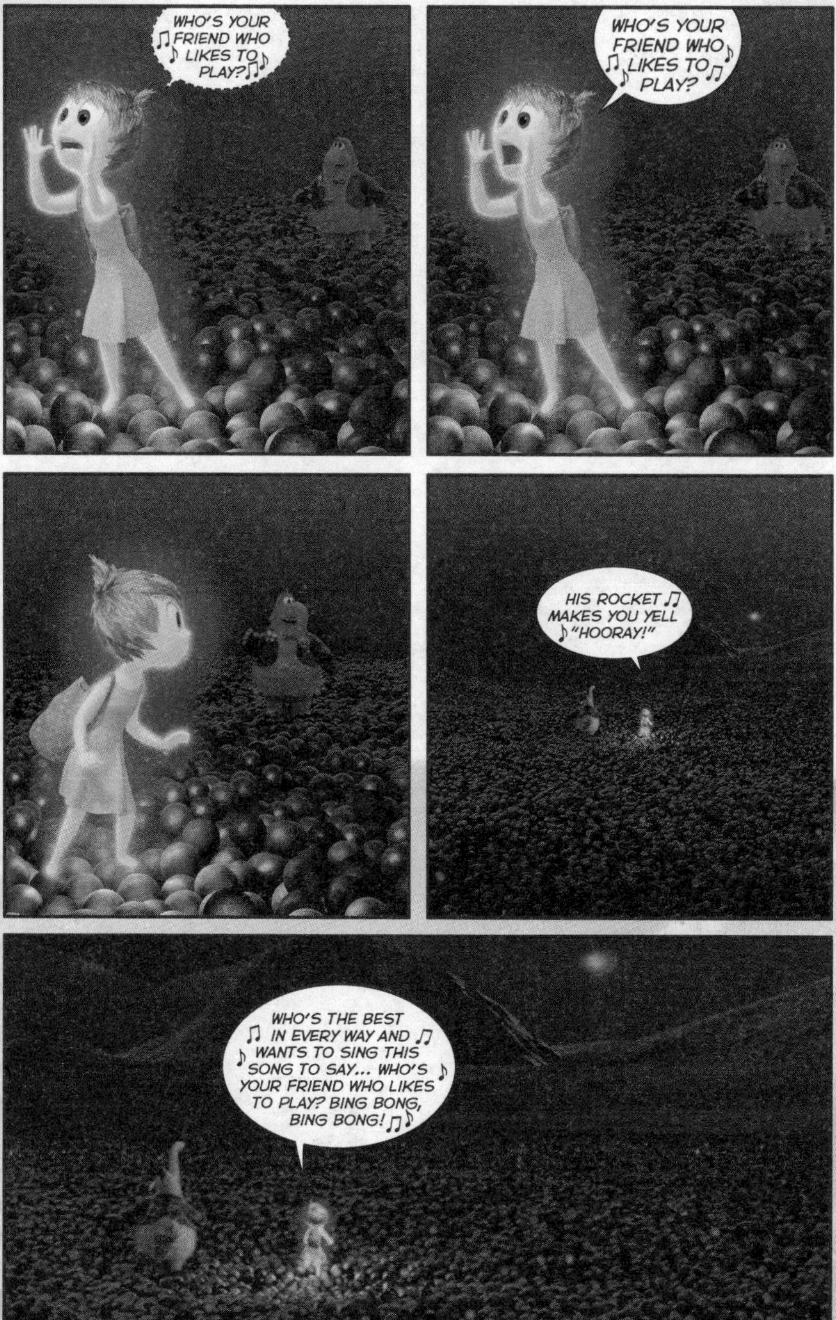
WHO'S YOUR FRIEND WHO LIKES TO PLAY?
WHO'S YOUR FRIEND WHO LIKES TO PLAY?
HIS ROCKET MAKES YOU YELL "HOORAY!"
WHO'S THE BEST IN EVERY WAY AND WANTS TO SING THIS SONG TO SAY... WHO'S YOUR FRIEND WHO LIKES TO PLAY? BING BONG, BING BONG!

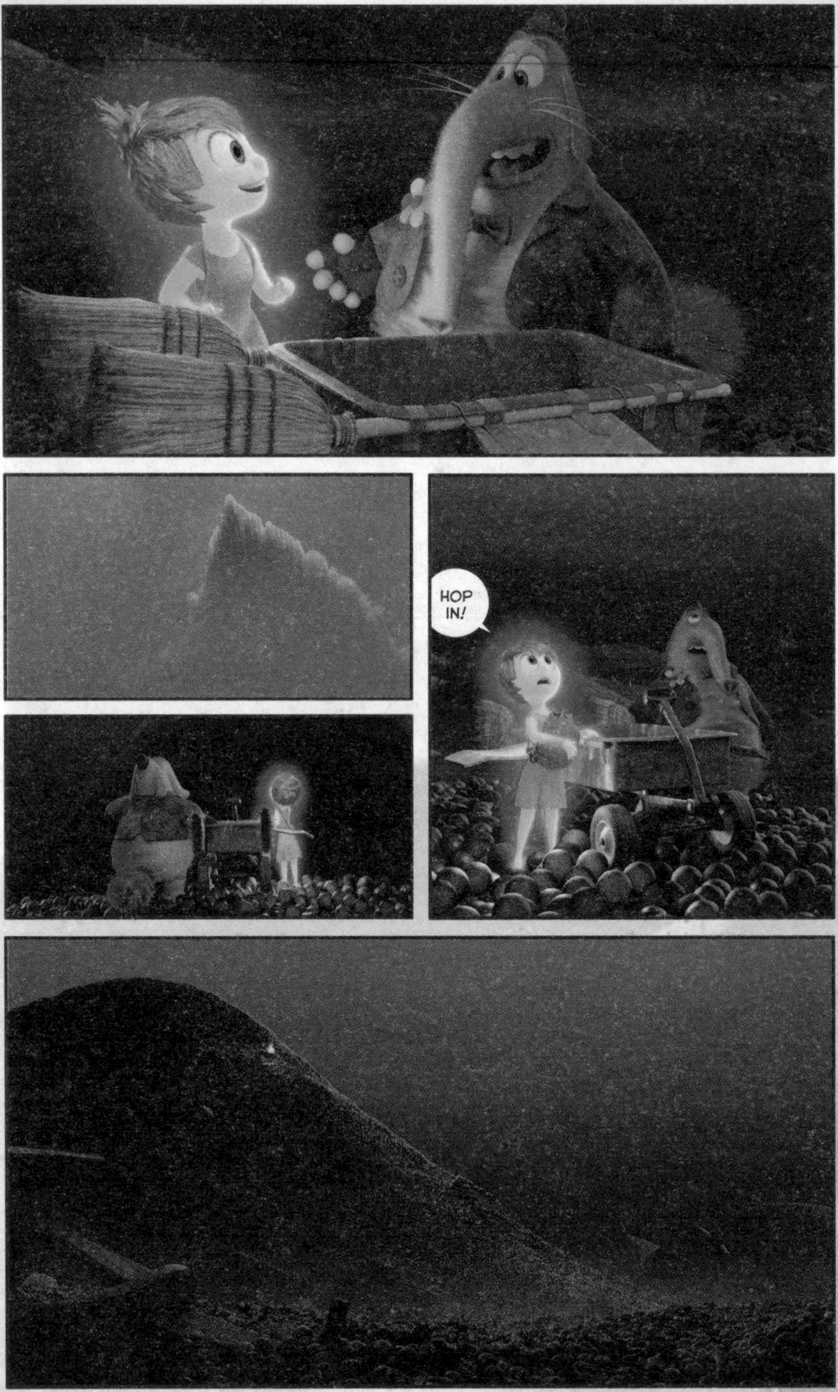
HOP IN!

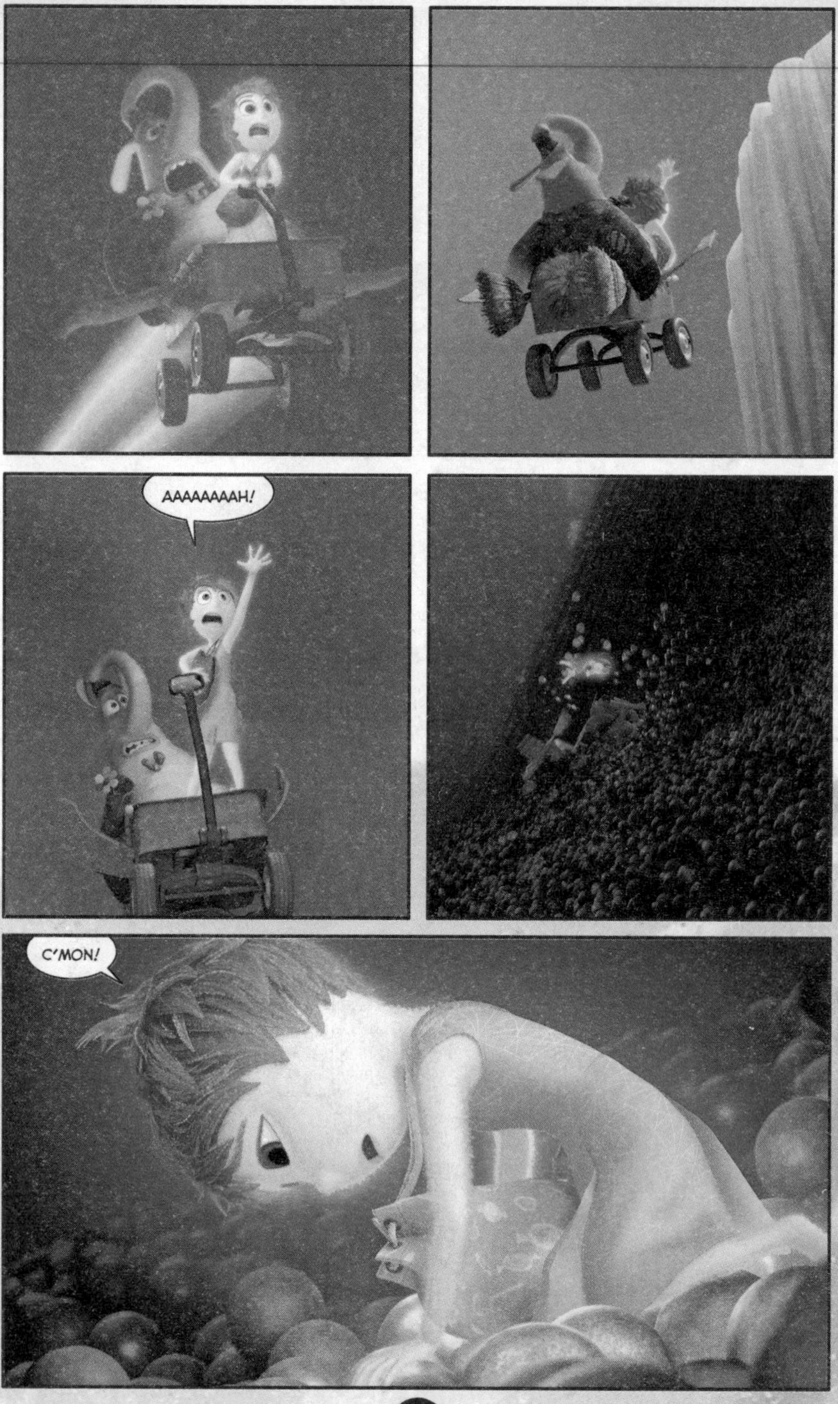
AAAAAAAAH!
C'MON!

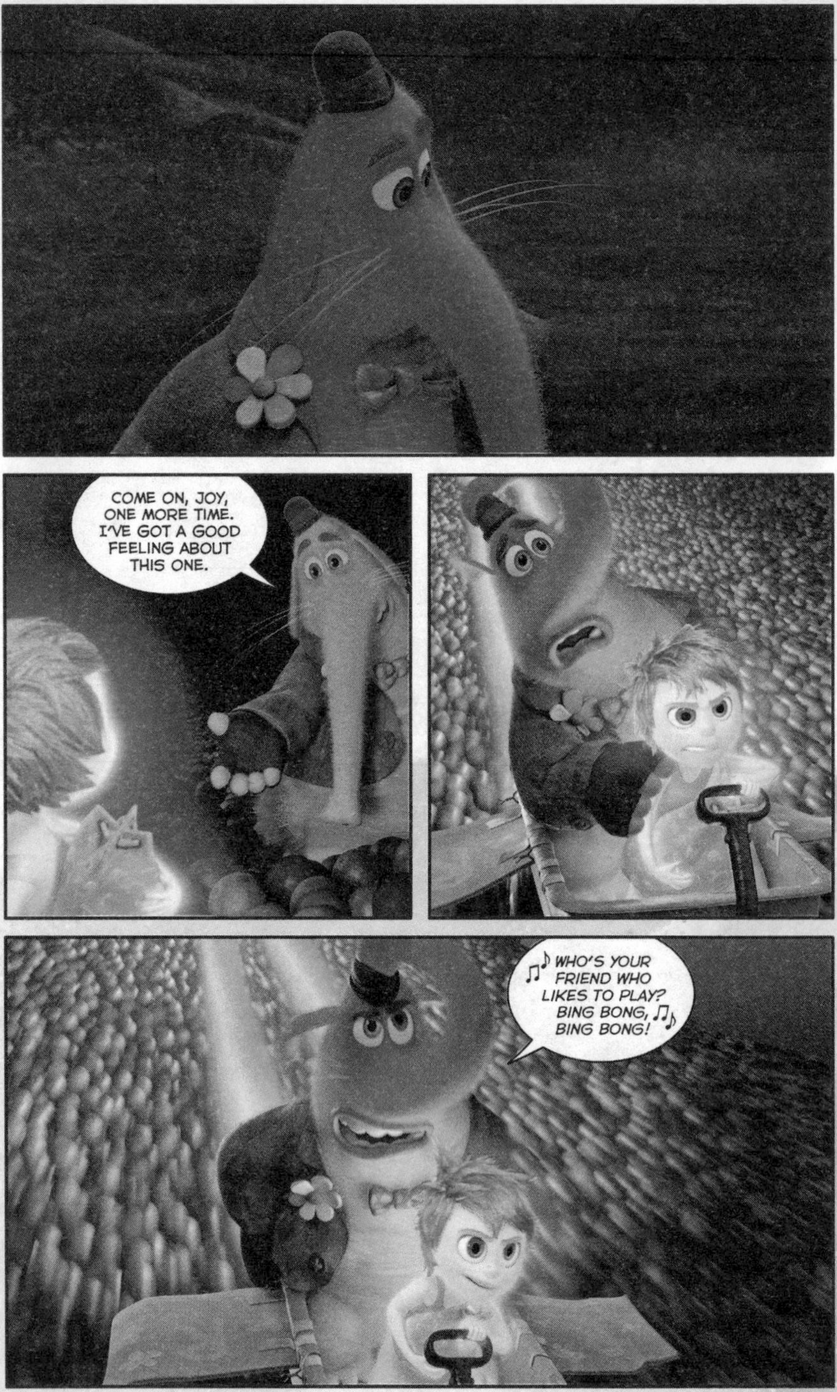
COME ON, JOY, ONE MORE TIME. I'VE GOT A GOOD FEELING ABOUT THIS ONE.
♫♪ WHO'S YOUR FRIEND WHO LIKES TO PLAY? BING BONG, BING BONG! ♫♪

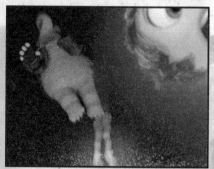

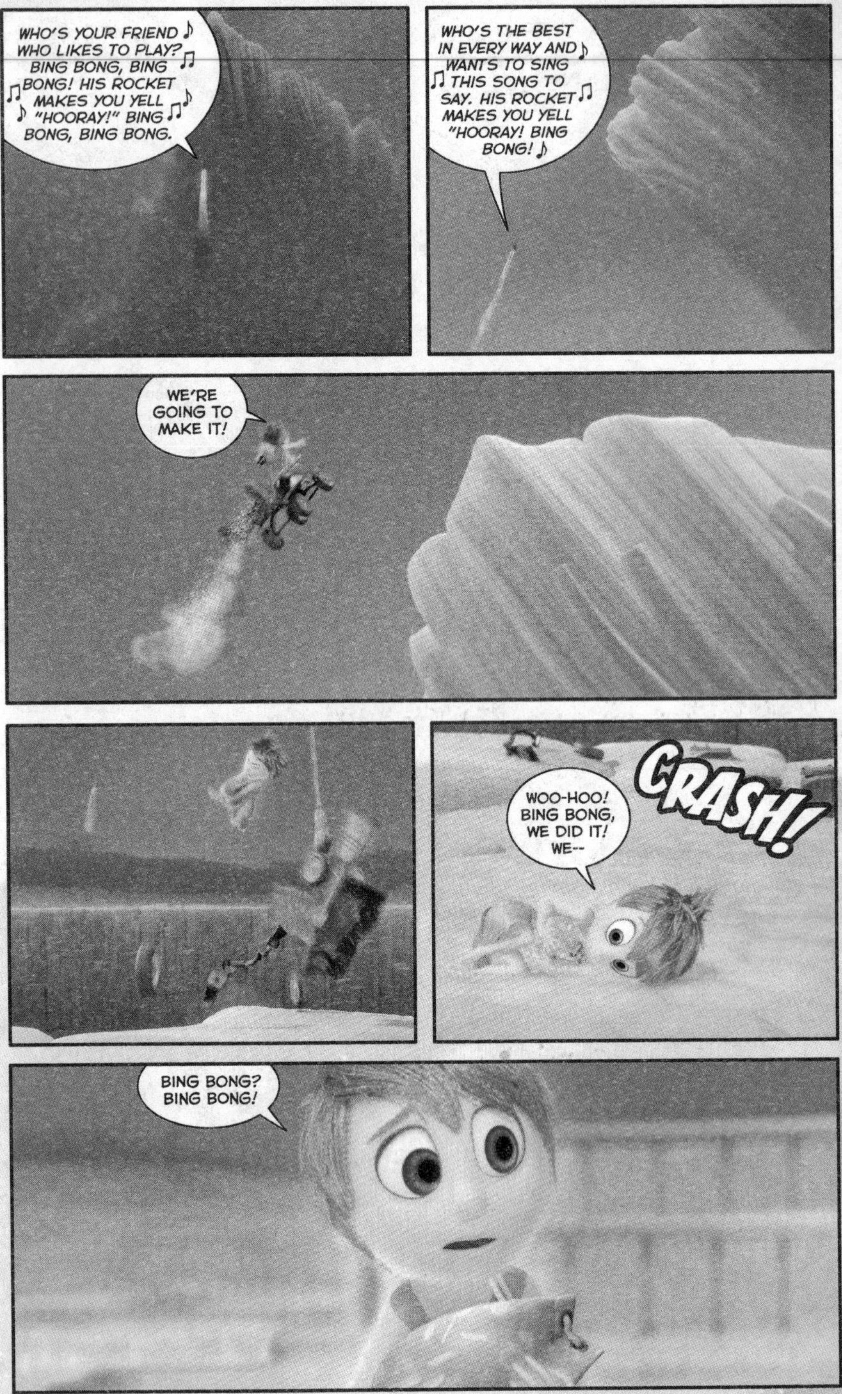
WHO'S YOUR FRIEND ♪ WHO LIKES TO PLAY? ♫ BING BONG, BING ♫ BONG! HIS ROCKET MAKES YOU YELL ♪ "HOORAY!" BING ♫♪ BONG, BING BONG.
WHO'S THE BEST IN EVERY WAY AND ♪ WANTS TO SING ♫ THIS SONG TO SAY. HIS ROCKET ♫ MAKES YOU YELL "HOORAY! BING BONG! ♪
WE'RE GOING TO MAKE IT!
CRASH!
WOO-HOO! BING BONG, WE DID IT! WE--
BING BONG? BING BONG!

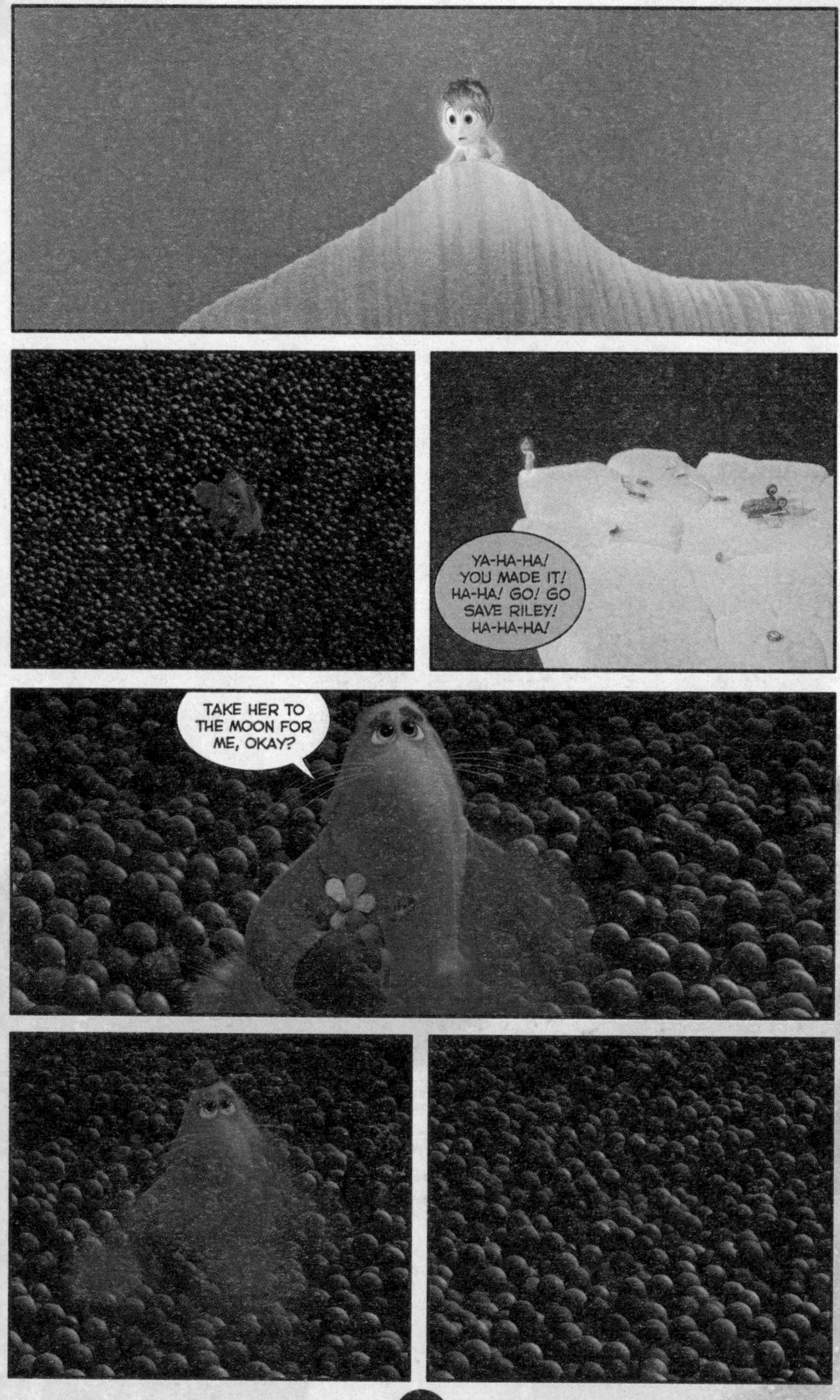
YA-HA-HA! YOU MADE IT! HA-HA! GO! GO SAVE RILEY! HA-HA-HA!
TAKE HER TO THE MOON FOR ME, OKAY?

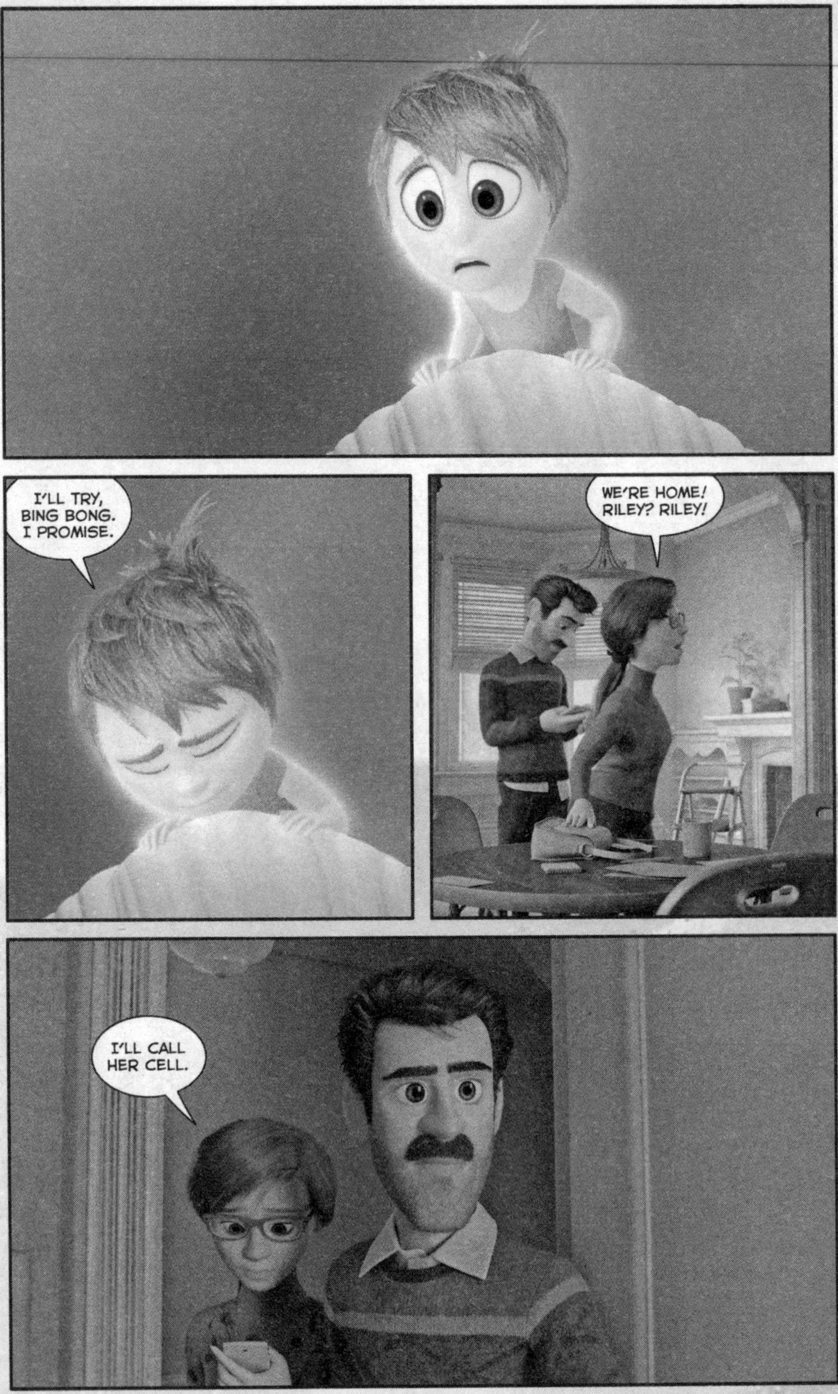
I'LL TRY,
BING BONG.
I PROMISE.
WE'RE HOME!
RILEY? RILEY!
I'LL CALL
HER CELL.

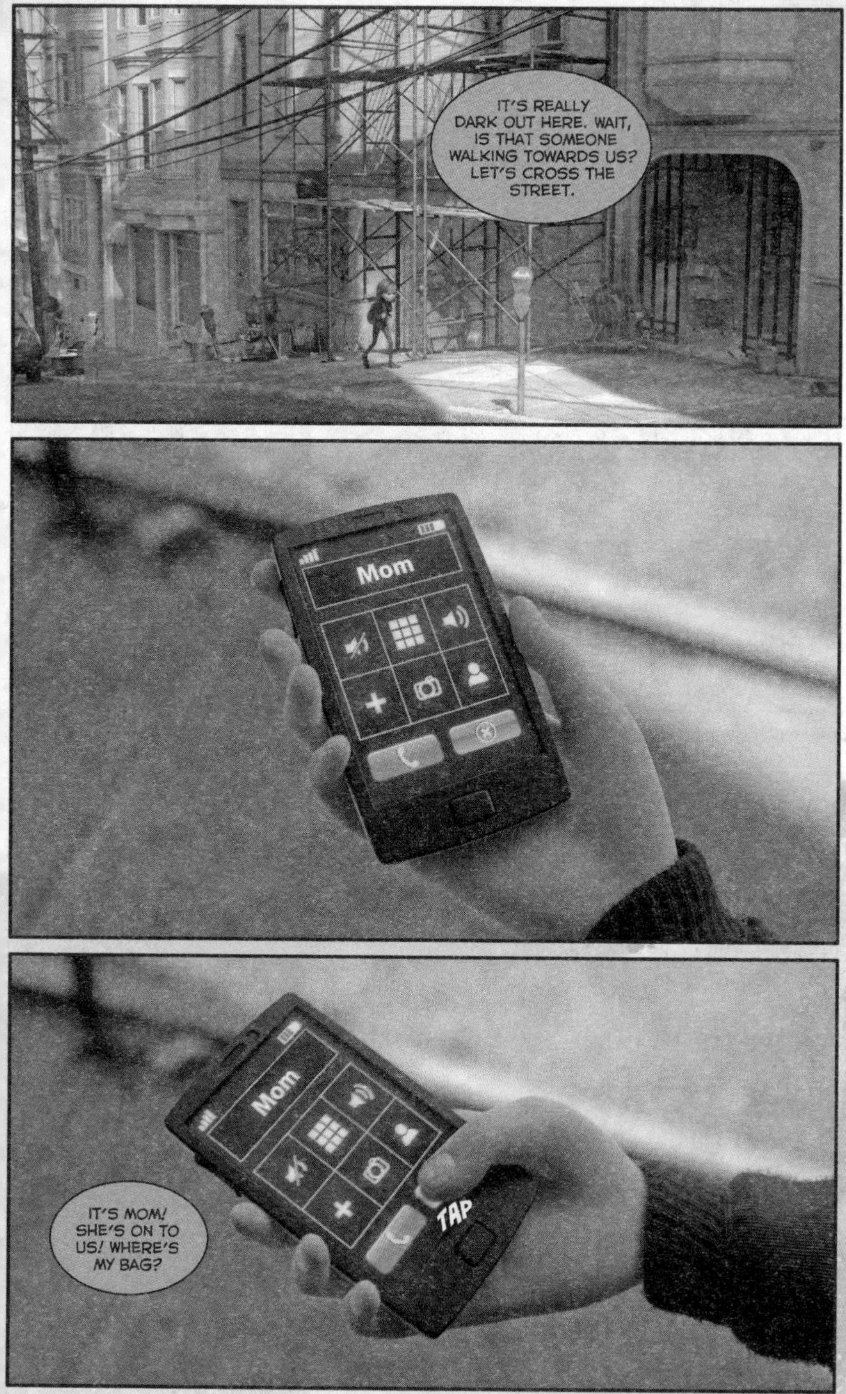
IT'S REALLY DARK OUT HERE. WAIT, IS THAT SOMEONE WALKING TOWARDS US? LET'S CROSS THE STREET.
Mom
Mom
TAP
IT'S MOM! SHE'S ON TO US! WHERE'S MY BAG?

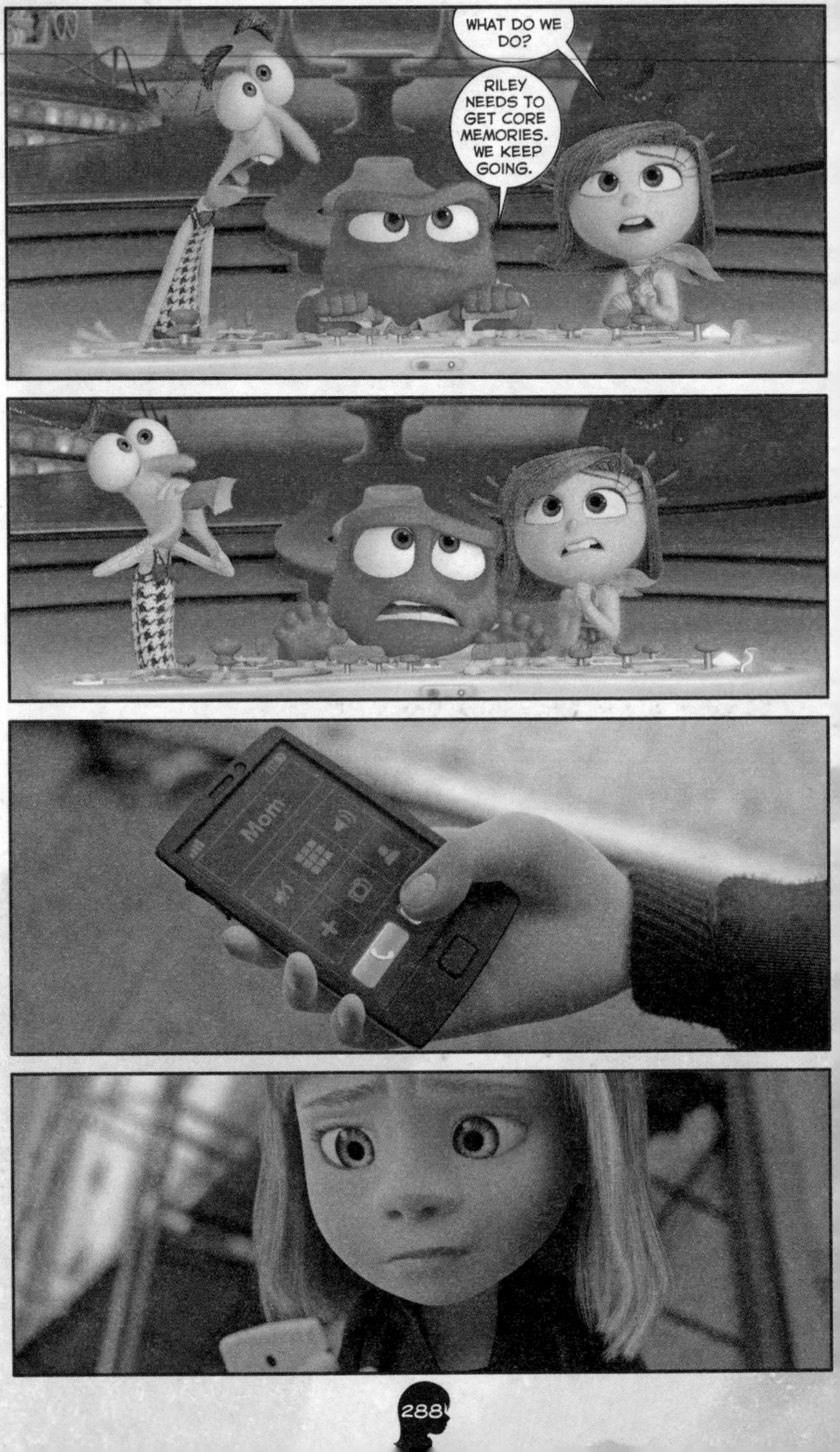
WHAT DO WE DO?
RILEY NEEDS TO GET CORE MEMORIES. WE KEEP GOING.
Mom

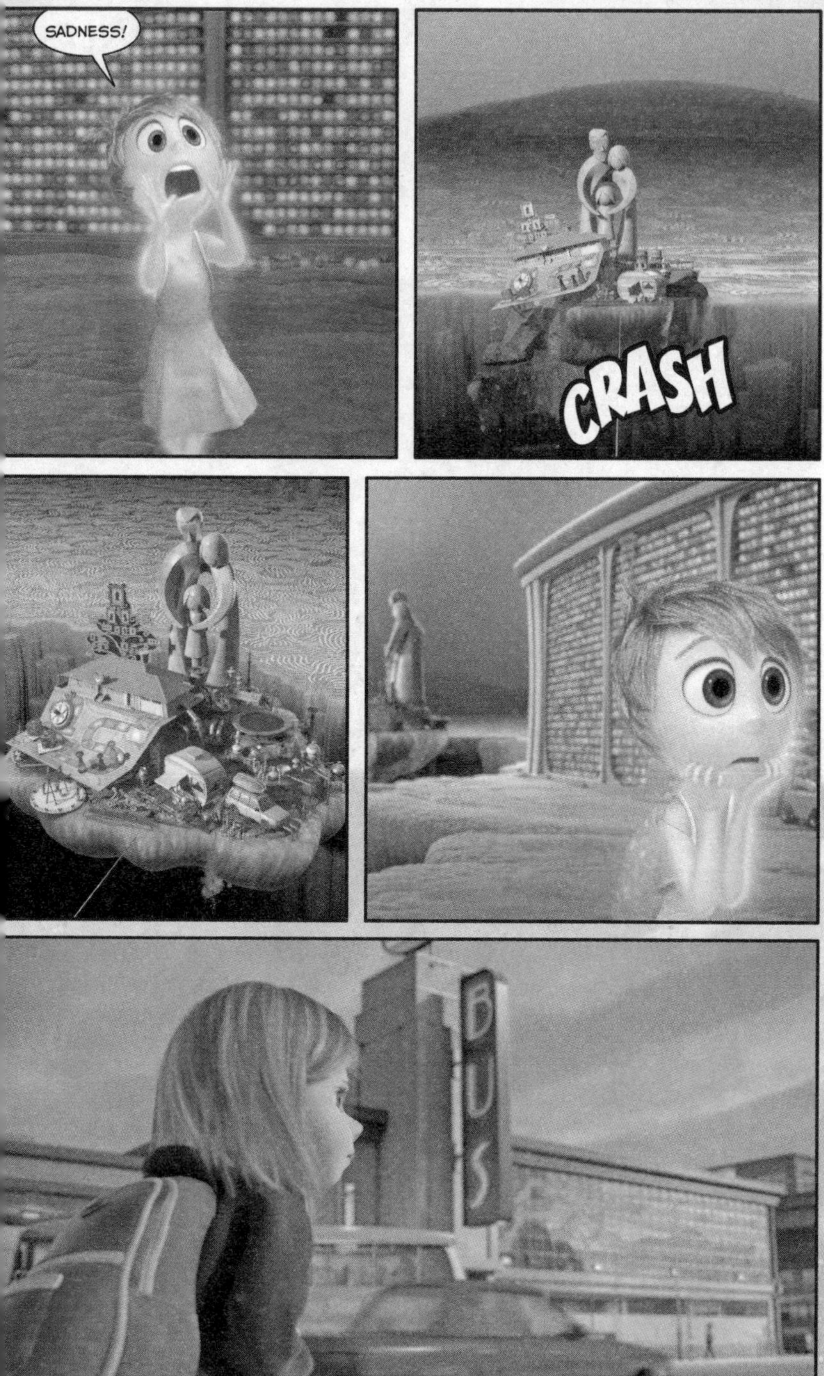
SADNESS!
CRASH

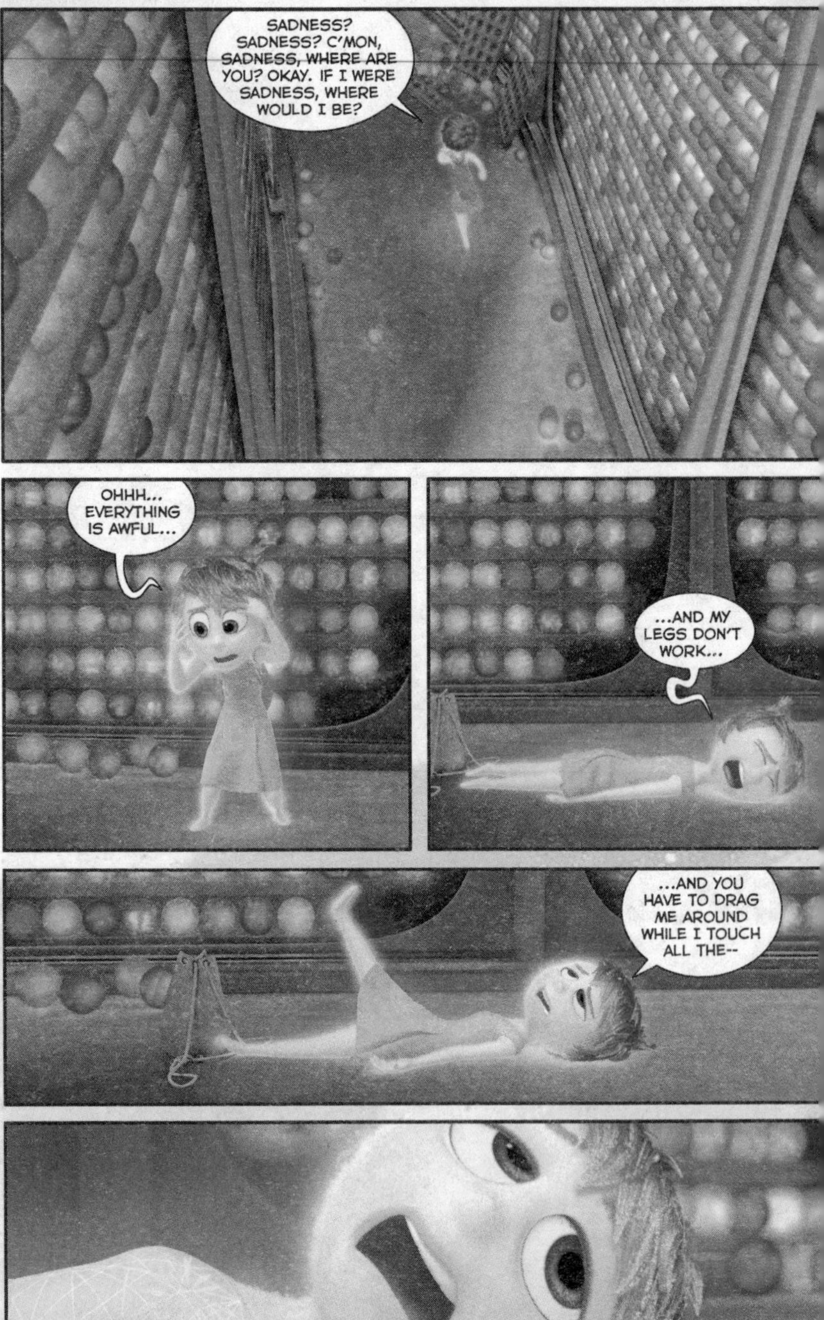
SADNESS? SADNESS? C'MON, SADNESS, WHERE ARE YOU? OKAY. IF I WERE SADNESS, WHERE WOULD I BE?
OHHH... EVERYTHING IS AWFUL...
...AND MY LEGS DON'T WORK...
...AND YOU HAVE TO DRAG ME AROUND WHILE I TOUCH ALL THE--

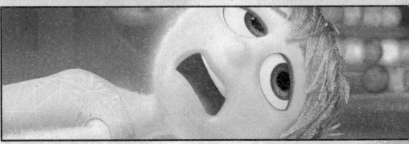

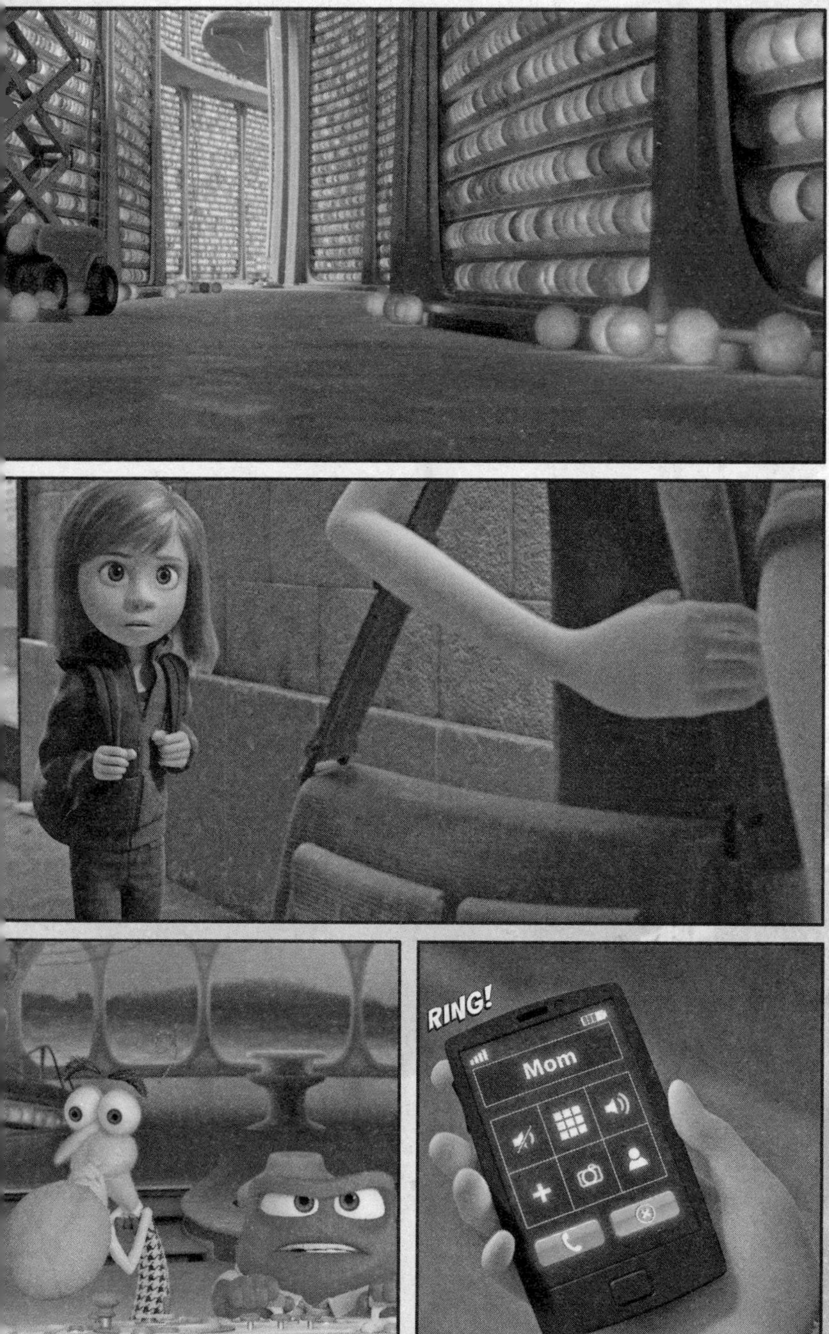
RING!
Mom

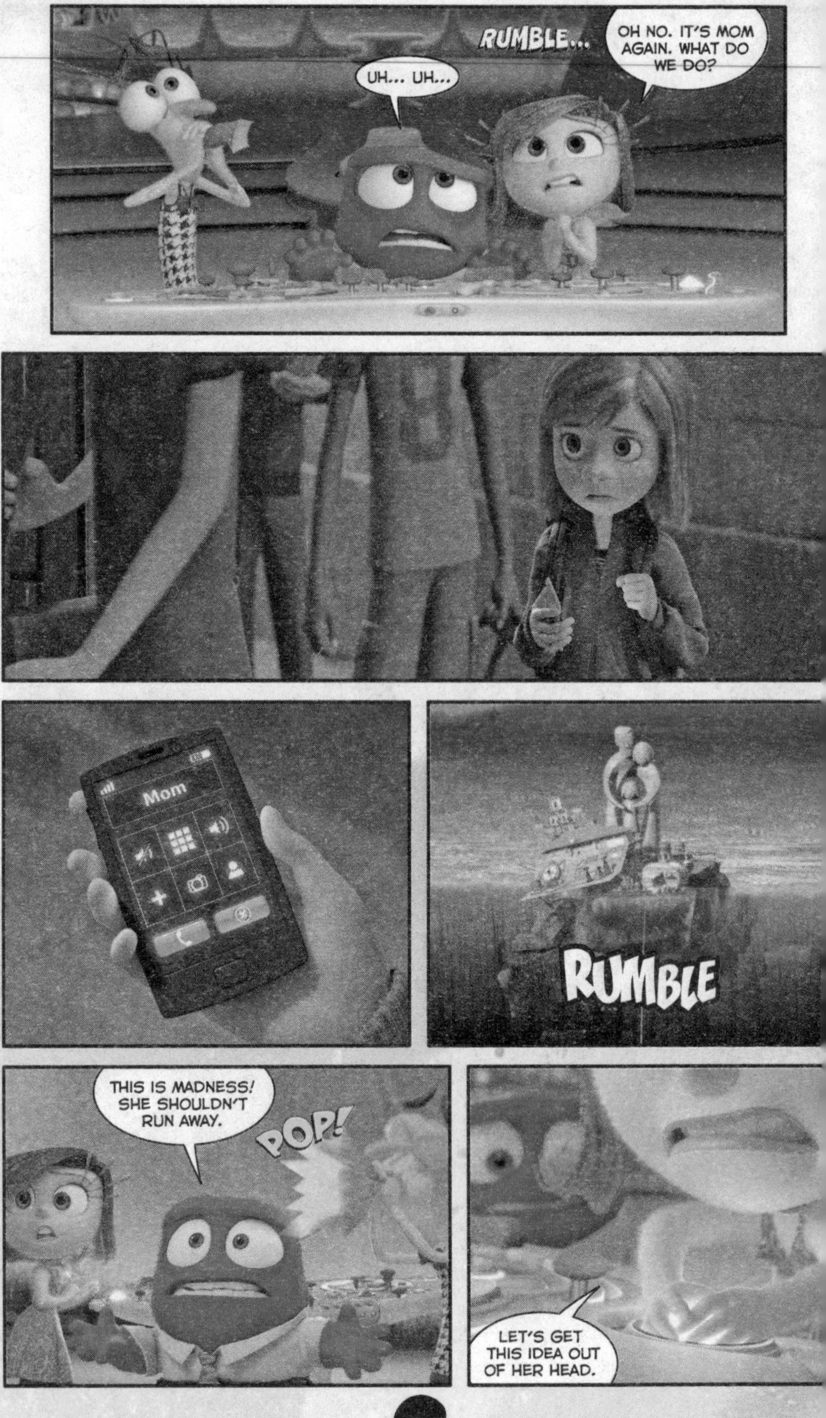
RUMBLE...
OH NO. IT'S MOM AGAIN. WHAT DO WE DO?
UH... UH...
Mom
RUMBLE
THIS IS MADNESS! SHE SHOULDN'T RUN AWAY.
POP!
LET'S GET THIS IDEA OUT OF HER HEAD.

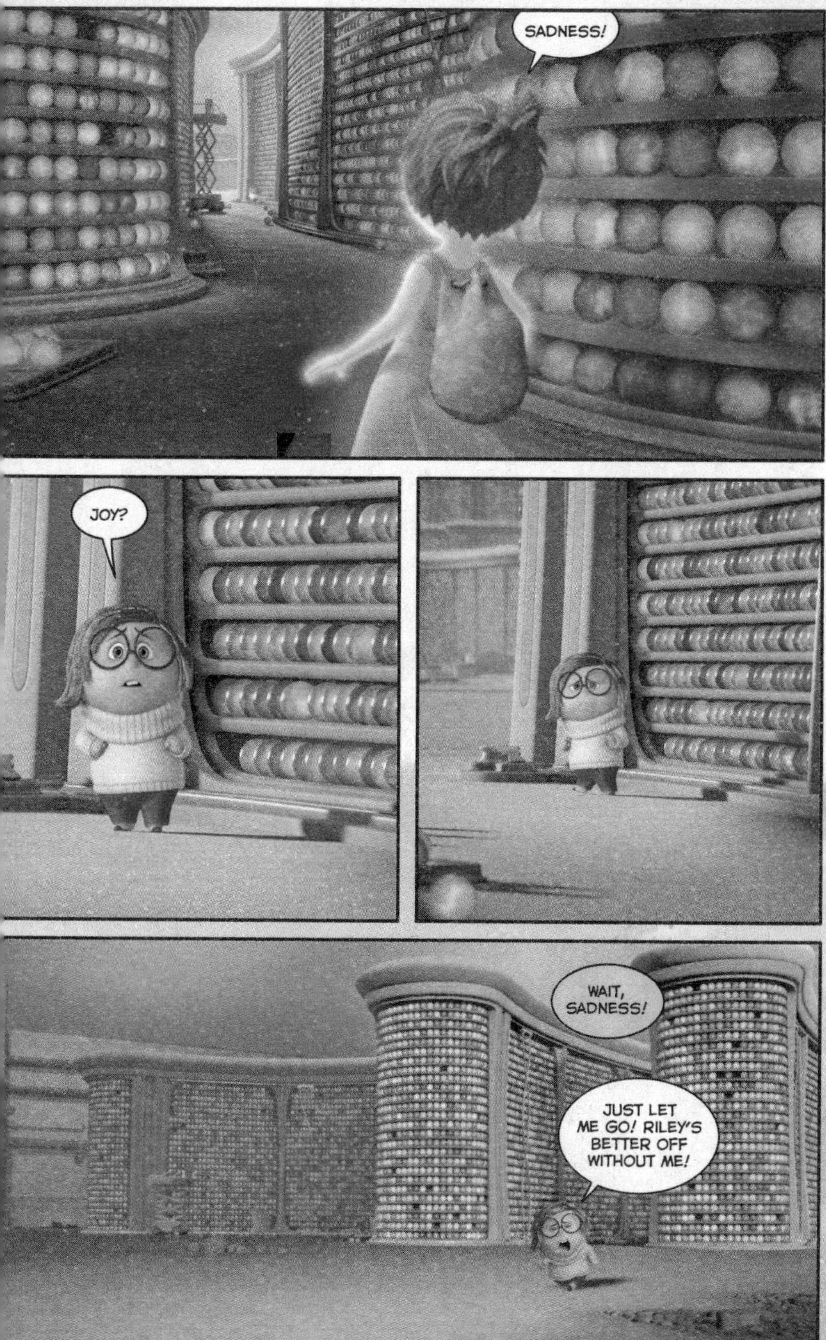
SADNESS!
JOY?
WAIT, SADNESS!
JUST LET ME GO! RILEY'S BETTER OFF WITHOUT ME!

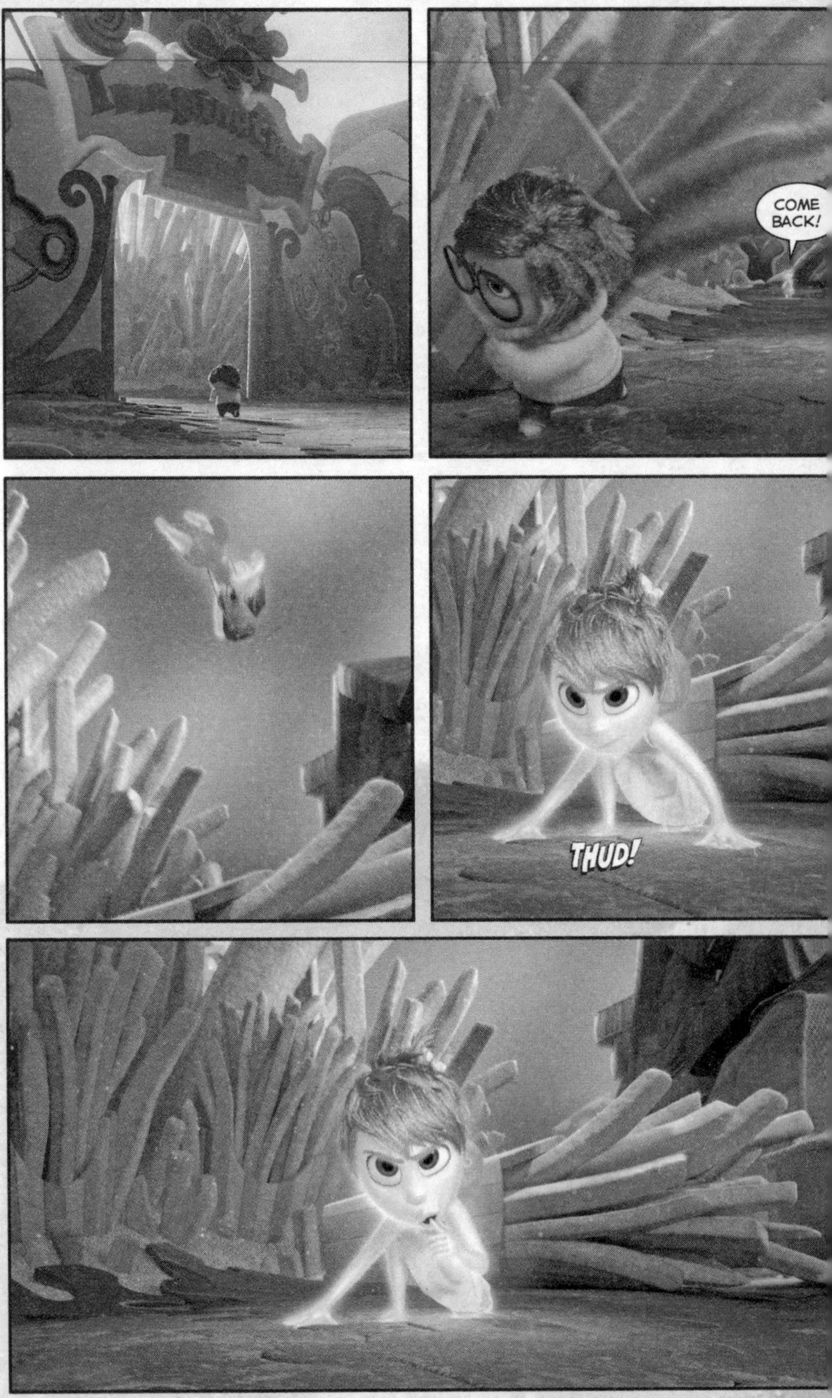
COME BACK!
THUD!

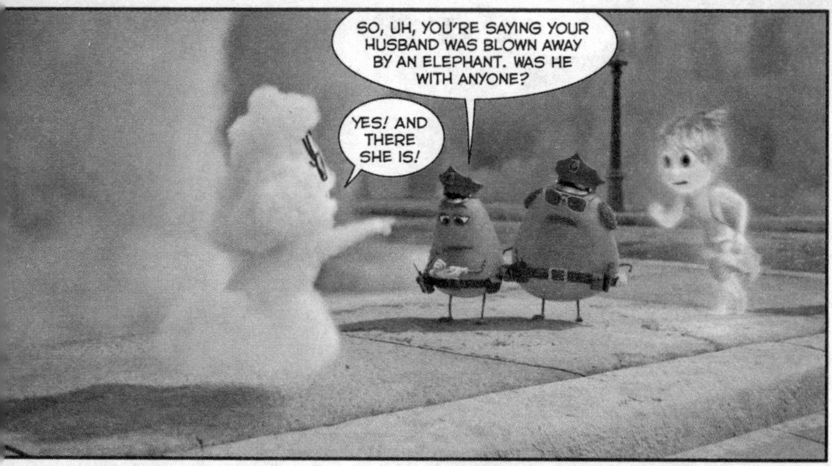
SO, UH, YOU'RE SAYING YOUR HUSBAND WAS BLOWN AWAY BY AN ELEPHANT. WAS HE WITH ANYONE?
YES! AND THERE SHE IS!

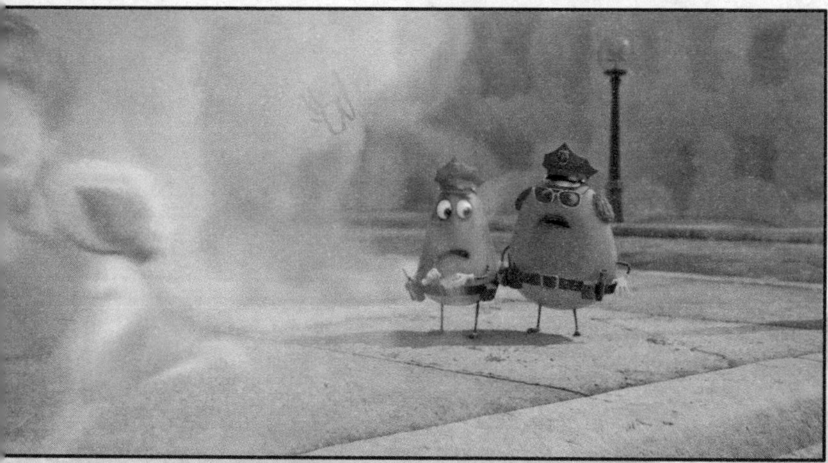

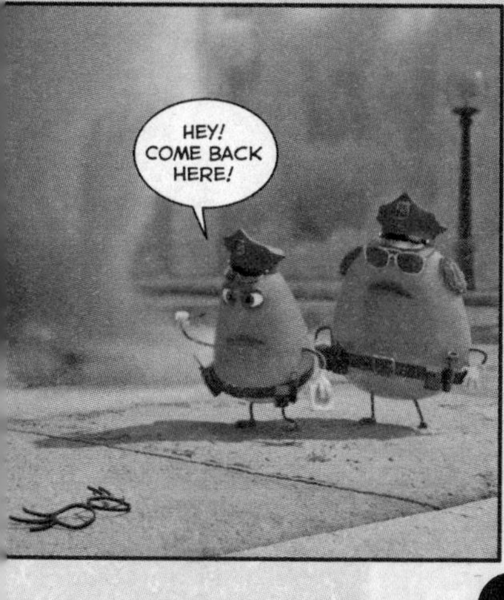
HEY! COME BACK HERE!

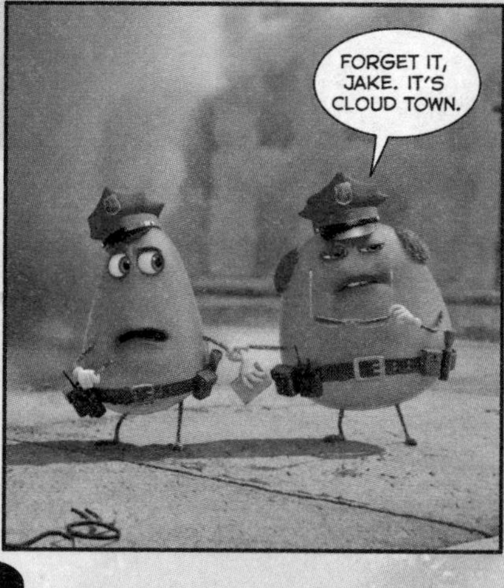
FORGET IT, JAKE. IT'S CLOUD TOWN.

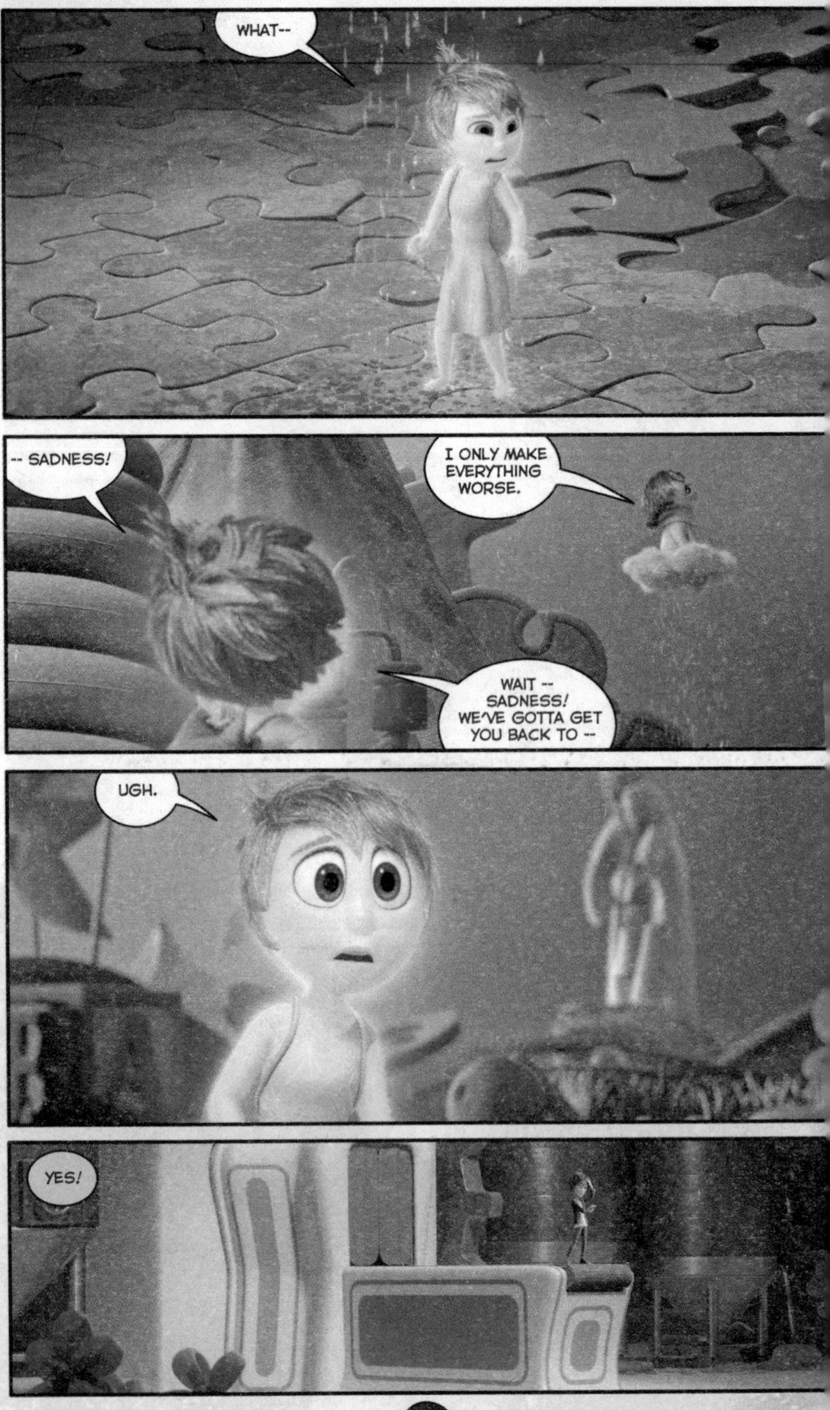
WHAT--
-- SADNESS!
I ONLY MAKE EVERYTHING WORSE.
WAIT -- SADNESS! WE'VE GOTTA GET YOU BACK TO --
UGH.
YES!

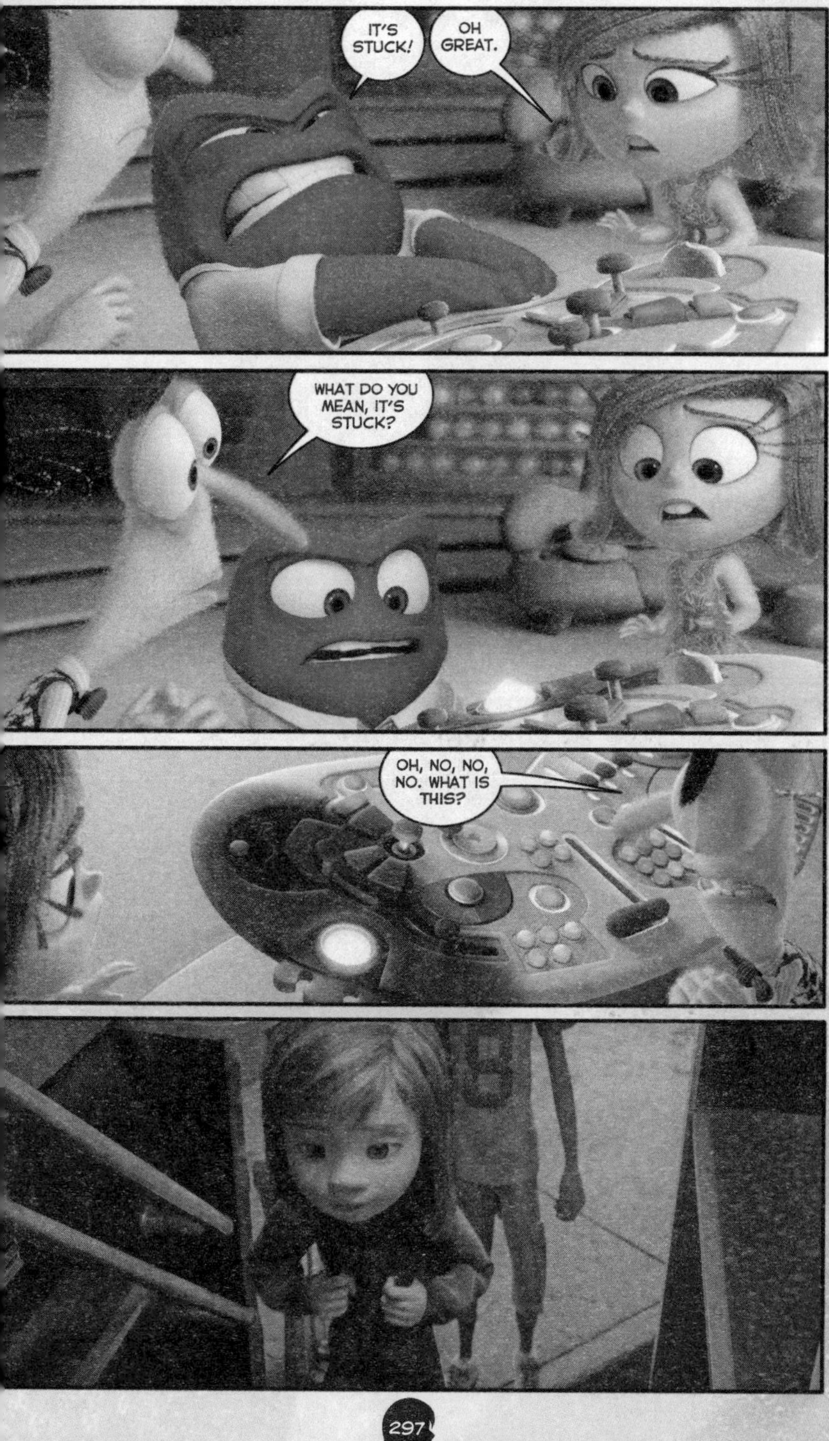
IT'S STUCK!
OH GREAT.
WHAT DO YOU MEAN, IT'S STUCK?
OH, NO, NO, NO. WHAT IS THIS?

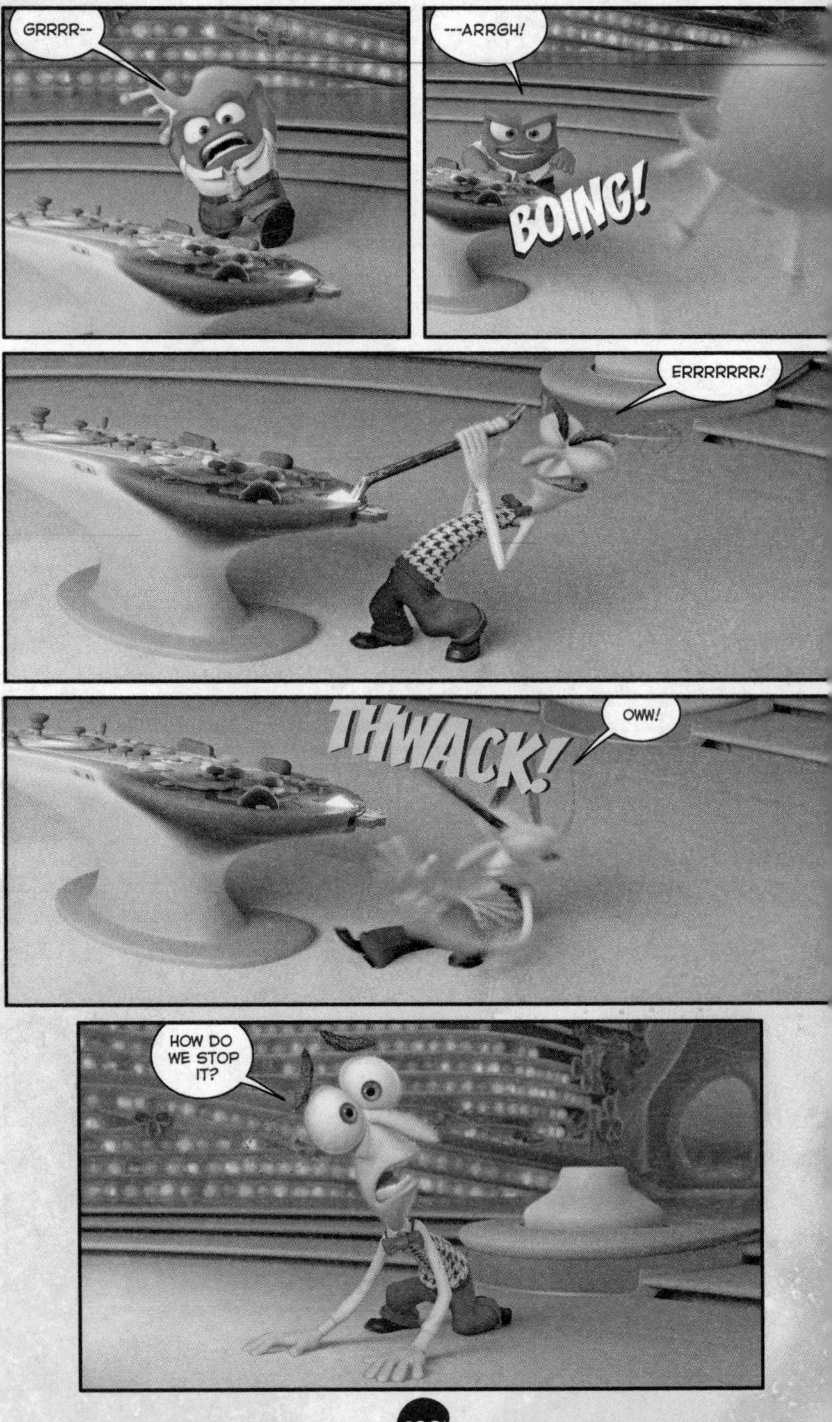
GRRRR--
---ARRGH!
BOING!
ERRRRRRR!
THWACK!
OWW!
HOW DO WE STOP IT?

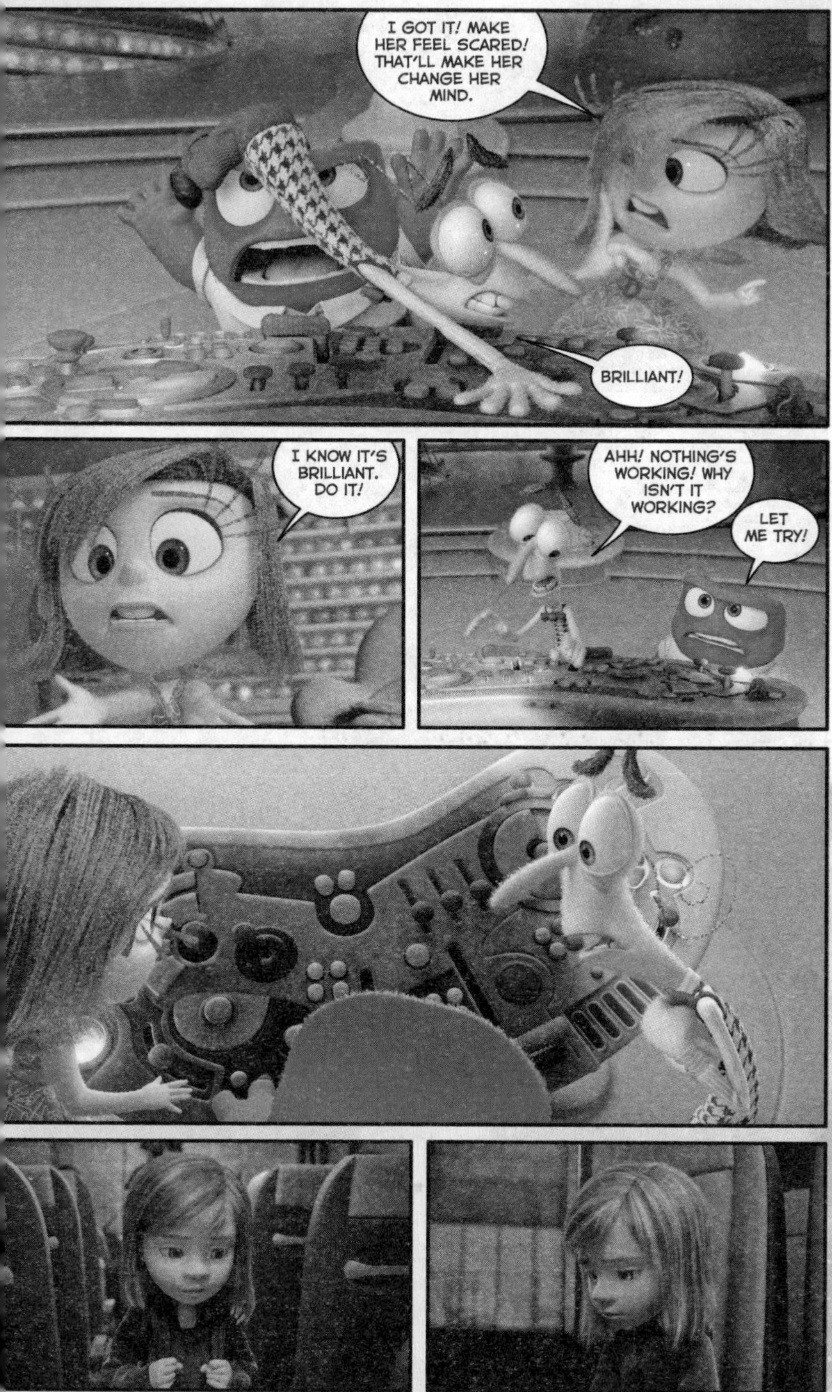
I GOT IT! MAKE HER FEEL SCARED! THAT'LL MAKE HER CHANGE HER MIND.
BRILLIANT!
I KNOW IT'S BRILLIANT. DO IT!
AHH! NOTHING'S WORKING! WHY ISN'T IT WORKING?
LET ME TRY!

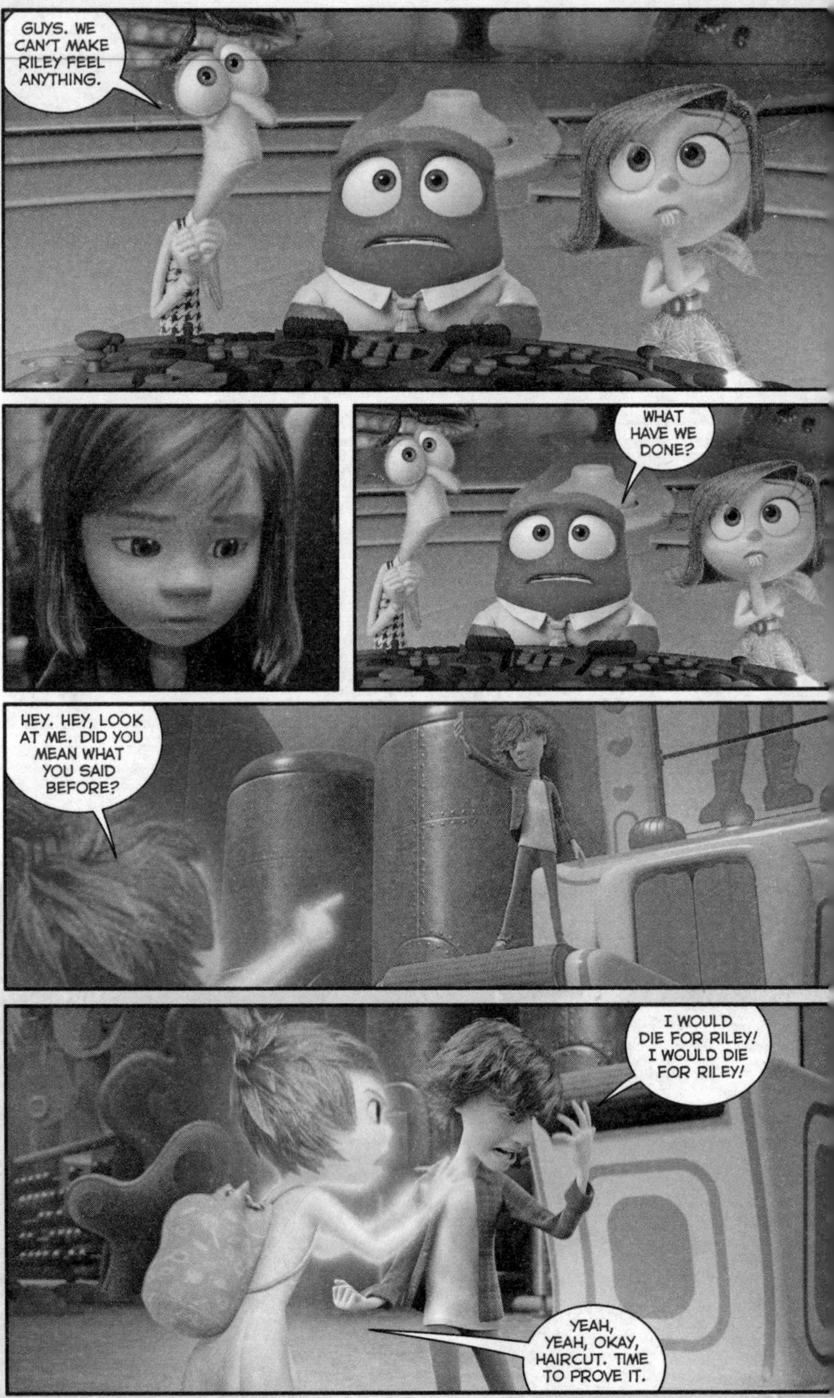
GUYS. WE CAN'T MAKE RILEY FEEL ANYTHING.
WHAT HAVE WE DONE?
HEY. HEY, LOOK AT ME. DID YOU MEAN WHAT YOU SAID BEFORE?
I WOULD DIE FOR RILEY! I WOULD DIE FOR RILEY!
YEAH, YEAH, OKAY, HAIRCUT. TIME TO PROVE IT.

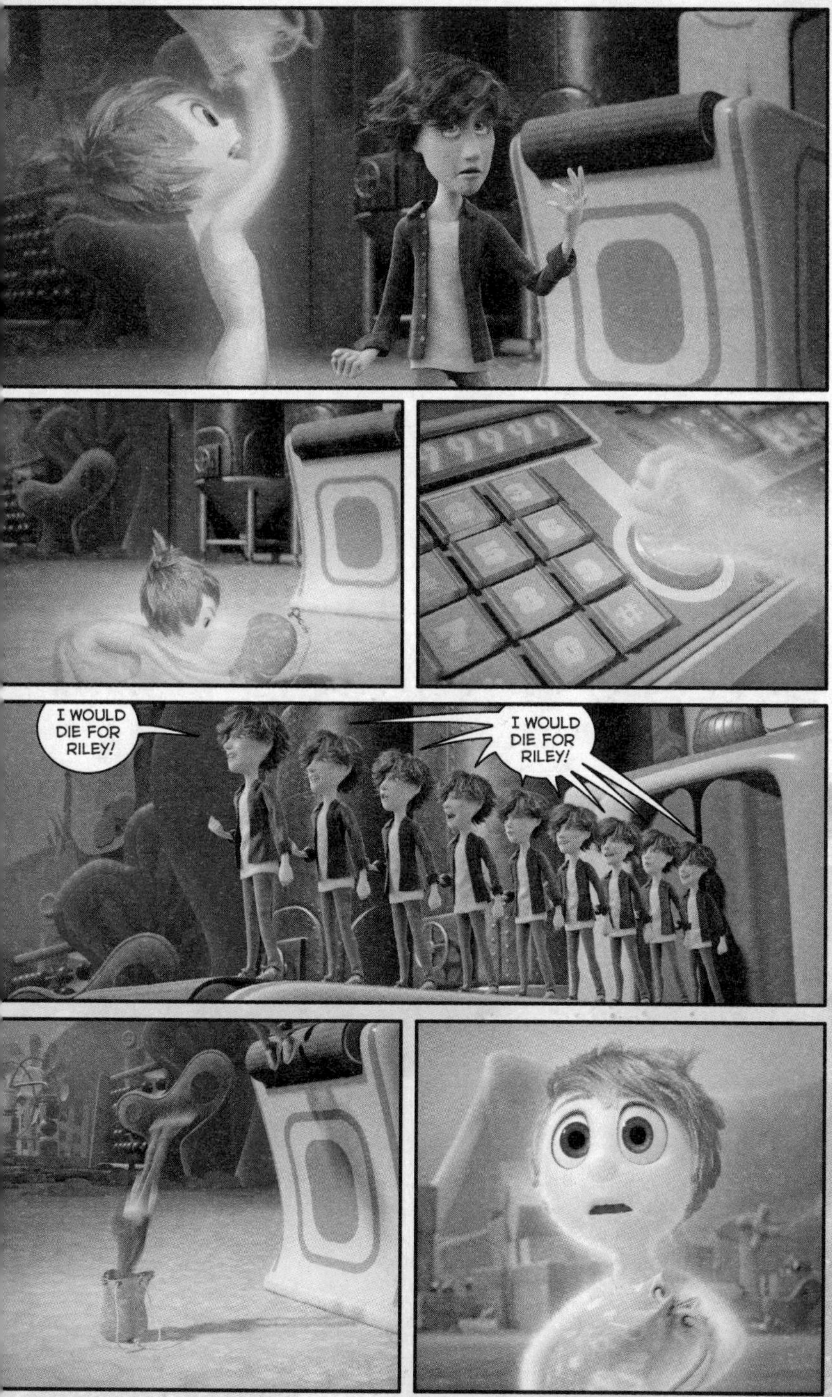
I WOULD DIE FOR RILEY!
I WOULD DIE FOR RILEY!

...RAIN...?

PTTHHTHPHTH!

THAT'S IT -- I FOLD!

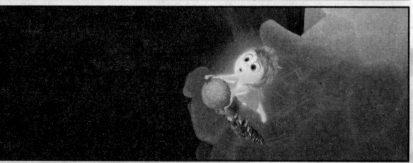

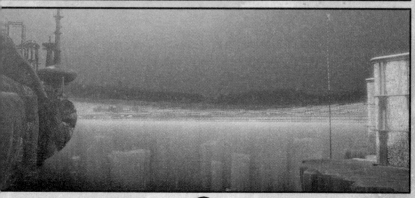

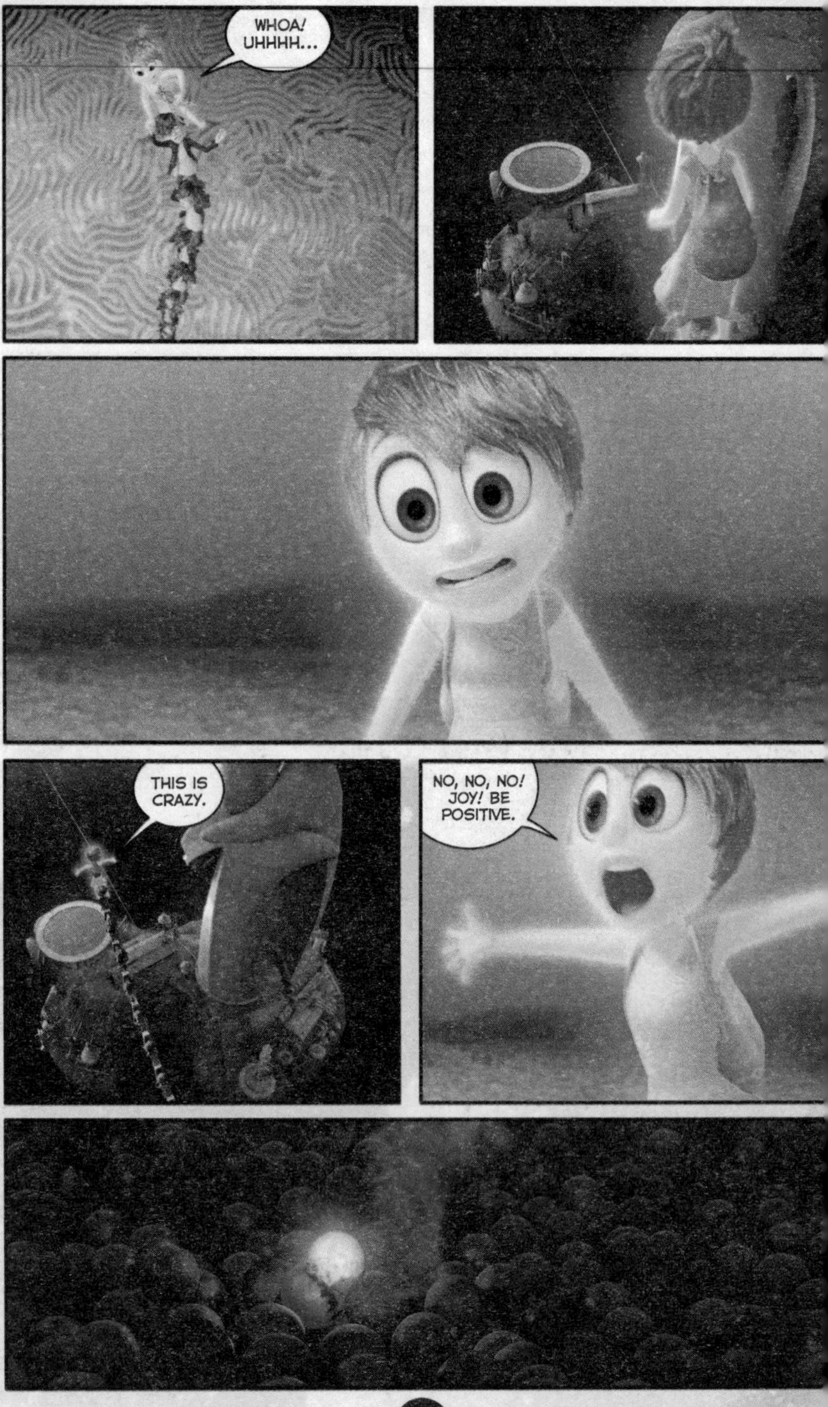
WHOA! UHHHH...
THIS IS CRAZY.
NO, NO, NO! JOY! BE POSITIVE.

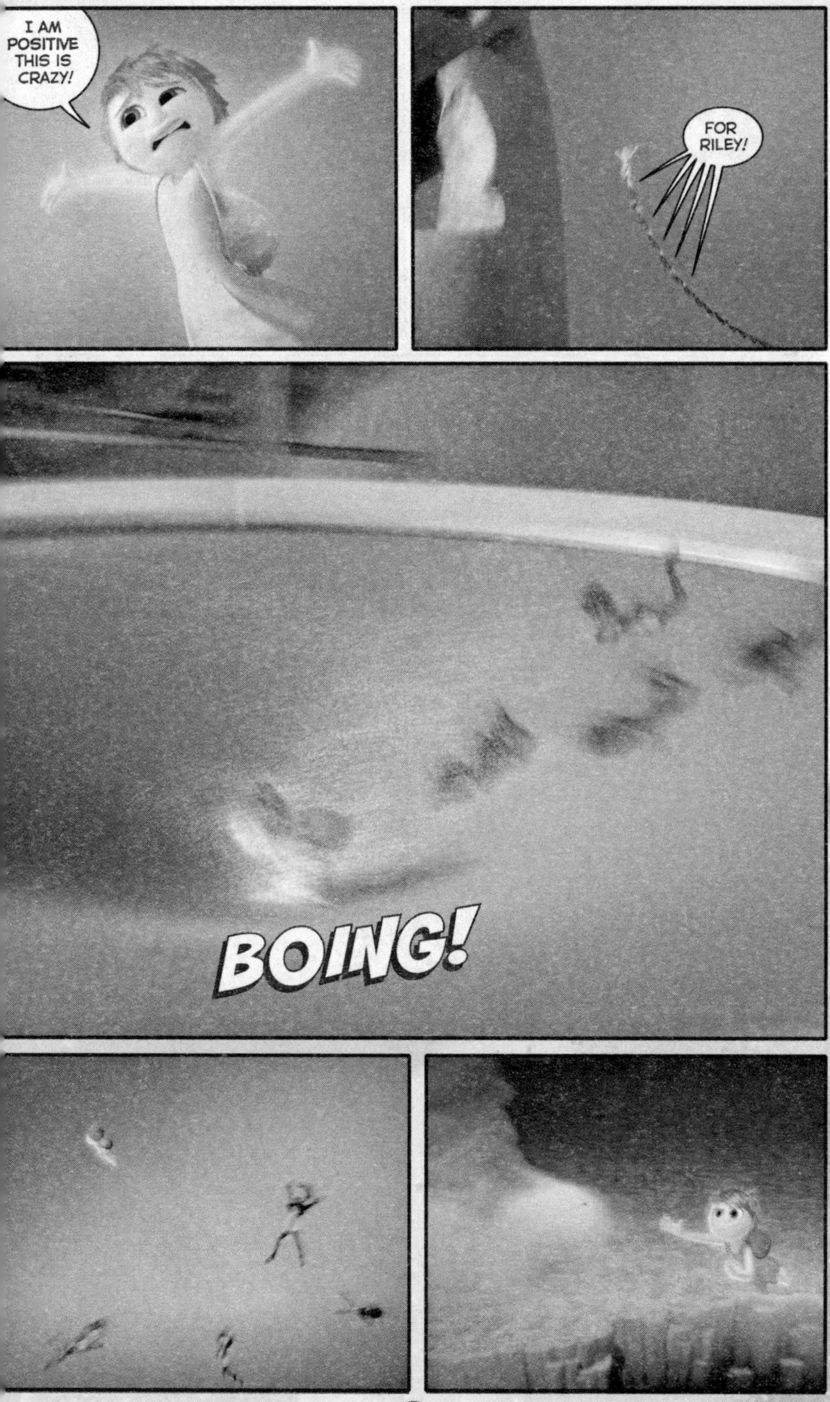
I AM POSITIVE THIS IS CRAZY!
FOR RILEY!
BOING!

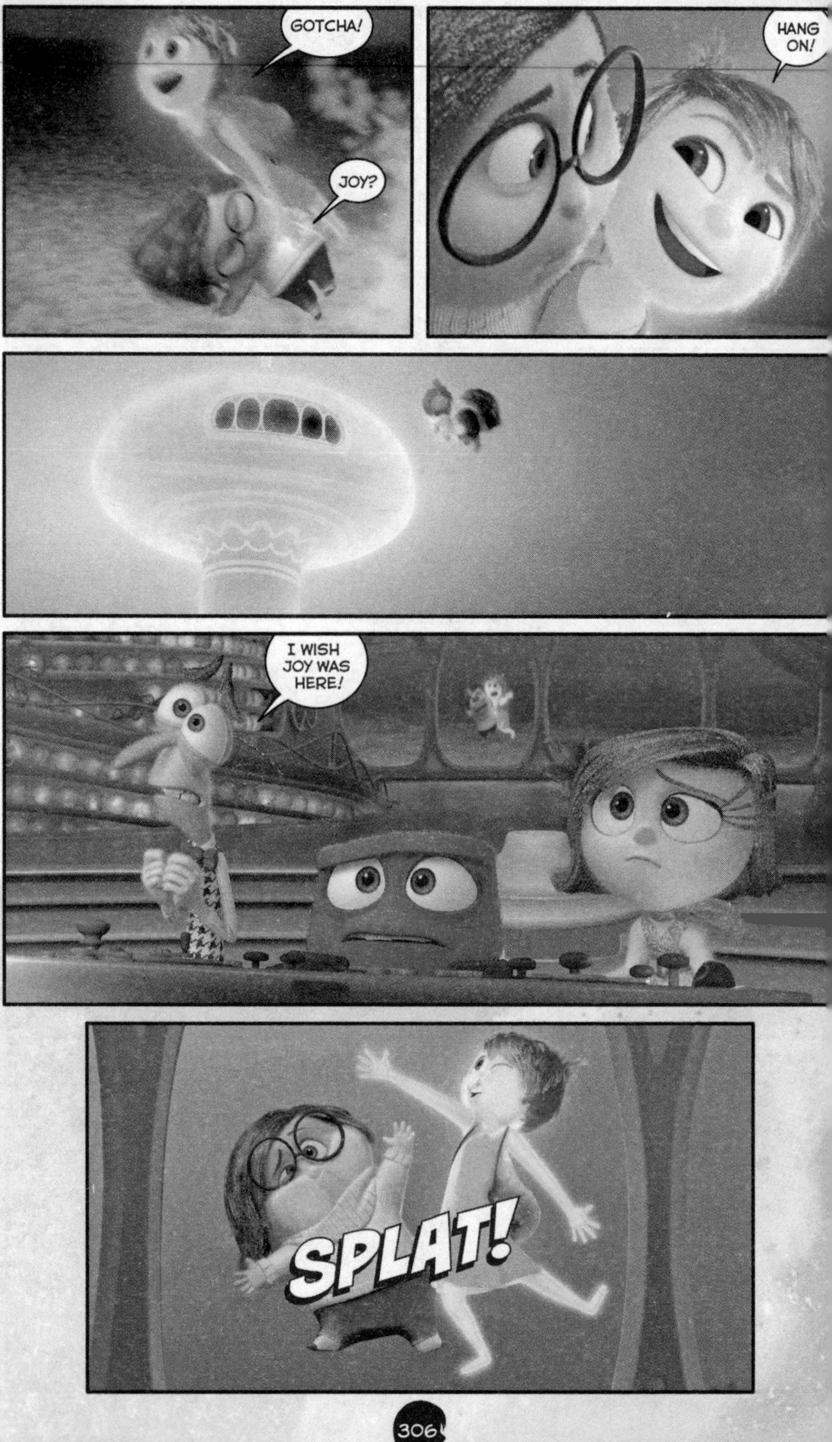
GOTCHA!
JOY?
HANG ON!
I WISH JOY WAS HERE!
SPLAT!

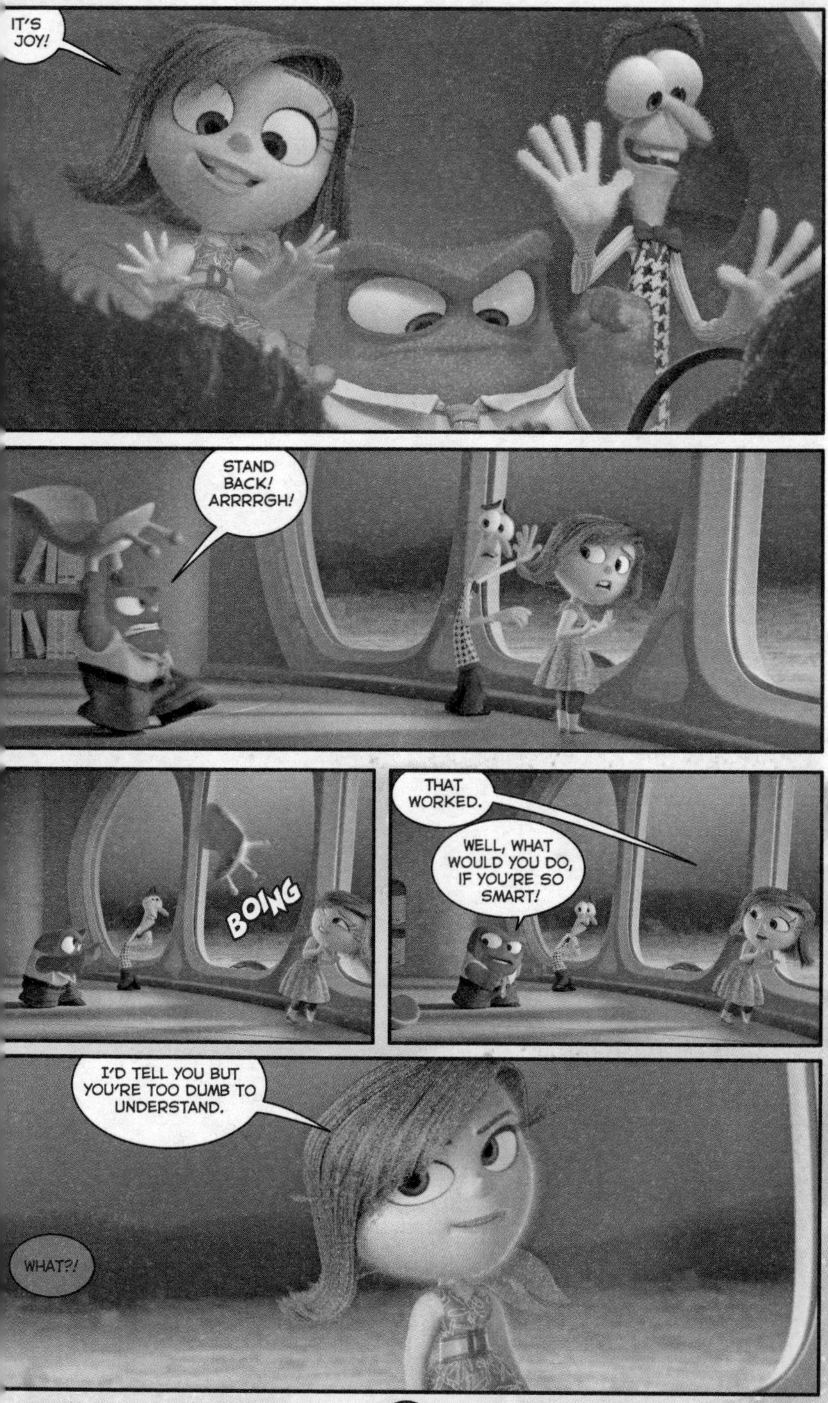
IT'S JOY!
STAND BACK! ARRRRGH!
BOING
THAT WORKED.
WELL, WHAT WOULD YOU DO, IF YOU'RE SO SMART!
I'D TELL YOU BUT YOU'RE TOO DUMB TO UNDERSTAND.
WHAT?!

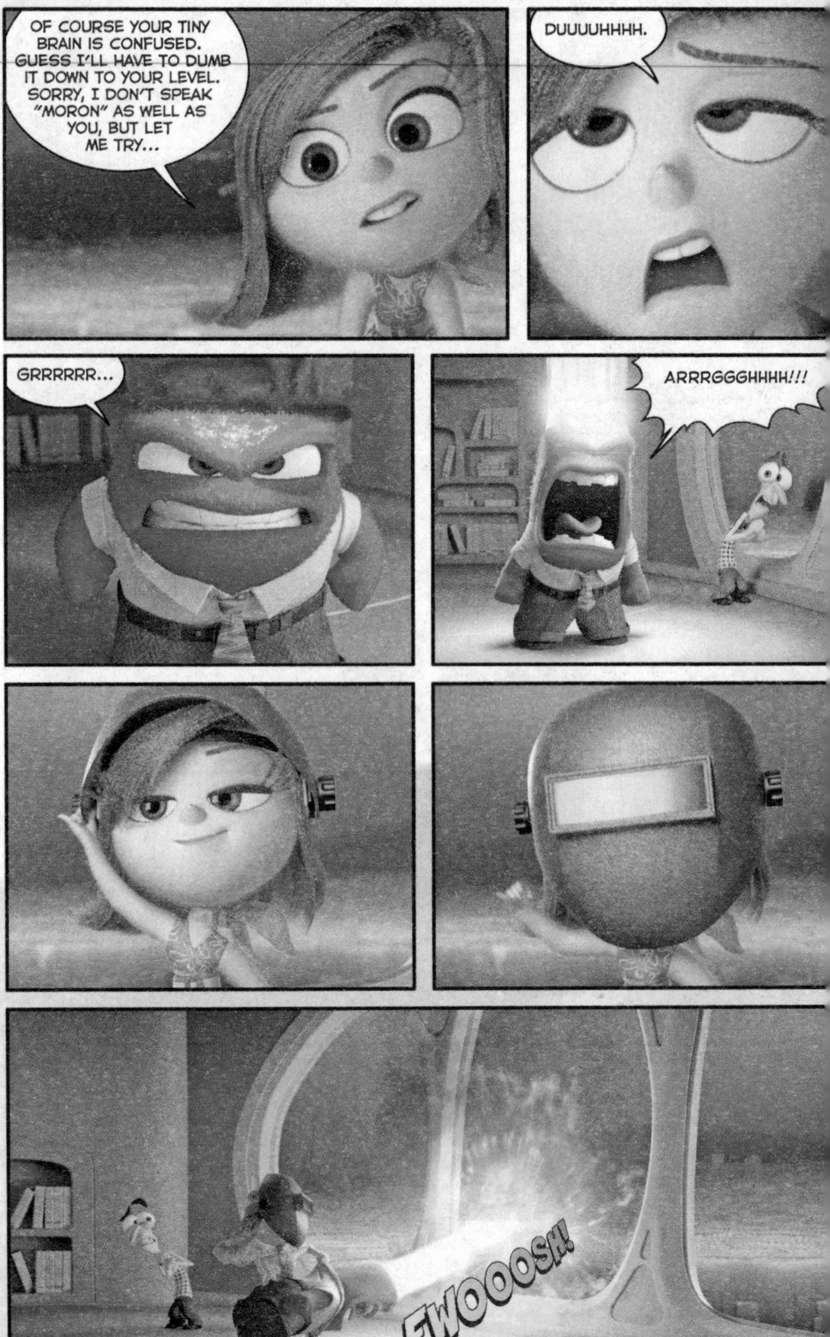
OF COURSE YOUR TINY BRAIN IS CONFUSED. GUESS I'LL HAVE TO DUMB IT DOWN TO YOUR LEVEL. SORRY, I DON'T SPEAK "MORON" AS WELL AS YOU, BUT LET ME TRY...
DUUUUHHHH.
GRRRRRR...
ARRRGGGHHHH!!!
FWOOOSH!

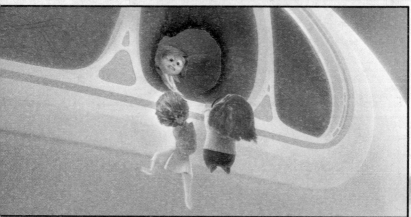

OH, THANK GOODNESS YOU'RE BACK.

THINGS ARE REALLY MESSED UP.

WE FOUND THIS IDEA, AND NOW RILEY'S ON A BUS HEADING FOR MINNESOTA!

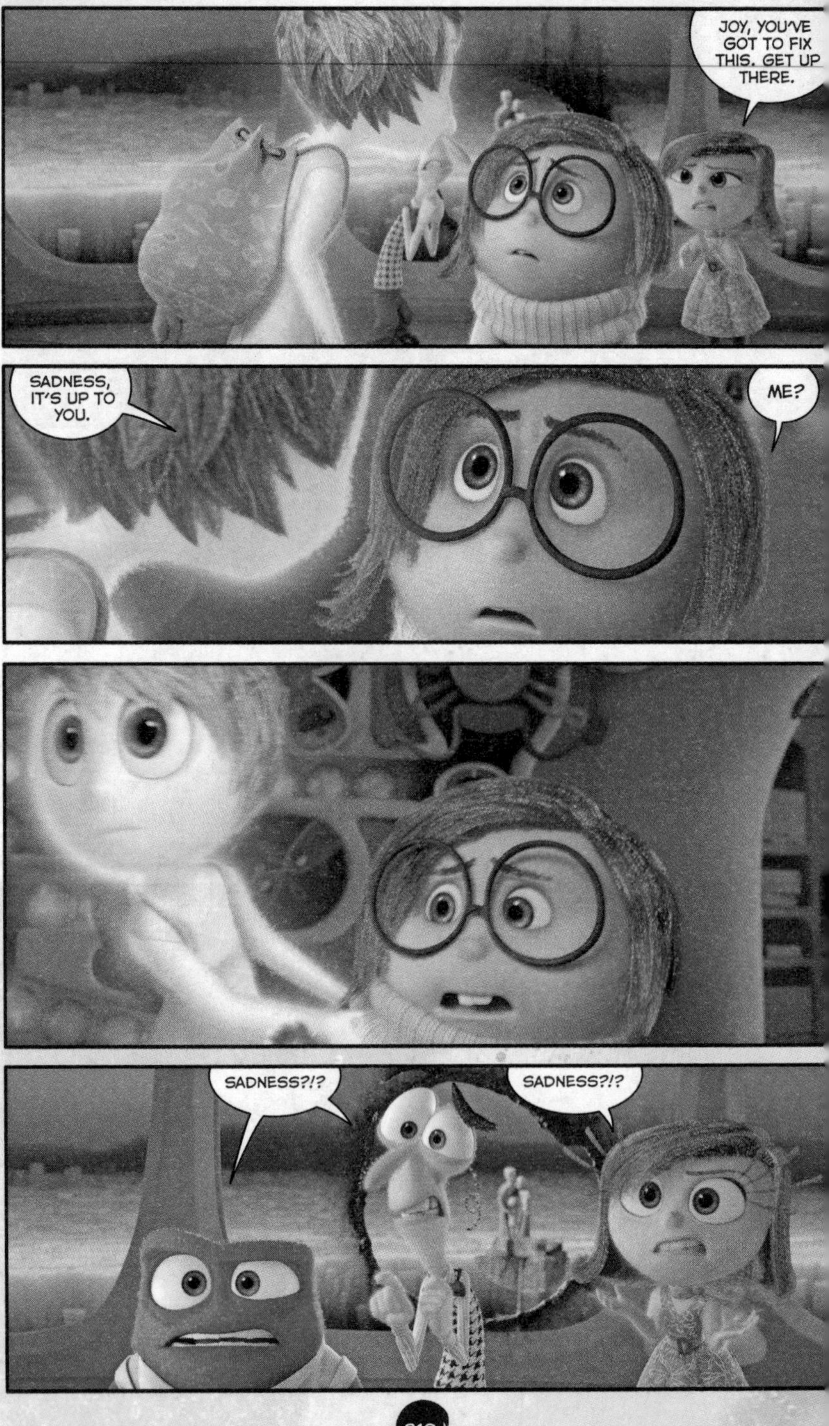
JOY, YOU'VE GOT TO FIX THIS. GET UP THERE.
SADNESS, IT'S UP TO YOU.
ME?
SADNESS?!?
SADNESS?!?

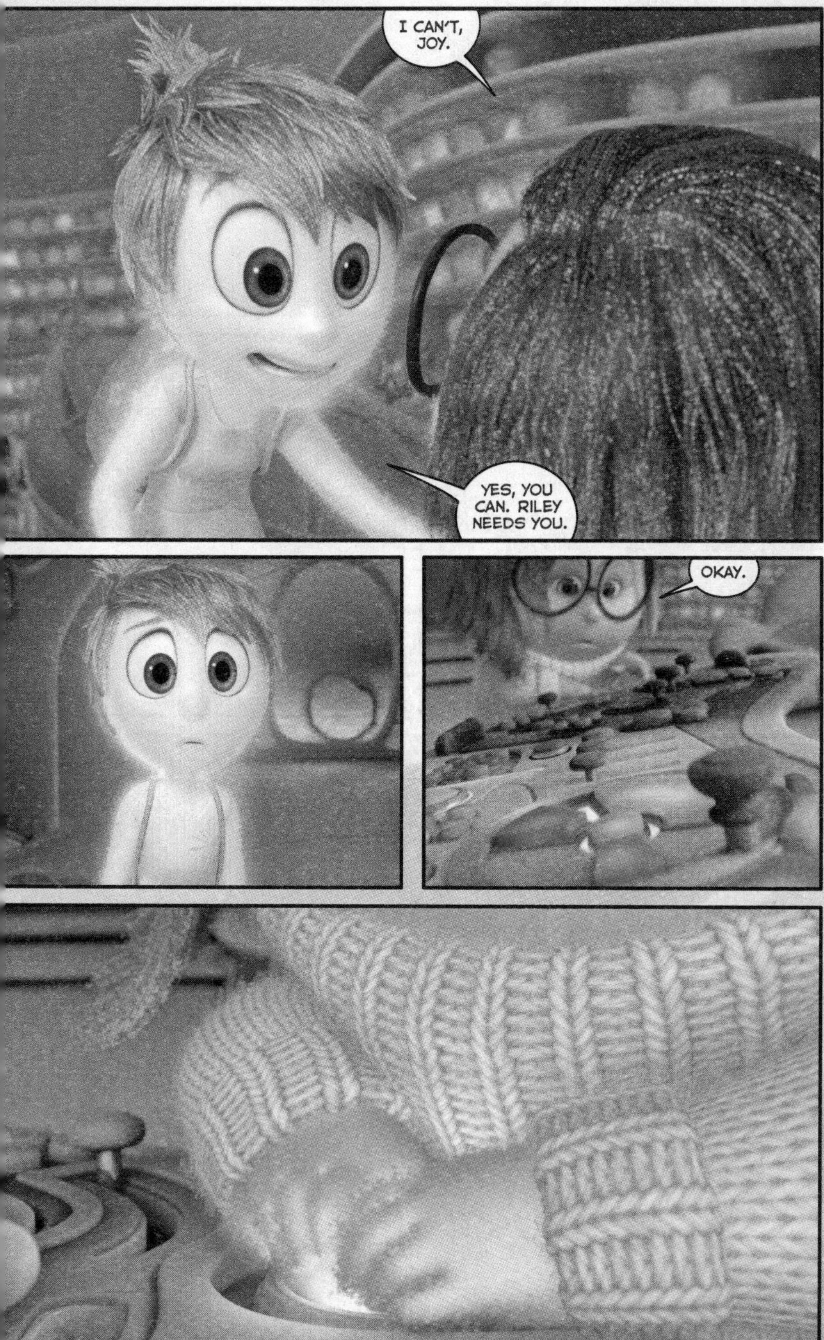
I CAN'T, JOY.
YES, YOU CAN. RILEY NEEDS YOU.
OKAY.

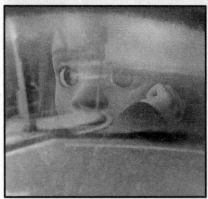

WAIT! STOP! I WANNA GET OFF.

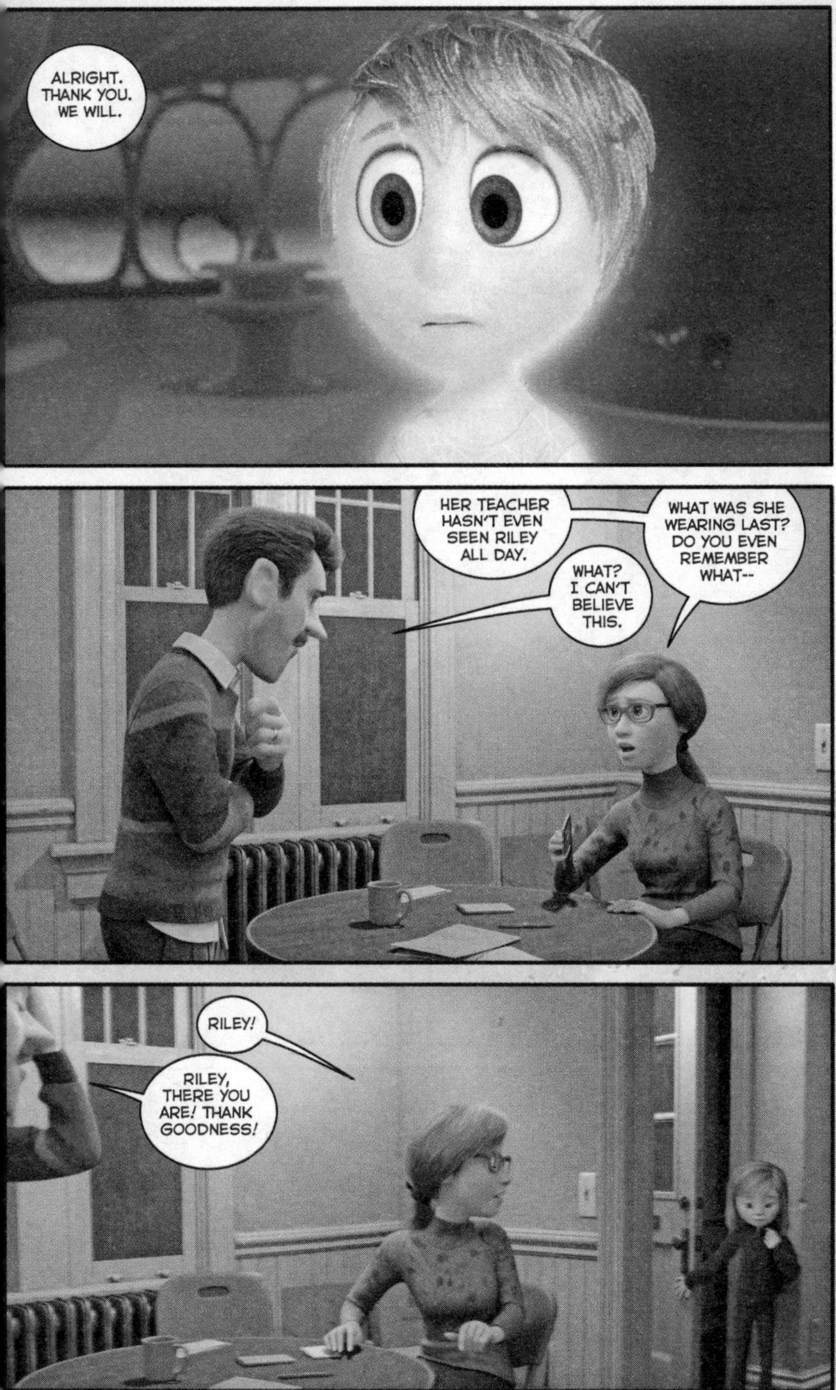
ALRIGHT. THANK YOU. WE WILL.
HER TEACHER HASN'T EVEN SEEN RILEY ALL DAY.
WHAT WAS SHE WEARING LAST? DO YOU EVEN REMEMBER WHAT--
WHAT? I CAN'T BELIEVE THIS.
RILEY!
RILEY, THERE YOU ARE! THANK GOODNESS!

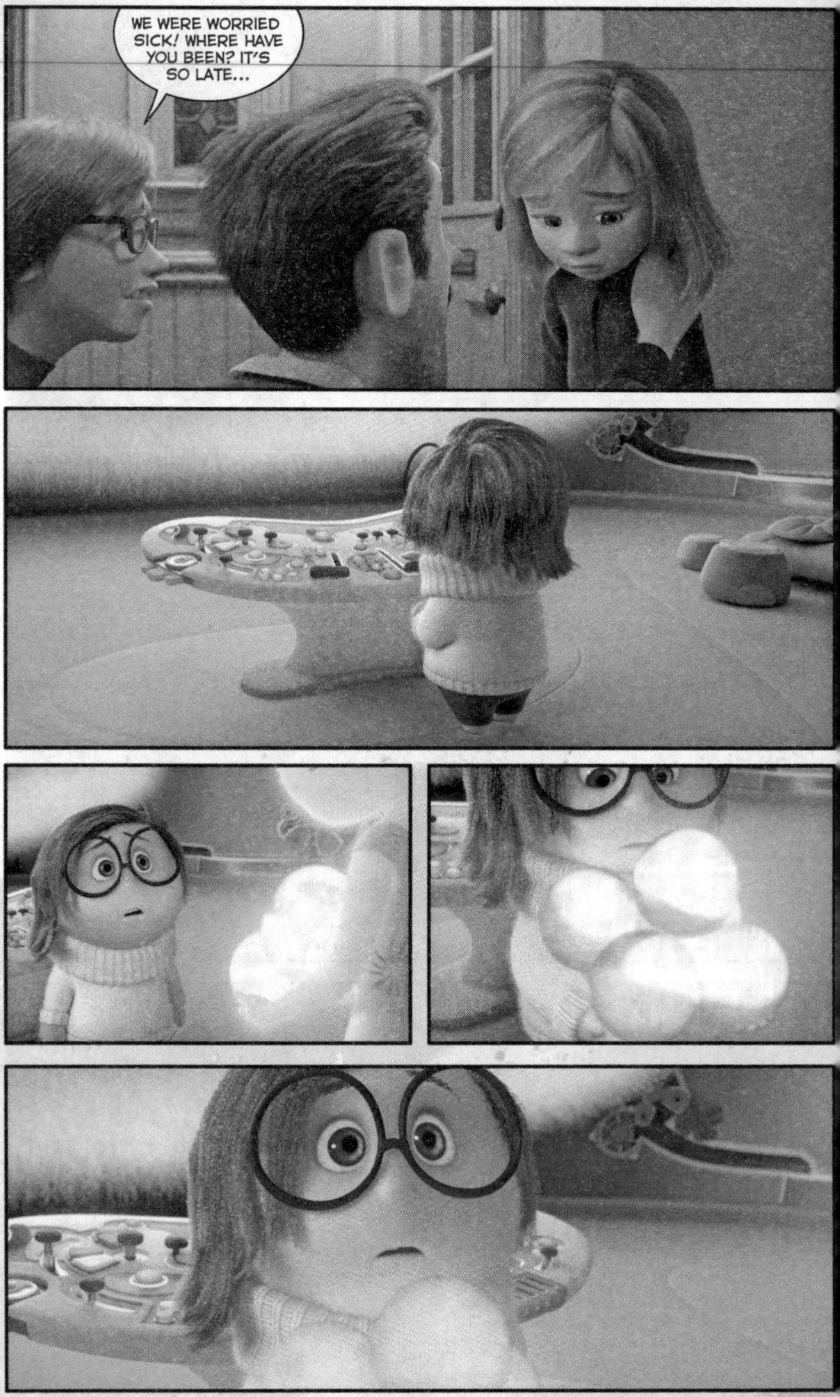
WE WERE WORRIED SICK! WHERE HAVE YOU BEEN? IT'S SO LATE...

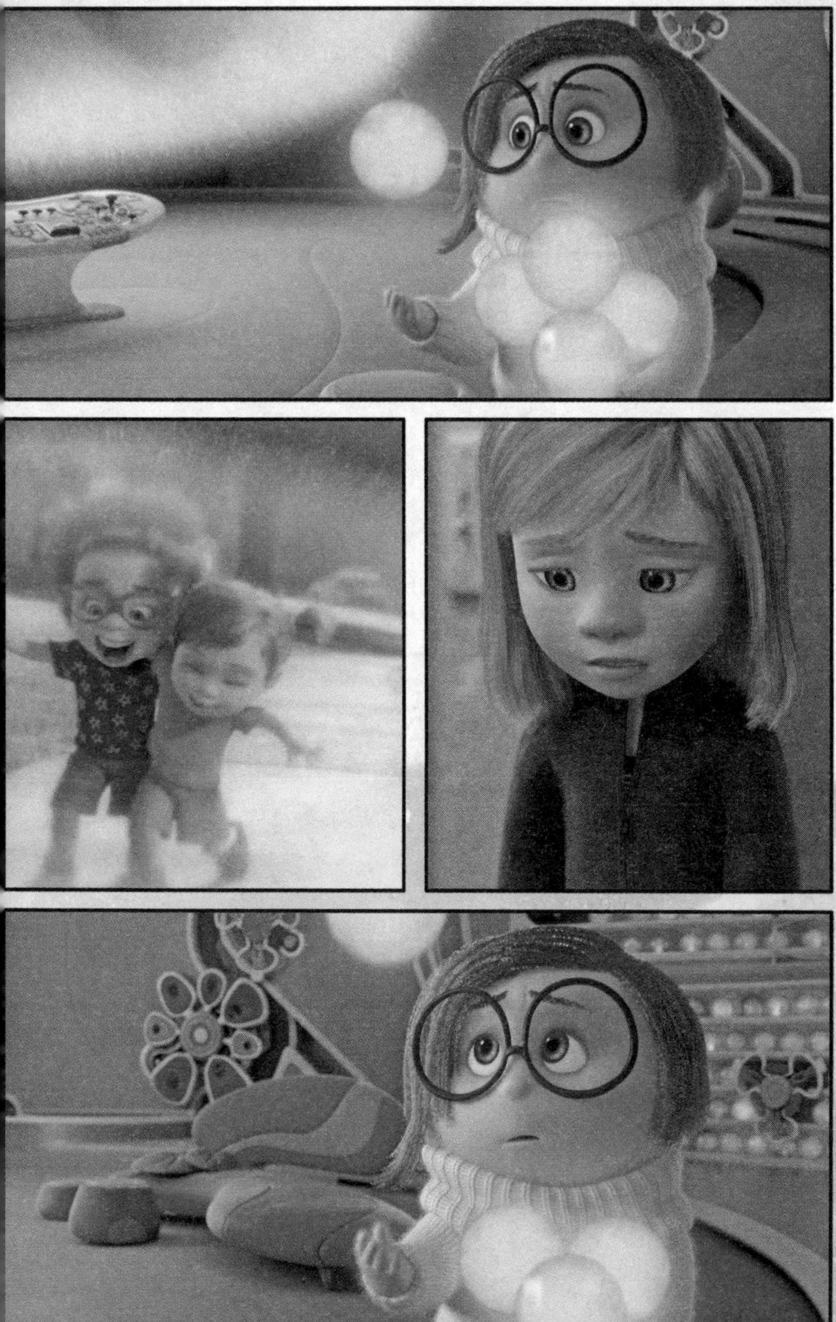

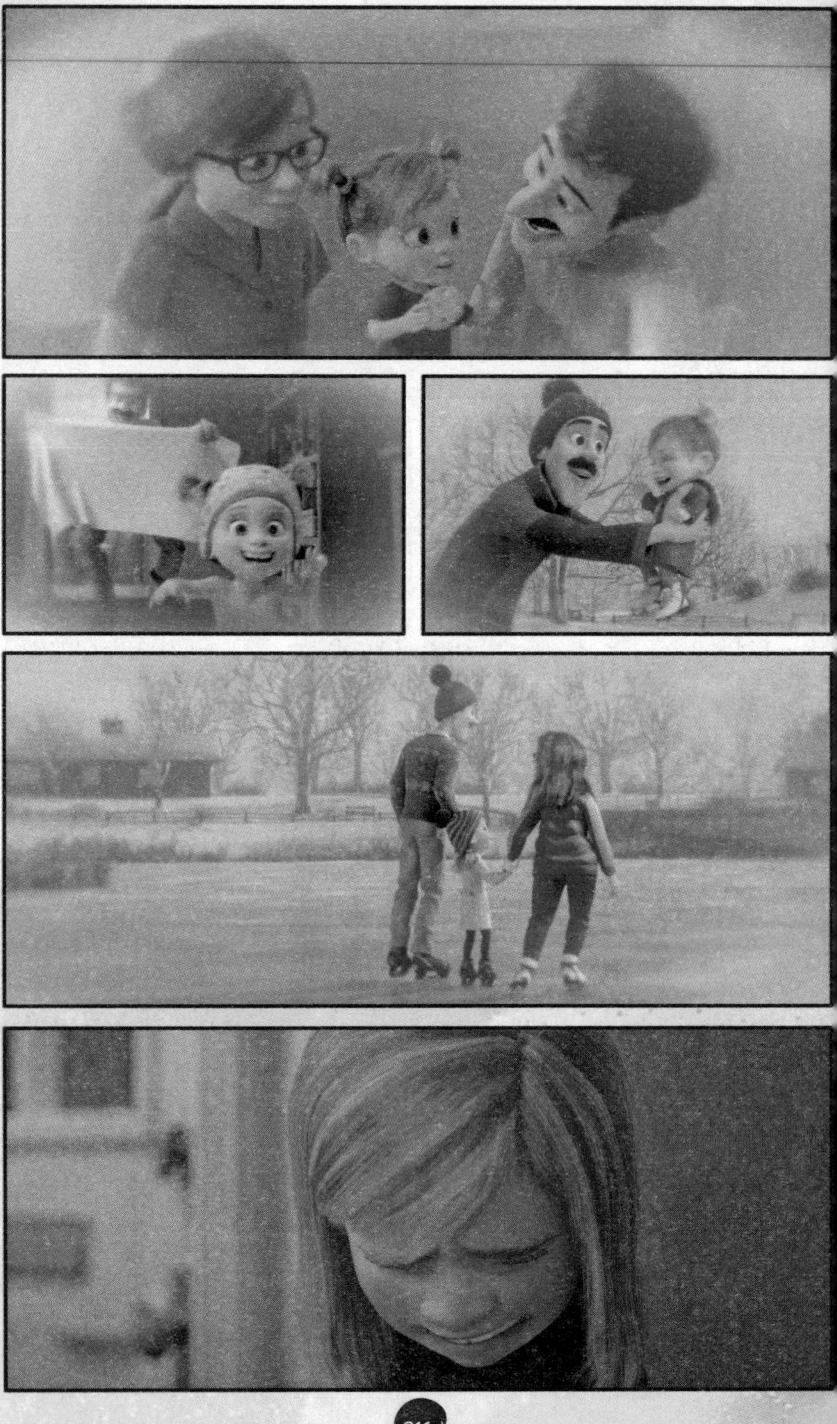

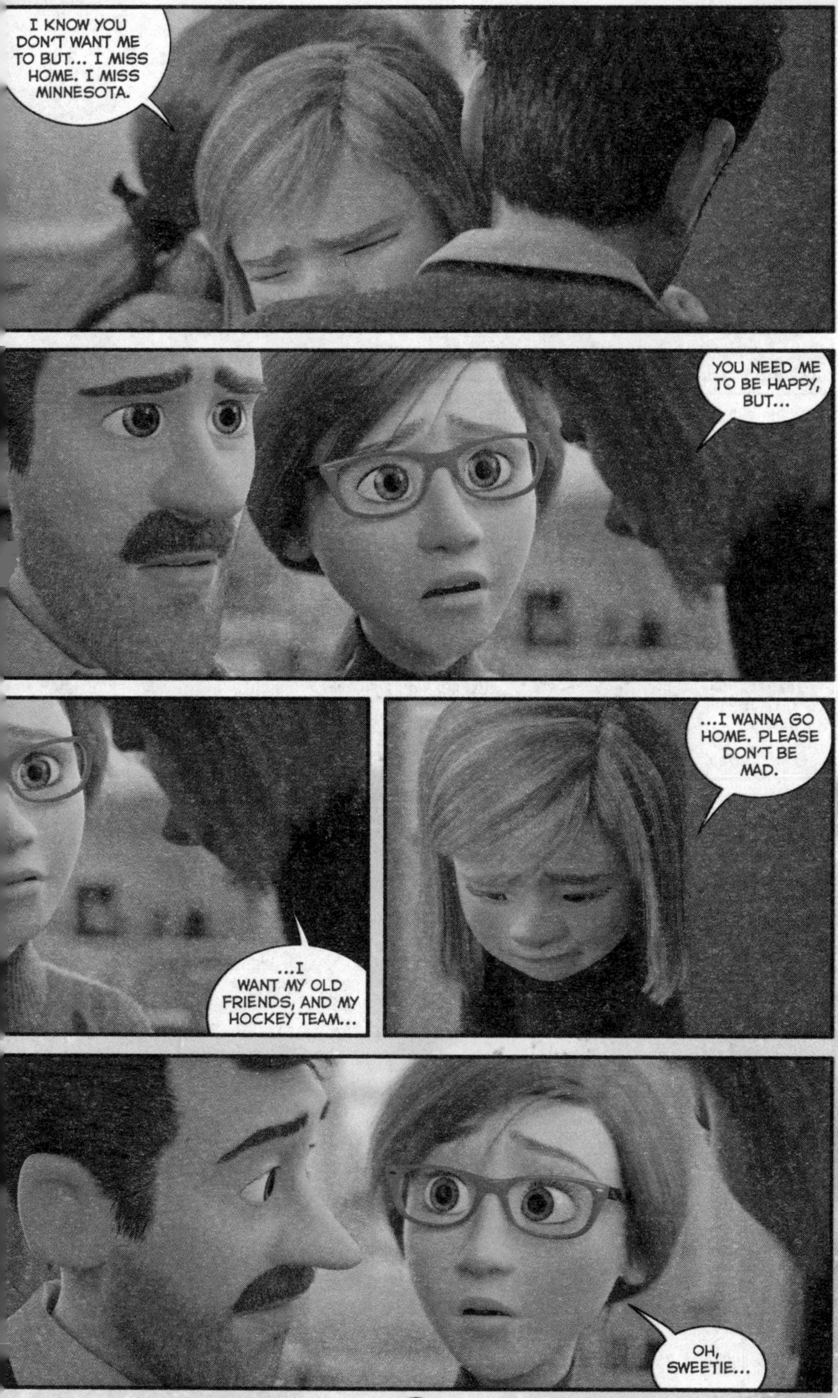
I KNOW YOU DON'T WANT ME TO BUT... I MISS HOME. I MISS MINNESOTA.
YOU NEED ME TO BE HAPPY, BUT...
...I WANT MY OLD FRIENDS, AND MY HOCKEY TEAM...
...I WANNA GO HOME. PLEASE DON'T BE MAD.
OH, SWEETIE...

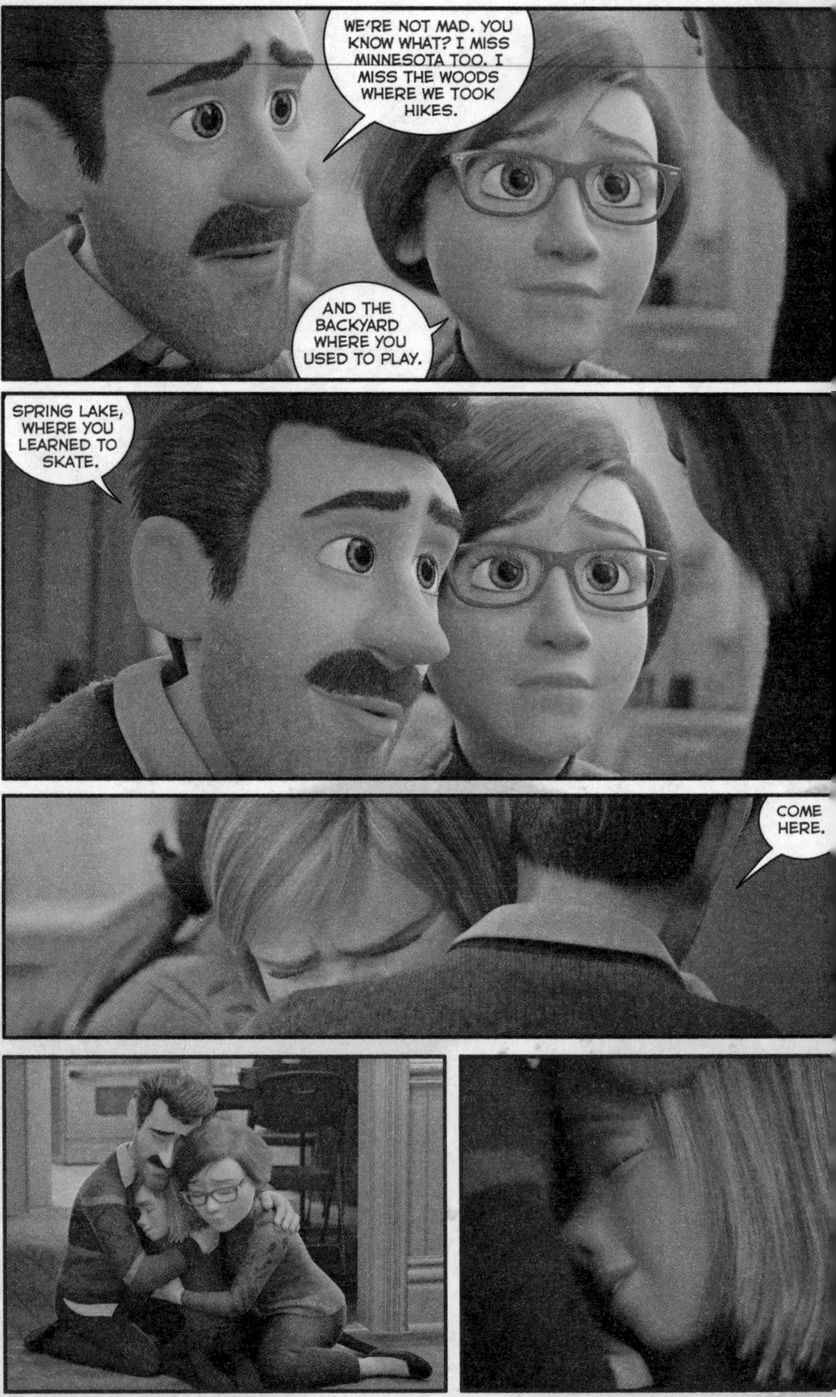
WE'RE NOT MAD. YOU KNOW WHAT? I MISS MINNESOTA TOO. I MISS THE WOODS WHERE WE TOOK HIKES.
AND THE BACKYARD WHERE YOU USED TO PLAY.
SPRING LAKE, WHERE YOU LEARNED TO SKATE.
COME HERE.

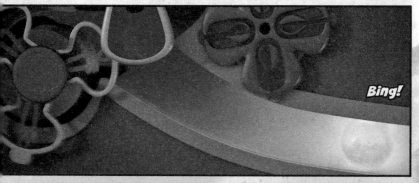

Bing!

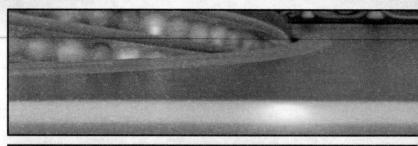

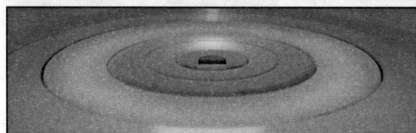

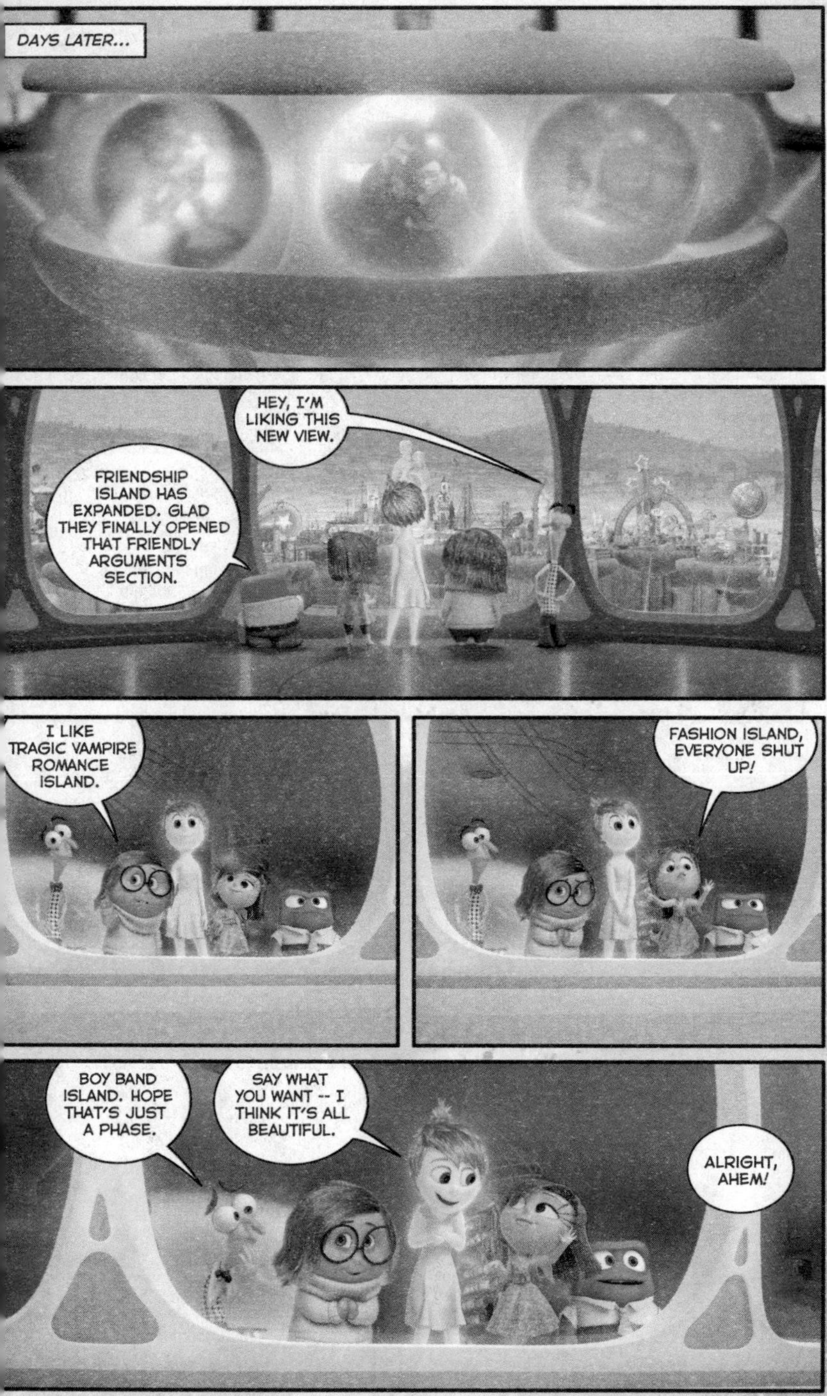
DAYS LATER...
HEY, I'M LIKING THIS NEW VIEW.
FRIENDSHIP ISLAND HAS EXPANDED. GLAD THEY FINALLY OPENED THAT FRIENDLY ARGUMENTS SECTION.
I LIKE TRAGIC VAMPIRE ROMANCE ISLAND.
FASHION ISLAND, EVERYONE SHUT UP!
BOY BAND ISLAND. HOPE THAT'S JUST A PHASE.
SAY WHAT YOU WANT -- I THINK IT'S ALL BEAUTIFUL.
ALRIGHT, AHEM!

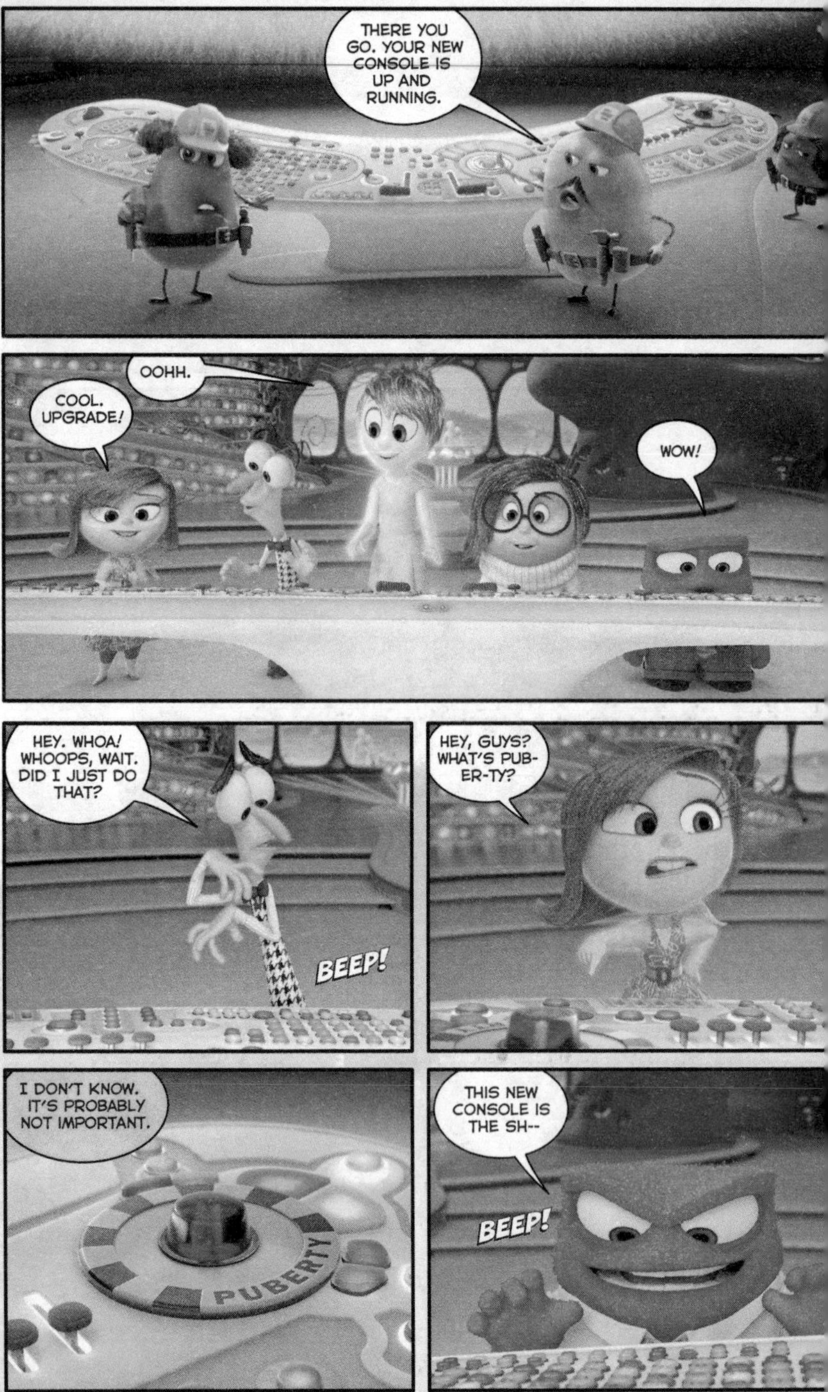
THERE YOU GO. YOUR NEW CONSOLE IS UP AND RUNNING.
COOL. UPGRADE!
OOHH.
WOW!
HEY. WHOA! WHOOPS, WAIT. DID I JUST DO THAT?
BEEP!
HEY, GUYS? WHAT'S PUB-ER-TY?
I DON'T KNOW. IT'S PROBABLY NOT IMPORTANT.
PUBERTY
THIS NEW CONSOLE IS THE SH--
BEEP!

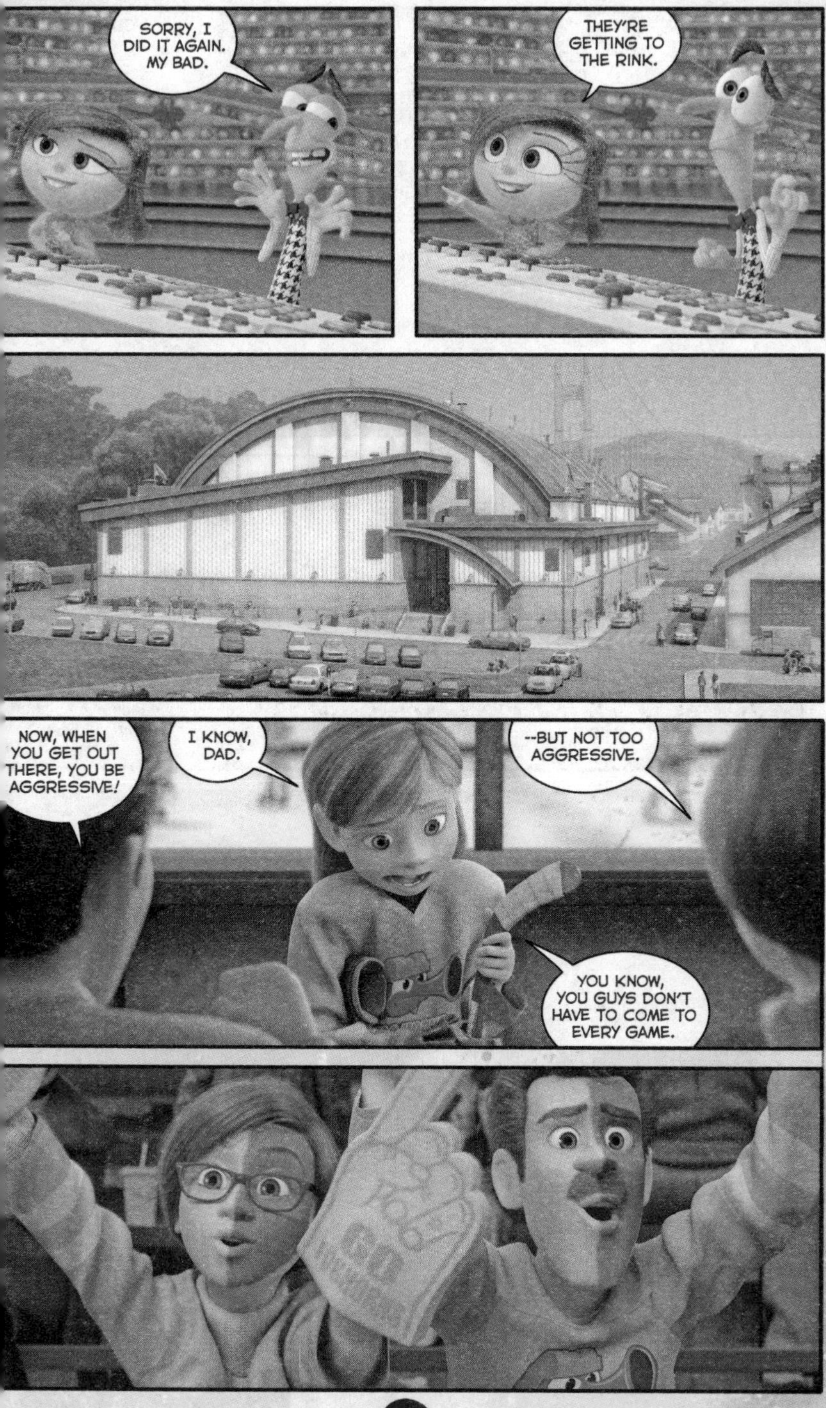
SORRY, I DID IT AGAIN. MY BAD.
THEY'RE GETTING TO THE RINK.
NOW, WHEN YOU GET OUT THERE, YOU BE AGGRESSIVE!
I KNOW, DAD.
--BUT NOT TOO AGGRESSIVE.
YOU KNOW, YOU GUYS DON'T HAVE TO COME TO EVERY GAME.

GO RILEY! FOGHORNS ARE THE BEST!
FOGHORNS
ARE YOU KIDDING? I'M NOT MISSING ONE! GO FOGHORNS!
OKAY, OKAY. I GOTTA GO.

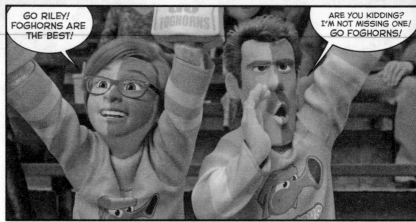

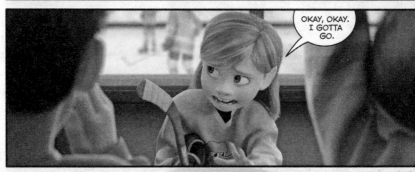

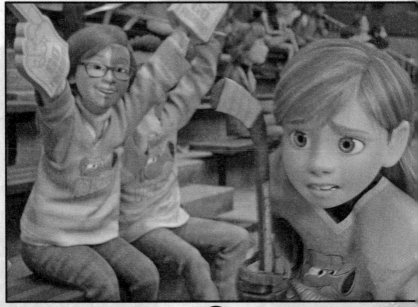

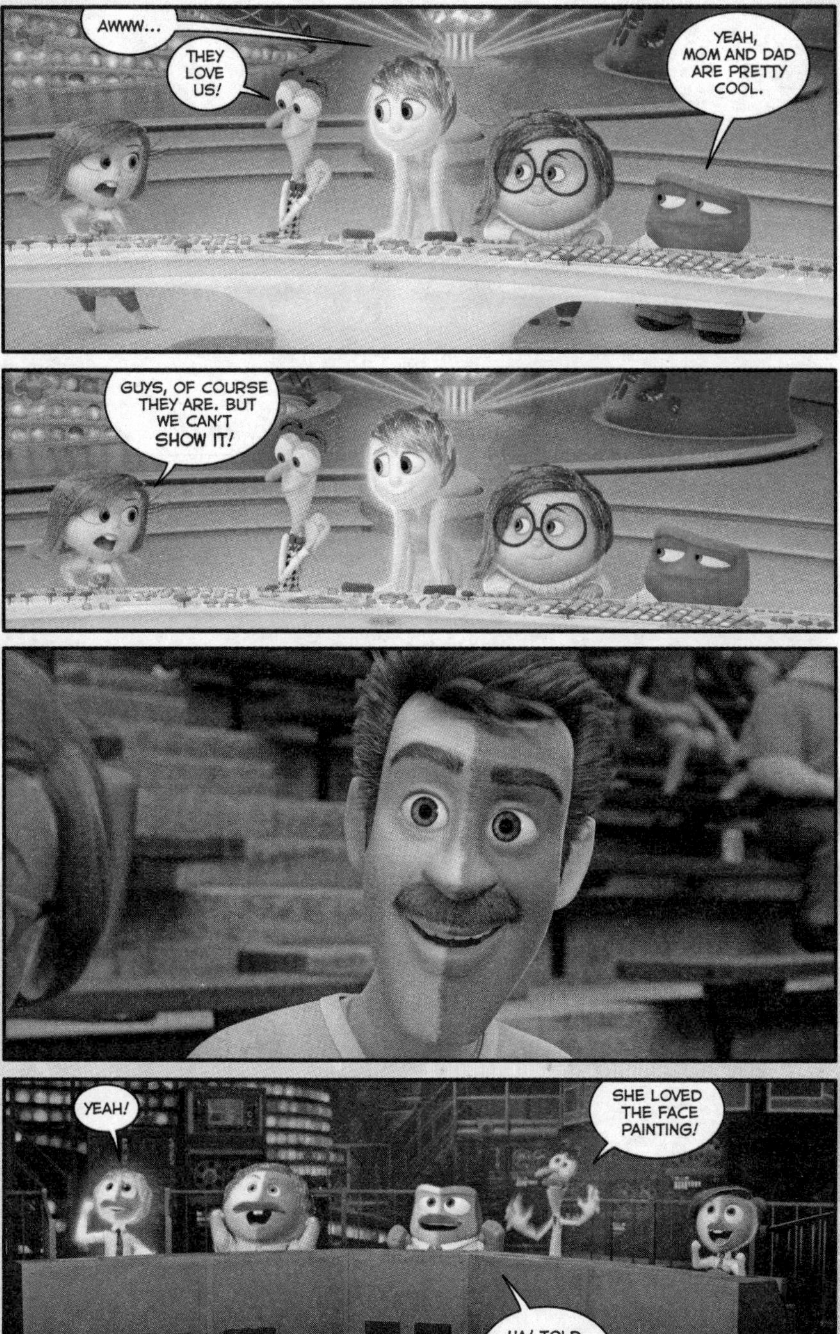
AWWW...
THEY LOVE US!
YEAH, MOM AND DAD ARE PRETTY COOL.
GUYS, OF COURSE THEY ARE. BUT WE CAN'T SHOW IT!
YEAH!
SHE LOVED THE FACE PAINTING!
HA! TOLD YOU IT WAS A GREAT IDEA!

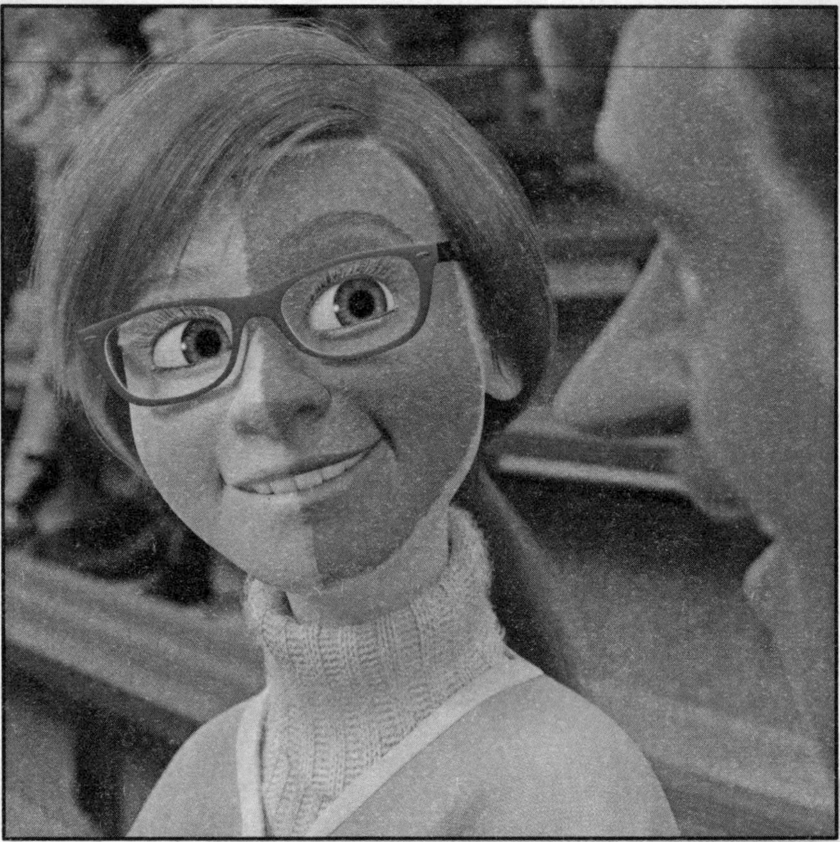

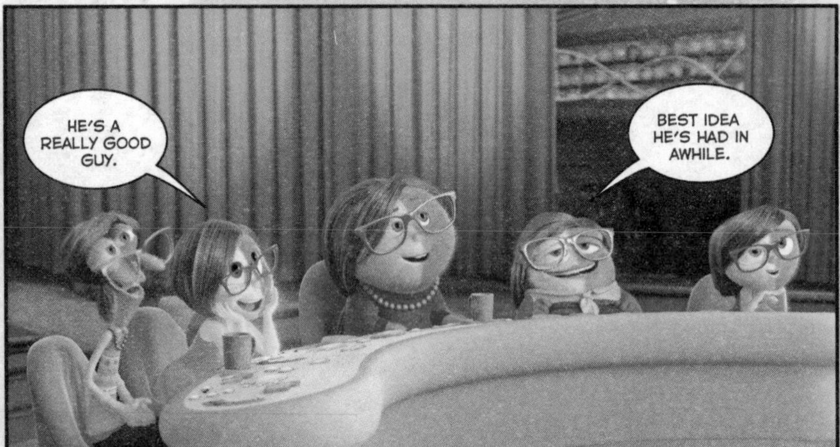
HE'S A REALLY GOOD GUY.
BEST IDEA HE'S HAD IN AWHILE.

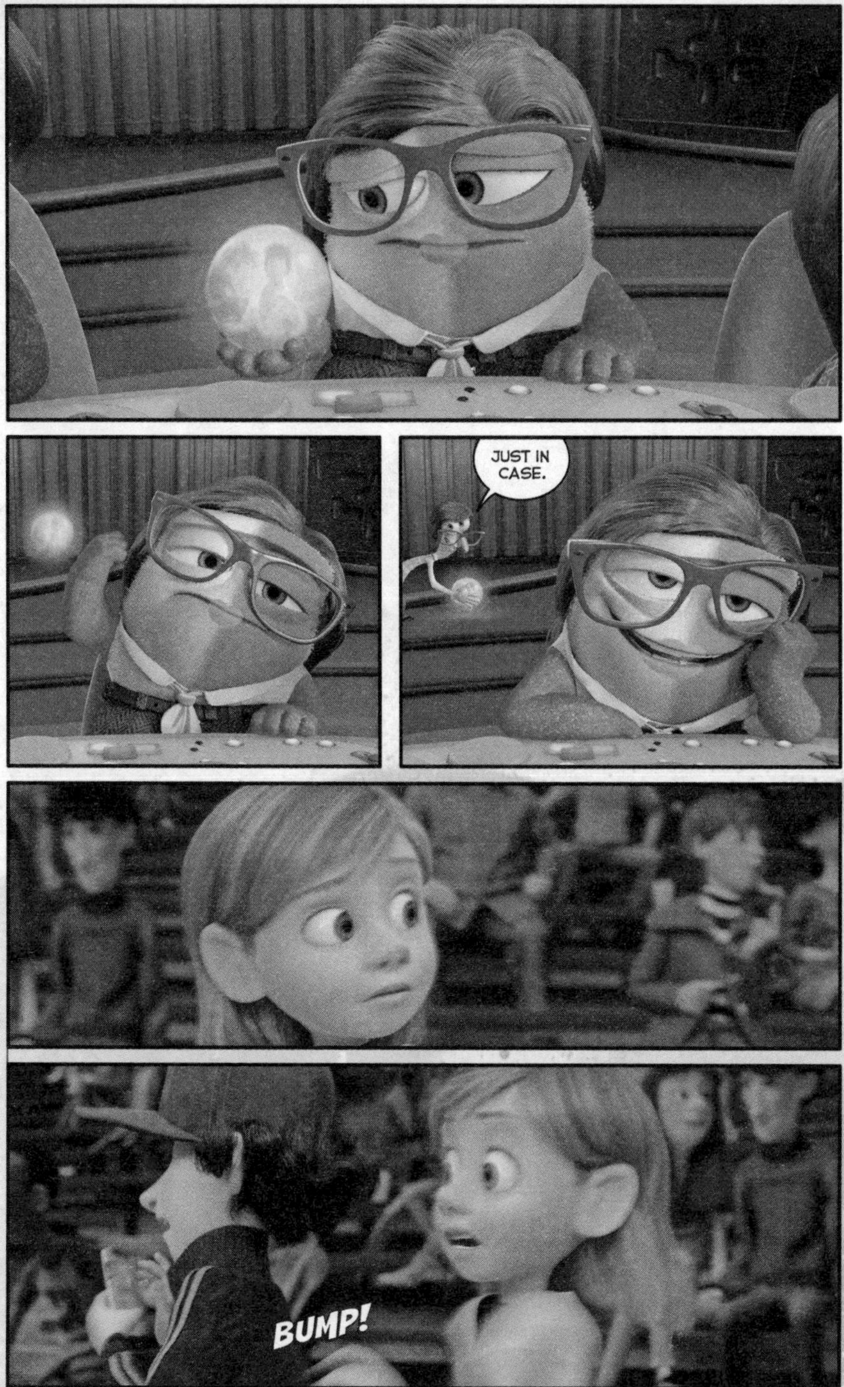
JUST IN CASE.
BUMP!

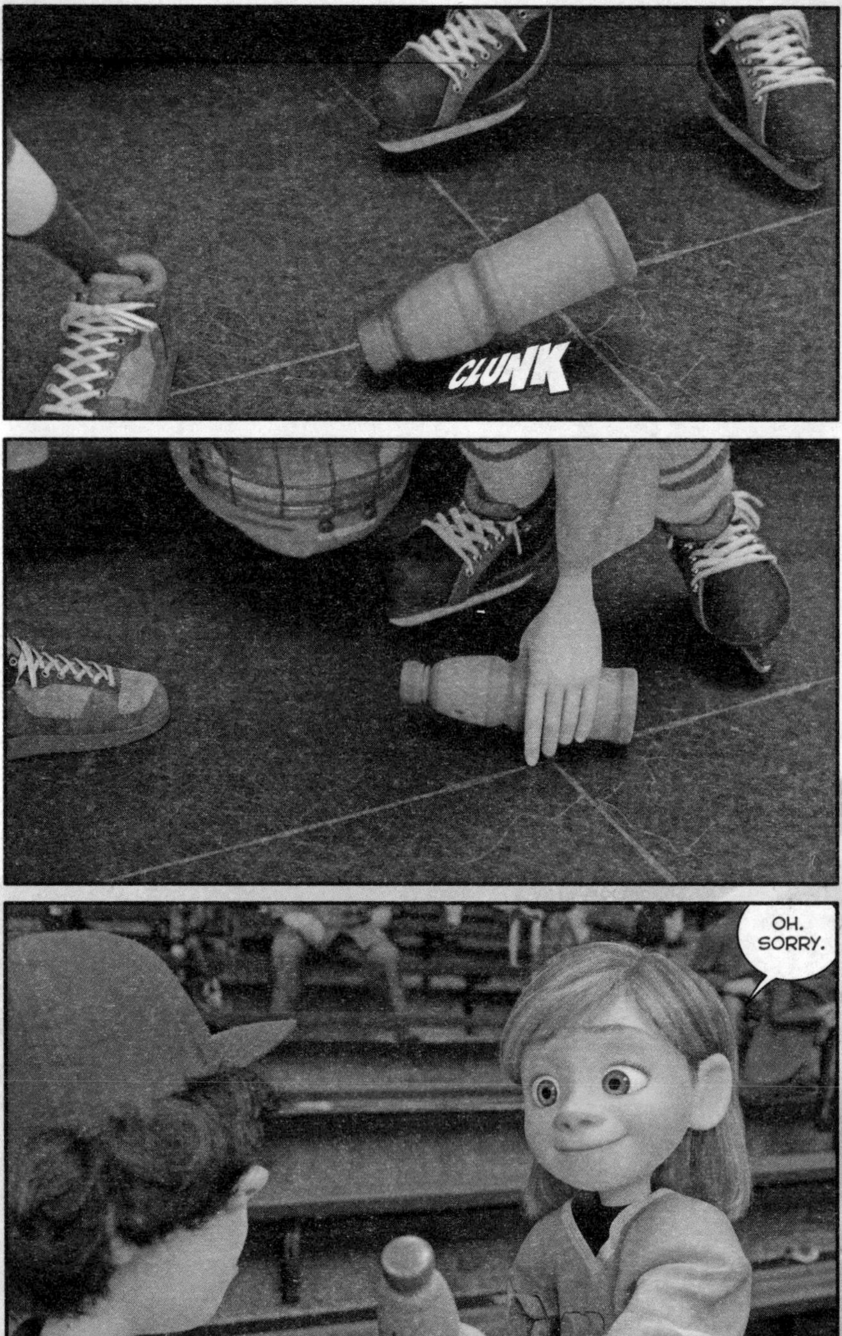
CLUNK
OH. SORRY.

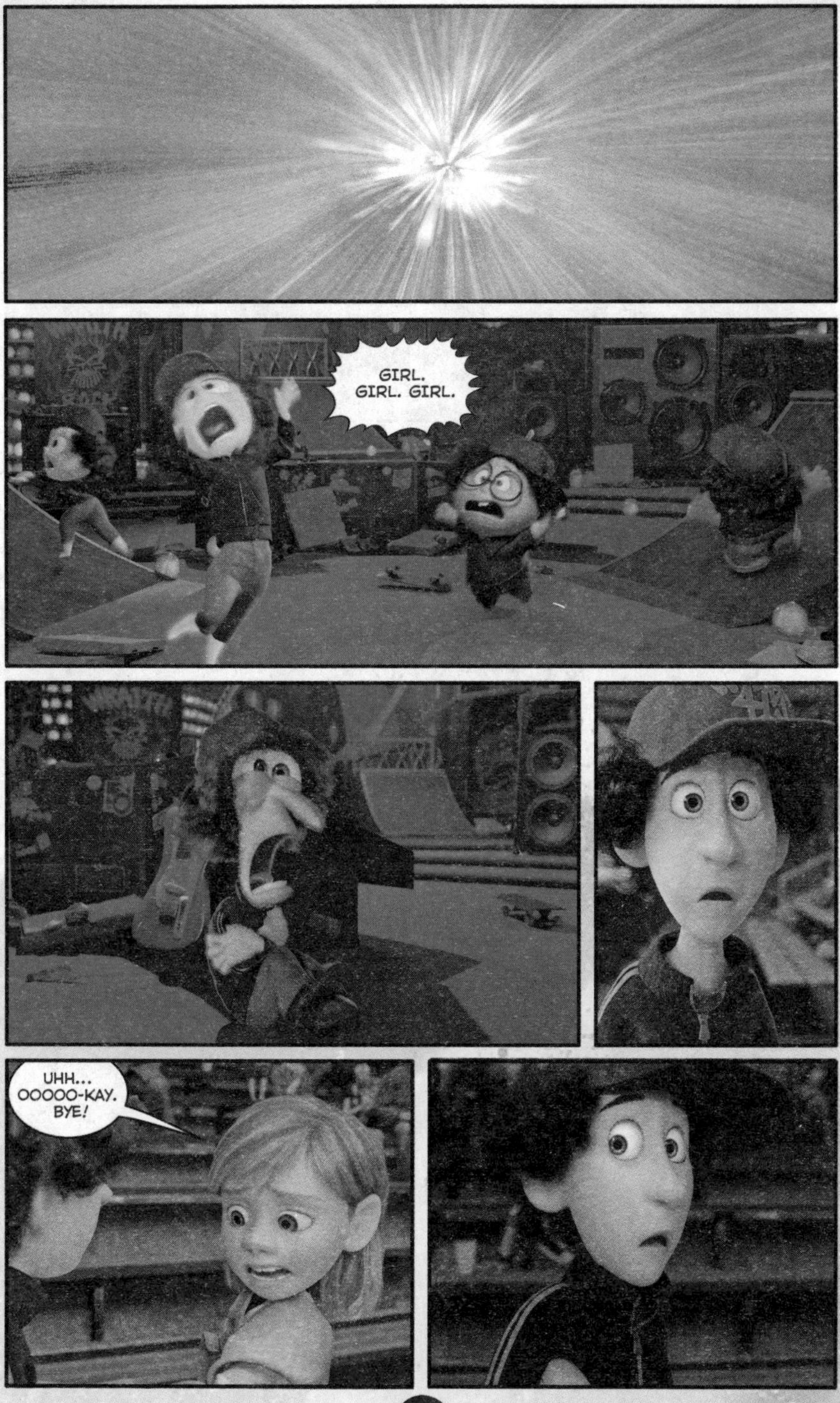
GIRL.
GIRL. GIRL.
UHH...
OOOOO-KAY.
BYE!

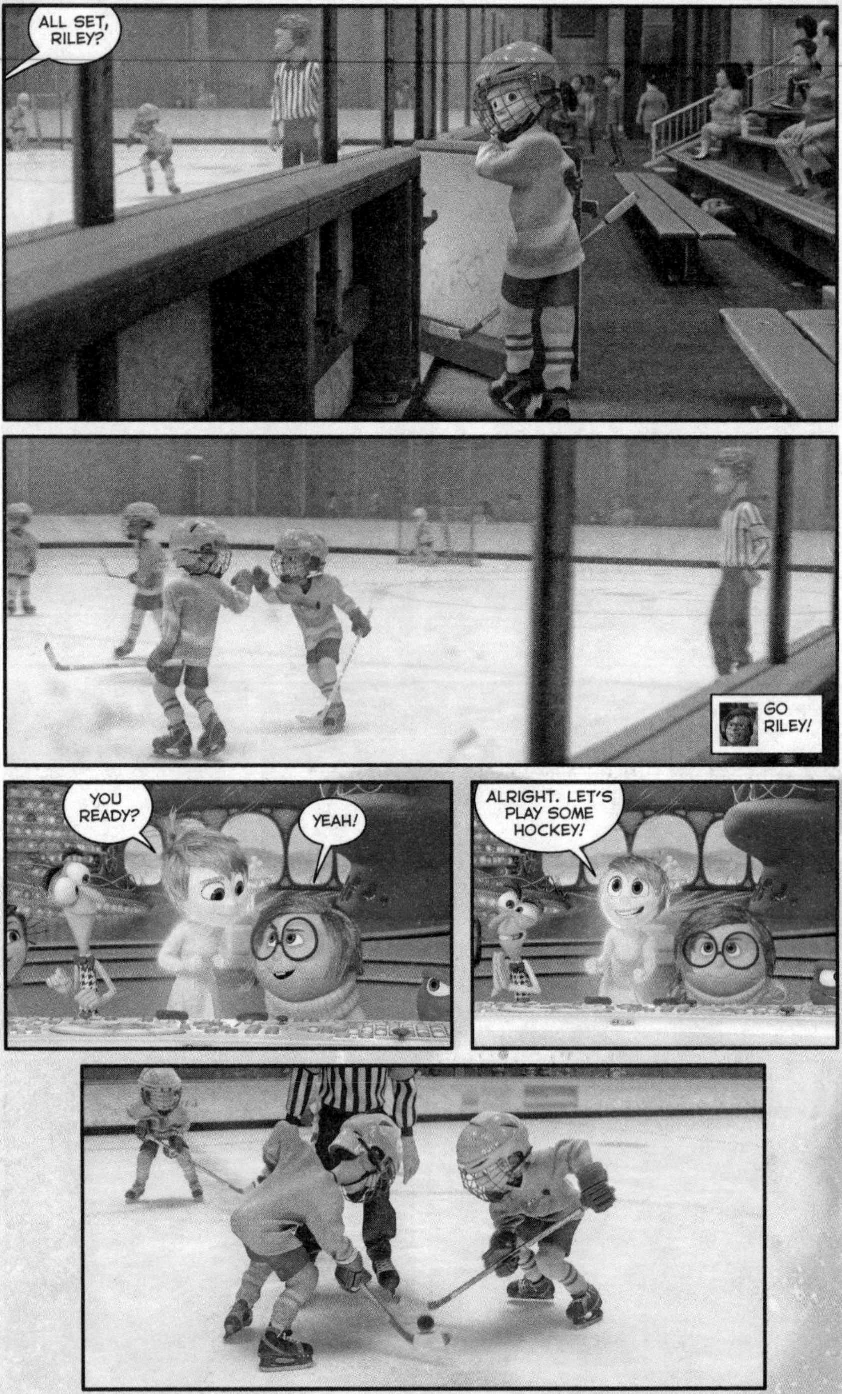
ALL SET, RILEY?
GO RILEY!
YOU READY?
YEAH!
ALRIGHT. LET'S PLAY SOME HOCKEY!

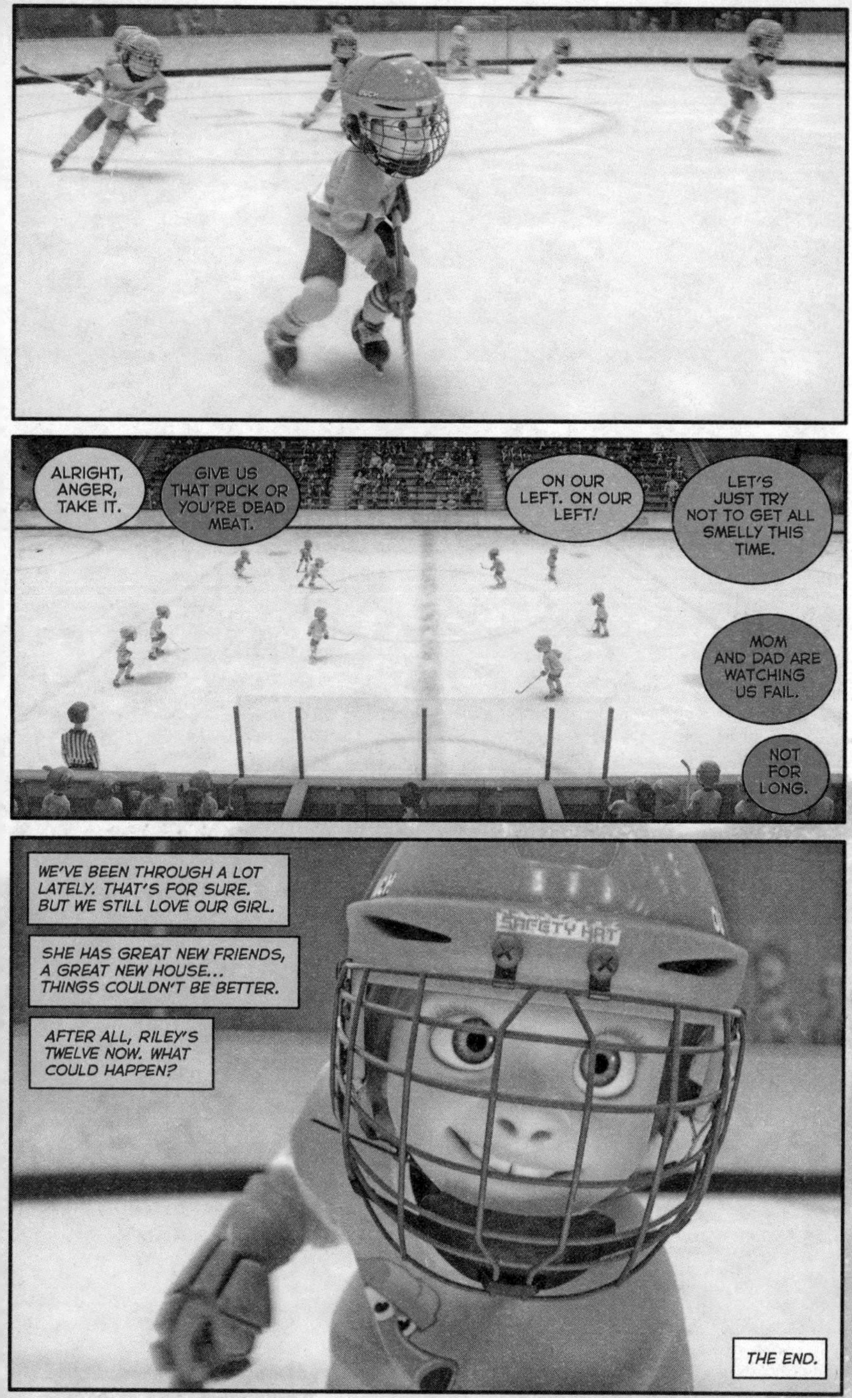
ALRIGHT, ANGER, TAKE IT.
GIVE US THAT PUCK OR YOU'RE DEAD MEAT.
ON OUR LEFT. ON OUR LEFT!
LET'S JUST TRY NOT TO GET ALL SMELLY THIS TIME.
MOM AND DAD ARE WATCHING US FAIL.
NOT FOR LONG.
WE'VE BEEN THROUGH A LOT LATELY. THAT'S FOR SURE. BUT WE STILL LOVE OUR GIRL.
SHE HAS GREAT NEW FRIENDS, A GREAT NEW HOUSE... THINGS COULDN'T BE BETTER.
AFTER ALL, RILEY'S TWELVE NOW. WHAT COULD HAPPEN?
SAFETY HAT
THE END.

directed by
pete docter

co-directed by
ronnie
del carmen

produced by
jonas rivera, p.g.a.

executive producers
john lasseter
andrew stanton

associate producer
mark nielsen

original story by
pete docter
ronnie del carmen

screenplay by
pete docter
meg lefauve
josh cooley

original score composed by
michael
giacchino

story supervisor
josh cooley

film edited by
kevin nolting, a.c.e.

production designer
ralph eggleston

supervising technical director
michael fong

production manager
dana murray

supervising animators
shawn krause
victor navone

directors of photography
camera
patrick lin

lighting
kim white

I smell food.

character supervisor
sajan skaria

character & sets supervisor
robert moyer

effects supervisor
gary bruins

simulation supervisor
edwin wooyoung chang

rendering supervisor
alexander kolliopoulos

global technology and
second unit & crowds supervisor
william reeves

second unit &
crowds animation supervisor
paul mendoza

character art direction
albert lozano

sets art direction
daniel holland

shading art direction
bert berry

sound designer
ren klyce

casting by kevin reher, c.s.a.
natalie lyon, c.s.a.

cast

joy amy poehler
sadness phyllis smith
bing bong richard kind
fear bill hader
anger lewis black
disgust mindy kaling
riley kaitlyn dias
mom diane lane
dad kyle maclachlan
forgetter paula paula poundstone
forgetter bobby bobby moynihan
dream director & mom's anger paula pell
subconscious guard frank dave goelz
subconscious guard dave frank oz
jangles josh cooley
mind worker cop jake flea
fritz john ratzenberger
helicopter pilot carlos alazraqui
clown's joy peter sagal
cool girl's emotions rashida jones

post production supervisor paul cichocki

production finance lead
& pre-production manager todd shaiman

production finance lead ryan broek

shot production manager michael warch

story

story manager samantha wilson

story artists
james s. baker jim capobianco
yung-han chang daniel chong
tony fucile manny hernandez
sam hood matt jones
vladimir kooperman valerie lapointe
tony maki tony rosenast
bobby alcid rubio j. garett sheldrew
domee shi shion takeuchi
j.p. vine

additional story material by michael arndt
simon rich
additional dialogue by bob peterson
bill hader
amy poehler
story coordinator isabel conde

editorial

editorial managers jesús martinez
becky neiman-cobb

second film editor jason hudak
associate editor kevin rose-williams
first assistant editor jason brodkey
second assistant editors jamie datz
jimmy lillard
additional editing john bryant
nicholas c. smith, a.c.e.
serena warner

production music & sound effects editor justin pearson
additional production music editor samuel lehmer
assistant sound editor kenny pickett

script supervisors mimi zora
emily zulauf

editorial coordinators leslie pao
alicia mooty
editorial assistant ben morris
reels coordinator jeremy slome
editorial interns lindsay armstrong
amber dupre
amy mcbeth

art

art manager **erik langley**

character artists **chris sasaki**
deanna marsigliese
daniel arriaga

set artists

kristian norelius **armand baltazar**
don shank **nelson "rey" bohol**
william cone **noah klocek**

previs artist **philip metschan**
sculptor **jerome ranft**
graphics art director **craig foster**
color artists **shelly wan**
chia-han jennifer chang

development artists

ricky nierva **mark oftedal**
bob pauley **richard thompson**
bruce zick

art coordinators **may iosotaluno**
pauline chu
art interns **janine chang**
jocelyn liang

camera & staging

layout manager **nick berry**

layout lead **adam habib**

layout artists

james campbell **robert kinkead**
colin levy **gregg olsson**
jan pfenninger **mark sanford**
leo santos **matthew silas**
derek williams **sylvia gray wong**

post-animation camera artist **sandra karpman**

layout coordinator **judy yi-inn jou**

animation

animation manager **courtney casper kent**

directing animator **jaime roe**
animation sketch artist **tony fucile**
animation fix lead **bruce kuei**

character development & animation

andrew coats **belen gil-palacios**
guilherme sauerbronn jacinto **amber martorelli**
bret parker **allison rutland**
kristophe vergne **priscila de b.vertamatti**
ron zorman

animators

dovi anderson **eric anderson**
evan bonifacio **shad bradbury**
jude brownbill **guillaume chartier**
michael chia-wei chen **simon christen**
christopher chua **claudio de oliveira**
robb denovan **paul f. diaz**
gwendelyn enderoglu **travis hathaway**
eliza ivanova **rob jensen**
patty kihm **jae hyung kim**
john chun chiu lee **wendell lee**
matt majers **michal makarewicz**
steve mason **cameron miyasaki**
dan nguyen **erick oh**
tim pixton **jayson price**
k.c. roeyer **nickolas rosario**
michael sauls **terry song**
matthew strangio **benjamin po an su**
jessica torres **ricky wight**
alon winterstein **stephen wong**
tom zach

animation tools lead **bret parker**

fix & additional animation

brendan beesley   shaun chacko
joshua dai   justin farris
graham finley   aaron hartline
carolina lopez dau   dave mullins
jordi oñate isal   bobby podesta
andreas procopiou   robert h. russ
stefan schumacher   mike stern

animation shot support

daniel campbell   june foster
robb gibbs   todd r. krish

animation coordinator   claire faggioli
animation technical & fix coordinator   sara trumpler
animation technical coordinator   daniella muller
animation fix coordinator   duncan ramsay

second unit & crowds

second unit & crowds manager   nick berry

second unit & crowds technical artist   michael lorenzen

second unit & crowds animation

james w. brown   arik ehle
joey gilbreath   richard gunzer
catherine hicks   shawn janik
holger leihe   tal shwarzman

second unit & crowds coordinator   andy sakhrani

characters

character manager   jaclyn simon

character articulation lead   seth freeman
character cloth lead   emron grover
character shading lead   jacob merrell

character modeling & articulation artists

paul aichele   jason davies
bernhard haux   michael honsel
jonas jarvers   tanja krampfert
alonso martinez   andrew h schmidt
ian steplowski

character cloth artists

chris griffin   fran kalal
aimei kutt   carmen ngai
edgar rodriguez

character shading artists

byron bashforth   philip child
sarah fowler deluna   masha ellsworth
jamie frye   alexander hessler
ana g. lacaze jordan   george nguyen
character groom artists   jacob brooks
kiki mei kee poh
ben porter

character coordinator   eoin convery bullock

sets

sets manager   deirdre warin

sets modeling lead   steve karski
set dressing lead   amy l. allen
sets shading lead   eric andraos
sets technical lead   michael frederickson
matte paint lead   david batte
additional sets supervision   alex harvill
john halstead

sets modeling artists

mike altman   andrew dayton
joshua mills   arnold moon
greg peltz   joseph suen
raymond v. wong

set dressing artists

nathan fariss   alison leaf
p. antonio piedra   michael rutter
frank tai

sets shading & paint artists

alec bartsch   chris bernardi
thidaratana annee jonjai   thomas jordan
alex marino   peter roe
shalin shodhan   richard snyder
peter sumanaseni   rui tong
yaa-lirng tu   andrew whittock
weera tom wichitsripornkul

sets technical artists

david dixon	omar elafifi
hsiao-hsien aaron lo	david luoh

matte painters
ernesto nemesio
paul topolos

matte paint technical
francisco de la torre
martin sebastian senn
matthew webb

additional shading leadership colin hayes thompson

sets coordinator anthony kemp
sets production assistant jon bryant

simulation

simulation manager sarita white

simulation artists

frank aalbers	henry dean garcia
emron grover	fran kalal
laurie kim	tiffany erickson klohn
sonoko konishi	aimei kutt
david lally	samantha raja
	edgar rodriguez

simulation coordinator isabel conde

global technology

global technology manager todd shaiman

global technology lead brandon kerr

global technology engineers

alexis angelidis	antony carysforth
bena currin	laurence emms
matt kuruc	heegun lee
ryusuke villemin	meng yu

global technology intern peter kutz

sweatbox

sweatbox coordinators stephen krug
eric rosales

lighting

lighting manager piper freeman

lighting leads sudeep rangaswamy
angelique reisch
michael sparber

master lighting artists

nick bartone	lloyd bernberg
alfonso caparrini	ye won cho
danielle feinberg	jesse hollander
steven james	josée lajoie
ken lao	andy lin
luke martorelli	ian megibben
vandana reddy sahrawat	jose l. ramos serrano
david shavers	philip shoebottom
	jeremy vickery

lighting artists

mimia arbelaez	katie bickley
maxwell bickley	brian boyd
mathieu cassagne	ed chen
charu clark	kathleen cosby
magen sara farrar	wen-chin hsu
sungyeon joh	jonathan kiker
emmanuel maniez	paul oakley
burt peng	maria powers
jordan rempel	julien schreyer

lightspeed lead tim babb

lightspeed technical directors

chris horne	james l. jackson
brandon kerr	jonathan penney
	reid sandros

lighting coordinators annie mueller
mimi zora

effects

effects manager	sarita white
development & effects artists	dave hale
	matthew kiyoshi wong

effects artists

alexis angelidis	amit baadkar
hosuk chang	sarah beth eisinger
christopher foreman	cody harrington
jason johnston	nick lucas
stephen marshall	leon jeongwook park
michael rice	ferdi scheepers
vincent serritella	tim speltz
	enrique vila

effects coordinator	lucy laliberte
effects intern	matthew benson

rendering

rendering manager	jaclyn simon

rendering & optimization artists

marlena fecho	robert graf
philip graham	donald schmidt

rendering coordinator	eoin convery bullock

production

assistant to the producer	elissa knight
assistant to the director	victoria manley thompson
production office manager	courtney bergin
feature relations manager	lee rase
feature relations coordinator	margo zimmerman
production office assistants	jon bryant
	candice kuwahara
	alyssa mar

additional production support

adrian ochoa	kiera mcauliffe
lorien mckenna	allison w. nelson

creative development

mary coleman	emily davis
kiel murray	karen paik
	james roderick

titles

title design	laura meyer
technical support	a.u.b.i.e
production coordinator	pauline chu

post production

director	cynthia slavens
post production supervisor, home entertainment	eric pearson
post production supervisor, ancillary	erick ziegler
senior scientist	dominic glynn
manager	robert tachoires
administration manager	beth sullivan
post production coordinator, theatrical	jeremy slome
post production coordinator	jeremy quist
management assistant	christine wilcock
mastering supervisor	robin leigh
colorist	mark dinicola
color grading operator	susan brunig
theatrical mastering specialist	erik anderson
post production engineering manager	andra smith
post production engineering lead	laura savidge
media systems architect	stewart birnam
software engineering	winston o. good
	brett warne
mastering coordinator	amy nawrocki
media control center operators	glenn kasprzycki
	cristopher knight
	richard pinkham
senior projectionist	john hazelton
projectionist	bryan dennis
projection scheduler	anthony david duran
post production assistant	rachael bigelow

international production

international production manager	cynthia lusk
international coordinator	megan alderson
international technical team	mark adams
	patrick james
international editorial	charles choo

stereoscopic 3d

stereoscopic supervisor	bob whitehill
stereo & international tech lead	jay carina
manager	danielle cambridge
rendering	jay-vincent jones
	yaa-lirng tu
production assistant	katherine gugger
director of stereoscopic production	joshua hollander

render pipeline group

manager	anne pia
technical lead	josh grant

team

kate cronin	nino ellington
boris krasnoiarov	yun lien
eric peden	zachary repasky
	eric salituro

production sound

original dialogue mixers	doc kane
	vince caro
dialogue recordist	jeannette browning hernandez

post production sound services by

skywalker sound

a lucasfilm ltd. company, marin county, california

supervising sound editor	shannon mills
re-recording mixers	michael semanick
	tom johnson
sound effects editors	david c. hughes
	jeremy bowker
	malcolm fife
supervising dialogue editor	daniel laurie
foley editor	thom brennan
first assistant sound editor	coya elliott
sound design assistant	nia hansen
foley artists	john roesch
	alyson dee moore
foley mixer	maryjo lang
assistant re-recording mixer	stephen urata
audio / video transfer	marco alicea
sound accountant	michael peters
client services	eva porter

skywalker sound executive staff

general manager	josh lowden
head of production	jon null
head of engineering	steve morris

additional voices

lori alan	carlos alazraqui
gregg berger	aurora blue
veronika bonell	lola cooley
john cygan	dani dare
ronnie del carmen	pete docter
keith ferguson	tony fucile
mary gibbs	randy hahn
carter hastings	jacob hopkins
emma hudak	evan hudak
dara iruka	molly jackson
daniella jones	sophia lee karadi
elissa knight	erik langley
dawnn lewis	sherry lynn
tony maki	mona marshall
laraine newman	bret parker
paula pell	phil proctor
murray pearl schaeffer	patrick seitz
paris van dyke	james kevin ward
lennon wynn	dash zamm

music

executive music producer chris montan
music supervisor tom macdougall
score orchestrated & conducted by tim simonec

additional orchestrations

peter boyer brad dechter
mark gasbarro norman ludwin
cameron patrick marshall bowen
jeffrey kryka

music editor stephen m. davis, m.p.s.e.
score recorded & mixed by joel iwataki
score coordinator andrea datzman
music production director andrew page
music business affairs scott holtzman
don welty
music production coordinator ashley chafin
music contracted by reggie wilson
assistant music contractor connie boylan
music preparation by booker white
score recordist tom hardisty
vincent cirilli
score recorded & mixed at eastwood scoring stage, warner bros. studio

scoring stage crew

ryan robinson richard wheeler
greg dennen jamie olvera

"grim grinning ghosts"
(otherworldly concerto)
written by
buddy baker & xavier atencio
performed by gaylord carter
courtesy of walt disney records

"exotico speedo"
written by
laurent lombard
courtesy of apm music

special thanks to the orchestra for bringing the music to life.

pixar studio team

administration

allysa amundson heather feng-yanu valerie graf meghan e. langham danielle rae levin
michelle moretta lightner gerisa macale cherise miller tanya oskanian john shannon
wendy dale tanzillo seth van booven

business & legal affairs

serena dettman richard guo jennie jensen brynn mohagen lara lesieur pendleton
jody weinberg

consumer products, interactive & publishing

kelly bonbright gigi dueñas catherine foreman mandy freund molly jones
jonathan rodriguez rob rowe jen tan scott tilley jay ward

craft services by luxo café

jennifer johnston vivian rodriguez andrea aleman melissa anderson clinton cook
daniel deitz aaron grimm derrick jones sara kosuth andreas merten
douglas monsalud matthew nydam tim power julio quintero zach schneiderman
glenn seto

documentary & home entertainment production

lauren conca sarah dunham christina f. julian tony kaplan erica milsom
taura musgrove chelsea walton

facility operations

patty bonfilio daniel alvarez james andereggen michael blackmon II marco castellanos
kyle charley michael douglass, jr. matt gagnebin michael hitson nick kolidakis
hsiao liu edgar a. ochoa joey roch ramirez peter schreiber brian torres

finance

mark joseph stephanie pham aganon megan albert nancy garretson case michelle lin chung
rachel ergas kristi gamble timothy glass valerie hathaway kentaro hinoki
heather d.c. jackson kheron jones-kassing kate lardiere michelle lopez kacy naylor
rosana neciuk karen perry kristina ruud-hewitt michelle simons shari villarde
deana walker annette wang sue williams

human resources

erica perkins kim diaz peggy dollaghan jennifer dunlap edwin fabian
elise foss nathaniel harting nancy howard ryan howe jennylyn mercado huynh
erin mcgarry krueger marcos navarrete allison parker rebecca pigg maggie m. randriamamonjy

marketing

jonathan garson britney best andy dreyfus lisa fletcher adam gates
cherie hammond holly lloyd sureena mann angela marie mistretta desiree mourad
shannon nicosia silvia palara kim ross david sameth laurie schrey
tasha sounart brian tanaka jesse weglein clayborn welch timothy zohr

pixar university & archives

elyse klaidman collin allen liz borges-herzog welburn trish carney leila chesloff
tony derose sharon dovas christine freeman brianne gallagher brian green
david r. haumann maren jones karen kiser tia wallace kratter shana levin
michelle lindsey radcliff adrienne ranft juliet roth erika schmidt tiffany taira
melissa woods jamie woolf

promotional animation

ross haldane stevenson	lindsay andrus	sequoia blankenship	kevin chesnos	keith cormier
tim fox	nicole paradis griudle	stephanie brooke hamilton	jessica harvill	ken kim
claire munzer	justin ritter	alli sadegiani	gini erus santos	raphael suter
rob duquette thompson	andrew vernon		nathan wall	brad winemiller

publicity

nicole albertson	krissy bailey	deborah coleman	briana gardner	susanne lally
	hasia sroat		chris wiggum	

renderman development

dana batali	katrin bratland	james burgess	per christensen	ray davis
julian fong	stephen friedman	ian hsieh	andrew kensler	charlie kilpatrick
david m. laur	trina m. roy	brian k. saunders	brian savery	brenden schubert
annabella serra	jonathan shade		adam wood-gaines	wayne wooten

brian smits (1968 - 2013)

renderman sales & marketing

christopher ford	renee lamri	peter moxom	dylan sisson	wendy wirthlin

safety & security

alana forrest	john bennett	marlon castro	paul chideya	richard cogger
mlinzi majigiza	cristina maurodopulos becker	arthur mcdade III	adrian rico-galvez	allan rivera
	joni superticioso		chris taylor	

software research & development

engineering & design leads

ryan burus	jeremy cowles	george elkoura	f. sebastian grassia	thomas hahn
jamie hecker	hayley iben	michael b. johnson	chris king	josh minor
daniel leaf nunes	cory omand	jack paulus	davide pesare	susan salituro
sarah shen	dirk van gelder		douglas waters	adam woodbury

management

gregory finch	dana frankoff	sue maatouk kalache	sowmya natarajan	sabine o'sullivan
	bill polson		david wehr	

infrastructure

robert eli	mckay farley		earl jon van arsdall	jack zhao

research

tom duff	kurt fleischer	florian hecht	mark meyer	jean-daniel nahmias
		tom nettleship		

pre production & asset based engineering

don bui	julian y.c. cheu	paul edmondson	philip floetotto	phred lender
aaron luk	edward luong	kyle mcdaniel	peter nye	lane pertusi
		stefan schulze		

look development

jim atkinson	joachim de deken	daniel chang	tolga göktekin	daniel lasry
shawn neely	arun rao	eliot smyrl	stephan steinbach	brandon wang
john warren	emily weihrich		magnus wrenninge	richard yoshioka

presto animation system & core engineering

david baraff	jonathan bianchi	malcolm blanchard	sunya boonyatera	andrew butts
juei chang	daniel garcia	matthias goerner	mark hessler	shriram neelakanta iyer
ryan kautzman	jason kim	manuel kraemer	venkateswaran krishna	doug letterman
brett levin	john loy	deneb meketa	alex mohr	gary monheit
corey revilla	florian sauer	chris schoeneman	chen shen	burton siu
ryan stelzleni	takahito tejima		david g. yu	florian zitzelsberger

systems

technical leads

dale bewley	lars r. damerow	joseph frost	grant gatzke	thomas indermaur
chris lasell	david nahman-ramos	wil phan	david sotnick	jim wilhelmi

management

joel bruck	tyler fazakerley	alisa gilden	may pon	m.t. silvia
		christopher c. walker		

support

administration & operations	data management	mac & windows	media systems	telecom
wesley callow	shaun brown	tlaloc alvarez	chris collins	shawn hovis
ling hsu	mark harrison	daryn cash	warren latimer	michael stewart johnson
jane murphy	heidi stettner	j. darion cnevas	joanna laurent	mark pananganan

animation support		james g. dashe	edgar quiñones	unix
robert hamrick	hardware	dan hoffman	steven ricks	peter kaldis
matthew muhili lindahl	ricky der	cory ander knox	jessica wan	nelson sette siu
sara sampson	leslie law	erin m. merchant	jason watkins	web development
ian westcott	financial systems	terry lee moseley		christine jones
backups	tiffany reno fung	benjamin rillie	storage	darla lovrin
jonathan hadden	peter plackowski		eric bermender	sean stephenson
jose richard ignacio	nicholas zehner		bryan bird	
bob morgan			andy thomas	
rudy jason vucelich			peter ward	

theme parks

anthony a. apodaca	keri cicolani	liz gazzano	roger gould	stephen gregory
heidi holman	donna quattropani		krista sheffler	carol waug

development

heather eisner	amy ellenwood	emily molienkopf	katherine sarafian	jenni tsoi

production babies

abril	adeline	ajáy	alexander	amelie	aria	arjun
aubrey	audrey	autumn	avery	axel	ayla mae	beatrice
benjamin	charley	christopher jd	christopher ru	cleas	colton	colton jace
delphine	eden	elaina	elise	elizabeth	ella	ellie
ellis	emery	eva	evan	evelyn	finley	fisher
gemma	georgia	grace	gray	greta	hannah	harper
hayley	hazel	imogen	isaac	julian	kalya	karter
kyle	laila	leia	lilly	linda	lucy	luke
madeline	madison	makena	marcus	matilda	matthew	maxime
maya	meara	mélodie	merritt	mia	mina	murray
oliver aquino	oliver chung	oliver lopez	oliver thomas	owen	penelope	riley
rj	robert	rosalind	rowan	ryan finley	ryan levin	rylin
sam	samuel	sanjay	sashi	seohu	shaan	shon
siena	tess	timothy	victor	walker	willa	william
willow	wyatt	wyatt ray	zachary	zoe	zoey	

3444

special thanks

flip phillips	tom mccarthy
diane disney miller	ron miller
sunrise farms llc	cassandra smolcic
lorne michaels & the snl team	katherine sarafian
laurel ladevich	lindsey collins
denise ream	john mulaney
daniel gerson	robert l. baird

and

the mortimer b. zuckerman mind brain behavior institute

special thanks to dr. paul ekman & dacher keltner
for guiding us through this emotional journey.

pixar senior creative team

| mark andrews | brad bird | brian fee | john lasseter | bob peterson |
| dan scanlon | peter sohn | | andrew stanton | lee unkrich |

pixar production senior managers

| lourdes marquez alba | andrew beall | pamela j. choy | gillian libbert-duncan | eben f. ostby |
| | susan tatsuno | | sophie vincelette | |

pixar senior technology team

| john kirkman | steve may | guido quaroni |

pixar senior leadership team

| ed catmull | marc s. greenberg | jim kennedy | lori mcadams | jim morris |
| | | thomas porter | | |

this film is dedicated to our kids. please don't grow up. ever.

animated with

presto
animation system

rendered with

RENDERMAN

no. 49510

DOLBY ATMOS
In Selected Theatres

DATASAT
DIGITAL SOUND
IN SELECTED THEATRES

Kodak
Motion Picture Film

sound created in dolby atmos
prints by fotokem®

original soundtrack available on

WALT DISNEY RECORDS

video games available from

DISNEP
INTERACTIVE STUDIOS
in stores now
on your favorite gaming systems

distributed by
**walt disney studios
motion pictures**

created and produced at
pixar animation studios
emeryville, ca

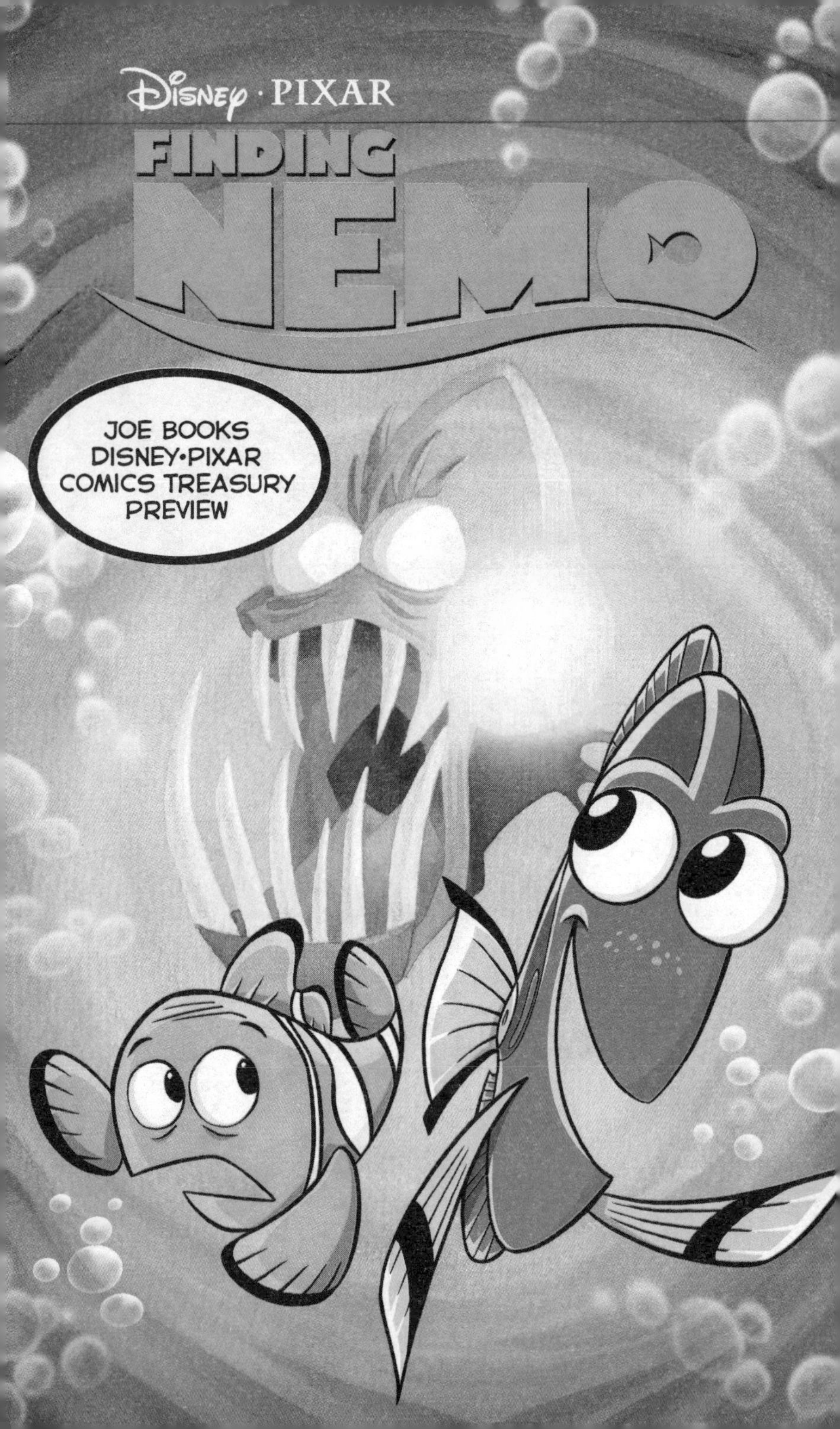
Disney · PIXAR
FINDING NEMO
JOE BOOKS DISNEY•PIXAR COMICS TREASURY PREVIEW

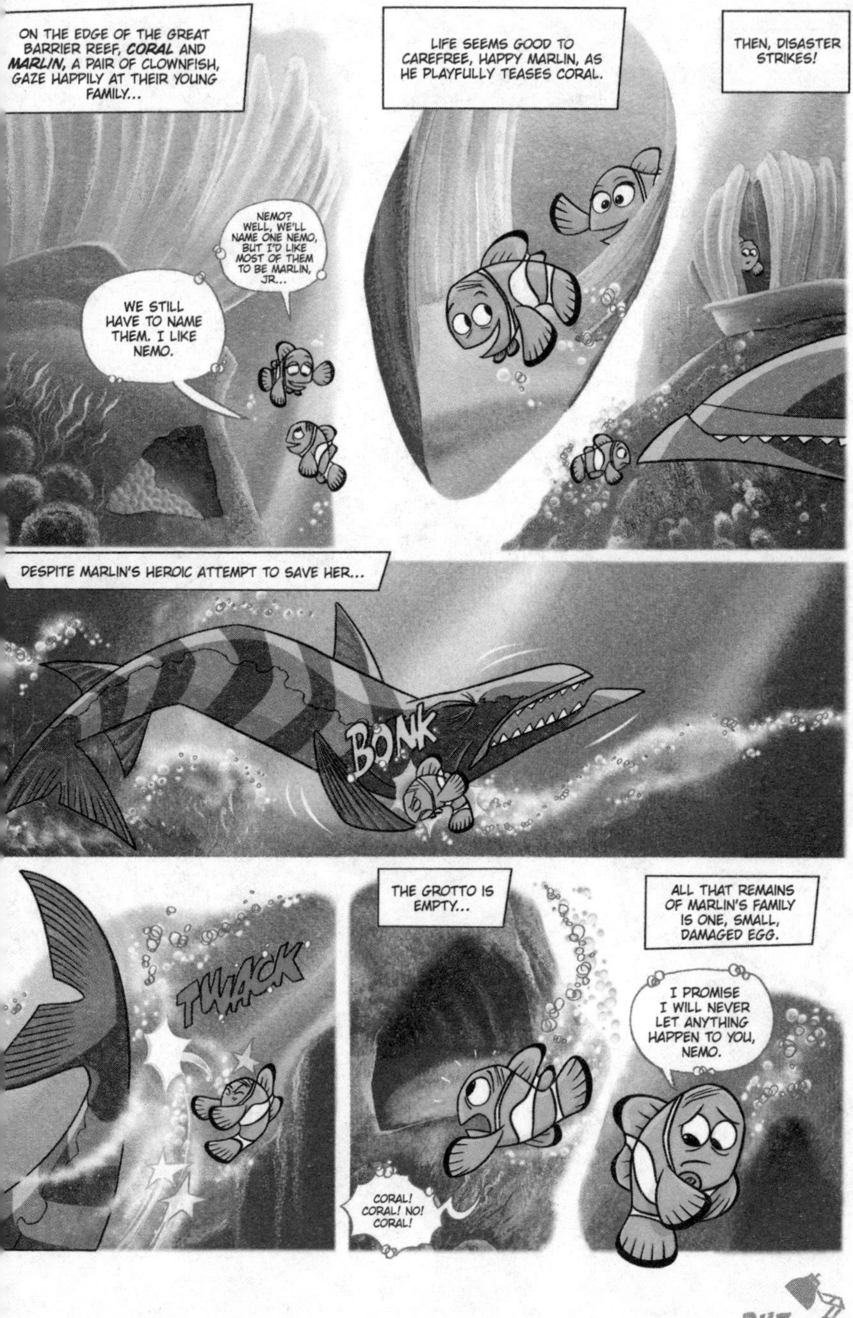
ON THE EDGE OF THE GREAT BARRIER REEF, CORAL AND MARLIN, A PAIR OF CLOWNFISH, GAZE HAPPILY AT THEIR YOUNG FAMILY...
WE STILL HAVE TO NAME THEM. I LIKE NEMO.
NEMO? WELL, WE'LL NAME ONE NEMO, BUT I'D LIKE MOST OF THEM TO BE MARLIN, JR...
LIFE SEEMS GOOD TO CAREFREE, HAPPY MARLIN, AS HE PLAYFULLY TEASES CORAL.
THEN, DISASTER STRIKES!
DESPITE MARLIN'S HEROIC ATTEMPT TO SAVE HER...
BONK
TWACK
THE GROTTO IS EMPTY...
CORAL! CORAL! NO! CORAL!
ALL THAT REMAINS OF MARLIN'S FAMILY IS ONE, SMALL, DAMAGED EGG.
I PROMISE I WILL NEVER LET ANYTHING HAPPEN TO YOU, NEMO.

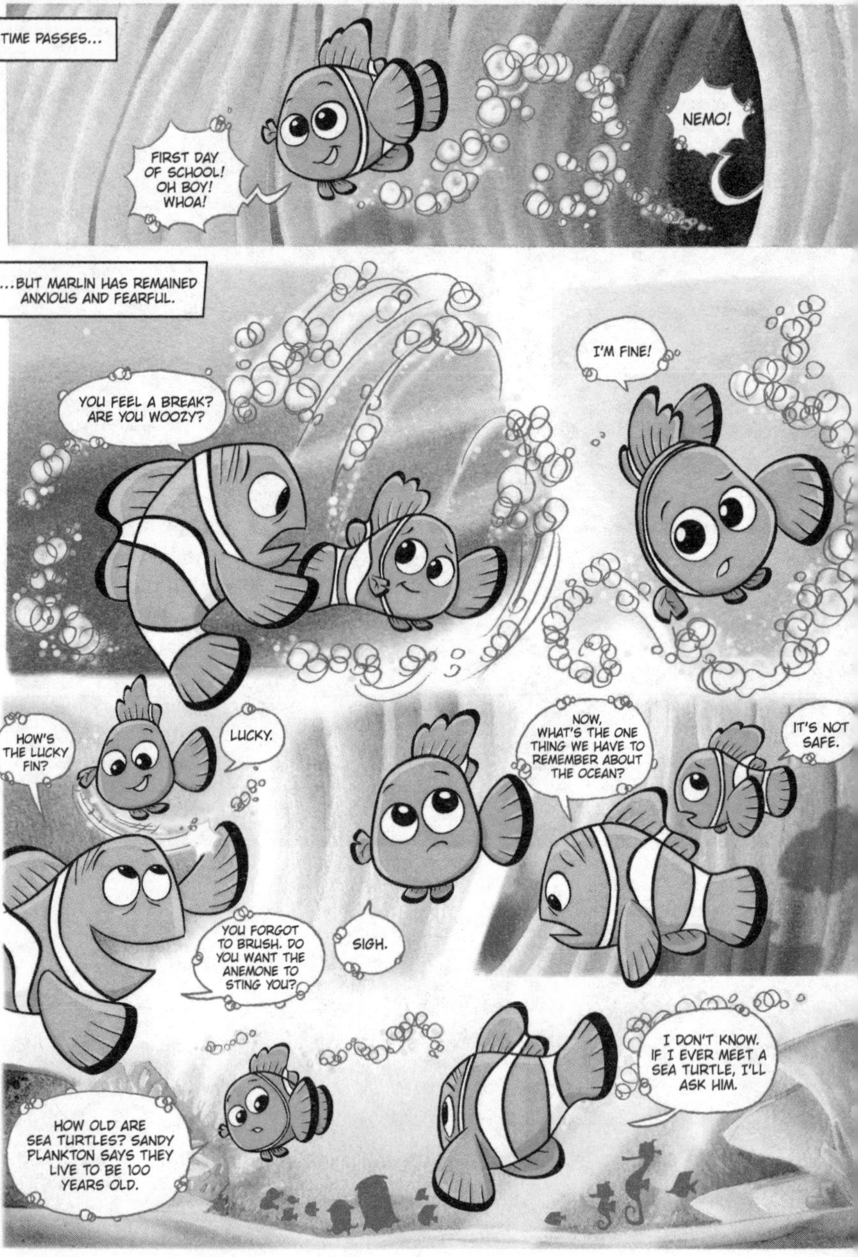
TIME PASSES...
FIRST DAY OF SCHOOL! OH BOY! WHOA!
NEMO!
...BUT MARLIN HAS REMAINED ANXIOUS AND FEARFUL.
YOU FEEL A BREAK? ARE YOU WOOZY?
I'M FINE!
HOW'S THE LUCKY FIN?
LUCKY.
YOU FORGOT TO BRUSH. DO YOU WANT THE ANEMONE TO STING YOU?
SIGH.
NOW, WHAT'S THE ONE THING WE HAVE TO REMEMBER ABOUT THE OCEAN?
IT'S NOT SAFE.
HOW OLD ARE SEA TURTLES? SANDY PLANKTON SAYS THEY LIVE TO BE 100 YEARS OLD.
I DON'T KNOW. IF I EVER MEET A SEA TURTLE, I'LL ASK HIM.

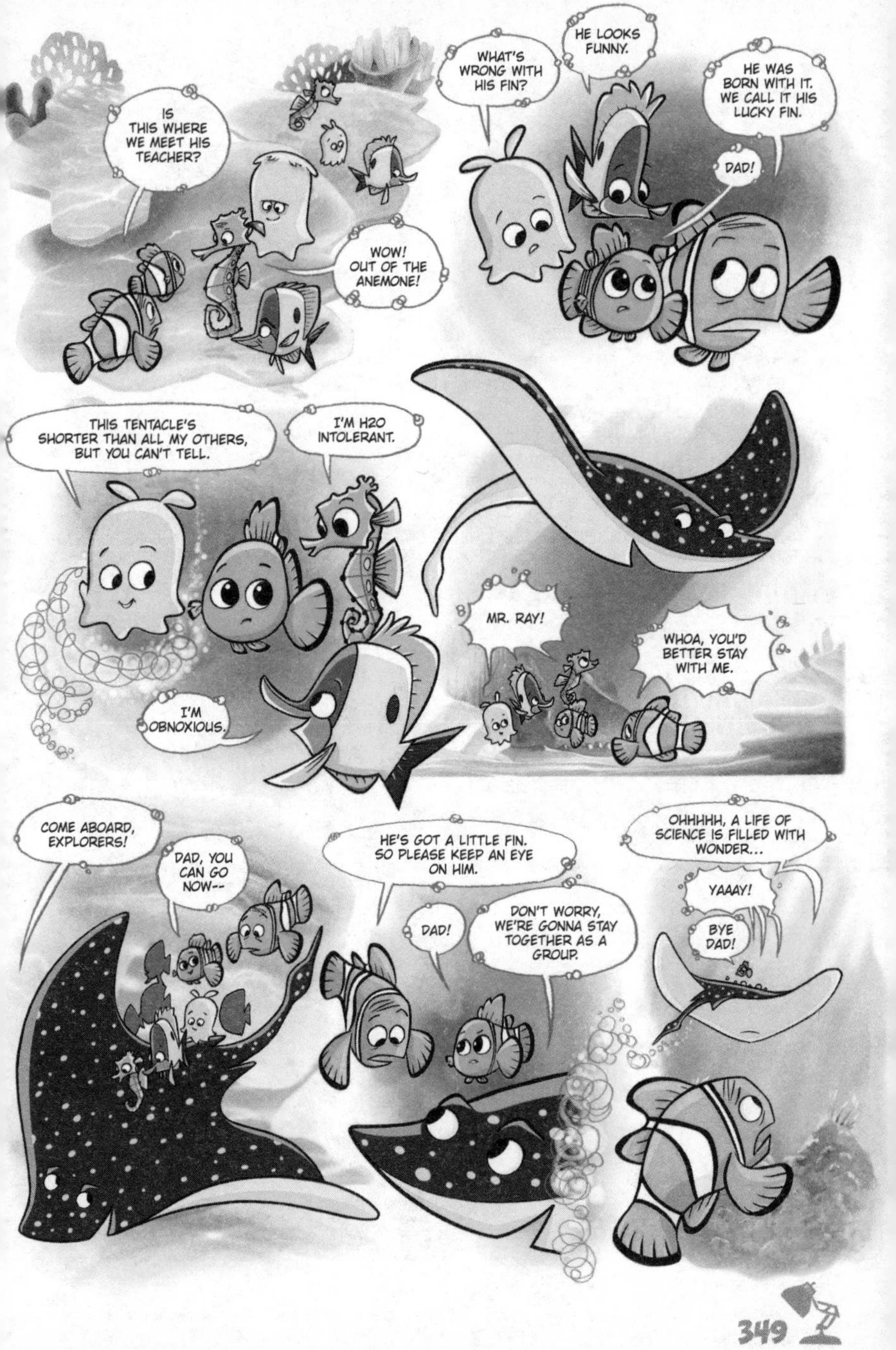
IS THIS WHERE WE MEET HIS TEACHER?
WOW! OUT OF THE ANEMONE!
WHAT'S WRONG WITH HIS FIN?
HE LOOKS FUNNY.
HE WAS BORN WITH IT. WE CALL IT HIS LUCKY FIN.
DAD!
THIS TENTACLE'S SHORTER THAN ALL MY OTHERS, BUT YOU CAN'T TELL.
I'M H2O INTOLERANT.
I'M OBNOXIOUS.
MR. RAY!
WHOA, YOU'D BETTER STAY WITH ME.
COME ABOARD, EXPLORERS!
DAD, YOU CAN GO NOW--
HE'S GOT A LITTLE FIN. SO PLEASE KEEP AN EYE ON HIM.
DAD!
DON'T WORRY, WE'RE GONNA STAY TOGETHER AS A GROUP.
OHHHHH, A LIFE OF SCIENCE IS FILLED WITH WONDER...
YAAAY!
BYE DAD!

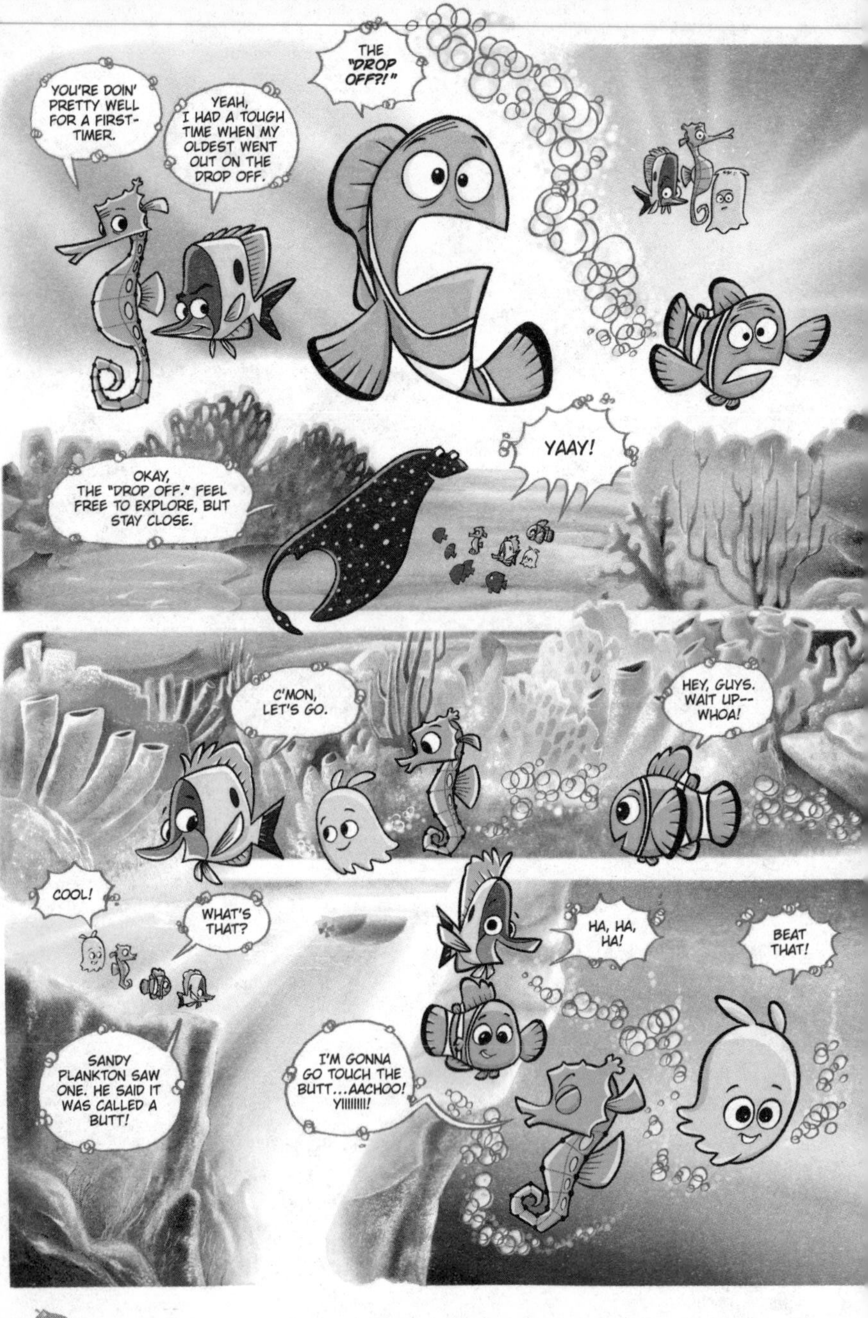
YOU'RE DOIN' PRETTY WELL FOR A FIRST-TIMER.
YEAH, I HAD A TOUGH TIME WHEN MY OLDEST WENT OUT ON THE DROP OFF.
THE "DROP OFF?!"
OKAY, THE "DROP OFF." FEEL FREE TO EXPLORE, BUT STAY CLOSE.
YAAY!
C'MON, LET'S GO.
HEY, GUYS. WAIT UP-- WHOA!
COOL!
WHAT'S THAT?
HA, HA, HA!
BEAT THAT!
SANDY PLANKTON SAW ONE. HE SAID IT WAS CALLED A BUTT!
I'M GONNA GO TOUCH THE BUTT...AACHOO! YIIIIIIII!

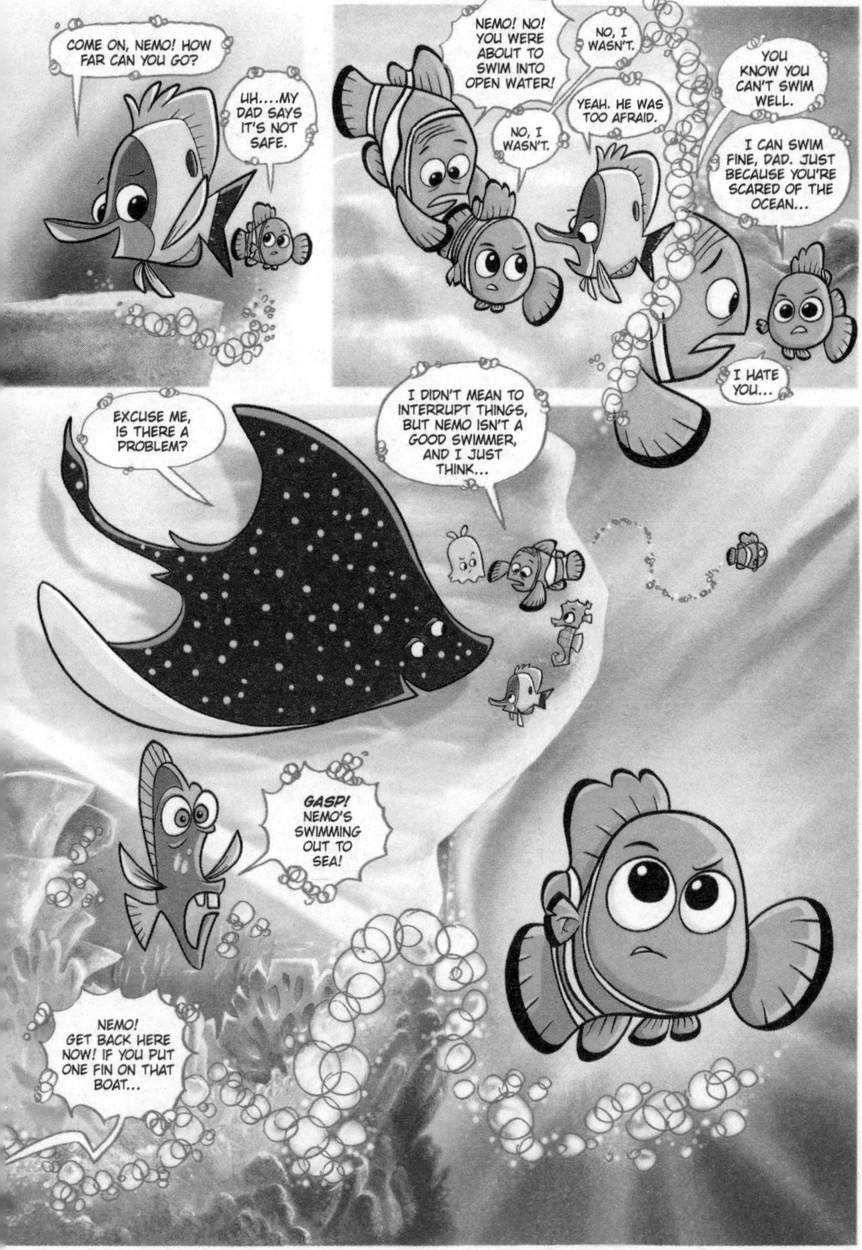
COME ON, NEMO! HOW FAR CAN YOU GO?
UH....MY DAD SAYS IT'S NOT SAFE.
NEMO! NO! YOU WERE ABOUT TO SWIM INTO OPEN WATER!
NO, I WASN'T.
NO, I WASN'T.
YEAH. HE WAS TOO AFRAID.
YOU KNOW YOU CAN'T SWIM WELL.
I CAN SWIM FINE, DAD. JUST BECAUSE YOU'RE SCARED OF THE OCEAN...
I HATE YOU...
EXCUSE ME, IS THERE A PROBLEM?
I DIDN'T MEAN TO INTERRUPT THINGS, BUT NEMO ISN'T A GOOD SWIMMER, AND I JUST THINK...
GASP! NEMO'S SWIMMING OUT TO SEA!
NEMO! GET BACK HERE NOW! IF YOU PUT ONE FIN ON THAT BOAT...

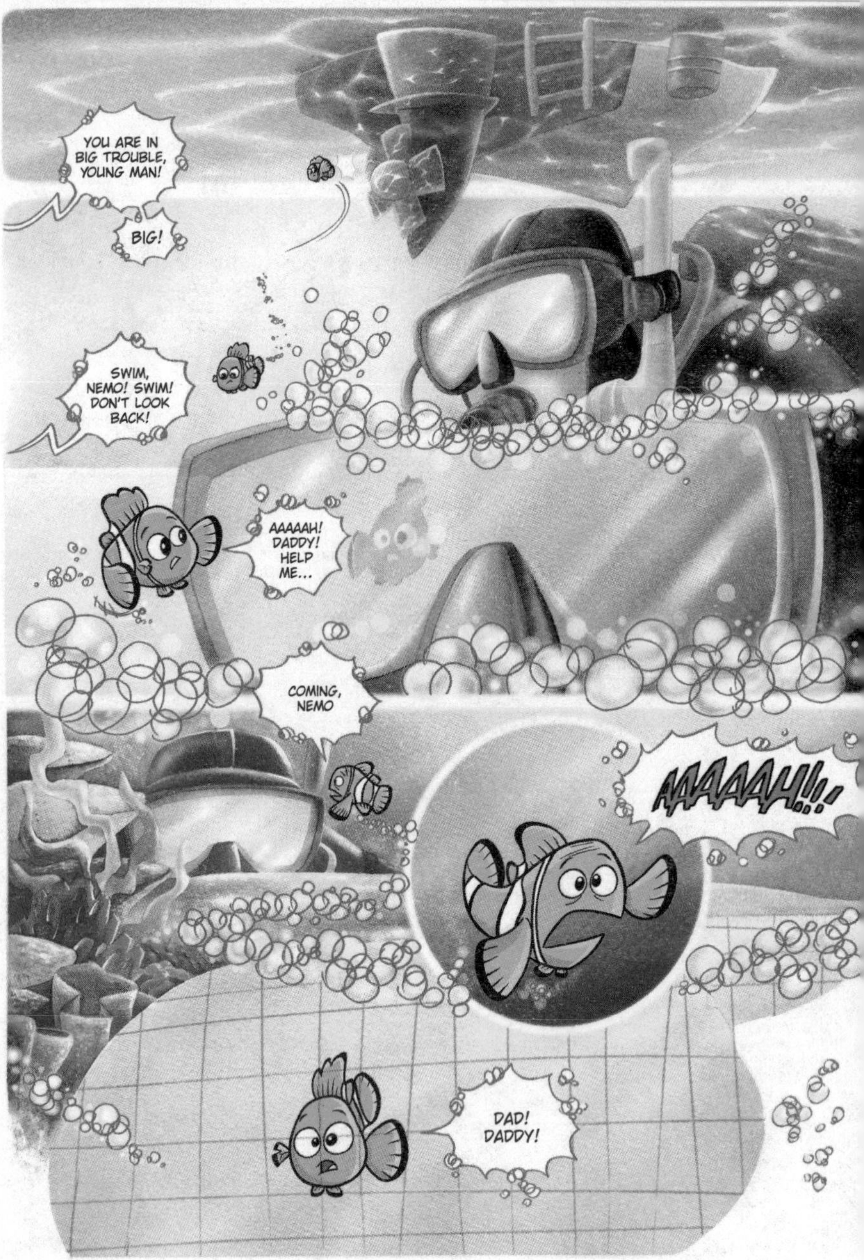
YOU ARE IN BIG TROUBLE, YOUNG MAN!
BIG!
SWIM, NEMO! SWIM! DON'T LOOK BACK!
AAAAAH! DADDY! HELP ME...
COMING, NEMO
AAAAAH!!!
DAD! DADDY!

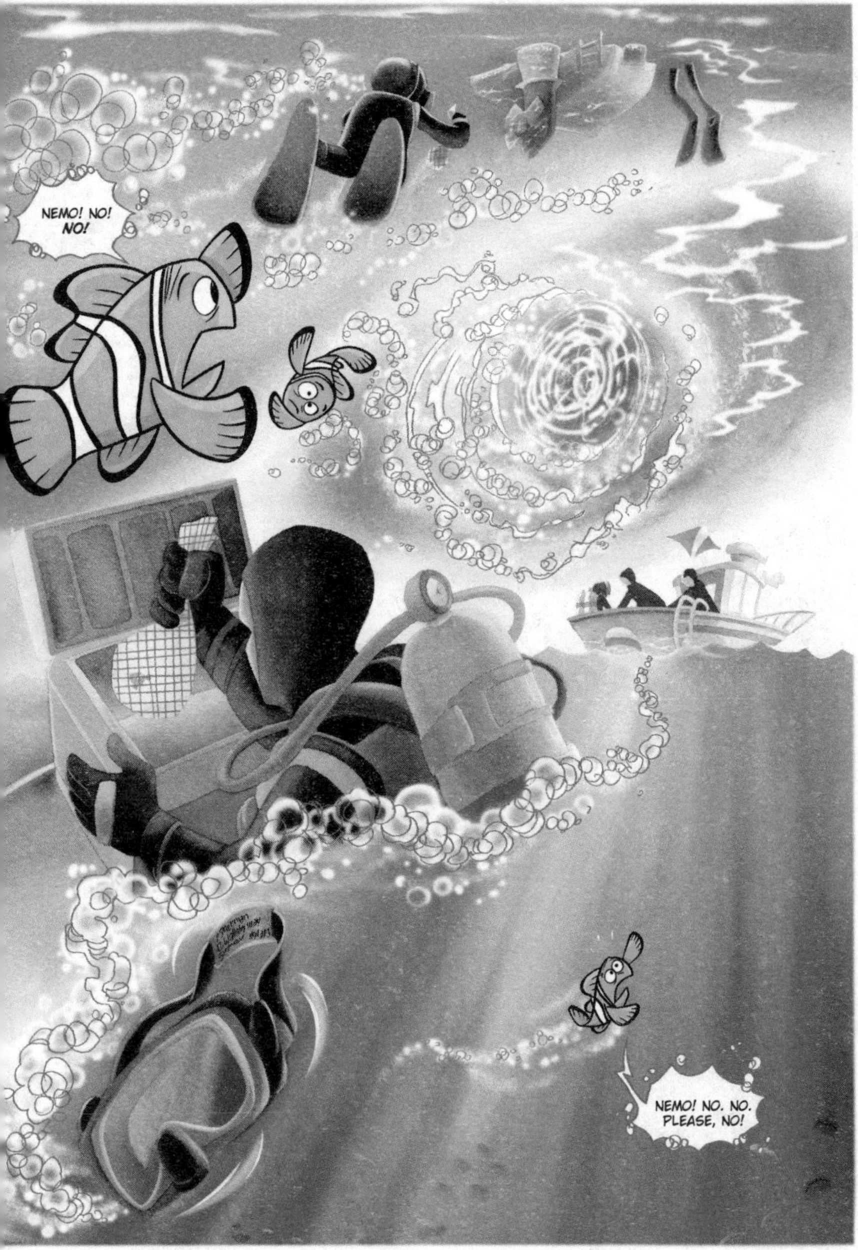
NEMO! NO! NO!
NEMO! NO. NO. PLEASE, NO!

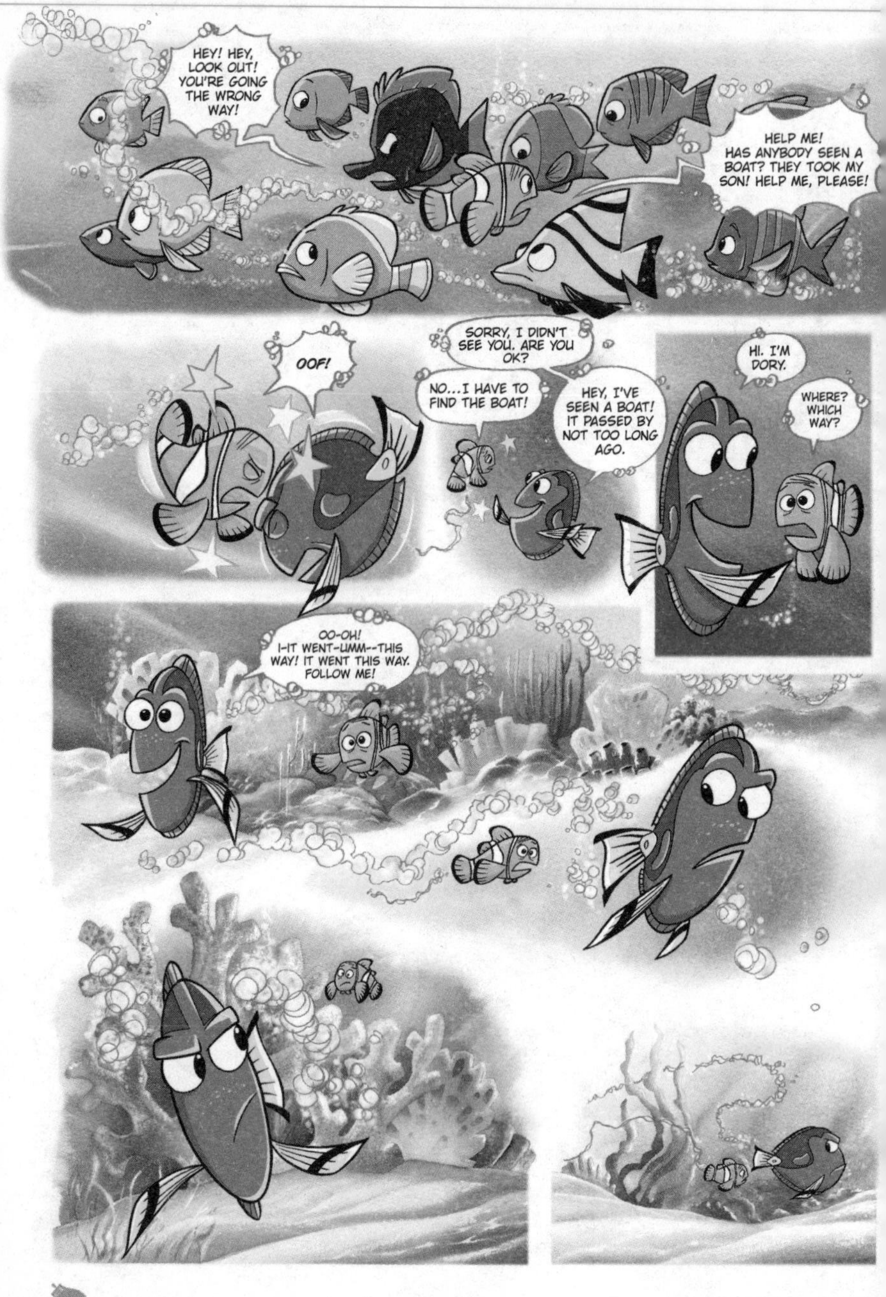
HEY! HEY, LOOK OUT! YOU'RE GOING THE WRONG WAY!
HELP ME! HAS ANYBODY SEEN A BOAT? THEY TOOK MY SON! HELP ME, PLEASE!
OOF!
SORRY, I DIDN'T SEE YOU. ARE YOU OK?
NO...I HAVE TO FIND THE BOAT!
HEY, I'VE SEEN A BOAT! IT PASSED BY NOT TOO LONG AGO.
HI. I'M DORY.
WHERE? WHICH WAY?
OO-OH! I-IT WENT-UMM--THIS WAY! IT WENT THIS WAY. FOLLOW ME!

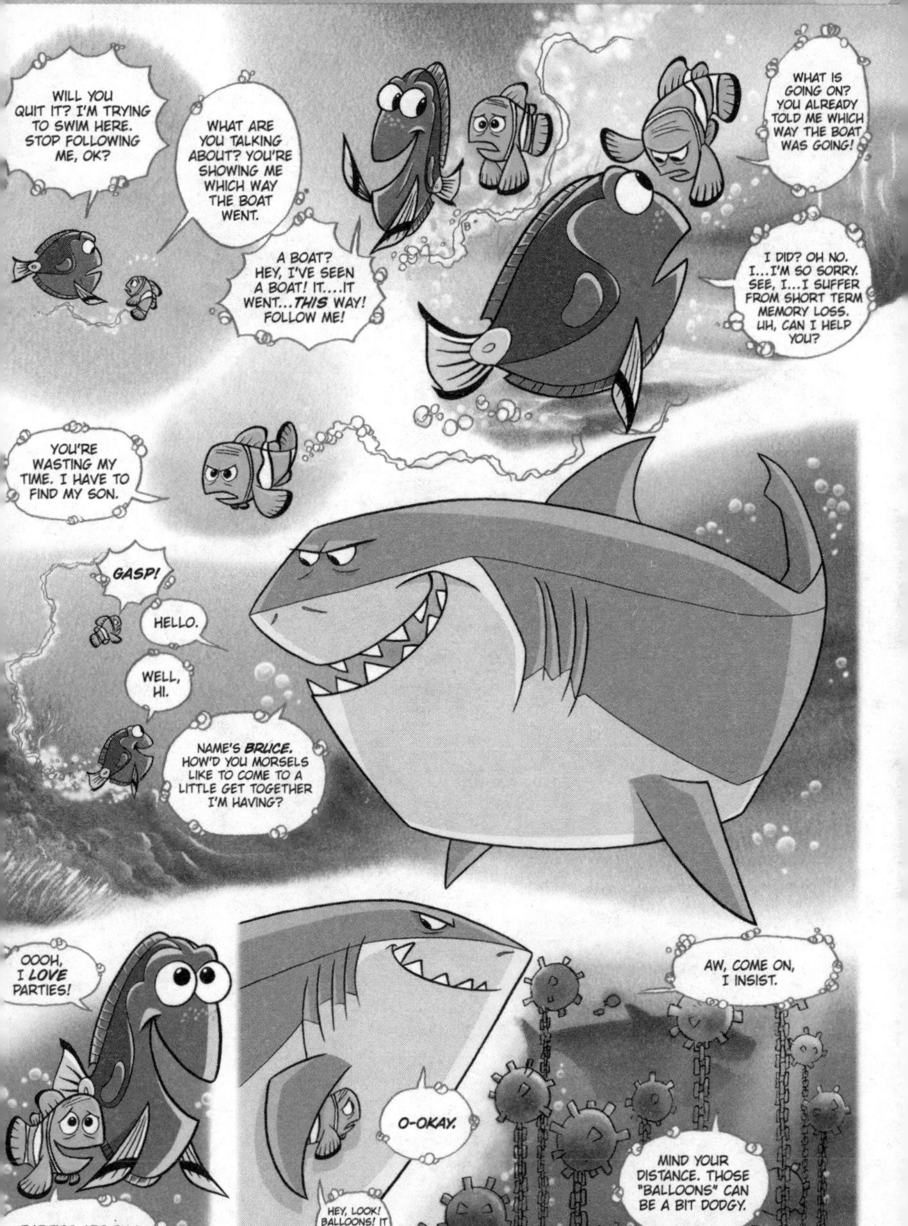
WILL YOU QUIT IT? I'M TRYING TO SWIM HERE. STOP FOLLOWING ME, OK?
WHAT ARE YOU TALKING ABOUT? YOU'RE SHOWING ME WHICH WAY THE BOAT WENT.
A BOAT? HEY, I'VE SEEN A BOAT! IT....IT WENT...THIS WAY! FOLLOW ME!
WHAT IS GOING ON? YOU ALREADY TOLD ME WHICH WAY THE BOAT WAS GOING!
I DID? OH NO. I...I'M SO SORRY. SEE, I...I SUFFER FROM SHORT TERM MEMORY LOSS. UH, CAN I HELP YOU?
YOU'RE WASTING MY TIME. I HAVE TO FIND MY SON.
GASP!
HELLO.
WELL, HI.
NAME'S BRUCE. HOW'D YOU MORSELS LIKE TO COME TO A LITTLE GET TOGETHER I'M HAVING?
OOOH, I LOVE PARTIES!
PARTIES ARE FUN, AND IT'S TEMPTING, BUT WE CAN'T...
O-OKAY.
HEY, LOOK! BALLOONS! IT IS A PARTY!
AW, COME ON, I INSIST.
MIND YOUR DISTANCE. THOSE "BALLOONS" CAN BE A BIT DODGY.

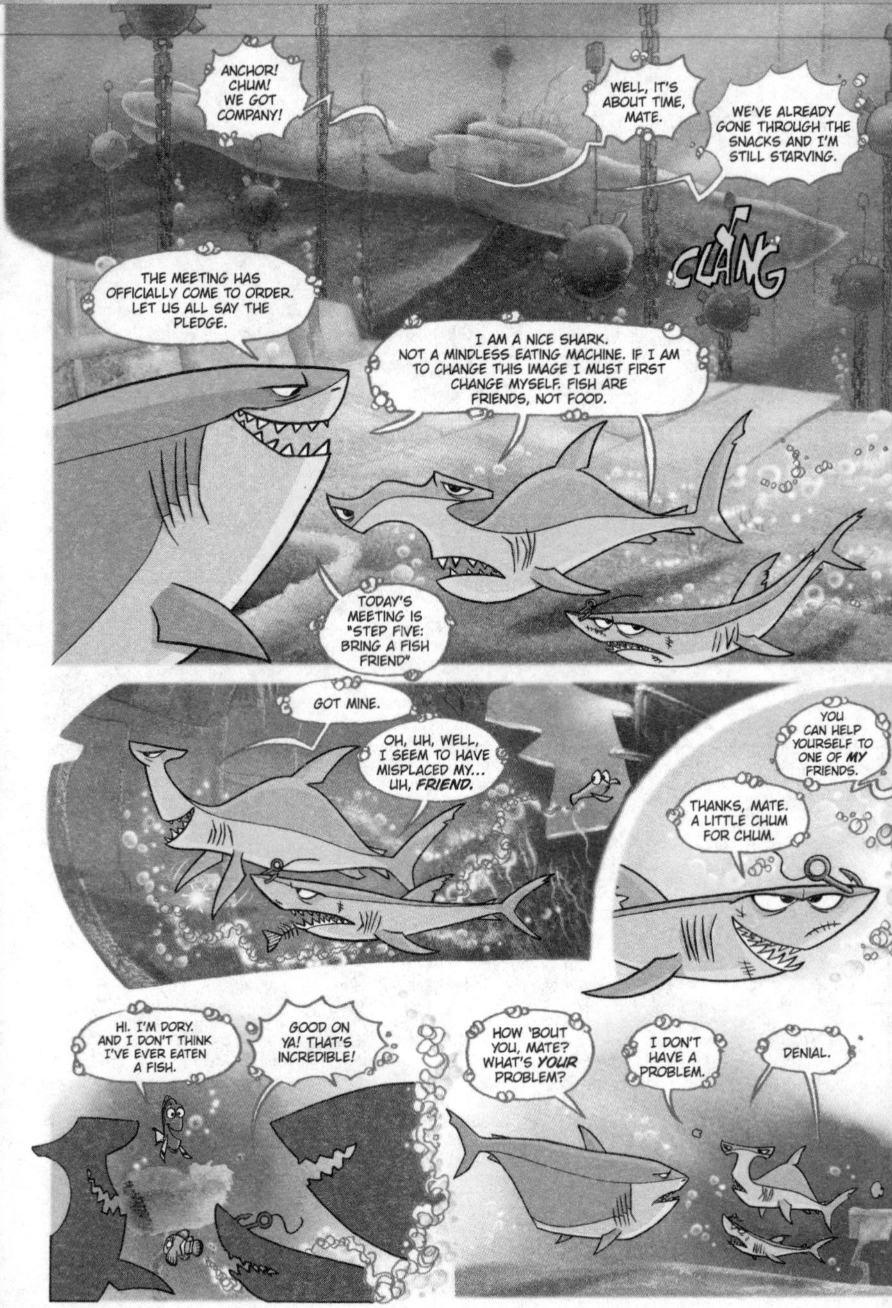
ANCHOR! CHUM! WE GOT COMPANY!
WELL, IT'S ABOUT TIME, MATE.
WE'VE ALREADY GONE THROUGH THE SNACKS AND I'M STILL STARVING.
CLANG
THE MEETING HAS OFFICIALLY COME TO ORDER. LET US ALL SAY THE PLEDGE.
I AM A NICE SHARK. NOT A MINDLESS EATING MACHINE. IF I AM TO CHANGE THIS IMAGE I MUST FIRST CHANGE MYSELF. FISH ARE FRIENDS, NOT FOOD.
TODAY'S MEETING IS "STEP FIVE: BRING A FISH FRIEND"
GOT MINE.
OH, UH, WELL, I SEEM TO HAVE MISPLACED MY... UH, FRIEND.
YOU CAN HELP YOURSELF TO ONE OF MY FRIENDS.
THANKS, MATE. A LITTLE CHUM FOR CHUM.
HI. I'M DORY. AND I DON'T THINK I'VE EVER EATEN A FISH.
GOOD ON YA! THAT'S INCREDIBLE!
HOW 'BOUT YOU, MATE? WHAT'S YOUR PROBLEM?
I DON'T HAVE A PROBLEM.
DENIAL.

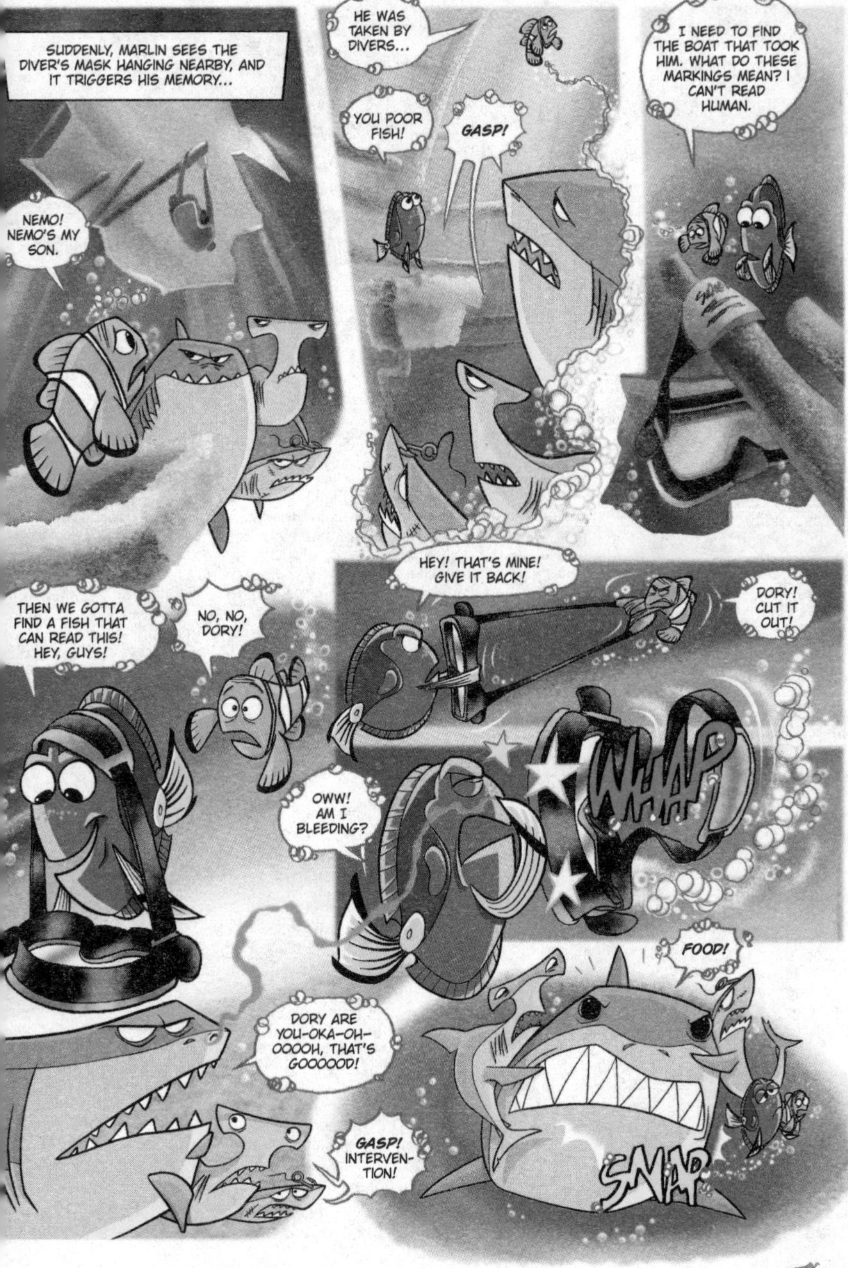
SUDDENLY, MARLIN SEES THE DIVER'S MASK HANGING NEARBY, AND IT TRIGGERS HIS MEMORY...
NEMO! NEMO'S MY SON.
HE WAS TAKEN BY DIVERS...
YOU POOR FISH!
GASP!
I NEED TO FIND THE BOAT THAT TOOK HIM. WHAT DO THESE MARKINGS MEAN? I CAN'T READ HUMAN.
THEN WE GOTTA FIND A FISH THAT CAN READ THIS! HEY, GUYS!
NO, NO, DORY!
HEY! THAT'S MINE! GIVE IT BACK!
DORY! CUT IT OUT!
WHAP
OWW! AM I BLEEDING?
FOOD!
DORY ARE YOU-OKA-OH-OOOOH, THAT'S GOOOOOD!
GASP! INTERVEN-TION!
SNAP

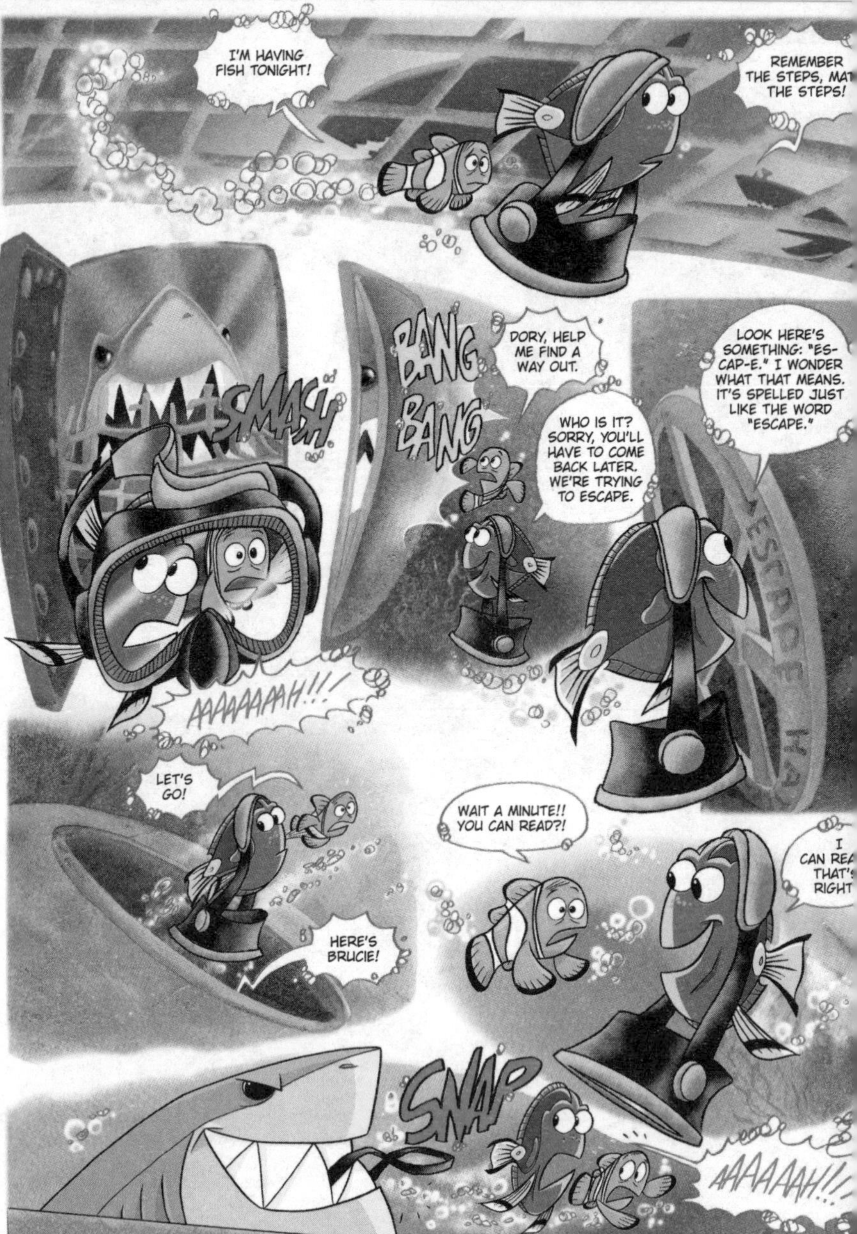
I'M HAVING FISH TONIGHT!
REMEMBER THE STEPS, MAT THE STEPS!
SMASH
AAAAAAAAH!!!
BANG BANG
DORY, HELP ME FIND A WAY OUT.
WHO IS IT? SORRY, YOU'LL HAVE TO COME BACK LATER. WE'RE TRYING TO ESCAPE.
LOOK HERE'S SOMETHING: "ES-CAP-E." I WONDER WHAT THAT MEANS. IT'S SPELLED JUST LIKE THE WORD "ESCAPE."
ESCAPE HA
LET'S GO!
HERE'S BRUCIE!
WAIT A MINUTE!! YOU CAN READ?!
I CAN REA THAT'S RIGHT
SNAP
AAAAAAH!!!

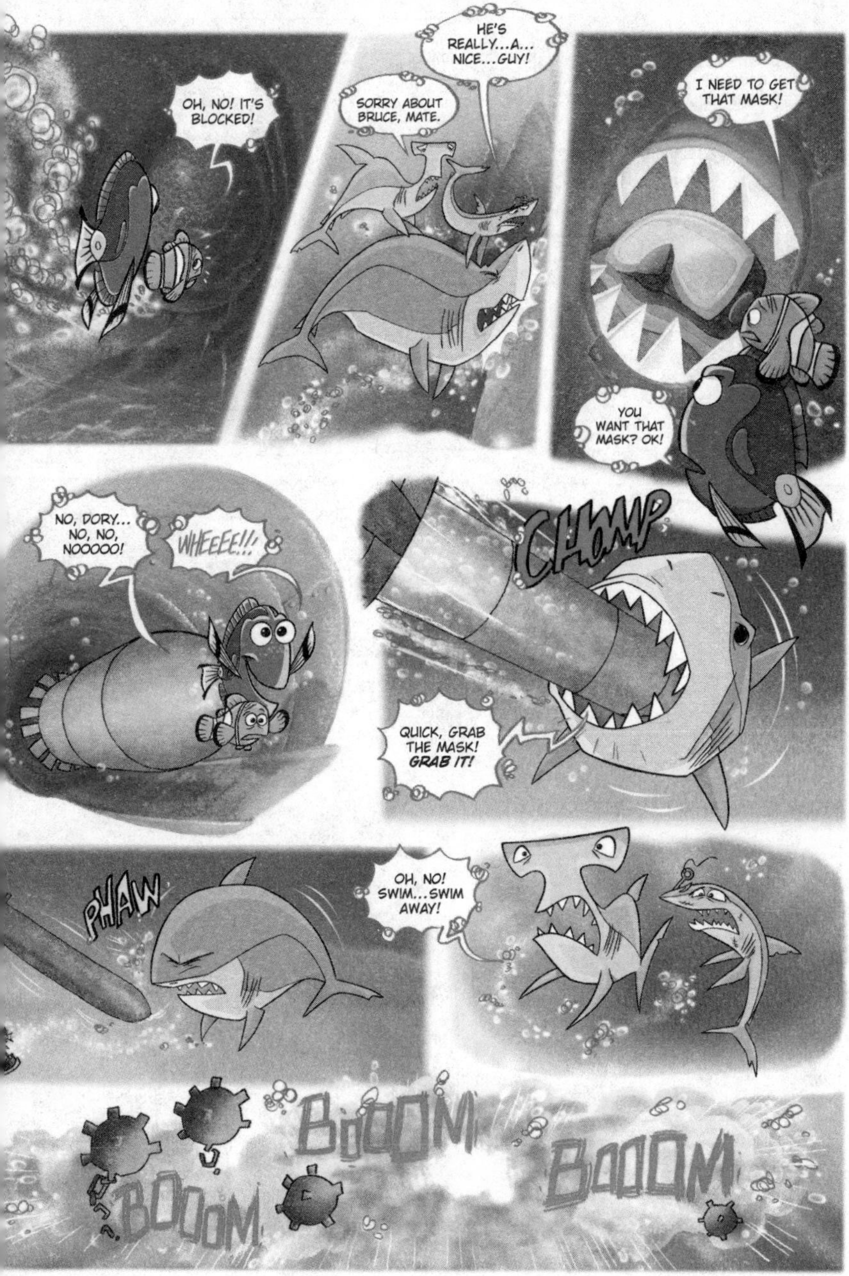
OH, NO! IT'S BLOCKED!
SORRY ABOUT BRUCE, MATE.
HE'S REALLY...A... NICE...GUY!
I NEED TO GET THAT MASK!
YOU WANT THAT MASK? OK!
NO, DORY... NO, NO, NOOOOO!
WHEEEE!!!
CHOMP
QUICK, GRAB THE MASK! **GRAB IT!**
PHAW
OH, NO! SWIM...SWIM AWAY!
BOOOM
BOOOM
BOOOM

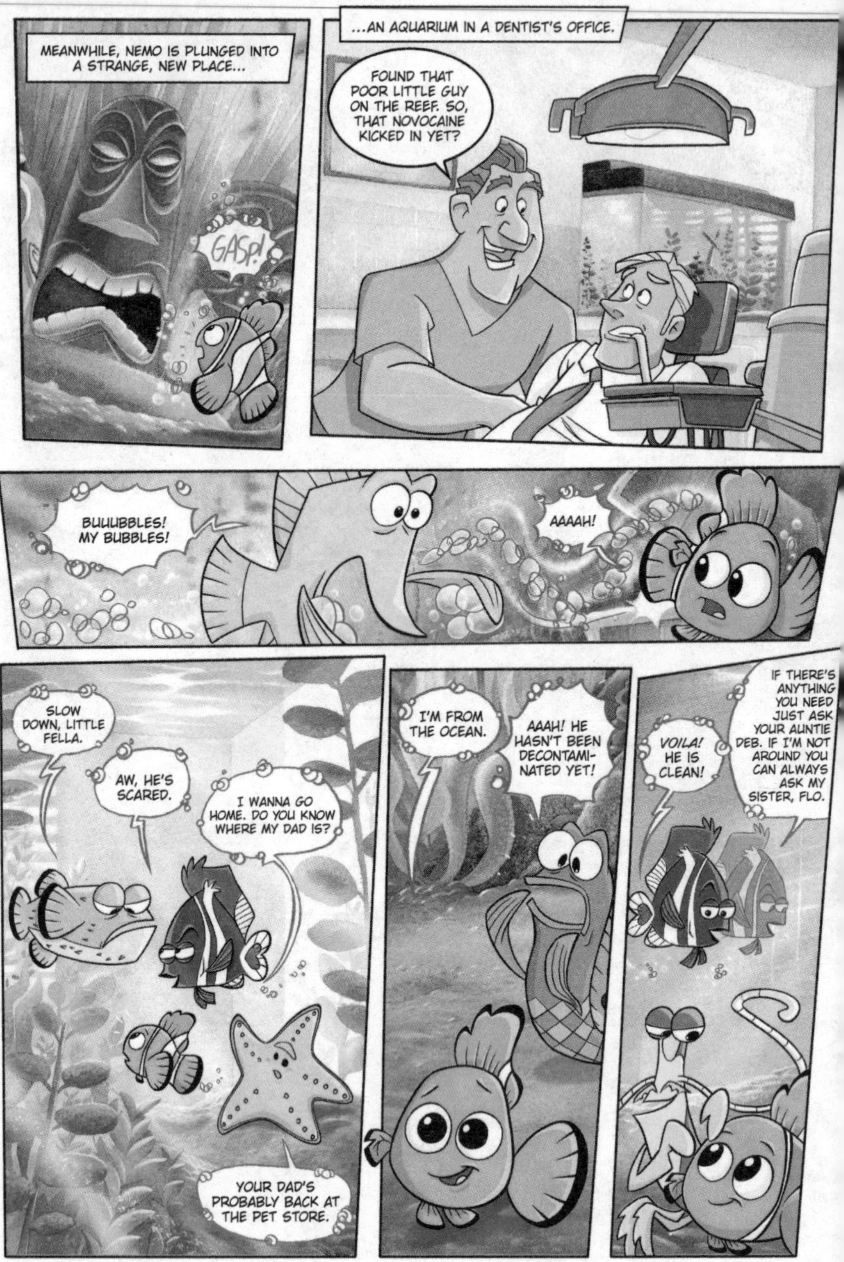
MEANWHILE, NEMO IS PLUNGED INTO A STRANGE, NEW PLACE...
GASP!
...AN AQUARIUM IN A DENTIST'S OFFICE.
FOUND THAT POOR LITTLE GUY ON THE REEF. SO, THAT NOVOCAINE KICKED IN YET?
BUUUBBLES! MY BUBBLES!
AAAAH!
SLOW DOWN, LITTLE FELLA.
AW, HE'S SCARED.
I WANNA GO HOME. DO YOU KNOW WHERE MY DAD IS?
YOUR DAD'S PROBABLY BACK AT THE PET STORE.
I'M FROM THE OCEAN.
AAAH! HE HASN'T BEEN DECONTAMI-NATED YET!
VOILA! HE IS CLEAN!
IF THERE'S ANYTHING YOU NEED JUST ASK YOUR AUNTIE DEB. IF I'M NOT AROUND YOU CAN ALWAYS ASK MY SISTER, FLO.

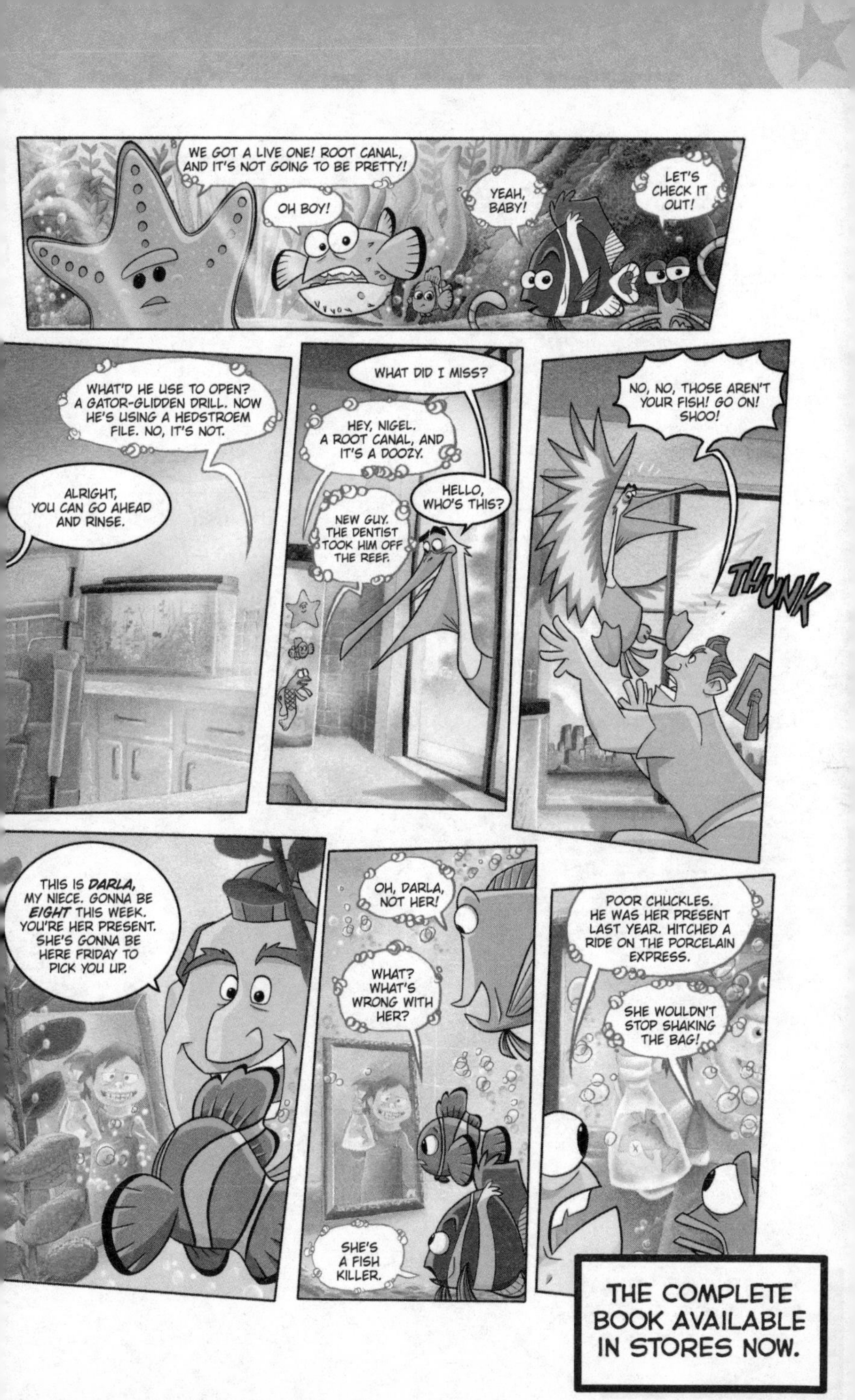
WE GOT A LIVE ONE! ROOT CANAL, AND IT'S NOT GOING TO BE PRETTY!
OH BOY!
YEAH, BABY!
LET'S CHECK IT OUT!
WHAT'D HE USE TO OPEN? A GATOR-GLIDDEN DRILL. NOW HE'S USING A HEDSTROEM FILE. NO, IT'S NOT.
ALRIGHT, YOU CAN GO AHEAD AND RINSE.
WHAT DID I MISS?
HEY, NIGEL. A ROOT CANAL, AND IT'S A DOOZY.
HELLO, WHO'S THIS?
NEW GUY. THE DENTIST TOOK HIM OFF THE REEF.
NO, NO, THOSE AREN'T YOUR FISH! GO ON! SHOO!
THUNK
THIS IS *DARLA,* MY NIECE. GONNA BE *EIGHT* THIS WEEK. YOU'RE HER PRESENT. SHE'S GONNA BE HERE FRIDAY TO PICK YOU UP.
OH, DARLA, NOT HER!
WHAT? WHAT'S WRONG WITH HER?
SHE'S A FISH KILLER.
POOR CHUCKLES. HE WAS HER PRESENT LAST YEAR. HITCHED A RIDE ON THE PORCELAIN EXPRESS.
SHE WOULDN'T STOP SHAKING THE BAG!

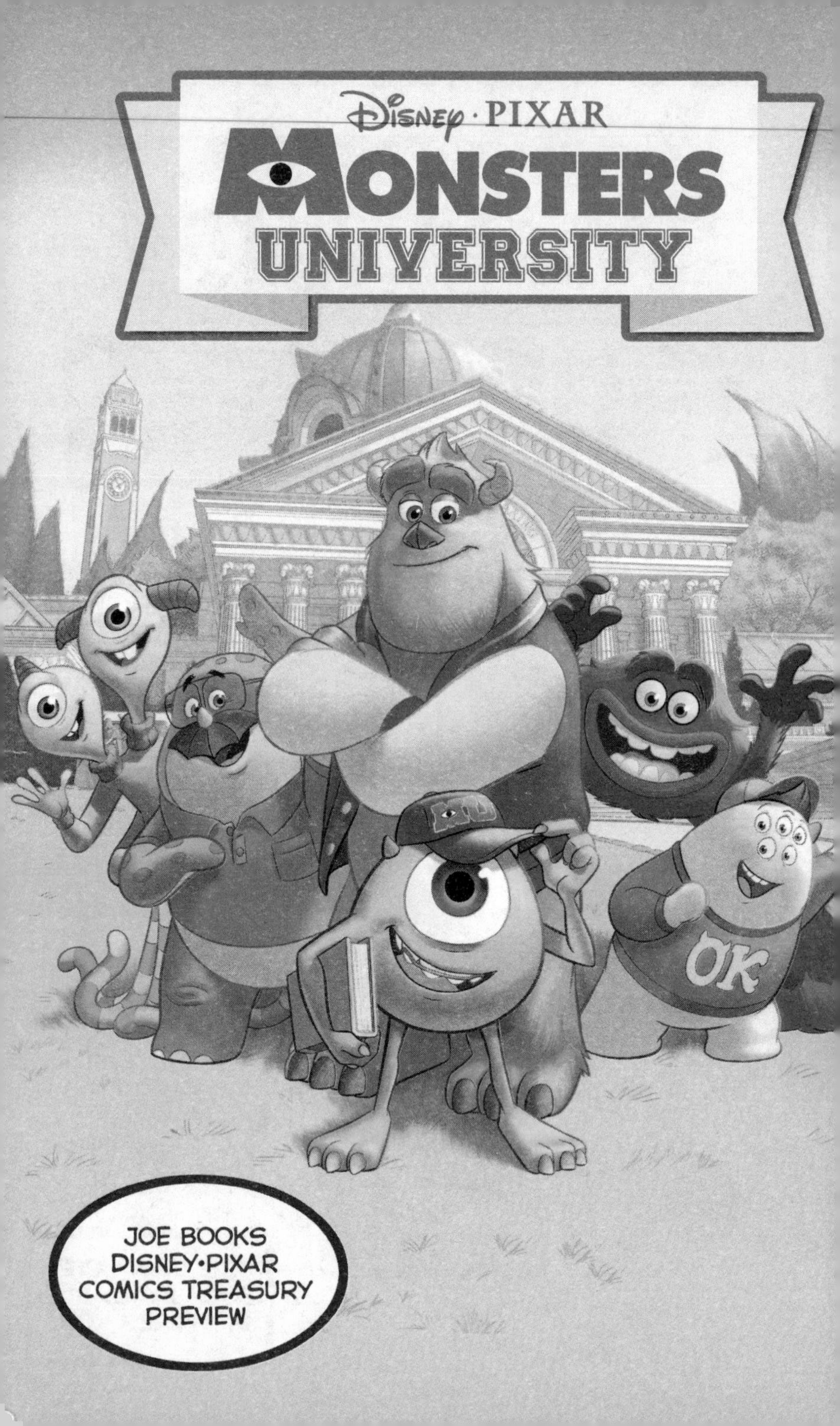
Disney·PIXAR
MONSTERS
UNIVERSITY
OK
JOE BOOKS
DISNEY•PIXAR
COMICS TREASURY
PREVIEW

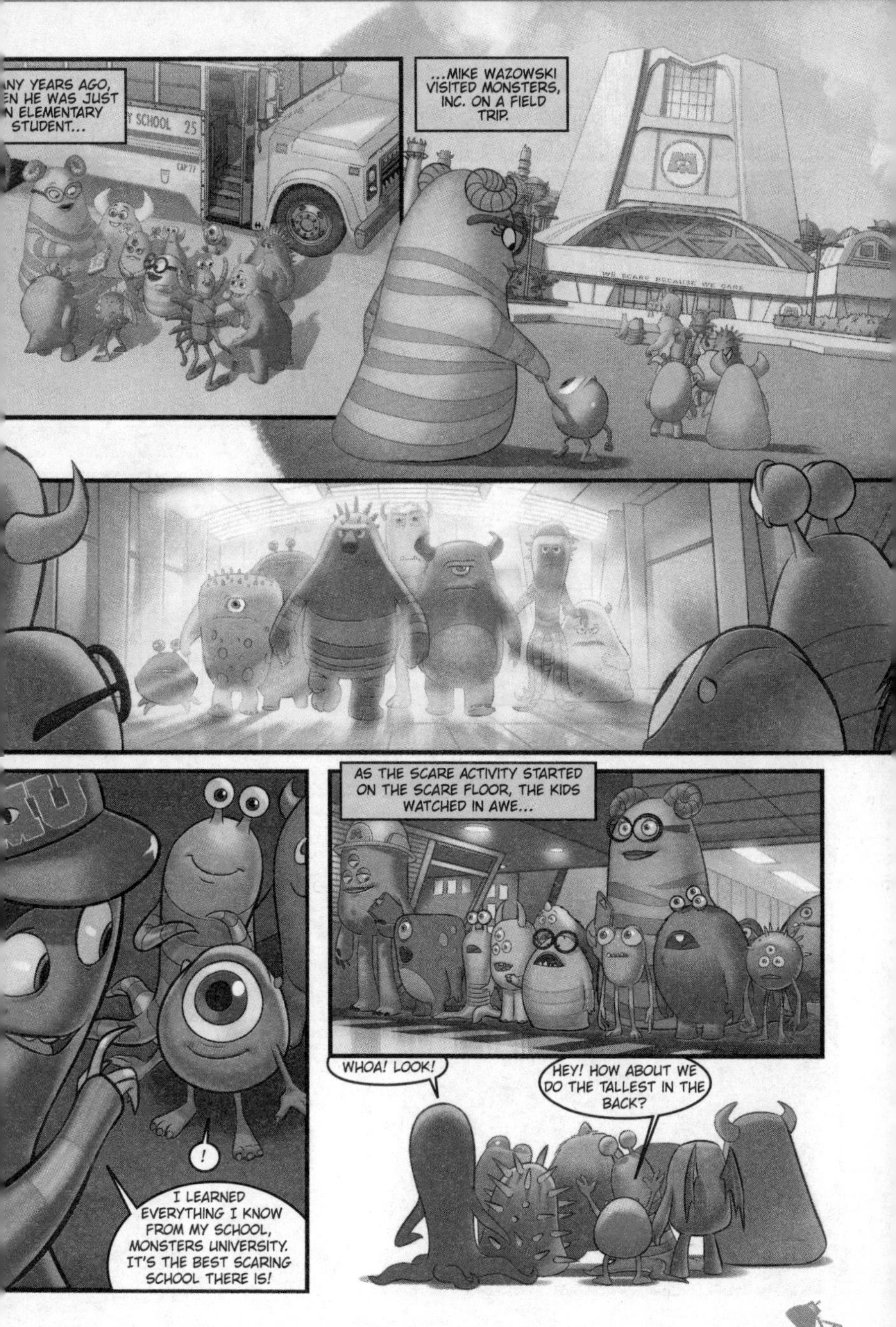
ANY YEARS AGO,
EN HE WAS JUST
N ELEMENTARY
STUDENT...
SCHOOL 25
...MIKE WAZOWSKI
VISITED MONSTERS,
INC. ON A FIELD
TRIP.
WE SCARE BECAUSE WE CARE
AS THE SCARE ACTIVITY STARTED
ON THE SCARE FLOOR, THE KIDS
WATCHED IN AWE...
WHOA! LOOK!
HEY! HOW ABOUT WE
DO THE TALLEST IN THE
BACK?
!
I LEARNED
EVERYTHING I KNOW
FROM MY SCHOOL,
MONSTERS UNIVERSITY.
IT'S THE BEST SCARING
SCHOOL THERE IS!

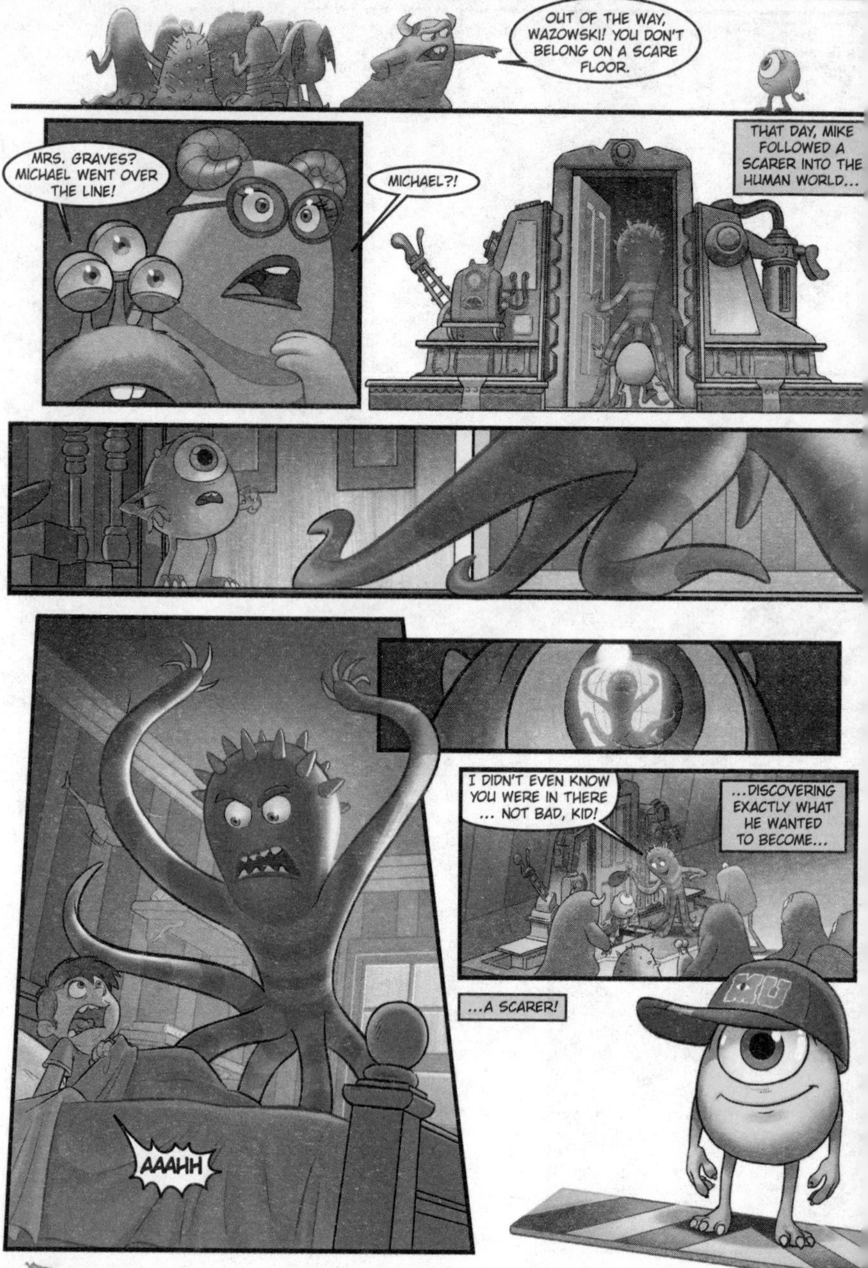
OUT OF THE WAY, WAZOWSKI! YOU DON'T BELONG ON A SCARE FLOOR.
MRS. GRAVES? MICHAEL WENT OVER THE LINE!
MICHAEL?!
THAT DAY, MIKE FOLLOWED A SCARER INTO THE HUMAN WORLD...
AAAHH
I DIDN'T EVEN KNOW YOU WERE IN THERE ... NOT BAD, KID!
...DISCOVERING EXACTLY WHAT HE WANTED TO BECOME...
...A SCARER!

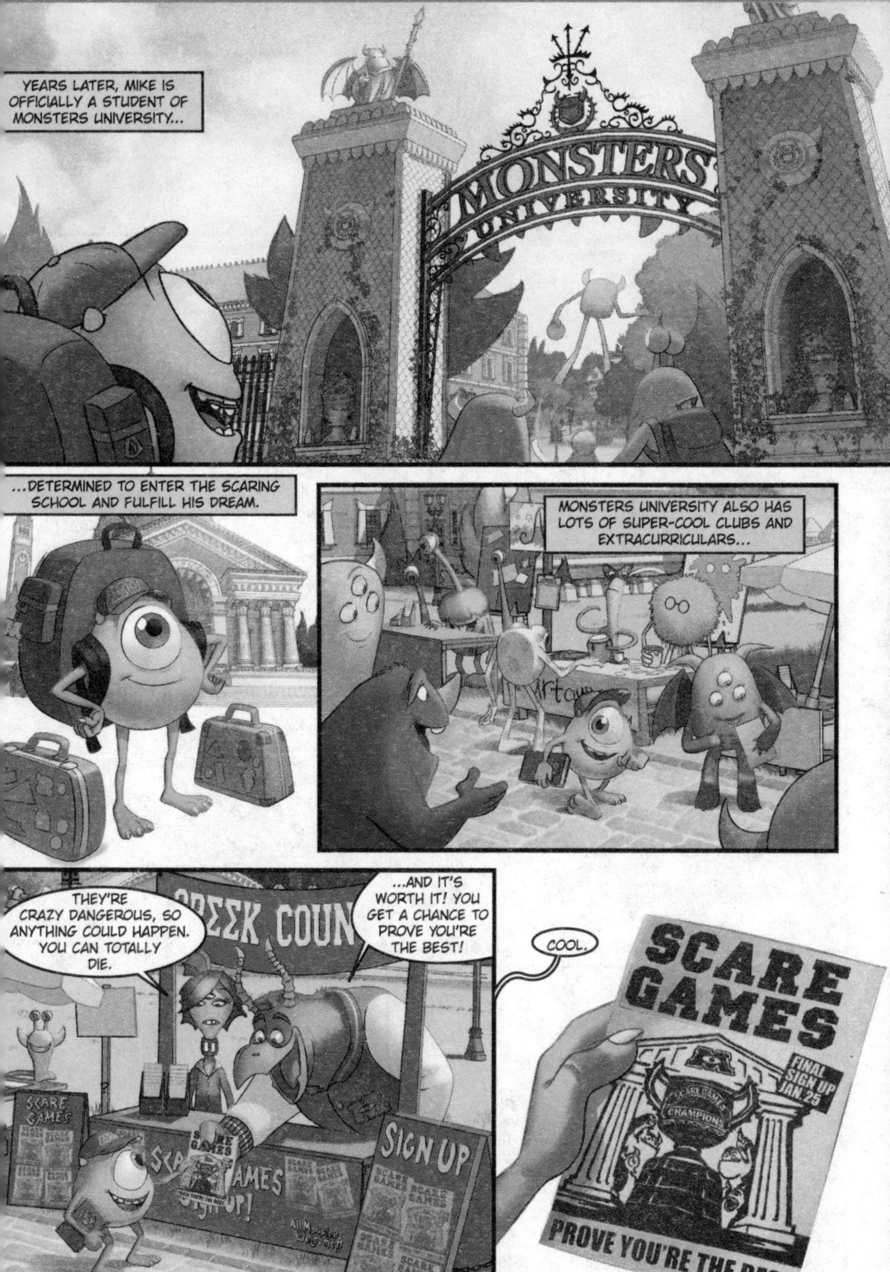
YEARS LATER, MIKE IS OFFICIALLY A STUDENT OF MONSTERS UNIVERSITY...
MONSTERS UNIVERSITY
...DETERMINED TO ENTER THE SCARING SCHOOL AND FULFILL HIS DREAM.
MONSTERS UNIVERSITY ALSO HAS LOTS OF SUPER-COOL CLUBS AND EXTRACURRICULARS...
THEY'RE CRAZY DANGEROUS, SO ANYTHING COULD HAPPEN. YOU CAN TOTALLY DIE.
...AND IT'S WORTH IT! YOU GET A CHANCE TO PROVE YOU'RE THE BEST!
COOL.
SIGN UP
SCARE GAMES
FINAL SIGN UP JAN 25
PROVE YOU'RE THE BEST

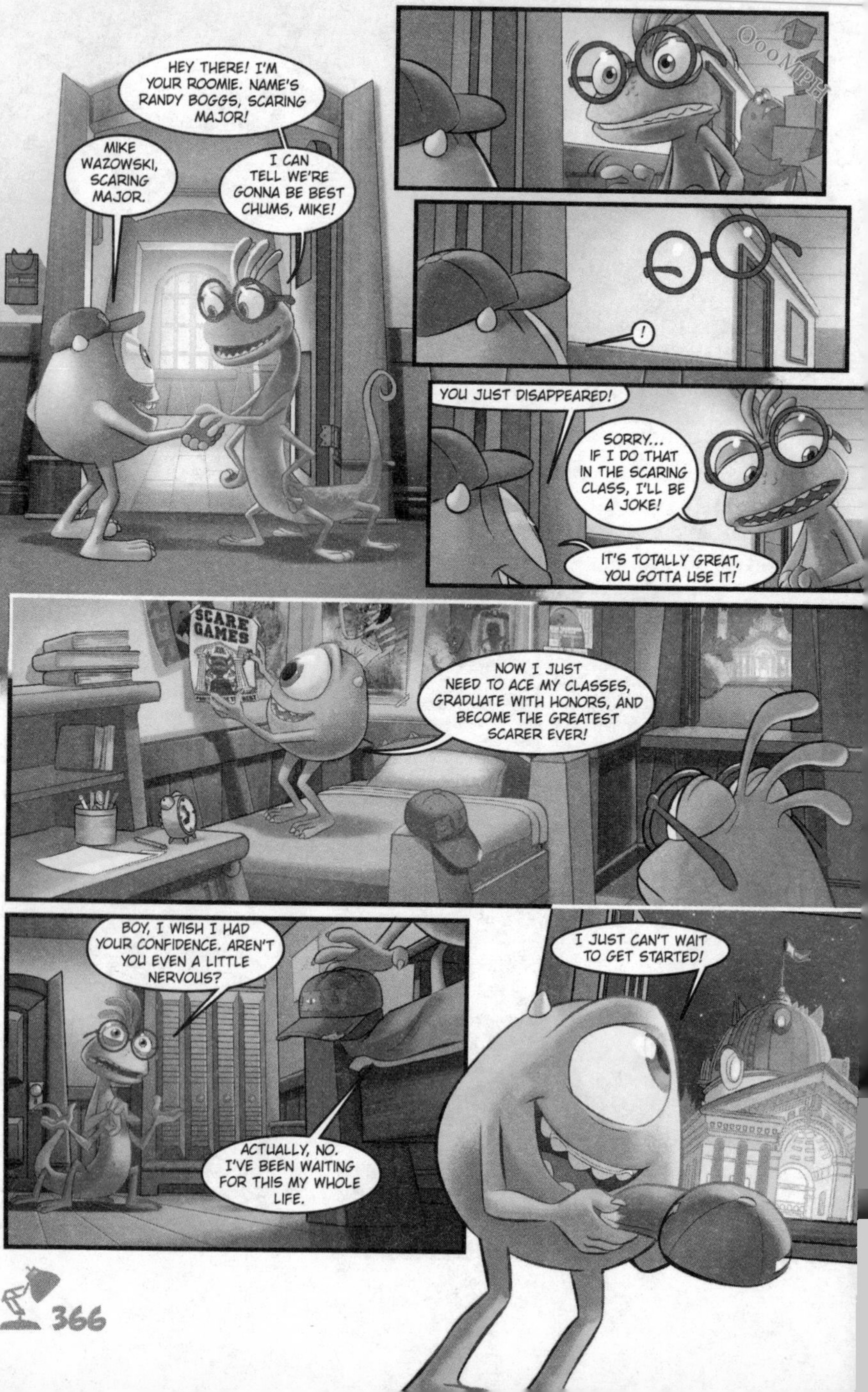
HEY THERE! I'M YOUR ROOMIE. NAME'S RANDY BOGGS, SCARING MAJOR!
MIKE WAZOWSKI, SCARING MAJOR.
I CAN TELL WE'RE GONNA BE BEST CHUMS, MIKE!
OooMPH
!
YOU JUST DISAPPEARED!
SORRY... IF I DO THAT IN THE SCARING CLASS, I'LL BE A JOKE!
IT'S TOTALLY GREAT, YOU GOTTA USE IT!
SCARE GAMES
NOW I JUST NEED TO ACE MY CLASSES, GRADUATE WITH HONORS, AND BECOME THE GREATEST SCARER EVER!
BOY, I WISH I HAD YOUR CONFIDENCE. AREN'T YOU EVEN A LITTLE NERVOUS?
ACTUALLY, NO. I'VE BEEN WAITING FOR THIS MY WHOLE LIFE.
I JUST CAN'T WAIT TO GET STARTED!

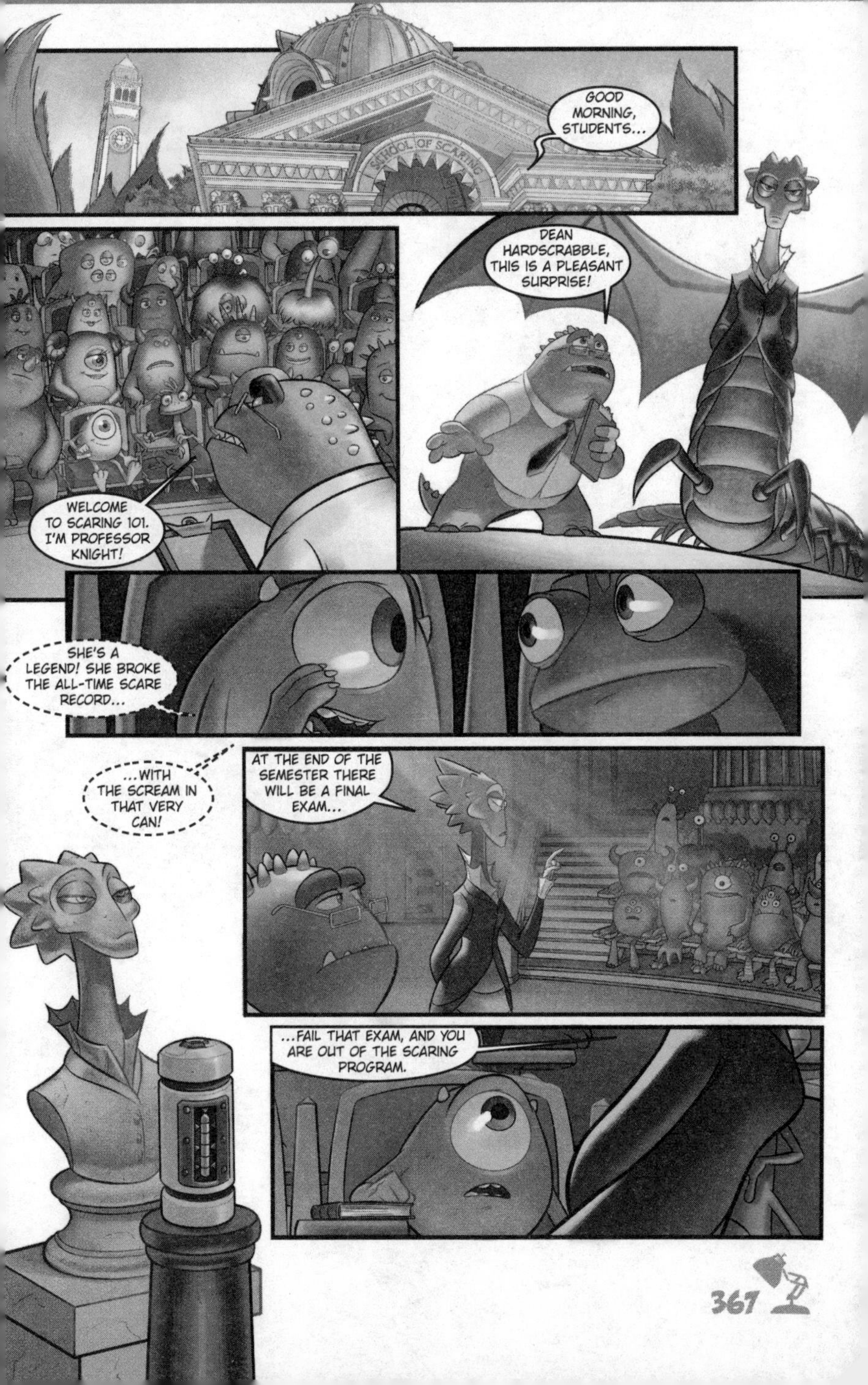
GOOD MORNING, STUDENTS...
SCHOOL OF SCARING
DEAN HARDSCRABBLE, THIS IS A PLEASANT SURPRISE!
WELCOME TO SCARING 101. I'M PROFESSOR KNIGHT!
SHE'S A LEGEND! SHE BROKE THE ALL-TIME SCARE RECORD...
...WITH THE SCREAM IN THAT VERY CAN!
AT THE END OF THE SEMESTER THERE WILL BE A FINAL EXAM...
...FAIL THAT EXAM, AND YOU ARE OUT OF THE SCARING PROGRAM.

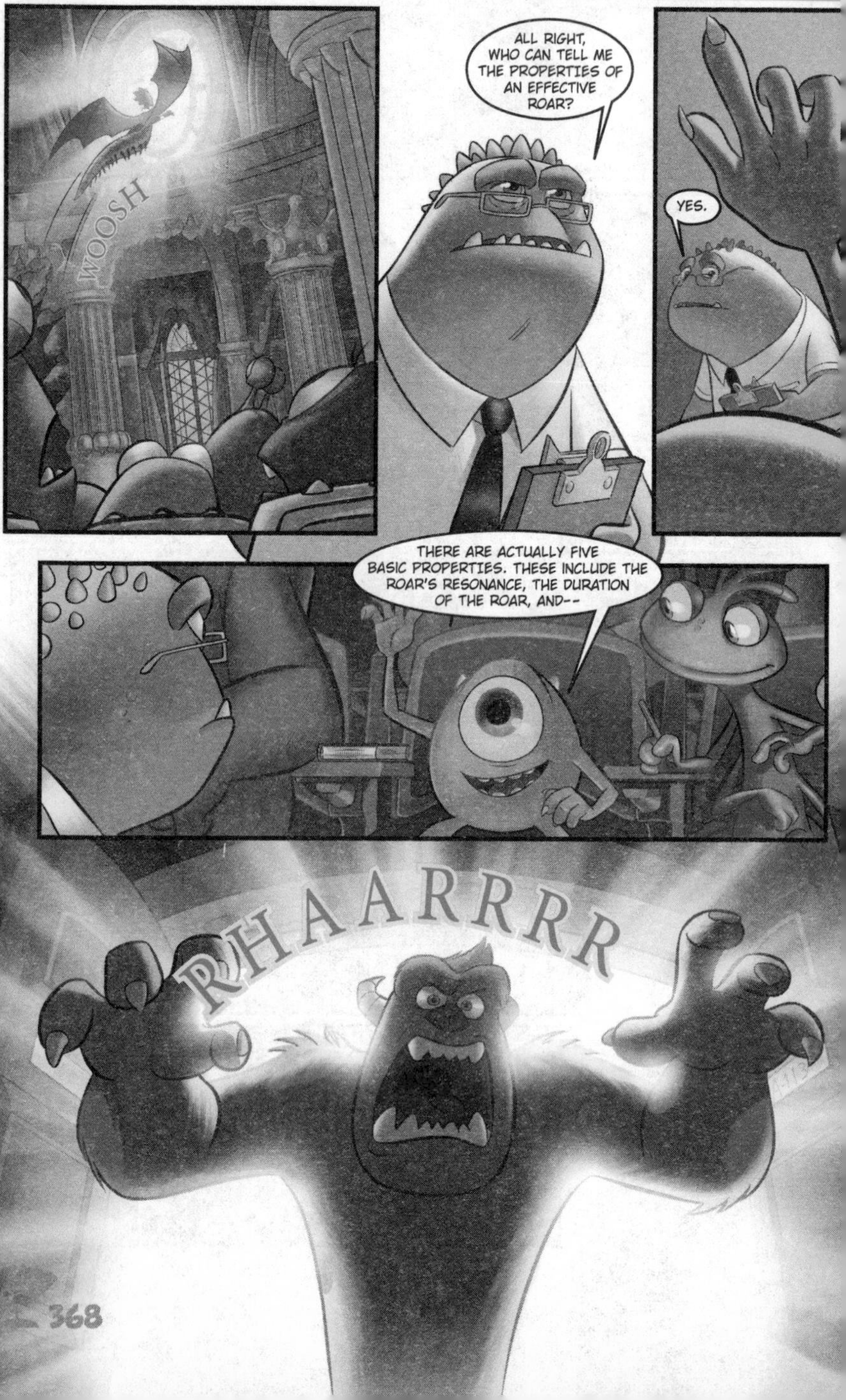
WOOSH
ALL RIGHT, WHO CAN TELL ME THE PROPERTIES OF AN EFFECTIVE ROAR?
YES.
THERE ARE ACTUALLY FIVE BASIC PROPERTIES. THESE INCLUDE THE ROAR'S RESONANCE, THE DURATION OF THE ROAR, AND--
RHAARRRR

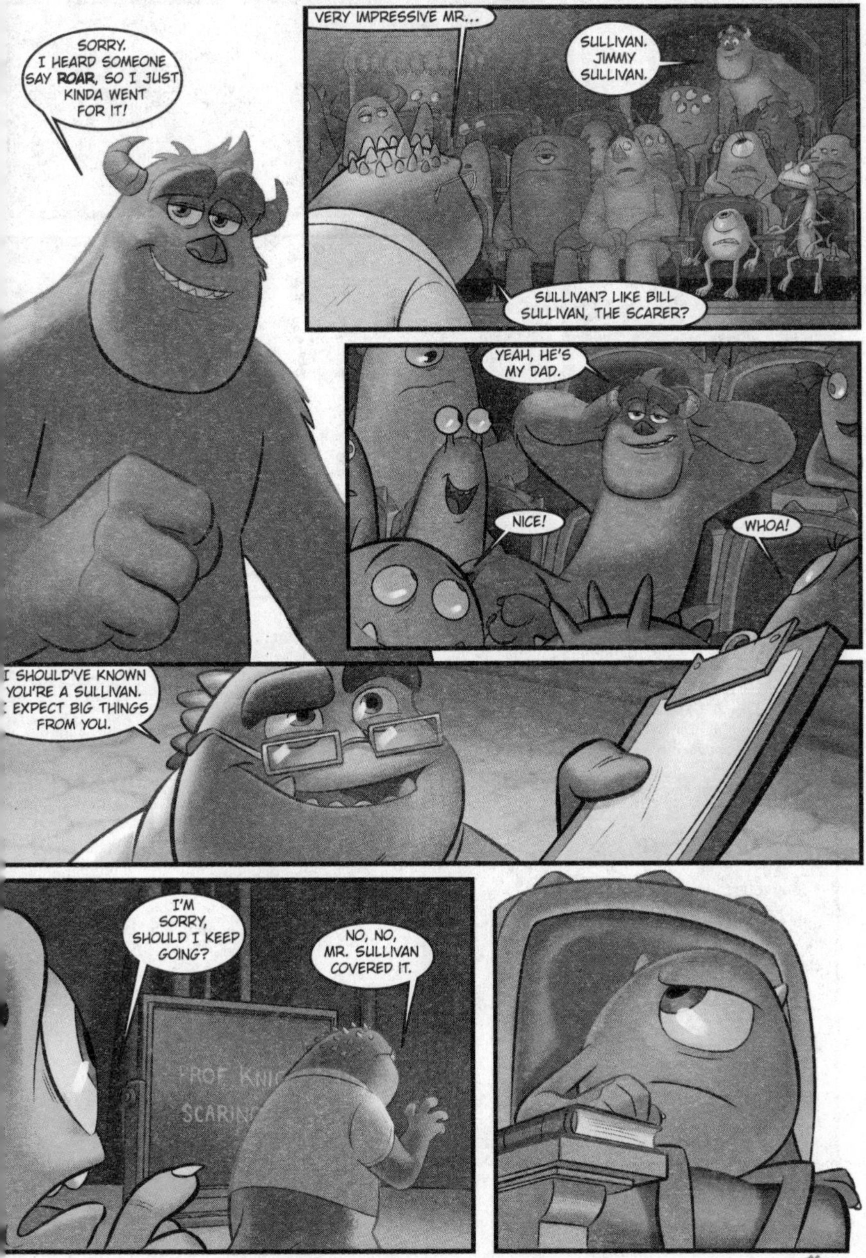
SORRY. I HEARD SOMEONE SAY ROAR, SO I JUST KINDA WENT FOR IT!
VERY IMPRESSIVE MR...
SULLIVAN. JIMMY SULLIVAN.
SULLIVAN? LIKE BILL SULLIVAN, THE SCARER?
YEAH, HE'S MY DAD.
NICE!
WHOA!
I SHOULD'VE KNOWN YOU'RE A SULLIVAN. I EXPECT BIG THINGS FROM YOU.
I'M SORRY, SHOULD I KEEP GOING?
NO, NO, MR. SULLIVAN COVERED IT.

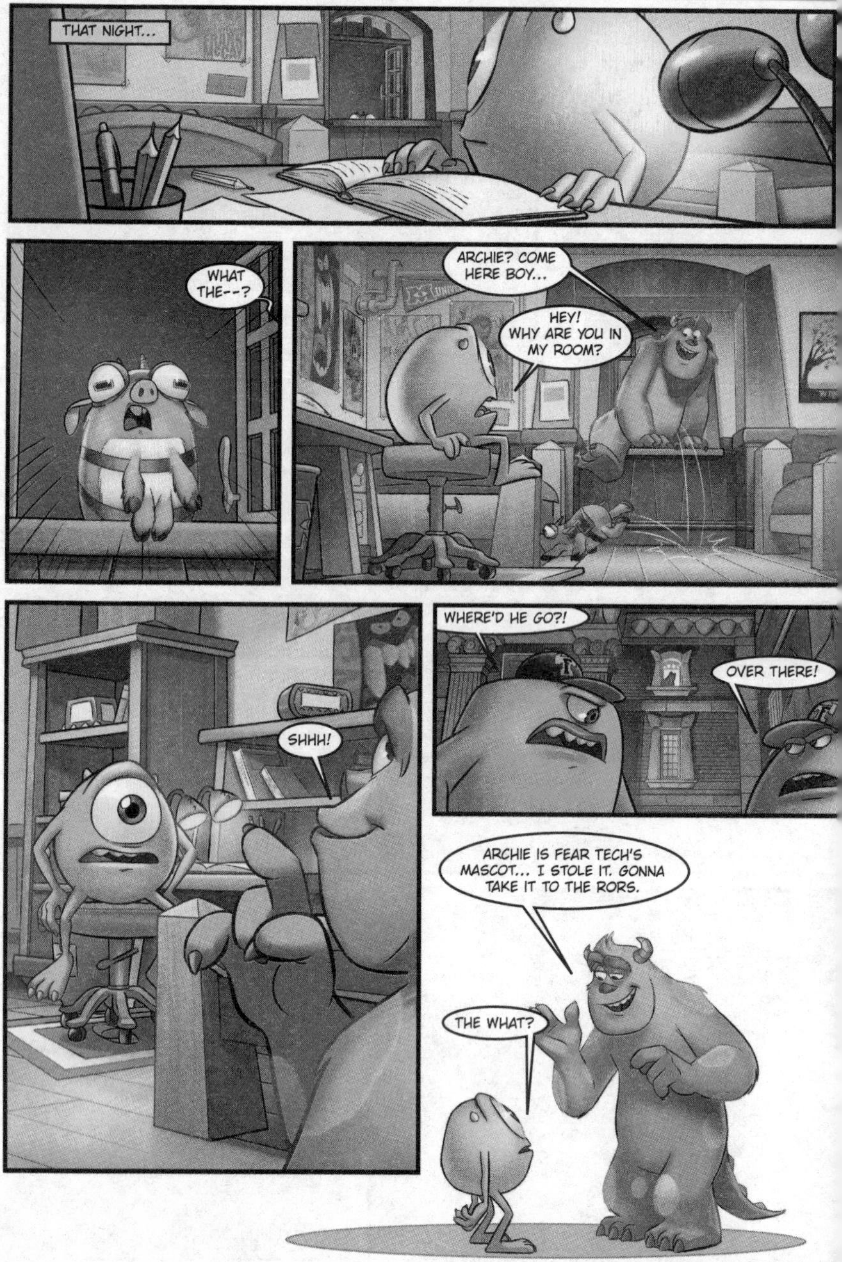
THAT NIGHT...
WHAT THE--?
ARCHIE? COME HERE BOY...
HEY! WHY ARE YOU IN MY ROOM?
SHHH!
WHERE'D HE GO?!
OVER THERE!
ARCHIE IS FEAR TECH'S MASCOT... I STOLE IT. GONNA TAKE IT TO THE RORS.
THE WHAT?

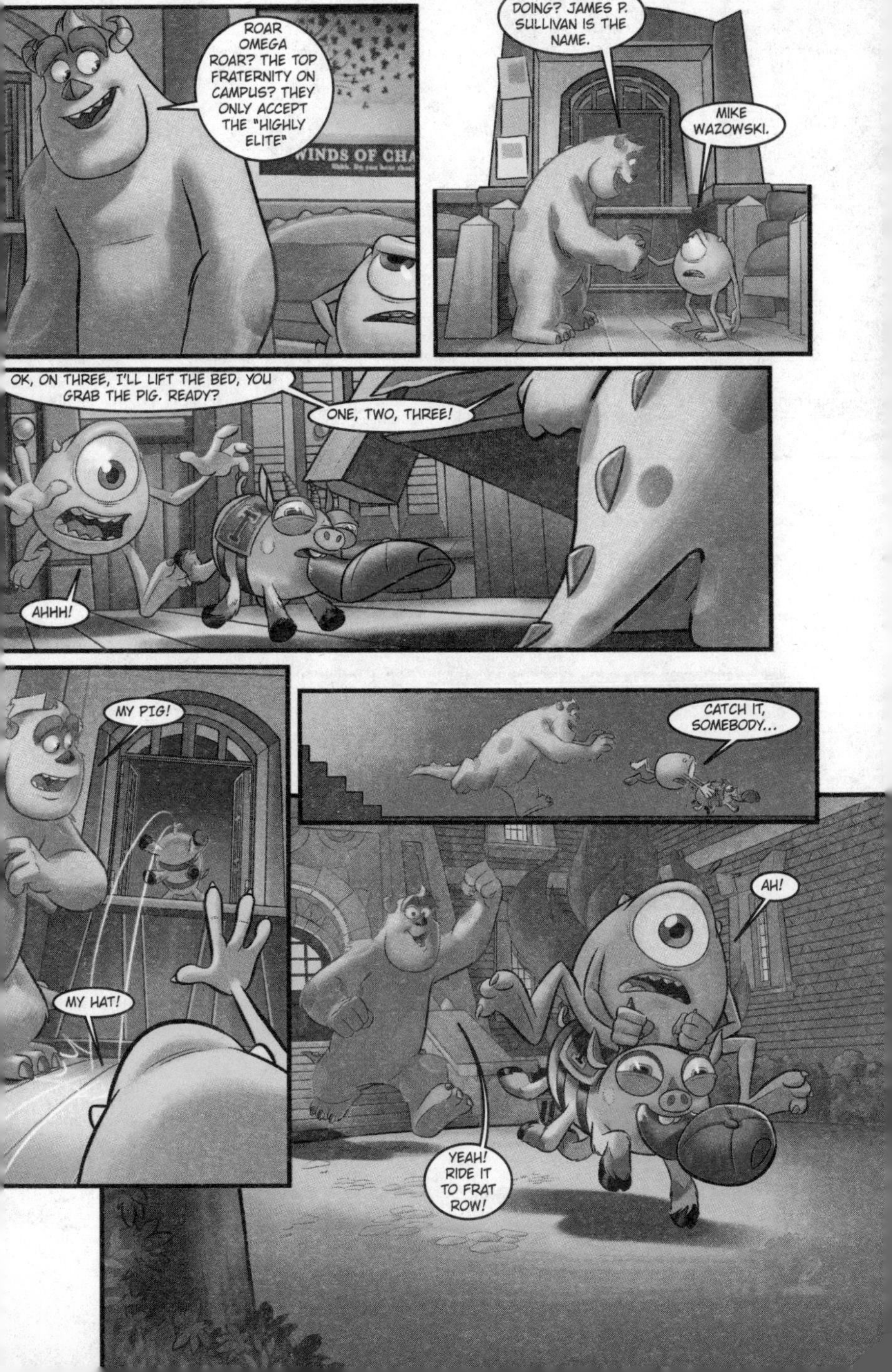
ROAR OMEGA ROAR? THE TOP FRATERNITY ON CAMPUS? THEY ONLY ACCEPT THE "HIGHLY ELITE"
WINDS OF CHA
WHAT AM I DOING? JAMES P. SULLIVAN IS THE NAME.
MIKE WAZOWSKI.
OK, ON THREE, I'LL LIFT THE BED, YOU GRAB THE PIG. READY?
ONE, TWO, THREE!
AHHH!
MY PIG!
MY HAT!
CATCH IT, SOMEBODY...
AH!
YEAH! RIDE IT TO FRAT ROW!

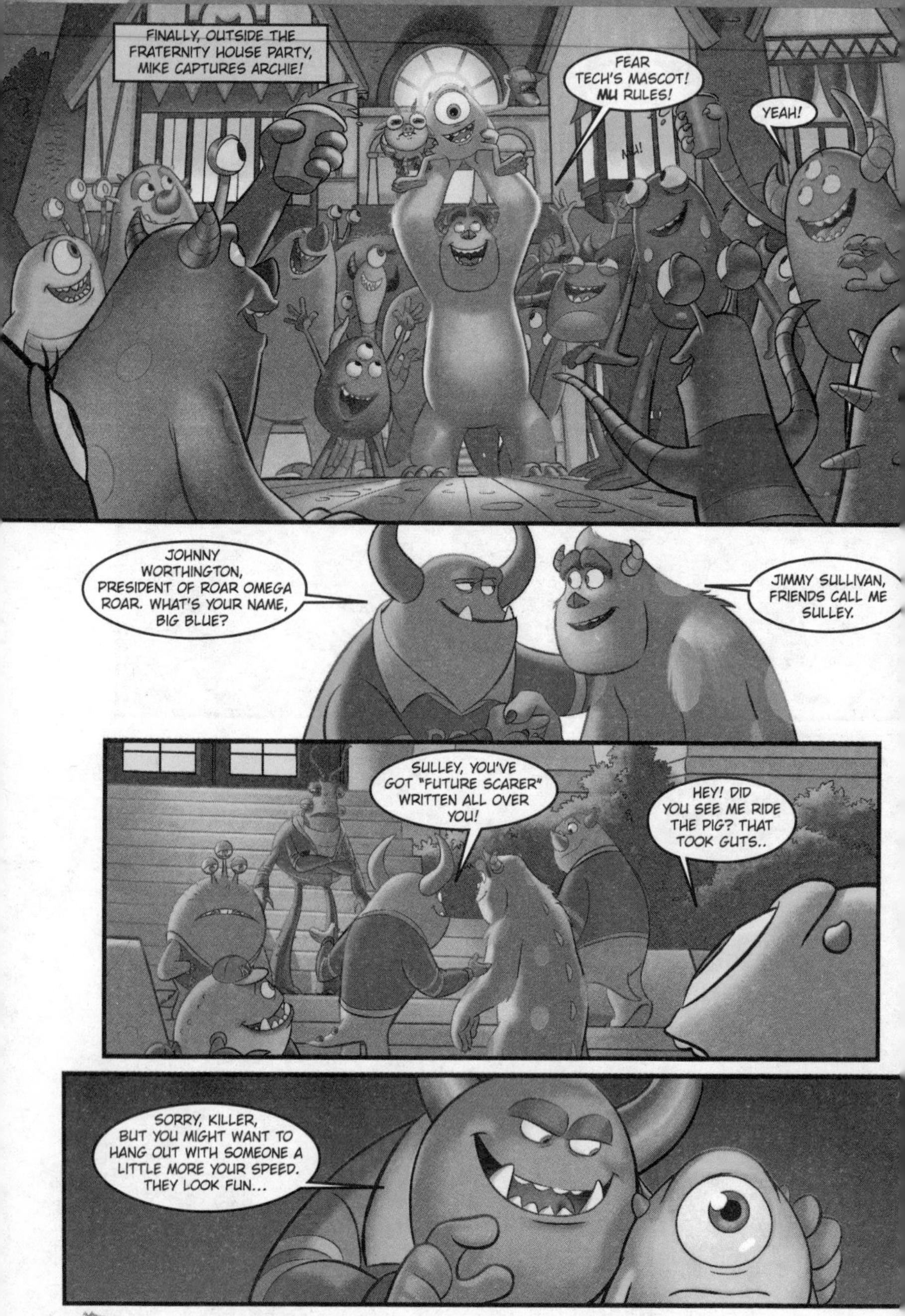
FINALLY, OUTSIDE THE FRATERNITY HOUSE PARTY, MIKE CAPTURES ARCHIE!
FEAR TECH'S MASCOT! MU RULES!
YEAH!
JOHNNY WORTHINGTON, PRESIDENT OF ROAR OMEGA ROAR. WHAT'S YOUR NAME, BIG BLUE?
JIMMY SULLIVAN, FRIENDS CALL ME SULLEY.
SULLEY, YOU'VE GOT "FUTURE SCARER" WRITTEN ALL OVER YOU!
HEY! DID YOU SEE ME RIDE THE PIG? THAT TOOK GUTS..
SORRY, KILLER, BUT YOU MIGHT WANT TO HANG OUT WITH SOMEONE A LITTLE MORE YOUR SPEED. THEY LOOK FUN...

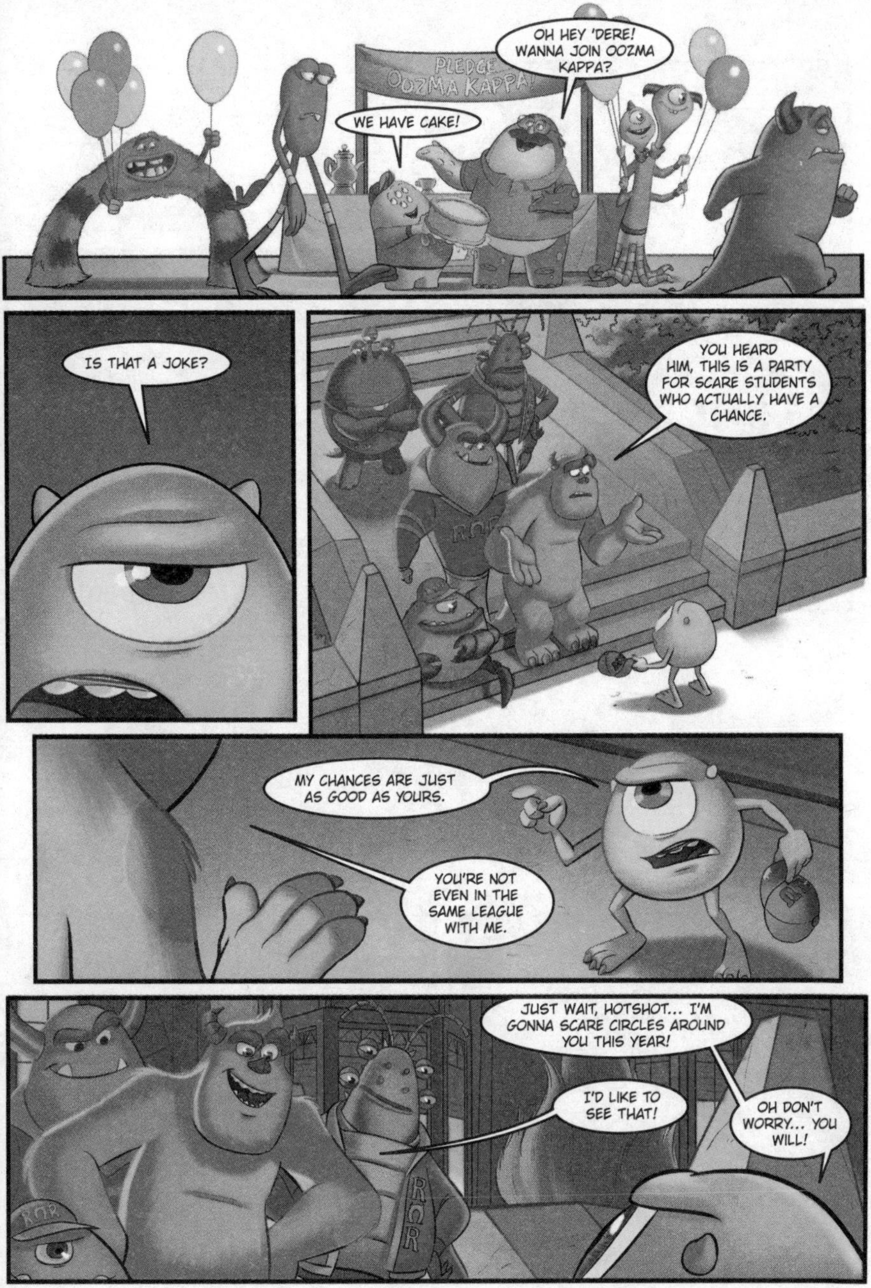
PLEDGE OOZMA KAPPA!
OH HEY 'DERE! WANNA JOIN OOZMA KAPPA?
WE HAVE CAKE!
IS THAT A JOKE?
YOU HEARD HIM, THIS IS A PARTY FOR SCARE STUDENTS WHO ACTUALLY HAVE A CHANCE.
MY CHANCES ARE JUST AS GOOD AS YOURS.
YOU'RE NOT EVEN IN THE SAME LEAGUE WITH ME.
JUST WAIT, HOTSHOT... I'M GONNA SCARE CIRCLES AROUND YOU THIS YEAR!
I'D LIKE TO SEE THAT!
OH DON'T WORRY... YOU WILL!

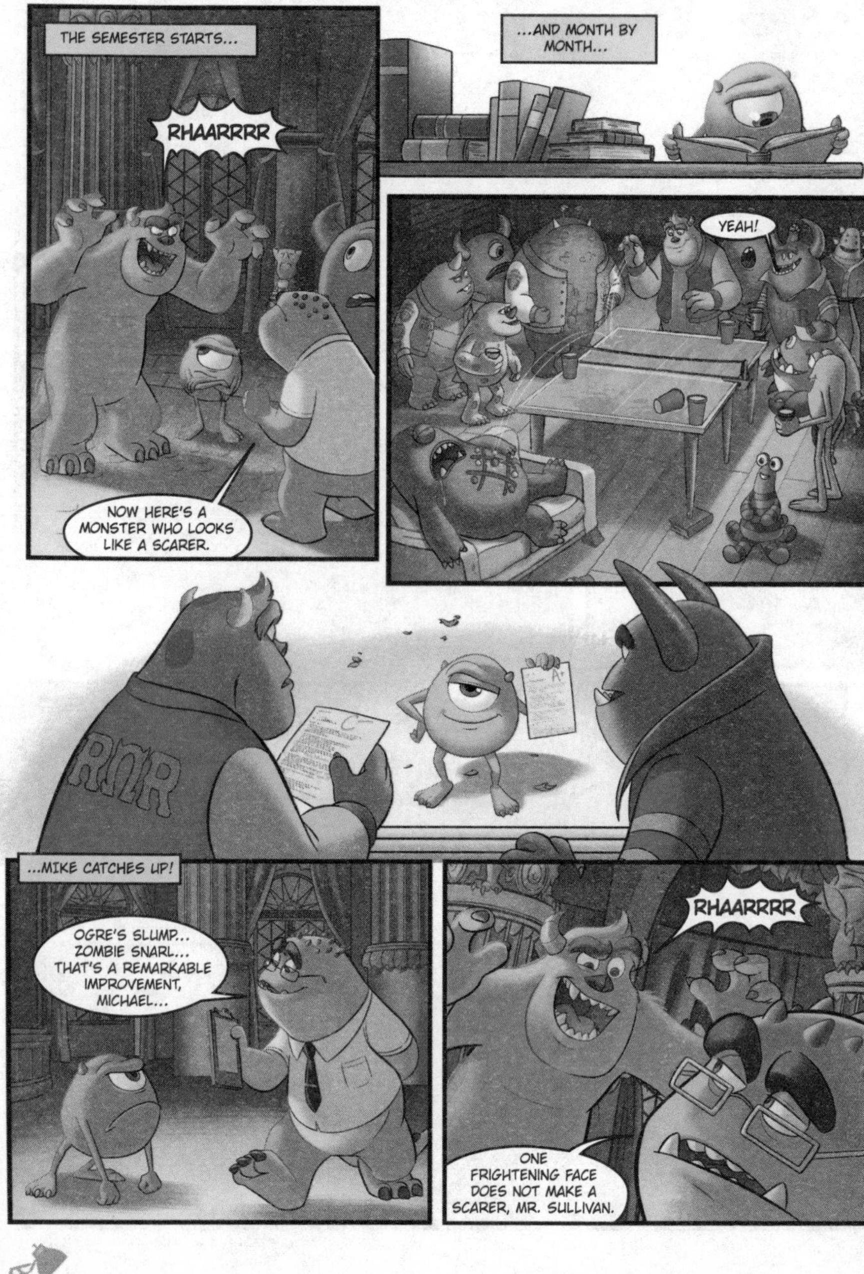

THE SEMESTER STARTS...
RHAARRRR
NOW HERE'S A MONSTER WHO LOOKS LIKE A SCARER.
...AND MONTH BY MONTH...
YEAH!
...MIKE CATCHES UP!
OGRE'S SLUMP... ZOMBIE SNARL... THAT'S A REMARKABLE IMPROVEMENT, MICHAEL...
RHAARRRR
ONE FRIGHTENING FACE DOES NOT MAKE A SCARER, MR. SULLIVAN.

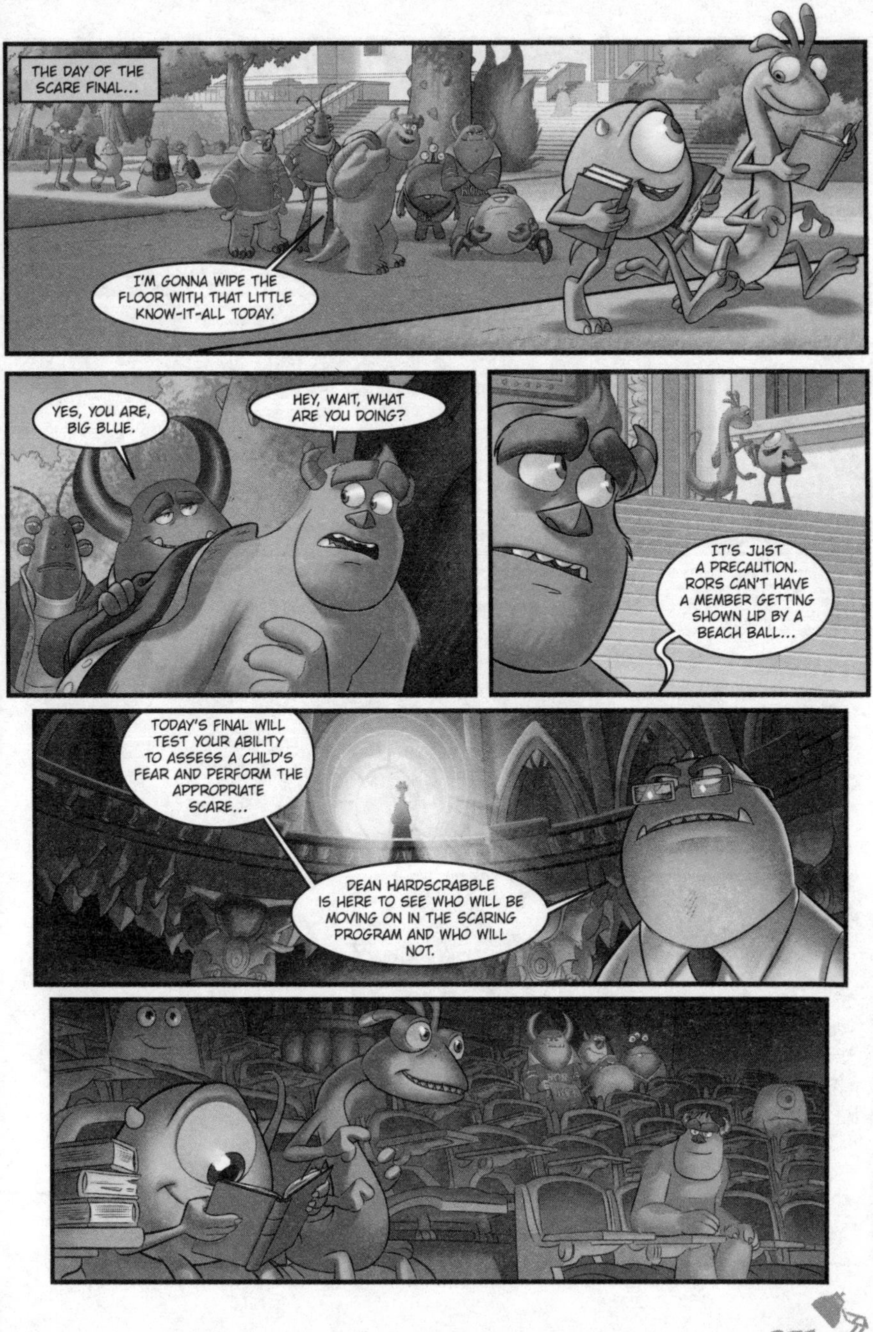
THE DAY OF THE SCARE FINAL...
I'M GONNA WIPE THE FLOOR WITH THAT LITTLE KNOW-IT-ALL TODAY.
YES, YOU ARE, BIG BLUE.
HEY, WAIT, WHAT ARE YOU DOING?
IT'S JUST A PRECAUTION. RORS CAN'T HAVE A MEMBER GETTING SHOWN UP BY A BEACH BALL...
TODAY'S FINAL WILL TEST YOUR ABILITY TO ASSESS A CHILD'S FEAR AND PERFORM THE APPROPRIATE SCARE...
DEAN HARDSCRABBLE IS HERE TO SEE WHO WILL BE MOVING ON IN THE SCARING PROGRAM AND WHO WILL NOT.

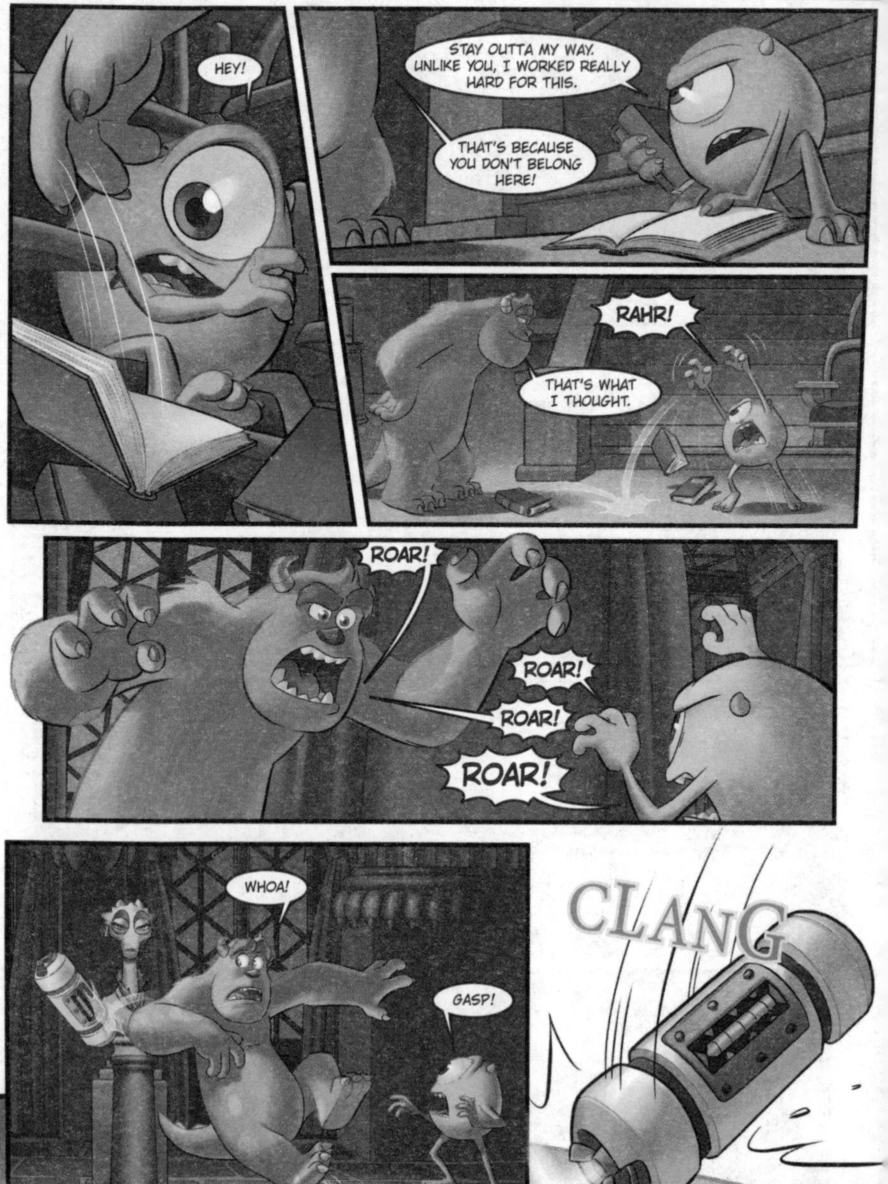
HEY!
STAY OUTTA MY WAY. UNLIKE YOU, I WORKED REALLY HARD FOR THIS.
THAT'S BECAUSE YOU DON'T BELONG HERE!
RAHR!
THAT'S WHAT I THOUGHT.
ROAR!
ROAR!
ROAR!
ROAR!
WHOA!
GASP!
CLANG

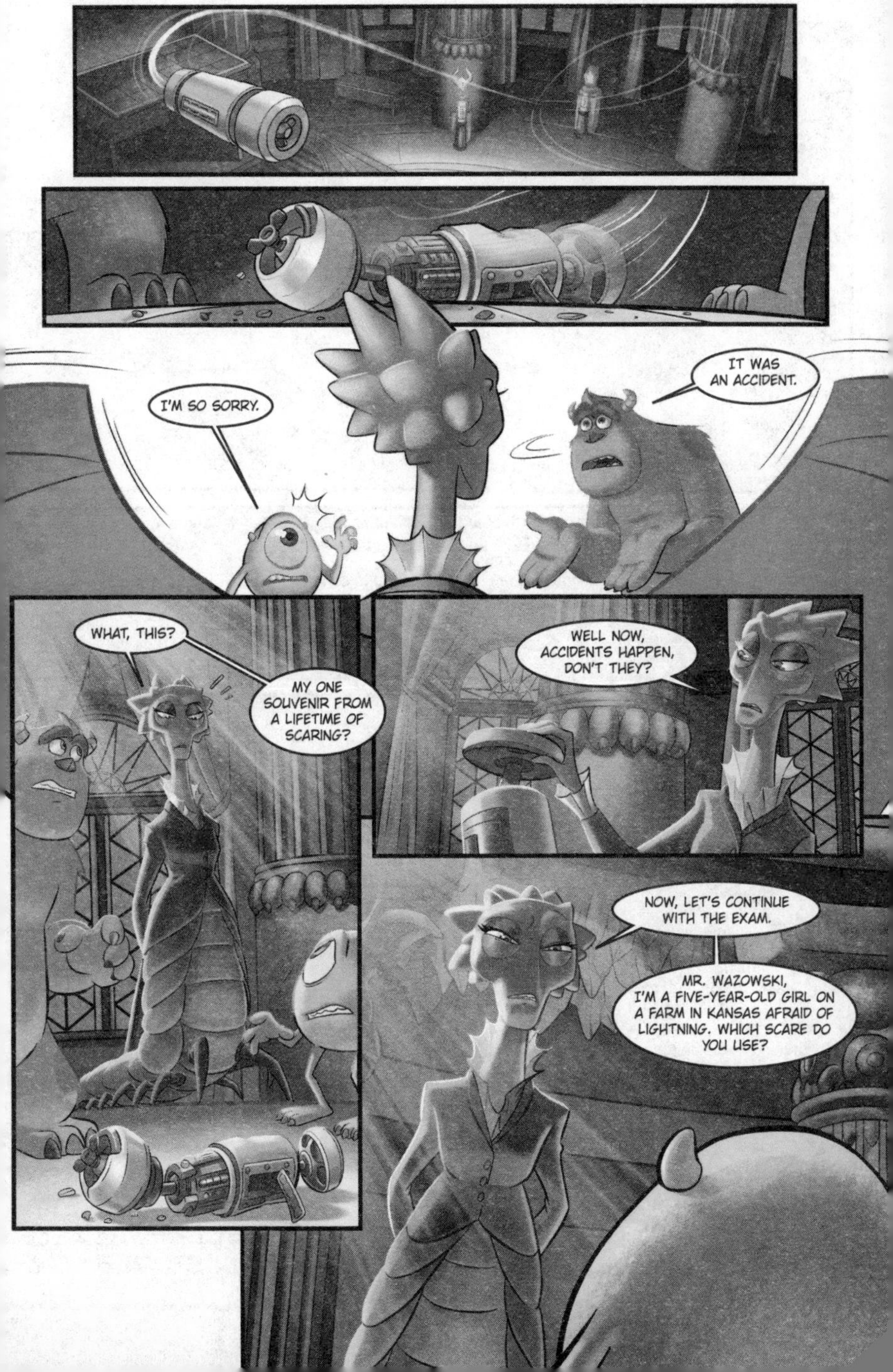
I'M SO SORRY.
IT WAS AN ACCIDENT.
WHAT, THIS?
MY ONE SOUVENIR FROM A LIFETIME OF SCARING?
WELL NOW, ACCIDENTS HAPPEN, DON'T THEY?
NOW, LET'S CONTINUE WITH THE EXAM.
MR. WAZOWSKI, I'M A FIVE-YEAR-OLD GIRL ON A FARM IN KANSAS AFRAID OF LIGHTNING. WHICH SCARE DO YOU USE?

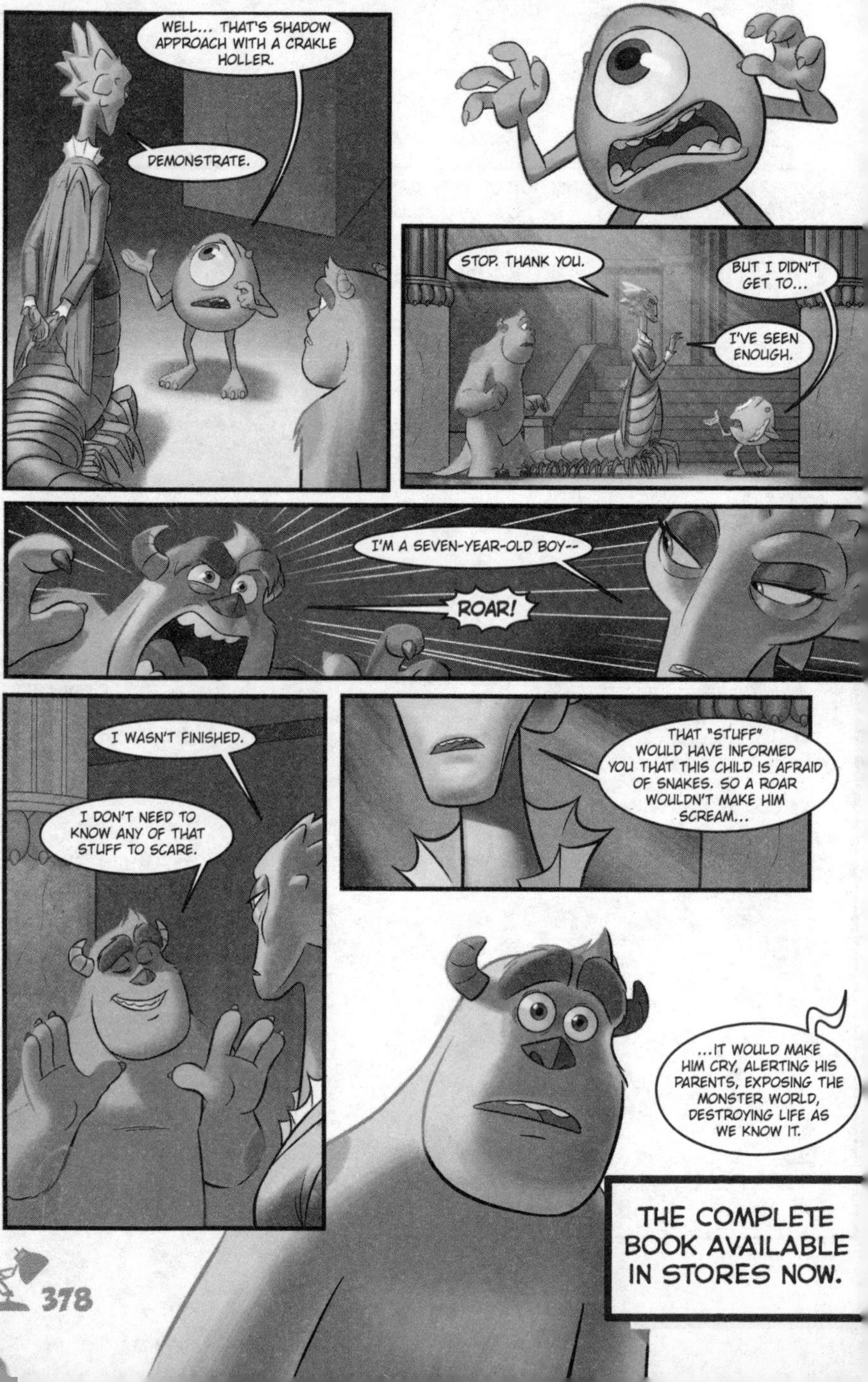

WELL... THAT'S SHADOW APPROACH WITH A CRAKLE HOLLER.
DEMONSTRATE.
STOP. THANK YOU.
BUT I DIDN'T GET TO...
I'VE SEEN ENOUGH.
I'M A SEVEN-YEAR-OLD BOY--
ROAR!
I WASN'T FINISHED.
I DON'T NEED TO KNOW ANY OF THAT STUFF TO SCARE.
THAT "STUFF" WOULD HAVE INFORMED YOU THAT THIS CHILD IS AFRAID OF SNAKES. SO A ROAR WOULDN'T MAKE HIM SCREAM...
...IT WOULD MAKE HIM CRY, ALERTING HIS PARENTS, EXPOSING THE MONSTER WORLD, DESTROYING LIFE AS WE KNOW IT.

THE COMPLETE BOOK AVAILABLE IN STORES NOW.